PRAISE FOR

Scandalmonger

"Handsomely constructed and politically sophisticated . . . *Scandalmonger* is solidly grounded upon Safire's wide reading, his meticulous scholarship and his careful weighing of conflicting evidence."

—*The New York Times Book Review*

"*Scandalmonger* is a smart, rollicking dramatization of the scandals that shook Thomas Jefferson's administration and barred Alexander Hamilton from the presidency."   —*The Christian Science Monitor*

"A gripping tale, a controlled and captivating web of carefully chosen truths and imagination."   —*Los Angeles Times*

"There's nothing like a vivid historical novel to bring to life the human reality of other times, and that's certainly what happens in *Scandalmonger*. William Safire not only knows whereof he speaks concerning politicians and the press, he's done the necessary reading, he's caught the temper, the vocabulary, of the vanished era of the Founders in a way equivalent to perfect pitch. His portrait of the little-known, much-scorned James Callender is one few readers will forget."

—David McCullough, Pulitzer Prize winner, author of *Truman* and *The Path Between the Seas*

"[*Scandalmonger*] is like a Safire column: It's tough, informative, colorful, and a good example of why we need scandalmongers—and newsmongers, too."

—*George Magazine*

"Maybe it takes one to know one. Whatever, who else but William Safire could tell the story of a scandalmonger (that's one word, please)? It's a gripping tale of scandal and sex and skullduggery, starring some of our history's best-loved Founding Fathers and Mothers. Safire is a superb novelist and it shows ever so clearly and entertainingly in this book."

—Jim Lehrer

"Mr. Safire has great fun with all this and tells his story well. . . . He allows the reader to relax into an amused and theatrical context of all the posturing and slander." 						—*The New York Times*

"*Scandalmonger* is clever and thought-provoking." —*The Wall Street Journal*

"*Scandalmonger* is one of the few works of fiction or non-fiction that I have encountered that is willing to confront the seamy and sleazy underbelly of the political life of America's founders. *Scandalmonger* is a story of real political hardball by America's founders in a period when the survival of the American Republic was at stake. *Scandalmonger* is a must read for anyone who wants to really understand the politics of America's founders."
						—Gerald W. Gawalt, Curator, Early AmericanHistory,
						Library of Congress

"[A] fascinating story that Safire not just retells, but recalls vividly from the historical mists." 						—*The Boston Globe*

"A pleasing fictionalized history text that demonstrates how sexual scandal is as old and venerated a tradition in American politics as kissing babies. . . . Richly researched and nicely paced: sure to satisfy readers with a healthy appetite for American history." 						—*Kirkus Reviews*

"This meaty, profoundly engrossing novel vividly illustrates episodes in the history of American journalism and government."
						—*Library Journal* (starred review)

"Catnip to history buffs." 						—*Publishers Weekly*

"The plot is fascinating, the issues raised are as crucial now as they were then, and the language used in the book, as one might expect from Safire's other role as a grammar maven, is terrific." 		—*San Francisco Chronicle*

"In a lively fictionalized version of historical fact, Safire shows how Callender, a transplanted Scottish journalist, pioneered the use of the poison quill. . . . Safire, as he did in *Freedom*, does a deft job of breathing life into stony faces we know from currency and monuments." —*Chicago Sun-Times*

"Early nineteenth-century colloquialisms and actual quotes transform the icons of American history with their powdered wigs into real human beings with personal frailties and political agendas. . . . Entertaining and informative."   —*Book*

"*Scandalmonger* is a fresh and thought-provoking look at the monument set: George Washington, John Adams, James Madison, Aaron Burr, Meriwether Lewis, James Monroe and other dead Colonial all-stars are brought to life in these pages."   —*Rocky Mountain News* (Denver)

"[Safire] has turned authentic letters, newspaper articles and court transcripts of the period into high drama. If our school teachers could have been as resourceful, we would now have a nation of American history experts."   —*The Tampa Tribune*

"A lively and enjoyable account of a turbulent period of American History . . . A historical novel that can delight both historians and ordinary readers seeking a political potboiler."   —*The Jerusalem Post*

"History, twistery, fact or fiction—whatever you label it, this is a polished piece of historical writing."   —*San Antonio Express-News*

"William Safire has fully mobilized his monumental talents as novelist, columnist and scholar of history to bring us this breathtaking and instructive tale of how a tangled series of seductions and betrayals, involving some of the greatest names in our pantheon, changed American history. So sure is Safire's mastery of historical fiction that as you race through these pages, you will have a hard time believing that he was not really there in the center of the drama when (almost) all of this happened."   —Michael Beschloss

"*Scandalmonger* has a surefooted timeliness about it. . . . Safire lays open the rivalries and intrigues that came close to shattering a new republic still in its infancy."   —William C. Davis, historian, author of *An Honorable Defeat*

William Safire

A NOVEL

A HARVEST BOOK
HARCOURT, INC.
SAN DIEGO   NEW YORK   LONDON

For

Timothy Thunderproof
and Peter Porcupine

www.harcourt.com

First published by Simon & Schuster in 2000

Library of Congress Cataloging-in-Publication Data
Safire, William, 1929–
Scandalmonger: a novel/William Safire.—1st Harvest ed.
p.   cm.—(A Harvest book)
Includes bibliographical references.
ISBN 0-15-601323-1
1. Callender, James Thomson, 1758–1803—Fiction.
2. United States—History—1783–1815—Fiction.
3. Hamilton, Alexander, 1757–1804—Fiction.
4. Journalists—Fiction. 5. Scandals—Fiction.   I. Title.
PS3569.A283 S33 2001
813'.54—dc21   00-048221

Designed by Amy Hill
Text set in Caslon Old Face
Printed in the United States of America
First Harvest edition 2001
A C E G I J H F D B

CONTENTS

PROLOGUE
1792
11

PART I
The Hamilton Scandal
47

PART II
The Sedition Scandal
145

PART III
The Jefferſon Scandals
263

PART IV
The Libel Scandal
371

EPILOGUE
What Happened Later
431

THE UNDERBOOK
Notes and Sources
445

Bibliography   489
Picture Credits   495

And there's a Luſt in Man no Charm can tame,
Of loudly publiſhing our Neighbour's Shame;
On Eagles' Wings immortal Scandals fly,
While Virtuous Actions are but Born, and Dye.

—Juvenal, *Satire IX* (c. A.D. 120)

TO THE READER

*T*he reader of historical fiction wonders: "What's true and what's not?" As docudramas blur the line between fact and fiction, the reader is entitled to know what is history and what is twistery.

In this novel, all the characters are real people who lived during America's Federal period at the turn of the nineteenth century. Much of the dialogue, especially that attributed to past Presidents, is based on contemporary letters, diaries and newspaper accounts. Accounts of trials are drawn from transcripts made at the time. A central romantic relationship is fictional.

For the reader interested in separating documented history from informed speculation and outright imagination, the author reveals his sources of all that's true in the back of the book.

Philadelphia, c. 1799

PROLOGUE

1792

December 17, 1792
PHILADELPHIA

"*T*he man now in jail who got me into all this trouble says he has enough on the Treasury Secretary to hang him."

The note from his former clerk startled Frederick Augustus Muhlenberg. Squinting at the familiar, crabbed handwriting, the member of Congress from Pennsylvania—about to begin his second term as Speaker of the House of Representatives—read on: "Reynolds claims to have proof showing that Hamilton secretly engaged in speculation in government securities."

Alexander Hamilton corrupt? Muhlenberg's well-ordered Germanic mind refused to entertain the scandalous thought. President Washington's Secretary of the Treasury had been General Washington's courageous aide-de-camp in the War for Independence. He gave unity to the Union by having the Federal government assume the debts of the States. Everyone knew that Hamilton was the Cabinet officer that the great man would rely on most heavily in the second term soon to begin. To suggest that this exemplar of financial probity was enriching himself at public expense was to shake the very foundations of the new Republic. And with war brewing between England and France, such a damning charge against Hamilton, an avowed admirer of the British, would be grist for the mills of the new anti-Federalist faction so entranced by everything French.

Muhlenberg was certain that Jacob Clingman, who had worked in his

Philadelphia mercantile house and later served as his assistant in Congress, was honest at heart. The unfortunate young man had become involved with a ne'er-do-well from New York named James Reynolds in a scheme to buy up the claims for unpaid past wages of the Revolution's veterans. After almost a decade, most of the old soldiers thought the claims would never be paid, and were selling them for 10 cents on the dollar. But some speculators, said to know of Hamilton's plan to pay the old debt in full, were avidly seeking the government's list of veterans and the amounts they were owed. Reynolds and Clingman were discovered impersonating claimants and jailed; only Muhlenberg's intercession, attesting to the young man's character, had allowed his former clerk to be free pending prosecution.

The Speaker laid the accusatory note on his desk. Muhlenberg was a "low" Federalist, not as all-out for central power as the Hamiltonian Federalists, but loyal to President Washington. He was relieved that the Republic's leader had consented to be re-elected, the month before, to a second term. Because the Pennsylvanian had long frowned on the emergence of a republican faction with ties to France, he was also glad that Washington was retaining that troublesome faction's leader, Thomas Jefferson, in his Cabinet as Secretary of State. By holding both the pro-French Jefferson and the pro-British Hamilton close to him, Washington could keep the United States united and neutral. Muhlenberg was convinced that the nation, not two decades from its Revolution, was wholly unprepared to fight another war.

But what if the outrageous charge that Hamilton was abusing the public's trust turned out to be true, or even partially true? The stain would not only sully the President's reputation but would discredit the entire new government. The farmers in Pennsylvania's West had already been infuriated by Hamilton's proposal for a whiskey tax, a scheme of Eastern moneymen that would punish Western growers of grain and distillers of its alcohol. The bankers in Boston did not seem to realize that whiskey was a more trusted medium of exchange than banknotes. A financial scandal in Hamilton's department, by adding substance to the republican suspicion that the Treasury Secretary was a secret monarchist, would tear the new nation apart.

A charge of corruption in the Cabinet should be brought directly to the attention of the President, Muhlenberg was certain, but not until the allegations were examined. This brief note slandering Hamilton could be merely a false accusation by some panicked wrongdoer. Did not a brave patriot, a national hero with a financial reputation as spotless as Hamilton's, deserve the benefit of the doubt—especially against the self-serving hearsay of an accused speculator?

But the letter from young Clingman required urgent action. "Reynolds's threats have borne fruit," his former assistant wrote. "Hamilton's Comptroller, Wolcott, has signed the order for Reynolds's release tomorrow morning. He will take his wife Maria and their child and sail for England. I have some letters you must see today."

That forced Muhlenberg to move quickly. A financial scandal, if such there were, would not vanish with the disappearance of one of its agents. The new pamphleteers, often working for the publications of what Washington himself disparaged as "self-created societies," were sowing disunity. They would see to it that every suspicious whisper and outright calumny would be repeated in print, breathing fire into the growing spirit of faction. Reynolds had to be interrogated before he got out of jail tomorrow morning, and his charge against Hamilton corroborated or put to rest.

The portly Speaker pushed himself out of his chair and buttoned his waistcoat. His political sense told him that one man alone could not conduct the investigation. He would need a companion to give at least the appearance of factional and geographical impartiality. Because Muhlenberg's own background was in the Lutheran clergy and the mercantile trade, he would need a colleague versed in the law.

John Adams, the Vice President? He had been known to call Hamilton "the bastard son of a Scotch pedlar." While that ancestral slur was true enough, it was unfair to hold Hamilton's low birth in the West Indies against him, and Adams's angry remark indicated he would have a personal prejudice.

Aaron Burr? Muhlenberg considered his friend Burr, Senator from New York, to be the sort of shrewd lawyer ordinarily perfect for such a mission. A good friend of Jemmy and Dolley Madison, too; indeed, Burr had introduced the longtime bachelor to the sunny widow. But a month before, when the Speaker had prevailed on the republican Burr to take him to see the Federalist Hamilton, the Senator's fellow New Yorker, to recommend leniency for the young clerk, Muhlenberg sensed a tension between the two. They were not only of opposing political factions but seemed to dislike each other in a personal way.

What about Jonathan Trumbull, who had replaced him as Speaker in the past term? No; "Brother Jonathan" was too close to President Washington, too ardent a Federalist, and was from Connecticut, which was too far north. Needed for balance in confronting Hamilton was a man of the Senate; a Southerner or Westerner, preferably a Virginian; a lawyer but not a sitting judge; someone trusted by Jefferson and the other anti-Federalists gathering around him.

James Monroe. The perfect choice. Muhlenberg knew the youthful Virginian had been Jefferson's law student, his political acolyte and the man Jefferson was even now urging Washington to appoint as his Minister to France. "Cool and collected," as Jefferson liked to say, prudent and correct, Monroe was not personally amiable, but had a reputation of being both high-minded and hardheaded.

The Pennsylvanian snatched up the troubling note and set out across the chambers for the Virginia Senator's office.

Monroe, the accusation from Reynolds's confederate in hand, was hardly able to hide his delight at what Muhlenberg, in his rich German accent, was telling him. Jefferson's break with Hamilton was absolute; the Secretary of State saw the Treasury Secretary as twisting the Constitution into a device for snatching power from the States and individuals in the name of "empire." For months, in general terms, Jefferson had been warning President Washington that Hamilton was guilty of dealing out Treasury secrets among his financier friends. The Treasury Secretary had countered that Jefferson was an incendiary promoting national disunion and public disorder. Now here was a specific case supporting Jefferson's suspicions of Hamilton's character to lay before the Chief Magistrate.

"The President must be made aware of this," Monroe told the Speaker firmly. "There is no offense more reprehensible, in an officer charged with the finances of his country, than to be engaged in speculation."

"Of course." But Muhlenberg hesitated. "Don't you think we should see Hamilton first, in case he has some logical explanation?"

Though eager to use the evidence to undermine Hamilton's influence with Washington, Monroe agreed. He considered it important to give the fair-minded Speaker every impression of his own impartiality. "And before we do," he suggested, "perhaps we should see the judge who ordered tomorrow's release of Reynolds. To see if Hamilton had a hand in that."

Muhlenberg shook his head, no. "The Attorney General of Pennsylvania signed the release order. I know the man. If we go to him, the news will be all over Philadelphia in a matter of hours."

Monroe reluctantly accepted the need for discretion. "The young man who wrote this note—when he was your clerk, was he reliable? Do you trust his word?"

"He's easily misled and I believe was duped by Reynolds. But in the years he worked in my store, Jacob Clingman never stole a thing. I'd vouch for him to that extent. I arranged for his release on bail, but I refused to do the same for Reynolds."

Monroe believed he could do with more evidence, particularly letters in Hamilton's handwriting, before he confronted the Treasury Secretary, who would surely deny everything. And he felt a need for some political basis for interceding in this affair. "The name Reynolds is familiar," he said, frowning as if to remember. "Is this man one of the Virginia Reynoldses?"

"He's a New Yorker, but I suppose it's possible he has family in Virginia."

"Could be a constituent of mine in trouble, then." He rose. "Let's see what letters your informant Clingman has. Then we can interview Reynolds." Monroe presumed that if Reynolds had incriminating documents from Hamilton, they would probably be at his home. Because this was to be his last night in jail, there might be an opportunity to visit the Reynolds domicile and speak to his wife or housekeeper without his presence, perhaps even to search his desk. "After we hear what this Reynolds says, then we can visit Hamilton."

The Speaker nodded his agreement. "At that point," he said, "we would be in a position to lay this before the President."

FREDERICK MUHLENBERG

Jacob Clingman, coatless—it was a mild winter in Philadelphia—was brought into the Congressional office. He was genuinely glad to see Speaker Muhlenberg, the only man of power who had ever befriended him. He did not recognize the tall, sharp-nosed, cold-eyed man with him, introduced by the Speaker only as "my colleague." Probably a lawyer, Clingman thought.

"I vouched for your good character, Jacob," said his business mentor, who had once been his Lutheran pastor, "but not that of Reynolds. I verily believe him to be a rascal."

"He is that and worse, sir. Reynolds says that he has it in his power to injure the Secretary of the Treasury, and I think that is why he is to be released tomorrow."

"That cannot be the reason Comptroller Wolcott gives," said the lawyer with the cold eyes.

"No. Wolcott is in a tight place," Clingman told his interrogators. "He was doing his job, investigating a fraud, and tripped over this much bigger speculation scandal involving Reynolds and the Secretary. Then, to save his superior any embarrassment, Comptroller Wolcott had to find reasons not to prosecute us. So Reynolds made full restitution of the money, and gave him the list of veterans that we used. He even told the Comptroller which Treasury clerks in New York had slipped him the list. That's when his case was dropped, and Reynolds gets out tomorrow all free and clear. But my case is still pending and I don't know why."

"Do you have any personal knowledge," the unidentified interrogator asked, "of a direct connection between Reynolds and Comptroller Wolcott's superior?"

"Hamilton, you mean?" When the lawyer kept looking silently at him, Clingman blurted out more than he had wanted to say. "In January, not quite a year ago, I went to Reynolds's house, and just as I came in, Colonel Hamilton was leaving. I knew it was him. It's a face everybody knows who does business with the Treasury."

"The colonel cuts a memorable figure, true. Do you recall any other time you saw them together?"

"Not exactly together." Now he was wading into deeper water. Clingman looked to Speaker Muhlenberg for reassurance, and received a friendly nod. "A few days after that, I was at the Reynolds house with Maria, Mrs. Reynolds, Mr. Reynolds being out." Hoping he would not be asked to explain that, he hurried on. "It was late at night and somebody knocked at the door. I got up and opened it and saw it was Colonel Hamilton. He looked surprised. Maria came up behind me. Colonel Hamilton handed her a paper and said something curious."

When he hesitated, trying to call up the exact words, Muhlenberg barked a quick, guttural, "Vot?"

"What Colonel Hamilton said was, 'I was ordered to give this to Mr. Reynolds,' and he turned and left."

"Why did you find that curious?"

"Because who could 'order' the Secretary of the Treasury to give anybody anything?" Clingman quickly retreated to his respectful demeanor. "That's the very question I asked Mrs. Reynolds, sir, and she said she supposed Colonel Hamilton did not want to be recognized. This was late at night."

"Did you see what was written on the paper?" the lawyer asked.

"No, it was in a blank envelope."

"Then why did you say it was a paper?"

Clingman felt his heart clutch into a tight fist. "I don't know. It was an envelope with a paper in it, I guess. It wasn't thick." At least they weren't asking him what he was doing late at night in the Reynolds house, alone with Maria.

"Surely you asked Mrs. Reynolds about Hamilton's visits?" Congressman Muhlenberg observed.

"She said he had been assisting her husband for some months. Only a few days before, her husband had received eleven hundred dollars from Colonel Hamilton." He had no cause to hold back: "She said her husband told her that the Treasury Secretary had made thirty thousand dollars by speculation, thanks to him."

"That is a very serious charge to repeat, young man," said the lawyer.

Clingman was eager to substantiate it. "When I must have looked as if I didn't believe her, Maria said her husband had applied to Colonel Hamilton for money to subscribe to the turnpike road at Lancaster, and received a note from him saying no."

"You asked to see that note, of course?" said the lawyer.

He looked uncertainly at Muhlenberg, who nodded encouragement. Clingman reached inside his shirt, took out a small packet of notes, and slid it across the table to the Congressman, who read the top one aloud: " 'It is utterly out of my power, I assure you upon my word of honor, to comply with your request. Your note is returned.' No signature. Well, if Hamilton wrote this, he did the right thing."

"But if that handwriting is Hamilton's," the lawyer said, "it does prove a certain connection. That's hardly the way he would turn down a request from a stranger." Three other cryptic notes, unsigned, were in the packet, with Reynolds's endorsement "From Sec. Hamilton, Esq." on them. "We'll hold on to these, if it's all right with you, Mr. Clingman." He asked for Reynolds's home address and Clingman told him. As the two men prepared to leave, the lawyer said, "What else can you tell us about Mrs. Reynolds? Is she young?"

"She's twenty-two, same as me. She comes from a good family, connected to the Livingstons, in New York." The connection was remote, but the Livingston clan was as powerful as the Clinton family in that state. He hoped they would understand that Maria was not at fault in all this. "She left her parents' home hurriedly, under trying circumstances, and in her marriage has been much abused." The clerk said nothing of her fine figger or elegant carriage or the way Maria's dark blue eyes could quickly fill with tears; all that they could find out for themselves. "Has a daughter named Susan, about five or six years old, a sweet child terrified of her father. The Reynolds family, sirs, is not a happy one."

The men from Congress took their seat in the warden's office, a sullen gray room with a poor painting on the wall of George Washington astride his white horse. James Reynolds was brought to them from his cell.

"I am Frederick Augustus Muhlenberg, Mr. Reynolds, and this is my colleague in the Congress."

"Does your colleague have a name?"

"I am Senator James Monroe of Virginia. Are you one of the Richmond Reynoldses?"

"No, I am a New Yorker."

"I was misinformed. Are you the man who claims to have a person in high office in his power?"

Reynolds showed them a sly smile. "Thanks to my associate in high office, who sometimes writes me the most abusive letters, I am getting out of this place tomorrow morning. Under this gentleman's influence, Comptroller Wolcott had no choice but to find a way to drop my prosecution. It would have embarrassed his superior."

"We are interested in examining those letters," said Muhlenberg.

"All in good time, perhaps. I will do nothing to prevent my discharge."

The Speaker pressed: "Will you meet us tomorrow morning as soon as you are released?"

"I'd be delighted." The prisoner added darkly, "And I'll have much to tell you about a prosecution that was commenced to keep me low, and oppress me, and ultimately to drive me away from this city. But not yet."

"Tomorrow, then," said Muhlenberg, to pin down an elusive witness. "We come to your home at three."

"Done."

Monroe, less trusting than the Speaker, suspected they had seen the last of James Reynolds. The chicken was likely to fly the coop as soon as the lid was lifted. If Hamilton had taken the chance to get Reynolds out of jail, the brilliant Secretary would not hesitate to get him out of the country before he could tell his tale.

Seated at a desk in the failing light of the warden's office, with the stout Speaker looking over his shoulder, Monroe wrote the first draft of a letter to President Washington reporting in detail the interviews just held with Clingman and Reynolds. He thought it important to get the testimony about Hamilton's perfidy down on paper while it was fresh in his mind. He intended to amend the letter the next day and make a copy to show to Secretary of State Jefferson, in utmost confidence, of course.

An hour later, with the troubled Muhlenberg in tow—Monroe assumed that the poor fellow must be worrying about how a corruption scandal in the Treasury would dismay his fellow Federalists—he directed the carriage driver to an address on South Fourth Street.

Monroe sat forward, most of his weight on his feet to absorb the bumps and ruts in the road. He found the port city of Philadelphia close and oppressive; it teemed with 55,000 Pennsylvanians, ten times the population of his native Richmond. In winter, one usually froze; in summer, at night one's ears were assaulted by the incessant croaking of frogs in the nearby swamps. He was glad to have voted to remove the national capital, eight years hence, to a place at the mouth of the Potomac River.

Curiously, that compromise on location was Hamilton's doing. In return for the South's willingness to let the national government take over all State debts, the Northern Federalists agreed to situate the capital near Virginia. Hamilton won his long-sought centralization of financial power, the basis for national empire; Jefferson won the presence of a new national capital near his home and far from the urban influences of Boston, New York and Philadelphia. Monroe knew that Jefferson and Madison thought the compromise would serve the anti-Federalists well in the long run, but the Virginia Senator was not so sure; Hamilton was dangerous because he understood the use of government power better than most and seemed to enjoy its exercise more than anyone. Like his New York rival Aaron Burr, he was fourteen years younger than Jefferson and would be around a long time.

The Reynolds house was in a pleasant neighborhood not far from Alexander Hamilton's home; one could hardly hear the frogs. Monroe stood back and let Muhlenberg rap on the door.

Maria Reynolds appeared and motioned them to enter as if she expected their visit and was resigned to it. The tall young woman's blue eyes directly engaged him; on first impression, she struck the Virginian as both capable and vulnerable. Dressed in a high-necked maroon dress with a tight bodice that had been the fashion a few years before, the striking young lady held herself proudly. Monroe presumed from the interview with Clingman that the two were having an illicit romance; if so, he decided, the sallow young man was getting much the better of the bargain.

He let Muhlenberg take the lead in gaining her confidence. Mrs. Reynolds offered them tea and served it with a relaxed grace that Monroe considered almost Southern. Though the teapot was respectable silver, the earthenware dishes were chipped, the pewter mugs were somewhat battered and the furniture in the modest home was inelegant. A general messiness suggested the presence of a small child and a lack of domestic help. Gentle questioning by the avuncular Congressman from Pennsylvania revealed that she was a Van Der Burgh from New York, related by marriage to the wealthy Livingston clan. Or so she said. Monroe wondered, but did not ask, what could have driven a young lady of such fine bearing and aristocratic attraction to leave home at a tender age and follow the fortunes of a blackguard like Reynolds.

"We have just come from your husband, who will be free to come home tomorrow," Monroe informed her. He did not essay a smile. "And we understand that Colonel Hamilton has been a frequent visitor in this house." He left the impression that the prisoner had told them that.

"I know," she said. "A friend of my husband's observed your visit at the jail and rushed here to tell me to expect two gentlemen from the Congress. I have been instructed to tell you nothing and—more important—to give you nothing."

"*Ach,*" said Muhlenberg, taken aback.

"But that is not your intent," said Monroe quickly. He assumed she would not have told them about being forewarned had she not intended to cooperate to some extent.

"I am reluctant, sir," the composed young woman replied, "to say anything that would renew Mr. Reynolds's difficulties with the law."

Monroe judged that she expected to be persuaded. "Let me be frank," said the Virginia Senator, to whom candor did not come easily. "Your husband is not the primary object of our concern. Tell us, as a good citizen, all you can about the visits of Colonel Hamilton and any written communication your husband may have received from him."

She took a deep breath. "My husband sent word to me to burn them and I did." Monroe instantly doubted that; if letters from Hamilton to her husband existed, it would be in the interest of both Reynoldses to hold on to them. "He said that Colonel Hamilton told him that he would provide us with enough money to leave the country as soon as he was released." That part, at least, sounded true.

"The person who came just now with a message from your husband—what else did he tell you, besides to tell us nothing?"

"He said Mr. Hamilton had enemies who would try to prove he engaged in some speculation, but that he would be shown to be immaculate."

"And what did you say?"

"I said I rather doubted that."

Monroe raised his eyebrows. "Why do you doubt it?" When she remained silent, he refined the question, presenting it this time more firmly: "What led you to believe Hamilton would not be 'immaculate'?"

She shrugged. "My husband often said he could tell of something that would make the heads of great departments tremble."

Muhlenberg put in a question that had not occurred to Monroe. "You say you burned letters to your husband from Hamilton. Did he send any letters directly to you, that you kept?"

For the first time, Maria Reynolds lost some of her poise. "Colonel Hamilton asked me to destroy those. I did. Last week, in that fireplace."

"You would recognize his handwriting, then?" asked Monroe. He lay before her one of the unsigned notes to Reynolds that Muhlenberg and he had taken from Clingman. "This is from Colonel Hamilton, is it not?"

She glanced at it and nodded.

"And this one?"

Maria Reynolds nodded again.

"But the handwriting on the two notes is not the same, Mrs. Reynolds," Monroe said, as if puzzled. He thought that he had caught her out in a falsehood, but he did not want to appear the aggressive questioner.

She showed no surprise, which surprised him. "In the first one, Hamilton tried to disguise his handwriting. He often did that." She hesitated, appearing to weigh the alternatives of trusting them or not. "I do have a note from Colonel Hamilton that arrived only last week—I haven't destroyed it yet." She went to the desk and took a sheet out of the middle drawer. "That's the Colonel's normal writing."

It was a brief note, dated the sixth of December, offering to be of help to her, and signed boldly "Hamilton." Muhlenberg reached for it, but Maria Reynolds did not part with it. After denying again that she had any other written communication from the Treasury Secretary, or that any money had been included with that last note, she rose and politely showed them to the door.

Jacob Clingman had been upstairs in the Reynoldses' bedroom throughout the interview. When he heard the door close, he raced down and embraced Maria to comfort her. After a few moments, she pushed him away and told him she had shown them the note Hamilton sent her a few days before.

"Did they ask you about us?"

She shook her head. "Only about Hamilton and my husband. They showed me the notes you gave them, and I said they were in Hamilton's writing, sometimes disguised."

"Did they ask about any relationship between you and Hamilton?" Clingman knew that the Treasury Secretary had taken advantage of her at least once, over a year ago. She had told him it was during her faithless husband's pursuit of another woman, when she found herself lonely and destitute, but she had assured him that she yielded to the handsome Hamilton only in a moment of passionate gratitude. Jacob believed her when she said it was a single occasion of moral weakness, not a prolonged affair.

She sat down. "They did not ask if he and I were lovers. They are gentlemen. They would never presume to inquire into indelicate matters."

"If this ever gets into the hands of newsmongers," Clingman warned her as gently as he could, "everyone will believe the worst."

"Jacob, that hateful man I was so foolish to marry when I was fourteen years old," she said, "now wants me to play the whore. I won't do that. Not to save him, not for the money I need so desperately, not for anything. I won't abase myself. I have a daughter—" She took the handkerchief from his breast pocket and covered her eyes.

Stroking her hair, Clingman asked, "Does Hamilton have letters of yours?"

"I never wrote him, never had occasion to. After Reynolds and I reconciled, I saw my husband write him often, pleading for money—the Colonel surely has those, if he hasn't destroyed them. But nothing from me."

"Then your reputation is safe. You don't have to worry." Clingman assumed she was protected from her husband's design to have her "play the whore" not only by her own past discretion, but by Hamilton's interest in keeping their brief amorous encounter secret, lest it bring dishonor to him and shame to his wife and children. It seemed like a safe bet.

December 18, 1792

At three the next afternoon, Monroe and Muhlenberg appeared at the Reynolds home to find the freed prisoner had come and gone. Maria Reynolds let them in and said Reynolds told her he was sailing to New Jersey. Her eyes were reddened, but she carried herself bravely. Muhlenberg expressed his indignation at her husband's deception of the investigators and his abandonment of wife and child. Monroe was unsurprised; in his eyes, Reynolds was a thief.

Clingman was there and had a useful piece of evidence for them. He said that Reynolds, unaware that his confederate was cooperating with the Congressional investigators, had left a mangled note for him: "Let me read it to you," Clingman said. " 'I hope I have not forfeited your friendship, Jacob . . .'—here three lines were scratched out—'I will have satisfaction from HIM.' The 'him' is Hamilton, of course. 'He has offered to furnish me and Mrs. Reynolds with money to carry us off. If I agree to go immediately, he will see that Mrs. Reynolds has money to follow me. That is all I can say till I see you.' He didn't sign it, but this is his writing."

"What was scratched out?" Muhlenberg asked.

"He scratched it out, not me," Clingman said, "so I don't know. Here's another note that came to me at home first thing this morning, from Comptroller Wolcott." The note was on official Treasury stationery, and read, "Mr. Wolcott will be glad to see Mr. Clingman today, at half after ten o'clock."

"And did you see him?"

"Of course, and he took me directly into Colonel Hamilton's office at Treasury. They wanted to know who I was seeing from the Congress and what was the nature of your questioning."

"You told them?"

"I told the truth, Speaker Muhlenberg. They made it clear they would reopen the proceedings and put me in jail if I didn't cooperate. I said I went to you—you're the only one who has helped me in all this, and Colonel Burr, a little. I told them you brought along this gentleman"— he indicated Monroe—"whose name I did not know, and still don't."

Monroe allowed himself a thin smile and did not introduce himself. Let Hamilton wonder who else was on his trail besides the Speaker, a mild Federalist as well as a generous soul, inclined to forgiveness. "What did Hamilton say to that?"

"He desired me to go into the Gallery, where I could see the Members of the House, and inquire of your name from the bystanders."

"Do that," directed the Senator, who would not be in that chamber. "And when you don't see me there, report that to Wolcott and his superior. In your meeting this morning, what else did they want to know?"

"Hamilton wanted—demanded—to know if I turned over any documents. I told him what I gave you, the three. He said I had done very wrong to do that." The former clerk looked back plaintively at Maria. "I'm caught in the middle." She put a comforting hand on his shoulder. Monroe sensed that she was in control of whatever they would do.

"Keep telling us the truth, Jacob," said Muhlenberg, "it's the only way you can keep the story straight in your head."

"Now that your husband has fled, Mrs. Reynolds," said Monroe, "is there anything you think we should know?" Certain that the conspirators would leave the investigators a false story to misdirect them, he was stunned by her answer:

"My husband told me he was received by Hamilton this morning."

Muhlenberg thundered some imprecation in German.

"Reynolds said that the Treasury Secretary was extremely agitated," she went on, "walking backward and forward, striking alternately his forehead and his thigh."

That detail struck Monroe as having the ring of truth. He had once seen Hamilton agitated, making such gestures unique to him; he remembered thinking it was lucky Hamilton did not carry a riding crop.

"Colonel Hamilton said he had enemies at work," Maria Reynolds continued, now at ease with her interrogators, "but he was willing to meet them on fair ground. Then he told my husband not to stay long in his Treasury office in case his presence might be noticed."

Monroe asked, "Did Hamilton give him any money, did Reynolds say?"

"He didn't say. There were times," she volunteered, "when Hamilton did give him money—as much as a thousand dollars at a time—but I don't know about this morning." She added, more wistfully than bitterly, "He surely didn't leave any for my daughter and me."

Outside, in the carriage, Muhlenberg exploded: "Can you imagine? Hamilton frees this criminal Reynolds and then secretly sends for him. Then the criminal breaks his appointment with us and disappears for good. Hamilton probably gave him hush money. Do you suppose the wife is part of the plot?"

Monroe thought that Mrs. Reynolds was a charmer who could keep a secret. He also guessed that, as a sensible woman, she had not been inclined to burn any letters that might become useful to her. She was also a disenchanted wife unlikely to follow her reprobate husband out of the country. Maria Reynolds was probably committing adultery with Clingman, and the testimony of both of them had to be evaluated in that light.

"In a curious way, she's protecting Hamilton," Monroe told his fuming fellow investigator, "even as she gives us information to discomfort him. I can only presume Mrs. Reynolds's motive is also to protect her husband. She may be feigning her irritation with his sudden departure. Perhaps she considers loyalty to be the greatest virtue."

The Speaker said he could hardly believe what they had found. "We have evidence that the Secretary of the Treasury has been colluding for months with a confessed speculator. Think of it! And this morning he obstructs a Congressional inquiry by freeing and sending away a material witness. Monroe, finish the letter you began last night to President Washington. We must take it to him right away."

Monroe shook his head. "That was my own first impulse, and you were right to restrain me, Mr. Speaker. Hamilton has been tracking us as we have been tracking him. I think he expects us to come and confront him." The Treasury Secretary was a formidable public figure, personally fearless, certain to present a vigorous defense. Monroe rather looked forward to Hamilton's explanation of his dealings with Reynolds, and to the report he would write of their confrontation to Jefferson, and then to the President. "I propose we do just that tomorrow morning. Then we can take both the accusation and his explanation to President Washington."

Muhlenberg saw the wisdom in knowing Hamilton's explanation before going to the Chief Magistrate. "We'll need copies made of everything—Hamilton's notes, his letters, our reports of each interview, the draft of our letter to Washington, Clingman's affidavit."

"Get your man Beckley to do that tonight, if he has to work all night." John Beckley was Clerk of the House. Monroe said "your man" as if to defer to the Speaker of that body, but he wanted Beckley, an intensely loyal Jefferson partisan, in charge of the copying. Those documents might—in good time, perhaps in a few years, before the next Presidential election—bring disgrace down on Hamilton's Federalists. Muhlenberg hesitated; apparently wondering whether it was wise to trust the journeyman Beckley. Then the Speaker nodded assent and gathered all their notes.

"This unsigned note," said Muhlenberg, laying down a letter as if it were a card in a high-stakes game. "Do you know who may have written it?"

Hamilton responded to their gambit by sacrificing a pawn. To deny authorship would add to their suspicions, but to assert it freely would begin to disarm them. "I wrote that. I tried to disguise my handwriting, but the note is from me."

"Why did you try to—"

Hamilton held up a hand. "The affair among us is now on a different footing," he said as if his initial indignation had been assuaged. "I always stand ready to meet fair inquiry with frank communication." He looked directly at Monroe. "As it happens, I have it in my power—with written documents—to remove all doubt as to the real nature of this business. I will be able fully to convince you that absolutely no impropriety of the kind imputed to me did in fact exist." He rose confidently. "You will not be forced to embarrass yourselves by making an accusation to the President that would be quickly shown to be false. Allow me to assemble some papers. Tonight at my house you will have the explanation that will lay this to rest."

"After dinner, then," said the icily correct Monroe, who Hamilton was convinced was keeping Jefferson fully informed of evidence that might lead to the removal of his Cabinet adversary. "We'll be there."

Oliver Wolcott, Comptroller of the Currency, the son and grandson of Governors of Connecticut, was the trusted subordinate Hamilton invited to be his witness and supporter at the meeting with the inquisitors. Wolcott had stumbled onto Reynolds's wrongdoing and then demonstrated his loyalty to Hamilton by finding a suitable excuse for not prosecuting the case. This action did not trouble his conscience because Reynolds had not only made restitution, but had revealed the name of the Treasury clerk who provided him illicit information, whom Wolcott promptly fired. In the more serious case of Hamilton's friend William Duer, who had misappropriated official Treasury warrants and used them as collateral for private loans, Wolcott had no choice but to refer the case to Richard Harison, United States Attorney in New York. Harison was a Hamilton appointee who investigated dutifully the complaints of hundreds of investors who lost money with Duer, but who let the case lapse without indictment.

Wolcott saw the political wisdom in that. Had Harison in New York allowed the Duer case to go forward, or had Wolcott allowed Reynolds to drag Hamilton's name through the mud, the scandals would be a burden to a Hamilton campaign for the Presidency in 1796, should the aging Washington decide to retire. Under a President Hamilton, Oliver Wolcott expected to serve as Treasury Secretary; Federalism would triumph over the disunionist agrarian faction; the nation's westward expansion would be properly financed, and the Jefferson republicans and other apologists for the bloody French Jacobins would be routed once and for all.

"The charge against me," Hamilton began, "is a connection with one James Reynolds for purposes of improper pecuniary speculation. The truth is that I have been wholly indifferent to the acquisition of property and am poorer today than when I entered public office. I have not more than two thousand dollars in the world."

"There are these letters," said Muhlenberg, "some in a disguised hand, which was in itself evidence of a need to conceal the truth, and which you admit now to be your own writing—"

"I will show you many more letters attesting to a connection between Reynolds and me. The fact of the connection is not in dispute. But the purpose of the connection is not what you suspect."

This was all news to Wolcott. He had never dared ask what hold this criminal Reynolds had on his superior.

"My real crime," Hamilton went on, "is a loose connection—an amorous connection, I should say—with his wife. More shocking than that, gentlemen, this amour was pursued for a considerable time with his privity and connivance."

That revelation was met with silence. Wolcott could imagine Hamilton's dalliance with Maria Reynolds—an undeniably beautiful and mysterious woman, with aristocratic features not unlike Hamilton's—but the notion of conspiring with her husband to seduce and entrap the Treasury Secretary stretched credulity. Could it be that the husband was the pimp and his wife the whore? And Hamilton was doing business with them? Wolcott made an effort not to appear profoundly shaken.

"That much I can prove with these documents here." Hamilton laid a sheaf of letters on the table. "These letters to me covering a period of eighteen months are from Reynolds and his wife. As you shall see, they show a combination with the design to extort money from me."

Since the investigators from the Congress were too dumbstruck to say anything, Wolcott put in, "Which you paid?"

"I paid and paid and paid. This confession," Hamilton said, "is not made without a blush. I condemn myself because if this were ever to become public, it would inflict a pain upon my wife, who is eminently entitled to all my gratitude, fidelity and love."

"When did the extortion begin?" Monroe asked, ignoring Hamilton's expressions of sentiment about his wife.

"Sometime in the summer of last year a woman called at my house here in Philadelphia and asked to speak to me in private. . . ."

June 17, 1791
PHILADELPHIA

As Hamilton chose to remember it, the slender young woman standing in the sunlight of a summer Sunday afternoon, her face shadowed by a fashionable hat, appeared to be distraught. She was well dressed, obviously not a mendicant.

"Colonel Hamilton, could I have a few moments of your time?"

Hamilton asked if whatever was troubling her could not be better attended to at his Treasury office the next day. She seemed on the verge of tears and in a choked voice replied that it was a personal matter; she did not think it proper to disturb him at the Treasury Department.

"My family is in the drawing room," he said, motioning her in, "so let me attend you in my study over here."

After declining a glass of sherry, she folded her hands in her lap and introduced herself. "I am the daughter of Edgar Lewis of New York, and sister to Gilbert Livingston, whose family I believe you know."

Hamilton nodded his recognition of this distinguished lineage; one Livingston was Governor of New Jersey, another a political and financial ally of his in New York. By "sister," she undoubtedly meant "sister-in-law." She also identified a brother as a longtime sheriff of Dutchess County. He felt a fleeting urge to tell the wellborn young lady that, in contrast, he was an immigrant at seventeen from the Leeward Islands, the bastard son of a freethinking mother and a deserting father, and had spent the past twenty years in America as revolutionary warrior and creative banker living down his shameful family background. He let it pass; in her fragile emotional state, his statuesque visitor with the near-violet eyes was too appealing to interrupt.

"I was married seven years ago, Colonel Hamilton, to James Reynolds." She was now hardly more than twenty, he estimated, and might have been forced by necessity of pregnancy to marry that young. Few women of her class were as courageously amoral as Hamilton's mother, willing to bear and rear a child out of wedlock. "His father was in the Commissary Department during the war with Great Britain, in which you so valiantly fought."

"The name Reynolds is familiar." It was a common name, and he did not recall the man, but she evidently felt the need for further familial endorsement.

"My husband is a cruel and dishonest man. He has abandoned me, and my daughter, to live with another woman." She searched for a handkerchief in her purse, avoiding his eyes. "He has left us destitute."

His surge of sympathy for her distress was genuine. The man who abandoned a woman of such breeding and carriage, not to mention good looks, was not just a rogue but a fool. "How may I help?"

She looked up with hope. "I desire to leave Philadelphia to return to my friends and family in New York. The cost of such a move is at present beyond my means, and I cannot take a position in commerce because my young daughter requires my care." She took a deep breath. "Because I know you are a foremost citizen of New York, I have taken the liberty to apply to your humanity for assistance."

As Hamilton was to recount it, he sensed something odd in the application; a New York background in common was more excuse than good reason for soliciting his help. Yet the simplicity and modesty in her manner of relating the story impressed him with its truth, and her beauty was undeniably affecting. Hamilton was eager to comply. He had thirty dollars in the house, the kind of substantial sum that would take her home to her relatives in New York, but he did not want to dismiss her so quickly. And his family was in a nearby room. "The moment is not convenient to me, but if you will tell me the place of your residence, I will bring or send a small supply of money tonight."

"I live at 154 South Fourth Street." That was a short walk away from Hamilton's home at Walnut and South Third. "Not five minutes from here. You are so kind."

After dinner with his wife and children, Hamilton announced he had an appointment at the George, a nearby tavern, and put a $30 bank bill in his pocket. He envisioned the day when banknotes would be issued throughout the nation by the United States Bank, backed by the full faith and credit of the Federal government, and not issued pell-mell by local banks that were all too often on the brink of insolvency.

Keeping his mind on his banking, Hamilton recalled how Congress had passed his bank bill over the objections of James Madison and the Jeffersonians, who argued that its powers could not be found in the Constitution. These believers in a rural society of yeomen and farmers had almost persuaded Washington to veto the banking legislation designed to finance an empire based on urban manufactures, but the President asked Hamilton to present the reasons for the validity and propriety of the law. Writing a memorial day and night for a week, Hamilton devised a new theory: he persuaded the President that the Constitution contained "implied powers" to carry out functions not expressly forbidden, and that Madison's strict construction of the document would strangle the infant nation in its crib. Washington signed the bill and, perhaps without fully realizing the strength he was gathering to the Executive, laid the foundation for financing a continental empire. That was a good week's work.

He walked quickly down Walnut Street, slapping his thigh nervously with one hand, fingering the bank bill in his pocket with the other, focusing his mind on his victory over Madison about implied powers to keep his expectations down about his meeting with the young woman from New York. Was he hoping too hard for an assignation? Did he overstep in suggesting he come to her house? Her assent was so quick—was he stepping into a trap of some sort? If her brother-in-law was Gilbert Livingston, and her half-brother was a former sheriff of Dutchess County, why hadn't she written to them for a small loan? Would he be played the fool?

Hamilton stopped in his tracks and composed himself. He was a Good Samaritan doing a good deed for a lovely woman in distress. If his fellow New Yorker responded to his gift with a cup of tea and a handshake of gratitude, he would wish her well and return home with dignity intact.

He suddenly found himself at the address the Reynolds woman had given him. A pretty child, not more than five or six, opened the door to the modest Fourth Street home, silently pointed to the stairway, and disappeared into the kitchen behind it. His eyes swept up the stairs to see Maria

Reynolds standing at the top, in a black dress that accentuated her slim waist and full bosom, beckoning him to come up. He bounded up the stairs and followed her into the master bedroom. More awkwardly than he would have liked, he took the bill out of his pocket and laid it on the dresser. She ignored it, stepping close to him with a look of excited expectancy that he was sure no gentleman could fail to fulfill.

"I am glad you turned to me," he said.

"I read the articles you signed as 'Publius.' And 'Catullus.' Why do you use so many pseudonyms?"

"A single voice is not enough. I am trying to appear to be a legion, a host of pamphleteers and newsmongers."

She laid the fingers of one hand lightly on the ruffles of his shirt. "You may remove your jacket if you wish. It's a warm evening."

As he did so, he watched her step out of her shoes. Because that was not enough to bring their eyes to an equal level, she sat on the edge of her bed and looked up at him. There was none of the coquetry about her of his sister-in-law Angelica Church, his current vision of attractive womanhood, who liked to tease him with her passionate letters from abroad. He let himself believe that this woman, Maria Reynolds, desired his closeness more fervently than she needed his help. Perhaps his fame and appearance so attracted her that she used a request for carfare home as a ruse to become his friend.

Stimulated by the directness of her gaze, even more than her evident willingness to follow wherever he led, he placed his hands on her arms, pulled her to her feet and turned her around to face the mirror. After a long moment reflecting on her figure over her shoulder, he unhurriedly worked his fingers down the long row of buttons on the back of her black dress. The elation he felt surging in him was the product of the discovery of a kindred soul, the aesthetic of a beautiful woman in the act of welcoming his intimacy, and the practical comfort of anticipating her total availability within a few blocks of home. He took his time with her; this was to be no transient or furtive affair. Only when he was certain she was quite ready for him did he commit himself. She took him into her with a long cry of unashamed delight, which pleasured him no end.

The lovemaking was worthy of his passion; she inspired him to heights and depths he had never reached before in a life of no mean experience with women. After he dressed and was about to depart, Hamilton took her naked shoulders in his hands and looked profoundly into those memorably deep blue eyes. "I will give you my assistance, Maria. There is no need for you to leave Philadelphia. But I require your promise—now that you have made me your friend, you must apply to no one else."

She gave Hamilton her promise. He began to think of the excuse he would give at home for his lateness. On the way out, she introduced him to her daughter Susan, who curtsied and vanished.

December 19, 1792

"This was more than a year ago. Some conversation ensued," Hamilton went on to tell his visitors in the study of his home, "from which it was quickly apparent that other than pecuniary consolation would be acceptable. And it would take a harder heart than mine to refuse a Beauty in distress." The men nodded their understanding. "After this, I had frequent meetings with her." He gestured at the walls. "Most of the meetings were here at my house, many right here in this room—Mrs. Hamilton with our four children often being absent on visits to her father."

Muhlenberg, slumped in the couch, closed his eyes and shook his head, as if feeling the presence of Hamilton's paramour in the room.

"She was, and is, a very pretty woman," Hamilton observed, as if in partial expiation of his behavior. He instantly regretted saying that; the quality and power of Maria's attraction was ill described as prettiness. This genuine beauty had brought back into his life the thrill of dangerous adventure. He regretted his need to strip away her privacy, but saw little danger to her reputation because his account would remain in this room. Certainly these men of honor would not want to cause pain to his family by revealing any of this.

"Mrs. Reynolds did not indicate to us any amorous connection with you," Monroe said.

Hamilton nodded grimly. "The variety of shapes that this woman can assume is endless. In a few months, she told me her husband had solicited a reconciliation. I advised her to do it and she did, though we continued our intercourse. Her appearance of a violent attachment to me, and the pathetic importunings in her letters, made it very difficult to disentangle myself." It was important to impress upon his visitors that the impetus to continue the

William Safire

affair, like its origination, came from her; Maria was the seducer, conspiring with her husband to blackmail Hamilton, their victim.

"Then she told me that her husband had been engaged in speculation in claims on the Treasury," Hamilton recounted. "She said he could give me useful information about the corruption of some persons in my department. That was when I sent for him and he came to see me."

When neither investigator asked the reason, Wolcott put in, "What did Reynolds want from you?"

"Employment in the Treasury Department. I may have used vague expressions which raised his expectations. My situation with his wife naturally inclined me to conciliate this man, but the more I learned of him, the more inadmissible his employment in public service became. I hazarded his resentment by refusing. Whatever the impropriety of my private behavior, my refusal to put him on the public payroll demonstrates the delicacy of my conduct in its public relations."

"I think we need proceed no further," said Muhlenberg, his discomfort obvious at prying into a man's private passion.

"On the contrary, Mr. Speaker, I insist that you see everything, to lay this to rest once and for all."

Hamilton proceeded to lay out letter after letter, written in a feminine hand and with egregious misspellings, that he said had come from Maria importuning him to meet her, professing her love, confiding her misery: "Let me once more see you and unbosom myself to you. . . ."

He interspersed these purported cries for his affection with near-illiterate notes from James Reynolds pleading for money. One proclaimed he had discovered their affair and forgave them, wanting only $90 for his pain, another that "she is determined never to be a wife to me any more" because of her love for Hamilton. Reynolds then in effect offered to sell his estranged wife's exclusive affections to her lover.

"This proves that they acted in concert, from the start," Hamilton concluded, "to entrap me."

Wolcott, eager to believe his friend, was not sure that such collusion in entrapment was proven; it would be fairer to say it was indicated. He hoped the investigators would be too stunned by the sexual revelations to pursue this point, and was relieved when they did not.

"They tried to use my own vile weakness," Hamilton concluded, "to extort from me the employment of Reynolds in a position where he could debauch the public trust. Not only that, but they tried to bleed whatever money they could from my personal funds, which they mistakenly thought were limitless."

Muhlenberg was shocked into an apology. "We need trouble you no more, sir."

Monroe, however, was not completely persuaded. "There is the matter of Reynolds's visit to you after his release from jail and then his disappearance," he said. "His note to Clingman, the one with the part erased, says you were providing money for his flight."

"Nonsense," Hamilton retorted, "and the 'part erased' casts suspicion on the note itself. How am I responsible for his disappearance? Isn't it probable Reynolds fled to avoid detection and punishment in other cases, and was deeply in debt? What more natural than after being jailed for a crime, to run from creditors as fast and as far as possible?"

"That's only logical," Muhlenberg agreed.

"My crime is moral, not pecuniary," Hamilton said in summation. "I have cheated my wife, and am profoundly ashamed of my behavior, but I have never cheated the public by engaging in or permitting speculation based on advance information of Treasury actions." He paused. "Do you think this indelicate amour—deserving personal censure, but not involving the public monies—is a fit subject to be brought before President Washington?"

"No," said Muhlenberg.

"I am inclined not to trouble him with it," Monroe agreed, to Hamilton's evident relief. "But I want to put together the complete record before making that decision final." He gathered up all the letters on the table. "May we have your notes as well?" Hamilton, determined to demonstrate that he had nothing to hide, offered up his original notes, asking only that copies be made and returned to him. "Your privacy will be respected," Monroe assured him. They were all, after all, men of honor. "The copying will be done by the Clerk of the House and given only to us."

"Your conduct toward me has been fair and liberal," Hamilton said.

In the vestibule, as the visitors were getting into their overcoats, Wolcott with appropriate casualness approached the subject Hamilton wanted him to raise with Monroe for ultimate transmission to Jefferson. "You defeated John Walker in your election to the Senate last month, did you not?"

Monroe nodded yes. Wolcott knew that on Jefferson's order the compliant Virginia legislature had chosen Monroe to represent the state. It had rejected the sitting Senator, John Walker, who was Jefferson's lifelong friend and Monticello neighbor. As a result, Jefferson and Walker were now estranged.

"We hope you will tell your friend in Virginia," Wolcott added, "that the matter of Mrs. Walker need never see the light of day."

"I don't deal in cryptic messages," Monroe snapped. "What does it mean?"

"To be honest, I don't know," Wolcott said lightly. "But your friend may know."

Outside, Muhlenberg said, "I see no need to burden the President with this. Reprehensible behavior by all concerned—*Gott in Himmel,* right in his own home, maybe on the couch I was sitting on!—but not affecting the public business." He added angrily, "What a Jezebel that woman is!"

"His explanation is plausible," Monroe said. It could be that their intercourse had been sexual and not commercial, but if that were true, why had Hamilton been so eager to make certain the male Reynolds could not be questioned? Because Muhlenberg was so obviously convinced by Hamilton's seeming candor, Monroe chose his words with care: "We left Hamilton under the impression our suspicions were removed. That's just as well, because he did not ask that all the correspondence, and his notes, be destroyed."

That removal of suspicion may have been Hamilton's impression, but Monroe chose to remain doubtful. The blackmail story was persuasive to the easily shocked Speaker, perhaps, but it was self-serving, effectively cutting off further inquiry. Moreover, it was contradicted by Mrs. Reynolds and therefore not conclusive. Were those incriminating letters in her own hand, or forged? Their egregious misspellings did not befit her well-bred manner.

He handed Muhlenberg the thick file. "Have your man Beckley deliver a copy of these to Hamilton and the originals to me. If I am assigned the embassy to Paris, I'll leave them with"—he did not want to say Jefferson, and so picked up the phrase used by Hamilton's man Wolcott—"my friend in Virginia." Muhlenberg would understand that to mean Secretary Jefferson.

"And I'll ask Senator Burr to keep an eye on that Reynolds woman," the Speaker said, "in case her husband returns." He took the file from Monroe, agreed to have it copied and returned to him for safekeeping at Monticello, and pressed again: "But it's not for Washington's eyes, I trust. He loves Hamilton like a son, even now calls him 'my boy.' This would sadden him unnecessarily."

"The draft report to the President, with these exhibits, will not be completed or sent," Monroe promised.

He was determined to be as good as his word. First, he would send for the clerk, Beckley, a man with loyal republican instincts and a legible hand, to make a copy of the letters Hamilton had been induced to give them, and to return the copies to Hamilton. Next, before sailing for France as Washington's Minister, Monroe would deposit his report of the investigation, with the original letters attached, in confidence with Thomas Jefferson, who would be identified in this business only as a "friend in Virginia."

He asked himself the central questions: Was Hamilton telling the truth about being seduced and blackmailed? Or was the confession of adultery an ingenious tale, perhaps with a salacious germ of truth, to cover up the nefarious abuses of the public trust by the Treasury Secretary or some of his friends?

Monroe was glad he did not have to make a decision on that, which would have required a prompt and full report to President Washington. Undoubtedly, James Reynolds was a scoundrel and Clingman his dupe, but Monroe was ambivalent about Maria Reynolds. She was either a duplicitous Jezebel, as Hamilton had convinced Speaker Muhlenberg she was, or the mysterious young woman was a pawn in an elaborate scheme of concealment her husband and Hamilton had concocted.

What about Hamilton? Although Monroe suspected that he might have passed along information that made possible profiteering by his Federalist allies, the Treasury Secretary's confession of adultery and blackmail provided a plausible explanation for his payments to Reynolds. Evidence of financial dealing by Hamilton for his own profit was far from conclusive enough to take to President Washington; indeed, the President, who treated Hamilton as the son he never had, might associate Monroe's patron, Jefferson, with the unproven charges that led to the embarrassing revelations. That would never do.

This might be a matter for another day, to be pursued only if Hamilton's Federalists stifled the rise of republican government. The secret investigation of Alexander Hamilton, Monroe believed—whether rooted in an adulterous affair, as Hamilton shamefully asserted, or in corruption he so vociferously and perhaps creatively denied—was a sword best kept in the scabbard, to be drawn only at a time of political danger.

December 20, 1792

John Beckley sanded down the sharp tip of his quill slightly so as to lay a strong stroke of ink on paper, easily read. The Clerk of the House, as directed by the Speaker, made a copy of the fascinating letters to and from Hamilton and delivered them to Muhlenberg overnight, to be given to the Treasury Secretary.

As instructed, he deposited the original documents with Senator James Monroe for safekeeping with his friend in Virginia. The Senator was a republican with whom Beckley was well acquainted, though one was a high-born Virginian and the other an immigrant Englishman who arrived at the age of eleven as an indentured servant. Monroe and he, Beckley liked to think, were joined by a dedication to the defense of the American citizen's right to be free of taxes, Federal restraints, and forced service in armies that would surely be required if the government were to follow the call of Hamilton's empire-building high Federalists.

As not instructed, Beckley made another copy of the letters, along with Monroe's unsent memorial to the President, for himself. That was not because he thought of himself as a librarian at heart, a safe repository of documents that deserved to be preserved in archives. On the contrary, he made the copies because he knew it would give him a guilty thrill to re-examine them. The notion that men in high places could fall prey to the basest impulses of sex or greed—or both—fascinated him. And who knew what use could be made of such deep secrets one day?

With a length of red-tape imported from England, the Clerk of the House tied his copies of the documents into a neat bundle and locked them in his official safe. He looked out the window to see the nation's representatives hurrying back to the House after lunch as snow was beginning to fall. Beckley wrapped a scarf around his neck, pulled on his woolen greatcoat and put on a fur hat given him by a republican candidate for Congress in Vermont, Matthew Lyon. That republican Vermonter had little chance of winning but had ringingly denounced the Hamiltonians for "screwing the hard earnings out of the poor people's pockets to enable government to pay enormous salaries and vie with European courts in frivolous gaudy appearances." Beckley liked that kind of oratory in campaigning and had sent Lyon one of the few useful anti-Federalist pamphlets to help him in his speeches. Wearing the losing Vermonter's gift hat, he set out for the Philadelphia docks.

He wanted to greet two arrivals, each of whom might be helpful in articulating the republican cause. One was an Englishman, William Cobbett, who had written Secretary of State Jefferson a few months before from Paris. The letter, nicely phrased, had been passed to Beckley: "Ambitious to become a citizen of a free State, I have left my native country, England, for America: I bring with me youth, a small family, a few literary talents and that is all." Jefferson's reply had been politely dismissive: "Public offices in our government are so few, and of so little value, as to offer no resource to talents." True enough—the total employment of the State Department was seven, including the Secretary—but Cobbett, undiscouraged, had come to America anyway. He was in Wilmington, teaching English to Frenchmen, and had written to say he was coming to Philadelphia today on the packet. Beckley wondered what trouble had caused him to leave England. He hoped it had been plenty; writers angry with Britain and friendly to France were what the republicans needed.

The second writer Beckley set out to meet at dockside had a more urgent reason for running to America: James Thomson Callender was a fugitive from Scottish justice. Not for his scholarly excoriation of Samuel Johnson's dictionary, or for the anti-British screed *The Political Progress of Britain,* a polemical history by the Scot that Beckley had enjoyed. He was on the run for writing a pamphlet that urged his fellow Scots to rise up and throw off England's chains. The warrant for Callender's arrest on the charge of sedition had been passed on to Beckley by one of the immigrant radicals as a perverse recommendation. It read that the rebellious Scot was "an Outlaw put to his highness's horn, and all movable good and gear were escheat and inbrought to His Majesty's use."

Beckley waited in the frigid barn on the docks where passengers of arriving ships passed through. He put up his sign—"Clerk of the House"—so they could recognize him.

First to appear was Cobbett. He was a robust, six-foot-tall Englishman, with ruddy face and close-set eyes, the beginnings of a paunch, and redolent with confidence. He warmed his hands on a pot of tea and, to Beckley's "Tell me about yourself," spoke proud and plain: "I am charged with being a troublemaker. The charge is true. As a lowly corporal and regimental clerk in His Majesty's service in Newfoundland, I discovered that the officers were stealing much of the soldiers' pay. I had read Thomas Paine's pamphlet *The Rights of Man,* and I wrote one like it—*The Soldier's Friend*—demanding the courts-martial of the corrupt officers. For that I was considered a snitch and made a pariah."

"Are you a fugitive, Cobbett?"

"No, because I resigned the army before they could drag me before a drumhead court. I sailed to France, where I taught myself the language. But that land is filled with revolutionaries eager to cut the throat of King Louis and hot for war with Britain, and hardly the place for an Englishman. So here I am in the Colonies."

"Family?" The imposing fellow appeared to be on the fair side of thirty, and respectably turned out in long jacket, bright red waistcoat, breeches and clean stockings.

"As soon as I could afford it, I brought my wife Nancy and our infant. The baby died." He waved aside Beckley's condolences with "No, no—she is with child again, and this time will be better. I propose to teach English to Frenchmen in this city, charging each of them six dollars a month, more than I can get in Wilmington." He pointed to the sign above them: "What does a Clerk of the House do?"

"I take notes of the debates and votes, and distribute them to the members of Congress." That was his position by day; at night, in the coffeehouses and taverns, Beckley plotted the political takeover of Pennsylvania by supporters of Jefferson. For that, he needed radical pamphleteers and newsmongers with a gift for writing in plain words.

They were interrupted by the arrival of Callender and family. The fugitive Scot appeared with his wan wife and three shivering boys, all too thinly clad for the snowy weather. Beckley judged the wiry Callender to be in his mid-thirties, a few years older and a few inches shorter than Cobbett—

hungrier-looking, with dark hair and piercing eyes, dressed in what appeared to be the cast-off clothes of a sailor. The Clerk made the introductions and ordered some hot mulligatawny soup, a peppery stew from a recipe brought to the Philadelphia docks by emigrants from East India. Two of the boys sat on Callender's knees, while the oldest hung on his neck from behind, looking up at Cobbett warily over his father's shoulder.

"What sort of country is this, Mr. Cobbett?" asked Callender.

"This country is good for getting money, provided a person is industrious and enterprising. In every other respect," Cobbett added, "the country is miserable, exactly the contrary of what I expected."

"That's not what we expect," said Callender, taken aback.

"The land is bad; rocky. The houses are wretched, the roads impassable after the least rain. I was a farmer before I was a soldier, and I judge that America has fruit in quantity but not to compare with an apple or peach in England or France."

"It's cold, too," said the boy behind Callender.

"Freezing!" Cobbett agreed heartily. "And the people are worthy of the country—a sly, roguish gang."

"You've only been in America a month," Beckley put in, "and this is your first day in Philadelphia."

"You'll see," Cobbett assured Callender, "the natives are by nature idle and seek to live by cheating. But the industrious foreigner can do well here, for even rogues like to deal with an honest man."

"I'm curious," said Beckley, thinking of the materials he had under lock and key, "what you think of our newspapers."

"Tupp'ny trash," Cobbett snorted. "But the Americans who read, read nothing else. The fathers read the newspapers aloud to their children while the mothers are preparing breakfast."

Callender's youngest whimpered at the mention of food, and his father signaled to the waiter to hurry with the soup. "I saw copies of your *Aurora* in Edinburgh, when I was keeping from starving as a recorder of deeds," the Scot said to Beckley. "It's wonderful what you can say here about the government. In America, it is your happy privilege to prattle and print in what way you please, and without anyone to make you afraid."

"Some say," Beckley offered, fishing, "that it gets too personal."

"No man has a right to pry into his neighbor's concerns," Cobbett stated firmly, "and the opinions of every man are his private concerns—so long as he keeps them so. But! But when he makes those opinions public; when he attempts to make converts, whether it be in religion, politics or anything else; when he once comes forward as a candidate for public admiration—then, I say, his opinions, his motives, every action of his life, public or private, become the fair subject of public discussion."

Beckley looked at Callender, who was looking with relief at the arriving bowls of steaming soup. "I agree," he said. "The conduct of men in public stations is fair game." He was solicitous about feeding his wife, who was apparently with child and in some distress after the long ocean journey. He reached behind him to scratch the back of his neck; Beckley remembered well that everyone who stepped off that ocean-crossing vessel must be afflicted with lice.

"But in your book *The Political Progress of Britain*," Beckley said, "you did not discuss personal character when you were excoriating their laws."

"You wrote that book?" Cobbett looked up sharply. "No wonder they threw you out. All that inflammatory nonsense about 'the six or eight hundred years of botching to produce a constitution that is a conspiracy of the rich against the poor'? Never read such seditious drivel."

"Glad you read the book closely enough to remember that line," said Callender mildly, "and that it moves you so."

"Wait." Beckley was confused by Cobbett's patriotism. "You're afraid to go back to England," he said to the bumptious British immigrant, "because you offended the British army's officer corps and you may be arrested for sedition. Yet you think this man's book, critical of British history, is seditious drivel?"

"I am an Englishman, a subject of King George III. His government may be in error, and his courtiers may be corrupt, but every loyalist knows he reigns over the greatest country in the world." Cobbett broke off a piece of stale Philadelphia bread, looked at it coldly and set it back down. "In my brief stay so far in America, I have not met an American who, in his calm and candid moments, did not admit that his country was much happier before the rebellion than it ever had been since."

"You have just met one happy to be independent of that damned tyrant," Beckley said heatedly. "And I think what you have said is a bald-faced lie."

Cobbett rose to his full height and reached for his greatcoat. "Sir, I have never lied in my entire life. I rue the day when I thought of writing to your

Jefferson." He bowed to Mrs. Callender. "Madam, your three boys are models of good behavior and I congratulate you on their proper upbringing. Unfortunately, their father and his new friend here are fools. Good-bye."

"A prickly fellow," Callender observed as the Englishman stormed off. "If he writes as vividly as he speaks, he'll do well."

"Not in Philadelphia. King George is seen here to be a great villain."

"As well he is, but you Americans are free of his despotism. We Scots are not."

The oldest boy looked up between spoonsful and asked, "You suppose the big man never lied, not once?"

"Let me tell you a story, boys." Callender leaned back in his chair and looked at the high ceiling of the barn near the docks, the crowd now thinning out after the passengers had debarked. "Charles the Second of England had an unruly horse. He proposed to give the horse away to any one of his courtiers who could tell the greatest lie."

The children and their mother stopped eating to listen, as did Beckley. "During the competition among the members of the King's court," the Scot continued, "a country fellow came into the castle, for Charles was quite accessible. The man was told of the King's challenge and invited to furnish the biggest lie he could think of. 'May it please Your Majesty,' the man said, all offended, 'I never told a lie in my life.' And the King said, 'Give that man the horse! For that is the greatest lie that any man can tell.' "

The boys all laughed and banged their spoons. John Beckley reckoned that was the sort of anecdote that would register with readers of popular pamphlets like Tom Paine's. "I know a family with rooms to let, Callender. We'll take your wife and sons there, and then I want you to meet a printer friend on South Market Street. Matt Carey's an Irishman, a good red republican from Dublin doing a new edition of *Guthrie's Geographical Grammar,* in installments. Maybe you could do a section. Ask for twelve dollars a week, or two dollars a printed page. That's the going rate, and it's a start."

"Why are you doing this for me, may I ask?"

"Writers are needed for the anti-Federalist cause. There may come a day when you'll want to help us."

PART I

The Hamilton Scandal

Chapter 1

*J*ames Callender was seething. "Peter Porcupine," five years after their first confrontation on the Philadelphia docks, was after him again. The newspaper written and published by the Englishman William Cobbett, *Porcupine's Gazette,* shook in his hand as the Scotsman read it.

It was not enough for Cobbett to call him "Newgate Callender," a pun on the schedule of trials put out by London's Newgate Prison. Nor was Cobbett satisfied with ridiculing "this abandoned hireling, Callender" as afflicted with *mania reformatio,* a fictitious disease caused by an empty purse: "When the purse is full, the intestines are in a correspondent state," wrote Porcupine, "and the body is inclined to repose and the mind to peace and good neighborhood: but when the purse becomes empty, the sympathetic intestines are immediately contracted, and the whole internal state of the patient is thrown into insurrection and uproar." To top it off, Porcupine issued an invitation to Callender's hanging: "If this malady is not stopped at once, by the help of an hempen necklace, it never fails to break out into Atheism, Robbery, Swindling, Massacres and Insurrections."

As the target of Cobbett's gleeful vituperation, Callender could almost feel the "hempen necklace" around his neck. Nor was the favorite editorial defender of the Federalists and their British allies finished with him. Porcupine went on to vilify "a mangy little Scotsman who has a remarkably shy and suspicious countenance; loves grog; wears a shabby dress, and has no hat on the crown of his head; I am not certain whether he has ears or not." Callender, object of this vitriol, was particularly infuriated by Cobbett's attack on his personal appearance: "He leans his head toward one side, as if his neck had a stretch, and goes along working his shoulders up and down with evident signs of anger against the fleas and lice."

"It's a pack of damned lies," he said to the paper clenched in his hands. Callender had not been troubled with lice since he stepped off the ship from Edinburgh and met the pompous Cobbett on their first day in Philadelphia, five years before. And if he cocked his head to the side when he was thinking, what was wrong with that?

More damnable, in the Scot's eyes, was the way everybody who counted for anything, on both sides of every controversy, read the British loyalist. Even republicans—who could read Callender's frequent paragraphs in Benny Bache's publication, the *Aurora*—surreptitiously bought Cobbett's new journal. They wanted to have a laugh at their own kind and to see what the other side was saying in such plain and mutton-fisted words of inspired ridicule.

The 3,000 paying subscribers to *Porcupine's Gazette* far surpassed the numbers for the staid *Federalist Gazette,* and worse, journals all up and down the nation reprinted Cobbett's colorful fulminations about France's conspiracies to undermine the government. In five years, as Callender struggled to write, usually with no byline, in newspapers owned by others, the irrepressible Englishman Cobbett had marched from irregular pamphleteer to writer-editor of the most influential daily sheet of news and opinion in America. Though the first census in 1790 showed fewer than 4 million people in all of the United States, this Englishman's twenty pamphlets had sold a half-million copies.

Particularly galling to Callender about Porcupine's success was that he knew from personal experience that Cobbett often stretched, squeezed and tortured the truth. The Scot was not mangy; he bathed as often as he could, considering that the hot water was needed for his family. Nor was his countenance suspicious, as Cobbett claimed; he thought the more accurate word for his expression was skeptical. He remembered how women in his youth in Scotland—when he was the passionate poet who signed his name "Timothy Thunderproof"—told him his face was darkly handsome and his nose aristocratic. True, he wore no hat, but neither did he wear any man's collar. His hatlessness was by choice—it made him feel free—and if his habit of dress was not that of a dandy, it was only because the needs of their boys kept Callender and his wife from buying new clothes for themselves. And though he liked his ration of rum as much as the next man—perhaps a little more because writers needed a freedom of spirit—he felt it unfair to write that "he loved grog," as if he were a common drunk.

The one Cobbett charge he could not deny or ameliorate was the permanent emptiness of his purse. Callender was habitually short of money. At this moment, he was on the very edge of bankruptcy and was dyspeptically aware that his "internal state" was in the uproar that Porcupine so vividly described.

But he never doubted his ability to survive. In the five years since he came to America, Callender had survived the loss of intermittent newspaper jobs as well as Matt Carey's patronage. He survived the loss of his one regular job as stenographer making a record of Congressional debates. Most important, he survived, with his wife and now their four boys, the scourges of yellow fever that had killed every sixth person in Philadelphia.

Through all that, and added to his unfortunate habit of making enemies in every endeavor, he had been forced to suffer the sustained abuse directed at him from the established Federalist press. After John Beckley had arranged the publication here two years ago of Callender's anti-British history, that pro-British pack determined to discredit him was led by Porcupine, who branded him "Citizen Callender"—using the honorific assumed by bloodstained French revolutionaries. Cobbett took particular umbrage when Callender was the first to dare criticize George Washington's expense account and his curious advances on salary, along with the revered President's undue deference to Hamilton and his New York banker friends.

Now, on a muggy Philadelphia June day in this first year of the rule of the Federalist President John Adams, the Scot sat glumly in the borrowed upstairs office of Snowden & McCorkle's print shop. He was stung more painfully than he would admit by his rival's invective.

Callender had completed writing the first four parts of his projected *History of the United States for the Year 1796* but had not found enough subscribers to persuade the printers to set type. Because of this uncertainty of publication, he was too discouraged to write further. Callender's despondency had reached the point a month earlier at which he had written to James Madison, who had just quit the Federalist-dominated Congress, for help in finding a position in Virginia as a country schoolmaster or a journeyman carpenter. Today's blast from Cobbett had deepened the sorrow he felt for himself.

McCorkle, in a folded-paper printer's hat, used a hand blackened by ink to push his door open. "You have a visitor."

Callender expected no visitors because nobody thought enough of him to come. He did the calling on others, and had already called on everybody he knew to subscribe to his projected book. "Send him up," he said.

"Maybe you ought to come down and bring him up, if he is who he says he is. He claims he's Tom Jefferson."

Hope surged, mingled with panic. "No, you go down and send him up." He used the thirty-second delay to clean away the dirty cup and mess of old newspapers and dust off the unused side chair. He wanted to be seen working at the manuscript of his *History of 1796*.

He greeted the tall, redheaded Vice President of the United States at the door and awkwardly ushered him in. Jefferson had run second to John Adams in the Electoral College vote for President; the prize for coming in second was the Vice Presidency. Like Adams before him in Washington's Administration, the newly elected Vice President had nothing to do but let others prepare to back him for President again four years hence. He, of course, could not appear to be interested. That would be unseemly and only confirm Federalist accusations that he was motivated by personal ambition.

Jefferson interrupted his effusions of what a great honor it was. "I thought you might be somewhat melancholy today, because Porcupine's quills are sharp, and this would be a good time for us to meet. I admire your writings."

Callender put on a modest smile; he was happily aware of that. He had already made much of a remark Jefferson was reported to have said about the abuses of English power recounted in the Scot's *Political Progress of Britain* after its publication in America: "The work contained the most astonishing concentration of abuse I have ever heard of." Jefferson's overheard remark was phrased confusingly—the abuse was by Britain, of course, not by Callender—and Callender didn't bring it up for fear Jefferson would deny having said it, or complain about Callender's self-serving use of his commendation in print. But praise from the writer of the Declaration of Independence provided an opening that cried out to be followed up.

"My writing is not very lucrative, I'm afraid, sir." Callender was eager to use this opportunity to press for financial help. His plea to Madison had gone unanswered; perhaps this visit had been stimulated by Madison passing his letter on to the Vice President.

To his surprise, Jefferson reacted positively to the hint that he needed money. "I'm concerned that the republican press in Philadelphia might totter for want of subscriptions. We should really exert ourselves to procure them," the Vice President said, "for if these papers fail, republicanism will be entirely browbeaten."

"And that goes for books, too, Mr. Jefferson." What did one call a Vice President? Excellency? That title went against his grain. He would stick to "sir" or "Mr." Though nervous, Callender tried not to fidget, lest he seem to be lice-infested; Cobbett's mean-spirited skewering kept everybody on the defensive. "I keep Tom Paine's *Rights of Man* right here on the shelf, sir, the American edition Benny Bache turned out in the *Aurora*'s printshop, with your endorsement."

Jefferson's expression clouded, but Callender reached for the book, opened it to the first page, and pointed delightedly to Jefferson's courageous endorsement of the work by the English radical so beloved by the French and despised by aristocrats in England and their Federalist followers in America. "Here, where you say that Paine's work published here will prove an antidote to 'the political heresies which have sprung up among us' "—Callender pointed to Jefferson's endorsing line—"that took great political courage. Everybody knew the heretic you had in mind was John Adams in his Federalist screed *The Doctrines of Davila.* "

The Vice President nodded glumly. "All I did was send Paine's pamphlet to a friend, with a brief note. But the printer published my note, to my astonishment, at the head of this edition of *The Rights of Man.* "

"But surely you are glad to be associated with Paine's work," Callender insisted.

"In my note I tell Adams freely that he is a heretic," Jefferson admitted, "but I certainly never meant to step into public print with that in my mouth."

Evidently, the new Vice President was not as courageous as Callender had hoped. Even so, at that expression of the great man's need for discretion, Callender felt drawn into his confidence.

"I understand from friends we have in common," Jefferson said, coming to the purpose of his visit, "that you have a book in work. How soon—"

"Here. Here it is, sir." Callender gathered the sheaf of pages, with his crabbed writing on them, spread out on his desk. "The printers are eager to set it in type. They're urging me to finish."

"May I be a subscriber?"

"That would help a great deal, Mr. Jefferson. Oh, yes. Not just in the number of books you order personally, but by virtue of your show of interest, others will surely follow." He was about to say how he would use Jefferson's name to get other subscribers but, in light of the admonition about discretion, cut himself short. He would do that first and apologize, if he had to, later.

Jefferson leaned back, reached into his pocket, took out three bank bills and laid them on the writer's table. "Send me however many copies fifteen dollars will buy."

Fifteen dollars would feed Callender's sickly wife and four always-famished boys for weeks. Moreover, the Vice President's presence in the office must already have impressed both Snowden and McCorkle. They would surely fling the news of the visitation in the face of Matt Carey, whose domination of republican printing they were eager to crack. Jefferson's name at the head of the printed subscribers' list, Callender knew, would bring in other republicans across the range of Paineites. These subscribers would range from Southern anti-monarchists to Western farmers who resisted Hamilton's whiskey tax, and from people put off by the self-importance of President Adams to all good American friends of the radical republicans of France.

"John Beckley might have some suggestions for other subscribers," the Vice President added. "Monroe is still on the high seas on his way home from France, but Madison, Israel Israel, and Marshall Smith of Pennsylvania should be interested in your work." Almost as an afterthought, and in an even quieter voice, he added, "And perhaps there is some assistance I can give you in a pecuniary way when the volume is finished. Are you almost done?"

"A week or two, no more. . . ."

"Are you getting all the information you need? I know that Beckley is somewhat troubled by the events of last week."

John Beckley had just been fired as Clerk of the House, though he had held the job since Speaker Muhlenberg's day. In the Presidential campaign of 1796, however, the tall, spare functionary, always dressed in black, became an active republican partizan, daring to derogate the retiring Washington's second term, organizing and ultimately carrying the State of Pennsylvania for Jefferson's candidacy. Such partizan agitation invited Federalist retaliation; when Adams won the Presidency, the Federalists in the House threw Beckley out of his job as soon as the new Congress convened. The new Vice President had no power to stop them.

So Beckley was Jefferson's choice to be go-between. Callender counted himself a journalist who knew a signal when he heard one. Every now and then, Beckley—enjoying a glass of rum with Callender in a bar or writing pseudonymously as "The Calm Observer" in one of the republican organs trying vainly to compete with Porcupine—would drop a hint that he had damaging material on a Federalist in high office. Cobbett had even teased Beckley in print about those sinister hints, and the Clerk had backed away. Now he was surely filled with resentment at his ouster, and at the glee with which Cobbett hailed the partizan deed by calling him "the first of the bricks to fall from the Temple of Anarchy." The longtime government functionary was now reduced to advertising for law clients in Bache's *Aurora*.

"That was a dirty deed of the Adams men in the House," Callender said fervently, "firing Beckley after eight years. Where were our republicans?"

"They were prevented by the suddenness of the call and their distance from being here on the first day of the session," said Jefferson. "And so we've lost the ablest clerk in the U.S. An outrage."

"To the Adams men, he was guilty of politicking in Pennsylvania for you," the Scot chimed in. While Jefferson had stayed serenely above the electoral battle, as was the custom, Beckley had delivered the votes that made Jefferson runner-up to Adams and Vice President. "There's no end to Adams's lust for vengeance," Callender told his visitor. "With Monroe recalled from Paris, and Edmund Randolph sent packing out of the Adams Cabinet, now the Federalists are reaching right down to the clerk Beckley. They have the power now, and no President Washington to even try to balance the scales. There's nobody left in the government but you, Mr. Jefferson, for those who believe in the rights of man." Callender faulted Jefferson for having quit Washington's Cabinet as Secretary of State, leaving Hamilton and his faction to dominate the field, but had never written that and was now thankful for his caution.

"The new changes excite a fear," the Vice President agreed, unwinding his long body from the chair, "that the republican interest has lost." Yet it seemed to the heartened Callender that the Vice President was hardly fearful. By virtue of this visit to a republican writer, and by the unexpected of-

fer of financial aid from himself and his political supporters—not to mention the suggested avenue of information to Beckley—Jefferson was hinting that the republican cause was far from lost.

The languid Virginian bid him farewell with a casual invitation: "I'm
staying at Francis's Hotel." He motioned for Callender to stay at his desk to
finish his book, and walked downstairs unescorted.

Callender waited until he heard the front door close. He bolted down
the steps, and waved the three $5 bills in the faces of both Snowden and
McCorkle, beginners in the printing trade who had never before assembled
a subscriber list. The Scot shouted, "He gave me a joe!"—the full value of a
Portuguese gold coin—and then made a beeline for a tavern near Francis's
Hotel, where Jefferson lodged amidst a nest of like-minded Congressmen.
Republican scriveners like Callender and agitators like Beckley had made
that convivial drinking place a second home.

Chapter 2

June 19, 1797 (Evening)

"Put James Madison down for twelve copies," Beckley
said expansively. He poured Callender and himself another glass of rum.
"I can speak for him. And another twelve for James Monroe, who should
be home from France any day now."

Callender knew that Beckley could indeed speak for Madison and
Monroe, Jefferson's two leading acolytes. He assured the former Clerk of
the House that all good republicans were aware that it was Beckley's skill at
press persuasion and political agitation that had made possible Jefferson's
surprising victory in Pennsylvania. Without those electoral votes, Jefferson
would not have come in second and been Vice President today.

"Jefferson's throwing a very grand dinner to welcome Monroe home,"
Beckley said. "It will be at Oeller's Hotel on the first of July. I'll be there, of
course, along with fifty republican members of Congress. Pity they don't
invite poor miserable scriveners, James, or you could come."

"Twelve copies for Madison, same for Monroe," Callender noted down, "and when you buy twelve, you get a thirteenth copy free. I have the addresses." He put aside the quill and took up his glass of Madeira. "To your success in the law."

"I'm broke, James," Beckley blurted with inebriated honesty, "forty years old and out of work. I co-signed some notes when I was Clerk, and now that I'm not, they're after me. And I have my family here and my family back in England to support." He slumped over the bar. "You know, the only time they removed anybody from clerical office was for misconduct. Never for faction. They changed the rules on me."

Callender was no better off financially, but now at least he had prospects. "I thought you owned land in Virginia."

"Greenbrier? Nobody wants to buy it. You want to buy ten thousand acres in the wilderness? Make a fortune someday. But it's worthless now. I'm advertising in the *Aurora* for clients as a lawyer. Benny Bache isn't charging me for it."

"You'll get them," Callender assured him. "You made a great record as Clerk and everyone knows that it was the Federalist politicians who turned you out."

"But then there's Cobbett. I think he's going to come after me in his filthy gazette, kicking me when I'm down. He's been asking about a little mistake I made in the House on the Jay Treaty."

"Don't tell me about Peter Porcupine." Callender poured his companion another glass and reminded him of their common enemy. "You saw what he wrote about me in his sheet today. Cobbett is still soreheaded about what I wrote about Washington after he signed that treaty."

"You were dead right about Washington, the old hypocrite." Beckley had given Callender the story of the President's extraordinary advances against salary. The Scot had written that Washington—who claimed at first he wanted no salary at all—was drawing money from the Treasury faster than Congress had authorized. The *Aurora* printed it and the President was said to have been furious. Served him right, Callender thought, for signing John Jay's treaty that served British commercial interests at the expense of the American farmer.

"Somebody had to criticize the President," Callender said. "The Federalists were hiding behind his famous 'integrity' up and down the country."

"You were right with us, Jimmy. Nobody else was willing to say that

Washington could no longer expect to be viewed as a saint. For God's sake, for four years running, the President was in debt to the United States!"

"If ever a nation was debauched by a man," Callender agreed, "the American nation has been debauched by Washington. Let's hope Adams will be an improvement."

They drank in silence awhile. "We took Washington off his pedestal," Beckley went on. "Probably why he didn't run for a third term, couldn't stand our criticism."

"You mention that blackguard Cobbett," Callender said, steering the conversation toward his object. Jefferson had said the Clerk had some information for his *History of 1796,* but Callender did not know if the cautious Vice President had directed Beckley to pass it along. He had a suspicion, however, about the subject. He extracted a couple of cuttings from an envelope in his jacket. "Here's something you wrote not long ago, as 'Calm Observer,' that intrigued me. You asked 'whether a certain head of a department was not in the month of December 1792, privy and party to a certain inquiry of a very suspicious aspect, representing real mal-conduct on the part of his friend, patron and predecessor in office?' I calculated that to be Treasury Secretary Wolcott and his predecessor, Hamilton. Right?"

Beckley would not say. "And then you went on to ask in this piece," Callender continued, " 'Why has the subject been so long and carefully smothered up?' "

Beckley nodded acknowledgment that he wrote it but offered nothing more. Callender held up a cutting from *Porcupine's Gazette* of only a week before. "Now here's Cobbett, saying you're bluffing. 'Pray, Mr. Beckley, if you are really in the possession of these valuable secrets of official misconduct in certain high characters, was it not your duty, long since, to have disclosed them?' Cobbett then goes on about 'such threats are either the ravings of approaching insanity or the fretful foamings of a weak mind.' The bastard."

"It's the real bastard who's at the root of it all," murmured Beckley.

Now Callender felt he was getting somewhere. He took that remark to refer to Hamilton, whose mother on the island of Nevis had been unwed.

" 'Fretful foamings,' " Beckley muttered. "That's what Porcupine says now. When the time is ripe, we'll see who's the mad dog."

"How soon might we see this information, John? No need to keep it 'smothered up,' as you say. It may be hard for you to practice law here in

Philadelphia, with the newsmonger that everybody reads hooting at you this way, for bluffing."

"Don't press me, Jimmy. Before I let any of that go, there's somebody I have to see first. It's too soon."

Who had to authorize Beckley to let slip the story he had been hinting at? Not Jefferson; Callender judged it was unlike him to ever let his hand show. Madison? That high-principled fellow would never dirty his delicate hands by touching the subject of mal-conduct. Monroe? "Would that somebody be anybody you could talk to tomorrow, to release you from any bond of secrecy?"

"No."

That direct answer pointed to Monroe. The ship bringing him home from France was not to arrive for three days. Callender could feel a thumping in his breast. Monroe was said to be a cautious and calculating man and, when he arrived, might well counsel Beckley to continue "smothering up." He might want to wait until a more propitious moment, such as during a presidential election three years hence, if Hamilton were a candidate. Or Monroe might fear, if a scandal were spread across the public press so soon after his return, being blamed for spreading it himself.

Whatever the republicans' interest, Callender was certain it was in the interest of his book that the news be in hand quickly, before Monroe arrived. Indeed, he could publish a part of the book on the day the Jeffersonians gathered to honor Monroe at Oeller's the next week. That would take some fast writing and typesetting, but it was not impossible—if Beckley would confide in him tonight or, at the latest, tomorrow.

"I don't want to press you, John, because your pledge of confidence is sacred. But in view of Mr. Jefferson's personal interest in my book, and the fact that you can trust me completely—"

"Stop. Not another word. I have to talk it over with someone first."

Callender, frustrated, finished his rum, bid his reluctant source good night and trudged homeward. He picked his way through the mud of Second Street, then over to Front Street, close to the Delaware River. The humid air was oppressive. He could hear the distant, nocturnal croaking of the frogs in the mosquito-laden swamps. At 64 Dock Street, he turned in to his house. His wife, the three older boys, and the new baby boy were asleep. What, he asked himself as he eased into bed, could induce Beckley to talk before James Monroe's ship arrived?

Next morning, Peter Porcupine struck again. His target this time was the ousted Clerk of the House of Representatives. Cobbett charged John Beckley with the most corrupt act that could be taken by a recorder of the votes of the House: deliberately miscounting a close vote as a tie rather than allowing the winning party to win. Nor was the vote run-of-the-mill legislation: The appropriation of money to implement the Jay Treaty was the most crucial vote of that year, following President Washington's most controversial decision about foreign intercourse. To impute chicanery to its count was to forever besmear the reputation of the official counter.

Quoting Beckley's feeble defense that the miscount had been only "a casual and unintentional mistake," Cobbett lit into the hapless republican: "Although I have never entertained a very high opinion of John Beckley's political principles, I confess I did not believe him to be that whining, pining, cringing, contemptible creature he has shown himself on occasion of his removal from office. He has merited his fate, and shame and contrition should stop his mouth . . ." With this broadside, Porcupine discredited the republican complaint that rank partizanship was the reason for the firing of a well-qualified official; the real reason, Federalists could now insist, was at the least the Clerk's ineptitude and at the most his corruption.

Callender showed up at Beckley's door with a copy of *Porcupine's Gazette* under his arm. The former Clerk, whose career as a lawyer now looked most unpromising, was in his sleeping shirt and unshaven.

"I read it already. I've been expecting you."

Newspaper delivery to the door before breakfast, a Cobbett innovation; another reason his *Gazette* was outselling the republicans' *Aurora*. They sat down over a pot of tea in Beckley's kitchen. After sympathizing as only a fellow victim of Cobbett's could, Callender offered the immediate opportunity of vengeance. The assault on the Clerk's integrity was rooted in Federalist politics and the counterattack had to be not personal but political. Callender assumed the subject of scandal had to be Hamilton because if it were Adams, it would have been used in the recent campaign. "Any assurances of secrecy given to Hamilton by any of our leaders no longer bind you, John. No man of honor, especially a Virginian, would expect you to suffer this slander in silence."

"Jimmy, that history you're writing," Beckley said finally. "If I were to make available some historic material, how soon could you put it out?"

"How soon do you want it out?"

"It would be good to distribute at Monroe's homecoming party at Oeller's. You'd have to start writing around the clock right away."

"If it has to do with Alexander Hamilton and wrongdoing at the Treasury Department," Callender said eagerly, "I won't have to sleep for a week. If even a part of what you give me sells, as I expect it to, I can put out the rest of the book later as Part Two."

"Oh, this'll sell, all right. And it will bring down a powerful man who would be President, maybe even King. But it's not the financial scheme that you think."

"Tell me what it is, then."

"You won't say who you got it from?" Beckley raised his right hand as if administering an oath. "Under any circumstances?"

"As God is my witness."

"And no mention will be made of Thomas Jefferson or James Monroe as the original repository of this material?"

"My solemn oath," Callender swore. "The Vice President, you know, is the first paid subscriber to my *History of 1796.* Fifteen dollars he put here"—he showed his palm—"in my hand. What is more, Jefferson promised he is going to help me in a pecuniary way later. But not a word of that can ever come out." As proof of closeness to the great man, the Scot was sure, nothing could impress the practical Beckley more than real money passed and pledged.

"The time has ripened, Jimmy. Wait here." He walked out of the kitchen in his bare feet and returned a few moments later in a robe and slippers, carrying a bundle. He unwrapped it, placing a sheaf of papers and letters, bound in ribbons of red-tape, on the table. "These contradictory documents need the interpretive eye of an historian."

"I am that, as you well know, John."

"And they also need the fine touch and the fearless nature of a genuine scandalmonger."

"I can be that."

Chapter 3

June 21, 1797

PHILADELPHIA

*N*ever in the hiſtory *of* the press anywhere in the world, Callender knew, had anyone written such a scathing blast at a public figure and been able to buttress the charge with damning documents. The journalist profoundly engaged in public political struggle—Callender now knew himself to be that, more than mere historian or pamphleteer—felt he needed some justification for exploding this bomb. A simple lust for political vengeance by a broken Clerk would not do.

The higher-minded reason he chose was the Federalists' recent vilification of America's Minister to France. A farrago of their insults directed at James Monroe, Jefferson's Virginia supporter, was crowned by his ignominious recall from Paris by President Adams. Callender had to ask himself: Would adopting this as his motive for exposing Hamilton make Monroe appear to be the source of his confidential documents? He shrugged that off; he owed Monroe nothing, and it was a good way of throwing Federalist hounds off the scent of Beckley. "The unfounded reproaches heaped on Mr. Monroe," he explained, "are my motive for laying these papers before the world." Tit for tat.

"We now come to a part of the work," Callender wrote, "more delicate, perhaps, than any other." He could hardly hold his quill for wanting to rub his hands. "In the arts of calumny and detraction, the publications of the Federal party exceed, beyond all proportion, those of their adversaries. Hireling writers like William Cobbett, whose shop is so often secretly visited by the British Ambassador, describe Mr. James Monroe, our late envoy to France, as 'a traitor who has bartered the honor and interest of his country to a perfidious and savage enemy.' The friends of *order*, for such they call themselves, set no limits to their rage and their vengeance. They cannot expect to meet with that tenderness that they refuse to grant."

They started it, he told himself, the British agent Cobbett and the rest of the stock-holding Federalist press. Now he, James Callender of British-enslaved Scotland, would give them back a taste of their own. Callender assured his readers with consummate delicacy that he would not tamper with the text of the long-secret memoranda and letters, despite his personal aversion to invective and expressions that harshly convey disgust. "They are here printed from an attested copy, exactly conformable to that which, at his own desire, was delivered to Alexander Hamilton himself."

With documents in hand, Callender could almost let the story tell itself. He began, slowly, with Speaker Muhlenberg—the Lutheran minister who carried great weight with the many Americans of German stock—printing his statement of how Jacob Clingman came to him with allegations of improper transactions of Treasury Secretary Hamilton. Then to Monroe's account of an interview in prison with James Reynolds and that culprit's false promise to tell the whole story to Congress's investigators as soon as he was released the next day. Next, Callender placed before the reader Muhlenberg's memo of the visit to Maria Reynolds, revealing her possession of notes from Hamilton. That included her testimony that she had burned many letters from Hamilton to her husband, the Secretary's offer of "something clever"—money, of course—if the Reynolds couple would just go away. Especially damning was Maria's expression of strong doubt that Hamilton would be found to be "immaculate" in his Treasury dealings. The editor wondered: Was that merely intuition on her part, or did she know something about him that did not appear in the documents?

He let the drama in the Hamilton papers unfold. Clingman's affidavit reported that Reynolds had told him Hamilton had made $30,000 by speculation, and had paid thousands to Reynolds for his help over eighteen months of secret communication. Most damaging was Clingman's report that the vanished Reynolds claimed to have the list of Virginia veterans whose claims were being bought up by the speculation ring conspiring with the dishonest Treasury Secretary.

Callender allowed himself some hyperbole in his summation of how Hamilton and his ring had bilked the public by taking advantage of a too-trusting Congress: "The funding of certificates to the extent of perhaps thirty-five millions of dollars, at eight times the price which the holders had paid for them, presents, in itself, one of the most egregious, the most impudent, the most oppressive, and the most provoking bubbles that ever burlesqued the legislative proceedings of any nation."

Callender, writing for the first time with exclusive documentary evidence of wrongdoing in hand, was satisfied he had made the most of what he had. "Are there more letters?" he asked Beckley, who had joined him in his office above the printers' shop.

"Not in the packet I had."

"Where is Reynolds now? Can I talk to him?"

"Disappeared. Hasn't been heard of for years."

"Did he take Maria Reynolds with him?"

Beckley said no. "I think she and Clingman are down in Maryland or Virginia. Don't confuse the readers with all that. Publish what you have."

"You mean she left Reynolds and ran off with Clingman?" Callender recalled the young man's testimony that he had been alone with Mrs. Reynolds late one night when Hamilton came to the Reynolds house with a message. "There's more to this, isn't there?"

Beckley was evasive. "Colonel Burr knows a lot about what happened to our fair Maria. He arranged for her divorce from Reynolds. But you have all I can give you, Jimmy. Make the most of it."

"But is there anything," Callender pressed, "any document you know of, that exculpates Hamilton? I don't want to be accused of suppressing anything. That's why I didn't cut a word out of the documents. Too much is at stake here."

"Are you worried about going to jail?"

Callender considered that. Nothing he wrote went beyond the evidence in the documents. But were the copies made by a clerk authentic? He was forced to trust Beckley, his only source, who was using him as a conduit without telling all he knew. "Who has the original letters, in the original handwriting?"

"When Monroe went to France, he left them with a friend. A respectable resident of Virginia."

Presumably, Jefferson himself. Callender came at his question obliquely: "Was Jefferson informed about all this five years ago, when it happened? Has he been keeping evidence of corruption in the Treasury to himself all this time?"

Beckley said yes, Jefferson had been kept fully informed at the time. He added that the copies were true copies of originals that he had personally seen.

Callender began to feel uneasy. Hamilton was a formidable figure in the world of power, a crafty player unlikely to crawl into a hole when Callender published. He would lash back with everything he had to make the journalist appear to be a vicious, libelous hireling of radical, seditious political enemies. The documents showed that five years ago, when Hamilton had only two days to prepare a defense, he had been able to persuade Monroe and Muhlenberg not to take the matter to the President, and indeed to cover up the entire episode. Who knew what sort of defense the articulate New Yorker would present now that he had these five years to prepare?

"I'm going to hold a little something in reserve," Callender decided. "We're going to publish in installments anyway, so let me keep this Monroe memorandum about his suspicions to myself for a while. Let's see how Hamilton reacts, and then we can return his answering fire with another broadside."

"You're holding back the juiciest part."

The memo he would hold back was Monroe's account of the evening at Hamilton's house. Part of it read: "Hamilton informed us of a particular connection with Mrs. Reynolds; the frequent supplies of money to her and her husband on that account; his duress by them from the fear of a disclosure."

Monroe was being discreet, Callender suspected, by referring only to a "particular connection." If Maria Reynolds had been committing adultery with Clingman, she could also have been committing it with Hamilton. Or not; perhaps Hamilton had deceived the investigators by falsely claiming that his sin was merely wenching with Mrs. Reynolds, not making great sums of money secretly with Mr. Reynolds. Callender suspected that might be how, on that night five years ago in Hamilton's mansion, the target of the investigation had been able to conceal the abuse of his Treasury powers— by appealing to the male code of discretion in an illicit affair. By throwing the dust of adultery in their eyes.

"Your friend Monroe was being a gentleman at the end, wasn't he, John?"

"A man of honor, but not a fool. Look at this line"—Beckley was intimately familiar with every nuance in the documents—"where it says, 'We left Hamilton under the impression our suspicions were removed.' That says to me Monroe was unconvinced by Hamilton's story. When the Colonel sees that, he'll go off like a bomb."

The best part of Callender's strategy of holding back the memo was that it boxed Hamilton in. No political figure in his right mind, he was certain, could claim publicly to be betraying his wife as a defense against betraying the public trust. How could he face his supporters? How could he face his wife and her whole influential Schuyler family? Callender did not want to be the one to suggest a peccadillo in this case, which might divert attention from the more serious matter. Financial wrongdoing, not adultery, was his focus.

"I would let all the documents out at once," Beckley advised. "Let the gossips do their work."

"No, no. Let's see what he says. And then we'll be in a position to hit back." More to the point, he could make more than double the money on a second installment. "Everybody who buys *The History of '96* will want to buy the supplement, if he takes the bait."

"Ah, Jimmy," said Beckley, the Calm Observer, "you're becoming a man of trade."

Chapter 4

OLIVER WOLCOTT

June 30, 1797
NEW YORK CITY

*W*hen **Secretary of the Treasury Oliver Wolcott read the** booklet that was Part V of *The History of the United States for the Year 1796* by James Thomson Callender, he saddled his horse and set out on the three-hour ride to the New York home of his mentor and predecessor. No messenger would do; Wolcott, who had been a witness to the confrontation five years before, knew he had to be at Hamilton's side when he read the publication that was being perused by every public man in Philadelphia.

"There's not a word in here about my explanation that it was all a blackmail plot," Hamilton snapped when he finished reading the detailed account, with many documents reprinted in full, of the secret investigation of five years before.

"That explanation, because of its delicate nature, was not recorded in the documents, if you recall," said Wolcott. "Apparently, this man Callender was given the papers but is not privy to what you told the investigators actually happened." That was just as well, he thought; he had never liked the notion of using one scandal to obscure another. Alexander Hamilton, the nation's first Treasury Secretary and architect of its financial system, stood accused of meeting secretly with thieving speculators and having enriched himself while in public service at the expense of veterans of the War. It seemed to Wolcott, his successor in that office in the Adams Administration, that such a charge was damaging enough without being compounded by a desperate defense that revealed a sordid marital infidelity.

Callender's booklet shook in Hamilton's hand. "This is James Monroe's doing. He gave me his word that night that it would all be kept confidential, and the scoundrel broke his word."

"The Minister must surely be angry at his abrupt recall from France," Wolcott conceded, "and he has cause to blame all Federalists, you in particular, for his humiliation by Adams. But Monroe arrived back from Paris only this morning. There wasn't time for him to give the documents to Callender and have them in print today. Do you suppose James Madison—"

"It was Monroe's doing, Oliver, whatever the timing. Madison is weak and somewhat honorable. He wouldn't have the stomach for this sort of thing. Monroe, with Burr and John Marshall and Lafayette, all served with me in New Jersey in the Revolution. He's as stiff and stubborn now as he was then. I wish we were still on the same side."

"What about Jefferson himself? He's probably the 'friend in Virginia' Monroe left the papers with when he went to France."

"No, Jefferson never dirties his hands. James Monroe has the motive and knew where the copies were." Hamilton paced the floor of the library of his elegant home, slapping the Callender booklet against his leg. "That night in '92—did you tell Monroe afterward that we knew about John Walker's wife, and direct him to inform Jefferson of that?"

"I remember passing along such a message." Wolcott was on the verge of asking what the reference had been to Jefferson's Monticello neighbor, but decided it was probably information that was better not to know.

Wolcott felt that Hamilton's initial reaction did not deal with the problem at hand. "How do you want to respond to that book you're holding? Not publicly, I hope." His own reputation, as Treasury's Comptroller under Hamilton at the time, was in jeopardy. Wolcott did not want to be tainted with any imputation of impropriety, of which he was totally innocent, especially since he was the one who first wanted to prosecute Reynolds. He was vulnerable to criticism only in one respect: letting the villainous Reynolds go to save embarrassment to his Treasury superior.

"First, I'll respond through you to Monroe," Hamilton said. "Go to him and demand a declaration from him now equivalent to that he made to me that night—that I was totally innocent of any financial wrongdoing."

"He'll say that his memory has faded," Wolcott said, being realistic.

"Then refresh it with a memorandum by you of exactly what transpired that night."

Wolcott frowned, trying to remember having written such a memorandum.

"Which we will write right now." He sat Wolcott at his desk and pushed forward a quill, ink and paper.

> In the month of December 1792, I was witness to an interview of Alexander Hamilton . . .
>
> The conference commenced with Senator James Monroe reading certain Notes upon which suspicion rested. Mr. Hamilton entered into an explanation and by a variety of written documents, ready fully evinced, proving that nothing in the transactions had any relation to speculations in claims on the United States, or any official transactions whatever.

"Now say how absolutely convinced they were."

> This was rendered so completely evident that Speaker Muhlenberg asked Mr. Hamilton to desist from exhibiting further proofs.

"But I wouldn't let up," Hamilton reminded him.

Mr. Hamilton insisted upon being allowed to read such documents as he possessed, for the purpose of obviating every shadow of doubt respecting the propriety of his official conduct.

"Until they said I was completely exonerated."
Wolcott wrote on:

> After Mr. Hamilton's explanation terminated, Messrs Monroe and Muhlenberg acknowledged

"Both acknowledged," Hamilton corrected. "Monroe is the key."

> both acknowledged their entire satisfaction that the affair had no relation to official duties, and that it ought not to impair the public confidence in Mr. Hamilton's character.

"They were sorry they even brought it up," Hamilton dictated.

> Mr. Muhlenberg expressed his regrets

"Monroe, too." Wolcott did not want to make a false statement that Monroe could refute, so assumed that Muhlenberg spoke for both, and wrote instead:

> They expressed their regrets at the trouble which the explanation had occasioned.

"I hope you don't intend me to backdate this," Wolcott said.
"Date it today, and sign," Hamilton ordered the Secretary. "Then go to Monroe and give him a letter I shall now write."

Hamilton told himself not to let his fury get the better of his judgment, but then ignored his own advice. He took the quill from his former deputy and wrote on a fresh page:

James Monroe, Esq.: July 5, 1797: I ask you to attest to this account of our interview. I shall rely upon your delicacy that the manner of doing it, will be such as one Gentleman has a right to expect from another.

Wolcott, looking over his mentor's shoulder, urged him to stop at that, but the infuriated Hamilton had to get in a rebuke about the unauthorized disclosure.

You must be sensible that the present appearance of the papers is contrary to the course which was understood between us to be proper and includes a dishonorable infidelity.

"He's not going to like that 'dishonorable,' " Wolcott cautioned. "Monroe's a Virginian—you know how important honor is to them."

"No more than mine is to me." Hamilton, anger at his tormentor rising with every moment, was aware that he might be taking the step that would precipitate a duel. Much as he despised the code duello, he did not care. On second thought, and as a concession to Wolcott's advice, he added a word making it "dishonorable infidelity somewhere."

Wolcott was trying to placate him further. "Monroe is sure to want to think it over, sir, and to talk to Muhlenberg. You know you won't get an immediate response from Monroe."

"Meanwhile, the whole country will be talking about this." Hamilton, who had shown his understanding of the need to mold public opinion in *The Federalist Papers* two decades before, was aware of how such word was spread. "Every republican sheet will reprint the worst of this part of Callender's book, and then commentary on top of that. The 'democratic societies' will post it everywhere. This slander cannot go unanswered. I have to make some kind of statement now."

"That would be unwise, Colonel. Stand above all this. Don't feed the fire."

"I know what I'm doing. Send up Fenno." Hamilton referred to John Fenno, the Philadelphia editor whose publication the Federalists sponsored. "I'll have a letter for his *United States Gazette* making clear that I was investigated and exonerated. And if that doesn't staunch the wound, I'll have more later. Much more."

Hamilton was aware that Wolcott departed for his Treasury office in Philadelphia with a sense of great unease. Hamilton was glad to have such a loyal friend with him in this, though he could have done without his successor's high-mindedness about backdating his memorandum.

No sense of guilt whatever attached to his personal financial dealings while in command at Treasury in Washington's Cabinet. At the time, he had even rid himself of valuable holdings at a loss rather than have it appear to be in conflict with his duties. He had been poorer when he left the government than when he went in, a statement few could make, including the tower of integrity Washington himself. Some of Hamilton's friends and family had been knaves, and in retrospect perhaps he might have been more severe with them, as Wolcott and Richard Harison had counseled at the time, but nobody could truthfully say that Secretary Hamilton was not personally honest to a fault.

But what did Callender, the hireling of the republican *Aurora,* care about truth? His only interest was in helping Jefferson and Madison and that icicle Monroe seize power from the government and distribute it to the States, returning the country to a loose confederation of sovereignties, encouraging disorder, abetting disunion. He slapped the writer's damned booklet against his leg a few times, pacing around the library. Who could contradict today the account he gave to Muhlenberg and Monroe five years ago? James Reynolds, he had been assured, was a sailor usually at sea and in deserved obscurity. Young Clingman knew nothing of importance firsthand. Maria Reynolds had obtained a divorce from her husband a couple of years ago in New York, represented by Aaron Burr, the republican New York lawyer who had long been a thorn in his side. Hamilton suspected that Burr and Maria had known each other all too well years ago; were they still friends? That could spell trouble.

He sat down on the maroon leather library couch. He thought again about that Reynolds woman, what she had done to and for him, and the poignant way she refused to argue with him five years ago, the last time he saw her. One of Hamilton's informants had reported that Maria and her daughter were living in Maryland, probably with Clingman. Though he could not be certain, he was willing to gamble that she would be disinclined to come forward now to dispute his account by claiming he had forged her letters. Though he had savaged her privately in his defense, he had never intended to brand her a whore and a blackmailer publicly; that would be Monroe's doing, and Callender's. But further notoriety could do her no good. All Maria could do now was to hide her identity and protect her daughter.

He tapped the rolled-up Callender pamphlet lightly against the arm of the couch. With his other hand, he stroked the supple leather seat of the only major piece of furniture he had transported from the library in his Philadelphia home. He had paid a foolishly large sum for its carriage when he returned to New York, but it was his souvenir of the unforgettable Maria Reynolds.

Chapter 5

July 3, 1797
PHILADELPHIA

*I*n his suddenly bustling office at Snowden & McCorkle, the most successful new printing establishment in Philadelphia, Callender read that morning's *Gazette,* edited by the Federalist hireling Fenno, with glee.

"Hamilton's decided to engage me," the newly invigorated Scot said. The former Secretary of the Treasury had confirmed the accuracy of the published documents and then tried to wriggle out of responsibility for his actions. "Listen to what Hamilton writes, McCorkle: *'The inquiry was politically motivated. Two of the most profligate of men sought escape from prison by the favor of party spirit. One of the inquiring Congressmen was my known political opponent'*—he means James Monroe, who went out of his way to avoid partizanship in this. *'A full explanation took place between the Congressmen and myself in which by written documents I convinced them of the falsehood of the accusation.'* "

Callender, finger trembling in his excitement, pointed to a key paragraph in Hamilton's quick response. "Now see this base canard, McCorkle, the lie that gives me my opening: *'They declared themselves perfectly satisfied with the explanation, and expressed their regret at the necessity which has been occasioned to me in making it.'* Hah!"

"What's the lie?" the printer asked.

"Oh, I wish Beckley were here, he'd see it in a minute." He rummaged through papers on his table for the original memorandum from Monroe, and held it up. "Here is what Monroe wrote just after the interrogation at Hamilton's that night. Look at this line: '*We left him under the impression our suspicions were removed.*' Does that sound like a man who, as Hamilton now says, was 'perfectly satisfied with the explanation'? Hamilton, five years ago, thought he got away with it—which was evidently what Monroe wanted him to think. But Monroe wrote down that he remained suspicious— Hamilton's explanation, whatever it was at the time, did not resolve all doubts."

A postscript to the investigators' memo of that night was the keystone of Callender's planned riposte. In it, Monroe re-introduced Maria Reynolds—how Callender wished he could have met that mysterious belle, who either manipulated men or was cruelly abused by them, he couldn't be sure which—with this passage: "*Mr. Clingman called on me this evening and mentioned he had been apprized by Mr. Wolcott of Hamilton's vindication. When he told that to Mrs. Reynolds, she appeared much shocked at it and wept immoderately.*"

"That postscript is the key. Why, McCorkle, do you suppose our beautiful Maria was shocked to tears when she heard about the presumed vindication of Hamilton?"

The sturdy printer was catching on. "Because she knew Hamilton's explanation was false?"

"Exactly! You're beginning to understand what you printed. Here's the investigators' report of what Clingman told them about Maria's reaction: '*She denied the imputation & declared it has been a fabrication of Colonel Hamilton, and that her husband had joined in it and even told her so. Reynolds had given Hamilton receipts for money and written letters, so as to give countenance to the pretense.*' You see? Hamilton and Reynolds conspired to make Maria seem to be the reason for their late-night dealings in stocks and government bonds. The money that passed was ostensibly for her assistance because of what Monroe called the 'particular relationship' Hamilton was supposed to have had with her."

"What's a 'particular relationship'?"

"It's what happens when a man and woman are in bed together, Mc-Corkle." Callender had to marvel at the daring of Hamilton, Wolcott and his fellow conspirators. "I'm only guessing now, but I think the explanation Hamilton gave the investigators for his dealings with Reynolds was that he was committing adultery with his wife."

"Do you suppose that was true?" The printer did not seem able to get his mind around the idea that one of the founders of the nation was confessing to such a sin, and that Callender, his attacker, was suggesting the confession might be untrue.

"Who cares if it was true or not?" Callender answered. "The explanation is a diversion intended to throw the investigators off the trail of Reynolds and the money. Remember, Clingman said—in a note made contemporaneously, not cooked up five years later—that Maria told him that her husband was with Hamilton the morning after he left jail. After that visit of Reynolds to Hamilton, the investigators found out that Reynolds had run off to New Jersey or somewhere. Obviously, he ran off at Hamilton's instigation, so he could not talk to the Congress."

Such encouragement of a witness to take flight, in Callender's mind, was damning. "Now here"—he brandished one of the documents given him by Beckley—"is Monroe and Muhlenberg in their conclusion: *'Clingman was of the opinion that Maria Reynolds was innocent and that the defense created by Hamilton and James Reynolds was an imposition.'* "

"What's an imposition?"

"A damned lie, McCorkle! The hint of adultery was a false story imposed upon the truth to mislead the unwary!"

"But nothing you've written makes the slightest suggestion of this, uh, imposition. Not a hint, even. That would be an awful libel."

"Fear not. The astute reader can infer any such odious explanation from the documents themselves."

Callender could hardly wait to see the next installment of his *History of 1796* in print. The book, by being published in a series of newsmaking pamphlets, was helping to make the history of 1797, because it was already pitting the Federalist Hamilton directly against the republican, democratic, anti-Federalist Monroe. No longer would the deep political differences between the factions be limited to printed debate in pamphlets, usually under pseudonyms, augmented on occasion through the hireling daily press of each side. Now the clash was out in the open and intensely personal, with the protagonists calling each other liars and a thirsty public lapping up the salacious details of a purported scandal.

"I hope Hamilton doesn't add to his reply with a barrage against us," said the worried printer. "He can really write, you know. It would be terrible if we were successfully refuted."

"Don't be a fool! Stop thinking like a printer and think like a newsmonger—this is an advertisement for our next installment."

"Can we get the same subscribers?" McCorkle was dubious.

"No time to get subscribers. Print first, and you'll have buyers lining up at the door. Every republican newsmonger in America will be scratching at the window for a copy."

"But this postscript that you set such great store upon, that had Maria weeping. Who wrote it?" asked McCorkle. The papers were copies, in a clerk's hand, and no signature was under the memo or the postscript. "It says only that *Clingman called on me.* Who was the 'me'—Muhlenberg or Monroe? That's important, isn't it?"

Callender revised his estimate of the printer's acumen. Even McCorkle was aware that the authorship of the postscript was vital, and the unsigned document provided no answer. Muhlenberg was no longer Speaker; having voted for Washington's unpopular treaty with Great Britain, he had been defeated in a bid last year for Pennsylvania Governor and his political career was finished. Monroe, on the other hand, was a figure of current controversy. He had been insulted by President Adams with his recall from France, and was an anti-Federalist known widely to be allied with Jefferson and Madison, and as such had become the darling of the repressed republicans.

"Of course the authorship of the postscript is important. Good for you for catching it, McCorkle. Let's print Monroe's name, alone, after the postscript, along with Maria's charge of forgery and conspiracy. It's obvious to me he wrote it." Putting Monroe's name under what Monroe had neglected to sign was not another instance of forgery, he told himself; it was merely informed attribution. And the printed signature would more likely draw a personal counterattack on Monroe from Hamilton, generating more controversy that would serve republican interests, not to mention the journalist's own.

Callender decided not to wait for Hamilton's promised reply in detail. That might take a month. Instead, he would take quick advantage of his adversary's blunder in falsely claiming that his explanation had convinced the investigators to exonerate him. The editor knew he had been shrewd to hold a little something back; a shocking revelation need not be a one-pamphlet thing. If the fish took the bait, a stream of booklets and articles could be developed, with circulation building at each new refutation and revelation in the scandal. Callender grinned, certain he had set his hook firmly in the great man's mouth.

Chapter 6

JAMES MONROE

July 5, 1797
NEW YORK CITY

$\mathscr{T}$he James Monroes arrived at a hotel on New York's Wall Street by stagecoach from Philadelphia. The grand banquet welcoming them back to America, held at Oeller's Hotel, had been a notable success, attended by Jefferson and every republican legislator left in the capital in mid-summer. Monroe knew the event was more than a personal welcome home; it enabled the anti-Federalists to conspicuously honor a diplomat known to be friendly to the French at a time they were denying President Adams the money he wanted for armed forces to oppose France.

The ostensible purpose of the Monroes' trip to New York was to visit Elizabeth's family after their long service in Paris. But the recalled ambassador was keenly aware that his presence in New York meant a confrontation with Alexander Hamilton.

A few days before, he had received Hamilton's letter demanding a sweeping exoneration, which the newly unemployed Virginian was not inclined to give. Muhlenberg, a Lutheran pastor and forgiving sort—and still a Federalist in good standing with Hamilton's party—was likely to accede to the former Treasury Secretary's wishes. But Monroe had no cause to make Hamilton's possible bid for the Presidency in 1800 any easier for him; on the contrary, any taint of scandal attaching to Hamilton would help Jefferson overturn the Federalists. Let General Washington's favorite, whose near-monarchist advocacy of "energy in the executive" had caused Jefferson such pain in the first Cabinet, suffer a little.

Unpacking at the lodgings took time because the stagecoach had been largely filled with dresses his wife had brought back from Paris and was eager to show New York friends. Elizabeth at thirty was seen to be a cool beauty, but Monroe admired her reserve, which was much like his own.

"You never told me about your investigation of Colonel Hamilton," she chided him. "All the ladies are buzzing about it, especially the hint of an affair with that Reynolds woman. I don't know one of my friends who doesn't find the Colonel powerfully attractive."

"It was a private political matter," he said, helping her open a trunk, "and I couldn't be sure the charges were true. Don't feel left out. We didn't tell President Washington, either."

"But you were genuinely surprised at the news when it appeared. Did it upset you?"

"Surprised, yes; upset, not really." Publication of most of the papers relating to their investigation of the association of Reynolds with Hamilton did not trouble him a whit. Let the man whose British sympathies undermined the Monroe mission to Paris feel some pain, if not of remorse at least of embarrassment. The Reynolds matter was never fully resolved, and only his and Muhlenberg's sense of fairness in giving the accused the benefit of the doubt prevented the documents from reaching the President or the press five years before.

"You'll be blamed for putting it out, you know," his wife said. "You have the motive."

"Impossible." Elizabeth graced any dinner party with her easy correctness and high fashion, and usually took little interest in politics—the perfect wife of a politician, offering domestic tranquillity. She was no Angelica Church, who entranced both Jefferson and her brother-in-law Hamilton with her good looks and worldly good sense, or Anne Bingham, who be-dazzled George Washington with her salon. "We were on the high seas when the documents were passed to Callender, my dear. There is no way I can be blamed for arranging for their publication."

Only recently had he learned that Jefferson was supporting the man's book with his subscription, and perhaps some other gifts of money through third parties. He had left all the originals of documents gathered in his investigation with Jefferson, who at that time and now showed an intense interest in the potential scandal. Monroe presumed the Vice President still had them in a strongbox at Monticello. There was irony in that: only when Hamilton asked for copies for himself had John Beckley, Clerk of Muhlenberg's House, become involved. Somebody—Beckley, probably—made an extra set, which Monroe presumed was the source of Callender's exposé.

There was always the possibility that Jefferson himself had passed the materials on to Callender, but Monroe set that disturbing thought aside. Most likely it was Beckley, acting on Jefferson's behest or what he thought was his behalf.

Evidently, the slandering pamphleteer did not have copies of all the documents. Monroe, the first installment of Callender's book in his hand, noticed that a key postscript was left out: his assessment of Clingman's testimony that would, if it ever saw print, prove most damaging to Hamilton. The unpublished memorial reported Maria Reynolds's dispute of the excuse Hamilton was presenting; her stunning suggestion that her husband and Hamilton were forging and imposing false evidence; and Monroe's own careful distancing of himself from any exoneration. He recalled writing that the investigators had only "left Hamilton under the impression" that all doubts were resolved. That, if published, would surely direct Hamilton's ire solely at him. The Virginian was just as glad Beckley had not passed that inflammatory memo along to Callender.

A messenger arrived from Hamilton with a note asking for an immediate meeting here in New York. Monroe replied he would be available at ten the next morning. Remembering Hamilton's wisdom in arming himself with a witness at their last encounter—Wolcott was a trusted aide who would furnish a detailed account, drawn to his former boss's specifications, five years later—Monroe wrote that Hamilton could bring anyone he liked this time as well, but made certain he, too, would have a witness of his own.

Who? David Gelston, a republican Congressman from New York with no personal animus toward Hamilton, came to mind, but Monroe wanted someone of a craftier nature to help deal with the most brilliant adversary of the Jeffersonians. Aaron Burr had recently been defeated for re-election to the New York Senate. A man of quicksilver ideology, Burr was useful to the republicans. Years before, Monroe had recommended him to General Washington to be Minister to France, but the President didn't trust him— some minor transgression during the Revolution cast a shadow over Burr in his mind—and that foreign assignment fell to Monroe. Jefferson was also wary of the man; Monroe remembered him cruelly calling Burr "a crooked gun whose aim or shot you could never be sure of." But Burr was a New Yorker, a political ally, sufficiently anti-Hamilton though not a Jefferson acolyte, and Monroe knew he would be eagerly available.

Hamilton strode into the room, introduced his brother-in-law, John Barker Church, and said, "I presume the motive and cause of this meeting is pretty well understood." At Monroe's nod, Hamilton sat, then rose again to pace as he launched into a lawyer's presentation of the case he made five years before.

After listening to twenty minutes of monologue, Monroe interrupted him. "Excuse me, but what does all this mean? I was there—all this history is unnecessary."

"Unnecessary?" Hamilton became visibly hot under his stiff collar. "I shall come to the point directly, then. I wrote you a letter. I expect an immediate answer on so important a subject, on which my character and reputation, and the peace of my family, is so deeply interested. Your delay is intolerable." Hamilton took a few deep breaths to help contain his anger. "Your postscript of five years ago, which I had never before seen until this morning, casts doubt on my explanation that it was blackmail, not financial speculation, that was the cause of my commerce with Mr. and Mrs. Reynolds."

"What postscript?"

"Right here, in that scoundrel Callender's latest installment. It arrived in the mail last night, probably on the same coach you took from Philadelphia." He handed it to Church, who handed it to Burr, who handed it to Monroe.

Reading the second installment for the first time, Monroe recognized the central document. Its postscript contained his line about leaving Hamilton "under the impression" that suspicions were resolved—but which in Monroe's mind, at least, had not been resolved at all. No wonder the proud and sensitive Hamilton was up in arms; all these years, the former Treasury Secretary thought he had persuaded the inquisitors of the truth of his story.

Callender had skillfully placed Hamilton's freshly published assertion that the investigators had been satisfied with his explanation next to Monroe's five-year-old memo with its damning postscript to the contrary. The effect of the juxtaposition was to catch Hamilton in a blatant lie. Monroe did not recall signing the postscript, but presumed he had, because his name appeared at the end of it in the printed version.

"If you would be temperate and quiet for a moment," Monroe rejoined, "I will answer you candidly. When I received your request in the post"—Monroe did not characterize Hamilton's tart letter as an insolent demand, which he thought it was—"I thought it proper to meet with Mr. Muhlenberg and answer you jointly. Unfortunately, he has not been in Philadelphia. When we can get together, we will reply."

"After my reputation is ruined?"

"I am not the cause of your present distress, Hamilton. After the meeting in Philadelphia that night five years ago, I sealed up my copy of the papers and delivered them to my friend."

"Who was—?"

Monroe was not about to reveal it was Thomas Jefferson. "A respectable character in Virginia."

"And how did they just happen to come recently into the hands of a scurrilous newsmonger?"

"I had no intention of publishing those papers." The former ambassador went further: "I declare, on my honor, that I knew nothing of their publication until I arrived from Europe and was sorry to find they were published."

"That's a totally false representation."

Hamilton's words hung in the air. Monroe stood up, as did his adversary.

"Did you just say I represent falsely?" Monroe had never in the thirty-nine years of his life been called a liar. And he had just made a declaration on his honor, which to a Virginia gentleman was as good as under oath.

Normally a controlled man, Monroe felt a fury surge in him, and told Hamilton what he really thought of him: "You are a scoundrel."

Hamilton rose as well and stared at him for a long moment. "In your recording of Clingman's last miserable contrivance, I think you were actuated by motives malignant and dishonorable." He issued his challenge: "I will meet you like a gentleman." Monroe was familiar with the code duello; those words meant a fight that often resulted in a death.

"I am ready," Monroe replied. Seeing himself as the challenged party, he took advantage of making the choice of weapons. "Get your pistols."

"Moderate yourselves, gentlemen, be calm," said Church, interposing himself between them. Placing his hand on Hamilton's chest, he told his wife's sister's husband: "I fought a duel last year, in England, and I can assure you it's never a good idea."

Burr also stepped in, as Monroe hoped he would, putting his hand on Monroe's shoulder and urging him to take a seat. "This is based on a misunderstanding. It need not become an affair of honor."

As Church managed to get his brother-in-law to a seat as well, Burr said, "If you please, Colonel, I would like to make a proposition."

Hamilton, ashen-faced, said to his New York political adversary, "By all means."

"Mr. Monroe has satisfied your inquiry as to that part of the business that relates to publication of the pamphlet," Burr reminded him. "He has said unequivocally that he had nothing to do with it. Surely you, on the word of honor of a gentleman, accept that." When Hamilton was silent, Burr hurried on, taking the silence as assent. "As to your wish for a written reply, Mr. Monroe should soon return to Philadelphia and expeditiously seek out Mr. Muhlenberg. The two of them should then satisfy your request promptly."

Burr then provided a moment's delay in a way that Monroe, regaining his composure and not eager to fight a duel, thought especially skillful. "Mr. Church, perhaps my proposition ought to have been made with more propriety to you." In the code duello, a second did not address the other second's principal; the momentary delay also reminded all the men in the room how close they had come to the presence of death.

"No need," said Hamilton, showing he understood Burr's subtlety. By choosing to accept Burr's direct address, rather than through a second, the former Treasury Secretary took a step back from the formal procedure leading to a duel. "When will you be returning to Philadelphia to see Muhlenberg?"

Monroe said in three days, on Friday, because he had to begin work on his own book refuting the calumnies heaped on him by Federalists here while he was trying to represent the United States in Paris. Hamilton gave a grunt assenting to Burr's proposition that his principal, Monroe, consult with Muhlenberg. He added he would be in Philadelphia on Sunday to get the inquisitors' joint reply.

"Any undue warmth that occurred here today," added Church, "or unguarded expression that happened during this interview, should be buried. It should be considered as though it had not happened."

Monroe caught Burr's quietly triumphant glance. He was relieved; though Burr was a crack shot, Monroe was not, and would have had to take lessons from Burr in the art of killing with a pistol if he had been required to face Hamilton. But now was not the moment to show relief; on the contrary, Hamilton's desire to pretend that the meeting had never taken place was to be a point of pressure.

"In that respect," said Monroe, not wanting to be seen as backing away from a challenge, "I shall be governed by Colonel Hamilton's conduct." He left unsaid that if any report of that scoundrel Hamilton's doubting of his word appeared in Porcupine's Federalist sheet, then Bache in the republican *Aurora*—or even the vitriolic Callender—would have the accurate account from Burr promptly.

"I think that any intemperate expressions should be forgotten," said Hamilton.

"Agreed," said Burr and Monroe as one.

"You understand," Hamilton added in a civil tone, "that your postscript implied that your suspicions that I speculated in government securities were still alive. That is intolerable to me."

"Whether the imputations against you as to speculation," Monroe replied, giving no ground on the key point, "are well or ill founded depends on the facts that appear against you and upon your defense."

"From that I infer a design to drive me to the necessity of a formal defense," said Hamilton, "while you know that the extreme delicacy of its nature might be very disagreeable to me."

That was Hamilton's problem and the anti-Federalists' hope: that Hamilton would fall into the trap he set for himself five years before. He was now faced with the need to make public his private defense of confessing adultery to assert his financial honesty. Monroe shrugged and left.

Chapter 7

*T*he full title was *Observations on Certain Documents Contained in No. V & VI of "The History of the United States for the Year 1796," in Which the Charge of Speculation Against Alexander Hamilton, Late Secretary of the Treasury, Is Fully Refuted. Written by Himself.* It immediately became known across a scandalized and titillated nation as "the Reynolds pamphlet."

As soon as he heard about it, Callender raced over to John Bioren's print shop to buy two copies. There was Hamilton's "confession" in excruciating detail. "The charge against me," he began, "is a connection with one James Reynolds for purposes of improper pecuniary speculation. My real crime is an amorous connection with his wife Maria, for a considerable time with his privity and connivance, if not originally brought on by a combination between the husband and wife with the design to extort money from me. This confession is not made without a blush."

Then followed thirty-five pages of self-justification, with a fifty-page appendix of letters and memoranda from the time of the investigation to the most recent contretemps between Hamilton and Monroe. Devouring it with his eyes, Callender grew more elated as the apologia went on and on. It excoriated Maria Reynolds as a "woman who could assume any shape"— no more than a conniving slut—and incredibly argued that his admission of adultery rather than dishonesty showed "the delicacy of my conduct, in its public relations."

Callender kept one copy to examine closely and refute the refutation, especially the passages that reviled him. He underlined "Does this editor"— Hamilton meant him—"imagine that he will escape the just odium which awaits him by miserable subterfuge?" Nothing could please Callender more than to be personally engaged by the object of his attack. He was no longer a mere historian; Hamilton had elevated him to the role of participant in the history of his time.

The other copy he delivered to Thomas Jefferson's lodgings with an excited note: "If you have not seen it, no anticipation can equal the infamy of this piece. It is worth all that fifty of the best pens in America could have said against him."

He underscored a footnote in which Hamilton slyly suggested that Thomas Jefferson, Vice President of the United States, had improperly corresponded with a distant Reynolds associate who was in debtor's prison and asking for money. Jefferson had written back politely declining, but Hamilton insinuated that the very fact of the correspondence suggested that the source of his troubles was Jefferson. Callender noted: "The most pitiful part of the whole pamphlet is his notice of you."

The excited Scot found Beckley sitting behind a glass of rum and an open copy of the Reynolds pamphlet at the bar of Francis's Hotel. Callender slid onto a stool next to his source for the documents that ignited Hamilton's self-immolation.

"This is good for President Adams, you know," said Beckley.

"How so?"

"Hamilton was planning to challenge Adams for the support of Federalist voters in 1800. Now Hamilton can never be President. A man who carried on with a whore in his own home when his wife was away? And then brought shame on his wife and children by confessing to it publicly, just to save his precious financial reputation? Never."

"It's immensely helpful to Jefferson," Callender reminded him. That was surely his own and Beckley's purpose behind the revelation of the corrupt speculation, now given ever-widening currency and an entire new dimension of scandal by Hamilton's incredible Reynolds pamphlet.

"Perhaps, perhaps not," said Beckley. "What strengthens Adams is not good for Jefferson or the republican cause. It's good for Aaron Burr, too—with Hamilton out of the way, he is now in position to carry New York by appealing to both Federalists and anti-Federalists."

"Quite a trick." Callender doubted that any political figure could prevail by being all things to all men, but Beckley knew more about elective politics than he did.

"Burr can be everybody's friend, you know. He represented Maria Reynolds in her divorce suit, and must have used what happened here"—Beckley tapped the pamphlet on the bar—"as her grounds for divorce. Defamation of character by her husband, reported and endorsed by Hamilton."

"How could she afford Colonel Burr's legal services? She's penniless, isn't she?"

"Ah, James, ever the innocent on matters of human passion. You can see venality in every politician of every stripe, but you impute virtue to every young woman."

Beckley had it wrong, and Callender was determined that he not be taken in by Hamilton's story. "I believe Maria Reynolds. Hamilton is lying about an affair with her and a blackmail plot. Don't you see? That's his way of covering up the damning evidence of his financial dealings with Reynolds at Treasury. So much correspondence by Hamilton could not refer exclusively to wenching. She's telling the truth, not him."

"What about the letters from her that Hamilton publishes in this pamphlet?"

"Forgeries, just as she claimed. He made them up himself to show he was the victim of a plot. Nobody's seen the actual letters from Maria."

Beckley had a good idea. "Why don't you ask Hamilton to show you the originals?"

"I will," Callender promised. The haughty New Yorker would probably reject any contact, but his very rejection of a challenge to produce the original letters from Maria would be part of Callender's answer to Hamilton's long rebuttal. "He won't, of course, because he doesn't have them. The so-called letters from Maria don't exist. Do you know where Maria is?"

"Burr stays in touch with his client. He says she's living with Clingman in Maryland."

"That means Hamilton could produce her before a magistrate to prove she is lying," Callender said. "He could force her to give a sample of her handwriting to compare with the notes from her that he claims he has. But he won't do that."

"How can you be sure?"

"Because his notes are forgeries and she is telling the truth. Hamilton is lying in his teeth, Beckley, and you know it. You know how he traded in Treasury securities on behalf of his brother-in-law, Church, when he knew what the price of bonds would be. He was guilty of making money from his place at the head of Treasury, and dreamed up this adultery story to cover it up."

"Nobody in the world is going to believe that, James. Not even President Adams thinks the Treasury was run dishonestly. Just the opposite—I hear he's telling friends that Hamilton suffers from"—Beckley took a breath, looking at the ceiling of the tavern to recall the exact phrase—" 'a superabundance of excretions which he could not find whores enough to draw off.' "

"A superabundance of excretions? Too much semen? Adams said that about Hamilton?"

"It's true. Sometimes men in the same party despise each other."

Callender knew he couldn't use that inflammatory phrase in a pamphlet; it would be denied and he'd be sued for libel, and lose. "But Maria is not a whore," he insisted. He groped for the softer word: "She's an adventuress, perhaps, ill used by powerful men. But we have to believe her if we are to refute Hamilton's defense."

That would be hard. Everyone would want to believe Hamilton's false confession of illicit sex because that was more delicious to gossip about than complicated Treasury theft. Hamilton had fashioned an effective defense, if his central concern was the probity of Treasury and not the feelings of his family or his future in politics. Even the President of the United States was taken in. "Did President Adams really say Hamilton suffered from 'a superabundance of excretions'?"

"Don't repeat it, for God's sake. I only tell you that so you know it's in Adams's interest to watch you destroy Hamilton, his rival next time. Don't make a fool of yourself. You brought down the man who was General Washington's right arm. You ruined the political future of the most brilliant political writer in the country, our Madison not excepted. Now let the matter lie."

Callender did not want to feel alone in his efforts. "We all brought him down together, John. You and me, and Monroe and Madison and Jefferson himself. I am the agent, the conduit, and proud to be—but not the principal here."

"When they come down on you, James, you cannot say you got anything from me."

Callender felt a chill. He made no pretense to himself or to the public, as Cobbett so often did, that he was a fearless voice for liberty. He had barely escaped being hunted down for sedition in Scotland, was still under indictment there, and had no desire to seek refuge elsewhere again. If Hamilton succeeded in changing the subject to sex, then it would be James Callender who would be identified as the man who revealed the most salacious scandal in the brief history of the Republic.

That was not his purpose. Callender saw himself as the heroic exposer of serious violations of the public trust, not the chronicler of personal sin. Abuse of great power was his enemy, not a public man's sneaking about with a private paramour. If Hamilton were believed, Callender would not be hailed for exposing crime in high office, but hated as the snitch that forced an honest man to reveal his weakness in betraying his marriage vow. Unless he refuted Hamilton's daring smother-up with more facts about financial chicanery, the pamphleteer would find himself under the "just odium" of the Federalists—and at the same time secretly despised by his own kind.

But Callender knew he was not totally naked to his enemies. He said nothing to Beckley about his personal contacts with Jefferson, or about the Vice President's direct financial help and warm encouragement, oral and written. That was between the great man and himself.

WILLIAM COBBETT

"Listen to this," William Cobbett said to his wife. "This woman comes to Hamilton's door, he says, and asks him for money. He says he will bring it to her house. Then, he writes: 'In the evening I put a bank bill in my pocket and went to the house. She conducted me into a bed room. I took the bill out of my pocket and give it to her.' Then comes a dash after the period, indicating an excision, I suppose because the printer was too embarrassed to offend the common decency with the next line in the manuscript. Then his printed confession picks up: 'Some conversation ensued from which it was quickly apparent that other than pecuniary consolation would be acceptable.' *Other than pecuniary consolation*—do you hear that, Nancy? What a turn of phrase! That milksop!"

"I think it cruel of him to burden his wife with the shame of a public confession," said Nancy Cobbett. "Not to mention the pain to the harlot Maria, if such she is. The moral guilt is his, the man of wealth and power, even more than his unfortunate paramour. She was probably pushed into a life of sin by her miserable thief of a husband."

"Noah Webster agrees with you." Webster, editor of New York's *Minerva*, was a low Federalist, suitably anti-French, and—though egregiously permissive in his softheaded opinions about a bastard "American language"—was usually in alignment with Cobbett in lashing the republicans. He turned to that day's *Minerva* and read aloud Webster's opinion: " 'What shall we say to the conduct of a man who could deliberately write and publish a history of his private intrigues, degrade himself in the estimation of all good men, and scandalize a family to clear himself of charges which no man believed! Such a man is unfit to administer the government.' Well said, I'm sorry to say, and from our side. Good English, at least, from Webster—that impudent vagabond juggler whose utmost exertion was the compilation of a school-book."

"Will you be writing about this awful affair, William?"

"As little as I can. Even if Hamilton is telling the truth about his financial purity, and I presume he is, a claim of sexual immorality is no defense. Adultery is just a different manifestation of dishonesty. And his panicked assertion of it is a sign of weak character." He felt, but would not admit to, a twinge of envy at Callender's coup. The seditious little Scot had done some original reporting that provoked the great Hamilton into a terrible blunder.

Cobbett decided to change the subject to moral abdication on a political level. He took up his pen: "When we view the second magistrate of the United States, Vice President Thomas Jefferson, erecting the standard of opposition to the Government; when we see him rallying around it a host of malcontents, and taking a position as the chief of a faction; when we see him openly vindicating the insults and aggressions of a foreign nation,

France—when all these shameful and degrading circumstances are reviewed, what are we to think of Jeffersonian morals?"

Determined to ignore the Reynolds pamphlet, he decided to follow that up with an attack on one of the host of republican malcontents. He had already characterized Matthew Lyon, an Irishman from the bogs of Hibernia elected Congressman, as "the beast of Vermont," suggesting he needed caging by loyal Americans. Cobbett identified Lyon as having been an indentured servant in Ireland, no better than a slave. The arrogant Irisher had refused to join the formal procession marching in deference to the new President's inauguration, claiming that such royalist ceremonies were not in keeping with a democratic republic. Peter Porcupine denounced that as the typical pap of French radicals. Lyon had also offended Cobbett by taking the side of the Society of Quakers protesting "the oppressed state of our brethren of the African race." Porcupine considered such sowing of dissatisfaction among the slaves to be a sly way of helping France to conquer the United States: if the war between France and Britain spilt over to the New World, France would count on a slave revolt in America to help in its invasion of the South.

Cobbett had learned from Robert Goodloe Harper, a Federalist Congressman who wanted to shut the door to aliens (and whose speeches Cobbett occasionally wrote in exchange for information), a nice tidbit about this low-life Irish England-hater. It seemed that Lyon had been abusing his franking privilege by sending out two hundred letters a week and enclosing in them copies of the *Aurora,* Bache's radical red sheet. Nobody in Congress had dared do that much for *Porcupine's Gazette.* But Cobbett had also been told that the strident anti-Federalist Lyon had a blemish on his record of service in the Revolution: "This is the redoubtable hero," Porcupine then wrote, "who, a few years after he was sold for his passage from Ireland, was condemned for cowardice in the American war by General Gates to wear a wooden sword."

He paused. Libelous? Surely it was, since it brought the man into disrepute. But it was true. Cobbett hoped it would partly distract the public's attention from Hamilton's troubles. It would also remind the Jeffersonians bent on destroying reputations that their own dirty linen would need to be washed.

"Sweet vengeance for my recall," said Monroe, "and for the partizan firing of Beckley—or so it will be interpreted by the Federalist press."

With Philadelphia in the grip of its dread summer epidemic of yellow fever—not as bad as the horror of '93, but bad enough to empty the city of all those who could afford to leave—he and James Madison had called on the Vice President at his Virginia home. Madison at Montpelier, thirty miles away, and Monroe much closer at Ash Lawn, in Albemarle County, were Jefferson's neighbors; the choice of Monticello as meeting place was a natural one. Even though Monroe was fully occupied with writing a memoir defending his embassy to Paris, he set his book aside to discuss the likely repercussions of the Reynolds pamphlet.

At first, Jefferson seemed concerned that he would be identified as the source of the material Callender published. Monroe assured his mentor that no danger of exposure existed. "I told Burr that it was John Beckley who caused the publication of the papers in question," he said. "By his assistant clerk they were copied for us. Five years ago, when Hamilton asked Beckley's clerk whether others were privy to the documents, the clerk replied that only Beckley was. Hamilton told him to tell Beckley he considered him bound not to disclose them. Beckley sent back word that he was under no injunction whatever and that if Hamilton had anything to say to him it must be in writing. Of course he never replied to that."

"But you told Beckley to keep them secret, didn't you?" Madison asked.

"Most certainly. And I never heard of the documents afterwards till my arrival from Paris. That if necessary will be declared by all."

Jefferson was curious about what Callender would say.

"Beckley says Callender will deny to his death Beckley was the source," Monroe assured him. "It's as if there were a code of honor among the pamphleteers. Its publication will never be traced to any Virginian."

"Are you in danger," Jefferson asked, "of a challenge from Hamilton under the code duello?"

"Burr thinks not." Monroe hoped Burr was right, and in the presence of Jefferson acted more confident than he felt.

"Burr inspires me with distrust," said Jefferson. "I know he is a good friend to both of you, but I caution you not to trust him too much."

Monroe did not argue the point about his friend Burr but went to the reason he did not feel immediately threatened. "Hamilton's aim in all this is not to kill me in a duel, but to force me to discredit Mrs. Reynolds's claim that he has fabricated her documents. That I will not do."

"Do you suppose Hamilton did that?" Jefferson asked. "That he forged her letters, that his whole story of the adulterous affair was a covering up of speculation inside Treasury?"

Monroe looked at Jefferson and shrugged. "We may never know. But we should never do the Federalists the favor of exculpating him. Indeed, Beckley tells me that Callender plans to attack Hamilton anew on the weakest point of his defense—the authenticity of Maria Reynolds's notes to him. Callender will charge they're all forgeries by Hamilton and—who knows?—he may be right. If Hamilton wanted to prove she wrote them, he would bring her forward and compare her handwriting with that on the notes. But he does not do that, which could be significant."

Madison suggested that the truth might lie somewhere in between: that Hamilton was an adulterer and a speculator as well. Monroe had to stop and think about that; it was not a possibility he had examined. "What do you think, Thomas?"

"Finding the strait between Scylla and Charybdis too narrow for his steerage," Jefferson said, "Hamilton has preferred running plump on one of them." The Vice President pondered this a moment and came down on the side of the most serious and damaging conclusion: "But his willingness to plead guilty as to adultery seems rather to have strengthened than weakened the suspicions that he was in truth guilty of the speculation."

"The publication of this Reynolds pamphlet is a curious specimen of the ingenious folly of its author," said Madison, shaking his head in wonderment. "First is Hamilton's error of publishing at all. Next is his forgetting that simplicity and candor are the only dress which prudence would put on innocence."

"He did seem to go into great and unnecessary detail," said Monroe. "Even I had trouble following some of it."

"Here we see every rhetorical artifice employed," said Madison, his eye on Hamilton's prose technique, "to excite the spirit of party to prop up his sinking reputation. While the most exaggerated complaints are uttered against the unfair and virulent persecution of himself, he deals out in every page the most malignant insinuations against others."

"Callender pointed out his pitiable notice of me," said Jefferson.

"The one against you is a masterpiece of folly," Madison agreed, "because its importance is in exact proportion to its venom."

"We should exercise caution in our relationship to both Beckley and Callender," Monroe said. Beckley was useful, but the pretensions of this immigrant to the stature of a Virginia gentleman were ludicrous to genuine gentlemen. Callender, a Scottish immigrant, was not even a citizen of the United States, and was said by Porcupine to have too great a reliance on the bottle.

Madison nodded agreement, but Jefferson did not seem concerned. Monroe assumed his reason was that there were too few champions of the republican cause willing to risk their livelihoods in this time of domination by Federalist leaders, unrestrained by Washington's even hand. Faction, so deplored by Madison in his contribution to *The Federalist Papers* he wrote with Hamilton and John Jay a decade before, was now a fact. Because the triumvirate of Virginians could not yet show their hand publicly, they had to depend to considerable degree on the denizens of the distasteful newsmongering world. But Monroe doubted that Jefferson could always explain away his support of Callender as purely charitable. It would not bear close scrutiny.

Chapter 8

"Congressional Pugilists," caricature, Lyon v. Griswold, 1798

January 30, 1798

PHILADELPHIA

*C*allender was at the *Aurora,* dropping off a couple of paragraphs about the way the Jay Treaty was enriching British bankers at the expense of American farmers, when a messenger came in with news of a ruckus about the press brewing in Congress Hall. He slipped and stumbled through the snowbound streets of Philadelphia to State House Square to see the spectacle for himself.

Matthew Lyon was denouncing the Federalist representatives from Connecticut. "You are acting in opposition to the interests and opinion of nine-tenths of your constituents," the Vermonter proclaimed in his rolling brogue. "You know the American people stand with the free people of

France in their war against the subjects of the English King. We remember who fought on our side in the Revolution against English tyranny." Callender nodded vigorously; he was certain that American popular sentiment, certainly in the South but even in the North, was with the red republican French. All of President Washington's popularity and prestige could not make popular the treaty his envoy, Chief Justice Jay, brought home from London, knuckling under to British interests. Washington had been ashamed to make the treaty public; Callender was proud that the *Aurora* editor, Benny Bache, surreptitiously obtained a copy and printed it. At the time, that flexing of the muscles of the opposition press caused an uproar of republican protest against the Federalists and the British bankers.

The people of the not-so-united States, in Callender's view, were dividing among North and South and West, and within those sections between rich and poor, religious and irreligious, early and late arrivals, and most divisive of all, between the governing and the governed. On that last score, he believed that the petulant and self-important Adams, the Federalist President saddled with the likes of Hamilton's Oliver Wolcott as Treasury Secretary, was out of touch with the sentiment of the majority of the people. That majority voice could be heard in the fierce tone and Irish accent of the radical Congressman from Vermont.

Lyon shook an admonitory finger at the Connecticut delegation, representing the hotbed of the American elite. "You are pursuing your own aristo-Tory private views without regarding the interests of the people of your districts, whose lackey press deprives them of another point of view. If I should go into Connecticut and manage a press there for six months, I could effect a revolution and turn you out." He could, too, Callender thought; the *Farmer's Library* in western Vermont, run by Lyon's seventeen-year-old son, made possible his own upset election victory.

"If you go into Connecticut, Matt Lyon," Callender heard one of the Congressmen fire back, "you had better wear your wooden sword." That he knew to be a snide reference to the item in *Porcupine's Gazette* calling into question Lyon's courage during the war. Lyon ignored the interruption and went on with his speech about the lapdog press in that Nutmeg State. Representative Roger Griswold, one of his targets, rose and went over to Lyon and laid his hand on his arm to make sure he would hear the gibe: "I asked if you intend to fight the people of Connecticut with your wooden sword."

Lyon, accused of cowardice, turned to Griswold, reared back his head, worked his mouth and spit in his tormentor's astonished face.

After gasps echoed through the hall, a Massachusetts member rose: "I move to expel Matthew Lyon for his gross indecency." Callender heard a shout from the gallery near him: "Throw the Irish scum out!" The Scot doubted that in the four previous Congresses there had ever been a breach of parliamentary decorum as egregious as this.

"I rise to express my abhorrence," said a New York republican, eager to dissociate himself from his colleague Lyon's action, "of such abusive insinuations. At the same time, I condemn the indecent reaction to indecent language." An angry man in the gallery stood up to say, in a loud voice that carried to the floor, "I feel grieved that the saliva of an Irishman should be left upon the face of an American." Callender—a fugitive from sedition court in Scotland but still a Scot—winced at the depth of the anti-immigrant feeling and wished Lyon had held his temper in check.

As member after member stood to revile the horrid act, only Albert Gallatin, the anti-Hamilton representative from Pennsylvania, attacked Lyon's attackers: "This whole proceeding," he said in his Swiss immigrant's French accent, "is nothing more than an affected cant of pretended delicacy, and the offspring of bitter party spirit." But a member of the Connecticut delegation countered by calling the expectorating Lyon "a kennel of filth" to be expelled from the dignified halls of Congress "just as citizens removed filth from their docks and wharves."

After the Speaker gaveled the unruly House into recess, Callender joined Gallatin in quieting the furious Lyon. "This will play into Porcupine's hands, Matt," the Scot whispered urgently. "You must apologize." Gallatin agreed: "There's a move already afoot to expel you, and we cannot afford to lose your vote. I'll get a Virginian to write your apology." Matt Lyon, muttering under his breath at the hypocrisy of the native-born, said he would write his own with Callender's help, and simmered down.

The dominant Federalist majority in the House sought to expel the man who became known nationally in the week that followed as "Spittin' Lyon." Federalist cartoonists, urged on by *Porcupine's Gazette*, pictured him as a lion with wooden sword in paw, trampling on scrolls labeled "Politeness," edging away from a prickly porcupine and spitting at a stately politician. The republican press limited itself to reporting Lyon's half-apology: "We do not always possess the power of judging calmly what is the best mode of resenting an unpardonable insult." But Lyon told Callender he would not grovel: "Had I borne that accusation of cowardice patiently, I should have been bandied about in all the newspapers on the continent, which are supported by British money and federal patronage, as a mean poltroon. The district which sent me would have been scandalized."

"You know your constituency," his new friend replied, "but look over your shoulder. I always do."

"I whipped the lawyers back home, you know. They hate me because I started no better than a slave and don't have their social graces. These Federalists are a set of gentry," said Lyon, "who consider the science of government to belong to only a few families. They think I can't buy my way in with the money I've made in trade. You saw Porcupine today?"

Cobbett had jeered at him in his *Gazette* as "our Lilliputian, with his dollars, gets access where—without them—he would not be suffered to appear." Callender, who always read *Porcupine's Gazette* first thing, said, "Nobody reads Cobbett any more." The fact was that every one of his damned pro-Government, French-hating pamphlets sold copies by the tens of thousands, and his *Gazette* was also thriving.

Meantime, Callender's fortunes were headed in the opposite direction. His big sale had come six months before, in his vigorous response to Hamilton's strange Reynolds pamphlet, and nothing had developed since. The public had largely accepted Hamilton's "confession" as true and dismissed Callender's refutation of that deliciously detailed account of adultery as that of someone spoiling its fun. Peeking through the keyhole of Hamilton's bedroom was more satisfying than examining the contents of the Treasury counting house. The Scot was astounded that nobody, not even the most rabid anti-Federalist, was willing to pull aside the veil of lies about sex and shame to examine the evidence of Hamilton's abuse of his Treasury position to line the pockets of his friends. Most people were content to take Maria to be a blackmailing whore and Hamilton to be too easily seduced, like so many other men, by a scheming adventuress. The Federalist leader had made his painful choice: he was willing to be seen to be a moral transgressor so long as he was known to be an upright public servant. Callender, alone in his contrary view, had gained no respect for having forced out such a ruination of reputation.

From the money earned by sale of *The History of 1796*, Callender paid his outstanding debts. A much-welcome payment of fifty dollars from

Scandalmonger

Thomas Jefferson supported him and his four boys and his wife. Bache paid him only a dollar for every piece he used in the *Aurora,* and that was limited to two or three a week. The Lyon spitting episode would be worth several more pieces, he estimated, especially if jousting with Cobbett about it kept reader interest up.

A two-thirds vote was required for the banishment of a duly elected member of the House. Gallatin sought to hold his minority of forty-four anti-Federalists firm with a cogent argument: "Congress is not a fashionable club. It is a representative body which has no right to deprive the voters of Vermont their representation because it doesn't like his manners."

Callender returned to Congress Hall to watch that vote. On the way, he noticed Griswold of Connecticut coming out of McCallister's store on Chestnut Street, a new, yellow hickory walking stick in hand. Inside the hall, Callender watched the vote and double-checked the count, remembering how Cobbett last year had flayed Beckley in print for an error.

Gallatin held his republican troops together. The vote to throw out Lyon achieved a majority but fell short of the necessary two-thirds. The Vermonter was humiliated but retained his seat. Though relieved at the majority's failure to oust Lyon, the observing Scot remained nervous about the degree of rancor, the outright hatred of immigrants, exposed by the episode.

After the failure to expel was solemnly recorded, Connecticut's Griswold rose to say, "The House by its decision has sanctioned violence within these walls." He then walked across the floor in front of the Speaker's chair, walking stick gripped firmly, toward Lyon's desk. The Vermonter did not see him approach.

"Matt!" Callender shouted. "Watch out!"

Too late. Griswold's stout cane cracked Lyon on top of the head, then across his back, again and again. More than twenty heavy blows rained down on his victim, who was groping for help in escaping along the floor, blinded by the blood spurting down from his scalp. Callender looked around frantically for a weapon, saw a fire tongs near the fireplace and slid it down the aisle toward Lyon, now crouched on one knee, absorbing the punishment with nobody to stop his attacker. Lyon felt the iron slide against his leg, grabbed the tongs and with a roar swung it at Griswold, knocking the bludgeoning cane out his hand. Before the bloodied Vermonter could maim his attacker with the heavy iron weapon, other Congressmen interceded, the Speaker pounded his gavel for order and Callender rushed to help Lyon to a doctor's house.

There, two days later, Callender reported to a still-steaming Lyon, head wreathed in bandages, that a committee had been appointed on the spot to consider the expulsion of Griswold and Lyon together for turning the House into a "gladiators' arena." Though Gallatin argued angrily that the Federalist's offense was significantly greater because the aggressor was the worse offender, the committee held along party lines that the two insults cancelled each other out, and the members agreed 73 to 21 to expel neither.

"They equate my spittin' in his eye after he called me a coward with his bashing me over the head twenty times with a hickory club?"

"They have the votes," Callender said. Reviled as a scandalmonger, now despised or feared by most, the editor was pleased to have made a friend.

"It's because those highborn lawyers call me an *arriviste*. They think they were born to rule. What are the people saying?"

"You're famous all across the land, Matt," Callender replied, putting the best face on the general revulsion. Cobbett, with his knowledge of French, had translated the word *arriviste* as "the name applied to the unwelcome arrival of a moneyed boor." Callender told the battered Congressman, "You'll never go anywhere without being introduced as 'the Spittin' Lyon.' "

"I'm thankful to you, James, for sliding down those fire tongs. Otherwise, I'd have been a dead man."

"We newspaper men have to stick together." Lyon had started a weekly sheet to support his political campaign; that made him a newspaper man.

The Vermonter rolled to his side in bed and reached for Callender's arm. "I have a piece of news for you that will embarrass the bastards. You know that delegation Adams sent to France after the French wouldn't receive his replacement for Monroe?"

Callender nodded. The Directory in Paris had ended the bloody revolutionaries' Reign of Terror; supported by Napoleon Bonaparte and guided by the diplomat Talleyrand, the new French government had rejected the credentials of Adams's ambassador as a Federalist too favorable to the British. The new American President, not wanting to become embroiled in the war between Britain and France, had consulted Hamilton, who Callender was sure controlled the Adams Cabinet from behind the scenes. Hamilton suggested a delegation of three eminent Americans led by John Marshall be sent to Paris to assure Talleyrand of our neutrality. Adams took that advice and dispatched the delegation; the nation had been anxiously awaiting word from them for months.

"The ship with their report to the President will soon arrive," Lyon confided. "The documents are in code. A seaman just in from France, a member of the United Irish, tells me the report contains a great shock."

"If it's good news for Adams," Callender said, worried, "making him look like a great diplomat avoiding a war, he'll make it public right away."

"That's my thought, too. But if it's bad news, he'll keep it secret. Our good French ally complained bitterly about the way we've been helping the damned English in their war, with Hamilton and the New York bankers makin' money on the side. I can't be certain, but I'm bettin' Adams will want to keep Marshall's report quiet because it makes our friends in France look good and his friends in Britain look bad. You be the first to find out what's in those dispatches, James me boy, and you'll have yourself grist for your mill."

Chapter 9

JOHN ADAMS

*T*reasury Secretary Oliver Wolcott, like all *of* Adams's Cabinet a holdover from service with President Washington, had never seen a Chief Magistrate so visibly upset. The agitated Adams smacked his fist on the deciphered documents, strode about the room set aside by Congress for the President's office, and fulminated at the insulting French.

"To me there appears no alternative—none!—between actual hostilities on our part and national ruin."

At this angrily expressed intention of asking for a declaration of war, Wolcott wondered what Hamilton would want him to advise. He suggested a middle course: "Perhaps we could adopt a policy of qualified hostility."

Adams wasn't listening. "What an insult! You know, the republicans brought this on us," the President said. "By professions of unqualified devotion to the French Republic, Jefferson and Monroe and that crowd encouraged Paris to believe a majority of Americans preferred the French government to their own. They'll be terribly embarrassed by this, and deservedly so."

Wolcott nodded agreement; that was the long-held opinion of Hamilton, whose idea it had been to send the Virginia Federalist John Marshall, accompanied by Charles Pinckney and Elbridge Gerry, to France on this mission of amelioration. Anticipating France's continued arrogance, Hamilton had even suggested sending Jefferson's man Madison, but that intellectual worthy wanted no association with the Adams Administration.

"Those French," Adams went on, bounding about the room, "with their cabals and corruptions, their employment of profligate printers and prostituted newspapers here. I tell you, if war is not to be declared, then we should at least pass a law prohibiting all commerce, intercourse and correspondence with France and all its dominions in every part of the world, upon penalty of treason!"

With his step back from war, Adams was apparently calming down. "I like that approach," said Wolcott, reflecting what he assumed would be Hamilton's moderate view, "because a recommendation to Congress for a declaration of war would require us to make public these extremely embarrassing documents. If we did that, France's Directory would surely react and perhaps endanger the lives of our commissioners."

Adams sat down glumly. "Abigail compares the three of them to Shadrach, Meshach and Abednego, sitting in the fiery furnace. Yes, they are potential hostages. We have to consider their safety if all this gets out." He flicked at the decoded documents with nervous fingers. "By God, it's humiliating."

"Let me draft a statement expressing your disappointment and resolve," Wolcott offered.

"Sure. Say the correspondence offered no expectation that the mission can be accomplished on terms compatible with the honor or essential interests of the nation, some pap like that."

"Exactly," said Wolcott, relieved.

"You know, it's a very painful thing for me to hold back these dispatches," Adams said. "The people deserve to know the baseness of the French behavior."

Wolcott recognized that making public the commissioners' report would inflame public sentiment against the French. It recounted how three French intermediaries—identified mysteriously as X, Y and Z—had sought huge bribes from the American envoys before they could even begin negotiations with Talleyrand. The arrant corruption would surely cause great consternation among the Jefferson men and their lackeys in the press who had been foolishly hounding Adams to favor France. But France's Directory had already announced its intention to seize all neutral ships carrying goods made in England, which had devastated American shipping out of Boston and New York. This latest insult would pour salt in the wound, offending the nation's pride in all regions. Wolcott considered the moment ripe to put forward the first element of Hamilton's plan: "We could respond to France's seizure of our ships by arming our merchant vessels."

"President Washington didn't want to do that."

"But you're President now and circumstances have changed."

Adams paced back and forth, looked out the window at the rain, returned to his writing table and smacked his palm down on it. "We cannot do nothing if they seize our ships. We'll arm the merchantmen. Put that in the statement."

Wolcott went on: "The second step would be to buy and build warships. And then, if the threat continues to grow from a Europe at war, you could create a standing army."

Adams winced. A navy would require new taxes, but the people might hold still for the building of ships to protect the nation's interest on the high seas. But Americans did not like the idea of a standing army; soldiers too close to home reminded many of the British occupiers. "That would require money. Taxation. Public opinion would have to be prepared."

Wolcott presumed Adams was thinking that the only way Americans would tolerate a standing army would be under the command of General Washington, now retired to Mount Vernon. Adams, who had spent a lifetime in Washington's shadow, would not want to be further beholden to him.

"You could send an emissary to Mount Vernon," he suggested tentatively.

"You know I love and revere the man," Adams said. "But it is his humanity only that I admire. In his divinity I never believed." The President seemed to force himself to be calm. "He possesses the gift of silence. One of Washington's precious talents is a great self-command. To preserve so much equanimity as he does requires a great capacity." He as much as admitted it was not in him.

Wolcott knew what lay behind Hamilton's plan. The need for a standing armed force, requiring General Washington at its head, would surely lead to the General's appointment of a man with military experience in the Revolution to be his chief of staff. That man would be Alexander Hamilton, always Washington's favorite. That would be the New Yorker's way to breathe new life into his political fortunes. By patriotically answering the call of military duty, he would wash away the sins of the Reynolds affair.

Adams, deflated, his coat unbuttoned, stared at the pile of decoded dispatches. He recalled to his Treasury Secretary how closely guarded the text had been of the treaty with Britain negotiated by John Jay. Only a few Senators were allowed a copy, but its ensuing appearance on the pages of the republican sheet *Aurora* had caused an outcry that only George Washington's prestige could overcome. Adams did not have such standing with all the people, or even with all his fellow Federalists.

The President silently gathered up the pages and put them under his arm to place them in a locked file. Lest France's slap in America's face inflame the unarmed nation with war fever, he determined that the public would not see his envoys' account of the XYZ affair. He passed up the temptation to embarrass Jefferson, Monroe and all the other Francophile republicans. Wolcott, often troubled by Adams's tendency to explode in anger, in this case had to admire his statesmanship and good sense.

"But I shall resist a recommendation that Hamilton be commissioned," Adams, as if reading his Treasury Secretary's mind, made clear. "This shall not be made the headquarters of fornication, adultery, incest, libeling, and electioneering intrigue."

Wolcott withdrew, shaking his head. He had heard all the others for years, but incest? What rumor had Abigail Adams heard and told her husband about Angelica Church, Hamilton's beautiful and flirtatious sister-in-law? Wolcott rejected the idea out of hand; that would be too much. And Adams, if Washington insisted on Hamilton as his chief aide, would surely come around.

March 11, 1798

PHILADELPHIA

Benjamin Franklin Bache, the editor that Cobbett had dubbed "Young Lightning Rod" to demean both the young man and the scientific findings of his philandering grandfather and namesake, took ill. He placed James Callender in charge of his *Aurora* for all of March 1798. Jefferson's friends supplied Bache the money to pay him.

Fully employed for the first time in nearly a year, Callender not only reported the shipping news and edited the incoming correspondence from abroad, but wrote the opinion editorials as well, with no one to restrain him. Busy, productive, earning $10 a week for engaging in provocative polemics, he was in his element.

"Why is the President afraid to tell?" demanded his *Aurora* editorial. The answer was obvious to Callender: Adams was keeping secret the dispatches from our envoys for the simple reason that they were favorable to France. The blame for the failure of the mission was squarely at the door of the Federalist President, whose bias toward England and antipathy toward France had endangered the United States. "People begin to see their madness in preferring John Adams and a French war," wrote Callender, "to Thomas Jefferson and a French peace." But he dismissed Adams as a mere cat's paw of the true culprit, Alexander Hamilton, "the son of a camp follower, a confessed adulterer and an avowed monarchist." If Hamilton chose to hide his financial venality behind a mask of adultery, the editor would remind the world of it at every opportunity. He sandwiched Hamilton's profession of adultery nicely between a reminder of his bastardy and a slight exaggeration about his being what Jefferson liked to call "the Consolidator."

When Adams issued his mealy-mouthed statement sorrowfully announcing the failure of the mission and the arming of merchantmen, probably drafted by the cautious Wolcott, Callender remembered his tip from Spittin' Matt and pounced: Where was the rest of the tale? Why was the full report being smothered up, kept even from the responsible committee of the Senate?

The drumbeat in the *Aurora* to reveal the report was taken up in the next few days by the rest of the republican press, and echoed in the Congress Hall. Southern Senators who knew and respected Commissioner John Marshall demanded that his full dispatch be submitted to the Senate forthwith. Vice President Jefferson, the *Aurora* reported, was "petrified with astonishment" at Adams's statement slyly derogating French policy and putting cannons on ships. His primary representative in the House, Albert Gallatin, passed Jefferson's word to republicans in Congress to resist Adams's proposal to arm merchant vessels and instead "to adjourn and consult with the people." An aroused populace friendly to France, he said Jefferson believed, would resist the Federalist trend toward war.

As a result, anti-Federalist John Beckley in Pennsylvania was organizing town meetings against war. His format was copied in Massachusetts, and Whig printing presses were set up in Connecticut. The message went out to all democratic societies: Delay. Speak out against war. Needed now was time for sober reflection, not precipitate action.

"Publish the commissioners' report!" boomed Matt Lyon in Congress Hall, taking his cue from Callender, whom he had directed to the issue of concealment. What information could not be ferreted out could be forced out. "Why can't the people know? Could it be that what the President implies is not supported by the full report?" Republican members forgot their embarrassment with him and cheered.

Albert Gallatin, however, the republican leader in the House, did not join in the taunting of Adams and his Cabinet. He slumped in his chair looking worried. Born in the French-speaking portion of Switzerland, he was aware of the nativist undercurrent that made the Connecticut bully's attack on Lyon dangerous to the new democracy. His own election to the Senate from Pennsylvania had been set aside because he had not met the length-of-residence requirement; that was why, even though his interest lay in the foreign affairs overseen by the Senate, Gallatin had made his political career in finance in the House. Porcupine had already charged him with being a French secret agent, and the word "sedition" was being used to describe his speeches in the House.

In Gallatin's judgment, something was uncharacteristic about Adams's behavior in this episode. Here was an Anglophile, a former Minister to Britain, and a man notable for his hot temper reacting in a relatively restrained fashion toward France's belligerence on the high seas as well as its diplomatic frigidity. Although Jefferson viewed the arming of our merchant vessels by Adams as an unconscionable step toward war, Gallatin thought it was the least the President could do in light of the provocation of a seizure threat. The most forceful advocate of republicanism on the House floor detected the hand of Hamilton in all this careful calibration of mildness. He suspected a political trap. Gallatin was not eager to see the report of the envoys to Paris made public until he read it himself.

When the President's proposal came to a vote, he noted worriedly that some well-informed Federalists joined the republicans in demanding publication of the dispatches. The resolution passed easily—too easily. Adams was forced to hand them over.

Benny Bache climbed out of a sickbed and returned to Philadelphia in a febrile fury. He at once confronted Callender with "You damn fool! Do you realize what a blunder you made?"

Callender, reading the dispatches that the Adams Administration had just released, nodded glumly. "Because Adams wanted to conceal them, I thought the French must have been friendly and forthcoming. I thought his commissioners did something that favored the British and provoked the French and put us at risk of war. I was mistaken."

Using the trumpet of the *Aurora,* the crusading Scot had blown down the walls of Federalist concealment. President Adams had been forced by the public outcry and the vote in Congress to make a full release of the decoded correspondence from his emissaries to the Directory in Paris.

The result, however, did not reflect badly on Adams; on the contrary, the news in the report was a terrible embarrassment to all American friends of France. The embarrassment to the Federalists in the Reynolds affair was as nothing compared to the damage to the republicans in what would surely be known as the XYZ affair.

With Bache looking over his shoulder, coughing and fuming, Callender re-read the documents. Talleyrand, "the fox of Europe," who had spent a year in America escaping the bloodthirsty Robespierre after the fall of the Bastille, was now back in power as the Directory's Minister of Foreign Affairs. Marshall's report recounted how he had admitted the American envoys to his house but told them he was "too busy" to discuss official matters. The feelings of the Directory were wounded, he claimed, by certain phrases in Adams's first address to the Congress. Until they were withdrawn, no progress could be made in improving relations between the two countries. Talleyrand also hinted he was looking forward to a *douceur,* a sweetener for himself. When the three eminent Americans replied it was not in their power to get the President of the United States to apologize for a speech, France's Foreign Minister coldly informed them he would grant them no further interviews.

"There's the part about X, Y and Z," Bache's finger jabbed at the papers. "Why did they make such a mystery about the names?"

"Marshall must have known it would add piquancy to the report," said Callender, "if he used symbols to keep them anonymous. The French names would be harder to remember."

Three unofficial emissaries from Talleyrand then approached the Americans. "Monsieur X" told them that the Foreign Minister would provide them an authoritative audience upon payment to him of a personal *douceur* of $250,000. Charles Pinckney induced X to put the demand for a bribe in writing. But that was only the entrance fee. X then ushered in a well-known confidant of Talleyrand designated by Marshall as "Monsieur Y," who explained that a successful mission would require a loan to France from the United States of $6 million. When Elbridge Gerry pointed out that would infuriate the British, Y came up with a complex arrangement to buy Dutch bonds that would wind up in France's coffers.

The Americans had replied that they were empowered to make a treaty but not a loan. In came "Monsieur Z" to try to split Gerry off from the other two Americans; Talleyrand remembered Gerry cordially, having met him in Boston when hiding from the Reign of Terror. Gerry was more susceptible to flattery and insisted they continue talking to the go-betweens, who kept saying, "It is expected you will offer money." At that point, according to the report, Pinckney shouted, "It is no, no; not a sixpence!"

"Imagine putting something as colorful as that in an official report," said Callender. Marshall was evidently a politician who knew the power of words.

"Now—right there—comes the part about the whore," said Bache, eyes tearing. He blew his nose into a kerchief.

An attractive feminine intermediary "well acquainted with Talleyrand" joined X, Y and Z to explain that the money was not a demand but merely a delicate suggestion. The Foreign Minister's mistress then pointed out the strength of the pro-French party in America led by the well-regarded former Ministers to France, Jefferson and Monroe. She was the messenger Talleyrand sent to threaten, in a gentle voice, that failure to pay the bribe and make the loan would lead to more than diplomatic disaster. It could lead to active French support of the replacement of the Federalists with a friendlier American faction—the Jefferson republicans.

Bache groaned. "How many copies are they printing of this?"

"Matt Lyon tried to hold it down to fifteen hundred," Callender, heartsick, replied. "We had the votes in the House to limit it to that, but you know how the Federalists run the Senate. They ordered fifty thousand copies for free distribution and now everybody who can read will read it." He thought of the hireling Federalist printer who constantly sniped at him and Bache. "Fenno will make a fortune."

The final words on the document, which took two months to cross the Continent and the Atlantic, were Marshall's and Pinckney's: "There exists no hope of our being officially received by this government, or that the objects of our mission will be in any way accomplished." They were on their way home. Talleyrand, the venal diplomat who represented France, a former ally, had treated the representatives of the United States with contempt and had thereby humiliated every American.

Callender hung his head. "What do you want to say in tomorrow's *Aurora*? I'll write whatever you want."

"Is there anything in this whole damned mess of messages we can use?"

"Marshall reports here that Talleyrand complained that the Adams government had manipulated the press in America to be against France. That's true enough—republican newspapers are outnumbered three to one."

"We can't use anything Talleyrand says, James," Bache said, biting off his words. "He's the villain in this, don't you see? He's done more to ruin us than anybody. That damn French fox may even achieve the impossible—he may make John Adams a popular president."

Callender looked more closely at one of the documents. "Here's Marshall's answer about the press. 'Among those principles deemed sacred in America,' he says, 'there is not one more deeply impressed on the public mind than liberty of the press. That this liberty is often carried to excess, that it has sometimes degenerated into licentiousness, is seen and lamented; but the remedy has not yet been discovered.' Let's hope they don't discover it now. Should we print this?"

"No. And by 'licentious' he meant you. Say it was wrong for Adams to publish the documents because negotiations are still going on—Elbridge Gerry is still over there, maybe a hostage." Bache grasped for another avenue of escape: "Maybe people will forget what you had us saying all last week. Write that it's all a Federalist scheme to start a war with France."

"Talleyrand is the villain," Callender added, "and the Directory might not have known what he was doing. Everybody knows he and Hamilton are close and both are monarchists. This is a Hamilton plot to push Adams into supporting the British."

"Yes, and you can imagine what Porcupine will do to us on all that. We look like fools, Callender, and God knows what you've done to the republican cause. Write for tomorrow, and I'll pay you what they gave me to pay you, and then I don't want to see you again."

Callender could not blame him. He had made a terrible mistake. Matt Lyon's misjudgment had led him there, but the fault was his in not recognizing the possibility that he might be mistaken. Why had Adams wanted to suppress the dispatches if they would do harm to the republican cause? Callender wanted to think it was a trick that had fooled him, but another possibility presented itself: what if Adams was genuinely concerned about a war fever raging through the body politick, at a time when America was without the means to wage war? What if this petty popinjay, the tool of the Hamiltonians, had put the interest of the people ahead of the need to crush his political opponents?

On occasion, a bad man did a good thing, and a weak man took a strong stand; motives sometimes conflicted, leading to inconsistencies. Callender had trained himself to think consistently and that is what had led him over the cliff on this. The pity was that the combination of a minority voice in the House, that of Lyon, magnified by the voice of the opposition press, that of Callender, had the power to lead an entire political movement over the cliff. That was what dismayed him even more than being dismissed for good reason from a position he had so long dreamed of and so briefly enjoyed.

He thought, too, of his four children and his wife, who had grown accustomed to eating regularly and dressing respectably. The security of regular employment was gone now. He reminded himself that sustaining his ailing wife and making a better life for his four boys was his first responsibility, coming before replacing this administration or changing the world. Newsmongering had its satisfactions, even its savage thrills, but the writing life made it hard for a family man to plant two feet firmly on the ground. Perhaps he could prevail on someone like Madison to get him a position teaching history. He also knew himself to be a fairly capable carpenter. Was it too late, at age forty, to begin again? He had the sinking feeling that it was. "You probably will see me again, Benny. We'll meet one day in jail."

June 16, 1798
PHILADELPHIA

Peter Porcupine, as William Cobbett was now universally known, did not believe it was proper to do business with politicians, but considered a fair exchange of talent for information to be entirely within propriety for opinionmongers. So it was that he developed an arrangement a few years before with Robert Goodloe Harper, a pugnacious lawyer and businessman elected to the Congress from the Up Country of South Carolina.

They were the same age, thirty-eight, avid readers of political pamphlets and attracted to public controversy. Although Harper came to Philadelphia inclined toward republicanism and France, he was educable. Cobbett saw in him a man of character and business acumen, if lacking in the skill of the quill, and knew that Harper saw in him an avenue to a wide public. Thus, Cobbett was to aid the budding politician in the preparation of speeches and papers, and Harper was to provide the journalist good report on the inner workings of the Federalists in Congress.

Their collaboration had begun three years before with a powerful tract published under Harper's name on the Jay Treaty with Great Britain. As Cobbett saw it, this was the first great foreign-policy debate to illuminate the growing split in the American politick. It separated the Federalists behind Hamilton who supported the treaty as averting war with Britain from the mobocrats behind Jefferson who denounced the treaty as subservient to British mercantile interests. The newcomer to Congress, Harper, astounded his colleagues and his rural constituents with a closely reasoned, plainly expressed document in strong support of the controversial treaty.

Thanks to the furor over the XYZ affair, that simmering controversy had reached a boiling point. Americans of all factions and regions were furious at the arrogant French treatment of their nation. Southerners especially were fearful of invasion; rumors swept the plantations of slave uprisings to support the arrival of French troops. *Porcupine's Gazette* warned of the kind of nation in store for property owners if the bloody-minded French radicals took over: "We do not wish to divide our property with idlers, nor daily to tremble at the guillotine."

Harper met Cobbett at the Porcupine print shop, and together they walked to the Federalist dinner and rally for John Marshall at Oeller's Hotel. This event far outdid the anti-Federalist dinner welcoming home James Monroe the year before. Six miles outside the city, at Frankfort, Adams's Secretary of State and a large party of dignitaries met the coach carrying Marshall down from New York, their greeting heralded by an artillery salute from a Pennsylvania regiment. An exuberant crowd was waiting in front of the hotel, and people waved banners from the nearby rooftops.

Cobbett was grateful for the invitation that Harper had wangled for him; the 120 invited guests included all the Adams Cabinet members and the justices of the Supreme Court. But Peter Porcupine was the only representative of the press. "These are not the shouts of a giddy populace," the journalist told the politician, looking up at the demonstrators hanging out of windows, "responsive to the flattering cant of a hypocritical demagogue. In your toast, Robert, you will want to say that this is an expression of gratitude toward a man—at hazard to his very life—who displayed fortitude in defending the honor of his country against the devious Talleyrand." Offhandedly, he added, "He came to see me two years ago, you know, when he was here, hiding from the revolutionaries."

"Talleyrand did?" The rotund Harper was impressed, as Cobbett hoped he would be.

"Yes, this modern Judas and I were seated by the same fireside. I had called him an apostate, a hypocrite, and expected that he wanted to expostulate with me at such severe treatment. Imagine my astonishment when he complimented me on my wit and learning, and asked if I had received my education at Oxford! As you know, I never went to any school—well, up to then, I kept my countenance pretty well at his flattery, but this abominable stretch would have forced a laugh from a Quaker in the midst of a meeting."

"What did Talleyrand want?"

"He wanted to pay me twenty dollars a month for English lessons. I had written my French-English grammar and was charging six dollars a month at the time, so his offer was obviously a bribe to get me to stop my hectoring of his nation."

"And you told him—?"

"That I was no trout and consequently could not be caught by tickling." Cobbett laughed heartily, then sobered: "He was a spy when he was here, for the Directory men who soon welcomed him home with open arms. And there are now hundreds of French spies flying about the country in every direction. They know exactly those in sympathy with the reds who are to be counted on in case of war."

"You mentioned my toast tonight. There will be fifteen other toasts," Harper said. "How do I make mine stand out?"

Cobbett had been thinking about that. "The most important moment Marshall recounted in his dispatches was Pinckney's exclamation when he rejected the bribe solicitations. He cried, 'No, no, not a sixpence!' There is much to be made of that. Your run-of-the-mine laborer understands such language more than any high-flown declarations of dull policy. Let me work on that."

"We'll meet in the barroom just before the dessert is served."

Harper was seated near the guest of honor at the head table. Marshall, the returned envoy, was a low Federalist, moderate as Adams but far less excitable. He was not in favor of war unless the French invaded the Carolinas or came up through the port of New Orleans. He also told those at the head table he was doubtful that Americans were prepared to pay the taxes that raising an army and building a navy would bring. Harper, on the other hand, was a high Federalist, hot for Hamilton and energy in the Executive, and eager to ride the wave of resentment that most members of his faction felt surging in their voters at home. He slipped out to pass what he heard to Cobbett and to get his idea for what he should say.

Thus, when it came his turn to raise his glass in a toast to John Marshall, it was Robert Goodloe Harper who came up with the rallying cry that reverberated in the room and would be carried around the nation by the press and shouted at parades in the coming weeks: "Millions for defense—but not one cent for tribute!"

June 25, 1798

PHILADELPHIA

"The press is the engine." Monroe had never heard Jefferson more certain of the best way to regain republican momentum and cool the war fever.

Monroe had ridden through the Virginia heat up to Francis's Hotel at Jefferson's request. He had been at his Virginia plantation writing his memoir justifying his years representing Washington in Paris, and was somewhat fearful of the news of a new onset of the summertime yellow fever in Philadelphia. But a summons from his leader at a critical time for the cause was not to be ignored.

James Madison joined them in a council of anti-war. The little former Congressman from Virginia (Monroe thought of him as little, though at five feet six, he was no shorter than John Adams) had been properly credited with fathering the Constitution nearly a decade before. Now he deferred to Jefferson as his political chief. Too much so, Monroe thought; with Jefferson always preferring to operate behind the scenes, there was a need for Madison to be more publicly engaged in public affairs. Fortunately, there was Albert Gallatin to take the leadership in pressing the republican cause in Congress. Though the Senate was hopelessly in the hands of Federalists, Monroe was pleased with the way Gallatin unified his minority of anti-Federalists in the House.

After some small talk about the time and money Madison spent on remodeling his home, Montpelier—and after he ordered 100,000 nails from Jefferson's home nail factory—they came to the subject endangering the Republic.

"The XYZ dispatches account for a state of astonishment in the public mind," Madison reported. "Its inevitable effect is to blast every chance of accommodation with France."

"Adams's message arming our merchant vessels is insane," Jefferson said. "Any resistance from our democratic societies?" These local political groups were modeled on the Jacobin clubs in revolutionary France, to resist the concentration of power in Philadelphia. Alexander Hamilton had written a message for George Washington denouncing such "self-created societies," but Jefferson, even while serving as Washington's Secretary of State, had encouraged them.

"In several places the people have turned out with protests," Madison replied, "against the war measures urged by the Executive. In our county in Virginia, a petition is to be handed about—"

"Not enough," said the Vice President.

Monroe said he thought Jefferson was being alarmist, and indeed used that French term, *alarmiste*. In his view, the Talleyrand request was just an experiment in swindling that did not represent France's policy, and he agreed with what Callender had written in his farewell appearance in the *Aurora:* that the horror registered by Marshall in his report would ultimately bring derision on our naïve envoys. As Jefferson's successor as Minister to France, Monroe had seen much petty corruption. When he arrived there, he had been shocked at the arrangement made by his predecessor as American envoy, Gouverneur Morris, to share Talleyrand's mistress in what was called a *ménage à trois*. Monroe assumed this new example of Gallic amorality—Talleyrand's bribe request—was merely an extension of such private corruption, and surely had not been approved by the four-man ruling Directory. Jefferson waved that excuse aside as unacceptable to an aroused American public.

"Public sentiment," Madison said with certitude, "is unquestionably opposed to every measure that may increase the danger of war."

Monroe sadly shook his head; he knew that to be wishful thinking. So did Jefferson, who looked at his intellectual partner and political acolyte as if he were living on another planet. "The irritation pouring in from the great towns is becoming unbearable," the Vice President pointed out. "Party passions are high. I receive daily proofs of it from angry people who never saw me, nor know anything of me but through Porcupine."

At Jefferson's mention of Cobbett's newspaper, Monroe placed a copy of *Porcupine's Gazette* on the table. "He's discovered you gave a passport to Paris to your friend George Logan. Claims it's proof of a Jacobin plot, led by you, to conduct foreign policy behind the back of the government."

Jefferson winced. "Dr. Logan's personal and unofficial venture was dictated by his own enthusiasm for peace, without consultation with me. But Porcupine gives me a principal share in it." He added, lest his friends think he was a regular reader of the sheet that most effectively kept republicans on the defensive, "I was told that. I never read his paper."

Monroe read aloud Cobbett's twist on Logan's trip: "'Watch, Philadelphians, for the *couteau* at your throats: when your blood runs down the gutters, don't say you weren't forewarned of danger.' No wonder the people are panic-stricken. Memories of the guillotine are too recent."

Madison stopped trying to put a hopeful face on the disastrous turn-around against France in public sentiment. "The success of the war party," he admitted, "in turning the XYZ dispatches to their inflammatory views, is mortifying. It suggests that the character of our citizens may not be enlightened." His face bore a sour expression as he rumpled the ruffles on his shirt.

Monroe had to smile at what to Madison was a terrible admission of his misplaced faith. Madison was brilliant, sometimes even inspired, when it came to drafting a Bill of Rights, but hopeless as a political realist. He had been dead wrong in his Federalist paper on the need for organized political opposition, and he was equally blind to this day in his trust in the serene sagacity of the public.

"To be realistic," Monroe countered, "let us assume we are not able to stem the tide toward war. That means President Adams would have to raise an army. That in turn means someone would have to be chosen to command that army who has the absolute confidence of all the people. Do you remember the last time that happened?"

"The Whiskey Rebellion of '94," said Madison instantly. The farmers around Pittsburgh wouldn't pay Hamilton's tax on grain they sold to make alcohol. When President Washington raised 12,000 troops, he brought his revolutionary aide-de-camp, Colonel Hamilton, back to be his second-in-command. "Washington and Hamilton scared off the Western farmers."

"And made good republicans out of them," Jefferson remembered. "That's why we carried Pennsylvania, and why I hold this curious office to-day."

"Put yourself in Adams's shoes now," Monroe went on, "and you saw how this war hysteria was making you popular for the first time in your life. You would not want the fever to end. To whom would you turn to head a costly army?"

"George Washington, again, of course," said Madison, looking worried at the prospect. "And though reluctant to leave his retirement at Mount Vernon, he is too much a patriot not to do his duty. He would surely bring back Hamilton again."

Jefferson was not so certain. "Adams would not want to do that. He wants so badly to be his own man."

"Surely he fears Hamilton as a challenge within the Federalist ranks," Monroe granted, "and he must know that most of his Cabinet gets their guidance from Hamilton. But Adams has no choice. If he is to maintain his popularity as defender of the national pride—if he is to ride the tide of war sentiment—then he must recruit Washington and suffer the public rise of Hamilton." A thought occurred to Monroe to bolster his analysis: "Perhaps that's why Hamilton suggested to Adams this trio of envoys in the first place. He was counting on them to fail in France so that he could get back in the saddle. I'll bet he's behind the 'Day of Fasting and Humiliation' next week. That's intended to whip up more hatred and fear of foreigners in our midst."

But Madison remained hopeful about Washington. "It is said, and I believe it, that the hot-headed proceedings of Mr. Adams are not well relished in the cool climate of Mount Vernon."

Jefferson shook his head; Monroe's dire forecast apparently made more sense to him. "Washington was fortunate to leave office just as the bubble is bursting, leaving others to hold the bag."

"In raising a standing army, the voice will be the voice of Washington," Monroe said, allowing himself a biblical paraphrase, "but the hand will be the hand of Hamilton."

Jefferson pulled himself out of his overstuffed hotel-room chair and, on his feet, addressed his lieutenants. "We cannot allow events to run such a calamitous course." The man Monroe knew to be essentially contemplative was being forced into action. "Though not one twenty-fifth of the nation, the Federalists command three-fourths of its newspapers."

Monroe tried to explain that was because most commercial newspapers, often titled "advertisers," were published in seaports and large towns interested in promoting trade with England and the kind of banking system Hamilton preached. The predominance of Federalist papers was a commercial outcome, not a political conspiracy.

Jefferson nodded and went right on. "We must marshal our support in the press. Bache's paper, and also Carey's and Cooper's, totter for want of subscriptions. We must really exert ourselves to procure it for them, for if these papers fail, republicanism will be entirely browbeaten."

The Vice President cited an example of previous support for the republican press: "As you know, I gave the State Department printing to Freneau when I was Secretary, but now his *National Gazette* is out of business." Jefferson had been criticized at the time for subsidizing an editor critical of his own administration, but had refused to cut him off. "His paper saved our Constitution, which was galloping fast into monarchy, and was checked by no one means so powerfully as by that paper."

Monroe hoped that in the future more gentlemanly editors could be found than those now being subsidized by republicans. Callender, Bache, William Duane and Thomas Cooper were as savage and low-class as the vulgar Cobbett was on the Federalist side. He knew that well-bred journalists like Samuel Smith wanted to establish a *National Intelligencer;* that was the sort of stable person to give a regular source of Federal income, if and when the time came.

Jefferson turned to Madison, who had returned to Virginia and all but abandoned public life, with a half-appeal, half-order. "Take up your pen against Hamilton." Writing under the pen name of "Marcellus," that all-too-brilliant New York lawyer was writing a series of articles in the Federalist press, giving an underpinning of intellect to the emotional anti-immigrant outbursts, thereby striking at the very heart of the republican popular support. Immigrants voted republican. "Hamilton's life has been a tissue of machinations against the liberty of his country. But he is a legion, a host in himself. You know the ingenuity of his talents and there is no one but you who can foil him."

He stood over the seated Madison, who leaned far back in his chair to look up at him. "For heaven's sake, take up your pen and do not desert the public cause altogether. "

"Perhaps if someone of your eminence—" Madison began, but had no chance to finish.

"At a very early period of my life," Jefferson said, "I determined never to put a sentence into any newspaper. I have religiously adhered to the resolution through my life, and have great reason to be contented with it. Newspapers are a bear-garden scene into which I will enter on no provocation. But you two should. Now what about Callender?"

"He was the one who brought all this down on us—" Monroe started to say, but Jefferson motioned him to forget about the editor's well-meaning misjudgment. Because the Vice President did not explicitly mention financial support for Callender, Monroe guessed that he had assumed that burden himself, which was fortunate because both he and Madison were financially strapped. Though Callender surely deserved sustenance for his large family after all he had done as the Jeffersonians' conduit to bring down Hamilton, the fugitive from Scotland struck Monroe as undisciplined. Remembering what trouble that note of transmission to Reynolds had caused Hamilton, he hoped that Jefferson was using the utmost discretion in helping Callender. He had already suggested the sending of banknotes only through a trusted intermediary, without committing anything to writing.

"Our Scottish friend is in a sorry state," said Madison. "When he came to importune me, he quoted Ossian, 'I am alone in the land of strangers.' Evidently an educated man, but guided by passion. And he's worried about the Alien bills." Federalists led by Harper proposed to give the President the power to deport aliens in peacetime as well as during a war. "There's a monster of legislation that must forever disgrace its parents."

"That's a detestable thing," Jefferson agreed, "worthy of the eighth or ninth centuries."

They were all aware that Callender was a fugitive from a sedition prosecution in Scotland. If the Alien bill passed, he was sure to be deported, then tried in English courts and probably imprisoned for a long time. Prime Minister William Pitt was cracking down on sedition as never before.

"Impress on Gallatin the need to moderate that Alien bill in the

House," Jefferson directed Madison. "Callender is the main object of it, just as Gallatin himself is the target of the naturalization bill." Harper and his fellow anti-immigrants were also proposing to change the waiting time for an alien to become a citizen from the present two years to fourteen years. Worse, they wanted to make the rule retroactive; that would remove Gallatin from Congress.

Monroe observed that Federalist leaders were aiming the current wave of hatred not just at the French living in America but at all foreigners, especially "the wild Irishmen" and Scottish opponents of Britain. "Spittin' Matt Lyon," fortunately, had been a soldier in the Revolution and was beyond the punitive bills' fourteen-year reach, but Gallatin and Callender were not. Monroe knew that although Virginia aristocrats and political philosophers led the republican cause, they relied for popular support on immigrants in the north recently escaped from tyranny abroad, and on farmers in the west resentful of taxes. Small wonder that the Federalists wanted to cut off the immigrant flow and to deny a vote to those already here.

"This is the season for systematic energies and sacrifices," Jefferson said. "The engine is the press," he repeated, looking hard at Madison. "Every man who believes as we do must lay his purse and his pen under contribution. As to the money, I may be obliged to assume something. As to the pen, let me pray and beseech you to set apart a certain portion of every post day to write what may be proper for the public. Send it to me here, and when I go to Virginia I will let you know to whom you may send it, so that your names will be sacredly secret."

Jefferson went to the window, hands clasped behind his back, and looked at the muddy street below. "There is now only wanting a Sedition bill," he predicted, "which we shall certainly soon see proposed. The object of that is the suppression of our Whig presses. We must resist that mightily."

"Perhaps there is enough virtue remaining in the public mind," Madison suggested in his optimistic way, "to make arbitrary attacks on the freedom of the press recoil on their wicked authors."

Virtue in the public mind? Monroe was less sanguine; people were more inclined to read the licentious press than to defend it. The United States under Adams, he feared, was entering its own Reign of Terror, perhaps without the guillotine, but similarly intended to repress all opposition to those in power. He saw coming the times, as Thomas Paine had written during an earlier American crisis, to try men's souls.

Chapter 10

THOMAS McKEAN

July 7, 1798
PHILADELPHIA

*T*he shame at having helped make John Adams popular was the least of James Callender's worries. More immediate was the yellow fever that had struck Philadelphia again and afflicted his wife. The epidemic struck every summer, seemingly heralded by the croaking of the frogs in the swamps around the town. This year, remembering the terrifying scourge of 1793, more than 1,500 families had fled the city. The Federal government was again moving to Trenton.

Like so many others, including women and children, Callender had taken to smoking cigars; the smoke was said to ward off the disease. The same preventive benefit was attributed to garlic. He bought two bulbs a day and carried cloves of the odoriferous plant in his pockets and every morning stuffed one in each of his shoes. Like everyone else determined to protect himself, he never went outside without a sponge impregnated with camphor and vinegar to wet his face and hands. The combination of smells was horrendous at first, but one got used to it, especially since it was the common practice. He had no idea if the smoke and the smell of garlic, camphor, vinegar and cigars protected anyone from the disease, but at least it discouraged the onslaught of the annoying mosquitoes.

At his fevered wife's urging, Callender had taken his older boys and their two-year-old brother, Thomas, born in America, to the home of

Thomas Leiper on a farm far removed from the swamps and town. That kindly soul, a snuff-maker and tobacconist, knew that Callender could not afford to pay board. He took his fellow Scotsman's children in not just out of his natural good nature, Callender reckoned, but because he was a good republican and liked what their father was writing about Jefferson. The payment of board would await an improvement in Callender's fortunes; when Jefferson was President, the Scot would not lack for subscribers or government printing. Postponing board was no hardship for Leiper; the sudden popularity of cigar smoke had trebled his business.

The boys, awed and delighted by the farm animals, did not at first feel lonely at their separation from their parents; they were happy to be away from the incessant botheration of the Philadelphia mosquitoes. Leiper urged the distraught father to find a way to get to Dr. Benjamin Rush, the foremost physician in America and whose services were in great demand, to save the life of his wife.

Dr. Rush was frequently the target of Porcupine's rages. That meant he was an outspoken republican, on the side of the French, and probably a friend of the anti-Federalists in Congress. Callender went to the City Tavern and found John Beckley and Matt Lyon, or "Spittin' Matt" as he was now known by friend and foe alike, conspiring in the bar. They did not shake hands; nobody in Philadelphia wanted to take a chance on contamination.

"You're an alien, James," Lyon told him before he could ask for medical help, "and you're in danger. The Alien Enemies bill will be passed in the House tomorrow. Harper, damn his eyes, says it's needed 'to purify the national character.' The Senate aristocrats have already given the President the power to ship the foreign-born back to where they came from. They're all tagged as troublemakers."

"You and your United Irishmen are the biggest foreign-born trouble-makers in this God-forsaken town," Callender reminded the Vermont Congressman. He reached for the bottle in front of them and poured himself a drink he sorely needed. His friends could afford it.

"But Matt's no alien," said Beckley. "He's a citizen, fought in the Revolution, and he has all the rights Madison put in the Constitution. You don't. It's not only the twenty thousand French they want to put on boats back to France. There's a few Scots they want to see back in Edinburgh."

The specter of deportation now loomed in his mind. His first thought was that his sick wife could not travel. His second was that, as a fugitive from Britain's sedition law, he faced certain imprisonment in Scotland, which meant that his wife and their boys would be sent to the poorhouse. The only Callender who could claim to be an American was Thomas, the two-year-old born here. That America that was now in the grip of war fever and yellow fever was a terrible place, but it was safer than any other place he could think of.

"Fortunately, you applied for citizenship years ago," Beckley was saying. That was not true; Callender had never sought to become an American, hoping instead to return to Scotland when it was free of oppressive British rule. But the Scot's long-range hopes of return seemed to concern Beckley less than the immediate danger to Callender's ability to wield his pen in freedom. "The date on your application is 1796," he lied, "two full years ago, and you can prove you have resided here for six years. A man in the State Department who remembers he owes me his job has your documents in order."

"And after you pick those up," added Matt Lyon, "there's a judge who harbors secret republican sympathies ready to swear you in as a citizen. The man who's taken in your children, Thomas Leiper, a man of property here, has agreed to be your witness. We've told him that Thomas Jefferson will hear of it and be grateful to him. Drink up, lad, you're a dirty Scottish interloper no more."

The deed was done. Callender was the newest American. He could smile when Lyon teased him with Cobbett's gibe at "Citizen Callender." His spirits rose further when Beckley told him that he knew Dr. Benjamin Rush well. "A great man, James. Signed the Declaration of Independence, you know. Hated Hamilton in the Revolution, introduced me to Colonel Burr. Saved thousands of lives, and I'm proud to say he spent many a happy hour by my bed and fireside."

Walking down the hall of the courthouse, the three naturalized citizens passed a crowded civil courtroom. Beckley, out of curiosity, stopped to look in, then motioned his friends quickly to come inside. "Cobbett's being charged for libel. This should be worth watching."

"He's one of that aristocratic junto," Lyon agreed, "trying to screw the hard earnings out of the poor people's pockets so the government can pay enormous salaries. I want to see the Porcupine get his comeuppance."

Callender saw the ruddy-faced Cobbett sitting in the dock, answering questions in a libel case brought by the Spanish Minister on behalf of the King of Spain. A grand jury of a score of citizens was listening.

"Is it not true, Mr. Cobbett," said the Pennsylvania judge conducting the interrogation, "that you caused to be published in *Porcupine's Gazette* an accusation that the King of Spain was 'a degenerate Prince whose acts were directed by the crooked politics of France'?"

"It is true that I wrote and published it," said Cobbett stoutly, "and 'crooked' is the true word for it. That I should be arrested for it and dragged into this court is proof of the low estate to which America's vaunted 'liberty of the press' has sunk." He noticed the entrance of Beckley, Lyon and Callender into the courtroom—all frequent targets of his— and nodded grimly at their presence, as if they were part of a conspiracy to silence him.

Beckley leaned across and whispered to Lyon: "The judge, McKean, is one of ours. Best republican in the State of Pennsylvania, helped me carry the state for Jefferson. And the Spanish Minister is soon to be his son-in-law. This should cost Cobbett a pretty penny."

McKean proceeded with his examination of the defendant. "And did your reference to the Minister Plenipotentiary here, in the same publication, as 'the little Don,' not hold him up to ridicule?"

"He is demonstrably small," said Cobbett. "Look at him. He's getting littler every minute. As for my writing, I have endeavored to make America laugh instead of weep."

"Everyone who has in him the sentiments of a Christian or gentleman," said McKean, turning to the jury, "cannot but be highly offended at the envenomed scurrility that is raging in pamphlets and newspapers printed in Philadelphia. Libeling has become a kind of national crime."

"And so it has," whispered Lyon, who had caught more than his share of abuse from Cobbett. "This judge is also the prosecutor. Porcupine will pay."

"This scandalous evil of scurrility and defamation," the judge went on, "is aimed at creating a rupture between the sister republics of the United States and France."

"Criminal intent," whispered Beckley, who had read law. "He has to prove criminal intent."

"The editor and printer of the most licentious and virulent of these publications," said McKean, "—the defendant Cobbett—has ransacked our language for terms of reproach and insult. His irritating invectives, couched in the most vulgar and opprobrious language, are designed to provoke a war with France. They seem calculated to vilify, nay, to subvert, republican governments on both sides of the Atlantic."

Callender was torn. He agreed with everything the republican judge was saying about the despicable Porcupine, and especially his intention of provoking a war with France. The XYZ affair had given him a whip that Cobbett used to flay the *Aurora*, Callender personally, Lyon and all the Jefferson men. And yet the editor was being sued for the way he presented his opinions, much as Callender presented his. Cobbett was more successful at it by far, and handier at invective, but they were in the same boat, in a sense. If the prickly Porcupine could be fined heavily for his use of invective, who would be next?

The judge rose from the bench and brandished his gavel at the jurors: "Gentlemen of the Grand Jury, it is for you to animadvert on his conduct. Without you these libels cannot be corrected. To censure the licentious is to maintain the liberty of the press."

Cobbett raised his hand for permission to speak. Judge McKean—Callender recalled that Cobbett had denounced him recently in his *Gazette* as "a vain, conceited, rusty old weathercock"—nodded yes. He smiled and sat back as if to enjoy the sight of the defendant further infuriating everyone in the courtroom.

Still seated, Cobbett said to the judge, "So pointed and personal a charge to a jury, I am bold to say, has never before been delivered from the bench in any country that has the least pretensions to civil liberty."

"Stand up when you address the bench," said the judge, "before I hold you in contempt."

Cobbett rose from his chair in the dock, turned away from McKean and addressed the jurors. "I will say that I have never attacked anyone whose private character is not, in every light, as far beneath mine as infamy is beneath honor. I defy the City of Philadelphia, respectable as are many of its inhabitants, to produce me a single man who is more sober, industrious, or honest; who is a kinder husband, a tenderer father, a firmer friend. Though it is unseemly for anyone to say that much of himself, I invite comparison of my character with the very judge who holds me to be the worst of miscreants."

"He'd better not lose the jury's verdict," Lyon whispered, "because he's just asked for hell itself as a fine."

"As to my writing," Cobbett continued, "I never did slander or defame any one, if the promulgation of useful truths be not slander."

Beckley whispered, "Ah, but there's the rub. Truth is no defense against libel." Callender nodded grimly; in England, the truth defense had made headway in changing the common law, but not here.

"I have, indeed, stripped away the close-drawn veil of hypocrisy," Cobbett boasted. "I have ridiculed the follies, and lashed the vices of thousands, and done it sometimes, perhaps, with a rude and violent hand. But these are not the days for gentleness and mercy. Such is the temper of the foe; such must be the temper of his opponent."

The editor of *Porcupine's Gazette* took out his billfold and extracted from it a pamphlet and a clipping from a newspaper. "I carry these," he said mildly to the jurors, "as an example of the correctness and accuracy of all you have heard from our distinguished judge on the subject of personal invective. By the way, I congratulate Judge McKean on his sagacity, and wish his famously beautiful, if otherwise limited, daughter well in her forthcoming marriage to the Minister of Spain, the complainant in this case."

"I wondered how he would inform the jury of that slight conflict," said Beckley.

"Here is an effusion from the editor Bache, hireling of the French and the Chief Judge's companion at civic festivals." The editor of *Porcupine's Gazette* pulled on his spectacles and examined the cutting from the rival *Aurora*. "He calls the King of England 'that prince of sea-robbers, head of a corrupt monarchy, a mixture of tyranny, profligacy, and brutality,' and says, 'I would heartily rejoice if the Royal Family were all decently guillotined.' Compare that diatribe, which went unchastised by this court, to my mild censure of Spain.

"And what did this same calumniator of Britain write of John Jay, Chief Justice of the United States, who negotiated a peacemaking treaty with your mother country? That he was, and I quote, 'a damned arch-traitor.'" Cobbett paused for effect. "Was his sheet, the *Aurora*, harassed with libel suits or for publishing Thomas Paine's infamous letter to George Washington with all its hellish malignity of Parisian cannibals?"

He looked out into the courtroom, as if seeking out his tormentors. "Paine's letter savagely maligned Washington, whose fame and character are now bleeding at every pore as a result of the attacks of these unrestrained scoundrels. And right over there"—Callender's chest constricted as Cobbett pointed an accusing finger at him—"seated there, to gloat at this travesty of Pennsylvania justice, is James Thomson Callender.

"That little reptile, who seems to have been born for a chimney-sweep and to be even now following the sooty trade, made his escape from the hands of justice in Scotland for publishing a string of infamous falsehoods."

Cobbett held up another page torn from the *Aurora*. "Here is what this fugitive has written about the one man this nation universally reveres. 'If ever a nation was debauched by a man, the American nation has been debauched by Washington. Let his conduct serve to be a warning that no man may be an idol, and that the mask of patriotism may be worn to conceal the foulest designs against the liberties of the people.'" Cobbett reminded his audience that Callender had proudly signed that defamation of the nation's first President. "And this from a writer who claimed in the preface to his 'history' that Thomas Jefferson encouraged him to publish an American edition of his perfidious work."

Judge McKean looked out into the audience, spotted his trio of anti-Federalist allies and motioned for Callender to stand. "You have been singled out for vilification by the defendant, Mr. Callender. Do you wish to tell the court what you think of this defense?"

"Here's your chance, James," said Beckley. "Remember, Cobbett's intent in what he wrote was to start a war. That pernicious purpose, that criminal intent, is what makes a libel."

Lyon joined in the hurried coaching. "And every man in the jury box will be taxed by the Federalists to pay for that war Cobbett wants against France."

Callender walked slowly to the front of the courtroom. He was thinking less of what he would say than of how he looked to the jurors, dressed as he was all in black, not that much unlike a chimney-sweep. It was a good thing he was hatless. He willed himself not to fidget or otherwise seem to be ridden with lice, as Cobbett had pictured him before, or reptilian, as he had caricatured him now.

He did not say what they expected. "If a man is attacked in the press," he told the jury, "he should reply through the same channel. In that way, he fights his antagonist with equal weapons."

Judge McKean looked sharply at him. Callender went on with what he believed: "The doctrine of libels has frequently been a screen for powerful and profligate men. When they are unable to meet their accusers on the fair ground of argument, they take recourse to law to overwhelm their accusers by the expense of litigation."

Nobody in the room was prepared for that. The republican judge directed a question to Callender: "You were speaking of private citizens. But what of libels against those entrusted with the conduct of public affairs? Does this not breed in the people a dislike of their governors, and endanger the public peace by inclining the people to faction and sedition?"

Sedition against the government, more than defamation of the character of individuals, was apparently where all this was headed. Callender stubbornly shook his head, even as he felt he was shaking in his shoes. "In all countries," Callender replied, "those who hold the reins of government are the persons who have most to fear from disclosure of the truth. Let the history of the federal government instruct us all, that the mask of patriotism may be worn to conceal the foulest designs against the liberties of the people."

From the defendant's table, Cobbett stared at him with his mouth open. Callender turned and trudged back to his seat.

Beckley said, "You damn fool, whose side are you on?" Lyon weighed in with "Have you forgotten what he just said about you? It's not like you to turn the other cheek. I'd have—"

"Spit in his face," Callender finished his sentence for him. "I'm sorry, Matt, but that's what I think." To him, liberty of the press went beyond a guarantee of no previous restraint, especially if the sword of later punishment hung over the head of writers. Freedom of speech even went beyond admitting truth as a defense against libel, which this judge rejected as not being part of the common law. As Callender saw it, the place for public disputation was in print, not in any law courts. You inveighed as vigorously as you could with fact and opinion, and then you lowered your head for the return attack in an opposing journal, and then, if you were still standing, you let loose a return broadside. An editor had a responsibility to print a target's answer, but that obligation was assumed voluntarily to encourage the cut and thrust of debate and to let the editor pose as an exemplar of fairness. Any government restriction on the right to criticize—especially to criticize national leaders, even in language chosen to call up outrage—diminished a country's freedom.

Callender's friends, disgusted with his political apostasy, strode out of the courtroom and left him there alone. With little else to do, he seated himself to await the decision of a grand jury that had been forcefully directed by the judge to indict.

In two hours, the nineteen members filed in and were polled. Nine voted for indictment of Cobbett, but ten—Federalists, probably, but joined by one or two republicans swayed by Callender—voted against. The clerk said, "The bill is returned Ignoramus by the grand jury."

The jurors, to the surprise of most spectators and to the evident irritation of the judge, had decided to ignore Cobbett's undoubted offense. There was to be no prosecution of *Porcupine's Gazette* for libel. Callender's reaction was mixed. He was glad that jurors had shown respect for an editor's right to criticize, even abusively, for that was a step away from sedition. At the same time, he was sorry that the pompous Porcupine, profiting handsomely from his abuse of the minority, had not felt the pain of monetary judgment.

Cobbett sought Callender out afterward. "You surprised me. I am in your debt."

"We reptiles and chimney-sweeps want no thanks from the likes of you," Callender told him sharply. "It's just that I believe it is the happy privilege of every American that he may prattle and print in what way he pleases, and without anyone to make him afraid."

"You think your republican judge, McKean, was not trying to make me afraid? Of course he was." Cobbett punched a finger into Callender's chest. "Here is the only difference between my Adams and your Jefferson on the liberty of the press: Adams wants to control republican newsmongers in the Federal courts, and Jefferson wants to control Federalist newsmongers in the State courts." Callender shook his head, certain his adversary was mistaken.

"You should be more careful about whom you befriend," Cobbett added. "Spittin' Lyon, you know, is head of the United Wild Irish who are plotting with the French émigrés to overthrow the government here. And that Jacobin milksop Beckley, him and his false vote counts, walked out on you, too—was he disappointed in your stand?"

Callender took offense at Cobbett's bullying gratitude. "Matt Lyon is as loyal to the Stars and Stripes as you are to the Union Jack. And John Beckley is my friend." Beckley was also the source of the pamphlet that made him famous, but that was not for Porcupine to know. "What is more, I need Beckley." He paused because his heart was beating too fast. "My wife is ill and he will introduce me to Dr. Benjamin Rush."

"The fever?"

"It is ravaging her." She had lost twenty pounds and looked like a skeleton.

"Callender, I have two pieces of advice for you. They are in recompense for the great favor you have done me today, the reason for which I cannot conjecture. Perhaps you spoke up out of some perverse consistency of principle."

"I don't need your advice."

"Yes, you do, and don't let your pride make you a fool. The first advice is fair warning: get out of Philadelphia immediately. My friend Harper tells me that tomorrow the House will pass his Alien bill. It's aimed at all your radical ilk, but you are the first one the government intends to arrest and deport. In fact, the bill ought to have your name on it."

"You're an alien, too, Cobbett."

"An alien, yes, but a friend to America's Tory government. I am not an agent on Talleyrand's payroll, as you are, ready to urge a legion of readers to rise up in support of a French invasion. You are the enemy alien."

Callender did not countercharge Cobbett with being on the British ambassador's payroll, though he believed that to be true. Certainly those two Englishmen were thick as thieves. Instead, he said, "I'm an American now," the words coming strangely to his tongue. "Since this morning."

Cobbett's light-colored eyebrows shot up, his close-set eyes widening. "Good for you. That was a deft maneuver. It will cause great gnashing of teeth among some of my dearest political associates."

"Harper, you mean."

"Robert Harper will follow his Alien and Immigration bills with a Sedition bill," Cobbett confided. "Your cadaverous Gallatin will fight it in the House, but the temper of the times is such that Harper will prevail."

"Harper's Federalists may not have a big enough majority in the House," Callender reminded him.

"Ah, but Harper will make some compromises to win over some republicans. And I," Cobbett said immodestly, "am suggesting a couple of those compromises."

Why would this English Tory want to soften the impact of sedition's blows in Federal courts? It occurred to Callender that Cobbett wanted to fashion some basis for defenses against libel in Pennsylvania State Court, thereby protecting himself from a renewal of today's attack.

"Gallatin is asking for truth to be a defense against a sedition charge," Callender offered.

"Right. And if Harper follows my advice, which it is his custom to do, Gallatin will get that. And he'll get something else from Harper: that a jury, not a judge, should decide the intent of the accused in a sedition trial."

Those concessions would make the monstrous sedition gag more palatable to a few republicans. Callender assumed it would also lay the ground-work for what Cobbett wanted: the acceptance of truth as a defense in State libel trials, and for the jury in those trials to determine if the defendant had been driven by a malicious intent. The ham-fisted Cobbett was subtler than he had thought.

"Your friend Harper wants my scalp," Callender said, knowing that for a fact.

"No, it is Alexander Hamilton, the greatest American alive, who wants your scalp. Also, President Adams, urged on by his meddling wife Abigail, wants your scalp. And to be brutally honest, if you still had a newspaper to write for, I would want your scalp. But Congressman Robert Goodloe Harper has something grander in mind than to squelch one noxious news-monger like you, or a handful of divisive papers."

Callender waited for Cobbett to vouchsafe the ulterior Federalist motive in pressing for a sedition law. Cobbett outwaited him, so Callender was forced to ask: "What's more delicious to the Federalists than silencing the opposition press?"

"Crushing the opposition itself, of course, at the very center of resis-tance to authority." The Englishman smacked his fist into the palm of his other hand. "At that moment, unity and stability will be restored to Amer-ica's political life. Enough—I am off to excoriate this rascal McKean in a pamphlet exposing the hypocrisy of American liberty of the press."

Callender held the sleeve of his jacket. "What do you mean, 'the center of resistance'? Are you talking about silencing the House of Representa-tives?"

"I've told you as much as your feeble mind can handle. You must re-member, of course, that I will continue to denounce, in what your radical friends call my vulgar and licentious way, anything you write in support of those incendiaries and disorganizers."

Callender expected as much and dismissed it with a grin. "What's your other advice?"

"A personal matter." He dropped his bantering manner and became se-rious. "Do not allow your loved ones to come under the care of Dr. Ben-jamin Rush."

"He's the most famous—"

"I know, the leader of the Philosophical Society, a pillar of the church, the cynosure of all medical eyes. But his remedy for everything is to purge and bleed. Rush's patients die, if not from the fever, from his murderous, quack treatment. He is a sneaking trimmer in politics, but more important, he's a doctor who kills his patients. Stay away from him."

Callender looked up at the imposing figure and shook his head. "I don't agree with you about anything, Porcupine. Beckley's my friend, and he would not direct me wrongly. Now I have to go after him and Spittin' Matt and say I lost my head in here. We are under the most vicious attack from you and your tyrannous crew, and we must stick together."

Cobbett shrugged, then cheerfully clapped him on the shoulder. "You Americans."

As Callender left, he heard Cobbett calling after him, "And by the bye, in your next turbid harangue, you really ought to do something about your figures of speech. When I see you flourishing with a metaphor, I feel as much anxiety as I do when I see a child playing with a razor."

Chapter 11

GEORGE WASHINGTON

July 9, 1798
MOUNT VERNON, VIRGINIA

"You saw that impudent letter from Paine?" said George Washington, who seemed to Hamilton to have grown much older in the year since he retired to Mount Vernon.

Hamilton nodded that he had. Bache had published in his *Aurora* an open letter from the revolutionary patriot, now living in France and still the patron saint of Jefferson and his Jacobin ilk. Tom Paine called his erstwhile hero, Washington, "treacherous in private friendship and a hypocrite in public life, an apostate or an imposter." Even worse, the author of *The Rights of Man* had addressed the President—defender of his dignity as the nation's founder—as "George." Hamilton had never even heard Washington's wife Martha call him by his first name.

Washington, notoriously thin-skinned when it came to criticism, removed his spectacles and pushed a newspaper across the tea table. "That's a production of Peter Porcupine, alias William Cobbett," the former President said. "Making allowances for the asperity of an Englishman, for some of his strong and coarse expressions, and a want of information of many facts, it is not a bad thing."

Hamilton glanced at the small but potent print in *Porcupine's Gazette:* "How Tom gets a living, or what brothel he inhabits in Paris, I know not. But men will learn to express all that is base, malignant, treacherous, unnatural and blasphemous, by one single monosyllable—Paine." Hamilton agreed with the point of view and admired the way that Englishman made his position absolutely clear. Cobbett, whom Hamilton knew to be more British Tory than American Federalist, had also joined the criticism of Washington on his expense accounts, but the great man's longtime aide and message-writer did not bring that up; few newsmongers were reliable in everything.

"Some of the gazettes," Washington went on, "have teemed with all the invective that disappointment, ignorance of facts and malicious falsehoods could invent." He shook his head slowly, obviously grieved at the licentiousness of the press.

"General." Hamilton liked to address him thus, recalling their days in the Revolution when he had served Washington as his chief of staff. The military title also introduced what he had in mind. "At the present dangerous crisis of public affairs, I make no apology for troubling you in your deserved retirement."

The former President, however, had his mind on his unfair treatment by the press and was not about to move to another subject. As his guest had to nod in sympathy, he continued full sail: "They have sought to misrepresent my politics and affections, and to wound my reputation and feelings. Their purpose was to weaken, if not entirely destroy the confidence the American people had been pleased to repose in me."

"But they failed abysmally, sir. Your good repute has never been sullied."

"It might be expected," Washington pressed ahead, "that at this stage of my public life I should take some notice of such virulent abuse."

"No. It's beneath you to notice those attacks." Hamilton wished he could get him off this subject. He knew that Washington's reputation for integrity meant more to him than anything, and he knew it was not mere vanity. Such stature inculcated the people's faith in their new government and gave permanence to the institutions of democracy. The French had tried to emulate the American experiment and had failed in the mob's lust for blood and bread. There was no guarantee that the American experiment in representative government would not similarly fail; if it did, nobody could foretell when the chance would come to mankind again. Hamilton knew that the people's trust in the political virtue of their leaders was central to Washington's plan. That was why he, when Treasury Secretary, was willing to present his tale of adultery and blackmail rather than admit to any hint of financial corruption.

"You're right, Colonel. I shall pass over them in utter silence." The cloud passed from Washington's expression. He became formally receptive, looking at once interested and aloof, the way Hamilton recalled him in Cabinet sessions. His longtime subordinate felt subordinated again. Hamilton's mission was manipulative, to use the General as his route back to power, but he at once felt the old tug of unchallengeable authority. The man had an uncanny ability to exude command; only that presence had kept Hamilton and Jefferson, with such differing views on the source of sovereignty and the centrality of authority, in harness in the nation's formative years. Power—perhaps because truly unsought—naturally flowed Washington's way.

"A powerful faction—a sect whose high priest is here in Virginia—wishes to make this country a province of France," he told his old commander. He presumed that Washington was well aware of Jefferson's machinations with Madison and Monroe in the middle counties of the state. "I foresee a serious struggle with that nation. It is the most flagitious, despotic, and vindictive government that ever disgraced the annals of mankind. You are aware of the disclosure of the XYZ perfidy?"

Washington acknowledged that he was, but was not at all surprised. "One would think," he said, "that the measure of infamy pursued by the French Directory required no further disclosure to open the eyes of the blindest."

That encouraged Hamilton to go on. "In the event of an open rupture with France, the public voice"—on behalf of which he felt free to speak to-day—"will again call you to command the armies of your country. You are again needed to unite the nation. Everyone says that you will be compelled to make the sacrifice."

"Open war is likely only if the French mounted a formidable invasion," noted the former President. "In case of an actual invasion by a formidable force, I certainly would not entrench myself under the cover of age and re-tirement. But there is no conviction in my breast that I would be the best choice to lead a new army." Hamilton shook his head and waited, knowing this was his leader's modest introduction. "If I were to serve, it would have to be unequivocally known that the nation's preference might not be given to a man more in his prime." That meant he wanted some insulation in ad-vance from the expected criticism from Bache and Callender and their re-publican ilk.

"How might you counter such an invasion, sir?" Hamilton wanted him thinking militarily rather than politically.

"During the Revolution, our plan called for time, caution and worrying the enemy," said Washington, warming to the subject, "until we could be better provided with arms and had better-disciplined troops. But in this case, the invader ought to be attacked at every step, not suffered to make an establishment in this country and acquiring strength from disaffected Americans and from slaves." He paused. "I would want to know who would be my coadjutors. Would you take an active part?"

Hamilton was hoping for just that invitation. "Sir, not only am I pre-pared to give up an extensive and lucrative law practice, but Governor Jay has just offered to appoint me Senator from New York, to fill the Hobart va-cancy. I have declined, in anticipation of the honor of serving as your sec-ond-in-command." That position as number two was central to him; with the aging Washington as titular commander-in-chief of the army, he wanted to be the de facto commander. "Perhaps as your Inspector General with line command. Frankly, I would expect rank proportionate to the sac-rifice I am to make."

As a major-general named before any others, he would in effect have control of a 20,000-man provisional force that could one day become Amer-ica's standing army. Such a force not only would put the pro-French faction in the central counties of Virginia to the test of resistance, but also would make possible a vast expansion of the United States. It was Hamilton's dream to compete with France in wresting control from Spain of all the Florida and Louisiana territories, thereby extending the nation south to the Gulf and west past the Mississippi. After that, a march southward through Mexico would ultimately bring South America under U.S. control.

The New World, in Hamilton's vision, would then be a unified empire, capable of challenging any empire in the Old. He disagreed with what he thought of as Madison's shortsightedness; a nation, as Hamilton conceived it, did not have to be compact to be responsive to the will of its people. Popular resistance to such a campaign to strike westward and southward, he was certain, would be minor; all Hamilton needed to overwhelm domestic division and unify two continents was an army. Such a hemispheric conqueror would be made President in 1800 almost by acclamation, in the Washington tradition. Some halfhearted, "low" Federalists might stick with President Adams when Hamilton's challenge came, but he was confident that the "high" Federalists loyal to him controlled the election machinery.

The former President rose and led the way to the front porch of Mount Vernon, overlooking the Potomac River. On its banks some of his slaves were washing clothes. Hamilton, looking up at him, was reminded of how commandingly tall and erect Washington was, even in his declining years. Physical size and carriage were helpful in dominating a roomful of men.

"If the President calls me into service," Washington said quietly, "I will tell him of my wish to put you first in my command."

Hamilton closed his eyes in relief and then thanked his chief for his confidence. "Harsh measures are in store as we raise this army," he reported. "An Alien Act has been passed to deport those suspected of secret machinations against the government. I hear a Sedition bill is on the way."

This did not bother Washington. "In many instances aliens are sent among us for the express purpose of poisoning the minds of our own people. They seek to sow dissensions among them, thereby endeavoring to dissolve the Union." But he cautioned Hamilton: "Of course, these could become the desiderata in the opposition."

That last was a politically wise observation; Hamilton agreed that if Adams became too fervent in his suppression of dissent, public sentiment could turn and the strict new laws then play into the hands of the Jeffersonians. The old man, always seen to be above faction, was not above recognizing the growing partizan reality.

"I agree, sir, of course. Although the mass of aliens ought to be obliged to leave the country, guarded exceptions should be made in the case of merchants and those whose demeanor among us has been unexceptional. We need not be cruel or violent." As Washington seemed to await more, Hamilton added, "Let us not establish a tyranny. Energy in the Executive is a different thing from the violence that would give body and solidity to faction."

Then the New Yorker pushed a pin into the ballooning fortunes of an irritant in his own state: "I fear President Adams, who may be an alliance in New York with Aaron Burr, will want him in a position of authority."

Washington shook his head, no. "Colonel Burr is a brave and able officer, but"—and the "but" was all-important—"the question is whether he has not equal talents for intrigue."

Hamilton took that to mean Burr was out, and with him any challenge to Hamilton's authority over the new army. President Adams would soon learn that when asked to save the country again, George Washington would do it on his own terms. And the key term would be the return to public life of Alexander Hamilton astride a white horse.

Chapter 12

July 11, 1798

EAST NOTTINGHAM,

CECIL COUNTY, MARYLAND

"You are well acquainted with Colonel Burr," Jacob Clingman said to his wife, the former Maria Reynolds. "He represented you in your divorce, and would take no fee. He told you to stay in touch with him. Now we need him again. Why are you reluctant to write?"

Maria was glad her young husband did not know that she knew Colonel Burr better than anyone suspected. She had met that dark-eyed New Yorker soon after she had left home at age fourteen, against her parents' wishes, to marry the handsome and seductive Reynolds. That was over thirteen years ago, two years before the birth of her daughter Susan. She had discovered that Reynolds was a ne'er-do-well and a cheat, unreliable and unfaithful; often brutish to her and of late too inclined to fondle Susan. But by then her unforgiving family had cut her off. Burr, contrariwise, was gentle and considerate, appreciative of a neglected young beauty, and opened her mind to a world of politics and intrigue; their secret intimacy blossomed into a deeper friendship that lasted to this day.

Had that trustworthy friend been in Philadelphia when Reynolds's brutality forced her to leave him, she would have solicited Burr's help in returning to New York in 1792; as it turned out, a stroke of unkind fate took her to Secretary Hamilton's door. She recalled how Burr helped extricate her from her husband's schemes after the flinty Monroe and the kindly Speaker Muhlenberg began their investigation, and later represented her in a divorce proceeding that made it possible for her to make lawful her mating with Jacob. Despite the scandal that reached the surface in 1797, and despite Jacob's inability to find a permanent position, Maria had remained a faithful wife and caring mother. She did not know where asking Burr this favor might lead.

"I am not reluctant to write him," Maria lied, quill in hand, the blank paper before her. "It's difficult to find the words to start."

" 'My dear Colonel Burr' is a good way to begin," he said.

She sighed and began. *"Because you were good enough to suggest that Jacob and I keep you informed about our lives and whereabouts, I send you these greetings from Cecil County in Maryland."* She knew that Burr did not care about the location of Jacob Clingman, a stockjobber with a tainted reputation; he cared about Maria. Her letter had to conceal their relationship from her second husband as well as from Burr's beloved daughter, who often read his mail. *"My daughter Susan and I are well. My husband Jacob is trying to make a career in finance but finds it difficult to overcome the enmity of Col. Hamilton."*

"It's General Hamilton now," he corrected, looking over her shoulder. "He's back in the saddle."

"That evil man will always be 'Colonel' to me," she said. Drawing the inkwell closer, she continued writing. *"We think that he has blacklisted Jacob Clingman among the securities dealers in commerce with New York banks, and his man at Treasury has done the same in Philadelphia. This has made it hard for us.*

"Jacob has written to a friend in London and hopes to get employment in England. If you would be willing to write to anyone you know in a bank or counting house there, we will be most grateful."

"That's it, good," said Clingman. "Burr is known to despise Hamilton and has been doing political business with James Monroe and the other republicans. That takes courage now, with the Sedition bill and all."

"*The newspaper here tells us that Hamilton has overcome the*"—she was about to write "scandal" but decided on "*episode*"—"*that bore my name,*" Maria continued, "*and is now second in command to General Washington in the new army. Do you really suppose they expect an invasion by the French? I remember your concern about the danger to liberty of a standing army, and I hope you remember my concern about the kind of man who would forge letters from me and place at risk my reputation to protect his own.*" That would stimulate an answer, she was sure, even if he had no help to offer in England for her husband.

"*Partly because of the settlement you were able to wring out of—*"

"'Extract' is better."

"*—my former husband Reynolds, we managed to keep our heads above water. I will never forget your many kindnesses.*"

"Offer to help him," Clingman suggested. "Politicians always need help."

She stayed her pen, thinking of the way her first husband, Reynolds, had often urged her to thrust herself on men of financial means or political influence. Though Jacob, she was sure, did not think of it in that way, renewed contact with Burr would mean temptation.

"*If your travels bring you to Maryland, or if you wish to see me anywhere else, I am at your disposal for any service to further your political career. I hope you will call on me for whatever I can do.*

"*Sincerely your friend, Maria Lewis Clingman.*"

"You'd better tell him I've adopted the name of James Clement. It will sound better to an English firm."

Maria sighed, adding that in a postscript. On second thought, she copied out the letter again, pointing out the name change as useful to her husband in starting a new life, and signing her own name as the one most likely to be her last: *Maria Clement.*

Chapter 13

ROBERT GOODLOE HARPER

July 14, 1798
PHILADELPHIA

*R*obert Goodloe Harper welcomed Cobbett to his cramped quarters in Congress Hall and cheerily held up his copy of *Porcupine's Gazette* for that sweltering summer day. "I see with great satisfaction that *Porcupine's Gazette* has driven the *Aurora* to the wall."

Cobbett was pleased. He had been told of the financial difficulties of Bache's paper by a friend in the Mayor's office, and had written with unconcealed glee of the failure of that strapped publisher to pay a $5 fine. On top of that, Bache was stricken with the yellow fever and the fool was being treated by Dr. Benjamin Rush, the bleeder. "You have news for me?"

"George Washington is with us," Harper said. "President Adams gagged a bit at having Hamilton rammed down his throat as second-in-command, but he's organizing a force of twenty thousand men. That gives us the flower of the country and puts arms into the hands of all our friends."

Cobbett was comfortable with that; even if the French did not invade, the war fever he had helped whip up with the unwitting aid of Callender would have a beneficial effect. Every nation's rulers needed a standing army to keep order and protect property. As one of Harper's lieutenants had openly declared, the only principle by which radical republicans could be governed was fear.

"I wanted you here today, William, to hear the debate on my Sedition bill. We are this close to passage"—the portly South Carolinian held up thumb and forefinger a half-inch apart—"but Gallatin has been able to muster resistance. I'll have to compromise on a couple of points."

The Englishman was quite prepared with recommendations. Sedition, in his eyes, was merely a special type of libel; it brought a government, rather than an individual, into disrepute. What was sauce for the goose of sedition could be sauce for the gander of libel, and it was the gander of libel that was honking at him. In Harper's sweetening of the federal Sedition bill to placate a few republicans would be Cobbett's defense against the libel lust of the state republican Judge McKean.

The editor raised one finger: "Malicious intent to weaken the government must be proved." Harper nodded approval.

He held up a second finger: "The jury and not the judge must decide on such malicious intent." Harper shrugged his agreement; apparently that did not seem to him to be much of a concession, but if it would please wavering republicans, fine.

A third pudgy finger joined the others: "And the truth of what is written or said about a public official must be a defense against a charge of sedition." If those principles were made part of Federal sedition law, Cobbett believed, they would inevitably become part of State libel law. He would then be much safer in the radical-red State Court of Pennsylvania from reprisal by irate friends of Jefferson like Dr. Rush, whom he had been calling a bloodstained quack.

"I'll use all three if I have to," said Harper hurriedly, "to overcome Gallatin's opposition. Come listen."

"Does the situation of the country require that any law of this kind should pass?" asked Albert Gallatin, as anti-Federalist leader, launching the debate on the floor. "Do new and alarming symptoms of sedition exist to require us to restrict freedom of speech and of the press?"

"Yes!" Harper shot back. "I have in my hand evidence of a dangerous combination to overturn the government—by publishing the most shameless falsehoods against the Representatives of the people." He brandished a fistful of clippings from the *Aurora*, the *New York Argus* and other newspapers. "These say that we are hostile to free governments and genuine liberty.

These say that we should be displaced and that the people ought to raise an insurrection against the government."

"Do you think, sir," said Gallatin, "that the people of America are ready to submit to imprisonment, or exile, whenever suspicion, calumny or vengeance shall mark them for ruin?" He waved off Harper's request to immediately reply. "No, sir, they will resist this tyrannic system! The people will oppose it, the States will not submit to it." Everyone in the chamber knew he was getting into dangerous territory with this argument, suggesting popular resistance and State opposition to Federal law. Nevertheless, he proceeded in his Swiss-French accent: "Whenever our laws infringe the Constitution under which they were made, the people ought not to hesitate which they should obey."

Cobbett, at the table for the stenographic clerks, raised his eyebrows. This republican had just dared to suggest that any man could interpret the Constitution in a way that permitted him to ignore a law passed by the Congress.

Harper caught it, too. "Beware what you are suggesting, sir."

"If we here exceed our powers, we become tyrants," Gallatin said, plunging deeper into rebellious rhetoric, "and our acts have no effect. Your Sedition bill will cause disaffection among the States. It will rouse the people to oppose your government. It will bring tumults and violations." He paused, seeking a way to express in coolly formal terms the most inflammatory idea yet to be expressed in the House. "It will bring a recurrence to first revolutionary principles."

"Do you talk of revolution? That, sir," said Harper in a menacing tone, "may border on an expression of sedition itself."

The customarily noisy House was hushed. Cobbett, at the clerk's table, caught Harper's eye and nodded approval. He knew that Harper's target only appeared to be the irresponsible press. Although in the case of Callender, it was, the hidden goal of the Sedition bill was far more daring: to suppress opposition in the Congress itself. The press was but the mouthpiece of party, and to silence the press would not totally crush the party in opposition.

"Those who oppose this law," warned Harper, "without carefully distinguishing between verbal protest and violent action, are insurgents and rebels themselves. Your statement just now, Mr. Gallatin, about 'first revolutionary principles,' is intended to produce divisions, tumults, insurrection and blood."

Gallatin stood his dangerous ground. "You suppose that whoever dislikes the measures of an Administration, and of a temporary majority in Congress, is seditious. You hold that whoever expresses his want of confidence in the men now in power is an enemy—not of the Administration, but of the government itself, and is liable to punishment. In this despotic bill, you seek a weapon to perpetuate your authority and preserve your present places."

True enough, thought Cobbett. Gallatin seemed to understand the essential purpose of the Federalist bill. Swatting the annoying mosquitoes of the press was incidental to the great goal of achieving a serene public order. The end being pursued was to preserve national unity even if it meant crushing all political opposition.

"You, sir," said Gallatin, taking the argument to his opponent, "in imputing sedition to me just now, have made the first attempt in this House to suppress the opinion of an elected Representative. I am not surprised. In your career, you have grossly attacked members for writing circular letters. Your next step is to make our speeches the subject of prosecution for sedition."

"You, sir, and not I," retorted the leader of the Federalists, "are the one to set up a doctrine that every man has a right to decide for himself what laws are constitutional. You and not I suggest that States have a right to combine and resist the laws passed by this Congress. Is that not a call for disunion? For anarchy?"

Good point; Cobbett always thought that a great weakness in the U.S. Constitution was its unanswered question: Who decides what is constitutional? The President? Congress? The States? The courts? The "people," in an unruly mob assembled? Because the founders had left that question of ultimate authority unresolved, he felt, Congress should decide it here and now.

Gallatin did not rise to Harper's bait. Instead he cited the First Amendment to the Constitution and James Madison's views about what laws the Congress was expressly forbidden to pass. But his Federalist opponent derided that interpretation as only one man's opinion of the meaning of one amendment; and as war threatened, the opinion of a former Representative now under Jefferson's sway carried little weight.

Cobbett had prepared Harper with materials to take up a charge he had published in *Porcupine's Gazette:* that Vice President Jefferson was working hand-in-hand with Bache, Callender and now William Duane, the editor and writers for the *Aurora*, to undermine government authority. He did not have long to wait.

"The evidence in my hand," continued Harper, "is from a newspaper—the *Aurora*—that sounds the tocsin of insurrection. But this is not an independent voice. This paper is supported by a powerful party. Its anonymous pieces contain the opinions of a certain great man." He did not mention the name of Thomas Jefferson, just as Cobbett had not in his *Gazette*. "Its inflammatory addresses to the wild Irishmen and other immigrant radicals is, therefore, understood by them to come clothed with high authority. They know he is daily and nightly closeted with these disunion-minded journalists."

His voice rose to fill the hall as he decided to reveal his goal. "This sedition is the work of a party, not a mere newspaper. That party assiduously disseminates this paper through the country. And that party is a faction controlled by the government of France, which is engaged in a most criminal correspondence with her agents here. The purpose of this Sedition bill, entitled 'an act for the punishment of certain crimes against the United States,' is to repress the criminal enterprises of this party."

Gallatin disputed this direct linkage of Jefferson to the *Aurora* and Callender.

"The gentleman uses the word 'closeted,' " said Gallatin, affecting a smile, "as if that were a sinister place of meeting by the Vice President. If the receipt of visits in his public room, the door open to anyone who should call, may be called 'closeting,' then it is true he is 'closeted' with everyone who visits him. In no sinister sense is it true."

"The press is merely the engine," Harper pressed, "through which this party conspiracy functions. This is not a free press, this is a party publication, and it is the party that bears the responsibility for seeking to undermine the government and subvert the security of the nation."

"The gentleman has forgotten," said Gallatin, "that laws against political writing have throughout history been used by tyrants, from the Roman emperors to the Star Chamber. They have been used as this Sedition bill will be used—to prevent the diffusion of knowledge, to throw a veil on their folly or their crimes. This odious bill will satisfy those mean passions which always denote little minds, and will be used to perpetuate their own tyranny."

That eloquently phrased tirade may be satisfying republican passion, Cobbett observed, but was not winning a majority of votes in the House.

Apparently, Gallatin sensed the same mood, and concluded in a more conciliatory way.

"I join with all of you in despising all malicious slander. But I submit," he reasoned, "that governments whose motives are pure have long been willing to listen to legitimate criticism. These good governments have realized that suppression of criticism is a confession that no other means could defend their conduct. Coercion is never the answer to calumny. The only proper weapon to combat error is truth. Let the public judge."

To Cobbett's relief, Harper seemed to soften. "In the spirit of comity," he said—to pick up a handful of votes needed for a majority—he would support some amendments in the House to the Senate's harsh Sedition bill. First, he struck judges from the category of officials protected from attacks in print; Porcupine, thinking of the infamous McKean, applauded that.

Then he struck the words "libelous or scandalous" from the Senate language and substituted the more specific "false and malicious." Perhaps without fully realizing it—as Cobbett, advocate of this point, most certainly realized it—he made truth a defense against a charge of sedition. In a single stroke, Harper set on its head the old English common-law notion that "the greater the truth the greater the libel." Under this amendment to the proposed law, if a statement attacking a government official was true, no matter how vicious or defaming, it was not sedition. And if a true statement was not sedition against the national regime, Cobbett would argue in State court, it was not libel against an individual, either.

To win over one more republican vote from Maryland, Harper offered another concession: that a jury, not a judge, would decide if a seditious statement were made with malicious intent. That satisfied the Englishman, whose experience led him to feel more comfortable with jurymen for his own libel defenses.

"Next, I will stipulate that this law is not to apply where freedom of speech is expressly allowed by the Constitution." That sounded innocent enough, but Cobbett was aware it contained a trap for republican Members. Harper knew that the first amendment decreed that "Congress shall make no law" to abridge freedom of speech—but it said nothing about the States making laws abridging speech all their legislatures liked. The only place the Constitution expressly protected even the most outrageous speech, putting it beyond the reach of the States' libel laws, was on the floor of Congress. But the canny Harper, by specifying that nothing spoken on the floor could be prosecuted for sedition, made vulnerable to prosecution statements the Congressmen made or letters they had written outside the protected halls. His was no real concession; on the contrary, it was a way to prosecute such loudmouths on the campaign trail as Spittin' Matt and his "wild Irish" cohort.

Enough of the republicans went along, in fear of popular revulsion against the French, to pass the bill as amended. They hardly noticed a small provision Harper included authorizing judges to bind the accused seditionist to "good behavior" during prosecution by posting bond. That was the only part of the bill that Cobbett would have changed. Fear of losing a large deposit would effectively keep indicted critics of government from further berating officials.

Porcupine scribbled a quotation from the poet Juvenal and had a page take it to Harper. The Federalist leader smiled at him, and used it to close the debate on the bill designed to end American disunion by making outspoken opposition a crime:

> On Eagles' wings immortal Scandals fly
> While virtuous actions are but born and die.

PART II

The Sedition Scandal

The President's House, North Front, c. 1800

Chapter 14

October 10, 1798

PHILADELPHIA

*H*e was a widower now. Defpite the miniftrations *of* Dr. James T. Reynolds, the medical man assigned to the case by Dr. Benjamin Rush, the frail mother of his four boys had succumbed to the yellow fever. Callender never felt more alone.

Though it ran against his Calvinist nature to see much good in anybody, the bereaved man thanked God for Thomas Leiper. At a time when "moderate" republicans in the Congress were shunning him; when too many republican editors saw fit to trim their sails in the patriotic storm, leaving him exposed to Federalist fury—here was a Scot blessed with an open heart.

As head of the St. Andrew's Society, the tobacco merchant provided aid to Scottish immigrants in need. He provided his former countrymen a sense of pride, too, when he carried the tobacconists' standard in the Grand Federal Procession in Philadelphia in 1788, celebrating the new United States Constitution. And the gray-haired, tall Scot had given Callender a much-needed financial lift even before either of them had met Thomas Jefferson, by getting his fellow merchants to sponsor Callender's *Short History of the Nature and Consequences of Excise Laws.* In retrospect, Callender was satisfied that his pamphlet in criticism of sales taxation was well argued, because the tax not only fell on the poor, but also harmed small merchants and local manufacturers who needed tariff protection against imported British products. Even those who condemned Callender now as a scandalmonger had to admit he was capable of serious analysis of the government's role in promoting domestic trade.

"I never needed you more than now, Thomas," he said, his voice breaking, "my boys are motherless. And they'll have to be fatherless, too, until I can make enough money to send for them."

Leiper took his fellow Scot by his narrow shoulders and shook him gently, sharing the grief of the loss of a wife to the fever that had again decimated Philadelphia. Not even the personal care of Dr. Reynolds, at the direction of Dr. Rush himself, bleeding off her poisoned blood to balance her bodily humours, had been able to save her. As she lay dying, the agonized Callender, rocking the wasted woman in his arms, had made a deathbed promise that their four boys would be safe with him in Virginia. They would grow up far from the dread roar of the frogs in the mosquito-infested swamps near Philadelphia, and far from the fury of Federalist politicians who wanted to put their father in jail.

"You see I have thirteen of my own," Leiper said to him, pointing across the expanse of his estate where the children of his first and second wives were playing. "What's four more? They all take care of each other."

At that poignant evidence of kindness, the writer could hold himself together no longer and broke down sobbing. After a time, the two Scotsmen, a generation apart but their political convictions akin, began to take the long walk toward their children. They talked of past times, when Callender as the poet "Timothy Thunderproof" had urged independence for Scotland. When England's prosecutors decided he was neither thunderproof nor arrestproof, their sedition indictment forced him to flee across the Atlantic. Now, even with his suddenly acquired American citizenship, he was being forced to run from a sedition law again.

"With the yellow fever and now the war fever, these are terrible times," said Leiper. "You heard the sad news about Benny Bache?"

Callender nodded; the editor of the *Aurora* had been taken by disease as well. He was not so regretful at the death of Bache, who had often denied him credit for authorship of his articles and had failed to defend him when Porcupine denounced his books. Recently and more damagingly, Ben Franklin's hot-tempered grandson put all the blame on Callender for bringing the public's wrath down on the heads of republicans by forcing President Adams to release the XYZ papers. Worst of all, when Bache ran a foolish letter in the *Aurora* calling the President "old, querilous, bald, blind, crippled, toothless Adams," the President's partisans assumed Callender had been the author. That was untrue, but Bache did nothing to protect him by setting the record straight. Now, armed with the Sedition Act, the President had a personal reason to want to prosecute Callender.

He asked his merchant friend: "Will republicans keep the *Aurora* going?"

"Tom Jefferson himself told me we must try. Bache's widow Margaret will be publisher and Bill Duane will write it. We hoped it could be you, but you're a marked man, James. There's no more safety for you in Philadelphia than in Constantinople."

"I'm menaced by prosecution and imprisonment," Callender agreed, "by the sorry understrappers of Federal usurpation, who have much in common with the savage Turks."

He wished he had been asked to take charge of the *Aurora*, if only for the satisfaction of turning it down. Callender had been warned that enemies frustrated by his last-minute escape from alienhood were investigating his fraudulent new citizenship. "Duane will do," he told Leiper. "Not much of a writer, and he doesn't really understand political arithmetic, but at least he's not afraid of Porcupine." He had heard that the red-bearded Irishman had served time in a Calcutta prison for annoying the local British authorities, which spoke well for his courage. But as a troublemaking immigrant, Duane would now be vulnerable to the Alien Act. His predecessor at the *Aurora*, the late Benjamin Franklin Bache, had at least the protection of being his revered grandfather's grandson.

A new wave of bitterness swept through the doubly exiled Scot-American. "I hope that this pestilence of yellow fever," he told his benefactor, "so justly deserved by so many of the male adults of this sink of destruction, will prove a check on a much worse one—the black cockade fever." He burned at the thought of the Adams mobs, parading in their cockade hats, reviling the ranks of persecuted republicans. "I mean the fever that, under the pretense of defending us from a foreign war, aims at promoting a civil one."

Leiper tried to lift his spirits. "Jefferson also wanted you to know you won't be friendless in Virginia. Stevens Mason will give you shelter in his plantation at Raspberry Plain."

Callender knew that was intended to be comforting to a man, now forty and with no prospects, dependent on the dole of a dwindling band of politicians under fire, heading off into the unfamiliar territory of the Southland. Again, he was "alone in a land of strangers." Virginia's Senator Mason was an ally: The legislator proved his anti-British mettle by slipping the text of the Jay Treaty to Bache's *Aurora* for publication even as President Washington was trying to keep it secret. Nothing so daring had ever been done in the press before.

"You will find Mason has fifty dollars there for you," Leiper added, "from Jefferson's correspondent in Richmond, his cousin George. And I was asked to give you this to help you keep body and soul together on your journey. As subscription for your next book, of course."

Callender put the five $1 bills deep in his pocket, shamed at taking charity but murmuring his gratitude.

"We republicans are on the run up here," Leiper said. "Some of the cowards in our ranks don't want to know you. But Jefferson knows how valuable you are, and there's hope and some protection where you are going."

"He said that to you, that I was valuable? You know him well, then?"

"I was his landlord when first he came to Philadelphia to be Washington's foreign minister. He rented one of my houses on Market Street." Callender, dreading the moment of parting soon to come, felt himself tearing up again and was glad that Leiper filled the moment with idle conversation. "He hung three of the paintings he brought home from Europe in the front parlor. Portraits of Sir Francis Bacon, Isaac Newton and John Locke. He told me that one day Colonel Hamilton came to call, and asked who they were. Jefferson told him, and said they were the trinity of the three greatest men the world ever produced. And Hamilton said no, the greatest man that ever lived was Julius Caesar. Shows you the difference in the men's vision of life, no?"

The writer, staring across the field, felt the tobacco merchant's hand grasping his arm firmly to prepare him for the coming separation. Callender's four sons, from age eight down to little Thomas, now three, came running toward them.

"Be brave now, James. No tears; tell them you'll see them soon. A little lying can be a kindness."

Callender admonished his sons to behave well on the Leiper farm while he made a home for them in a happier clime. "First, down in Virginia, as soon as I can settle in and get a home ready for you. And someday, I promise you, we'll see a land and a seacoast and a people whose beauty will leave you breathless, as soon as matters clear up on the other side of the Atlantick."

He started south on foot, figuring he could reach Lancaster, Pennsylvania, in two or three days' walking. There he planned to use one of his dollars to buy a seat on the stagecoach to Richmond.

His left foot soon blistered. Limping along the dusty roadway, cutting across fields of late-summer corn to save steps, Callender reminded himself that he was a severe critic but not a commonplace railer. He had asked hard questions, and closely studied documents, and listened to debates in Congress, and then he wrote the truth. And then, by infusing the facts with his opinion, he conveyed a much deeper truth. Because he had a way with words, his truths hurt and angered the men in power who confused themselves with the government itself. And what was the result? He was a stranger in this country and not six people cared a farthing if he were gibbeted.

He was originally a poet, he reminded himself, and one day would be a poet again. Trudging along, favoring his blistered foot, he recited some of the couplets he wrote as Timothy Thunderproof in his youth: "Such is the in-born baseness of mankind / A grateful heart we seldom hope to find." For every kind person like Leiper, he saw a score of cruel Cobbetts; for every political inspiration like Jefferson and Tom Paine, he saw the long shadow of Hamilton and the hateful Goodloe Harper. Nor did he expect fame from his poetry, writing then as he ruefully remembered now: "Modest Merit rarely meets her due / Happiness recedes as we pursue."

What would his famed uncle think of those modest lines? James Thomson Callender firmly believed himself to be the namesake and nephew of the great Scottish poet James Thomson, though he had never met his uncle. That meant that running through his veins was the blood of the most celebrated poet of the century, Alexander Pope excepted. Although the sensuous imagery of his uncle's work ran counter to Callender's prudish upbringing, he remembered how one Thomson poem—*Liberty*—had the ringing theme that the freedom attained in ancient Greece, lost in the Dark Ages, was reborn in Britain. The great poet's nephew, a fugitive from British justice, wished that it were so. Perhaps if he could bring his boys back to Scotland, they would live to see Scottish freedom's day.

Callender came to a brook and was able to bathe his sore foot. He believed he was born to defend the unfairly attacked: after Dr. Samuel Johnson derogated the great Thomson in his *Lives of the Poets,* Callender excoriated the critic as "Pomposo" in a reply critique. Nursing that grudge, he later wrote a pamphlet exposing Johnson's *Dictionary* as a collection of stolen definitions and confused judgments. Such a passion of loyalty to his family, his nation, his political beliefs, was at his heart's core. Callender hoped he would never forget that. Like his satiric hero Jonathan Swift, he trusted the individual man but suspected the motives of all collections of men, including his own set of browbeaten Philadelphia republicans. Tom Paine would call these cautious trimmers "summer soldiers and sunshine patriots"; Porcupine would call them milksops.

As a professional polemicist, Callender recognized that he took more than a little pleasure in delivering a stinging riposte. At the same time, he knew himself to be no fearless Porcupine, reveling in the cut and thrust of literary political combat. Cobbett had even placed a picture of King George III in his Philadelphia bookshop window and then stared down the infuriated republican mob that Beckley had sent to intimidate him. Callender would never go out of his way to taunt a crowd like that; on the contrary, in the flesh he was as privately fearful as on the page he was fierce. But he told himself that it took more courage for a mild and medium-sized man like himself to be seditious than it did for Cobbett, born pugnacious and grown tall and strong.

Thus it was, when he arrived in Lancaster, Pennsylvania, and went to the shop of Barton & Hamilton, printers he knew, looking for a recent newspaper, he felt the familiar twinge of anxiety. He picked up a copy of *Porcupine's Gazette* of a few days before and saw the news he dreaded: "Vermont Representative Arrested for Sedition. 'Of Depraved Mind and Wicked and Diabolical Disposition,' says Indictment. Matthew Lyon Incited Hatred Against Government and President." He read Porcupine's ominous urging: "When the occasion requires, the Yankees will show themselves as ready at stringing up insurgents as in stringing onions."

Callender had not expected the Federalists to move immediately on the elected opposition in Congress. Lyon accurately predicted that everyone not in favor of the mad war with the French was to be branded with the epithet of Opposer of Government, Disorganizers, Jacobins, and if not silenced, jailed. As soon as the Sedition Act was passed, he had warned that "people had better hold their tongues and make toothpicks of their pens." Gallatin was right in underscoring Harper's purpose: to enable the dominant party to strangle nascent opposition in its crib. But Callender had presumed the first to be silenced would be the pens of the *Aurora* and not the tongues of men duly elected to the legislature.

Lyon was standing for re-election as Vermont's representative in Congress against the Federalist editor of the *Rutland Herald*. When that editor-candidate charged Lyon in print with disloyalty and refused to print a letter from his opponent defending himself, Lyon started a newspaper of his own. He called it the *Scourge of Aristocracy*, which Callender thought was a fine name for a newspaper. Cobbett quoted that republican paper's announced list of targets, proud that his Porcupine led Lyon's list: "Every aristocratic hireling from the English Porcupine at the summit of falsehood, detraction and calumny in Philadelphia, as they vomit forth columns of lies, malignant abuse and deception."

Cobbett enjoyed quoting fulsome attacks on himself, Callender knew; it was a good way to call attention to yourself while posing as impartial. But the Sedition Act concerned itself with more than newsmongers savaging each other. Further down in the report, he saw the words in Lyon's new newspaper that had asked for trouble: "The public welfare is swallowed up in a continual grasp for power, in an unbounded thirst for ridiculous pomp, foolish adulation or selfish avarice. When I see the sacred name of religion employed as a State engine to make mankind hate and persecute one another," wrote Lyon, the frequent target of bigotry, "I shall not be this Administration's humble advocate."

That was sedition, plain and simple, in the act's definition: a statement intended to incite the hatred of the people toward their government leaders. And it was not spoken on the floor of Congress, where the Constitution guaranteed Lyon would be safe. Callender assumed he was deliberately challenging the law, inviting his arrest and trial. Didn't Spittin' Matt realize that these Federalists were serious about crushing the opposition? Couldn't he imagine how delighted they would be to make an Irish-born Catholic Congressman their first case?

He saw that several men in the print shop recognized him. When one of the printers pointed to the report of the Sedition Act and said, "Callender, they must mean you," a customer who seemed more like a ruffian left hurriedly, presumably to spread the word that a prime object of the Sedition Act was in town. The printer suggested that his plan to await the stage to Richmond might be dangerous for him.

Callender never pretended to himself that he was as personally courageous as the Vermont curmudgeon. He had no appetite for a confrontation
with a mob urged to string up seditionists like onions, or a group of Federal
lawmen at the depot ready to arrest him. Having been beaten senseless
more than once in Scotland for what he had dared to write, he did not look
forward to such heavy corporal punishment in America.

He asked directions for his journey southward. He was told to take the
road to York, down to Hagerstown in Maryland, then to the new town
named for Washington where the Federal capital was being built. There he
could get a ferry across the Potomac River to Alexandria, walk a day or two
back up to Leesburg, finally out to Virginia's Loudon County where he
could ask the way to Senator Mason's home at Raspberry Plain. Exchanging his valise for a backpack, he set out again on foot.

He despaired that America, supposed land of refuge and freedom, offered refuge no more and was ready to strip him of his freedom. He had
run from prosecution for sedition in Scotland only to instigate prosecution
for sedition here. Callender could not deny that many republicans held him
responsible for his new country's turn toward tyranny. If he had not revealed Hamilton's secret passing of money to Reynolds and refused to accept, as most others did, the false excuse that it was merely blackmail to
conceal adultery; if he had not hectored Washington as "debauched" and
been on the staff of a newspaper that roiled the current President of the
United States by deriding him as old, querulous, toothless, etc.; if he had
not given the Federalists the excuse to publish the XYZ dispatches that led
to the national anger at Talleyrand's France—if, if, if—then he would not
be running from arrest or assault today.

No; such self-flagellation was foolish. He told himself his present sorry
state was not his fault. He turned his hypotheticals around. If he and his
fellow seditionists had not shown the courage to bring the men who controlled the government into disrepute; if a virtuous philosophy that rooted
sovereignty in the people could not at least challenge the despotic notion
that rooted it in the government—then the American Revolution, the hope
of dissidents here and radicals in Scotland, Ireland and France, would have
been for naught.

But who would speak up for the opposition now that public sentiment,
insulted by the French, had swung behind the government? Was popular
government to be equated with government that was popular? Who would

dare speak out against public sentiment now that even elected Representatives could be prosecuted for what they said in an election campaign? The victory of the revolutionaries in France degenerated into their Reign of Terror, a blow to radical democrats everywhere. Callender asked himself how it could be—only one generation after the victory of the revolutionaries in America—that opposition to government would lead to sedition trials of Congressmen, the silencing of the press, and a bloodless reign of terror.

The reaction to the revolutionary victory in France was violently antipathetic to dissent. If that turned out to be true in America, the rule of the mob crying "order and unity" would be worse, and far bloodier, than the rule of an aristocracy.

He decided that discretion dictated that this was a good time for dissidents to hide. The men in the saddle were never more arrogant in their power. Unlike Spittin' Matt, who had a yearning to become a martyr, the "moderate" republicans had no heart for the fight. James Thomson Callender, with a talent for invective and a hunger for the truth, could offer a megaphone to a leader, even propound ideas to a leader, but had no illusion of being a leader himself. He would follow Jefferson, if that believer in liberty would come out into the storm and absorb the lightning. Meanwhile, a rejected and despairing Timothy Thunderproof would crawl under a Southern rock and hide.

Chapter 15

THOMAS JEFFERSON

"You remember what Ben Franklin uſed to say about John Adams," said Madison. " 'Always an honest man, often a wise one, but sometimes wholly out of his senses.' He must be in the grip of that last phase now."

John Beckley agreed. He was tempted to recall another remark of Franklin's—that America had cut into the apple of freedom and found the worm of slavery at its core—but he was back in Virginia where such sentiments were frowned upon. He had come to Monroe's farm for this meeting with Madison and Thomas Jefferson because their gathering could not be kept secret if held at Monticello. Amateur spies were everywhere these days, even in Virginia, eager to curry favor with Hamilton's high Federalists leading the charge for national defense. Jefferson had cautioned all his lieutenants not to use the postal service for fear that their messages would be intercepted and read by Federalist postmasters, who were chosen for their loyalty to the government that appointed them. As architect of the republicans' unexpected victory in Pennsylvania in the last election, Beckley knew his presence at this meeting placed him in the inner circle of sedition and made him a prime target of Federalist prosecutors. It was worth the risk.

As an accountant and lawyer, he also knew just how deeply he was in debt. Not even the republican Israel Israel, influential among merchants, had been able to find clients for him to replace the income lost when he was fired from his House clerkship. (Curious, he thought, that a man with a name like Israel Israel was not an Israelite. Probably descended from one.) Beckley was hard-pressed to afford a place his wife could stay outside of Philadelphia to have her baby safely away from the fever. His hope for financial salvation lay in Judge Tom McKean, whose campaign for Governor of Pennsylvania Beckley was organizing. That great jurist, whose attempt to break the savage Porcupine was applauded by all good republicans—with the untimely exception of Callender—would surely put some patronage Beckley's way. Madison at his Montpelier estate was all but penniless, too, he had heard; Monroe and Jefferson, at least, were plantation owners with a valuable stock of slave property and had been able to keep up appearances.

"The news from the North is bleak," he reported to the Virginia triumvirate. Though twice elected Mayor of Richmond in his twenties, Beckley considered himself a Philadelphian now. "Four thousand dead in Philadelphia. John Adams left the city months ago and tries to stay in touch by mail from Massachusetts. I was a pallbearer at Benny Bache's funeral, along with my friend Dr. Rush, but most of the bodies are carted away for burial without being shriven. Now it's getting cold, thank God, and the plague is retreating, as it always does when the frogs stop croaking in the swamps. The government will soon return from Trenton. All the political talk there among our friends is about the conviction the other day of Lyon in Vermont."

"Convicted of sedition?" said Monroe, unbelieving. "A member of Congress?"

"The judge said that made it worse for him—he said the defendant, as a Federal legislator, was fully aware of the law he violated. Matt was forced to defend himself. No lawyer would take the case on such short notice, and everyone knew the jury was packed with friends of the man who's running for his seat."

"What defense did Lyon put forward?" Madison asked.

"First, that the Sedition Act is unconstitutional."

"As it surely is," said Jefferson hotly. The Vice President could not understand how most people seemed to placidly accept it: "This is an experiment on the American mind. If this is swallowed down, we shall immediately see another act of Congress declaring that the President shall continue in office for life."

"Matt conceded, Mr. Jefferson, that it was possible to defame a person or individual official and be tried for libel, but argued that there was no such thing in a free country as defaming a whole government." Sedition, as Lyon and the republicans understood it, was libeling a whole government—a right of speech which the very first amendment of the Bill of Rights forbade Congress to abridge. "The judge threw that constitutional defense out right away," Beckley reported, "because Congress, in its wisdom, decides what the Constitution means. Then Matt argued that he had no bad intent when he wrote that Adams had 'an unbounded thirst for ridiculous pomp.' "

"That describes John Adams, all right," Madison put in.

"The judge directed the jury to find Lyon guilty of bad intent," Beckley continued, "because he could not have had any other intent when he made the President appear odious and contemptible."

"Did anybody point out that what Lyon wrote was absolutely true?" Monroe wanted to know. "I think of the 'Day of Humiliation,' when Adams came out on the porch of the President's house dressed in full military regalia, with sword and black cockade, to salute the ruffians demanding a war with France."

"Lyon tried using truth as a defense," Beckley reported, "which Gallatin was able to include in the law, as you know. Matt even called the Federalist judge to be a witness to the fancy nature of the Adams dinner service, because the judge frequently dined with Adams." Noting the beautiful silver service and crystal glassware from France in the Monroe home, Beckley was sorry he brought that up and hurried on. "But the judge testified that Adams lived plainly and simply. The jury found Matt guilty and sentenced him to a thousand-dollar fine and four months in jail. And then they threw him in the oldest jail in Vermont, in a cell with horse-thieves, runaway slaves, the worst kind of criminals."

"I don't know what mortifies me more," Jefferson said angrily, "that I should fear to write what I think—or that my country is forced to bear such a state of things. Lyon's judge and his jury are striking fear in the heart of the nation."

"Sentenced to four months in that jail," said Monroe, focusing on Congressional elections three weeks ahead. "That means he cannot campaign to keep his seat. And if we lose just a few seats in the House, Harper will have a huge majority. Then not just the Presidency, but the Senate and the House will be in the hands of the Federal party. And the courts, too."

"Yet the body of our countrymen is substantially republican through every part of the union," a frustrated Jefferson said from the depths of his chair. "But we are completely under the saddle of Massachusetts and Connecticut, and they ride us very hard." One of Monroe's female slaves entered the room and gracefully served tea and biscuits. "Do you know what brought about this unnatural situation? It was the irresistible influence and popularity of Washington, played off by the cunning of Hamilton, that turned the government over to anti-republican hands."

Beckley nodded eagerly at his chief's analysis. Not only had he supplied Callender with the documents from Monroe that ruined Hamilton's reputation two years ago, but the political manager could point to a proud history of anti-Hamilton activity. Years before, Beckley—writing as "the Calm Observer"—had exposed Hamilton's register of the Treasury, Joseph Nourse, as one who juggled the books, making Hamilton look good by ignoring the interest on the national debt. Now the corrupt Nourse lived in a fine stone house named Piedmont near Charles Town, where Washington and his wealthy family owned land, and Nourse had even entertained Washington there at dinner—while Beckley had no roof over his head. He broke off brooding about Fate's injustice to direct an answer to Monroe's despairing observation. "Matt Lyon has a strange plan that you should know about. He says he will continue to stand for election to keep his seat in the House."

"From a jail cell?" Madison asked.

"Exactly. It's never been tried before," Beckley said. "But nobody's been silenced for speaking his mind against the government before, either."

"But how will he make his views known to his constituents?" Jefferson asked. "He cannot speak to them. They cannot visit him." The teacup rattled in his hand. "The right of freely examining public characters and measures, and of free communication among the people about them, is the only effectual guardian of every other right."

"He has started a newspaper and made his son editor," Beckley answered, avoiding a mention of the name of Lyon's new sheet, the *Scourge of Aristocracy*. He was sensitive to the deep split in the republican forces: one element was made up of the workers and small merchants of the North, including many recent immigrants, in alliance with the farmers and trappers of the West. The other element—of a much higher and different culture—was represented by those meeting here in Monroe's elegant home. This was the aristocracy of the South that had its own local, ragtag scourges to worry about. Beckley knew the amalgam of these disparate elements made for awkward moments in a national party, but the republicans, rich and poor, did have a unifying theme: resistance to central Federal authority, and opposition to a standing army with the oppression and taxation it would bring.

"Matt's son, editor of his newspaper, tells me," Beckley relayed to the triumvirate, "that Congressman Lyon will not be talking to the voters about the folly of war with France. He won't appeal to national pride, or the unfairness of the Alien Act to the Irish, or the unconstitutionality of the Sedition Act in his case, or the theoretical danger of central power to what was a compact of states."

"What is there left?" asked Madison.

"Lyon will be campaigning against one thing—taxes."

The Virginians looked at each other in dismay. Beckley assumed they were concerned that the high-minded concerns of political philosophy—the human freedom through representative government for which the Revolution was fought—were being slighted in Lyon's unprecedented jail-based campaign.

"I know it seems simplistic and a crass appeal to self-interest. But in New England," Beckley recalled to them, "the stamp tax imposed by King George was a source of great resentment. And in western Pennsylvania, the Whiskey Rebellion that Washington and Hamilton and Harry Lee repressed was about taxes on grain." The experienced politician added a fact he knew would hit home to Virginia planters: "It's not as if we're putting a tariff on goods from England. Harper in the House proposes to raise $2 million with internal taxes—direct taxes on property, especially land and slaves."

Monroe, in Beckley's eyes the most coldly practical of the three, was first to catch the national significance of Lyon's thrust. "The prospect of taxation to pay for warships may cool some warlike ardor. But John, 'Spittin' Matt,' as they call him, stands accused of cowardice during the Revolution and his wooden sword is the butt of every Federalist caricaturist. Will he make a suitable political martyr for the republican cause?"

Beckley wanted very much to associate himself with his wellborn superiors, though he avoided the presumption of calling them by their first names. "Lyon is hardly one of our kind," he said as snobbishly as he safely could, "and I would not make much of his plight here in the South. But as a victim of arrogant government, this naturalized citizen—a properly elected official—could prove useful in arousing public sentiment, even in defeat." He could see that thought registered with Jefferson, who had a keen sense of the public mind.

The Vice President explained that the reason he had assembled his closest aides, and the necessity for utmost secrecy in their gathering, went to the essence of power in a democracy. It had to do with an issue not addressed in the Constitutional Convention: When a dispute arose between the Executive and Legislative Branches, or between the several States and the Federal government, about the meaning of the Constitution, who shall decide?

Though he had been serving in Paris and had not been at that convention, as Madison had, Jefferson seemed certain of the answer: "The States did not unite on the principle of unlimited submission to their General Government," he said, laying a draft of a resolution in his handwriting on the table. "Nor was the government created by the States' compact made the final judge of the powers delegated to itself.

"Congress was not a party to, but merely the creature of the compact that is our Constitution," Jefferson went on. "When it exceeds its power, every State has a natural right to nullify such assumption of power."

Talk like this, Beckley was aware, would be taken by Federalists as not just sedition but treason. He looked at Madison, who knew more about what had been in the minds of the writers of the Constitution than any of them. Madison shifted his slight build in his chair and said he was uncomfortable with the word "nullify."

Jefferson ignored that and pressed on. Such Congressional abuses as the Sedition Act of that compact among the States were, in Jefferson's view, "not law, but utterly null, void, and of no force and effect."

He had a plan to carry out his bold proposal of State nullification of Federal action. It was to give his draft of a resolution secretly to friends in North Carolina or Kentucky and back it up with a similar resolution, to be put in different words by Madison, which would be passed by the Virginia legislature. Those resolutions overturning the Alien and Sedition Acts would then be presented to every other state. Beckley estimated that the

Pennsylvania legislature, which would not take the lead in this unprecedented challenge to Federal authority, might well go along.

Madison slowly shook his head. He said he was certain that the Sedition Act was not only expressly forbidden by the First Amendment, but transgressed the Tenth Amendment's limitation on the power of the Federal government. Even so, he was not prepared to go as far as outright nullification, directly pitting individual states against the central government. Perhaps, Beckley thought, Madison was thinking of General Alexander Hamilton at the head of an army recruited mainly in the north enforcing Federal law in Virginia. Perhaps Madison could envision the dangerous notion of nullification leading one day to wars among the States, or civil war between a group of States and the Federal Union.

"Not 'nullify,' " the little Virginian said. He searched for a milder term. "Perhaps 'interpose.' We should say that the states have the right, or even the duty, to interpose themselves between the people and the tendency to transform the present republican system of the United States into an absolute monarchy." That would make a State government appear to be peacefully standing between its aroused populace and a national government reaching for absolute power. It was the first time Beckley had seen Madison resist the leadership of Jefferson, but the Vice President was all but inviting Hamilton's army to march on Richmond.

Jefferson, to Beckley's relief, deferred to Madison's caution. "We need not commit ourselves absolutely to push the matter to extremities," the Vice President allowed, but refused to close off that option if Adams and Harper drove him to the wall: "We should remain free to push as far as events render prudent."

Monroe asked Beckley, as the one among them who best read public sentiment in the North, if he thought New England States would follow the lead of Virginia and perhaps Kentucky.

"No," Beckley said without equivocation. "This will be seen as a step toward secession and disunion." Into the worried silence that followed, the politician added, "But such a powerful assertion of the rights of States will certainly draw close scrutiny. It is a warning that the Alien and Sedition Acts could lead to civil war, which nobody wants. This might embolden our candidates to criticize the government in these final weeks until the November elections."

Madison directed a correction of emphasis to Beckley, who assumed it was his way of instructing Jefferson: "These resolutions are not to assert the rights of the States," he said, "as much as to assert the ideals of the Revolution."

It was agreed; Jefferson's incendiary resolution challenging Federal authority would be copied in another hand, revised by Madison for Virginia, given to at least two state legislatures for passage. Jefferson's authorship and Madison's revision would remain secret. What was left of the republican press would be given the documents and told to disseminate the official—and therefore presumably not seditious—opinion of objecting States throughout the nation.

Beckley wished he had Bache and Callender to lead the charge. One was dead, however, and the ardor of the other was dampened. He had heard that Jefferson had arranged for Stevens Mason, the Virginian who represented republican interests in the hostile Senate, to offer Callender sanctuary and the use of a library at his Raspberry Plain estate. He hoped that James was not drowning his despair in rum or otherwise abusing the good Senator's hospitality.

Jefferson closed with a warning about secrecy: "During the next twelve-month, I will cease to write political letters. A campaign of slander is now about to open upon all of us. The postmasters will lend their inquisitorial aid to fish out any new matter of slander they can to gratify the powers that be."

Beckley pledged to refrain from sending him correspondence that might cause embarrassment. "Our enterprise is risky," he observed to his political superiors, "but with all dissent in Congress and the press about to be crushed, what is there to lose?"

Chapter 16

Porcupine's Gazette

Maſon the Senator, and Callender the Runaway

STEPHENS MASON the Senator is the man who, contrary to his duty and his oath, three years ago made a premature disclosure of the contents of Gov. Jay's Treaty with the British. He caused the treaty to be published in the Aurora by a hireling of France, with the evident intention of exciting a clamour against it, in order to prevent its final ratification by the Senate. He has constantly, since that time, been of the French faction, and has uniformly opposed every measure calculated to protect this country against the infamous designs of the savage despots of Paris.

JAMES CALLENDER on his arrival in America, boasted that he had escaped the gallows in Scotland, and that his comrades were then in Newgate Prison awaiting their final doom. The wretch, with the encouragement of JEFFERSON and others, throve for a little while; but his drunkenness, his rascality in every way, led him from den to den, and from misery to misery, till he, at last, took shelter under the disgraceful roof of BACHE, hireling editor of the Aurora, now deceased. Fearful of rightful prosecution for his sedition, this runaway alien with a false set of papers claiming United States citizenship has left the city. CALLENDER buried a poor, abused, broken-hearted wife and left behind four ragged, half-starved children, to be sent to the poor-house.

"Birds of a feather flock together." CALLENDER and MASON contracted such a friendship for each other that they were inseparable while the Senator was in this city. The Senator went home before this year's fever struck, but hankering after his companion, he sent an invitation to come and pass the summer season at his house in Virginia. He forgot, however, to send a horse, for the poor rascal to ride upon; he was, therefore, like a true vagabond, obliged to tramp it.

The wretch CALLENDER has a most thief-like look; he is ragged, dirty, and has a down-cast look with his eyes. Notwithstanding this appearance, his munificent friend received him with all the affection of a brother. Soon after his arrival, however, he was found drunk in the neighboring distillery. Judging from his villainous look, the people suspected him to be a felon who had made his escape from the convict wheelbarrow gang on the Baltimore roads. On that suspicion, they conducted him before a magistrate, where the scape-gallows declared his name, said he was a printer at Philadelphia (which was a lie), that he came into Virginia in consequence of an invitation from Stephens Thomson Mason, one of the Virginia Senators in Congress, and that he then resided at the Senator's house, where his identifying papers were lodged.

In consequence of this declaration, CALLENDER was allowed until five o'clock to produce his testimonials. At that hour, MASON appeared in his behalf, produced a certificate of his naturalization, and said he was a man of *a good character!!!* An account of this affair was published in the Columbian Mirror, an excellent paper published in Alexandria. MASON later denied some of its details, which gave his neighbours an opportunity of proclaiming him for an atrocious LIAR.

—*William Cobbett*

October 24, 1798
CECIL COUNTY, MARYLAND

Maria Clement, formerly Clingman, read of Callender's arrest in the Virginia newspaper distributed in the Maryland town that she and Jacob (now calling himself James) temporarily called home. She promptly posted that *Columbian Mirror* to Colonel Burr in New York; she knew he had a continuing interest in the republican writer so despised by Alexander Hamilton, Burr's longtime political rival in that state. So that he would know the truth of the matter about Callender, she included her own quite different account of the episode that she had heard from Cecil County neighbors.

According to them, Callender, fleeing south from Philadelphia to escape the sedition police, was set upon by a gang of toughs in Leesburg, Virginia, and badly beaten. A couple of the gang's confederates then "rescued" him, wiped the blood off his face and torn clothes and offered him alcoholic spirits to relieve his pain. When the writer was well liquored, his new acquaintances took him to the Federalist magistrate, ostensibly to help him complain about his assault. It was then that the staggering Callender was charged with vagrancy and public intoxication. The magistrate sent for Senator Mason, to embarrass him publicly by having to stand up in court for his drunken houseguest. At the same time, the toughs alerted a reporter for the *Mirror,* who came to court. The edition describing Callender's disgrace was mailed to Federalist papers around the country—including, of course, *Porcupine's Gazette*—as the varied election days approached.

A week later, a somewhat battered-looking James Callender appeared at the door of the woman that he had made famous as Mrs. Reynolds.

Maria was not surprised by his visit. Now that he was within a day's ride of her home, she had assumed that he would probably want to meet the woman fiercely maligned by Hamilton as not just a loose woman but a blackmailing prostitute. Callender surely had some questions about the letters Hamilton claimed she had written. She had long been prepared with her answers.

"My name is James Thomson Callender," he introduced himself formally, looking up at her in unfeigned wonderment. She was surprised by his deferential and soft-spoken manner; from his writing she had supposed him to be strident and accusatory. He was of medium height, slightly shorter than Maria, eyes almost as dark as Burr's, with a loose cap covering a bandaged head. He wore a black coat and trousers. "Do I have the honor of addressing Maria Reynolds?"

She opened the door wide and smiled him inside. "Not many would consider it an honor, Mr. Callender. And Reynolds is not a name I use any longer since my marriage to Jacob Clingman. We are trying to put the past far behind us. Our name is now Clement."

"First, Mrs."—he paused, getting it straight—"Clement, I want to apologize for any suffering that my writing may have caused you." Her daughter Susan, now entering her teens but still fearful, peered at the stranger from behind the kitchen door, then slipped away. The writer added, "Or any embarrassment the public attention subsequently brought upon your daughter. Was that she?"

"That is Susan. I do all I can to protect her."

"As well you should, Madam. I have four sons of my own. Mr. Cling-man is—?"

"Mr. Clement is traveling to New York. We are hopeful that he may be able to obtain suitable employment in England." Jacob, friendless and at wit's end, wanted to run away from his reputation as fraud and prisoner. Her friend Burr had consented to see him and send letters of introduction. Tired of the torrent of slander heaped on her after Hamilton's excuses became public, Maria, too, was eager for a major change of scene. It would be especially good for Susan.

She served tea properly, as befitted a member of the New York Livingston clan, using a silver pot and her best bone china, complete with slop bowl. She took her time about it, assuming he would want a strong brew with sugar and milk, and did not show her amusement at his evident discomfort. "You're not at all what I suspected 'that scoundrel Callender' to be," she told him lightly.

"I am more fierce in print than in person," Callender admitted, making an effort to stop fidgeting. "It is easier to wield the hammer of truth from afar than to brandish it in someone's face."

"You were the only one to write the truth about Maria Reynolds. Why does nobody else believe my account of what happened between Colonel Hamilton and me?"

"Perhaps because they have not taken tea with you," he said, sipping awkwardly from the small cup, "served from a silver pot. All they know of you is from those half-literate letters he says came from you. They are not the letters of a lady of your breeding. And your accuser is believed because he is a great general now, on a high horse again, soon to be at the head of a powerful army." As Callender talked politics, she noticed that the tightly coiled writer became more at ease. "It is more convenient for most people to believe Hamilton's story that you seduced him, Mrs.—"

"Maria," she said. She knew that he, and the rest of the world, would always think of her as "Mrs. Reynolds" and of Hamilton's long, misleading apologia as "the Reynolds pamphlet."

"—Maria, than it is for them to believe what you say. Which is, that he is using you to conceal his thievery of the public purse."

"But you are certain that Hamilton is lying and I told the truth." She leaned back in her chair, crossing her arms, glad that she happened to be dressed so chastely and had her long hair braided and pinned tightly back. "Why, Mr. Callender? You are famous as a fearless pamphleteer, suspicious of everyone. Does service from a silver teapot, and a modest daughter behind that door, persuade you that I am not a common slut?"

"I was hoping you could help me persuade others of that," he said. "That is why I left the safety of Senator Mason's library to come here."

"James. I call you by your Christian name because I think of you as a friend, surely my only friend in the press. You may ask me anything, however indelicate. I will hold nothing back." She had much to hold back about her relationship with Hamilton and with Burr as well, but relied on his apparent courtesy not to pry too deeply.

"There is a writer and printer in Philadelphia named Richard Folwell," he began. She remembered the man well. "He reprinted my book, *The Political Progress of Britain,* which you may have heard of. And last year he wrote a *Short History of the Yellow Fever.*" He paused. "The disease that recently claimed my wife."

Maria reached across the tea table and squeezed his arm in sympathy. "Your children?"

"Four boys boarded with a friend near Philadelphia. I miss them." He came back to his line of questioning. "Folwell says you boarded with his mother when you first came to Philadelphia. True?"

"Yes. I came to that city to find Reynolds, who had deserted us. I found him just released from jail. He developed some habits of brutality in prison and turned out to be impossible to live with."

"Folwell says that you—with the most innocent countenance—told his mother that so infamous was the perfidy of Reynolds, that he insisted that you insinuate yourself into the confidence of influential men." Callender looked closely at her, as if seeking permission to go on. Maria braced herself. "He says you told Mrs. Folwell that your husband wanted you to endeavor to make assignations with them." He breathed deep. "I know this is indelicate, and it comes third- or fourth-hand. But Folwell says, that his mother said, that you told her that your husband Reynolds was trying to get you to prostitute yourself to gull money from men of influence. Did you tell her that?"

She shook her head vigorously, no. "I stayed for a week with Mrs. Folwell. I left when her son, who tells you this terrible story, tried to force his way into my bed." She remembered vividly how she had jabbed her knee sharply into his groin and almost crippled the odious little man, but did not pass along that memorable detail to Callender. "He hates me, and this is his way of striking at me."

"Folwell is also an ardent Federalist, and wants to work for a newspaper Hamilton may be starting," said Callender. "He was honest in his dealings with me, but I had the impression he hated immigrants. He thinks cheap white labor from abroad would undermine the institution of slavery."

"Would it?"

"Of course not. How many whites would work in the hot sun picking cotton?" He focused on the matter at hand. "And now to the letters that Hamilton says you wrote to him pleading for money." Callender took the infamous Reynolds pamphlet out of his jacket pocket and opened it to a page he had dog-eared. "He printed them in his pamphlet, but showed no-body, not even the printer, the originals. I spoke to the printer and he said he worked from copies."

"There were never any 'originals,' " she said. "The printed letters are forgeries. And they make me out to be a low-class woman with the educa-tion of a scullery maid. Just the sort to seduce an innocent Treasury Secre-tary."

"Do you have a pen and a jar of ink, Mrs.—Maria? And some writing paper? We can conduct an experiment."

"You don't believe me," she teased.

"I am the only one who does," he replied seriously, "but I need your help to make others believe."

"I can give you samples of my handwriting easily enough," she said. "But what letters of mine, supposedly held by Hamilton, do you have to compare them with?"

"None. I wrote to Hamilton asking permission to examine the originals of your letters to him, which he said he lodged with William Bingham, a trusted friend. My letter was polite, not polemical. I promised that if the originals appeared genuine, I would publish an apology to him. You know what Hamilton wrote across my letter? I'm told he wrote 'Impudent Exper-iment' and then in capital letters, 'NO NOTICE.' "

"Then you went to his friend Bingham," she assumed. Callender was a newsmonger; she had heard that was the sort of thing they did. "You pre-tended you had Hamilton's permission, and asked Bingham to show you the originals of my letters supposedly in his keeping."

"Of course," Callender smiled conspiratorially. "You would have made a good pamphleteer. But Bingham said he never had them. He told Hamilton the same, which caught the Colonel in a palpable lie."

"Then why do you need to see the way I write, James?"

He looked uncomfortable. "Indulge me, madam."

She rose to her full height, arched her back and stretched, unconcerned about that movement's effect on her visitor. Her lower back gave her pain, a trouble that began soon after the publication of Hamilton's pamphlet and returned during moments of tension. She brought back the writing materials and looked directly at him, waiting.

"Write these words for me," he said, dictating *"Write, much, most, pillow, knees, greatest, alone. "* She did, handed him the sheet, and he put the sheet of paper to one side. "Take a new page, harder words this time. *Anguish, inexorable, insupportable, adieu. "* She wrote them down and handed that page to him. She hoped that would be the end of the experiment; paper was expensive and she did not have much left.

He studied them and then compared them to what had been printed in Hamilton's Reynolds pamphlet. "Here—see where the letters he claims come from you have mistakes in the simplest words. 'Write' is 'rite.' 'Much' comes out 'mutch,' 'most' is spelled 'moast,' and 'pillow' is 'pilliow.' And 'alone' is printed as two words—'a Lone.' But here, in the list you just did for me—all the spelling is correct. Hamilton was trying to make you seem uneducated, almost illiterate."

"What about the list of difficult words?"

"Those words were spelled correctly in his printed pamphlet, which struck me as odd. How could a person who ignorantly wrote 'mutch' for 'much' also spell 'inexorable' correctly?" Callender cocked his bandaged head in a way that struck her as appealing. "Even I have trouble with 'inexorable.' "

"If the hard words were spelled correctly in the forgeries," she asked, "why did you just have me write them out?"

"It was a way of making doubly sure." He smoothed the bandage on his head and contemplated the pamphlet on the table.

"You didn't trust me, James." She liked that skepticism in him. He made certain, but not in a sneaky way.

"Most times I don't trust myself. But do you see what our experiment shows us? Hamilton had only one night to forge these letters from you—

Monroe and Muhlenberg were coming to see him the next day. So he misspelled the easy words but had neither the wit nor the time to make deliberate spelling mistakes in words he regularly used. Literary words, the words of a writer. Let me ask you—what would you call something that could not be stopped, that just kept coming on and on?"

"Unstoppable?" That seemed obvious, so she reached for another word. "Relentless?"

"Good. Would you ever use 'inexorable'?"

"I think I know what it means," she said, "but no, it's not a word I would use."

"And if you did not use it in speech, you would not use it in a letter, which is the written spoken word. No—'inexorable' is a writer's word, one that often appears in Hamilton's writings."

"What are you saying, James?"

"That the King of the Feds is a total fraud," he said. "No wonder he called my request for the documents impudent." He grinned triumphantly, head bandage and all. The boyish smile transformed his usually intense expression into one she found winsome.

He held out his cup for more tea. She took the proffered cup instead, placed it in another saucer, and poured, asking, "And what does Mr. Jefferson think, James? Colonel Burr tells me that you and the Vice President are in closer touch than most people know."

"Strange Burr should know that. Years ago, when Thomas Jefferson was Secretary of State, he told President Washington that his Treasury Secretary, Hamilton, was corruptly speculating in securities. But Washington wouldn't listen to Jefferson on that. Then as now, Hamilton was the apple of his eye."

"And what does Mr. Jefferson think in my case?" she pressed.

"Jefferson told me that Hamilton's willingness to plead guilty to adultery," Callender confided, "strengthened rather than weakened his suspicions that the Treasury Secretary was in truth guilty of corrupt speculations. That means Jefferson believes you, Maria. I am as sure of that as I am sure that after this national madness about a war passes, he will be our next President."

Maria, satisfied, slipped off her heeled shoes so as not to tower over him as he left. When she rose, she shook hands solemnly and then touched his scarred face as she expressed condolences in his bereavement. "You will see

[*171*]

your children again soon, James, I know it. Cobbett has been even crueler to you than he has been to me."

"Porcupine's quills never bother me," he said stoutly, which struck her as plainly untrue, though the man might find comfort in deluding himself. He stared for a while into his teacup, examining the dregs, and veered off the subject to ask: "You keep in touch with Colonel Burr?"

She should not have mentioned that Burr had told her that Callender was in communication with Jefferson; she worried that it made it seem as if she was part of an intrigue. "He represented me in my divorce five years ago," she explained. "And now he's helping my husband Jacob find a position. I'll always be grateful to him."

"You knew him before the investigation by Monroe and the others took place." Because he seemed to state it as a fact, she did not want to contradict him. And yet she did not want him to know about her relationship with Burr in New York, starting even before she went to Philadelphia and had to seek out Hamilton for help.

"In New York. I am related to the Livingston family, and Colonel Burr and his wife Theodosia were part of that social set." When he waited, saying nothing, she felt the need to shift the subject slightly to "He was devastated when she died."

"Was Hamilton aware, when he was dealing with your husband Reynolds seven years ago, that you were acquainted with Burr?"

"I have no idea."

He shrugged as if it was of no importance, and she was glad when he did not continue down a road that might make her seem to be a manipulator of men. "Do you know the one line, in this curious pamphlet of Hamilton's, that I will never forget?" the writer asked. "It's about you. Here—'The variety of shapes which this woman could assume was endless.' "

She had re-read and puzzled over that line as well. In a way, it was true: with Hamilton, she had been supplicant, mistress, confidante, supporter, stimulant, changing as their mutual needs changed. But she refused to accept his portrayal of her in his infamous pamphlet as assuming the shape of prostitute, blackmailer or betrayer. That was what made it so difficult for her to tell the whole truth about her relationship to Hamilton to her husband Jacob, or to this journalist, with whom she would like to be honest. If once she were to admit Hamilton's account of an affair, that would make believable his entire story about blackmail. Her dilemma was that she could not tell the whole truth without adding credence to her former lover's falsity. She had to refuse to admit their adultery to keep Hamilton from using it to cover up his corrupt financial dealings with Reynolds.

"Do you see me, James, as capable of assuming an endless variety of shapes, like a jealous goddess or a demon?"

"Of course not. It's a flagrant lie," he assured her, "but poetic in its imagery. Evil men like Hamilton can be brilliant writers. Porcupine, damn his eyes, is another."

"I'm glad you recognize that I am incapable of such duplicity, James. Wait—you'll need a sample of my writing beyond the words in your spelling test."

She extracted the Reynolds pamphlet from his hand, took up her pen and wrote out a line she remembered from Shakespeare: "This above all— to thine own self be true, and thou canst not then be false to any man." She added, "—or any woman. For James, with the trust and affection of Maria."

Callender swallowed and said nothing more; he slid his cap over his bandages and left. She leaned back against the closed door, concerned about her dilemma, wondering if she could count on his belief in her or whether it would change as he delved further into her past. Susan came out of the kitchen and asked if the serious man in black was likely to return.

"Without a doubt, my darling," Maria replied. "It's inexorable."

Chapter 17

MATTHEW LYON

October 27, 1798
VERGENNES, VERMONT

*J*abez Fitch, marshal in charge of the impriſonment of Congressman Spittin' Matt Lyon, proudly claimed that his penal facility was the darkest, stinkingest, most loathsome jail in all of western Vermont. He made certain that his new political prisoner received treatment hitherto reserved for lowly and violent charges.

Huddled in his overcoat, Lyon sat on a stool in the corner of the small cell farthest from the stench of the "necessary." No glass was in the barred window and the late October cold snap chilled the prisoner to the bone. "Cheer up, Mr. Congressman," Fitch called in to him, "the colder it gets, the less it stinks in there. Count your blessings. Tell that to the mob of your friends out there."

The Green Mountain Boys, veterans of the Revolution that had served with Lyon under Ethan Allen, were massing outside the jail this Election Day to break him out. Lyon knew that such an unlawful assault was exactly what his jailers wanted; indeed, they had brought him to such humiliating and painful surroundings just to provoke a small rebellion. At the first sign of a riot, the militia would be called in, heads broken, his own jail term extended for years, and Inspector General Alexander Hamilton would have all the more reason to lure more recruits into his expensive standing army.

Standing on his rickety stool, the prisoner grabbed the freezing bars and shouted to the men outside: "Go home and vote! Obey the damn law! They're treatin' me fine in here!"

"I'm glad you appreciate our hospitality," said Jabez Fitch outside the cell door. "You disunionists and opposers will get to spend a lot of time with us."

"It is quite a new kind of jargon," snapped Lyon, "to call an elected Representative of the people an Opposer of the Government just because he crosses the view of the Executive." The worst he anticipated at his trial was a fine; he was astounded at the prison sentence with a $1,000 fine on top of that. Most republicans, Lyon included, had assumed the Sedition Act was directed at Callender and the other writers of defamatory pamphlets and newspapers, and not at duly elected officials. But now the purpose of the act was becoming clear: Unity required one party. Two parties meant disorganization, disunion, and secession. Therefore, all organized opposition was sedition and the opposers would be jailed.

The first Congressman convicted of sedition in America had to be careful about what he put in letters. He knew that Marshal Fitch would summon a Federalist lawyer to go over each one he wrote or received, hoping to find some new evidence of defaming the government on which to base a fresh arrest. That would permit months of detention pending another trial. When the *Vermont Gazette,* a Jefferson organ, castigated Fitch as "a hard-hearted savage, who has, to the disgrace of Federalism, been elevated to a station where he can satiate his barbarity on the misery of his victims," the Marshal's judicial allies promptly clapped its editor in jail to await trial. That effectively shut down that anti-Federalist paper through this election of 1798.

Only his son Jim was allowed to visit Lyon in prison, lest the people of Vermont be infected with red sedition or religious heresy during the month candidates stood for election. His son brought the one candle that the prisoner was allowed per day. Jim also brought a message from the republican almost as oppressed by the Sedition Act as the man in jail.

"Callender will be holed up for the winter in the home of Senator Stevens Mason," the younger Lyon reported. "He sends word from Virginia that Mason is collecting the money to pay your thousand-dollar fine. That'll be his own and from other republicans who can afford it."

It was as if the Scot were sliding the Wild Irishman another set of fire tongs to help him beat off his newest attackers. Lyon's jail term was supposedly for four months, but if the landowner could not get up the cash for the huge fine, the Adams men could keep him incarcerated for long afterward. "We can raise the money ourselves, lad. I'm not looking for charity." His son was selling his Fairhaven land at distress prices to whatever buyers he could find. "Show me our newspaper."

He lit the candle and avidly perused the *Scourge of Aristocracy*. He liked the statement of purpose in the first issue under his own signature: "to oppose truth to falsehood . . . to prepare the American mind to resist degrading subjection to a set of High Mightinesses in our own country, and a close connection with a corrupt, tottering monarchy in Britain."

Better than that, he liked the way his son tied the foolish fervor for war closely to a sobering distaste for taxes. A standing army with the necessary barracks and forts, added to the purchase or construction of new vessels for a navy, would cost the farmers and workmen of America $14 million in taxes—"more than three dollars a head for every man, woman and child in the United States." That brought the issue home. He hoped that such an appeal to the voters' simple selfishness—more viscerally gripping than his own example of martyrdom to civil liberty—would help him make a respectable showing at the polls. The inmate-candidate was prepared to lose but did not want to be humiliated.

November 2, 1798

VERGENNES, VERMONT

Lyon could hear the shouting outside and again climbed up to warn the demonstrators through the window's bars against taking the law into their hands. He was interrupted by Jabez Fitch, his face mottled with anger, who brought surprising news. "The people of this district have taken leave of their senses, Lyon. You were elected again."

His son Jim brought in details of the astonishing victory: 4,576 for the "caged Lyon," as his supporters called him, to 2,444 for his Federalist opponent. A secret message from Jefferson through Mason and Callender hailed his "great majority," and saluted Vermont for instilling new spirit in republicans in races not yet finished across the country. An Episcopal minister, who joined with Methodists, Roman Catholics and Baptists to resist the persecution of the established Congregational Church backing the Federalists, had gone to Philadelphia with a petition signed by thousands of

Vermonters. It asked President Adams to pardon the popular Representative of the people and rescind his heavy fine.

"What did His High-and-Mightiness have to say to that?"

"The President asked if you had requested the pardon yourself, Father. The minister had to admit it was his own idea. The President then told him 'Penitence must precede pardon.' "

"He'll get penitence from me when Hell freezes like this damn cell!"

"So he wouldn't pardon you. And Treasury Secretary Wolcott had the minister investigated and jailed for non-payment of an old debt. You're stuck in here for another month, and that's assuming Senator Mason can come up with the money for the fine. You like this leading sentence on the front page?"

Lyon had difficulty seeing the type, and his son read it aloud with great pride: "Three months ago, twelve political enemies and an angry Federal judge gave their verdict: Matthew Lyon guilty of sedition. Today, 4,576 free citizens of the free state of Vermont gave their final verdict to the forces of oppression: Matt Lyon Not Guilty!"

Lyon sat down on the hard bench under the barred window. For the first time in as long as he could remember, the voluble Congressman could not speak.

ALBERT GALLATIN

February 2, 1799

Senator Stevens Mason was outside the cell door. Lyon could hear his friend arguing with Marshal Fitch. "I paid one thousand dollars in gold to the Registrar in Rutland and here's the signed receipt and order for release. His sentence ends today, noon, which is now. You have no right to hold him one moment longer."

"He stands accused of five new acts of sedition in his newspaper," the jailer snapped back. "I have an order for his re-arrest the minute he comes out of that door. And no damned Senator from Virginia can tell me what I can't do here in Vermont."

"My good man," Mason said in a voice Lyon could hardly hear, "it happens that my father, George Mason, wrote the Virginia Declaration of Rights. That document became the basis of our Declaration of Independence—yours and mine. He later led the fight against ratifying the United States Constitution because it failed to contain a bill of rights. That is why I always carry a copy of the Constitution, complete with the ten amendments, here in my pocket."

"That's got nothing to do with—"

"Let me read you Article I, Section 6, paragraph 1. 'Senators and Representatives . . . shall be privileged from arrest during their attendance at the session of each of their respective Houses *and in going to and returning from the same.*' " Lyon, glad that Mason had skipped over the exceptions to the privilege about Representatives who commit a felony or breach of the peace, heard Mason shout through the door: "Hey, Representative Matthew Lyon, do you hear that? Where are you going right this minute?"

"I am on my way to Philadelphia to take my place at Congress in session!" He rattled the cell door. The new Congress had been in session for nearly two months and he was eager to get into the debates.

"Marshal Whatever-your-name-is," Mason barked, "if you so much as lay a hand on my colleague on his way to take his seat, you will be in contempt of Congress. I will have you arrested and hauled before a Federal judge. And as an example of the punishment that awaits anyone who challenges the Congress and refuses to respect the United States Constitution, I will personally see to it that you will rot in your own hellhole of a jail."

Lyon heard the welcome jangling sound as the key turned in the lock. Outside, the Green Mountain Boys led a parade that marched him to the state capital in Bennington, where the Federalist Governor grudgingly handed him his credentials. He was serenaded by thirty choristers singing a ballad entitled "Patriotic Exultation on Lyon's Release from the Federal Bastille in Vergennes," and he enjoyed these stirring lines: "Come take the glass and drink his health / Who is a friend of Lyon / First martyr under Federal law / The junto dare to try on."

His triumphal parade continued all the way to Philadelphia's Congress Hall. Toasts to "Lyon and liberty" hailed him down through Vermont, through New England, at rallies sponsored by republican societies in a dozen cities. It seemed spontaneous but was all too well organized; Lyon suspected Beckley must have had a hand in it, especially as his caravan approached Philadelphia.

Smiling and nodding to all, the freed convict took his seat in the House. He was startled to be greeted by a resolution by James Bayard of Delaware to expel him as "a notorious and seditious person." The expulsion proposal was warmly seconded by his aristocratic enemies from Connecticut, the same tightly knit Congregationalists who looked on Baptists and Catholics as scum. It seemed to Lyon, slowly shaking his head, that nothing had changed; most Congressmen were out of touch with the people. Election meant nothing to them. But this jail of Congress was one he wanted to stay in.

Albert Gallatin rose to speak against Bayard's resolution to expel. "This elected representative from Vermont has been wrongfully tried for a political offense. He has suffered grievously. His constituents have spoken. To expel him from this House would be an act of political persecution."

Lyon looked around at his colleagues. Most were stone-faced; "Spittin' Matt," the Wild Irishman, had few personal friends here. Gallatin recognized that sympathy would not be forthcoming. He tried a new argument to persuade his wavering moderate republicans to rally behind their unpopular colleague.

"You have passed a law that says that truth is a defense against a charge of sedition. The crime can exist only if the government can show the falsity of the statement," the republican leader maintained. To many in the House, his argument was as offensive as his French-Swiss accent. "But Lyon's words were expressed as opinions, not stated as facts. Do gentlemen say opinions can be false? Men's opinions are as various as their faces, and the truth or falseness of these opinions are not fit subjects for the decision of a jury. Opinion is not susceptible of proof by evidence."

Gallatin's new theory broke fresh ground in the intellectual resistance to sedition, but as Lyon anticipated, changed no minds. The vote was taken. The Clerk of the House—the Federalist who had been given Beckley's old job—announced the result: A majority of 49 voted "yea," to expel Matthew Lyon from the Congress, and 45 voted "nay," to allow him to stay.

"Because a two-thirds vote is required to expel a member," intoned the Clerk, "the resolution fails." Though rejected by a majority for a second time, Lyon was able to keep his seat.

Gallatin came over, shook his hand, and expressed his regret that not all the republicans supported one of their own.

"These damn fools in this House don't realize it yet," Lyon replied, "but we've won. The people are with us. I'm a damned martyr, is what I am, and there's a new wind blowing. You keep pipin' up for liberty of speech, Albert—I liked that part about no opinion can be proven false. Our press will report it through the length and breadth of the land, and the people will read and attend. You just hold our side together, and you'll see how their side will split apart."

Chapter 18

February 5, 1799
ALBEMARLE COUNTY, VIRGINIA

*B*uoyed by the news of Matt Lyon's triumphant jail-house campaign, Callender decided to borrow one of Senator Mason's horses and ride from Raspberry Plain to Monticello. He would consult Thomas Jefferson about his future as one who reported history and was uniquely equipped to help make it.

His head had recovered from its battering three months before in Leesburg. His reputation, however, would not soon recover from the humiliation of being accused of public drunkenness. Recently, after only one article he had placed in the *Richmond Examiner* denouncing President Adams's "conspiracy against the liberties of this country," he had been threatened by the local Federalist gentry gathered in the Swan Tavern. They called themselves "the Richmond Associators" and conspired to visit the newspaper office and run the immigrant radical out of town. Senator

Mason promptly went to the Mayor, who organized and armed a group of strapping young republicans. When the Richmond Associators found Callender well protected, the bullyboys turned and went home.

Mason's elegant and extensive library had been a tonic to him. The Scot had never before had the leisure to browse through the wit of Swift, the rousing courage of Paine, the more recent *Federalist Papers* of Hamilton, Madison and Jay; also at hand, he was proud to note, was a volume of James Thomson's poem *The Castle of Indolence.*

Although he could not afford more months of indolence, he was fearful of returning to Philadelphia. The war fever was beginning to subside, but the summer's heat would soon bring back the yellow fever. Perhaps he could get a permanent writing assignment in Richmond and send for his children. He missed his boys and wrote them every other day; Thomas Leiper arranged for his own eldest daughter to help them write him back, and she had shown the youngest, Thomas, how to make the mark of a *T,* which wrenched the father's heart. Much depended on Jefferson's plans: if the Vice President was prepared to stand for the Presidency next year, Callender would have not just a patron to sustain him but a political cause to awaken his spirit and enliven his mind.

Ever since Jefferson had walked into his McCorkle print shop office in Philadelphia almost two years before, the Scot felt a political presence in his life that gave it an underpinning of meaning. Politics until then, both in Scotland and America, had been an interplay of injustice and resistance. Now he felt his political newsmongering could be ennobled by a leader— an accessible man, one that his own writing talent privileged him to get instruction from, offer ideas to, and take up his pen in support of.

Thanks to Jefferson's personal interest in him, Callender could see himself as no common railer, but as the most vigorous voice in the press of a great movement enlightening the world to assert the rights of man. The Vice President, author of Virginia's statute of religious freedom as well as the nation's central document asserting the equality of man, validated Callender's buffeted beliefs. That validation of his intellect's long-ago choice of "red" philosophy, even more than the tangible sustenance he drew from the Virginian, made him a Jeffersonian to his core. He had little security, but felt secure in this: that the man he was going to see, and who would welcome him in his magnificent home as an intellectual equal, was the era's personification of personal freedom.

Riding his elderly horse slowly down toward Monticello, Callender's thoughts turned from hero-worship to heroine-analysis. He could not get Maria Reynolds out of his mind. Just thinking of her made him straighten up and try to appear taller. Was she, as Hamilton portrayed her, a demon capable of assuming any shape pleasing to the person she wished to manipulate? Or was she, as Callender alone had the temerity to have suggested in print, a virtuous and vulnerable wife and mother—used and betrayed by a venal husband and his high-level confederate, who blackened her reputation to cover their shady dealing?

Callender savored the time he spent thinking about her and evaluating the evidence on both sides of the conundrum. One fact was indisputable: all variety of men, from the most powerful like Hamilton and Burr to the ineptly crooked like Reynolds and the young Clingman—and even to himself, he had to admit, after one brief meeting—were drawn to her. That did not necessarily substantiate Hamilton's claim that her mysterious attraction, and not his own greed and venality, was the cause of his late-night meetings with the crooked Reynolds. But it lent at least the color of truth to Hamilton's smother-up story.

Certainly, Maria was literate and well bred; Callender had seen that with his own eyes, and tested it to his satisfaction. As a result, he had little doubt that the letters that Hamilton claimed to have received from her were forgeries. This judgment was reinforced by the inability of the former Treasury Secretary to produce the originals. Hadn't the close friend to whom Hamilton claimed he gave the originals for safekeeping flatly denied possession, or ever having seen them? That was the gaping hole in Hamilton's story.

Callender was glad he had not acted merely as a conduit for the documents Beckley gave him. When Monroe's documents first came into Callender's hand, the Scot had gone to the address in Philadelphia where Maria had lived before reuniting with her husband Reynolds. It was not a rooming house, as Hamilton has suggested, where adventurous women could have assignations; on the contrary, it was a residence in a good neighborhood, where people observed one another's coming and going. The lady of the house remembered Maria and her daughter as respectable roomers.

Contradicting that was what Folwell, the printer and writer, had said about the tall woman with the level violet eyes: that she revealed to his mother schemes to entrap men of high station into liaisons and then blackmail them. Callender turned over in his mind his recollection of her appearance when he had confronted her with this assertion. The slightest furrow had appeared in her brow and her neck colored; she stiffened in pain—something may be wrong with her back—but the expression of her eyes and the set of her mouth did not change as Maria suggested Folwell was a resentful rejected suitor, almost a rapist. But Callender knew Folwell had no such reputation; in his dealings with Callender publishing his annual register, the printer and writer—although a Federalist and friend of Hamilton—had shown himself to be trustworthy enough.

Callender then considered the visit he paid Folwell after Hamilton alluded to him in the Reynolds pamphlet. What was it the printer said about Colonel Burr? Something about bad blood between Burr and Hamilton tracing back to 1791, when the Treasury Secretary began to tell friends that Burr was "not to be trusted in public or private affairs." That was when Hamilton's affair with Maria supposedly began; Callender had the impression that the printer was hinting that the two New York political leaders might have been competing at that time for Maria's adulterous affections. If that were the case, it would help explain one cause for the genuine distaste the two men had since shown for each other. More to the point, it would lend credence to Hamilton's story that she was a manipulative slut.

Callender shook his head. He considered himself a fair judge of people, and Maria struck him as a fine woman done evil by powerful men. He sensed passion in her but dignity and probity as well. Moreover, as a pamphleteer and newsmonger, he had a major stake in her version of what had happened. He had every professional reason to continue to believe her; she bolstered his theory of the case. If she were lying, then Hamilton would be innocent of improper speculation and guilty only of the adultery he admitted—nay, asserted. That would make Callender a dupe and a laughingstock. Porcupine would crow for months, and Jefferson and his allies would be forced to distance themselves from the easily duped journalist.

He came to a crossing and stopped his horse to consult a rough map. One road led to Monroe's plantation, the other to Monticello, and he directed his mount to the latter.

It all struck him as most unfair. Though regularly denounced by Federalists as a "scurrilous scandalmonger," the scandal that interested him was financial and not sexual; the revelation of adultery was Hamilton's doing, not his.

William Safire

He faulted himself, however, for not being an aggressive digger-up of information. Openly invited by the candid Maria to ask the most indelicate of questions, Callender had not been able to bring himself to probe into any relationships that might have begun the friction between Hamilton and Burr. He faulted himself further for not pressing his question about her earliest meetings with the man who became her divorce lawyer. And he had failed completely to ask if Hamilton's account of their sexual encounter on the day they met was true. Callender kicked himself for that failure to probe, because if Hamilton was telling the truth about that, it was at least possible that the Treasury Secretary was indeed being blackmailed.

ALBEMARLE COUNTY, VIRGINIA

The north end of Monticello was without a roof. "It seems as if I should never get this house habitable," Thomas Jefferson told his visitor, steering him to the study and a strange-looking chair that Callender presumed he had designed himself.

"The violence mediated against you," said the republicans' leader, "excited a very general indignation in this part of the country."

Pleased at this show of concern, Callender told the Vice President, "I am in danger of being murdered when I go out of doors." He touched his scalp; his hair hid the scar of the wound inflicted by the ruffians of Leesburg.

"I'm concerned about your welfare," Jefferson said. "Those who attacked you tried to take out of the hands of the law the function of declaring who may, or may not, have free residence among us." That struck him as most un-Virginian: "Our State of Virginia, from its first plantation, has been remarkable for its order and submission to laws."

Two large dogs with white and gray markings ambled their way into the library and settled at their master's feet. Their hair covered their eyes; Callender wondered how they could see at all. "Sheepdogs," said Jefferson, stroking one. "I brought the breed back from France." He quickly returned to his subject. "I can recollect only three instances of organized opposition to law in Virginia. The first was Nathaniel Bacon's rebellion against the British overlords a century ago. The second was our Revolution. The third was this Richmond Associators club-law to deny you residence here."

[*184*]

It dawned on Callender that what offended Jefferson most was not the actual attack by ruffians in Leesburg, but the aborted attack by respectable gentry in Richmond. He saw the first as a nasty trick by hooligans, but the second as a serious conspiracy by the sons of plantation owners to deny him his freedom to live where he liked. The Leesburg beating, which hurt him, was politically insignificant; but the Richmond threat, which did not harm him physically, had meaning he had not before imagined. Jefferson's historical perspective made Callender feel he had a place in the long line of American patriots.

"Unfortunately, Mr. Jefferson, you and I were about the only ones outraged by the reversion to club-law." He had not heard the expression "club-law" before and would make use of it one day. For the present, however, he wanted to guide this angry sympathy into an offer of employment as a writer. "Yet the re-election of Spittin' Matt"—he corrected himself—"of Congressman Lyon—"

"Wasn't his majority great?"

"Yes, but the injustice done him by the Sedition Act would not have caused public indignation without a local newspaper voice. His newspaper roused Vermonters against the tyrannous law. An outraged public begins with an outraged editor."

Jefferson, to his surprise, was more outraged by the Sedition Act than anyone suspected. "We must rally the people around the true principles of our federal compact," Jefferson said, "or we may have to sever ourselves from that union we so much value."

Callender could hardly believe his ears. Did the Vice President from Virginia really say "sever ourselves from that union"? The ultimatum struck the Scot as deliciously close to treason. Could Jefferson actually be thinking of dissolving the federal compact formed at the Constitutional Convention?

"The Alien and Sedition Acts," Jefferson reminded him, "is an exercise of powers over the States to which we have never assented."

Callender was in no mood even to discuss civil war, especially with Hamilton at the head of a Federal army. Jefferson would surely back away from such an extreme position on the rights of States after Monroe and Madison had a chance to reason with him. He wanted to steer Jefferson back to his personal needs.

"If I could move down to the James River near Richmond," he said, "which I take to be one of the paradises of nature, perhaps I could write in safety." Because Jefferson had seemed receptive to personal confidences, and had sent him $50 on account of a future book, the writer felt he could indulge in sharing his fond dream of philosophizing in a bucolic setting. "I would dearly like to find fifty acres of clear land, and a hearty Virginia female that knows how to fatten pigs and boil homminy, send for my four little boys and then adieu to the rascally society of mankind."

That was intended to get his leader to urge him not to retire. As Callender hoped, Jefferson waved aside such unrealistic detachment in a time of crisis. He asked what newspapers in Richmond could carry the sort of writing that Callender had recently sent him for his next book. "I thank you for those proof sheets. Such papers as yours cannot fail to produce the best effect." There was earnest encouragement in Jefferson's voice. "We have to inform the thinking part of the nation and set the people to rights."

His guest expressed the hope that republicans could soon get guidance in writing—in public prints or private letters—from the cause's leader himself. Jefferson shook his head and explained why he could not take up his own pen publicly: "When I correspond with you, Callender, the letters will come without a signature. The curiosity of the post offices makes that almost habitual with me. Indeed, a period is now approaching during which I will discontinue writing letters as much as possible. That's because I know that every snare will be used to get hold of what may be perverted in the eyes of the public. I think it useful to keep myself out of the way of calumny."

Jefferson's reference to "a period now approaching" meant the election of 1800, and Callender wanted to find out if the Vice President was conversant with the details of politicking. "For my information, sir, what was the mode adopted by the several States in choosing the electors at the last Presidential election?"

Jefferson leaned forward and became quite professional. "Georgia, North Carolina, Tennessee, Kentucky, Virginia, Maryland and Pennsylvania choose their electors by the people directly. In New Hampshire, Rhode Island, Connecticut, Vermont, New York, New Jersey, Delaware and South Carolina, the legislature names electors. In Massachusetts, entitled to sixteen electors, the people chose seven last time and the legislature nine." Callender was impressed; the scholar of philosophy was certainly versed in the details of politicks, apparently having learned the tactics from his narrow loss to Adams in 1796.

Callender knew that in Pennsylvania, Tom McKean—the republican judge who tried Cobbett and was threatening to have him tried again—was now Governor, making it easier for John Beckley to organize support for Jefferson throughout that key state. The writer was aware, too, that Jefferson had ordered Monroe to take the Governorship of Virginia, which he dutifully did. With fear of French invasion and a slave insurrection fading, the rest of the South was at last turning anti-Federalist. In New England, Lyon of Vermont could now deliver at least half of that state's electors. John Adams's Massachusetts was hopelessly Federalist, but Jefferson felt that Hamilton's New York might be vulnerable.

"I declined the editorship of the *New York Argus,*" Callender said, which stretched the truth only a little. "Hamilton and Adams will surely use the Sedition Law to jail whoever takes that job, and I was not about to suffer through that. You say that in New York, the legislature, not the people, decide on Presidential electors. Who do we have to split New York's electoral votes?"

"Burr," said Jefferson. His Tammany Society was becoming a political force in the city. "If the city of New York is in favor of the republican ticket, the victory will be republican."

He surely grasped the details; Callender suspected he had in mind a grand design to rally public sentiment. In the elections of 1798, Matt Lyon had shown politicians in Congress the way to marshal new support; his dramatic acceptance of punishment had turned many against a regime determined to suppress free speech in the name of quashing scurrility. In next year's Presidential election, Callender suspected that Jefferson, both in his idealistic exhortation and practical financial support, would ask him to show the way for America's journalists by risking prosecution for sedition.

The French sheepdogs heard a noise outside, roused themselves and bounded out of the room. Callender came to the point of his visit. Meriwether Jones, a Jefferson friend, was starting a new Richmond newspaper, the *Examiner.* And Matt Lyon's son James was on his way down from Vermont to start a southern edition of *Scourge of the Aristocracy.* Should Callender take on the job of building a Southern version of the *Aurora?* Would he have Jefferson's blessing?

"Take up your pen." Jefferson would not only bless him but, if need be, back him with subscriptions.

Callender decided he would enliven the two newspapers in Richmond run by Jefferson's friends with his unique mix of fresh fact and slashing comment. He would do it not just for the combined $14 a week offered, though a regular income was needed if he was soon to see his boys, but because this inspiring man deserved his help. He felt a welcome breeze of returning idealism: he, James Thomson Callender—fugitive from Scottish justice and despised slanderer of revered American statesmen—would sound the tocsin to the army gathering behind Thomas Jefferson to defend the rights of man.

"I will take up the hammer of truth," he pledged. He felt obligated to warn Jefferson of retaliation from newsmongers inclined to twist the truth to besmear their opponents.

"I fear no injury that any man could do me," Jefferson assured him. "I never have done a single act, or been concerned in any transaction, which I feared to have fully laid open, or which could do me any hurt if truly stated."

That was reassuring. Callender was ready to run the small risk of another beating by ruffians in that noble cause. If violence were directed his way, he would publish the details of such intimidation to the far frontier. Moreover, he was already inured to whatever new vituperation Porcupine could fling at him. He knew himself to be neither flea-bitten nor reptilian, and the drunkenness was exaggerated. Of one risk he was uncertain: was he up to suffering the denial of his own freedom, if the long arm of John Adams reached out to silence him? He hated the thought of being clapped in jail for the crime of speaking out for freedom. Others could dismiss as remote the possibility of a Virginia judge applying to a Jeffersonian writer the Federal government's Sedition Law, which so outraged Virginians. But it was precisely that civil disobedience and unjust suppression, in Lyon's case, that did so much to turn public opinion around in the recent Congressional elections.

Jefferson, in a solemn way, went on to make a remark that both thrilled and chilled his Monticello guest. "To preserve the freedom of the human mind, then, and freedom of the press, every spirit should be ready to devote itself to martyrdom."

Scandalmonger

Chapter 19

Porcupine

June 5, 1799
TRENTON, NEW JERSEY

Cobbett jabbed the tip of his quill into the wood of his writing desk, ruining the pen and defacing the desk. He was furious at the duplicitous John Adams for losing heart in pursuing the undeclared war between America and France. Did the President not realize that the ambition of Napoleon Bonaparte was not limited to the conquest of Europe, but reached westward to the subjugation of Britain and ultimately the New World?

He saddled his horse and rode from the office of *Porcupine's Gazette* in Philadelphia to Trenton, where the government had again decamped to escape the yellow fever. At the temporary hall of Congress, the Federalist leader Robert Harper was as stunned as Cobbett was at the sudden diplomatic move by President Adams.

"He's sending an envoy to France to make peace," said Harper. "To Talleyrand, and after the XYZ incident discrediting the republicans played right into our hands. I don't know what got into him."

"Where is Alexander Hamilton?" Cobbett demanded. "He's your power behind the throne. He controls the Cabinet. How could he let that popinjay Adams do this to us?"

Harper accepted the copy of the *Richmond Examiner* and spread it out on his desk. "It could be that Adams really wants to be President in more than name only, and this is his way of declaring his independence from Hamilton and all of us high Federalists." He shook his head. "But it splits our government right down the middle."

"You see this?" Cobbett jabbed his stubby index finger at the lead story in Callender's new sheet. "It's Talleyrand's first letter to Pichon, his minister in Holland—not the innocuous later one that Adams showed your Congress. This damnable document proves that Adams chose the very ambassador that Talleyrand wanted. It was all arranged by that traitor Logan, Jefferson's friend."

"How did Callender get the letter? It's internal French correspondence."

Cobbett despaired of Harper's blindness to the ways of newsmongers. "Talleyrand wanted it published here, don't you see? He sent a copy to Monroe or Jefferson in Virginia, who set up this newspaper for Callender. The French Directory is coming apart and Talleyrand never stays with the losing side. He'll make his deal with Bonaparte, and Napoleon will ally himself with the Americans against Britain."

"There won't be a French invasion of America then," Harper said, Cobbett thought somewhat densely. He did not have a high opinion of the Congressional leader's mental powers, and hoped for Harper's sake that his courtship of Kitty Carroll, daughter of the wealthiest man in America, would be successful; the thickheaded fellow would need the money.

"That means Hamilton won't have his army," Cobbett told the leader of what he hoped would become the strong Hamilton faction of Federalists in the House. "And your government won't be able to keep order in this country when Virginia decides to secede, or worse—to put Jefferson and his ilk in the seats of Federal power. Does your friend Hamilton realize what Adams is doing to him?"

"Colonel—that is, General Hamilton thinks the President is 'an old woman unfit to be President.' He told me that this morning, in those very words, on his way to see Adams at his hotel."

"What brings Adams to Trenton?" Cobbett asked. "He's never at the seat of government, where he belongs. He prefers to watch over his beloved Abigail in Braintree, Massachusetts."

"He's here now, meeting with John Marshall and all our low Federalists," Harper reported. "I worry about Marshall."

As well he should, Cobbett thought. The Virginian Marshall was a Federalist, and Jefferson's principal political rival in that generally republican state. Though he had opposed Adams's Alien and Sedition Acts, Marshall was likely to be named Secretary of State or War in the Adams Cabinet; the President apparently felt the need for the presence of an independent legal mind to counter Hamilton's influence.

"Do you suppose this new Richmond sheet with Callender in it will be successful?" Harper was saying, turning the page.

"If you let it," the editor of *Porcupine's Gazette* replied. He had to keep educating Harper to the ways of American political journalism. "This latest Richmond paper is part of a vast enterprise dedicated to the overthrow of your government. The chief juggler, as you know, is Jefferson. The money men are Leiper, Israel and Senator Mason. Of the four grand departments Jefferson assigned the task of influencing the people, all are headed by radical runaways." The disorderly, pro-French radicals from Ireland, Scotland and England he preferred to call "runaways" and "haters of the Crown"; Cobbett thought of himself as in temporary exile from his beloved Britain.

"Four departments?" Harper was obviously ignorant of the conspiracy.

"The Eastern department is run by the Irishman William Duane of the *Aurora,* who took over for Bache. I am reliably informed, by the way, that Duane is bedding the dead wretch's widow. The Northern department is run by the Irishman 'Spittin' Matt' Lyon and his *Scourge of the Aristocracy.* The Western subversion of your Union is run by Thomas Cooper, an Englishman who seems to think that the abolition of slavery is the way to the hearts of the pioneers." Although Jefferson was a slaveowner, Cobbett judged him practical enough to put up with a newsmonger like Cooper who opposed the slave trade, so long as the abolitionist took part in the overthrow of the Federalists. "The red Southern department is now headed by the Scottish runaway Callender, the most dangerous of all because he writes with a rapier and digs up dirt like this." He snatched back his copy of the *Richmond Examiner.*

"What can only four newspapers—"

"They feed their poison to a hundred newspapers and pamphlets around the country," Cobbett reminded him. "Callender must be writing for a half-dozen publications and probably has a book in work—and everything the rascal writes is reprinted all over." The Scot had almost caught on to Cobbett's technique of personal ridicule, making up colorful nicknames and bestowing false titles, but the Scot's books were often grounded in facts and theories about trade that gave confidence to republican lawmakers.

"We're doing what we can with the post offices," Harper said. "Our postmasters throw the republican sheets away. Believe me, William, not only do we read their mail but good Federalist postmasters destroy many of their pamphlets and newspapers."

Cobbett could not applaud that government interdiction of the press, lest it be used at some later time against his own national circulation. He was already reaching 3,000 paid subscribers daily, by far the largest in the nation, by post from Georgia to Canada, and was circulated to lawmakers in Philadelphia or in Trenton by his small army of "barrow boys." "Good. My circulation is up strongly in New York and Pennsylvania."

"Those are the two states where Federalism is having the most trouble," Harper noted. "Burr and his Tammany Society have Hamilton's Federalists worried in New York, and your old enemy McKean, the republican judge, may just win the Governorship here in Pennsylvania. It's hard to puzzle out—how do you explain why Porcupine, the strongest voice for Federalism, is gaining circulation where Federalism itself is doing poorly?"

"Where our Federalists are most worried, they turn to me for reassurance." But the Englishman confided a fear to the Carolinian about disorder in English-speaking governments on both sides of the Atlantic: "I have strange misgivings hanging about my mind, that the whole moral as well as political world is going to experience a revolution."

Sometimes it seemed to Cobbett that the orderly, rural world he remembered in the England of his youth, as well as the self-reliant cottage industry he admired so much here in America, was being overwhelmed by the growth of a wen of mob-infested cities. He shook off his unaccustomed pessimism and asked Harper what he planned to do about Jefferson's propaganda apparatus. Though the Vice President took great pains to seem to remain above the battle, his minions in the press were rallying public sentiment behind him.

"The republicans seem to keep gaining ground among the less respectable elements," the politician said. "What should we do?"

"Recognize the danger to order. Stop disunion before it gets out of hand and the United States go the way of France, from revolution to a reign of terror and then to a dictator." Porcupine, though a newsmonger himself, took a deep breath and put first things first: "Shut those four seditionist editors down."

Harper eagerly agreed. "I'll talk to Justice Chase on the Supreme Court. Sam sees the danger. He'll ride circuit and do anything for us."

"You had better talk, too, to John Adams, France's new friend." Now that the initial shock of the President's betrayal of principle had worn off, he was looking forward to engaging Adams as a new adversary, and with his usual jovial ferocity. "You know, Robert, I started *Porcupine's Gazette* almost three years ago, just as the Adams Presidency began. My principal object was to render to his Administration all the assistance in my power." Cobbett tilted back his chair in the dreary temporary office, folded his hands across his vested stomach and allowed himself to ruminate aloud. "I looked upon John Adams as a stately, well-armed vessel, sailing on an expedition to combat and destroy the fatal influence of French intrigue and the French principles of the tyranny of the mob. But now he has suddenly tacked about and I can follow him no longer. From this day forward," he pledged with a nice sense of anticipation, "it is the turncoat Adams who will feel the quills of the Porcupine."

ALEXANDER HAMILTON

June 6, 1799

TRENTON, NEW JERSEY

President John Adams did not enjoy being in Trenton. He did not think it necessary for the nation's Chief Magistrate to be in the nation's capital even when it was meeting in Philadelphia. Nor did he look forward to suffering through the summer heat in the Southern swamps of the new capital now being readied, named after Washington. On the contrary, except for necessary ceremonial occasions like inaugurations, Adams found it more to his liking to preside over the affairs of the nation from his home in Massachusetts.

However, the President had heard troubling word from his Secretary of the Navy, one of his few Cabinet members not held over from the Washington Presidency, and that only because the Navy was new. According to this Adams man, in the President's absence from the temporary capital, "artful designing men" were busily at work undermining his initiative to send an envoy to make peace with France. That warning brought Adams hurrying to Trenton at last.

As the President expected, Alexander Hamilton, the chief artful designer himself, entered the hotel room being used as the Presidential office to pay his disrespects.

Adams pointedly did not rise. He motioned the elegant New Yorker to a chair and continued to read a newspaper. "Is there no pride in American bosoms?" Adams asked aloud. "Can their hearts endure that Callender, Duane, Cooper and Lyon should be the most influential men in the country—all foreigners and degraded characters?"

"The scurrilous Jacobin editors are not the only ones to find fault with our leadership," said Hamilton. "Porcupine, who up to now has been our government's staunchest defender, has turned on you as a result of your incredible *volte-face* in foreign affairs."

Adams, determined to appear serene and good-humored in the presence of his Federalist rival, smiled and nodded. "Ah, yes. Here is what Peter Porcupine has to say about me now." He read the column underlined on his desk. "He calls me a 'precipitate old ass,' and accuses me of 'having abandoned every idea of consistency and every principle of honor and freedom.' Imagine that," he said mildly, determined not to let his pique show. "And to think he was Abigail's favorite newsmonger, though she always thought he was a bit on the vulgar side."

"Cobbett uses the word 'precipitate' to describe the suddenness of your change of policy, and that is hard to argue with," Hamilton said. "The notion of sending an inexperienced envoy to France, with no assurance that he will not be humiliated as the others were, came as a complete surprise to your Cabinet and myself."

Adams did not feel the need to justify his action to his Cabinet. On the contrary, he took some delight in having surprised and embarrassed the New Yorker. He remembered well how the retired George Washington, as the price of returning to military service, had forced him to appoint this arrogant monarchist to be second in command of the army. "Mr. Cobbett is an Englishman," the President replied obliquely. "I could have him arrested and deported under the Alien Act."

"You cannot be serious."

Adams pretended to give that serious thought before dismissing it with magnanimity. "But I will not take revenge. I don't remember that I was ever vindictive in my life." At his guest's raised eyebrow, he added, "Though I have often been very wroth." It would not be credible to pretend he never exploded. "However, the reaction to my appointment of an envoy to France, though hostile from my erstwhile supporters, does not leave me vexed or fretted."

"Your policy is a terrible mistake." Hamilton was vehement. "To reach out to France's ruling despots now is the height of folly. They are weak and will be toppled in a month. Britain's Prime Minister Pitt is growing ever stronger and will help the Bourbons set Louis the Eighteenth on the throne of France. Your precipitate blunder will have gained us the enmity of both nations."

Adams disagreed and, as former Minister to Britain, could draw on more experience in foreign affairs than Hamilton. It seemed to him that the Bourbons were a lost cause, and this fellow Napoleon would be too busy redrawing the map of Europe to invade America. "Do not become all heated and effervescent, my dear Hamilton," he said with determined serenity. "General Knox described your paroxysms of bravery at the battle of Monmouth, which served the country well, but such emotion is out of place as we talk of peacemaking."

The President then allowed a bit of his own agitation to show. "As for your predictions: I should as soon expect that the sun, moon and stars will fall from their orbits, as events such as you describe should take place in any such period." He took some satisfaction in the way his critic blanched. "But suppose such events as you fear took place. Could it be any injury to our country to have an envoy in Paris?"

"They disdain and insult and seek bribes from our envoys," Hamilton snapped back, "humiliating our nation and you."

"And if France will not receive our envoy, does the disgrace fall upon her or upon us?" Adams thought that point well taken.

Hamilton brushed it aside. "If you had taken the trouble to discuss this beforehand with the British Minister—"

The President, annoyed at that suggestion of subservience to any foreign power in his foreign relations, cut his visitor short. "I have heard how the British minister remonstrated with you about how disagreeable my measure was to him. He is wise not to try that with me. The United States is an independent nation. No other nation has a right to dictate to us with whom we form connections."

"I was not absent from the field when we fought for our independence," Hamilton said acidly, "nor did I provide legal representation to British soldiers who massacred our citizens."

The President bridled; during the Revolution, he had been the primary force for independency, and had been dispatched abroad to raise money for the war. "Absent from the field" was an imputation of dishonor that he deeply resented. Moreover, his legal defense of the British soldiers, the most hated defendants in America after the Boston Massacre, was one of his proudest moments, helping establish the rights of the accused to representation in a United States court of law.

"You are inviting Britain to retaliate by resuming attacks on our shipping—" Hamilton continued, "attacks that were stopped by the Jay Treaty negotiated under your great predecessor. The effects on our commerce will be especially felt in Massachusetts. Explain it to your impoverished neighbors there." He vaulted out of his chair, turned on his heel and left without a farewell.

Adams had not felt better in a year. For the first time, he felt he was his own man, neither in thrall to Washington nor to his favorite, Hamilton, an illegitimate brat with aristocratic pretensions and no concern for the effect of his adulterous lechery on his adoring wife. Adams crumpled *Porcupine's Gazette,* threw it in the waste bucket, and paced happily around the office. He was aware what this peacemaking with France and estrangement from Britain might cost him: a split in his government, perhaps his re-election next year. Hamilton would probably try to replace him as the Federalist's choice. Not with himself, of course—that was impossible after he admitted whoring with the Reynolds woman in his wife's drawing room—but with Charles Pinckney or another Hamilton acolyte.

Let him try. Let the alien Porcupine and his seditionist newspapering cohort rage to their black hearts' content; there were now laws to control that abuse of the liberty of the press. Adams was convinced he had done the right thing for the nation in avoiding war, no matter if it divided his political support and jeopardized his position. Four years in the heat and mud of the new Federal city and its unfinished barn of a light gray "palace" held no great attraction for him. He had acted as a patriot in the Revolution and would continue to act as a patriot as President.

He sat down and let his rush of noble-spiritedness subside. Every political coin had two sides; it could be that this peacemaking would have its electoral reward. It meant the end of the standing army, headed by the ambitious Hamilton, with its huge cost. The people, including staunch Federalists, did not like to pay the taxes for that army's upkeep. Adams drummed his fingers on the table. In time he would ask Hamilton, as his patriotic duty, to disband the army in an orderly and efficient manner. And his contemptuous fellow-patriot and founder of the nation would, he was sure, do that onerous duty. John Adams could hardly wait until Alexander Hamilton, too, would be absent from the field.

November 7, 1799

PHILADELPHIA

Cobbett arrived back in his printing room above the bookstore in Philadelphia to learn a disturbing political development. His judicial nemesis, the republican Judge Tom McKean, had been elected Governor of Pennsylvania. This despite having been denounced in *Porcupine's Gazette* as "a degraded wretch, persecutor of the inoffensive Quakers, corrupt resident of a confiscated house, and so great a drunkard that after dinner, person and property were not safe in Pennsylvania." In the language of Porcupine, that was a standard salvo, based on well-known facts; nothing out of the ordinary. Cobbett wished he had been more forceful.

However, his election could mean trouble for *Porcupine's Gazette.* The vindictive McKean was an intimate friend of Dr. Benjamin Rush, the most eminent physician in the nation. Cobbett relished denouncing Rush as a Dr. Sangrado, the foolish physician immortalized in the novel *Gil Blas,* bleeding his patients until they died of the treatment rather than the disease.

When Rush threatened a libel suit, Cobbett had laughed it off. But now with McKean appointing the state judges and prosecutors, and with the juries being selected by radical republicans, his exposure of the quack doctor might cause him trouble.

He was cheered, however, by a pamphlet called the *Porcupiniad* by the republican printer Matt Carey. He settled by the fire and read it aloud to his wife: "Listen, Nancy: 'The style of *Porcupine's Gazette* is unquestionably the most base and wretched of any newspaper in Christendom,' this wild Irishman writes."

"You do enjoy it when you provoke their rage."

"True. Here: 'There never was a Gazette so infamous for scurrility, abuse, cursing, swearing and blasphemy. Cobbett, when hard pressed in an argument, calls his opponent rascal, scoundrel, villain or thief and by this eloquent mode triumphs over his adversaries.' You see? He concedes defeat." Smiling, he read on silently.

"Why does that seem to please you so, William?"

"It increases my *Gazette*'s circulation, for one thing," he told her. "But it illuminates the shallowness of Matt Carey's style. I don't describe Callender, for example, as a mere 'rascal'—I brand him a 'runaway wretch,' a phrase that fills the mouth even as it reminds the reader that our drunken Jimmy escaped the rope in Scotland. And the republican hero Dr. Benjamin Rush is no mere 'villain' to me—he is, in my *Gazette*, a full-fledged quack, which no less a prose stylist as the essayist Addison has defined as 'a boastful pretender to physic.' But Matt Carey has no sense of the poetry of slander. None of them do." At his wife's questioning look, he amended that: "Well, maybe Callender does, but there is no joy in his scurrility, no cheery buoyancy to his invective."

"That reminds me. Someone pointed out his Maria Reynolds to me on the street the other day. The woman who caused all that trouble for Colonel Hamilton? There was a mention in the *Aurora* of her being here."

"Oh?" Cobbett had given his wife permission to read Duane's sheet in his absence for just this purpose of keeping him informed. Nancy was loyal, strong, and above all, trustworthy. When he escaped to America, he had left her behind with 20 pounds for upkeep, and when she rejoined him here a year later, she brought the entire sum unbroken with her. He knew her sensible mind would not be affected by exposure to the republican poison.

"The *Aurora* printed something about a group of ladies calling a constable to eject 'that Maria' from some respectable establishment," she reported. "I accosted her in a friendly way because I supposed you would want me to."

"Good for you, Nancy. What did she say?"

"She was selling some property here and then was on her way to New York to see her attorney, a Colonel somebody. She separated from her husband in England and was looking for a position here."

It could not be Colonel Hamilton, Cobbett thought; perhaps his rival, Colonel Burr. "How did the Reynolds hussy strike you? As a person, I mean."

"More of a lady than I would have supposed from that shocking pamphlet of Hamilton's. Not a slut at all, the way he made her out to be, or a hussy, as you call her. Well spoken, in fact, and carries her height well."

"Good manners?"

"Oh, yes. And grateful that I treated her with respect. The daughter with her was more than a bit shy."

Cobbett shook his head; his wife's intuitive judgment about the character of Hamilton's accuser—and Callender's heroine—did not fit into his own notion of a great man who was temptable and a loose woman who was contemptible. The brilliant and strong-willed Hamilton had been a friend to Britain ever since the end of the unfortunate Revolution; anyone who called his integrity into question was worthy of nothing but scorn. He would have to straighten Nancy out.

He instructed his wife about the political significance of the Reynolds affair. Hamilton was the last barrier to the takeover of Federalism by Adams and his tepid lot. Hamilton still had George Washington firmly behind him, as Adams did not, and the Englishman reminded his spouse that the revered Washington's backing counted for much in the minds of most Americans. The victorious general, by comporting himself with such dignity and reserve after the Revolution, had given legitimacy to the new government. And years later, the former President, by refusing a King's crown, had given the new nation the chance to learn how to transmit executive power to the next Administration without turmoil. In refusing to become the Sovereign, he had confirmed the sovereignty of the people.

"Thornton at the British ministry told me," Cobbett recounted to Nancy, "that George III, informed of Washington's self-restraint, called him the greatest leader of the age." The editor did not disagree with his monarch's sweeping assessment of the general who—with the decisive help of the French fleet—defeated Lord Cornwallis at Yorktown in Virginia. In a mysterious way, Washington's public prestige, royal aloofness, and imperviousness to the need for power conferred a sense of national self-confidence on his fellow citizens. For the present, that reduced their need for reunion with the mother country. But as the primary rebel passed from the scene, could the nation created around "the greatest leader of the age" survive the division threatened by the disorganizing faction led by Jefferson? Cobbett doubted it.

Chapter 20

AARON BURR

December 16, 1799
NEW YORK CITY

"The entire nation is in mourning," said Aaron Burr, sitting up in bed, to Maria lying next to him, "except me." He set aside the *New York Argus,* with its columns edged in black recounting the death of George Washington. It featured prominently the eulogy to the first President by his comrade in arms, General "Light-Horse Harry" Lee, delivered by Representative John Marshall, as "first in war, first in peace, first in the hearts of his countrymen."

Her longtime lover and constant friend rolled out of bed in the frigid room, re-lit the fire and returned under the coverlet. He looked positively pleased at the news of the death of the great man that had shocked and saddened just about everyone else. "This removes an obstacle from my path. And it is a terrible blow to your former friend, Hamilton."

She yawned and luxuriated in a long stretch; her back pain, despite the strenuous activity through the night, was not troubling her this morning. Maria was comfortable in her nudity after a tumultuous reunion with her widower friend. The year she spent in England was not a success; she had returned with her daughter, leaving her young husband, Clingman/ Clement, behind for good. Thanks to Burr's introductions and his own sly business ways, Jacob had become both successful and insufferable and was glad to be rid of them. She had sailed back to Philadelphia, disposed of what little property Clement had, and was jolted by the disapproving stares of the vindictive ladies of that city. Only Porcupine's wife, of all people, treated her decently when they met. That city was no place for her, and the notoriety left her daughter shaken. As soon as she could, Maria came to the home and bed of the only man who never failed her.

"Colonel Hamilton was never my true friend. And that was eight long years ago." Hamilton had been a passionate lover, fiercely demanding and then eager to satisfy his partner; ridden by guilt but excitingly willing to take chances on being discovered. Not at all like Burr. Then as now, Burr was discreet and controlled, taking his time, with incredible stamina in his lovemaking, watching in the long looking-glass and always slightly detached, as if both participant and observer. "What did you mean, remove an obstacle?"

"Washington's death strips Hamilton of his only influence over Adams," Burr said. "The President needed Washington to head the standing army, ostensibly to fight France. Washington's price was to put Hamilton in effective charge of that army, and your old friend then blocked me from a high commission." He smiled. "But now George Washington is no more. Let us all join in singing Hallelujah to his memory."

She reached across his wiry body to retrieve the newspaper. "This is a republican paper, is it not?"

"The *Argus?* Yes, it's one of ours. We tried to get Callender to be the editor, but Jefferson needed him in Richmond."

She studied the front page. "But it seems to be genuinely grieving the loss of a great man."

"Washington was not a great general," Burr said, emphasizing the last word. "I thought General Horatio Gates, his rival, would have won the war far sooner. Washington suspected some of us under his command thought that, and so he gave me none of the opportunities he gave his sycophant, Hamilton." He fell silent for a while, watching her read the encomiums. "But yes, Washington was a great man. Nobody else could have pulled the Colonies together into a united States, or fused a union as he did in his Presidency. Give him that. And he had a presence, when people were in a room with him, that made them trust him and defer to him. I wish I knew how to do that."

"Maybe it was just because Washington was so much taller than everybody." She had seen him once, at a party that Reynolds had taken her to in Philadelphia, and been struck by the President's height and imposing bearing. "He liked to dance. Do you suppose he ever—"

He laughed aloud and poked her intimately. "Mrs. Bingham, his favorite party-giver? Charming lady, far more appealing than his dowdy Martha, but I doubt it. Our man Beckley instigated both Callender and Porcupine to challenge Washington on expense accounts, but I never heard a whisper about adultery. If there had been, Callender would have found a way to sneak it in the *Aurora.*"

"The *Argus* says here that the late President expired despite the efforts of a pupil of Dr. Rush."

"That means they bled him for days, probably quarts of blood. That's Rush's treatment for fever."

"But Porcupine has been saying that treatment kills rather than cures," she noted. When her daughter, now downstairs with Burr's daughter Theodosia, caught the fever, she refused to let the doctor bleed Susan, and the fever passed. "Cobbett says Dr. Rush is Dr. Death, and I bet he'll blame Rush for the death of Washington."

"He surely will. That's because Cobbett knows that Rush is a good republican. You saw where he called the doctor 'a poisonous trans-Atlantic quack'? We might be able to use Cobbett's attacks on the most respected physician in America to shut down *Porcupine's Gazette.* And it would have nothing to do with the Sedition Act." He explained that John Beckley had already discussed a libel suit with the new Governor of Pennsylvania, Tom McKean. That good republican was now in a position to arrange the proper judge and jury to fine *Porcupine's Gazette* out of existence.

"Public sentiment seems to be everything," Maria said. She recalled how Hamilton had miscalculated when he thought the public would forgive adultery more readily than financial chicanery. That is what induced him to assail her as a strumpet and worse. "I suppose that's why the newspaper writers and pamphleteers are so important. All of you great men use them to shape sentiment to your views."

"My dear Maria, you are completely mistaken," he replied, rolling out of bed. "Get dressed. The opinion of the general public does not determine who becomes President." When she shot him a look finding that hard to believe, he continued, "Do you know who chooses the President, Maria? The electors make that choice. And do you know how they are chosen? In '96, two-fifths of them were chosen by state legislators. In 1800, two-thirds of the electors will be picked by legislators."

"But the people elect the legislators."

"The legislators are almost all respectable men of property. They don't stand for office on any ideology, but on their local reputations, their family connections, and on local issues. The people choose them for their character and standing, but not specifically to elect one man or another President. That means the President is chosen by the politicians, not the people."

"Oh. I was taught to think of our government as a democracy."

"It's a republic, Maria, not a democracy. The people elect respectable state representatives, wellborn and well educated, to choose whoever they think would be the best President, and to choose Senators as well."

"But public sentiment must surely have a great effect—"

He was pulling his trousers over his white stockings. "Not as much as everybody pretends. Even Jefferson, who wrote about 'a decent respect for the opinion of mankind,' told his legislators in Virginia to elect Monroe Governor and they did. Mankind's opinion in Virginia had very little to do with it. And for the Presidency, less and less."

She frowned. "Then someone like Hamilton, who is disliked by many people like me, could become President."

"No, not him. You and Monroe and Callender made it impossible for electors to even consider a confessed adulterer. The only way he can take over is at the head of an army, but now Washington is dead and Adams is not stupid. He'll never tax the people to pay for a standing army with Hamilton at its head."

"Then John Adams will be re-elected President, as Washington was?"

"The English dress you arrived in last night does not become you," he said, tossing it at her. "Buy a new one today. No, by making peace with the French, Adams has made friends with the people in the street but cut his own throat with the politicians who elect Presidents. The high Federalists will choose some puppet of Hamilton's instead of Adams."

She placed his proffered bank bill in her handbag and quickly dressed. She could use the money to clothe her daughter. "If the politicians rather than the people are to choose," she said, not wanting to leave the subject, "and the Federalist leaders are split—you are suggesting that Thomas Jefferson is sure to be our next President."

He half-nodded. "Or Aaron Burr," he said quietly.

She would have to think about that. He was a serious man and had already been a Senator. If his plans were to take him to the new capital, the District of Columbia, it would not do for her to be so far away in New York. As he buttoned his long jacket in the cold room, he said briskly, "Now to the business at hand. You have made up your mind about Susan?"

She nodded firmly, yes. Her daughter was approaching fourteen, the age at which Maria had married, and though not as tall, she already bid fair to exceed her mother's attractiveness to men. Clingman, like Reynolds before him, had shown too great an interest in her, and the sailors on the ship home ogled the girl mercilessly. "I want her in a seminary. I want her protected from my reputation and raised to be a respectable lady."

"You are prepared to be parted for a time?"

"I am." Susan was not. "She knows that I think that is best."

He nodded. "There is a seminary in Boston that I know will welcome her. I will take care of the financial arrangements. Nobody will know who her parents are. The name you want her to use?"

"Susan Lewis." Reynolds was a badge of shame, and notoriety was what she was determined her daughter escape.

"Done. I have been thinking about a proper situation for you. There is an eminent physician in Richmond, Dr. Thomas Mathew. Fine man, widower, in his early sixties, wealthy. He has a large house and needs a housekeeper, someone with an organized mind to keep track of his practice. Perfect for you. I'll write him today."

Richmond was a far voyage down the coast from Boston, but nothing like the trip they had just taken across the Atlantic. A clear separation was necessary if her daughter was to start life unburdened with the association of parents marked by scandal. Maria trusted Burr, who always had her best interests at heart, and who was solicitous of the daughter of his own he was rearing alone. And she preferred the South to New York, with its unhappy family memories, or pestilential and gossipy Philadelphia.

"I have a friend in Richmond, too," she noted. "James Callender."

Burr smiled. "Jefferson has arranged for Callender to put some life into the local republican newspaper. You'll enjoy reading the *Richmond Examiner.*" He led her down to breakfast with their girls. "And the name I will send to Dr. Mathew?"

"Maria Clement." She had used that in her letter to him and liked the sound. Not only was it her legal name, but it meant "mild weather"; she was looking forward to more of that in her life.

Chapter 21

The Governor's manſion in Richmond was draped in black throughout the month of national mourning. James Monroe thought this properly honored the Virginian who bravely led the American Revolution against British tyranny, but who had failed to see the meaning to mankind of the subsequent French radicals' revolution against the Bourbon kings.

In Europe, that revolution to win the struggle against the kings and generals had failed; the Jacobins had been turned out and their red radicalism replaced by the new First Consul, General Bonaparte. Only America carried the hopes of Paine's Rights of Man, and even here, Monroe believed, democracy had been stultified by the Federalist oppression. Even the word "democrat" had become an epithet used by Porcupine to remind Americans of the Reign of Terror; Monroe could use only "republican" to define Jefferson's approach to government. Their dream of a worldwide alliance of free peoples lay in a grave deeper than Washington's.

He received John Beckley with a handshake as cordial as the dour Virginian planter could convey. That was because he considered the former indentured servant from England to be the republicans' most useful political instrument. Beckley had already demonstrated in Pennsylvania how to organize voters in their local villages to elect legislators. These officials would then pick the electors who would choose Jefferson President, if all went as planned.

Monroe accepted the political agitator's congratulations on his election as Governor by the Virginia legislators. He was aware that Beckley knew the Governorship was little more than a Jefferson-Madison appointment, and spoke quickly to pre-empt the inevitable request for patronage: "The Vice President gave me a letter for you, John, to give to Governor McKean of Pennsylvania. It endorses your proposal to become a state official there."

The new Governor of Virginia remembered well how Beckley had lusted for vengeance when Federalists had turned him out of his job as Clerk of the House of Representatives. The ousted functionary had taken his copy of the memorials Monroe had given him about the Reynolds affair and passed them on to Callender. That began the ruination of Alexander Hamilton's chances of ever becoming President, though it was surely Hamilton's indiscreet over-reaction that caused his downfall. He recalled with distaste how that arrogant financier's demand for support of his claim of honesty had almost led to a duel between them. But he did not blame Beckley, the perpetrator of the publication of the Hamilton scandal; the deed might have been a year or so premature, but had been useful in curtailing the Presidential ambition of Jefferson's most brilliant rival.

Beckley was effusive in his thanks for Jefferson's endorsement and Monroe's obvious part in it. "It's a sinecure, of course—hardly any work involved. But it will give me an income and pay my expenses in organizing supporters for the election of electors for Jefferson." Monroe nodded coolly: he knew Beckley had tried to become a landowner and thereby to rise above his station, but his speculations in Greenbrier land were unsuccessful. "By the way, Governor, your book on foreign affairs was very well received throughout the nation, despite one purely politically inspired review."

Monroe took that as a reminder that Beckley had performed a personal service to him in helping distribute and sell his book defending his service as Minister to France. President Adams had slandered him publicly as "a

disgraced minister, recalled in displeasure for misconduct," an insult that
called for detailed response in book form. The review Beckley mentioned
was by a Connecticut Federalist writing under the name of Scipio. "I have
repeatedly thought I would answer the flimsy, scurrilous papers of Scipio,"
he told Beckley with a sigh, "but whenever I took up the subject it really laid
me up with a headache."

He had a greater headache facing him as Governor: rumors of an im-
minent slave uprising in Virginia. Inspired by the success of the black
leader Toussaint L'Ouverture in San Domingo, the talk of black rebellion
was causing much unease among plantation owners. If the conspiracy led to
a riot, the Governor would have to apprehend and hang the leaders. No
lesser punishment was possible, and Monroe was not looking forward to it
because such punitive action would hurt the Jefferson cause in the North.
Federalists led by Porcupine were already mocking the Virginia republicans' eloquent protestations of belief in liberty and equality while they were
defending human slavery with its often attendant cruelty. Because Beckley
was the one who published Thomas Paine's radical works in this country,
Monroe said nothing about his concerns about an uprising.

"Let me tell you how I am organizing the campaign in the North,"
Beckley said. "I won't presume to discuss your efforts down here, which is
surely our stronghold."

"We take nothing for granted here," Monroe responded. "The resolutions in Virginia and Kentucky against the Alien and Sedition Acts, which
you know sprung from Jefferson's brain, were not taken up by other states.
To be truthful, they have not been too popular among the people here, either. And President Adams's appointment of John Marshall as Secretary of
State won him Federalist support here in Virginia. We will prevail, I am
sure, but not overwhelmingly."

"Then strong victories in New York and Pennsylvania are all the more
important," said Beckley. "In New York, I am working closely with your
good friend Aaron Burr. He understands political organization and despises Hamilton for some personal reason. He is, I'm sure, a loyal Jefferson
man. In Pennsylvania, I'm using the technique that worked so well to carry
the State for Jefferson in '96."

Monroe was aware of Beckley's zeal. When the Federalists passed a law
prohibiting the distribution of printed ballots, Beckley's troops wrote out
by hand 50,000 handbills with voting instructions. Beckley paid local lead-

ers and farmers to pass the word to come to evening meetings at which he harangued the populace for Jefferson. They denounced the Federalist belief that "the rich, wellborn, and well educated must be preferred to office." Although that was a credo that Monroe privately agreed with, he could see the political wisdom in the popular attack upon it by lower-class republicans campaigning against Federalists in the North.

"And I'm finishing a biography of Jefferson in time for the campaign," the politician concluded, "to be sold in the meetings and advertised in the handbills. Callender here in Richmond, besides his newspaper articles, is writing a new book analyzing the failures of the Federalists and hailing Jefferson as the next President we need. His work sells very well, you know."

Monroe knew all about the sales of Callender's works. He had some hints about his subsidy by republicans, including payments from Jefferson himself. That had to be done discreetly because Jefferson, the Vice President, wanted to be thought to be above crass politicking. It would not be seemly for him to be caught undermining the continued authority of President Adams. Even worse would be any evidence of Jefferson having supported newspaper and pamphlet attacks on George Washington's government in its final year.

Callender was one of the few journalists who had dared to question Washington's financial probity at the time that the President was using his reputation for honesty and fidelity to unify the new nation. Monroe knew that Washington's ambition had not been to acquire power or money, though he did both; his primary goal was to gain and hold the good repute of his countrymen. Vanity was part of that concern of Washington's with reputation, but the stability that came to the new nation with the assurance of a leader of pristine personal character and rock-solid financial integrity was the greater part. When Washington spoke of the need for Americans to have "a standard to which the wise and honest can repair," he thought of himself as that high standard. Because the rare newspaper attacks on him endangered that standard of stability, he had been infuriated by them. Now that one and all were elevating the dead President to sainthood, any politician who had contributed to criticism of him would be in trouble. Monroe hoped that Jefferson had not taken Beckley into his confidence about payments to the hard-hitting writer.

"A book by Callender is not enough," he told his visitor. "That will not come out until the fall, but the electors will be chosen in New York this summer. We need to stimulate public sentiment now."

"He's editing the *Richmond Examiner* here," said Beckley. "At the same time, he's writing for the new monthly that Spittin' Matt Lyon's son is publishing—"

"Strongly enough, you think?"

Beckley was taken aback. "Nobody ever suggested that James Callender wrote weakly about anything."

Monroe frowned; he did not want to put his thought into quotable words, but he wanted Beckley to grasp the maneuver he had in mind. "You mentioned James Lyon. I recall that the arrest and trial of his father, the Congressman from Vermont, had a great effect on public opinion in the North. It discredited the Sedition Act decisively when he won re-election, running from jail."

Beckley fell silent. After a bit, he observed, "Writing from jail is dramatic, no doubt. Whips up the emotions of people, especially when the trial is patently unfair, as those sedition trials always are." At Monroe's encouraging nod, he went on: "And the younger Lyon would be the perfect person to publish another inflammatory Callender book, this time with the author writing from behind bars."

"That would surely be a cause célèbre. I'm told that the Supreme Court Justice Samuel Chase is on his way to Virginia on behalf of the Federalists," Monroe observed, "to investigate seditious practices here."

The Governor was pleased to see that Beckley did not need further instruction. He was certain that the political operative understood that the sure way to infuriate Southerners against Adams was to stimulate overzealous prosecution of the Sedition Law by the Federal government. It was not so much a concern for liberty of the press that angered Virginians as the reach of the powerful Federal arm into the rights reserved to the States.

"I'm to have a glass or two with Callender tonight," said Beckley. "He reacts well to incitement from his friends."

"I'm firing through four portholes at once!"

Callender, his words published in more outlets than ever, could not have been happier to see Beckley's face in his *Examiner* office. He felt wedded, in a way, to the former House clerk who had not only been his source of the most stunning scandal exposure of the decade, but also had a few years before helped him escape deportation from America to certain prison, if not worse, in Scotland. "I sign five columns a week of politicks under 'A Scots

Correspondent.' This paper has doubled its advertising and gained four hundred subscribers in the six months I've been here—we've just about driven the *Virginia Federalist* out of business. On top of that, I do a monthly article under my name for Lyon's *Scourge of Aristocracy* that's circulated all over the South and West."

"And in Philadelphia?"

Callender winced. "Duane doesn't run me in the *Aurora* any more, but that's just because he's jealous of the way I write. Makes his own prose seem feeble. But the *New York Argus* takes my articles, and at night I work on my book, *The Prospect Before Us.*"

He took a bottle of rum out of his desk drawer, poured out a couple of drinks and toasted the campaign of 1800: "To the downfall of His Majesty John Adams—he likes that 'majesty' title, you know—the apostle of royalty and aristocracy, and the blasted tyrant of America."

"Strong words, Jimmy. I've not seen you put them in print."

"I will, I will. I've had to pull out of the press a few choice comments I was to make about that hypocrite George Washington—did you know he authorized the robbery and ruin of the remnants of his own army? I hold back only because it's not done to speak ill of the dead, and I don't want a mob of Virginia war veterans throwing rocks through my windows. But Adams is fair game, the blasted tyrant. I think he must be a British spy."

"You'll write that? Not many Americans with the courage to put that in print, Jimmy. Here's to you." He sipped his rum, darker and tangier than the kind they used to imbibe in the taverns of Philadelphia. "I take it you're not worried about the Sedition Law."

"Not down here. That's why I'm in Richmond, out of reach of the Federalist rascals. Took an awful beating from some ruffians in Leesburg last year, but that's northern Virginia. You see these proofs?" He proudly brandished the first chapters of the book that he was sure would crush all argument against a Jefferson victory. Beckley took them and perused the pages. "Kind of skips around," he noted.

"That's to capture the reader's attention." He hated to admit it, but he had learned this technique of holding the readers' attention from reading Cobbett. "I'm always afraid of saying a great deal at once, upon any one subject, for fear of becoming tiresome. When you cannot guess what is to come in the next page, your mind is kept more upon the watch."

"Isn't that a trick of Porcupine's?"

"Thomas Jefferson has seen this," Callender changed the subject, "and thinks it's a work of genius. Told me that himself: work of genius. Sent me fifty dollars against delivery of the first copies, through an intermediary of course." He flashed a letter of Jefferson's at Beckley that encouraged him to have confidence in his "power to render services to the public liberty." Jefferson had added that because of "the curiosity of the post offices," he would have to curtail his letter-writing in the future.

"Our Tom is not like Jemmy Madison," said Beckley. "I ordered a dozen copies of your last book in his name, but when they were delivered, the little skinflint wrote 'Not Authorized' across the bill and wouldn't pay."

"What's wrong with Madison, anyway? Jefferson wants him to take up his pen and join the fray, but he won't. For that matter, neither will Jefferson himself. At least Monroe turned out a book, crabbed as it was."

"They're above the battle, you know," said Beckley, grinning. "Gentlemen do not get down in the muck and mire of politicking. No dirtying of skirts, not even to present their views directly on great issues. They leave that to 'a Scots Correspondent' and 'the Calm Observer'—the likes of you and me."

"Just as well. Provides work for scribblers."

"You just get this book finished and printed before they start to pick electors for President this summer. I'll get the people to vote," Beckley promised, "if you get them all riled up with what you write about Adams. You say he's an English spy?"

"In effect," Callender hedged. "About my last book, the copies I sent to Madison—where did you get the money to pay for them?"

"From Israel Israel."

"A Jew?"

"He's not a Hebrew. Grandfather was, maybe. Monroe sent me to him. He's been an important supporter of republicans all over, the way Jefferson's relative George is down here, or Tom Leiper in Pennsylvania. Leiper tells me the boys you left with him are fine, by the way."

"They're coming down to visit me," Callender reported happily, "all four, as soon as school is out. Then I'm sending them back to finish, until I'm ready for a move. Richmond is no place to rear children, John."

The town of 6,000—less than a thousand white adult males—was safe from Federalists, he felt, but not from immoralists. Callender's puritanical upbringing made him recoil from the raffish, frontier spirit of the place.

Gamblers thrived on brutish animal blood sports. One tiny Episcopalian church was, as one shocked visitor put it to him, "spacious enough for all the pious souls of the region."

The newspaper offices had grown dark. Callender felt the need to get a little boozy and assumed his companion did as well. He motioned to Beckley to bundle up against the cold January night. To give his friend some idea of the moral degradation going on beneath the surface of Southern culture, the "Scots Correspondent" took the "Calm Observer" out for an evening's entertainment at a "black dance."

The festivities took place in a barn on the town's outskirts, near the James River. They could hear the thump of kettledrums and the merry sound of a couple of fiddles as they approached on horseback across the shallows near the riverbank. About a hundred slaves, mostly female, chanting and clapping, ringed the edges of the barn. Everyone with finery, certainly all the women, displayed it lavishly, the color red predominant. Over the pulsing sound and flashing lanterns and bonfires, Callender pointed out the dozen or so planters' sons and a sprinkling of hired plantation overseers. These youngish whites, smoking long cheroots, surveyed the scene, a few joining the dancing but most observing the sinuous movements of attractive black and mulatto dancers. The white planters made their choices of the women and paid each other the necessary rentals.

"This is where white and black mix," said Callender darkly. "I hear miscegenation is rampant. Do you remember this from your days when you were here?"

"Wasn't old enough, I guess, before the Revolution. We raised tobacco over by the York River. We indentureds weren't much above the slaves ourselves." That was a recollection he rarely shared. "Later, when I was Mayor here, these dances were just getting started."

"That fellow over there is buying himself a Negro girl for the night," Callender told him. "See him pointing her out—she's the light-skinned one, a quadroon or even an octoroon. He'll take her out to one of those shacks in the woods and use her any way he likes. She has no right to say no, and gets none of the money for saying yes. More often than not, he'll impregnate her. These white men don't just work their slaves, they breed with them. That's why you see so many shades of brown in the children here. Sometimes straight red hair, too."

"You're better off sticking to politicks, Jimmy. A black dance is no place for you Calvinists."

"Think of it—here in Richmond, the capital of the biggest state in the South, the races are intermingling." Callender, genuinely shocked, was surprised that his friend took it all in stride. "In the plantations, the field hands are separate from the whites, but this cross-breeding goes on all the time with the household help. And they say it goes right up to the plantation owners themselves. That's your Southern culture, John. Tyranny by day, a kind of sexual equality at night, except when some fellow won't pay and takes a black woman by force. That's immoral, slave or not. Makes my blood boil."

"Let's just listen to the music, Jimmy. And look at that gal dance. You won't be going soft on Adams in your book, will you?"

"I'll raise such a tornado as no government ever got before."

Chapter 22

SAMUEL CHASE

June 3, 1800
RICHMOND

*F*ive months had paſſed since Juſtice Samuel Chaſe attended the funeral of his friend George Washington. A generation before, as one of the Revolutionary "Sons of Liberty," Samuel Chase had led the attack on the British public offices in Baltimore to protest the Stamp Act. The pugnacious, heavyset Marylander was one of the signers of the Declaration of Independence. He was proud to have forced a group of Tory malcontents, including his own father, to swear allegiance to the Continental Congress. Now, a generation later, he had been appointed a Justice of the United States Supreme Court, and was pleased to be called "the hanging judge."

Chase had earned that sobriquet after the trial of John Fries, the ringleader of a Pennsylvania Deutsch clan who led an assault on a Federal prison to free a group of his kinsmen. Their crime had been to refuse to pay the property tax passed by the Adams government to fund Hamilton's army; high Federalists called the resulting riot an act of insurrection and charged Fries with treason. Riding circuit, Justice Chase tried the case with dispatch and sentenced the troublemaker to death by hanging.

Unfortunately, in Chase's view, for the nation's need of respect for order—not to mention its ability to raise the revenue to pay for an army—President Adams got cold feet and pardoned the miscreant. Although the pardon was received with great relief by most of the public, the judge thought it had been a craven act by the President that had little to do with justice and much to do with currying political favor with German-born farmers.

Sedition was not treason, a hanging offense, but to the Federalist judge the severe application of the Sedition Act was needed to stem the tide of disorder before it swept disunion in with it. Criticism of the Constitution itself, such as committed in James Callender's new book, *The Prospect Before Us,* did not merely bring the government into disrepute—the crime of sedition—but was only a step short of treasonably urging the overthrow of Constitution and government.

Chase had received a copy of the book from an incensed member of the President's Cabinet. The copy had been sent to Adams by Callender himself, in what could only be an act of calculated contempt. At the frequent stops on the stagecoach to Richmond, Chase read it with rising indignation.

"The reign of Mr. Adams," the judge read in Callender's book, "has been one continued tempest of malignant passions. The grand object of his administration has been to calumniate and destroy every man who differs from his opinions. Adams and Washington"—Chase braced himself for the writer's sacrilege against the departed father of his country—"are poltroons who raise an affected yelp against the corruption of the French Directory, as if any corruption would be more venal, more notorious, more execrated than their own."

The judge slammed the damnable book shut. "Poltroon" was another word for "coward." After drawing several deep breaths to calm his heart, Chase opened it again: "You will choose in this election," wrote Callender, "between a hoary-headed incendiary who has deserted and reversed all his principles, and that man whose predictions have been converted into history. Take your choice, then," exhorted the seditionist, "between Adams, war and beggary—and Jefferson, peace and competency. Let us, by one grand effort, snatch our country from that bottomless vortex of corruption and perdition which yawn before us."

Outrageous! Folded in the back of the volume sent to Chase were two clippings. One was from the *New York Spectator,* signed "Marcellus," which Chase knew to be a pseudonym of Alexander Hamilton. It ringingly denounced the Callender book's "falsehood, sedition and calumny" and charged—self-evidently, in Chase's firm opinion—that its nefarious republican purpose was the destruction of the Constitution.

The second clipping was from the *Richmond Examiner.* That sheet featured an article signed by Callender protesting the seizure of all copies of the book in Philadelphia by the government in that city. "If the author has afforded room for *an action,*" Callender challenged, "do prosecute him. But do not take such pitiful *behind-the-door measures* in order to stop the circulation of the truth."

"Some truth," Chase growled, reinserting the clippings that proved the seditionist's guilt. Apparently, Callender thought he had sanctuary in Virginia, far from the reach of Federal authorities. If prosecution was what the foul-mouthed disunionist wanted, the judge vowed, prosecution was what he would get.

Chase turned to the court clerk assigned to him. The young man had been introduced to him as the brother of John Marshall, the anti-Jefferson Virginian that Adams named Secretary of State to spite the republicans as well as to declare his independence from Hamilton. "Where is the damned rascal now?"

"The Anti-Callender Society, a Federalist group here, reported that he was hiding out in the Jefferson mansion in Monticello. But Callender writes in today's *Examiner* that such a statement is a sulphurous lie, and that he is resident in Petersburg."

"They should have hanged him when they caught him in Leesburg two years ago," muttered the judge. "Well, we now know where he can be arrested." He paused to wonder: Why was the culprit Callender so eager to taunt potential prosecutors? Why did he advertise his whereabouts? The judge sensed mischief afoot in this challenge to prosecute, but decided it must be rooted in the colossal arrogance of the press.

June 4, 1800

Three men entered Callender's cell.

"Governor Monroe sends his compliments," said the tallest one. "We are to be your attorneys."

"I cannot afford one lawyer, much less three," Callender said mildly. He was filled with the satisfaction of having been chosen the Adams government's primary target, but his pockets were, as usual, empty. Beneath the bravado he had shown since he had been arrested was the realization that he was unique in his jeopardy: angry authorities on both sides of the Atlantic wanted to put him away for the rest of his life.

"The Governor asked the Vice President of the United States if it would be proper to assign public counsel to defend you," the tall lawyer was saying, "and thereby vindicate the principles of the State of Virginia. Mr. Jefferson replied in writing that it was his wish that you be substantially defended by employees of the State of Virginia."

From that Callender understood this case was not primarily about an individual versus the law. It was about the State of Virginia against the Federal government in Washington. "Do you all work for the State?"

"I am Philip Nicholas," said the tall one, "Attorney General of the State of Virginia. This is William Wirt, clerk to the House of Delegates. We will represent you on behalf of the State. And this is George Hay, a private attorney working *pro bono publico.*"

Callender thought he recognized the third man. "We've met before at Monroe's plantation."

"Governor Monroe wanted me to tell you," the youngest and huskiest of the three said, "what he has made clear to the press throughout Virginia. That is, although this case presents a clash between State and National authority, Governor Monroe will not interfere with the orderly enforcement of the Federal Sedition Law in the Old Dominion."

Callender was well aware what that meant. His challenge to the Federalists to prosecute had been accepted, and Virginia would allow the Federalist judge and a Federalist prosecutor to choose a jury of twelve Federalists to try him. Both Richmond and Washington, for quite different reasons, were looking forward to a conviction.

"I'm glad sedition is not a hanging offense," Callender said, forcing a smile. "What is my exposure?"

"If found guilty," the Attorney General replied, "you could be sentenced to jail for at least as long as the Act is in force. The Sedition Act, unless extended by the next Congress, expires on the day this President's current term of office ends."

"That's ten months from now," said Hay. "You face that long in this jail if Jefferson wins the election. If you're found guilty, however, and if the judge gives you a longer sentence—and if the Federalists win this fall— there's no telling at this moment how long you'll have to serve." He did not seem troubled by that prospect.

The Scot had been assured by Beckley that when Jefferson became President in ten months' time, he would veto any attempt to extend the odious law. Callender and anyone else convicted of sedition would be pardoned, he was told, and any fine remitted. But if Adams won re-election? "No telling how long" could mean a long, long sentence. Adams was known to be a vindictive man with a meddlesome wife who despised his detractors.

He chose not to think about that. Callender had written what he had written knowing the possible consequences, crossed his Rubicon and was prepared to make whatever personal sacrifice was necessary to place a great man in the seat of power. Callender may have come by his citizenship slightly fraudulently, but the United States was his country now. He felt a certain nervous satisfaction in taking an action that, one day, patriots would say was honorable, even noble. His sons would all be proud of him.

"And there could be a fine," added Attorney General Nicholas. "Justice Chase is very heavy-handed with the imposition of monetary penalties. He has put two republican editors in jail so far this year and fined them each over a thousand dollars. It bankrupted their publications."

Callender nodded grimly; one of Chase's convicted editors was his friend Thomas Cooper. But Cooper told him that Nicholas had subsequently bought a hundred copies of his latest tract, *Political Arithmetick,* to distribute to county committeemen. Monroe's men took care of vulnerable allies. "You know I don't have any money."

The clerk of the Virginia House, Wirt, whom Callender knew to be close to the aged Patrick Henry and to James Madison, suggested in a low voice that the republicans had friends who would pay any fine. Callender took that to be a guarantee.

As the attorneys left the cell, Monroe's man Hay remained behind for a moment. "The Governor wanted you to see a note he received about you the other day."

Callender took up the papers and recognized Jefferson's handwriting, so familiar to him now. "I know that sometimes it is useful to furnish occasions for the flame of public opinion to break out from time to time," Jefferson wrote Monroe, "and that that opinion strengthens and rallies numbers in that way."

The Scot swallowed. Not just in his words, but in his person, the occasion of Callender's trial was to be the spark to ignite what Jefferson, with his usual eloquence, called "the flame of public opinion." He asked the strapping lawyer if he would take a message back to the Governor to pass on to his famous friend, whom he knew to be in Richmond that day. He wrote it out on a sheet of paper, folded it and told the Governor's aide to read it aloud.

" 'He who cannot submit to a few years of incarceration for the good of his country,' " read Hay, " 'degrades the Dignity of Man.' " At the cell door, he turned to say, "Mr. Callender, it is an honor to defend a true patriot."

The writer turned back to his cot and sat down heavily. He was profoundly moved. Friend and foe had called him many things, but nobody in Scotland or America had ever called him "patriot" before.

JOHN MARSHALL

June 5, 1800

A regiment of Virginia militia was assembled in the Common outside the jam-packed Richmond Circuit Court, standing at ease in the springtime sun. This unit of State troops, made up mainly of Federalists, was dispatched on Governor Monroe's orders, to prevent any provocation inside that would enable the U.S. Supreme Court's Justice Chase to call for Federal troops. Chase had heard that Vice President Jefferson was in the city, taking an interest in the proceedings but evidently not inclined to show his face at the trial that pitted Federal power against the arrogant nullifiers of Virginia.

Chase saw John Marshall dismounting and tying his horse to one of the many posts outside the courthouse. Adams's Secretary of State was a good Federalist and rival of Jefferson in the Old Dominion, but it was widely known that Marshall had opposed the Sedition Act. Chase would teach them all a lesson in order, the law and the need to bow to central authority. Chase nodded a greeting to his fellow Federalist; though he considered Marshall a pettifogging weakling, he was pleased to see an observer with legal training who could report to the President how the cream of the Virginia bar was taught a lesson in the new Federal law.

The Justice wedged his large frame into the seat behind the raised bench, set his wig on his head and surveyed the spectators. They were a motley throng, some well dressed in knee-britches and shoes with buckles, others in farmers' dusty garments. His purpose was not merely to silence a single disunionist editor. He intended to send a clear message to the farthest borders of Virginia that sedition would be prosecuted to the fullest extent of Federal law, defiant State resolutions threatening interposition notwithstanding. He crooked a finger at the marshal, who brought him a list of the names of the panel selected to try Callender. In a low voice, he asked, "Any of those creatures called republicans on it?"

The court clerk, John Marshall's brother, paused. "I didn't discriminate, Your Honor."

"If there are any of that description, strike them off. We're going to teach the lawyers of Virginia the difference between liberty and the licentiousness of the press."

The clerk explained that his search for jurors had taken him to plantations up to twenty miles outside Richmond, and he was sure the panel was made up of good Federalist citizens. He regretted that only eight had shown up that day. Chase called them in.

Wirt, one of the defense counsels, rose to request that he be permitted to examine the jurors for prejudice against the accused. Chase shook his head; he could not afford to lose a juror. "Submit your interrogatories to me," he ruled, "and I'll see if they're in order."

The defense counsels were dumbstruck. The court clerk looked over to his brother in the back of the room; the Secretary of State shrugged at the unprecedented procedure. Chase swore in the jury and nodded to the prosecutor to read the indictment.

"James Thomson Callender, by his writings attached hereto," read the prosecutor, Thomas Nelson, "has maliciously defamed the President of the United States, John Adams. The accused is a person of wicked, depraved, and turbulent mind and is disposed toward evil. He has written and caused to be published these words with the bad intent of bringing him into con-

tempt, and to excite the hatred of the people against him and their government."

He then read out twenty selections from Callender's book *The Prospect
Before Us* without naming the book itself in the indictment. That omission,
Chase understood, was to make sure that if these selections failed to per-
suade the jury to convict, twenty more could be introduced at another trial.

George Hay, a defense counsel, rose to object. "Ever since the unhappy
prosecutions for libels began in England," he said, "the whole work has
been specifically named in the indictment. In that way, the charge is for one
act and there can be but one prosecution. By breaking this up into twenty
charges—"

"Overruled," the judge said.

"If found innocent by the jury," Hay continued to argue, "the prosecutor could go through the book again and submit new charges, in effect a
double jeopardy. If convicted, he could be prosecuted again as soon as he
finished his sentence, and kept in jail forever."

Chase motioned for him to sit down. "It takes very little legal ability to
demonstrate that the title of the book need not be recited. The defendant
can be tried at some other time for other statements in the book. Proceed
with your case, Prosecutor."

"The Sedition Act," Nelson told the jury, "requires that I show the defendant to have written these words with 'bad intent.' Therefore, when I
show that the matter is libelous, scandalous and malicious, it must follow
that his intent was wicked and criminal, and you must find him guilty."

"No," Hay bounded up again. "That's presumptive intent, with no
standing in law."

"The malice is self-evident," Nelson shot back. "This disputatious foreigner writes that 'the reign of Mr. Adams has been one continued tempest
of malignant passions.' Is this true? What evidence does Callender have it
is true? If untrue, with what intention has he published it? Was it not to excite the contempt and hatred of the people against their elected President?"

"You cannot prove bad intent by merely presuming it. That flies in the
face of the United States Constitution."

"If I may continue without interruption," Nelson replied, with a nod of
approval from the bench, "the Sedition Act also introduces into the law the
defense of truth. That means the defendant Callender must prove the truth
of each and every one of his libelous statements." Chase was delighted with

that argument; no prosecutor in his previous sedition trials had thought to use it. "It is not for the government to disprove; it is for the libeler to prove the truth of his libel."

"But that turns on its head the presumption of innocence—"

"Sit down," Chase ordered the heavyset counsel. "Prosecution, continue."

"He can never prove the truth of this, for example. He writes in this book—" The judge noisily cleared his throat. The prosecutor looked up at the judge, caught his glare, and checked himself before making the mistake of referring to the whole book. "Excuse me, he writes this sentence: 'So great is the violence of the President's passions, that under his second administration, America would be in constant danger of a second quarrel.' This is the same as saying, 'Do not re-elect the present President, for he will involve you in war.' It predicts the future. How can that be true? Therefore, it must be false, scandalous and uttered with malicious intent."

"It is an opinion," countered Hay. "A political opinion does not purport to be a fact. It can be neither true nor false."

"Your objection is irrelevant," Chase snapped.

"Your Honor," Hay pressed, "are you ruling that it is against the law to have an opinion, to speak your mind during the Presidency of John Adams?"

"Your argument is disrespectful, irritating and highly incorrect," Chase told him severely. "I will have no more of that, young man."

Hay gathered up his papers noisily, stuffed them in his leather envelope, and announced: "Let the record show that I am not being permitted to defend my client, and I protest the injustice being perpetrated here today. I am forced to withdraw from this case." He turned about, nodded significantly to the press in its section of the courtroom, and stalked out. The audience applauded, until Chase threatened to clear the room of spectators.

The judge had been wondering why the Virginia Attorney General, Jefferson's man, was letting a young co-counsel carry the defense. Now he knew: Hay had been assigned to provoke him into error and to curry favor with the audience in the room before departing dramatically. The republicans had used the same device in the trial of the editor Cooper, the English radical, in Pennsylvania the previous month. That had been a show the Federalists put on to strike fear into the hearts of Northumberland County republicans, just as his presence in Virginia now was intended to send a message to this State's friends of disorder and sedition. The senior defense counsel was probably waiting until the summations to make some rebellious assertion; the Court would meet that challenge to Federal authority and slap it down when the time came.

After the prosecutor went through each of the counts, Chase asked the defense attorneys if they had any witnesses to call to prove the truth of Callender's calumnies.

"The defense calls John Taylor, former United States Senator from the State of Virginia, presently the leader of the Virginia Assembly."

Chase had heard of him. The white-maned Taylor, one of Jefferson's acolytes, was a popular figure locally and might be effective with the Virginia jurors. "What do you hope to prove with this witness?"

"The truth of Mr. Callender's statement that the President was 'a professed aristocrat,' the twelfth charge in the indictment."

The judge was uncomfortable with that. The aristocratic Taylor may have heard Adams identify himself as an aristocrat, even if only in jest. Or perhaps the President, who Chase knew from Revolutionary days was inclined to sound off like a damn fool, had seriously called himself an aristocrat within Taylor's hearing. He did not want the jury infected with doubt about any of the twenty charges. "Let me see a list of questions you intend to ask this witness."

"In all my years of the practice of law in the Old Dominion," said the Attorney General, "I have never been asked for such a list by any judge."

"You have now, and by a Justice of the Supreme Court of the United States, presiding over a Federal trial in a Federal court about a Federal law. We will stand in recess for ten minutes while you draw up that list."

The judge was pleased to see that the Virginia lawyer, shaking his head, dutifully wrote out several questions that he planned to ask the witness and brought them up to the bench.

"The term 'aristocrat' is one of those vague, indefinite terms," Chase observed, glancing at the questions, "which admit not of precise meaning, and are not susceptible of proof."

"Of course you're right, Your Honor," said Nicholas smoothly, "but the whole term 'professed aristocrat' has a specific meaning. It says plainly that President Adams conducted himself in such a way as to cause others to think him aristocratic—"

"Vague."

"—or perhaps once identified himself with that specific word to the witness. If so, that would be conclusive proof of the truth of Mr. Callender's assertion in his book *The Prospect Before Us,* the single source of the many libels charged."

Chase read over the count in the indictment and saw an opening. "Your client Callender wrote, 'Adams was a professed aristocrat; he had proved faithful and serviceable to the British interest.' Can your witness testify to the truth of that whole charge?"

"We propose to demonstrate that what Mr. Callender reported about 'professed aristocrat' was a fact—"

"No, just a part of it. Your witness's testimony would deceive and mislead the jury. An argumentative justification of a trivial, unimportant part of a libel would be urged before the jury as a substantial vindication of the whole."

"I respectfully—"

"Such illegal testimony would destroy public faith. No such illegal excuse can be allowed to undermine the law."

"Then I propose, Your Honor, to prove the first part with this witness, and prove the latter part about the British interest with other evidence."

"You cannot prove the President of the United States acted in the British interest. Yours is a popular argument," Chase charged, "calculated to deceive the people, but irregular and subversive of every principle of law."

"I take that as personally insulting, Your Honor." The Attorney General promptly took up his papers and strode out of the courtroom.

Justice Chase instantly regretted his use of "deceive," in effect calling the Attorney General a liar. The republican press would make much of the injudicious temperament of the visiting judge. He was aware that the Constitution had a clause in it giving the House authority to impeach Federal officials, and did not want to become the first judge so attacked if the radical left ever became a large majority in both houses of Congress.

"You still have one lawyer left, Mr. Callender. Mr. Wirt, do you have a witness?"

"I am not inclined to submit questions in advance to the Court about any witness," said Wirt, whom Chase took to be a Virginia gentleman-politician. "Can Your Honor instruct me as to any precedent in Federal court for a judicial demand for defense questions in advance?"

"Your client is on trial here, not the Court. I take it you have no other witnesses."

"I would like to address the jury about the constitutionality of the Sedition Law."

"Denied. It is not for the jury to decide what the law is. The jurors will take their instruction on the law from the judge."

Callender's last remaining lawyer turned to the jury. "Not only is this defendant denied the right to present witnesses in his defense. His counsel is not even permitted the opportunity to ask you to consider the unfairness of the law suppressing the right of this man"—he laid a hand on Callender's shoulder—"to write in freedom. I would like to say a personal word about Justice Chase."

"Take care. The Court has extensive powers of contempt."

"Justice Chase here took his life in his hands to sign the Declaration of Independence, an act that King George considered treason. Can you strip from this writer, James Callender, the right to free speech won by our patriot fathers in the Revolution?"

A nice touch, Chase had to admit. "You are raising the specter of anarchy, counselor. Do you propose that juries around this nation select which laws they wish to enforce? That would truly undermine our system of justice."

Callender's last lawyer started to walk out of the room and leave the editor undefended. That would not do. "Please to proceed, sir. You will not again be interrupted by me. Say what you will."

But Wirt kept walking down the center aisle and out the door in silent but effective protest. The crowd in the courtroom was becoming unruly, and the judge gaveled them silent, rising from his seat to shout after the departing counsel, "As you please, sir!"

Chase knew that the walkout of all three defense attorneys, seriatim, did not make for a good trial record. Perhaps, in retrospect, he should have made sure his temperament was more judicial. He composed himself. Remembering how Matt Lyon's jury in Vermont had chosen to ignore the evidence, to ignore the judge's charge, and instead to vote against the Sedition Law itself, Chase was careful to address the jurors soberly about their responsibilities.

"Hear my words. I wish the whole world to know them. My opinion is the result of mature reflection." The room became silent. "You are aware of the pernicious Virginia resolution complaining about the Sedition Law. That resolution, whose author we know not"—Chase was sure it had been Jefferson and Madison—"was rejected by all the other thirteen States, excepting Kentucky, which is willing to nullify Federal law and thinks it can secede from the Union. Of course it cannot."

Chase was speaking not just to the jury, but to the leaders of Virginia in the courtroom, to the press that would carry his words out across the South, and to Secretary of State John Marshall, who had good repute among lawyers. "Just as no State legislature has the right to express an opinion on the constitutionality of Federal law, no jury has the right to nullify that law by refusing to carry it out."

He reviewed at some length, with careful logic and no bombast, what he considered to be a necessary new doctrine of judicial review. At present, he had to admit the Supreme Court was the least important branch of government. Chase knew that he and his fellow Justices were reduced to hoping that Congress would allow them to meet in a room of the new Capitol. He knew, too, that George Washington, with his neutrality declaration, had set a precedent that it was the President, not the Congress or the courts, who had the power to interpret the Constitution.

Chase hoped, however, that a stronger assertion of the Court's power would be articulated soon—by a chief who would refuse to drift off on ambassadorial assignments like Jay to London and Ellsworth to Paris. A full-time Chief Justice was needed, one with enough political influence to make it possible for the Judicial Branch to interpret Congress's laws, to show the courage to say what the Constitution meant. With the re-election of Adams, that Chief might well be Samuel Chase. Not, of course, with the disunionist Jefferson, who would probably want each State to interpret the Federal compact.

Chase returned to the need to enforce the Sedition Law at hand. He charged the jury: "You must decide first, if defendant Callender wrote the words which you saw in his handwriting and printed under his name. Then you must decide if those statements are false and were intended to defame our President. Whatever you think of the Sedition Act, you must not substitute your judgment about the law for that of the Congress and the President and the Courts. I know you will do your duty."

. . .

Callender, having played no part in the proceedings, forlornly awaited the jury's return. He had been talked about but never directly addressed or asked to speak. Because he was far less eloquent as a speaker than as a writer, and because he was a newcomer to Richmond, Jefferson's attorneys had not sought his testimony. He could understand that, but for once wished he had been born an orator. He sat mute, feeling like the corpse at his own funeral, listening to the preachers and the mourners talk about him in the past tense. The verdict was a foregone conclusion. He would be found guilty, sentenced and fined, the latest martyr to the Sedition Act.

He knew he should be pleased at the way Judge Chase fell into the trap of squelching justice in Virginia. The harsh rulings, the evident unfairness, even the final insult to the jury forbidding them their right to nullify the law—as the courageous Vermonters did—would be used against Adams and in support of Jefferson. And the lashing-back against Federalist injustice would be felt not only in the South, but in New York and Pennsylvania, where voters would surely be discomfited by detailed reports of what Callender hoped would be seen as the present-day version of the Salem witch trials.

Beckley had organized a campaign of letters written from Richmond to leaders in legislatures across the nation, and especially to the Tammany Society in New York, where Aaron Burr was faced with the early election of Presidential electors. Much of the future direction of the young nation hung on the ability of Beckley and Burr to put the right electors in place; Chase's bullheadedness combined with Callender's sacrifice here in Richmond would help them advance the Jefferson interest in crucial Pennsylvania and New York.

Yet the courtroom was not his world. He was at a loss sitting isolated in the dock with nary a lawyer sitting near him to offer solace. Now that the first flush of incipient martyrdom had worn off, Callender realized how little he looked forward to going to jail. He had been assured that he would have a private cell with a table and writing materials. Matt Lyon's son James—a fine, sturdy lad, one of the few honest printers he ever met—promised regular visits to bring him the news and to pick up his copy for publication. On the debit side, he would not be able to go forth on a lonely evening and drink himself into blessed oblivion. Perhaps the coming enforced abstinence was just as well; because he had fallen into the habit of drinking alone, he had promised himself to cut down on the rum.

In the solitude of the crowded courtroom, the Scot found himself thinking about Maria Reynolds. It comforted him to see her in his mind's eye leaning forward, pouring tea, confiding in the visitor who had believed in her when so few others did. Was she settling down to married life with young Clingman in London? More likely, he assumed, she had already left him for a stronger and more prosperous protector for herself and her daughter. Or would she return to America? He hoped so, and that he would be free to meet her, if only to solve the mystery of Hamilton that still nagged at him.

What possessed the Treasury Secretary to shame his loving wife and family? What moved him to damage forever his hopes of the highest office, with a concocted story of infidelity and blackmail—merely to escape the hard-to-prove charges of financial speculation? His seventy-six-page defense was so excessive as to be irrational; that was not in character for a mind that could write *The Federalist Papers* with Madison. Years ago, Callender had been gleeful at Hamilton's confessional folly, but now he wished he could discuss more deeply with Maria the motive for the man's complicated deception.

That Hamilton's covering story was a lie Callender had no doubt. He believed Maria and her crooked husband, Reynolds, when they said the Colonel was making relatively small amounts of money unethically, though perhaps not illegally. Most others, including the most anti-Federalist writers, believed Hamilton for a simple reason: no man would so humiliate himself and his family to defend an abstract principle of Treasury integrity.

He started to come at the question through the prism of George Washington, Hamilton's hero and mentor. To Washington, probity was all. The Scot had heard, though not firsthand, that the President exploded at "that scoundrel Callender" in front of his Cabinet after a fairly mild criticism in the *Aurora* about cheating on his expense accounts to the Continental Congress. Why was Washington so sensitive to anything written about his personal finances, when he so coolly brushed aside criticism of his generalship or denunciations of his foreign policy? Perhaps it had a practical aspect, unrelated to vanity or pride. Perhaps the first President felt he embodied the trust of the nation in its leadership, and was fearful that anything that scandalmongers did to sully that personal trust subtracted from the small deposit of legitimacy in the new government.

In that case, figured Callender, with nothing to do but wait for the verdict, what was Washington's ambition? Obviously not the accumulation of power; the man resolutely turned down a King's crown. Washington's ambition apparently had been to conduct a pure Administration, free of partizan strife, free of personal bickering, free of criticism, and certainly free of bribery, theft, or any kind of governmental corruption. His Holy Grail was Good Repute. If Washington could maintain that reputation for public integrity; if by his studied aloofness he could lend an aura of personal majesty to the position of Chief Magistrate, he could then succeed in transferring the legitimacy of executive power to his successor, and that man to the next.

Hamilton must have understood Washington's concern for his Administration's good repute. Callender ruminated on the criteria of political reputation: honesty was at the top; morality was at the bottom. For Washington and his acolyte Hamilton, corruption was unpardonable but sin was forgivable. Dishonesty in office struck at the vitals of legitimacy, at the heart of the sovereignty America so violently and recently seized; but the shame of marital infidelity, though it could destroy families, did not shake the foundations of the republic. Callender remembered that Hamilton had made that point in *The Federalist Papers,* writing about the impeachment of a President—that it had to be a "high" crime or misdemeanor, like treason or bribery an offense against the public, harming the government system itself.

Members of the jury were filing back in slowly, but the defendant's mind was racing. Washington had been trying to replace the monarchic "the King could do no wrong" with a democratic "the President would do no wrong." If the Treasury Secretary had been personally speculating in securities—or, more likely, corruptly helping his associates make money on the foreknowledge of government information—Hamilton would have done anything to keep any imputation of such government-crippling dishonesty from reaching President Washington. The Treasury Secretary must have known that his idol, that rock of integrity, would have turned on Hamilton savagely—no matter that he was his good right arm, or substitute son—and fired him on the spot, prosecuting him and ruining him forever to reassert the good repute of the government.

What, in such a fix, would Hamilton do to keep Monroe and Muhlenberg from taking the charges of financial corruption to Washington? He would invent a blackmail scheme, covering all the real payments and notes to Reynolds, spicing it with an imagined affair with his wife and compounding it with nefarious blackmail. Never mind how painful or embarrassing it was or who it hurt; never mind that it would block his own future candidacy to succeed Washington—that concocted story of personal betrayal was as nothing compared to the revelation of a betrayal of the public trust. Hamilton took his moral standing down to perdition, but did not stain Washington's new American government. That was the reason for Hamilton's shame-filled cover-up in 1792, and that was the reason for his distracting and salacious Reynolds pamphlet five years later, when Callender dug up what he was sure was the truth about official wrongdoing.

Under that theory, it dawned on Callender that Hamilton had not reacted foolishly at all. On the contrary, the former Treasury Secretary did the only thing he could do to protect what was most important to George Washington, the man most important to him. Falsely betraying his wife was insignificant compared with truly betraying his country. The fallen patriot had responded as a patriot should, drawing enemy fire on himself rather than letting it bombard his government.

The defendant slumped back in his chair, shaking his head in wonderment at what he was certain was his flash of insight. He had at last reached a reasoned verdict on Hamilton.

"Guilty."

Judge Chase nodded his head in agreement toward the eight men of the jury. It had taken less than two hours for them to come to the correct conclusion. "Your verdict is pleasing to me, because it shows that the laws of the United States can be enforced in Virginia, which was the principal object of this prosecution."

He turned to Callender and motioned for him to rise. The editor struck him as a small and unworthy person to be the cause of so much stress between the nation and its component parts.

"President Adams is far from deserving the character which you, sir, have given him," said Chase. "You are a well-informed observer, and surely know of the President's long and eminent service to his country, and yet you represented him in blacker colors than Sejanus himself. Your attack on him is an attack on the people of this country, for any people who could elect so infamous a character as you pretend Mr. Adams to be must be depraved and wicked themselves."

Callender swayed in his place, and Justice Chase spoke slowly so that his words would be taken down by the press and sent across the land. "If your calumny, defamation and falsehood were to be tolerated," he intoned, "it would reduce virtue to the level of vice. There would be no encouragement to integrity, and no man, however upright in his conduct, could be secure from slander." Chase stopped glowering long enough to give the convicted man a last chance. "Do you have any contrition to express that might bring about a diminution of your sentence?"

The defendant started to speak but could not because of the evident dryness of his throat. The judge motioned the marshal to give him some water.

"I understand that government officers believe that government is strengthened by good repute," Callender told the judge. "But let me say something about the complicated robbery that is a hallmark of every government." The felon's reedy voice was not easy to hear, causing Chase to lean forward and the spectators in the courtroom to fall silent. "In collecting the national revenue, every customhouse officer and exciseman has opportunities, more or less, of filching. In the spending of those tax monies, every colonel and sergeant in the army, every contractor for a plank of wood or a barrel of beef, has a squeeze at the public purse. This always has been the case, because in all ages and nations, human nature is the same.

"Thus, you see, corruption is one of the first elements of government," Callender continued. "This proves the necessity for an impartial and independent press, because government exists but by the support of public opinion, and the press is the axis around which public opinion may be said to revolve." His voice gained some strength. "I may be insolent. I have written some words that may be abusive. But the insolence and the abusiveness of liberty, sir, are far preferable to the groveling decorum of this Court and the funereal silence of despotism."

The "hanging judge" had become aware, as the trial progressed, of the Virginians' plot to make their man Callender seem a martyr. He was troubled by Governor Monroe's ostentatious display of State protection of the Federal presence. He was annoyed by the walkout of the three defense attorneys, which was sure to be hailed as evidence of his unfairness in the press and perhaps even before the Congress. He was determined now to ameliorate the public reaction sure to come if he gave the convicted man the Draconian sentence he deserved.

"You will serve time in the Richmond jail until March 4, 1801," he pronounced, which was the day the Sedition Act was to lapse and the next Presidential term would begin. A mere nine months was not half the length of time this libelous hack ought to sweat in the Richmond jail. And because he knew that Callender could be portrayed by his friends as the penniless father of four destitute boys, Chase thought it wise to be relatively lenient on the fine. "You will pay a fine of two hundred dollars."

He gaveled the trial of Callender for sedition to an end. As he slowly exited the courtroom, accepting the congratulations of the prosecution and Federalist spectators, Chase could see the shorthand note-taker whispering to the prisoner and several newsmongers. They would most likely print the transcript of this trial in a pamphlet and mail it to every election district soon to choose Presidential electors. Virginia had deferred most politely to Federal authority in this case but the Virginians, he suspected, had a political plan in mind to exploit the "groveling decorum" in his court. Chase made a mental note to tell Robert Goodloe Harper that his plan to use the courts to systematically suppress criticism of the government might just have the opposite effect.

Chapter 23

August 19, 1800

"*J* don't know how Burr did it," said Albert Gallatin to John Beckley, "but his slate of Presidential electors was able to snatch victory from the Hamilton men in New York City. Imagine—the city, the bastion of Federalism."

They were in the republican leader's office in Congress Hall. Boxes of records were stacked to the ceiling in early preparation for the move of the nation's capital from Philadelphia to the muddy new town in the Federal District carved out of Maryland and Virginia.

Beckley was elated. News of the upset election in New York was trumpeted in that morning's *Aurora,* along with a savage bit of doggerel that its editor had been using to whip up sentiment against the Federalist judge for jailing Callender: "Cursed of thy father / Scum of all that's base / Thy sight is odious / and thy name is Chase."

Beckley had smoothed over the petty jealousy between the editor, Duane, and the unjustly but usefully convicted Callender. Now the *Aurora* was one of the many portholes that the Scot, more productive than ever in his Richmond jail cell, was firing through.

"Burr must have used some of the organizing methods we won with in Pennsylvania," Beckley speculated to Gallatin, the only republican he considered capable of matching Hamilton's brilliance in financial affairs. "Hamilton must be having fits. Now the New York Governorship is Burr's for the taking."

"Jefferson is certain he cannot win this winter without New York's electors," the angular republican responded. Beckley had heard Madison say the same. "That's why we failed four years ago. Can Burr bring the unanimous support of the New York delegation to us?"

"Not unless he is our choice for Vice President." Beckley knew Burr's reputation for a combination of shrewdness and ruthlessness in driving political bargains. "But I've heard Jefferson call him a 'crooked gun.' Doesn't trust him." It was one of the few judgments Jefferson and Hamilton had in common.

"Is the mistrust misplaced, Beckley, in your view? A crooked gun, when you fire it, explodes in your face."

The Clerk thought that Gallatin—and, for that matter, Jefferson and Madison—lacked political practicality. To his mind, the only member of the republican gentry who possessed an understanding of the need to compromise one's purity on occasion to win election was James Monroe. "We can count on Burr to defeat Hamilton's slate of electors," he replied narrowly.

"Is there another New Yorker, besides Colonel Burr, who could bring Jefferson the whole crowd of them?"

"Governor Clinton, I suppose. He's getting old, though."

"Here is what I would like you to do." Gallatin was the son-in-law of an eminent New York banker who was close to the political powers of the State. His wife was that month staying with her elderly father in their William Street home. He directed Beckley to see his wife and her father and find out who were the two or three republicans in that State who would best stand for Vice President alongside Jefferson for President. Then Beckley should sound out each of the two possible candidates, without, of course, making a commitment.

Beckley was sure Gallatin was aware of the blind spot in the Constitution that had been causing such trouble. The founders' idea was for the electors to cast votes for individuals running for the two highest offices, and the two men with the most support would be President and Vice President. Unforeseen was the notion of parties, each presenting a pair of men for the separate posts harnessed together like a team of horses. In the founders' theory, the second man would be nearly as capable as the first; in the practice of the factions, however, the second man was now to be decidedly inferior and running only for the secondary post.

Both parties were eager to avoid the sort of two-headed result in the 1796 election: the Federalist Adams, President, and the anti-Federalist Jefferson, Vice President. Not only did they work against each other, but if the President died or was assassinated, power would be wrenched by one party's hands from the opposition's, inviting civil war. Another problem that bothered Beckley was the possibility of a tie: in 1796, if Adams and Jefferson had tied, the election would have been decided in the House of Representatives by a vote of the States, and perhaps a compromise unknown to the people would be chosen. Madison and the other founders had thought only of individual candidates, and not of entire political factions, competing. The irony was that it was Madison who helped create an opposition faction behind Jefferson that left the initial national election process in a mess.

"There's another matter, while you're up in Hamilton's neighborhood," said Gallatin. "Robert Harper, not the brightest of our adversaries, let slip a remark to me that bears further examination. Something about a letter that is being sent from Hamilton, perhaps in pamphlet form, to a select group of Federalist leaders around the country. All very secret. I could not show too great an interest in it to Harper without engendering his suspicion, but if it has to do with Hamilton's disagreement with President Adams about war with France—"

Such a letter, if properly exposed, could split the Federalists. "Maybe Colonel Burr knows something about it. A printed pamphlet, you say?"

"I cannot be sure. You now know as much as I do about it."

If Hamilton wanted to circulate his strategy for the coming election to the key high Federalists, Beckley estimated, his list would include about sixty men. They would range from Harper in the House to Treasury Secretary Wolcott, the last of the Hamiltonians left in Adams's Cabinet. That many letters would be difficult to copy out by hand, if the letter was long, and Hamilton tended to write at great length. If this covered more than forty pages and sixty copies were needed, it would make sense to have it printed—if you trusted the printer. He assured Gallatin that on his trip to New York he would snoop about.

August 20, 1800
NEW YORK CITY

A large and ill-painted portrait of Tamanend, the Delaware Indian chief, in full-feathered headdress and beaded regalia, hung above the saloon bar at the Tammany Society. Over a glass of beer with one of the sachems in the political clubhouse in Martling's Tavern called the Wigwam—derided by the city's aristocrats as "the pig sty"—Beckley marveled aloud at the way Tammany had been able to bring to the polls such a number of republican voters. The system of district captains with money in hand for "expenses" on Election Day was familiar to him—he had pioneered the technique four years before—but the politician was intrigued by a few of Burr's original maneuvers. Voters had been canvassed door-to-door, and each voter's name was written on a card at the Wigwam, with his political background, family desires, and needs for transportation on Election Day.

"New York aristocrats put in a property requirement to vote," said the ruddy-faced sachem behind a brimming stein of ale. "You have to own a twenty-pound freehold, or live in a house that pays forty shillings in rent, to have the right to cast a ballot. Hell, the only things most of us own are our tools."

"You circumvented that law? And got away with it?"

"Colonel Burr found the way. Months ago, some of us gathered up forty, fifty laboring men or poor law students, and got them to club together and rent a house to live in. It's called a tontine. Then they could put down their address and every man jack of them was qualified to vote. We did that ten times." He took a satisfying swallow of the ale. "Tammany brought over five hundred votes to the polls that way, surprised the bejeesus out of everybody."

Armed with that and other electioneering tips, Beckley made for the town house of Aaron Burr. This was not Burr's elegant estate, Richmond Hill, overlooking the Hudson, but the modest quarters that included political offices at 30 Partition Street at the corner of Church Street. He presented the New Yorker with a congratulatory letter from the republican leaders in the House, added his own professional regard, and asked what the secret of the electoral success had been.

"Great names," Burr said immediately, making no mystery of it. "Up to this last election, nobody of any important station ever ran for elector. The office is insignificant, beneath the dignity of successful men or famous soldiers. After Hamilton put up his list of nonentities, all his lackeys, I offered the people of New York our most famous names. General Horatio Gates, for one—some of us know he rivaled General Washington in military sagacity—and Governor Clinton, and Judge Livingston."

"How did you get them to agree to stand for election?"

"I said it would irritate Hamilton and Adams, and it would not take any of their time, and that Thomas Jefferson and I would appreciate it. They found it amusing to stand for such an inconsequential and momentary office. Nobody turned me down, though Clinton—the 'Old Incumbent'—thinks Jefferson is a bit of a trimmer. And the people recognized the names on the ballot. They were impressed and voted for them, setting aside their politicks, and now we will have electors ready to vote for the republican candidate."

"Brilliant," said Beckley, smiling at the simplicity and audacity of the scheme. "I understand that the surprising result of the election set Hamilton off in a rage."

"He cannot stand to lose," said Burr, enjoying the thought. "He wrote to Governor Jay demanding that the selection of electors by the new legislature be changed. He suddenly, belatedly, wanted the direct election of the Presidential electors by the people." That was revealing to Beckley; direct election was what republicans sought wherever entrenched Federalists blocked them. "He said that Jefferson was an atheist and a fanatic and it would not do to be over-scrupulous in stopping him. John Jay's a good Federalist—they wrote *The Federalist Papers* together, remember?—but changing the rules after the election was asking too much. He ignored him."

Beckley made admiring noises about Burr's sources of information and then asked what he thought Hamilton would do next.

"Adams has accomplished his 'move to the middle,' where most of the people are." In Burr's analysis, Hamilton would have to find another Federalist—General Pinckney came to mind—to stand alongside Adams as Vice President and get the same number of electoral votes. "Then, when the House meets to break the tie and re-elect Adams, Hamilton and his high Federalists will arrange for some States to withhold their votes for Adams so that Pinckney would win in a most Constitutional coup."

Could such a convoluted scheme ever succeed? Would the people stand for it? It struck Beckley that Burr, a born conspirator, was remarkably adept at reading Hamilton's mind. "But that will come as a terrible surprise to the people, Colonel. They will have thought the Federalists wanted General Pinckney only as Vice President, and suddenly he'll be their President."

"That's Hamilton's plan. I'm sure of it. Such a coup won't be easy to bring off," Burr observed, as if finding the plan academically intriguing, "but what else can he do? Adams despises him and is stripping away his influence. He cannot desert Federalism and support Jefferson. He cannot run himself; you and Callender and that Reynolds woman saw to that. He can't make himself dictator, because Washington is dead and Adams took away his army. So what would you do if you were General Alexander Hamilton?"

"Attempt an electoral coup," Beckley found himself saying. So that was why the Federalist caucus in Philadelphia had voted to demand that all Federalist electors from every state vote for both the party's candidates. It had seemed so fair-minded that the republican caucus had done the same. But there was a plot at its core—a plot to arrange a tie within the party and then to have the second man win in the House. Beckley had to shake his head in wonderment at the chicanery in store.

But he had a specific task to perform for Gallatin in coming to New York. "You mentioned former Governor George Clinton. You indicated how widely respected he is here. There's republican talk of him, you know, as the possible candidate for Vice President with Jefferson."

Burr turned cold. "Not around here, sir. You are misinformed. The elderly Mr. Clinton—he must be past sixty now—is enjoying a well-earned retirement. Mr. Gallatin and Mr. Madison might like to know that the talk here is of Aaron Burr."

"You would be interested in the Vice Presidency, then."

Burr rose from his chair, picked up a long silver letter-opener, and examined it closely. "No, Mr. Beckley, you may tell your principals that I do not seek the Vice Presidency. Indeed, a far more important office, Governor of New York, might afford me a chance to do greater service."

Beckley expected such routine coyness from political figures, but thought it wise to probe for this practical man's purpose in holding back. "There has to be good reason for your reluctance, Colonel."

Burr was frank. "In '96, when I stood for national office, I was misled by the republican electors of Virginia and South Carolina. They promised they would cast their ballots for me, but reneged. Before I would accept any offer this time, I would have to be assured at the highest levels that the republicans of the South would not betray me again."

Beckley remembered well how the Virginians embarrassed Burr in 1796, at Jefferson's direction. "I will convey that to my colleagues in Philadelphia with absolute clarity," he assured the Colonel.

Walking to the door, Burr said, "What happened to Peter Porcupine down there? I read his *Gazette,* but he seems to have lost his Federalist fervor."

"That evil British agent has not been the same since his former hero Adams moderated the war fever against France," Beckley reported with relish. "Cobbett spends most of his time now railing at Dr. Benjamin Rush for bleeding George Washington to death."

"I see he's arguing with Noah Webster of the *Commercial Advertiser* here about Adams's peacemaking with France. It's good to see, with the election coming up, the Federalist editors fall out."

Beckley had an amusing piece of gossip to pass along. "Cobbett and Webster, though on the same side, bear each other some kind of grudge about the English language. Cobbett offered to pay for a new portrait of Webster at the front of his spelling book—said the present one is so ugly it scares the children from their lessons." The vain Webster had turned purple at that thrust, Beckley heard, and didn't know how to respond to the Porcupine's ridicule. "But the best news is that our new Governor, Tom McKean, is out to close down *Porcupine's Gazette,* with a libel suit."

He did not forget the last part of his mission. "Speaking of the newspapers, Colonel, I noted your reference to a role I may have played in the public exposure of Hamilton's peculation, or as he prefers it, peccadillo."

"Maria Reynolds was my client in her divorce, you know." Beckley did not know. "She tells me that you were the one who passed Monroe's copies of the Reynolds documents to Callender. True? I'm asking because I was the one who had to avert a duel between Monroe and Hamilton."

A thought crossed Beckley's mind: Did Burr have anything to do with an entrapment of Hamilton, using the Reynolds woman? The two political leaders were said to despise each other—Hamilton was known to have said it was his "religious duty" to oppose Burr's career. The roots of such fierce enmities often ran deep into men's pasts and involved women. He put that aside and dealt with the question at hand: "Let's just say I have friends in the press, but would never pass them private documents." He then exploited the opening. "One of them has asked me if I knew of a very recent letter, perhaps in the form of a printed pamphlet, that Hamilton is privately circulating to his wide circle of high-Federalist leaders. Have you heard anything about such a letter?"

"What does it look like? How thick?"

From that question seeking a better description, Beckley suspected that Burr had a spy in Hamilton's house—a faithless servant or clandestine visitor—who could be directed to find a specific item. "My guess is the size is octavo, same as his previous pamphlets under various pen names, perhaps twenty or thirty pages. My further guess is that the document has to do with his rift with Adams and what Federalists should do in the election. I stand ready to be the conduit to the press of any such document, which cannot be truly private if printed. Especially if it proves embarrassing to the writer."

Beckley enjoyed seeing Burr's conspiratorial smile. It was a pleasure to deal with a genuine political savant.

Chapter 24

September 28, 1800
RICHMOND

Callender, incarcerated in the Richmond jail, envied the *Aurora*'s William Duane. He was still at large in or near Philadelphia and avoiding his arrest for sedition, while Benny Bache's widow, soon to be the new editor's wife, published the paper. Unlike the imprisoned Scot, the fugitive Duane was still at the center of political action. He could be the recipient of John Beckley's confidences, including private documents that embarrassed Federalist politicians and made the journalist the center of controversy.

With direct financial support from Monticello, Callender was finishing Volume II of *The Prospect Before Us.* He was certain it would become the bible of the republicans supporting Jefferson for President. The sales of Volume I had been boosted by his famous sedition trial three long months before: in republican papers around the nation, Chase was the villain and Callender the hero. Advance excerpts from Volume II were being printed in the *Richmond Examiner,* and when offered for sale elsewhere were being snapped up by eager anti-Adams editors.

He did not like his surroundings at all. After the first few days, the exhilaration of writing from a prison cell, with its sense of being a martyr to the Jeffersonian cause, evaporated. Contrary to his expectations, writing in this monastic atmosphere was far from ennobling. The Africans in the cells downstairs, arrested for drunkenness or rebelliousness, made an awful racket with their Baptist hymns at all hours of the night. And the drunks: "I can hardly go on for the bellowing of the banditti downstairs," he wrote to Jefferson, "who should have been carried directly from the bar to the gallows." Through the hot summer months in the oppressive heat of Richmond, the stink from the ill-ventilated prison toilets often made him ill. An early autumn cold snap brought surcease from that, but caused other discomforts: the frigid nights in the jail with no fireplace or stove brought on chills and fever.

His writing hand frequently shook. Fleabites—not the imaginary kind that Cobbett had charged him with constantly scratching, but the damnable real things—mottled his skin. The febrile Callender prose, however, never wavered or cooled. Sweet indeed were the uses of adversity, he told himself, writing page after page, except for the noise and the smell and the itching.

For the past week, he had to suffer the close proximity of a black giant named Jack Bowler. The heavily fettered slave, blood and mud still caked on his freshly scarred skin after his recapture, was one of the ringleaders of an aborted insurrection. The warden, fearful of leaving him in the large cell with the other blacks lest he organize a riot and jailbreak, put him in Callender's cell upstairs.

"You really thought a slave uprising could succeed?" the Scot asked him. "Against all the guns of the Virginia militia?"

"Toussaint won his war," said the Negro on the floor. Callender had heard that slave quarters throughout Virginia were stirred by the story of Toussaint L'Ouverture, who had led a bloody uprising against their white rulers in Haiti and crowned himself Emperor. He threw out the British and allied himself with France's Jacobin faction, but the black leader now had another war to fight against Bonaparte, who wanted to enslave the islanders again. This fellow Bowler apparently thought he could be another Toussaint, establishing a black empire in America, perhaps with whites as slaves. No wonder Governor Monroe would want to hang him. "We could have taken Richmond," said the rebel, "but we were betrayed."

"I read that your conspiracy got caught in a downpour and it flooded you out," said Callender. His *Richmond Examiner*, taking the side of the alarmed white population, had given the matter two columns on the front page.

"Wasn't the storm. Slave named Pharaoh was the traitor, told the masters."

Callender tossed his cellmate a piece of hard-baked dough and watched him consume it angrily. "What do your people say about the American government?" the Scot asked. "Do you just think of us as whites, or do you know that there's a difference between us?" When the black, swallowing the dry food, did not answer, he added, "Federalists against republicans. Abolitionists up north and"—he groped for a neutral phrase to describe slave-owners— "the plantation people around here. Have you heard of Thomas Jefferson?"

Bowler nodded, his neck iron tilting. "Heard of Jefferson. Heard of Marshall. Talk about freedom, but they beat us and use our women."

"Not cruelly, though." A look at the man's wounds caused him to modify that. "At least they don't beat the women."

That drew a bitter laugh. "Jefferson uses one of our women to breed with, make new slaves, get richer. Marshall, too. Ever'body knows that."

"You're a liar. And you'd better not talk that way or you'll swing for sure." Callender thought of the way the white plantation youths had their choice of the black women at the barn dancing. He condemned such mixing of the races, but could not close his eyes to the sexual "use" of the female slaves by the white owners. Not Thomas Jefferson. The gossip might be directed at the Federalist John Marshall, the Virginian now serving Adams at State, maybe, but not Jefferson. He refused to listen to Bowler's taunts about the man who wrote the Declaration of white Independence while owning hundreds of slaves and ordering those he liked into his bed. Callender put the repugnant thought out of his mind and was half-glad the slandering insurrectionist would soon be permanently silenced.

October 1, 1800

Governor Monroe himself came to visit Callender in his cell, a newspaper in hand. The issue of the *Aurora* carried a full report of a secret document that Hamilton circulated to other Federalist leaders. The prisoner read the title and it made his newsmonger's mouth water: "Letter from Alexander Hamilton Concerning the Public Conduct and Character of John Adams."

"You will note," said the Governor, his thin lips exhibiting a small and unaccustomed smile, "what Colonel Hamilton has to say about the President of the United States there on page three."

Callender read it avidly. "He calls Adams 'a man of disgusting egotism, liable to paroxysms of anger, which deprive him of self-command and produce very outrageous behavior.' "

"Hamilton is trying to write the way you do, Callender."

"I welcome his emulation." He read more deeply into Hamilton's extended tirade: it dissected every mistake Adams ever made, demeaning his character throughout. Its unintended publication in the gleeful *Aurora* would, Callender was sure, rip asunder the Federalist party.

One twist at the very end, however, struck Callender as curious. The long letter seemed to have no conclusion, no clarion call to action. The vengeful Hamilton seemed about to condemn the President's candidacy for re-election, but then swerved away. He argued instead that "to support Adams and Pinckney equally is the only thing that can save us from the fangs of Jefferson," whose election, he warned, would subject the country to "a revolution after the manner of Buonaparte."

Why—if John Adams was as deranged and disgusting as he said—did Hamilton continue to urge his Federalist followers to support Adams for President, along with Pinckney for Vice President? Callender suspected the New Yorker had a scheme in his devious mind to advance his private interests. Did Hamilton expect his private letter to be discovered and published? Did he arrange for it to find its way instantly to the press—and did he insert that ostensibly loyal line at the end to protect himself from charges of political apostasy? And what did "support Adams and Pinckney equally" mean? He wished he could write to Beckley in Philadelphia to ask about this, but the mails were not safe.

"I would like to entrust this letter and package to you for delivery to your neighbor, Thomas Jefferson," he said to Monroe. Because the letter was already sealed, he said, "In it I express my thanks for his unfailing encouragement and attach the latest pages of my book. And I tell him, frankly, that the thing that vexes me most in this business is my being prevented from seeing my four boys. I am not free to get up to Leiper's farm in Pennsylvania, and I would not want them to see me in these circumstances here."

Lest he become sentimental in front of the resolutely unemotional Governor, Callender skipped to another subject of his concern. "The people here in your Virginia, Monroe"—he would continue to address his fellow henchman that way, despite his high and mighty new title—"seem to me buried in a kennel of servility. Richmond needs the aid of a local political apostle, a newspaper that can carry the Jefferson message day in and day out. If we succeed in turning out the aristocracy, I contemplate starting a press of my own. It could not fail of plenty of business. But I would need some capital to start, and a sinecure on which to build."

The part-time political sinecure Callender had in mind was Richmond postmaster. The job was currently held by a hack writer for the Federalists who rarely showed up to fill his official position, and whose main responsibility was to intercept and read the letters of prominent republicans. If power changed hands, it would be only right and proper to replace the Adams appointee with a republican loyalist. He would not only do the postmastering better but—supported by the public salary and with plenty of time to write—could advance Jefferson's cause.

There was surely precedent for it. After election as Governor of Pennsylvania, the good republican Tom McKean had punished all the Federalist officeholders by throwing them out of office. Not only did McKean take care of John Beckley at Jefferson's personal request, but that forthright tormentor of the evil Cobbett studded the state's government with other loyal republicans. Official recognition of his connection to the Chief Magistrate would help Callender's new paper attract advertisers. He knew that on his own, with his strong, vituperative style and well-known signature, he could attract and hold readers.

"Certainly, Richmond could make good use of a man of your talents, Mr. Callender," said Monroe. "Continue to take up your pen, as the Vice President likes to tell us—indeed, redouble your efforts. We will know the results of the election in two months. Nobody will ever forget all you have done for your adopted country."

The Governor took the letter and book pages and signaled to the jailer to open the door. "About your boys. If someone in authority were to explain to them the noble reason for your being incarcerated, I should think they would be quite proud of your political martyrdom. We'll see what Mr. Jefferson can do."

Afterward, Monroe evidently had a word with the warden. The celebrated prisoner was moved from his cell into a small apartment, allowing him to work and sleep in different rooms, and pace back and forth for exercise between chapters. No more unwanted cellmates like the hulking black Bowler bleeding all over the floor and sullying the atmosphere with his heinous imaginings.

The barred windows of his improved quarters were still a source of melancholy, but the forced solitude and regular food enabled him to do what the Governor and Jefferson urged. He took up his pen.

Callender set about turning out a stream of informed and stirring polemics that he was certain would be avidly read by everyone eager for ammunition to denounce the Adams Administration. Electors were being selected in different states on different days, and the voters needed to be exhorted by a writer unjustly denied his freedom. He did not have much time; on the first Monday in December, the Electoral College would cast its ballots for President and Vice President, as the Constitution directed.

In the light of two candles, he contemplated his pot of ink. He thought it could be considered the wellspring, in a sense, of rational argument and emotional fervor to be printed in Richmond and reprinted in newspapers up and down the country. By his example of martyrdom and through his written cry from jail, he saw himself as an historian helping make the history that he would later write. It was almost enough to make a man forget the fleas and lice and criminal company.

Chapter 25

Cobbett had promised long ago to quit the state of Pennsylvania if the libel-driven republican judge, Tom McKean, was elected Governor. As always, the proprietor of *Porcupine's Gazette* was true to his word. He had established a newspaper with the largest circulation in the nation. That was accomplished without any of the base and parasitical arts by which government patronage was generally obtained. He then closed down the paper.

"I congratulate myself," he declaimed to his wife Nancy, "on being persistent." He took a deep breath. "In spite of calumny, threats, prosecutions and savage howlings of the republicans on the one side; and in spite of the praises, promises, caresses and soothing serenades of the Federalists on the other side—in spite of all these, I have persisted in openly avowing my attachment to my native country and my King."

She agreed, as she turned the key on their home and printing shop and bookstore, that he had surely infuriated most of the neighbors. "The memory will never leave me," she said, "of the day you hung a picture of King George in this shop window just to upset the Americans."

"I succeeded," he reminded her. "Drew a mob and I faced it down. Showed them the mettle of an Englishman." With their five-year-old daughter Anne and two-year-old son William, and the valuable stacks of books that made up his bookseller's inventory, the man who had gained fame and infamy in Philadelphia as Peter Porcupine sailed to the port of New York. There he took up residence above his shop at 141 Water Street in what he thought would be a strong Federalist redoubt.

He soon discovered it was not. The war between Hamilton and Adams had riven the party. Republican Aaron Burr's Tammany Society had stolen a march on the Federalists by selecting pro-Jefferson electors in the looming Presidential election. However, Cobbett was not saddened by his departure from Philadelphia. Sales of *Porcupine's Gazette* had fallen off with the decline in Federalist popular support, and much of the city's political life was preparing to move to the new capital down South. The newspaper no longer satisfied his zest for combat because he was bereft of a hero: Adams had gone sour, Jefferson was worse and the admirable Hamilton had no future.

Fortunately for his finances, sales of his pamphlet about the atrocities committed by the French in southern Germany, *The Cannibal's Progress*, had reached 100,000. That was thanks to the anger of the Pennsylvania Deutsch about what had been happening in their ancestral home. Nobody since Tom Paine at the height of his revolutionary popularity had sold as well. Cobbett had demonstrated there was a market in America for lively controversy on emotional subjects written in a plain and buoyant style, spiced with personal invective and amusing ridicule.

As soon as he had settled in New York, preparing his bookstore for buyers and his print shop for the production of pamphlets, he paid a call on the one American whose politics he trusted.

"Hamilton, your country is going to the dogs," he said, coming immediately to the point. "You must do something about it or this nation, with all its promise, will sink into the radical bog."

"Have you read my letter to the Federalist leaders? It seems everyone else has."

"I presume you arranged for a copy to be stolen and delivered to Burr," the editor told the politician. "He would have given it to Beckley, who would have delivered it to Duane at the *Aurora*. That's how these things are done. You could then pretend to be outraged at the interception of your private message."

Hamilton smiled broadly. To the tall Cobbett, he seemed a small man, with a handsome English face, and a smile and aristocratic air that struck him as winsome. Hamilton indicated to Cobbett to sit in a Queen Anne chair in his study. The editor was pleased that his host expressed a concern about the libel judgment being sought against the Porcupine in Philadelphia by Dr. Benjamin Rush.

"I wrote the truth about that quack's purge-and-bleed cure for the yellow fever. His cure kills all his patients."

"You're certain?" Hamilton exhibited some lawyerly caution. "He's the most famous physician on this side of the Atlantic."

"I am a farmer's son, General Hamilton. I have cut the throats of scores of geese and little pigs, and I have always perceived that the moment the blood was out of the body the poor creatures died."

"Who's representing you in court down there?"

"Robert Harper. He's leaving the Congress for private practice of the law."

Hamilton looked troubled. "A great legislator, we'll miss him. But I'm not certain how he will fare in a courtroom, especially with a judge that McKean chooses to deal with you."

"Harper is trying to have the case moved to a Federal court, since I'm a British subject."

"McKean can block that easily. And he can see to it you have all republicans on the jury. See here, Cobbett, if there should be a judgment against you, they'll have to come after your assets in New York. In light of all you've done for America's cause, I'd be glad to represent you here. For no fee, of course."

Cobbett was aware of Hamilton's professional reputation as an attorney. He also had a way with New York judges, most of whom he helped get their appointments. Hamilton had planted a seed of doubt in his mind about Harper's ability and he was relieved at the generous offer.

"And now to politics," the editor said briskly. "I take it your secret plan is to promote the candidacies of Adams and Pinckney. Then at the last minute, with the two of them tied with the most number of votes for President, you will arrange for some of those electors to withhold their votes for Adams, slipping Pinckney in as the choice for President."

Hamilton seemed stunned. "Is the secret plan, as you call it, that widely known?"

"It's all there in your letter-pamphlet, for anyone who takes the trouble to read between the lines. Brilliantly written piece of work, by the way, Hamilton, I congratulate you on it. You really should publish a newspaper."

"I may, one day. Assuming *arguendo* that might be my plan, to surprise Adams—do you think it is feasible?"

"No. I am convinced it is doomed to fail." The man was entitled to an honest and forthright view, Cobbett felt; though he was probably surrounded by sycophants, Hamilton must be a realist at heart. "The States have already chosen most of the electors. Adams and Pinckney will have about sixty votes each. Jefferson and Burr will each have about seventy. Then Burr will refine your secret plan and use it himself."

Hamilton steepled his long, fine fingers and studied Cobbett closely. "How?"

The English editor enjoyed instructing the American on American politics. "Burr, too, will arrange for all the republicans to vote equally for Jefferson and himself. That's not hard to do because it's what the people expect. Then the matter will be thrown over to the House of Representatives, as called for in your Constitution. Each State has one vote." He added, "as you know better than I, of course," because, after all, the man had written the best of the *Federalist Papers*.

"But surely Burr would then defer to Jefferson—"

"Would he? If you say so. You know the ambitious Colonel Burr far better than I do."

Hamilton, frowning, thought that over. "You are suggesting, Cobbett, that some of our low Federalist friends would seek to make a deal with the republican Burr. To head off Jefferson."

"That's what I heard in Philadelphia. I'm surprised it has not been vouchsafed to you. It's a daring plan, to go against the will of the people that way, but—again, as you know better than I do—it would be quite constitutional. You really should do something about your Constitution, by the way. It's not very good about elections." The editor was pleased to be engaged in the manipulation of the political system rather than merely writing about it. Yet it was true that desperate Federalists were talking this way, and he saw no harm in making their case to the man most concerned. "A Federalist arrangement with the republican Burr would stop Jefferson and his radical French supporters from taking power—if Burr could be trusted to govern with Federalist support."

"This is not the sort of thing we had in mind," Hamilton mused. The editor presumed Hamilton was thinking of Valley Forge, American independency and all the tedious varieties of fuzzy Lockean philosophy that had transfixed the colonials.

"Come now, sir. You were willing to ask the New York Governor to set aside the recent election of electors." Cobbett had heard of Hamilton's desperate plea, ignored by Governor Jay. "Indeed, you are once again planning, even as we speak, to substitute your man Pinckney for Adams—in what the average farmer in the field would consider a dastardly trick. You have shown yourself willing to take extraordinary measures because your nation faces a terrible crisis with a Jefferson triumph."

"I know, I know. I have been fighting our home-grown radicals far longer than you have been here in our country, Mr. Cobbett."

"No time to give up now. Unless you stop the republicans, you will have a wholly different banking system, with that Swiss cadaver Albert Gallatin in charge, to keep you backward for generations. Think of it! A foreign policy encouraging mob rule abroad with Tom Paine himself dining in the new Executive Mansion. That would mean an end to your 'energy in the executive' and instead, all power diffused to the States, especially to sleepy Virginia."

With each salvo, Hamilton seemed to shrink into his chair; the notion of Gallatin at Treasury seemed especially hard for him to take. Cobbett rather enjoyed the experience of flaying his closest ally. "The American people need to be saved from themselves, from turning into the bloody-minded sans-culottes and away from their English heritage. This is hardly the moment, General, for democratic scruples."

He watched Hamilton give that some thought. "If there be a man in the world I ought to hate," the New Yorker said finally, "it is Jefferson. He has always been a hypocrite. With Burr I have always been personally well." Cobbett's eyebrows rose at that; he had heard, to the contrary, that Burr and Hamilton despised each other cordially. "But the public good must be paramount to every private consideration."

That last platitude struck Cobbett as the too-discreet mouthing of a political man worried about being quoted. He rose to take his leave.

"If I do start a newspaper here," Hamilton said, walking him to the door, "it would be about public policy, and not about the private concerns of public men."

Cobbett hoped the competition would sink the newspaper run by Noah Webster, the pompous fool, but assumed that such a lifeless publication as Hamilton described would be doomed. "No man has a right to pry into his neighbor's private concerns," he conceded, "and the opinions of every man are his private concerns, while they are confined to his family and friends."

"I agree," said Hamilton.

"But when he makes those opinions public," Cobbett said, admonishing Hamilton as he had Beckley and Callender years before, "when he once comes forward as a candidate—then his opinions, his principles, his motives, every action of his life, public or private, become the fair subject of public discussion."

Hamilton shook his head. "I know from your writing that you are a student of Roman history," he said. "You are familiar with Catiline."

Cobbett nodded; every self-educated man knew the history of Catiline, the defeated candidate for the consulship of Rome who plotted a military coup, was exposed by Cicero and killed. Down through the ages, his name had become a synonym for conspiracy.

"Whenever I think of Burr," said Hamilton, "I think of Catiline."

Chapter 26

ALBERT GALLATIN

February 4, 1801
WASHINGTON, D.C.

*A*lbert Gallatin had thought that on Election Day, laſt December 3, the electors would carry out the will of the people and name Thomas Jefferson President and Aaron Burr Vice President. The electors gave Jefferson and Burr 73 votes each, defeating Adams and Pinckney, each with 65.

Burr was not supposed to get 73 republican votes. Madison had assured the Jeffersonians that it was arranged for several republican electors to cast one vote for Jefferson and no vote at all for Vice President. That would have given Jefferson the most votes and therefore the Presidency.

But it had not worked out that way. Some electors, perhaps stimulated by friends of Burr, had lied to Madison. The two candidates were tied and nobody was the new President. The people had spoken and the electors had not listened. That profoundly disturbed Gallatin, but he knew all was not lost: the House of Representatives, on this frigid day of February, was to decide who would be the next President.

Meanwhile, the vengeful Adams, rattling around the huge new President's house down near the swamps of the new capital city, was appointing Federalists to lifetime judgeships. The Supreme Court's Chief had resigned, and Gallatin had feared Adams would name Samuel Chase; to his relief, the President chose John Marshall, despite that loyal Federalist's opposition to the Sedition Act. Jefferson detested his fellow Virginian, but Gallatin had found him a worthy intellectual adversary in Congress, a vast improvement over Harper.

Gallatin picked his way across the frozen mud of Pennsylvania Avenue to Conrad and MacMunn's boardinghouse. It was on the south side of Capitol Hill facing the Senate wing of the Capitol, the only part of the projected structure that was ready for occupancy. Jefferson had sent for him to come to Conrad's and meet with Madison about the election of the President in the House.

Each of the thirteen States had one vote, with nine required to elect. Gallatin knew he had only eight States lined up for Jefferson. Nine ballots had already been taken and the process was frozen at eight States for Jefferson, six for Burr. But within the State delegations, in individual votes cast, Burr led by 55 to 51; that meant it would be hard to get that last State.

Monroe would not be in the war council because he was assembling the Virginia militia to counter any usurpation in Washington. One rumor was that the Federalist Senate would pass a law placing the government in the hands of its president pro tem. If they tried that, Gallatin knew, the Middle States' militias would march on the capital.

Jefferson had a sitting room as well as a bedroom at the inn. That was better than Gallatin's lodging, a small room that he had to share with another Congressman. The Vice President nodded to his worried colleagues and put a sharp question to Madison: "Why have we come to this? You said you had a couple of electors who would withhold their votes from Burr. What happened?"

"At the critical moment," the short Virginian replied, "false assurances were dispatched to the electors of South Carolina that the votes of another State would be different from what they proved to be."

Jefferson, frustrated, shook his head in wonderment. "The contrivance in the Constitution for marking the votes works badly. It does not enounce precisely the true expression of the public will."

"We didn't think of everything," Madison murmured. "Maybe we could get Burr to join us in a proclamation calling the newly elected Congress into session rather than have this decided by the old Congress. I realize that might not be strictly regular under the Constitution, but—"

"Not a good idea." Gallatin cut him short because Madison did not seem to grasp the political cause of the impasse. "First we have to determine if Burr is trying to use this flaw in the Constitution to usurp the Presidency. You said you were given false assurances about the electoral votes. Jemmy—who gave you those assurances?"

Madison didn't want to say. Gallatin presumed that the betrayal was centered in South Carolina, where Robert Goodloe Harper was making mischief on behalf of Burr. Fear of a French-inspired slave uprising, whipped up by Harper during the XYZ madness, had given the Federalists surprising strength in what should have been a Jeffersonian state.

"I'm assuming that Harper prevailed on republicans in his South Carolina delegation to betray their commitments." When the discomfited Madison did not contradict him, Gallatin took that as confirmation of his fears. "He's become Burr's leading henchman. That answers my question. Burr will not step aside. That damned Harper will offer him Federalist support for President if he will guarantee them a share of power."

"I'll write Burr a letter," Jefferson suggested. "I'll offer him a post in my Administration more suitable to his talents than mere Vice President. If we could not get gentlemen who possess the public confidence, as Burr does, into the Cabinet, then the evil genius of this country"—they all knew he meant Hamilton—"may realize his avowal that he will beat down this Administration."

"A letter from you to Burr would not injure our cause," said Gallatin, assuming it would do little good. "But I think he would vaguely pledge his loyalty to you and see what the Federalists offer him and what the House decides." However, this evidence that Jefferson was ready to make a deal by offering a Cabinet post gave a practical politician an opening. "Of course, if I have your permission to negotiate with the Federalists on offices in the new Administration—"

Jefferson shook his head and struck what to Gallatin seemed an unnecessarily noble pose. "Many attempts have been made to obtain terms and promises from me. I will not go into this government with my hands tied."

Gallatin wished Monroe were there instead of Madison. Only he could drum some political sense into the mind of the writer of the Declaration of Independence.

"You are right about Hamilton being the evil genius of this country," Madison observed, slightly off the point. "Noah Webster said the same thing about him. It could be that Hamilton is the one behind this."

February 5, 1801
NEW YORK CITY

Hamilton was faced with a horrendous political dilemma. Having fought Jefferson in Washington's Cabinet, having twice bitterly opposed Jefferson's election to the Presidency—could he now reverse himself completely and throw his support to the advocate of France and a weak central government? Contrariwise, if not Jefferson, could he entrust the nation in whose Revolution he fought, and whose Constitution he shaped, to the hands of a shrewdly calculating Burr—a voluptuary he knew to be worthy only of the deepest distrust?

Because he asked himself the right question, he did not have to agonize long. That question was: what would his lifelong mentor, George Washington, advise? He knew the answer. Forced to choose between Jefferson and Burr, Hamilton unhesitatingly chose the man whose philosophy he opposed over the man whose character he despised. The nation would be misled, its economy damaged, by the agrarian Jefferson; but it was in danger of being seized and the American system profoundly changed by the power-hungry and more energetic Burr. Sitting alone at his desk in New York, three hundred miles from the center of political action, Hamilton turned his mind to electing Jefferson and to destroying Burr.

He knew he no longer controlled the Federalist party as he once did. Noah Webster was no match for the high-Federalist Cobbett or the low-republican Callender, but he was the best writer the low-Federalist Adamites could offer. Webster wrote in an impassioned response to Hamilton's pamphlet that he was "the evil genius whose conduct will be deemed little short of insanity, and who brought about our overthrow and ruin." But Hamilton felt sure he was not without influence with some of the Federalists who were tempted to follow the bumptious opportunist, Burr's Robert Harper, into a deal to maintain at least some of their power.

[*253*]

He drew a stack of stationery toward him and began to write letters to the men in the new capital city to whom he felt closest and who owed him the most.

To those of a religious bent worried about Jefferson's supposed atheism, he did not try to disabuse their fear because he, too, suspected that the man was godless. He countered, however, with his personal witness that he had heard Burr "talk perfect Godwinism"; that tied the irreverent Burr to William Godwin, the English dissenter who publicly denied God and married the notorious feminist Mary Wollstonecraft, whose antitraditional "rights of women" Burr also alarmingly embraced.

To friends doing business with England, he wrote that the French-loving Burr "could not abandon his scheme of war with Great Britain as the instrument of his power and wealth." To moralists—the few who stuck by him after the Reynolds pamphlet—he denounced Burr as a "profligate and a voluptuary in the extreme," which he knew him to be from several mutual women friends, especially Maria Reynolds. To associates in the law, he condemned the unlearned attorney as a kind of legal criminal—"an extortionist in his profession, insolvent and dangerous."

Hamilton found it much easier to denounce Burr than to find a word of praise for Jefferson. He had to begin by not appearing to spin about completely in putting forward Jefferson. "I admit that his politicks are tinctured with fanaticism, that he is not scrupulous about the means of success, nor very mindful of the truth, and that he is a contemptible hypocrite." He had to smile at his own words; this was hardly an introduction to a Presidential nomination. "But"—and here he forced himself to make his modest positive case—"Jefferson is not so dangerous a man because he had at least pretensions to character. There is no fair reason to suppose him capable of being corrupted."

What he could not say openly was what he long suspected: an effete, almost feminine quality in Jefferson would make him a flaccid executive. He was a languid sort, a dilettante in science and architecture, willing to use others to gain his ends but too much the aesthete to grapple with the foe in the arena. Hamilton thought Jefferson capable of writing with great ferocity about the need to spill blood to defeat tyranny, but was devoid of the force of character or executive energy to carry out the radical democratic principles he espoused. Better a weak Jefferson than a strong Burr.

He considered writing to Harper but dismissed that as a hopeless cause; that duplicitous Carolinian and Burr were birds of a feather. What about John Marshall, who he knew considered Jefferson immoral for his underhanded disparagement of Washington? An appeal to principle might persuade him at least to remain neutral: "Burr has no principle public or private," he wrote, "and disgrace abroad and ruin at home are the probable fruits of his elevation." Marshall, an intelligent attorney, would understand that "no private principle" meant "dishonest and immoral." Hamilton was glad Adams had skipped over Samuel Chase to appoint Marshall Chief Justice; the Federalist Virginian had the mental acuity to keep Jefferson in his place.

The final letter he wrote was to James Bayard, the only Delaware Federalist who would cast his State's vote for President. He recalled to Bayard that when he was Treasury Secretary, Burr had come to him with a dubious scheme. When turned down, Burr had said in French to Hamilton, *"Les grandes âmes se soucient peu des petits moraux"*—translating for Bayard, "Great souls do not worry about petty morals." He begged Bayard to desert Burr and switch to Jefferson: "No engagement that can be made with him can be depended upon. While making it, Burr will laugh in his sleeve at the credulity of those with whom he makes it. For heaven's sake, exert yourself to the utmost to save our country from so great a calamity."

He put down his pen and pushed aside the unused sheets of writing paper. He had no doubt that he had chosen the lesser of two evils. Burr was shrewder and tougher than Jefferson was, more purposeful and ambitious, and thus far more dangerous to the balance of powers the founders had so carefully constructed. Hamilton told himself that he acted not out of personal dislike for Burr. It had nothing to do with Maria Reynolds. Nor was he moved by selfish concern that the rise of the competing New Yorker would cause the fall of his own adherents in New York. Rather, Hamilton was certain, he acted out of love of country. He could look with equanimity at the painting of General Washington on his wall.

That reminded him of Lord Cornwallis surrendering at Yorktown and the day the band played "The World Turned Upside Down." Hamilton's Federalist world was being turned upside down, and he was poignantly aware that he was helping in the turning. After a decade's battle with Jefferson for the soul of the union, this was his surrender. He could truthfully assure himself there was no dishonor in it.

Of course, patriotism could always be alloyed with practicality. He took up his quill again. If Federalists were going to refrain from blocking Jefferson's ascendancy, they surely deserved some gesture in return from the man whose Presidency they did not deny. To Samuel Smith of Maryland, he wrote: "Obtain from Jefferson assurances on certain points. The maintenance of the cardinal articles of public credit, for one; a navy, for another; and neutrality between Britain and France." He reflected a moment before adding one more: "And the continuance in office of all our Federalist appointees."

GOUVERNEUR MORRIS

February 6, 1801
WASHINGTON, D.C.

Jefferson announced to his worried lieutenants that they all needed some fresh, cold air. Gallatin followed the Vice President and Madison out of Conrad's, up the hill to the steps of the Capitol. As Jefferson gazed down the street named after Pennsylvania, expounding on the genius of the planner, Gallatin took a more down-to-earth, Swiss view of the vista: he counted one shoemaker, one printer, a grocery shop, a small dry-goods establishment, seven boardinghouses and an oyster bar. In the distance, down toward the swamp and the river, was the President's mansion, where he had heard that Abigail Adams was complaining mightily about the accommodations. She would not have to put up with them for long.

Gulping deep breaths of the cold air in the February sunshine, they were accosted by Gouverneur Morris. New York's portly Federalist Senator was a cordial acquaintance of Jefferson's who had succeeded him as Washington's envoy to Paris. Though they disagreed profoundly about Louis XIV, Gallatin knew the two founders had a bond of love of language: Madison said that just as Jefferson had been the chief writer of the Declaration, Morris had been the man most responsible for the final literary style of the Constitution.

The dashing bon vivant, perched on his one leg and a cane, cheerfully told them that Federalists in the House were bargaining with Burr for offices in exchange for their support. Morris was sure that if Jefferson would show some interest in a compromise, that support would be his and the country would be spared much ill feeling.

"No," said Jefferson. "Many attempts have been made to obtain terms and promises from me. I will not go into government with my hands tied." Morris shrugged at this rejection of a sensible idea and wished Jefferson well in his additional four years in the demeaning Vice Presidency. Leaning on his heavy oaken cane, he started to limp laboriously down the marble stairs. Gallatin looked at Madison for help in reasoning with the rigid Jefferson, but the little Virginian, who so rarely crossed his leader, looked away.

"Morris could fall on that ice," said Gallatin, and left the group, ostensibly to help the lame Federalist leader down the slippery steps. He knew that Morris had been too close to the royalists in France, and had pressed in the Constitutional Convention for naming a President for life. But at that convention in Philadelphia a decade before, the anti-democratic Morris also struck the compromise between Hamilton and Jefferson that became the basis for a national currency. More to the point of the present crisis, Morris was a New Yorker who would know intimately the machinations of both Burr and Hamilton. Gallatin quickly caught up with him and asked, "May I help in any way?"

"The way you can help is to ignore that mule up there and talk to Sam Smith of Maryland," Morris told him in a low voice. "He and I have been in touch with Hamilton, and he knows what is needed from your side. Sam is close to Bayard of Delaware, and Delaware is your necessary ninth state."

Gallatin had been told that Bayard of Delaware, long a Hamilton ally, was the key to blocking Burr's usurpation. "Where is Hamilton in all this?"

"Jefferson has no stronger supporter in this than Hamilton," said Morris, "and I can hardly believe those words have passed my lips. Here—" He took out a letter; Gallatin recognized Hamilton's elegant handwriting. "Men never played a more foolish game than will do the Federalists if they support Burr," it read. Morris thrust Hamilton's letter to him back in his pocket. "But Robert Harper has broken with Hamilton, claims to be Burr's intimate friend, and is whipping my Federalist friends in behind Burr."

"On what theory? Burr is a republican. He built the organization that defeated the Federalists in New York."

"Harper is telling us," said Morris, "that Jefferson is so deeply imbued with false principles of government that nothing good can come of him. But"—he rested on the peg that replaced his missing leg and raised his cane—"he thinks that Burr's even temper and malleable disposition give an ample security for conduct hostile to your dangerous democratic spirit. That's why Harper is making them all promises in Burr's name."

Gallatin felt the Presidency slipping out of their hands. Despite the efforts of Hamilton, the evil genius, in support of Jefferson—in itself an incomprehensible turnabout—the will of the people was being foiled by fanatic Federalists. That could easily break apart the compact of the States; New England would march out. Drastic action was needed. "Jefferson is not interested in personally making such promises, as you heard. But I am, on his behalf. What is needed?"

Gouverneur Morris had the list. "First, the Adams and Hamilton appointees to keep their jobs, especially all the tariff collectors and postmasters." Gallatin knew how much that would infuriate the republican rank and file; without telling Jefferson, he and Monroe had made promises about rewards to loyal republicans, from national Cabinet posts to local postmasterships. Morris went on: "Next, keep building a navy." That would not be difficult; though Jefferson opposed the challenge to France on the high seas, Gallatin was sure he could be talked into providing American vessels naval protection from ships of both Britain and France. "And finally, Albert—you, of all people, must pledge to stay with Hamilton's plan of public credit."

Gallatin winced; he saw Hamilton's financial plan as the Federalist way to build ever more power at the center, in Treasury. That clashed with Jeffersonian principles about the sovereign rights of States. The Hamilton men saw the future of the nation as founded on the expansion of manufactures, with public credit and tariff protection, in contrast to the republican vision of a nation of self-reliant farmers and craftsmen selling their products to a hungry world. This was no technical argument about political arithmetick, Gallatin knew; it had to do with the future character of the people.

They reached the bottom of the steps. "Don't play into Harper's hands," Morris said, leaning on Gallatin to wave his cane in farewell to Madison and Jefferson at the top. "You know I think your man is an awful bore. Five minutes with him is like two hours. But better a bore than a knave. Keep on being obstinate and you'll be responsible for President Burr."

Thirty-six ballots, and the House of Representatives, in session to choose the third President of the United States, was still deadlocked. Neither Jefferson nor Burr had the needed nine States.

John Beckley had prevailed on his friends in the House to appoint him to an honorary post on the Committee of Correspondence. This gave him access to what no reporter—not even Jefferson's new favorite, Smith of the *National Intelligencer*—was allowed to see: the workings of the House chamber during the interminable balloting of each State to elect the new President.

Beckley wondered why Aaron Burr was nowhere near the place of action. Was he so confident of surreptitious victory? Did he want to be able to deny any participation in the coup if it failed? Or was he waiting to see what Fate would bring, unwilling to turn away from the prize if it should come his way? Then Beckley figured it out: Burr already had most Federalists without making a public move. He could only hope to get a majority by winning the votes of a few republican States, and those republican electors would resent any overt move he made to gain the Presidency from Jefferson. By avoiding the appearance of trying to snatch the prize, Burr might yet win the necessary republicans over.

Beckley became Gallatin's runner, taking messages to Jefferson at Conrad's. "If no President is chosen by March 4 when Adams leaves office," he reported to Jefferson, "they want to pass a law placing the government in the hands of a President pro tem. Neither you nor Burr nor Adams, but one of their own."

"In that event," said Jefferson coldly, "the Middle States would arm to oppose the usurpation." Beckley knew that Governor Monroe was ready-ing his militia to march on the new capital. He showed Jefferson a Federal-ist newspaper that demanded: "Are the republicans then ripe for civil war, and ready to imbrue their hands in kindred blood?" The Vice President was pleased to see that; the signal of readiness to fight was getting through.

"A new Constitutional Convention will be called to organize the govern-ment," said Jefferson, "and amend the Constitution. Tell that to Gallatin to pass along."

Beckley raced back across the icy mud to relay his leader's belligerent message: if the Federalists attempted usurpation, they would trigger civil war. At the very least, a new convention would drive them out of govern-ment, perhaps forever. That raised the stakes to what the republicans hoped would be an unacceptable level.

Gallatin, with Beckley trailing behind, went over to Sam Smith of Maryland. He delivered the Vice President's harsh message and watched from the door to the cloakroom as it was passed around the floor. As Beck-ley hoped, a half-hour later Gallatin sent a more conciliatory message for him to give to Smith, the noted deal-maker: "Regarding the assurances you seek, Mr. Jefferson is prepared to see you now." Beckley accompanied the Marylander over to Conrad's, where both Smith and Jefferson lodged.

Beckley, sitting just behind Gallatin, marveled at the way Sam Smith of Maryland had worked it out: not a single Federalist in his State would vote for Jefferson in the final ballot—or for anyone else. The shift began as Bay-ard cast Delaware's vote with a blank ballot, followed by Harper for South Carolina. Members from Vermont and Maryland who had been voting for Burr cast blank ballots as well, effectively switching Maryland's vote to Jef-ferson. Gallatin leaned back and whispered, "Here ends the most wicked and absurd attempt ever tried by the Federalists."

As the roll call of the thirteen States reached toward the bottom of the alphabet, Beckley could see what was coming. Eight States were now in Jef-ferson's column, with nine needed to elect.

The clerk said "The State of Vermont." A single Congressman from Vermont walked slowly down the aisle to the clerk to cast his State's vote. He handed over his ballot and turned to the members.

"The State of Vermont casts the vote of its proud and free people," he called out, "for Thomas Jefferson, thereby electing him President of the United States!"

Beckley leaped to his feet and joined in the great cheer. He only wished Callender in jail could be there to see it and to flourish symbolic iron tongs in triumph. The deciding ballot had been cast by the Irishman who came to America as an eleven-year-old indentured servant. He was another loyal Jeffersonian who suffered imprisonment for sedition, one of the two who turned public sentiment against the forces entrenched in power—the reviled and despised Spittin' Matt Lyon.

PART III

The Jefferson Scandals

A PHILOSOPHIC COCK

Tis not a set of features or Complexion
Or tincture of a Skin that I admire

Chapter 27

"*I* am a loyal subje&t *of* His Maje&ty the King *of* Great Britain," Cobbett told the Pennsylvania State Court, Judge Shippen presiding. The Englishman could feel the hostility in the courtroom rising at those words. "In addition, I am now an alien resident of the State of New York. Therefore, I petition the Court to remove this libel action for trial in the Circuit Court of the United States."

Cobbett was certain that the Act Establishing the Judicial Courts could not be clearer: aliens were to be tried in Federal court for disputes exceeding $500. Once in a Federal court, with a Federalist judge choosing a Federalist jury, he was equally sure he would make short work of the libel suit brought in this republican State by Jefferson's friend Dr. Benjamin Rush.

"Petition denied," ruled the judge.

"But it says right here," Cobbett persisted, "in the U.S. Constitution, Article III, Section 2, that 'the judicial power of the United States shall extend to all controversies between a State, or citizens thereof'"—that's Dr. Rush—"and foreign States, citizens, or subjects'—that's me."

"Denied," repeated the judge, giving no reason.

Cobbett turned to his lawyers, Edward Tighlman and Robert Goodloe Harper. "How can he do that? What chance does a Briton have in a court in a State in which the Governor bears me a mortal grudge? Protest."

"Don't anger him," said Harper. "He wants Governor McKean to appoint him Chief Justice of Pennsylvania, and he knows McKean wants him to try this case here."

Cobbett snorted in disgust. McKean was the Jeffersonian judge who tried to silence him years before on a libel charge and was frustrated by an honest jury. After that reprobate was elected Governor of Pennsylvania, thanks to John Beckley's nefarious organizing skill, Cobbett had declared in *Porcupine's Gazette* that he would never live under that foul drunk's gubernatorial sovereignty. But even after he closed the newspaper and moved his book inventory to New York, Cobbett was being pursued by the bleeding and purging Dr. Rush in the State courts McKean controlled.

"The charges laid against the defendant," the judge noted, "are that he repeatedly calls the plaintiff a 'quack'; that he charges him with intemperate bleeding, injudiciously administering mercury in large doses in the yellow fever; that he puffs himself off by styling himself the Samson of medicine; and that he has been murdering thousands of his patients."

Harper rose to address the Court. "Defendant acknowledges he caused such accusations to be printed in his *Gazette,* but without malice."

Cobbett reached up and pulled him to his seat. "Why are you admitting anything? Let Rush prove who wrote it and who published it. Take him months. As for the word 'quack' . . . " The defendant rose. "Your Honor, the good-natured advocate of the bleeding doctor"—here he pointed to Moses Levi, the bearded lawyer for Rush—"has kindly saved me the trouble of defining the word 'quack.' He has accepted the definition of Joseph Addison of London's *Spectator,* who stated a quack to be 'a boastful pretender to physick; one who proclaims his own medical abilities and nostrums in public places.' "

Cobbett brandished a handbill. "Here is an advertisement written by this vainglorious quack. Allow me to read a portion of it. 'The almost universal success with which it has pleased God to bless the remedies of strong mercurial purges and bleeding for the yellow fever,' Rush claims, enables him to assure us 'that there is no more danger to be apprehended from it than from the meazels.' This was while the bodies of a hundred nineteen people a day who were treated by this quack and his followers were being hauled away in carts to cemeteries."

"I wouldn't get into arguing the case yet," whispered Harper.

"To establish quackery," said Cobbett, ignoring his counsel, "the man must not only boast of his nostrums, but must do so in publick places. This piece of puffery was published in all the newspapers, given away in the apothecaries' shops, handed about the streets, and stuck upon the walls, houses and public pumps! Is this not quackery? Does not this demonstrate the truth of the accusation that Rush is a quack—one whose murderous nostrum was the cause of the bleeding to death of your revered President Washington?"

"Now you've done it," Harper complained. "The judge is furious."

Cobbett was pleased when his other defense attorney, Tighlman, popped up and asked for copies of all the supposed published libels. These might take weeks to gather. He also called on the Court for a continuance, which was required to be granted. The judge, looking toward Rush's counsel, who was also Governor McKean's nephew, announced he would set the trial date in due course.

"That should cause that damned quack to possess his soul in patience," Cobbett said approvingly.

"Stop repeating that word, William," Harper cautioned. "Rush is a distinguished physician, and 'quack,' no matter how you try to justify the word, is a libel."

"But we never admit that," countered Cobbett's other lawyer, who struck the defendant as being more interested in representing a client's interests. Cobbett had added his Federalist ally Harper to his defense to assure favorable treatment when the case was referred to Federal court, but now that did not seem to be likely. "Mr. Cobbett, just for safety's sake, have you removed your assets from Pennsylvania?"

"Everything but my printing press, which is too heavy to move, some large pieces of furniture and the unbound pages of my twelve-volume sets of *Porcupine's Works*. Otherwise, my wife and children and I are New Yorkers. Is it all right if I return there tonight?"

"The trial won't be for months," Harper assured him. "We'll send for you."

DR. BENJAMIN RUSH

February 28, 1801

The trial suddenly took place three days later. Cobbett, unaware of the prosecution's plan, had returned to New York and was not on the scene to lend his vigorous presence to the defense. Richard Harison, a law associate of Alexander Hamilton who happened to be in Philadelphia on other business, heard of the snap hearing and observed the proceedings from the back of the room.

This observer, a former United States Attorney in New York, thought that the corpulent Harper, either from inexperience in the courtroom or eager to curry favor with McKean's dominant republicans, was giving away his client's case. Harper not only admitted to the publication from Cobbett's press but also admitted that Cobbett was the author; worse, he freely acknowledged that the printed accusations were untrue. On top of all that, Harper expressed his high regard for Dr. Rush's international reputation. He argued only that the libels were not malicious. Cobbett's other lawyer, Tilghman, vainly sought a delay to bring Cobbett back into court. He seemed at his wit's end at the tactics of his concessionary co-counsel, who soon became a favorite of the judge. At one point, observers could hear the plaintiff Rush saying to his own lawyer, "No, I'm not paying a fee to Harper."

The plaintiff's argument was all but taken over by the judge. He addressed the jury with a summation of the evidence. "Defendant's counsel has acknowledged that the newspaper allegations against Dr. Rush were false, but not malicious. But these words themselves import malice, and the proof lies on the defendant to show the innocence of his intentions."

Tilghman stood up and the judge generously waved him permission to speak. "Another ground of defense, your Honor, is constitutional. The subject of this dispute is of public concern because it relates to the health and lives of our fellow citizens. By the words of the United States Constitution, and also of the Pennsylvania Constitution, every man has the right to discuss such subjects in print."

"The liberty of the press," responded the judge piously, "ought never to be unduly restrained." He leaned across the bench. "But when it is perverted to the purposes of private slander, it then becomes a most destructive engine in the hands of unprincipled men. Our State constitution expressly declares that every person availing himself of the liberty of the press should be responsible for the abuse of that liberty." He turned to the jury. "Offenses of this kind have much abounded in our city. It seems high time to restrain them. To suppress so great an evil, it will not only be proper to give compensatory, but exemplary damages. That will stop the growing progress of this daring crime."

The associate of Hamilton noticed that the judge looked for approbation to John Beckley, a well-known republican political operative working for Governor McKean, who was in the courtroom conferring with Harper. Smiling, the republican judge added, "I hope no party considerations will ever have place in the administration of justice. I entreat the gentlemen of the jury to banish any thought of party from their breasts."

March 3, 1801

NEW YORK CITY

"Five thousand dollars!"

Cobbett was thunderstruck not so much at the verdict of guilty—that was foreordained—but at the size of the judgment against him. Slowly, he said to Alexander Hamilton, "That is a sum surpassing the aggregate amount of all the damages assessed for all the torts of this kind, ever sued for in the United States, from the first settlement of the Colonies to the present day."

"And three thousand dollars in court costs and legal fees on top of that," reported Harison, who had hurried back with a full account of the proceedings.

"A ruinous and therefore a rascally judgment," Hamilton agreed. He

William Safire

was familiar with libel law, having successfully sued the republican *New York Argus* the year before. That sheet had reprinted an erroneous charge that he sought to silence the Philadelphia *Aurora* by arranging for its purchase by Federalists. He had put a journeyman printer in jail for four months as a warning to republicans that Alexander Hamilton, Esq., could not be trifled with in New York courts. In the back of his mind, however, was the idea of starting a newspaper in New York City that could attack Jefferson, who would take the oath of office on the morrow. He might switch positions soon, as an ethical lawyer could, to champion liberty of the press.

In Hamilton's judgment, Cobbett was clearly guilty of libeling Rush; "quack" was arguable, but "murderer" stepped over the line. The British subject, however, had a right as an alien to be tried in Federal court. And certainly the fine was both unprecedented and outrageously vindictive.

It did not surprise Hamilton that republicans like McKean, once in power, would behave no differently than Federalists did when under newspaper attack. But he gave them credit for being shrewd enough to avoid a Federal sedition law, which pitted government against the individual. Jefferson, he assumed, would rely on State laws of libel to put the anti-Administration press under pressure from maligned republicans. That would be a more popular way of suppressing criticism of government officials.

"I should never have announced the closing of *Porcupine's Gazette* in Philadelphia," Cobbett grumbled. "Now that they are relieved from all fears of my future writings, the dastardly wretches at last ventured on the execution of their revenge. So much for your laws about liberty of the press."

"I never thought much of fine declarations in a Constitution that 'the liberty of the press shall be inviolably preserved,' " Hamilton said frankly, recalling his argument with Madison about including it in an amendment. "It's impracticable. The security of the press must altogether depend on public opinion, and on the general spirit of the people and the government."

"In that regard, your lawyer Harper did you no good service," Harison told Cobbett. "He and John Beckley, McKean's man, were constantly conferring."

Hamilton remembered Beckley well. He suspected that he was the Jefferson apologist, years before, who passed the Reynolds dossier to James

Callender, probably on James Monroe's orders and with Jefferson's connivance. The commonality of their enemies made him sympathetic to Cobbett and eager to save him from financial ruination.

"Harper, that walking ball of tallow streaked with lampblack," the editor of the now-defunct *Porcupine's Gazette* was raging, "has gained the popularity of the new government by traducing his client. He made certain I would not be present to defend myself."

"That's what happened, " Harison confirmed. "All three referred to you as a scandalmonger."

"They accuse me of being given to scandal," Cobbett snorted. "If I had published one-hundredth part of the anecdotes Harper supplied me with, I should have set the whole city of Philadelphia together by the ears."

Hamilton turned to his gray-haired partner. "Was any of Mr. Cobbett's property in Pennsylvania seized after the judgment?"

"Yes, there was an immediate auction, sir. Household furniture, a device for cooking outdoors—"

"An excellent roasting jack," Cobbett noted glumly, "which I should have brought with me."

"And a complete printing press. The total raised and claimed by Rush was six hundred dollars."

"What about the works on the press, the thousand copies of twelve volumes of my collected works? That's the summation of a lifetime's writing."

Hamilton, who had been informed beforehand by his law partner, knew that news would be painful.

"I'm afraid, sir, it was all sold off as waste paper and destroyed."

The editor slumped in his chair, benumbed at the atrocity. Hamilton, who had high regard for the sanctity of an author's pamphlets and books, knew better than to try to comfort the man. After an interval to let Cobbett collect his thoughts, he changed the subject.

"I take it you do not have eight thousand dollars in the bank," he said. "What about the contents of your bookstore here?"

"Perhaps the inventory is worth half of that." The editor could not get over Rush's vindictive act. "Waste paper!"

"You have friends who will want to come to your aid, Cobbett," Hamilton said. "Not overtly. Through a discreet intermediary, I could arrange a flow of funds that would pay your debt."

He had in mind the British Minister, Robert Liston. Certainly the government of Great Britain, whose interests had been stoutly defended for years by this fearless loyalist, should be ready to arrange for his succor in his hour of financial peril. The rescue would have to be done secretly, lest Cobbett appear to have been a paid agent, as the republicans had long claimed and which the newsmonger had steadfastly resisted. If the money passed through other hands, Porcupine himself need not know its source. Hamilton would take no fee for this, but presumed that Cobbett's advice would be helpful in bringing to birth the newspaper of Hamilton's own. He did not offer him the editorship of the *New York Evening Post* because Cobbett wanted to return to England to start anew. Like Hamilton, this embodiment of John Bull had lost his American crusade; Jefferson and the French had won.

The editor snapped out of his benumbed state. "To say I do not feel this stroke, and very sensibly too, would be a great affectation. But to sink under it would be an act of cowardice."

"Nobody would accuse you of that," Hamilton assured him.

"Callender would, but that spiteful viper counts for nothing now that the Outs are the Ins. I warned him about Rush and his kind, but he let those butchers bleed his poor wife to death. Today in his jail the wretch may think he is a hero to the Jeffersonians. But he'll soon discover that the Italian, Machiavelli, was right—that only a fool counts on the favor of princes."

Hamilton did not agree. It pained him to think how James Callender, the only pamphleteer to claim his revelations about Maria Reynolds were a mask for financial dishonesty, would now be freed and lionized by grateful republicans as a martyred loyalist. As with the Spittin' Lyon, his stupid jailing and inspired railing had helped turn public sentiment against Federalists everywhere. Were Callender not a scrivener and an immigrant, he would rate high appointment by the republicans; even so, he would surely be rewarded for hatchet work savagely done and nearly a year's incarceration suffered.

Cobbett rose to his full height, towering over Hamilton and his partner, and related a story. "I knew an Englishman in the Royal Province of New Brunswick, when I served in His Majesty's forces up there. He had a very valuable house, which was, I believe, nearly his all, and one day it burnt to the ground. He was out of town when the fire broke out, and happened to come home just as it exhausted itself. He came very leisurely up to the spot, stood about for five minutes looking steadily at the rubbish, and then, stripping off his coat, said, 'Here goes to earn another!' and immediately went to work, raking the spikes and bits of iron out of the ashes."

Cobbett, shoulders squared, walked to the door of Hamilton's office. "This noble-spirited man I had the honor to call my friend, and I shall follow his example."

Chapter 28

March 5, 1801

ALBEMARLE COUNTY, VIRGINIA

Callender was free. His releafe juft two days before came on schedule, like the birth of a human child, nine months after his jailing began. He was freed in time to savor the happy event for which he had labored so long and suffered so much: the inauguration of Thomas Jefferson as President. He felt, as Tom Paine had written, "We have it in our power to begin the world all over again."

The talk about an attempted usurpation by Burr and the defeated Federalists had not overly worried him. Governor Monroe, Callender was certain, would have mustered his militia and marched on the new capital, just across the Potomac, at the first sign of the denial of the people's will. Monroe was not a political leader to be trifled with: he had hanged twenty-five of the slaves involved in the Gabriel insurrection, disregarding Jefferson's suggestion to deport the rebels. Callender, though an abolitionist when in Scotland, far from the problem, had come into all-too-close contact with one of those insurrectionists in jail. That exposure to the reality of race war brought his views closer to those of other white Virginians toward the threat of African speculators in fire and blood.

What did worry him was the $200 fine he had been forced to pay before being released. The friends of Jefferson who had pledged to raise that money to pay his fine had reneged. He had cut back on food and rum, denied himself a decent suit of clothes and even purchased the cheapest kind of writing paper to put that sum together to send to Leiper for his children's board. It was as if the jail had charged him rent; the need to buy his freedom had wiped out those savings.

Duane in Philadelphia, no longer a fugitive from the Sedition Act, had promised to take a hundred copies of *The Prospect Before Us*, but was failing to advertise them in the *Aurora* and could not afford to pay Callender for their cost. Nor had he been paid a farthing for all the newspaper articles published under his name in the *Richmond Examiner*, the *Aurora* in Philadelphia, and in Matt Lyon's papers in Vermont. He was strapped and urgently needed to get that $200 back. The republicans had promised it to him. His nine months of lost freedom could never be repaid, but a return of his money was the least they could do.

That reminded him of the woman who surprised him with her visit to his jail the month before. Maria Reynolds, with her striking looks and proud bearing, wearing a dress and complex hat of the best British make, had appeared at the prison and had been ushered to his writing apartment. She said she had returned from England the year before, placed her daughter in a seminary and had become housekeeper to a fine doctor in Richmond. Callender had been uplifted when this elegant lady—he was more certain than ever she was a lady, and not the whore Hamilton had made her out to be—told him she had been reading his articles and wanted to pay her respects to an unjustly imprisoned patriot. He remembered every word she said in that visit, especially her invitation to call on her when he was released.

Now that he was free and could hold his head high in society, Callender wanted to be able to afford a decent suit of clothes and the price of a good meal for two at the best tavern in Richmond. He had never treated his late wife to that and regretted the years of denial he had inflicted on her. It had taken all his courage to invite Maria to join him at the dinner celebrating the republican triumph.

At the Price Tavern in Albemarle County, seat of the Monroe and Walker and Jefferson plantations, that dinner was held to hail both the new President's ascension and his loyal editor's release. Callender, embarrassed by the shabbiness of his clothes, escorted his well-dressed companion to their table in the tavern's large hall. He was proud to see how the statuesque woman who went by the name of Maria Clement, her brunette tresses done up in what he assumed was the latest European fashion, turned more than a few heads of the Virginia gentry.

At the tables was that day's edition of the *Richmond Examiner* with the new President's inaugural address prominent on the front page. "Go ahead and read it," the understanding Maria said, and struck up a conversation with the man to her left. Callender perused it avidly.

He was disappointed in the tone of Jefferson's address. Instead of boldly charting a new course toward republican principles, it struck him as unduly conciliatory toward the routed Federalists. "Every difference of opinion is not a difference of principle," Jefferson told a nation so recently riven by genuine disagreement about the form and extent of government. "We have called by different names brethren of the same principle. We are all Republicans; we are all Federalists."

Water-gruel pap! Callender told himself to calm down; Jefferson intended to avert disunion, not to abandon principle. The new President did have something to say in favor of liberty of the press and the diffusion of information, which the writer took to be an acknowledgment of his efforts, and in favor of freedom of religion, which he took to be a subtle slap at the militant Congregationalists and all those who slandered him as an atheist. But the overall tone of the address was to cool passions, not to set a new course; Callender hoped that did not augur ill for the republican cause. What would Hamilton have said if it were his inaugural? Surely not "we are all Republicans."

In Jefferson's home county, however, the mood was joyously partizan. Edward Moore, a plantation owner who had been a captain in General Washington's army, rose to toast the guest of honor.

"To James Thomson Callender," he said, glass of good red wine in hand, "who came to us from Scotland with all the fire and genius of lovers of freedom there—and who looks down on his persecutors with their merited contempt!"

The crowd of Virginians, rich and not so rich, came to their feet and applauded and cheered their imported champion. That had never happened to him; the only time he had moved a crowd was in Leesburg two years before, where a mob of ruffians beat him up.

"You have to respond," Maria whispered to him.

"I haven't written anything."

"Say what you would write. But speak up, so all can hear."

Callender forced his voice to speak loudly enough to be heard throughout the tavern. "To me, writing and printing form not only the business, but

the pleasure of my life," he said. That was not an especially stirring beginning, but the crowd, eager to show its appreciation for his sacrifice, applauded anyway. Warmed by the reception and the feeling of a glass of wine
in his hand, Callender pressed on. "I would not, for all the money in the
world, be divested of the elation I feel tonight—for having been able to go
straight through this great national crisis, without looking back on one moment of trimming or flinching."

That drew cheers. Not many of these hardy followers of Jefferson,
Madison and Monroe, he knew, counted themselves among the pleaders of
compromise with the defeated Federalists. Encouraged, he plunged
deeper: "You and I know there are some republicans who have shown the
most wretched timidity and sycophancy over this past decade. They are the
trimmers, trucklers, apostates"—derisive synonyms for moderation came
easily to him—"turncoats, halfway hobblers, and water-gruel republicans.
Let them make their peace now with their consciences, if they have any."

Callender's voice was giving out, but he was not to be stopped from giving the Federalists the back of his hand, and from urging a clean sweep of
the Federal offices. "Those of us who have been the victims of the Federalists' partizan zeal," he said, just loudly enough to be heard, "will never forget the long nights in cold cells. Nothing can be an act of more exquisite
justice than that, as the poet Thomson, my uncle, phrased it, 'these tyrants
should feel the pangs they gave'!"

"What will you do now, James?" she asked. Bundled in overcoats against
the late-winter cold, they were riding with two other couples in the late
coach back to Richmond.

"I will give the men of the new administration a week to find their new
offices," he said, still excited by the reception to his speech. He wished that
Cobbett could have been there to hear it; that would have blunted a few of
the Porcupine's quills. The Scot had been pleased to hear at the dinner that
the British lackey had been driven out of Philadelphia and had to seek the
protective arms of Hamilton in New York, but he thought better of expressing that thought aloud in the crowded coach. "Then I shall go up to
the District of Columbia, which hardly existed when I was sentenced, to
pay a call on the new President."

"Will you ask for a pardon? The Sedition Act lapsed when Adams left office, and it's hardly fair that you should have a conviction against your good name."

"Matt Lyon and I have been promised that," he said, acutely aware of his leg pressing against hers in the tight carriage seat, "but I have two more important matters in mind." Two hundred dollars and the postmastership in Richmond were not too much to expect for the years spent on the republican ramparts. The talent that ignited what Jefferson called "the flame of public opinion," and the nine long months spent in solitary confinement helping to fan that flame into the blaze of victory, deserved the fine back and much more.

The stage driver stopped his coach in front of the portico of the Richmond home of Dr. Mathew. Callender hopped out and offered his hand to Maria, who stepped down carefully, wincing a little. They walked up the steps to the door and he awkwardly shook her hand, not having thought beforehand what to say at parting.

She took off her hat and shook her hair free. Leaning forward, she kissed him lightly on the cheek and said she was his lonely friend and hoped he would call on her at teatime some afternoon soon. He swallowed and nodded vigorously, not wanting to ask what time teatime was.

Chapter 29

April 6, 1801

WASHINGTON, D.C.

*M*uch as he found the profpect diſtaſteful, James Madison could not avoid seeing Callender. The man Jefferson had just appointed Secretary of State had not originally been an advocate of faction—indeed, had thought excessive partizanship would be a threat to the comity necessary to the workings of good government. Although the emergence of what Jefferson liked to call Whig and Tory factions demonstrated the inevitability of political conflict, Madison clung to the hope that the clash of ideology in America would be moderated. To his mind, this Scottish immigrant Callender—as passionate for liberty as his English counterpart Cobbett lusted for order—represented much that was mean and vindictive in American democracy.

"I am here because Tom Jefferson wouldn't see me," Callender began by saying. Madison bridled at the editor's calling the President of the United States by his first name. "He sent out his secretary, a Captain Lewis, to say he was busy with affairs of State."

"I'm sure he is." Madison knew Meriwether Lewis to be the former officer that Jefferson had in mind for a mapmaking study, perhaps leading to Western exploration. The man, a Virginia neighbor, was entirely trustworthy. As secretary to the President, he could be counted on to keep the likes of Callender at a distance from the Chief Magistrate.

"I marvel at Jefferson's ostentatious coolness and indifference," said Callender.

"Not so indifferent as to fail to sign your pardon, Mr. Callender." Madison noticed how the man's hands and voice were trembling. Too much rum, he supposed; the editor, like so many of the Scottish and "wild Irish" radicals, had often been accused by Cobbett of being a hard drinker. "Pardoning you and Matthew Lyon were two of President Jefferson's first acts in office, and I was pleased to countersign them."

He went to a table stacked high with the "midnight appointments" that Adams had made of scores of Federal judges just before departing. The Senate had confirmed them just before adjournment, thereby hoping to pack the judicial branch with stalwart Federalists. But the Secretary of State would not sign their commissions nor would the new President administer the oath of office. The Federalist John Marshall had been sworn in as Chief Justice of the Supreme Court in the nick of time as Adams's final insult to Jefferson.

Madison withdrew Callender's pardon from the drawer under the table and presented the doubly signed document to the fully pardoned man. "You can truthfully say you have no stain on your record as a citizen of the United States. No man can call you a felon." What stains there were on his record for sedition in his native Scotland, the Secretary of State did not add aloud, remained unpardoned.

Callender glanced at the parchment and stuffed it in his jacket pocket. "It is now seven weeks since I had a written message from Jefferson," he said, "with his solemn assurance that he 'would not lose one moment' in re-mitting my fine. His cousin George read it to me and then threw the note in the fire, lest I have proof of the promise. The President took unusual pains to make his promise both explicit and guarded."

Good for George Jefferson, the President's reliable kinsman, thought Madison; discretion was important in these sensitive dealings.

"I happen to know," added Callender, "that one week ago, Governor Monroe reminded Jefferson of his promise in Charlottesville. And still nothing."

"The order was given to Marshal Randolph to remit your fine," Madison reported. He knew that to be true; when the order would be carried out was another matter. Randolph was an Adams appointee and would proba-bly do all he could to delay the repayment for months, perhaps years. If Callender had to wait, he would just have to learn to be patient.

"On the strength of Jefferson's promise to return my money," said Cal-lender, "I wrote up to Mr. Leiper that I would send him two hundred dol-lars for the support of my boys. I do not want them to be sent off to a poorhouse or forced to work in the fields. I have now found it necessary to write him thus: 'Mr. Jefferson has not returned one shilling of my fine. I now begin to know what ingratitude is.' And I do."

"Ingratitude or gratitude has nothing to do with this. The pardon in-cluded a remission of your fine. These things take time."

"My story should reach the heart of a millstone," said Callender bleakly, "but I might as well be speaking to Lot's wife." He drew a deep breath. "I am obliged to speak plain, for necessity has no law. Does the President reflect upon the premunire into which he may bring himself by the breach of an unqualified promise that he volunteered? Does he reflect how his numerous and implacable enemies would exult in knowing this piece of small history?"

Madison understood the writer's reference to a premunire, or writ, in English law against one who procured charges against the crown. He thought Callender's legal threat was absurd. Would this ardent republican dare to go to court and reveal Jefferson's promise to repay his fine, and claim that promise was one of the inducements that caused him to attack President Adams? And yet, if he had it in writing from Jefferson, that might be awkward.

"Gentlemen do not make threats," was all Madison said.

"I never hinted a word of this to any human being but yourself," Callender said sharply. "Notwithstanding the occasional rattle of my tongue, I can keep a secret as well as anybody. Jefferson has repeatedly told me that my services were considerable; that I made up the best newspaper in America." He shook his head in wonderment. "I had no more idea of such mean usage of me by him now that he is in power than that the mountains were to dance a minuet."

Madison observed silently that the man spoke as colorfully as he wrote.

"But you, Excellency—you say I am not a gentleman."

"I never said—"

"I am not, to be sure, very expert in making a bow," said Callender in sarcasm, "or at supporting the sycophancy of conversation. I speak and write what I think; God made plain speech a part of my constitution." He left his chair and placed his knuckles on Madison's table, staring him close in the face. "But Mr. Jefferson and you should recollect that it is not by beaux, and dancing masters, or by editors who would look extremely well in a muslin gown and petticoat, that the battles of freedom are to be fought and won."

"You are unduly upset, my good man." He motioned for his visitor, whose face had turned ashen, to resume his seat. Madison, dressed as was his custom in silk stockings and black breeches and with powdered hair, did his best in surveying the disheveled Callender to conceal his repugnance. "But you must consider the propriety of repaying the debt to you here in Washington. That is a matter to be handled locally."

"Payments to me were never made on the basis of geography. Jefferson paid me in Philadelphia and Jefferson sent money to me in Richmond. Now you say no payment can be made in this holy capital? Can it be, sir, that you now disdain support of the member of the press who has most loyally supported you?"

"My views about the liberty of the press are unchanging." Madison restated them for this troublesome upstart: "I have said often that it is to the press alone—chequered as it is with abuses—the world is indebted for all the triumphs which have been gained by reason and humanity over error and oppression."

"I had not heard you say it with that qualifying clause before," said Callender with discomfiting accuracy. "How little you complained of 'abuses' when they were directed at Hamilton and Adams."

Madison had to concede that point and it irritated him. Porcupine, Duane, Callender and the lot of them kept referring to him in print as "Little Madison." He stood five feet six inches, exactly the same as John Adams, and few called Adams "Little."

Callender's defiance suddenly dissolved. "I have gone to such desperate lengths to serve the party." Madison, glad that his coolness had produced a good effect, nodded agreement; he acknowledged that the editor's trial and jail service had indeed rallied support for republicans. "But I believe your friend designs to discountenance me," Callender pleaded. "I fear that he and you intend to sacrifice me as a kind of scapegoat to political decorum and as a compromise to Federalist feelings."

Madison could not respond to that with more than a shake of the head because he knew it to be true. It was not in his nature to dissemble.

"It's hard to believe," the distraught writer went on. "Surely a wiser man than Jefferson does not exist. His probity is exemplary. His political ideas are, to the minutest ramification, precisely mine."

"Perhaps not precisely," said Madison carefully, "at least in terms of party spirit. You are, you must agree, far more of a passionate partizan."

"I read his Inaugural Address," said Callender, anger surging back. "One line was unforgettable. 'We are all Federalists; we are all Republicans.' Is that his new political philosophy? You and he now see no difference between Tories and Whigs, or between the farmers in Richmond and the bankers in Boston? How do we stand in war between France and Great Britain—are we foursquare for both?"

"The newspapers, unfortunately, capitalized words that led to a misimpression," Madison informed him. "I can assure you that in President Jefferson's own handwriting, the words 'federalist' and 'republican' were not capitalized. He was referring to the principles of federalism, about which Hamilton and Jay and I wrote many papers in support, and to republicanism, the nature of our government."

"Ah, now there are three of us who understand that nicely. But the message to the rest of the country is that there is no difference between those who stood for tyranny and sedition with Adams and those who fought for the rights of man with Jefferson."

Madison gave him what he hoped would be taken as a look of cold disdain.

"I can remember Jefferson saying that the cherishment of the people was our principle, and the fear and distrust of the people was the principle of the other party."

Madison squirmed in his chair and could not dispute the point. Who knew what Jefferson might have said to this man? That may have been said in the heat of a political contest; but in governing, civility and accommodation were more appropriate.

"It forms one of the topicks of Mr. Jefferson's self-approbation," Callender said, "that in his whole life he never wrote a single article for a newspaper."

"That's true. President Jefferson is proud of that." Madison sensed the irony in his admission. In the pseudonymous newspaper harangues early in the Washington Administration, it was Madison who had to counter the potent pen of Hamilton; Jefferson could never bring himself to take on the task, even under a pen name. Madison understood where Callender's argument was headed.

"Jefferson's duty, then, is to be thankful to the persons who did write for the public in his behalf. For four years, with a sinecure salary as Vice President of five thousand dollars a year, he chose to stand neuter. Like Nero, he fiddled while Rome burned. Today, ensconced at the center of all power, he should at least have the decency to thank those more adventurous citizens who rushed to defend the ramparts of liberty."

Madison pointedly looked at the clock on the wall. Callender seemed to take this as an additional affront.

"There's a contrast between you and me," said the editor, and Madison could not help but nod agreement. "Twelve years ago you wrote a book. The publication of your volume would have been of infinite service towards the resistance of Federal usurpation and rapine."

Madison bridled; Callender was broaching a subject he found most personally sensitive. The extensive notes that Madison had scrupulously taken on the debates in the Constitutional Convention a decade before remained under lock and key. The time was not ripe for their publication.

"Maybe you were dissatisfied with the part you and your friends played in the course of your narrative," Callender, who apparently knew too much, went on. "Or maybe you were afraid of provoking the revenge of the Federalist party. But as the result of your fear, your notes on the convention remain in your safe. You sacrificed the interest of your country to the wise but sordid consideration of personal tranquillity."

Too much. "Your presumption is outrageous." It was true enough that he did not want to become the object of criticism from his colleagues by making public who said what at that secret conclave. But Madison was simply holding those historical notes for publication at a more propitious time—perhaps a decade or two hence, when passions had cooled. He told himself with indignation that he felt no guilt whatever at the continued suppression of the debates at the formation of the Constitution. "What are you trying to say?"

"You must have despised the temerity of those writers like me who exposed themselves to the talons of the Sedition Act."

"Do you forget the Virginia Resolution?" Madison snapped back. He did not want to admit to this man that he and Jefferson had written his State's opposition to the Sedition Act, but his authorship of the courageous document was now a source of pride.

"You wrote that in the name of the General Assembly of Virginia," Callender countered. "You knew you did not run the smallest chance of personal danger. You gratified your sensibilities without the peril of persecution or the chance of six months of imprisonment."

Madison felt unfairly assailed. His place had always been as a voice of reason behind the scenes, and not, as the hot-eyed Callender wished, with the calumniators on the ramparts.

The writer lashed out again. "You would not take the chances that you wanted us to take. You suppressed the foul deeds and shameful compromises of the Convention that drew up your Constitution in secret. You shrink to this very day from your sacred duty both as a historian and a citizen. How can a man write what he durst not publish?"

Madison would not deign to answer the insulting question, nor would he allow his fury to show. Never before had he felt the slightest twinge of guilt at protecting the confidences of his colleagues making history at the Convention. He looked again at the clock.

Callender apparently realized he had overstepped and had harmed his own cause. He rose to take his leave. "I would also like to add that we in Richmond have a most wretched postmaster. The whole town is horribly tired of him."

That was it; the purpose of the visit was not just to get back his fine, but to seek office. When Madison did not show any interest in pursuing that subject of patronage, a dispirited Callender said, "If my visit breathes an unbecoming asperity, sir, I entreat you to recollect what lengths I have gone to serve the Jefferson cause, and in what way it now appears to be serving me."

The unwelcome visitor moved toward the door. "I am not going to set myself up in argument against you. There is something superior to argument, and that is the feelings and voice of mankind. What will be said of Mr. Jefferson's promises when I return to Richmond without my money? The world will examine not your argument but the fact of your rejection." His hand on the doorknob, Callender muttered words that the Secretary of State could barely hear: "I am not the man to be oppressed or plundered with impunity."

"What was that?"

"Putting principles and feelings aside, it is not proper for Jefferson to create a quarrel with me."

Madison and his wife Dolley were staying in the President's house until they could find an agreeable country residence in the new District. He crossed the road from his State Department office to his temporary home, picking his way through the new furniture and draperies that Abigail Adams had ordered installed in the President's light gray Virginia fieldstone palace. There he laid the matter of Callender's unremitted fine before Jefferson.

He recounted his painful conversation with Callender in detail, leaving out only the interchange about his suppression of the notes of the Constitutional Convention. "It may take months for him to get the money," the Secretary of State concluded, "to which he is entitled by law. He seems to be in genuine distress."

When President Jefferson heard about Callender's need for payment of board for his four boys, he was sympathetic, as Madison knew he would be. He called Meriwether Lewis into his office and asked for his account book. Madison nodded a greeting to Lewis, who came from Albemarle County, near Monticello and less than a two-hour ride from Madison's Montpelier estate. Jefferson took the account book from him, made a notation about a charitable contribution, dug in his pocket and handed his secretary five $10 notes.

"Inform Mr. Callender, Captain, we are making some inquiries as to his fine, which will take a little time. Lest he suffer in the meantime, I'm sending him this."

Madison didn't know if the President's personal advance was such a good idea, considering the veiled threat Callender had made about exposing his previous financial support. But Jefferson's motive was pure and he had marked it down as a charity, which it surely was. Certain that nobody could fairly call the aid to the distressed supplicant any form of payment of blackmail, the Secretary of State said nothing.

MERIWETHER LEWIS

April 7, 1801

After making inquiries at several rooming houses that were newly built and already run down, Captain Lewis consulted a rude map he had drawn of the District. Near the President's mansion was the building housing the State and War Departments and the square brick Treasury building. To the east, a half-dozen houses were grouped close together for safety's sake, because there were robbers in the new city but no police. Southward through rows of stumps and swamps was Georgetown. Roughly northward, a stone footway ran a mile and a half alongside the rutted Pennsylvania Avenue up to the Capitol. Approaching it, only the avenue named for New Jersey, headed south, suggested a city a-building, but the steep drop down toward the Anacostia River made it difficult for wood and coal carters to bring the loads up to the offices of the Congress. That was not good planning. After walking briskly up the stone footway for less than a half-hour, Captain

Lewis found James Callender in a pub designated for their meeting near the Capitol.

"The President has sent me to you, sir, with his compliments," he began. Callender, behind a bottle of rum, glared at him through bloodshot eyes and murmured a form of greeting or curse.

"President Jefferson has been expediting the remission of your fine, as you know. Secretary Madison spoke with him after your visits—"

"Three visits," said Callender, "one night after the next. I traveled a hundred and fifty miles, a painful and expensive journey, in search of performance of Jefferson's promise." He shuddered, though it was warm in the tavern. "Where was Little Jemmy's pen when we needed it? Too frightened of Adams to put words to paper, and now Little Jemmy is high and mighty. He seems to think he's become a sort of semi-divinity, and that I'm not worthy to be his footstool."

"—and the President was concerned lest you suffer in the meantime," Lewis persisted. "Therefore, he sent me along to find you and give you this fifty dollars, in the spirit of charity."

"Charity?" Callender grabbed the extended bills and jammed them in his pocket. "Charity? This is my due, young man. This is nothing but hush money."

Lewis did not know what to say and so remained silent. But he was familiar with the phrase "hush money": it was what you paid a blackmailer, just as Alexander Hamilton had paid to an extortionist in a famous case a few years before. "It's given to you to alleviate your suffering," he said with emphasis, though avoiding the incendiary word "charity" lest the man be insulted to be considered a beggar.

"I'm in possession of things," the editor said, his words slurred, "which I can make use of if need be. Three separate solicitations of the disdainful Little Jemmy, and Black Sally was fluttering on my tongue's end, but with difficulty I kept her down." He patted his pocket. "And this'll shut me up for a few days, hush me up like they want, but it's not the whole two hundred dollars."

"I doubt whether you can expect more from this source," said Lewis, choosing his words with care. "It's from the kindness of his heart."

"You tell old Kindheart that he knows full well what I expect. A certain office down in Virginia that handles the mail. Held today by a damned Federalist politician. Intercepted our letters and handed them over to Adams and Marshall, he did. We all had to be cir—circumspect. You couldn't tell what we meant half the time from just reading the letters."

The President's secretary listened to the writer rail about Jefferson's sudden remoteness and Madison's lack of generous feelings for a few more moments. As one who knew the black moods of the hypo himself on occasion, Lewis was inclined to be sympathetic; the man was surely in the depths. But when Callender began claiming that the Secretary of State was "hiding behind the hedge of hypocrisy, like the bull frog in the bottom of the ditch," Captain Lewis had enough.

"I'll be leaving you now, Mr. Callender. Is there any message of thanks you would like me to deliver?"

"I lost five years of labor. Gained five thousand personal enemies. Got my name inserted in five hundred libels. And in the end got in trouble with the only friend I had in Pennsylvania, now holding my boys hostage, practically. All for your Tom Jefferson, who sought me out in the first place at McCorkle's print shop. Tell him that. Tell him I'd be a better postmaster than the Federalist spy in Richmond would today. Tell him—"

Lewis about-faced and marched out of the bar. He would tell the President plenty about the danger in doing a good deed for this miscreant.

Chapter 30

April 9, 1801
WASHINGTON, D.C.

*G*overnor James Monroe dropped his duties in Richmond and rushed to the President's house in Washington as soon as he received Jefferson's worried message about Captain Lewis's interview with Callender.

He found the President steaming, more in a rage than he had ever seen. "I am really mortified at the base ingratitude of Callender. It presents human nature in a hideous form. Hideous!" Jefferson could not stay seated; the normally languid man paced the room in unconcealed agitation. "He told Lewis in very high-toned language that he received my fifty dollars not as charity but as his due, in fact as hush money." He almost choked on the last words and flung himself into a chair. "Such a misconstruction of my charities as 'hush money' puts an end to them forever."

Monroe was dubious about Jefferson's characterization of monies paid to Callender as charity: that generous explanation was a flimsy cover for the years of subsidy to the most savage attack dog the republicans had found to set on their powerful enemies. "Callender didn't make any threats to you directly, did he? He didn't say anything, or write you anything, that could be construed as a warning?"

"Well, yes. To Madison, both in person and later in writing. In no uncertain terms. Even so, Madison thought that a longtime supporter in distress deserved some help."

Monroe's heart sunk. Madison knew how to write drafts of a Constitution, and might yet turn out to be a capable Secretary of State, but as a political operative with some grasp of potential scandal, he was an innocent lamb to be led to slaughter by the press. For him to suggest the President of the United States to pay any money to a man who had just made threats to reveal past subsidies was naïve to the point of stupidity. Hamilton's Reynolds pamphlet immediately sprang to mind: the attempt to smother up payments to Callender with another payment would be seen as more troubling than the original act.

"It gives me concern," Jefferson added, "because I perceive that the monetary relief which I afforded him on mere motives of charity may be viewed under the aspect of employing him as a writer."

That was putting it gently. Because he did not want his friend to feel he had handled the situation wrongly, Monroe did not ask the obvious question: then why pay him more money after his broad hint of extortion? To assess the republican vulnerability, the Virginia Governor began to probe the Jefferson-Callender relationship. "How did you first become aware of this man's existence?"

"When *The Political Progress of Britain* first appeared in this country," Jefferson recounted, "it was in a periodical publication called the *Bee*. That's where I saw it. I was speaking of it in terms of strong approbation to a friend in Philadelphia, when he asked me if I knew that the author was then in the city. He was a fugitive from persecution on account of that work and in want of employ for his subsistence. That was the first I knew that Callender was author of the work."

"That must have been about four years ago," Monroe estimated, "soon after you became Vice President. And you expressed a willingness to see him?"

"I considered him a man of science fled from persecution, and assured my friend of my readiness to do whatever could serve him."

Monroe, respecting Jefferson's circumspection, did not ask who the friend was. He assumed it was John Beckley, their political operative who used Callender to great effect as the outlet for the Reynolds papers Monroe had left in Jefferson's safekeeping before sailing for France to be Minister in Paris.

"And when did you and Callender meet?"

"Probably not until years later, in 1798. I think I was applied to by Mr. Leiper to contribute to his relief. The next year, Senator Stevens Mason applied for him, and I contributed again. Callender had by this time paid me two or three personal visits."

Monroe, from his conversations with Callender in the Richmond jail, knew that recollections would differ. According to the Scot, it was Jefferson who paid him the first personal visit, in the summer of 1797, and he had vividly remembered the place: witnesses could probably attest to that meeting above the printing plant of Snowden & McCorkle. Journalists in the hire of Federalists could make much of the way Jefferson, then serving as Vice President to Adams and always striving to appear above the political battle, was secretly supporting the most virulent newspaper diatribes and pamphlets inveighing against the Federalists.

"You exchanged occasional visits over the years," was the way Monroe rephrased the meetings of statesman and scrivener. "Would he have any physical evidence of getting money from you? I know we used your cousin George as a conduit, which was wisely discreet, but might you have written Callender any letters mentioning money?"

"Two, I think. One in answer to the supplication for his relief from Senator Mason, enclosing fifty dollars. The other in answer to questions Callender addressed to me."

Monroe presumed the questions were to elicit scandalous information about Adams's men. If that correspondence ever came to light, it would show Jefferson's complicity in the newsmonger's abusive writings. "About—?"

"Whether Mr. Jay received salary as Chief Justice and envoy to Britain at the same time," Jefferson recalled with evident difficulty, "and something relative to the expenses of an embassy in Constantinople." Both had been hawked in the press as embarrassments to the Federalists in power, and both could now be traced directly to Jefferson as the source.

"No letters from you privately praising his attacks on Adams, or Washington?" Monroe felt Jefferson did not grasp the seriousness of the danger, and so he used specifics, as surely the newsmonger would. "Nothing from you that he could twist into praising him for calling President Washington a traitor or Adams a 'hoary-headed incendiary'?"

Jefferson winced at the vivid phrase, which Monroe thought all too accurately described Adams, and could not recall any. "I think those were the only letters I ever wrote him in answer to the volumes Callender was perpetually writing to me."

Monroe found some slight encouragement in that. He would pass the word if necessary that any claims by Callender of written encouragement of the most vicious of his writings were false. The contention that all the payments were meant only as charity, though patently a lie, was internally consistent. It could be maintained as true, and those who wanted to believe their President would believe it.

Jefferson put forward something else that might be seen as exculpatory. "Callender's writings last year in Richmond had fallen far short of the quality of his original *Political Progress* and the scurrility of his subsequent work began to do us mischief. As to myself, far from wanting to encourage his writing, no man wished more to see his pen stopped, even though I considered him still a proper object of benevolence. It is long since I wished he would cease writing about politicks, as he was doing more harm than good."

Monroe shook his head. Nobody would find credible the notion that Jefferson, in the heat of such passions as the XYZ affair, would have wanted to see Callender's much-needed pen stopped. And everyone who could read knew how much damage that pen had inflicted on the Federalists. Calling the years of subsidy "charity" was stretching credulity, but pretending to have wished he would cease his writing would snap it completely.

"That is the true state of what has passed between him and me," the President insisted. "I leave to your judgment what use can be made of these facts. What do you think, James?"

"It is to be regretted that Captain Lewis paid the money," Monroe replied, "after the intimation by Callender of his threat." But he assumed that neither Lewis nor Madison, properly forewarned, would say anything about that meeting. Jefferson had spoken of one day sending Lewis on a scientific expedition; Monroe hoped it would begin soon and take him far away. "It might be well to get all your letters, however unimportant, back from Callender."

Jefferson went to his desk and drew out a large file. "I have a letter file here that lists all letters I have written by the date." He ran his finger down the pages, then picked up a quill and made notations. "I wrote to Callender on October 11, 1798, and then in 1799 on September 6 and October 6. I'll get my secretary to search for the copies."

Three letters, expressing encouragement and possibly transmitting money. How to get them back from the recipient? Perhaps as some part of a settlement; no, Monroe guessed that any attempt along those lines would add fuel to a blackmailer's fire. "Your resolution to terminate all communication with him from now on is wise," he said. He hoped that Jefferson's recollection of those letters to Callender—presumably supplying objective answers to the questions of a reporter, but in no way urging him on—was accurate. But they should not cut off indirect communication, especially about remission of his fine. A postmastership would be a small price to pay. "However, it would be well to try to prevent a serpent from doing one an injury."

"As soon as I was elected," Jefferson responded, "Callender came on here wishing to be made postmaster at Richmond. I knew him totally unfit for it, and however ready I was to aid him with my own charities—and I gave him the fifty dollars you know about—I did not think that public offices were anything I could give away as charities. I think that rejection is what has given him mortal offense, far more than the delay in remission of the fine."

Monroe saw that Jefferson was adamant about refusing the appointment and did not press the matter; in fact, in these abrasive circumstances, it would seem like bribery. He recalled how he had led Callender in prison to believe he would be a good candidate for the postmastership, and thus would gain social acceptance for himself and commercial advantage for his newspaper in Richmond. But he found no need to say anything to the President about that. There had been no witnesses, nothing in writing, and if necessary he would simply deny hinting at a Federal appointment. "In case he comes to Georgetown," he cautioned, "be assured that Madison and yourself cannot be too circumspect in your conversations with him. Every act of charity he will attribute to improper motives, and he will pervert it to your injury."

Jefferson readily agreed. One thought nagged at Monroe, however. Nearly a decade before, during the visitation to Hamilton about the Reynolds affair, the Treasury Secretary had said something about passing a message to Jefferson. He tried to call up the exact words but could not; it had to do with a relationship with their Virginia neighbor, John Walker. Monroe had presumed at the time it was a threat to reveal something embarrassing about Jefferson if the republicans ever dared made public Hamilton's dalliance with Maria Reynolds. Monroe considered that threat to be idle. He knew that Walker was the only close neighbor who bore Jefferson a grudge, and that was merely about politicks. A decade before, Walker had been given an interim appointment as Senator from Virginia and wanted to continue, but Jefferson had snatched the nomination away from him and given it to Monroe.

"Beyond the charity offered to a man who was constantly importuning you," Monroe asked about Callender, he hoped delicately, "is there anything you suspect that he knows that might possibly be twisted into something embarrassing? We speak, as always, as men of honor." That "men of honor" phrase, as all Virginia gentlemen knew, was meant to assure absolute confidentiality about any hint of any affairs of a romantic or sexual nature.

Jefferson understood and replied without hesitation, "Callender knows nothing of me which I am not willing to declare to the world myself."

Governor Monroe leaned back in his chair and allowed himself to sigh in relief. Then, reviewing in his lawyerly mind the way Jefferson had carefully couched his denial—limiting it to what Callender knew—he wondered: who else might know something about Jefferson's past that the President was not willing to declare to the world? Who was in their Virginia social set, and knew Callender, and was a political opponent not to be trusted? John Marshall came to mind, and the Chief Justice was probably irritated at having to plead for a place for his Court to sit, but he was not a vindictive sort. Then he thought of Light-Horse Harry Lee.

"I have heard that Harry Lee was in Richmond the other day," he told the President, "and related to a mutual friend about a conversation he had with Aaron Burr up here. Lee told Burr that he knew all the arrangements of your Cabinet, and Burr replied with apparent resentment that he had never been consulted on a single point by you, or expected to be." When Jefferson attested to the truth of that last, Monroe went on: "Harry Lee also told my friend that if Burr had come forward and favored the views of the Federalists who supported him in the recent election in the House, he might be President today."

"You are sure Lee said that?"

"Yes, and it's important that you and Madison know it. I was always aware there would be much difficulty in the management of these men," Monroe said firmly. This report suggested that Burr might not have been as duplicitous in the election as Jefferson had suspected. But Lee knew all the gossip in their Virginia social set, was now out of power and out of sorts, and probably was in touch with Callender. "Nobody is likely to give you more trouble."

JAMES MADISON

June 1, 1801

Washington

Private
Jas. Monroe Esq.
Dear Sir

I have recd. Your favor of the 23 Ult.

Callendar made his appearance here some days ago in the same temper which is described in your letter. He seems implacable toward the principal object of his complaints and not to be satisfied in any respect, without an office.

It has been my lot to bear the burden of receiving and repelling his claims. What feelings may have been excited by my plain dealing with him I cannot say, but am inclined to think he has been brought by it to some reflections which will be useful to him. It is impossible however to reason concerning a man, whose imagination and passions have been so fermented.

Do you know too, that besides his other passions, he is under the tyranny of that of *love*. Strange as it may appear, this came out, under a charge of *secresy*. in a way that renders the fact unquestionable.

The object of his flame is in Richd. I did not ask her name; but presume her to be young, beautiful in his eyes at least, and in a sphere above him. He has flattered himself & probably been flattered by others into a persuasion that the emoluments and reputation of a post office, would obtain her in marriage. Of these recommendations however he is sent back in despair.

With respect to the fine even I fear that delays, if nothing more may still torment him & lead him to torment others. Callendar's irritation produced by his wants is whetted constantly by his suspicion that the difficulties, if not intended, are the offspring of indifference in those who have interposed in his behalf.

Intelligence has come thro' several channels, which makes it probable that Louisiana has been ceded to France. This is but little wonderful. You will readily view this subject in all its aspects. If any ideas occur on it that can be of service, favor us with them.

Mrs. M. joins in the most respectful salutations to Mrs. Monroe & yourself. Adieu Yrs. Affly

James Madison

Chapter 31

WILLIAM COBBETT

June 5, 1801
NEW YORK

"Prime Miniſter Pitt is going to be delighted to welcome you back to England, William," said the British consul, Edward Thornton, in his second-story office facing the Hudson River. "You have become quite the hero at home. William Windham told the Commons a golden statue should be erected in your honor."

"I left there nine years ago under threat of prosecution for sedition," Cobbett reminded him. "Frankly, I would prefer to stay here in New York and start *Porcupine's Gazette* again. But the choice is not mine. General Hamilton's partner—the scholarly fellow, Harison—advises that the bleeding doctor is coming after my stock of books to drive me out of business entirely."

"Dr. Rush will stop at nothing, it seems," the diplomat sympathized. It struck him that Cobbett's recent pamphlets excoriating the doctor in ever-more-libelous terms only stimulated the medical man's desire for vengeance, but Thornton was not about to try to influence the Porcupine's virulent opinions. "His destruction of your collected works—selling them for waste paper—added insult to injury."

"Rush will be remembered by Americans, thanks to me, as the man whose quack treatment killed George Washington. One of Rush's bleeding acolytes diagnosed a 'malignant sore throat' and 'lack of strength' and then bled his patient to death."

That often-repeated, abusive charge of Cobbett's—Thornton had no idea of its veracity—surely infuriated the eminent physician. But on the other side of the ocean, the unprecedented libel judgment against the only English journalist in America to stand up for King and Country had been taken as proof of republican hypocrisy. With all its talk of liberty of the press, America had shown how easy it was to bring a critic of the government to the brink of ruination, or so the tame British press liked to think.

"Mr. Pitt's government controls two daily newspapers," Thornton said, "the *True Briton* in the morning and the *Sun* in the evening. Pitt is prepared to turn over to you either one you choose—its printing press, the building, subscribers, everything. You would be sole owner."

Cobbett went to the large table in Thornton's office that held a stack of American newspapers and began perusing the ones from the South. "You know, my dear Edward, that I have always turned down any pecuniary assistance you have offered me in the past. I have often accused the likes of Bache and Fenno and Callender of being hirelings of their favored republican politicians. Though they accused me often enough of being recompensed by the Crown, I have been resolutely independent. You know that."

Thornton nodded agreement. Cobbett had frequently turned down offers of subsidy. He had made a financial success of his publications by his vividly plain, mutton-fisted style of writing, his corrosive humor, and the outrageousness of his personal vilification. But at the request of Alexander Hamilton, who was acting secretly as Cobbett's attorney, the British legation had quietly supplied the $8,000 needed to pay the egregious fine and court costs laid against the loyal editor. Hamilton had made a point that nobody, including Cobbett, was to be told of this; the story agreed to was that the legation had urged British loyalists here to help pay the fine.

"Let me remind you of the fable of the wolf and the mastiff," the editor continued as he turned the pages of the newspapers, apparently searching for something. "One night, when loose, the mastiff rambled into a wood. He met the wolf, all gaunt and shaggy, and said to him, 'Why do you live this sort of life? See how fat and sleek I am! Come home with me and live as I do, dividing your time between eating and sleeping.' The ragged wolf accepted the kind offer and they trotted on together till they got out of the wood."

Cobbett found an article in one of the papers that set him off to another stack, presumably looking for another writer's approach to the same account. Thornton waited, and then could not help himself: "You were saying about the wolf. And then what happened?"

"Yes. The wolf, assisted by the light of the moon—the beams of which had been intercepted by the trees—spied a crease, just a little mark, round the neck of the mastiff. 'What is your fancy,' said the wolf, 'for making that mark round your neck?' 'Oh,' said the mastiff, 'it is only the mark of the collar that my master ties me up with.' 'Ties you up!' exclaimed the wolf, stopping short. 'Give me my ragged hair, my gaunt belly, and my freedom!' And so saying, the wild and hungry wolf trotted back to the wood."

The consul smiled. "I shall inform Mr. Pitt that your support of his government will come through the pages of your own new *Porcupine's Gazette.*"

"You take my point. For me to do the government any service, I must be able to say that I am totally independent of it in my capacity of proprietor of a newspaper. Ah, here's what I'm looking for." He extracted a page from the pile. "My old adversary Callender, that flea-bitten and besotted fugitive from Scottish justice, is eager to make friends with his old foes. He writes here in the *Richmond Examiner,* in the spirit of Christian charity, that he is now willing to live and let live, and wishes to be let alone. He wants no more quills from Porcupine or my imitators in the Federalist press. Peace and good will and all that. Do you believe he means it, Edward? I don't."

It occurred to Thornton that these gladiators of the press, though different in personality and point of view, were intimately familiar with each other's methods and might have much more in common. "What's his game, William?"

"He is fishing for respectability, some sort of respite. They say there is a woman above his class he is eager to impress, and a postmastership would have done that for him in Richmond. But Jefferson properly denied it to him because he is a drunk and a rogue. His current posture of good will is either a manifestation of the glow of romance or a ruse. I suspect his true nature will manifest itself in time."

"Your thought is that Callender will engage the Federalists again?"

"What Federalists? The Tories here are finished. Jefferson has not only defeated them but also gobbled them up. 'We are all Federalists, we are all Republicans'—that means the Whigs and the Tories have become Tory-

Whigs. American politicians are now all thin-gruel radicals, middle-way quiddists, and in a few years time they'll be at war with England to save France, with nobody here to object."

"Surely the press," said Thornton, "with no fear from sedition law, will support an anti-government faction."

"Do you see another Porcupine around? No, they've driven me out, and Jefferson will not soon let another worthy opponent arise. The press was his engine to ride to office, Edward, and he knows its power. You'll see, with this State Libel Law of his, and miscreants like Governor McKean to protect him, the Jefferson men will crack the press's skull soon enough. I'm well gone."

The British consul told the editor he could not agree. He was convinced that the colonists had patterned themselves on the lines of English politicks—staunch Federalist Tories and radical republican Whigs—and the twain would not be joined.

"Only unless someone with the mind of Hamilton can find his way back," Cobbett amended, "or some hero on horseback sweeps the republicans out. Or a writer with a streak of meanness like Callender turns on them and ruins Jefferson as he ruined Hamilton."

"But I thought you said Callender is a drunk and a rogue."

"All that, but more than that. Callender is Ishmael," said Cobbett, "born to be an outcast."

"Ah," said the diplomat.

"You are thinking, my friend, that I cast Callender in that mold because I am an outcast myself. Not so. I am an oppositionist; he is an outcast. Peter Porcupine finds joy in doing battle against the hypocritical rousers of the rabble; but Timothy Thunderproof, as that fugitive from Scottish justice styled himself, is vengeful to the core, a dark spirit who chews the cud of his rejection." He contemplated the Hudson River boats, the mail packets and the stately, oceangoing *Lady Arabella,* in the docks that could be seen from the legation window. "I suspect that his innate rebelliousness will conquer his Tom Paine principles. A writer with a nose and an ear and a taste for scandal will ferret it out to satisfy the rage and hunger within. Callender will set his traps, gather up scandalous tidbits, and use them against his erstwhile allies in the next election. If the angry mob lets him live that long."

Cobbett stared at the stack of newspapers and offered the consul a bit of advice to pass along. "If Hamilton starts that newspaper after I'm gone, tell him to consider this: Callender, the dagger that Jefferson used to stab him, could in another hand become a weapon to cut a trail to his own presidency."

Thornton found most interesting Cobbett's description of himself as an oppositionist. That was surely true of his role first in the British army, in opposition to a corrupt officer corps. Then it was true here in America, as he stoutly opposed not only republicans, but the French, the Irish, the Scots, Methodists, Jews, Catholics, bleeding doctors, paper money, women's rights and all resisters to authority except himself. Cobbett had not often inveighed against blacks mainly because he found in their servile state an example of the Americans' hypocrisy about all men being created equal. Because Cobbett's loyalty to the Crown gained luster only as a lonely defender abroad, the diplomat wondered how long it would take him to find fault with the English government that welcomed him home.

"I sail for London on the *Arabella* tomorrow," the editor announced. "I'm sorry we delayed so long because I am apprehensive that some vile wretch will conceive the idea of hampering me at my departure."

"General Hamilton heard that Vice President Burr planned to send a gang of his ruffians from Tammany Hall to mar your leave-taking, but I have taken care of that," the consul assured him. "A group we have assembled of your supporters, and a contingent of New York police, will be at dockside to assist you and Nancy, and little Anne and William, aboard. When the *Arabella* stops in Halifax before the ocean crossing, there will be a proper reception and dinner in your honor by Sir John Wentworth."

"The Governor himself? You know me too well to suppose I am puffed up by all of this. When I was last in Halifax," the somewhat puffed-up Englishman recalled, "I helped, as a soldier on fatigue duty, to drag the baggage from the wharf to the barracks. And when my Nancy was there last, she was employed in assisting her poor mother to wash soldiers' shirts."

Nancy Cobbett stood dutifully beside her husband on the wharf, her hands holding those of her son and daughter. She thought of Halifax, their first stop on the trip back to England, and that called to mind the first time she laid eyes on her husband-to-be. He was twenty-four, already a sergeant-major, stationed at Saint John in New Brunswick, keeping the company's books and teaching himself the rudiments of English and French grammar. She was thirteen, daughter of a sergeant in the Royal Artillery. It was in the dead of winter, with the snow several feet deep on the ground, at first light in the morning. He was walking briskly up the hill to the barracks with two friends, and saw her standing in the snow scrubbing out a washing-tub. Their eyes met for a long moment, and as the men walked past, she heard him say, "That's the girl for me."

Years later, William told her he never had a thought of her being the wife of any other man, "any more than I had thought of you being transformed into a chest of drawers. I formed my resolution at once to marry you as soon as I could get permission," he said in his unwavering way, "and to get out of the army as soon as I could." They had to part when her father was transferred back to England, and William gave her 150 guineas, all his savings, to keep her from doing heavy work as a housemaid while they were separated.

That separation lasted four long years, whilst she never looked at another young man; when William finally was discharged and came across the Atlantic to claim her, she was able to hand him back the money unbroken, as she had drudged to save for their first home. Although she could then neither read nor write, in loyalty and industriousness she felt they were much alike. She knew his mixed feelings today about leaving America, where he had succeeded and yet failed, and where they had heartbrokenly buried two infants but happily could bring two healthy children back with them.

Her husband had a few remarks ready for the crowd on the dock. About fifty Tories, twice that number of hooting republican ruffians from Tammany Hall, and fifty police protectors had come to the shipside to await the *Arabella*'s sailing.

"As I have long felt the perfect indifference to the majority of the people here"—Cobbett's opening met with a chorus of catcalls—"I shall spare myself the trouble of a ceremonious farewell. Let me, however, not part from you in indiscriminating contempt." More boos.

"If no man ever had so many and such malignant foes, no one ever had more faithful friends. If the savages of the city have scared the children in their cradle, these children have been soothed and caressed by the affectionate, gentle and generous inhabitants of this country." Nancy drew the children closer to her, and the noise stopped.

"In a very little time," he said in his gruff voice, "I shall be beyond the reach of your friendship and your malice. But being out of your power will alter neither my sentiments nor my words. As I have never spoken anything but truth to you, so I will never speak anything but truth of you. The heart of a Briton revolts at an emulation of your baseness, and although you have as a nation treated me most unjustly, I scorn to repay you with injustice."

He turned to the Tories whose loyalty he shared. "To my friends, I wish that peace and happiness which I greatly fear they will not find. And to you lot"—he faced the surly Tammany crowd—"I wish you no greater scourge than that which you are preparing for your country.

"With this I depart for my native land, where neither the moth of Democracy nor the rust of Federalism doth corrupt, and where thieves do not, with impunity, break through and steal five thousand dollars at a time."

As the crowd applauded and jeered, Consul Thornton, standing near her, said something that struck Nancy as curious: "And the hungry wolf trots back to the woods."

Chapter 32

*C*allender was relieved that Maria took the initiative to put their time together on a regular schedule.

"I could spend every Saturday here with you, James," she said, drinking her tea in his room, a candle on the writing table between them. "And most evenings during the week, you would be most welcome to take dinner with me in the kitchen of the doctor's house."

At the nadir of his harsh existence, Callender found it hard to comprehend such gentle stroking of good fortune. A beautiful and statuesque woman, raised in gentility but accustomed to hard work, had unaccountably befriended him. Though the world had believed the slander of her name by a man of great power, Callender was one of the few who believed that she had been unfairly maligned. He had championed her cause before they had ever met, for reasons of his own, but now was more certain than ever that she was courageously honest. He began to let himself think of her as an experienced mother who could one day provide a loving home for his long-boarded children. This unknown presence from the heyday of his career had appeared, like an unfrightening apparition, to rescue him from the helplessness of despair. Maria was offering to share her company, her good food—and, once a week, he hoped, his bed—in an association with a solitary, itinerant writer who had no friends in power or prospects of success. The notion that she requited his love, or at least shared his need for affection and companionship in a place of refuge, stunned and exhilarated him.

"I will never take a glass of rum alone again and I will bathe in hot water every week," he volunteered in all sincerity. "I will give up newsmongering for good work like teaching, or the law. I am also a fair carpenter."

Maria Lewis Reynolds Clingman, now going by the name of Maria Clement, formerly of New York and Philadelphia and London, smiled. Her smile, less an expression of mirth than an overcoming of sadness, stirred his hopes and made him feel less like a man standing on a trapdoor. She did not take up his promise to change.

"You will continue to be the man you are," she told him. "You believed me when nobody else did, long before you befriended me. Now we will protect each other, and my daughter and your sons."

He had absorbed the story of her life into his own. Her second husband, Jacob Clingman, had fallen in with a swindler in London as predatory and clumsy as James Reynolds had been in America. The weak young fellow was now in Newgate Prison and Maria was well and truly finished with him. She had brought her daughter back with her the year before and again sought the aid of her attorney and friend, Colonel Burr. That generous man had arranged for the religious education of young Susan at a Boston seminary and found a respectable position for Maria with Dr. Mathew as his housekeeper and factotum in Richmond.

"You know I sent the whole two-hundred-dollar fine they finally repaid me up to Francis Leiper." His snuffmaker friend had fallen into financial difficulty with the drop in the price of tobacco, and that money, plus Jefferson's fifty dollars, did not cover the board for the four boys for the two years. Even if it had, his room above Henry Pace's printing shop did not have living space for his youngsters. "And little, pasty-faced Jemmy Madison, our

great Secretary of State, told me to forget about being postmaster. He said
I made too many enemies while fighting for Jefferson, and my appointment
would upset the Federalists here." He embellished the rejection a little.
"He gave me to believe they look down on me as a radical immigrant who
has never been to a dancing master."

"I won't tell you not to be bitter, James."

He understood that was her way of telling him not to be bitter. She had
as great an occasion for bitterness as he, but did not seem to hate anybody,
not even Hamilton. On impulse, he leaned across his writing table to kiss
her cheek, and she turned her head slightly to meet his lips with her own. In
all his married years and after, he had never done anything so romantically
impulsive. He prided himself on being a dour Scot and Calvinist moralist,
in whose world such impulsive expressions of pleasure were frowned upon.
He was determined to maintain, cherish and refine his political bitterness,
because the ingrates for whose cause he went to jail had, on assuming
power, betrayed him. And a ready supply of spite would add necessary pun-
gency to his prose. But Callender vowed to force back his bile for the time
being: above all, he would make an effort not to let it show to the woman
who had re-introduced tenderness into his life.

Callender was hopeful, however, that Maria's suggestion meant that
they would be living in sin. That both excited and troubled him. Not that he
cared what Virginians thought of his morals, because the sexual carousing
of the Virginia gentry with their slave women after the lascivious dances
made hypocrites of them all. But living together out of wedlock for any
length of time would offend God's law, invite the hellfire, and set a bad
moral example for his boys and Maria's daughter.

Two weeks before, here in this room, they had consummated their love.
He had never dared to imagine himself entwined with a woman so beautiful, passionate and gentle. Though embarrassingly clumsy the first time he
had made love since his wife's death, he improved on the second Saturday
and tonight he felt comfortable that his manliness would match her woman-
liness. Though he was not sure he deserved her, he was sure that neither of
them deserved to be alone; besides, they were old friends in an odd way because their lives had intersected long before they met. Marriage to Maria,
of course, was not possible now; any divorce from a man across the ocean
would surely take years and more expense than they could afford.

"I will not be bitter," he said. He was ready to promise anything.

" 'Vengeance is mine, saith the Lord,' and is not for mortal man to seek on earth."

"Your writing is best when you are angry," she said. He was glad she did not take his no-bitterness pledge too seriously. "And the Federalist press still blames you for bringing down Hamilton and President Adams. You won't respond to the terrible things they write?"

"I have declared a truce. The battle is over. I'll forget old scores." At least until the next election campaign. Or until the time he had a newspaper of his own, when his work would not be under the control of editors like Bache or Duane of the *Aurora* in Philadelphia, or Jones of the *Examiner* here.

"Your enemies may not be so forgiving," she said. "You know Hamilton as well as I do. He has a newspaper now."

The *New York Evening Post* had already suggested that Jefferson had been the source of Callender's exposé of Hamilton. That speculation, though annoying, was true. But what bothered Callender more now was what was untrue: Hamilton's pretense four years ago that he had been seduced and then blackmailed by Maria in 1792. That was a screen of smoke to conceal his financial dealing with her husband Reynolds, but the clinging stigma of shame was the reason Maria lived under an assumed name and her daughter had to be cloistered in a seminary. He put out of his mind the possibility that any assignation between Hamilton and Maria might have taken place.

"I shall place another article in the *Richmond Examiner,*" he decided. Meriwether Jones was still paying him a pittance for his writing, but it was the only money he could earn. Jones had made plain to him that any whisper of his support by Jefferson through the years would end even that small stipend; that meant he was being paid for what he tacitly agreed not to write. "It will be an open letter to my old foes, even more conciliatory than the one I wrote a little while back. I will quote Scripture: 'The righteous shall rest from their labors, and their works shall follow them.' The Federalists are determined that my works, righteous or not, follow me, and they bandy my name about. In the name of charity, I will ask those good folks to let me alone."

"And if they do, James—unlikely, I fear—what will there be for you to be angry enough to write about?"

"Not politicks." Now that the smoke of the campaign had cleared, he was beginning to think that the difference between the factions was not as important as he had thought. The weakness and moral ambiguity of men in the seat of power—whether radical commoners or royalist aristocrats—was more at the root of the trouble with government. Men as much as measures needed constant monitoring. "Tom Paine wrote that government, at best, is a choice of evils, a complex constable hired to keep the peace and nothing more. He argued that government is to society what a bridle is to a horse, or a dose of salts to the human body." What a pleasure it was for him to talk like this to a woman who understood it.

Maria rose and cleared their cups off the table, placing them on the pewter lining of his dry sink. She moved toward the sleeping alcove and motioned for him to wait before following her.

He waited for her to undress, explaining, "That is why both parties bear a great deal of watching, but it is not something that I have to do. There is not a prodigious difference between the moral characters of one party and the other. Individual leaders matter more. Washington, despite what I wrote at the time, was a great—that is, necessary—man." That reminded him of Dr. Rush and the bleeding of the General. Another thought followed of Cobbett's warning not to let Rush's associate, Dr. James Reynolds, no kin to Maria's husband, treat Callender's dying wife for the yellow fever. Wrong memory for the moment.

"When I do get back to writing for newspapers," he said, blowing out the candle and stripping off his clothes, "it will be about the wrongs being done all around us. The gambling, for example." He climbed into the narrow bed beside her, feeling the warmth of her skin and the length of her legs in the darkness against his hard body. "Do you have any idea how much these people gamble, and how many duels it causes? Can you imagine what all the evil associated with gambling debt does to their morality?" He felt her fingers on his lips and he quieted.

Chapter 33

"**J** cannot make a success of my *Recorder*," its editor, Henry Pace, told Callender. "There are not enough Federalists here any more to support a newspaper. Jones at the *Examiner*, with all his crowing about the wonders of Jefferson and republican government, is driving me out of business. You must help. I need readers."

The Scot was pleased at the compliment. Pace had come from England two years before, running from sedition charges there, a good credential for a newsmonger. Callender thought him to be a capable enough printer but with no idea of the soul of a newspaper. His *Richmond Recorder, or Lady's and Gentleman's Miscellany* was lifeless. Its columns lay inert on the page, creating no talk among its readers, no response from its subjects. Nobody felt required to read it lest they miss news that their neighbors would know. The *Recorder* lacked the spice of controversy and, unlike Jones's *Examiner*, shied away from personalities.

"I'm no Federalist, as you are, Henry," Callender said, glad to be starting a negotiation. He needed the work. An occasional item to pay for the right to sleep upstairs was no longer enough.

The *Examiner* had cut him off. Callender presumed that its editor, Jones, a longtime admirer of Jefferson, no longer thought he posed a threat to the new administration. Perhaps Monroe had passed the word that the rejected Scot was so impressed with the popularity of the new regime that he no longer needed subsistence as a writer, much less his due reward of postmaster. Though Callender had a score to settle with the republican leaders, he was not about to adopt Federalist principles that he had fought against so fiercely for so long.

"I just want to sell enough newspapers," said Pace, "to let me make a profit on my printing business. Everybody knows your name and you can write like Porcupine himself. Become my partner in the *Recorder*."

They struck what Callender considered his first fair deal in business: each would draw $15 dollars a week and share any profit from the newspaper. Pace, who put up all the capital, would keep all the additional printing profit that the newspaper would bring to his press.

"We shall neither calumniate nor flatter men in office," Callender said, sitting at a table to write his opening announcement. "We shall neither defame nor worship men who are out of office."

His new partner was dubious at the careful balance. "What will we do, then, to gain a readership?"

"The public will soon see," his new partner assured him, "that from whatever political or commercial quarter deceit and falsehood may come, it shall be our ambition to blast them with—" He paused: The hammer of truth? He had used that metaphor before, but you did not blast with a hammer. "—blast them with the lightning of truth." He swung into a rhythm of rhetoric long familiar to him. "We have no personal obligations to any party, though we are willing, if need be, to contend for political principles. We shall never prostrate ourselves to the fanaticks of either party."

"That's good to say," said the printer, "but don't we have to ally ourselves to readers on one side or the other?"

"The game is in the middle now," Callender instructed, "and each side offers little to oppose except in the way they use their power. I'm known to be a republican, but of the sort that challenges tyranny from any source to inflict its utmost, and never to flinch." If an angry mob came around with torches to burn down the press, Callender knew, he would flinch soon enough—physical bravery was for soldiers and fools—but in the *Recorder*, he would invite attacks in print from other newsmongers. Those angry builders of circulation he would prominently reprint, and wear the most vituperative of them as a badge of honor. "If we seem to bear hardest on the men presently in office," he wrote fluidly, "it is only because they are more formidable and dangerous than their defeated adversaries." He thought a moment and penned a line that expressed his new credo: "Neither the Ins nor the Outs ever deserve implicit confidence."

First as a pamphleteer, and later as an occasional writer for the *Aurora* and the *Examiner*, he had always been restrained by an owner's hand. Now, with the printer Henry Pace needing him and giving him carte blanche, he could express himself freely every week. He was no longer merely the submitter of copy, but the editor who decided what would appear.

"If you're not going to start a fight with the republicans," said Pace, "maybe you could start a fight with the *Examiner*?"

Callender considered the notion of a small war between newspapers. He could feel his competitive spirit—so long beaten down by the ungrateful Jeffersonians and then softened by his life with Maria—begin to rise like the head of a bear coming out of hibernation. Electoral politicks, and the ammunition he had saved for use in it, would await the coming of the next Presidential campaign. Now was the time to fight the local battle against the corrupt culture infecting the region, centered in Richmond.

What better way than to declare war on the owner of the competing newspaper? The *Examiner*'s Meriwether Jones, acting on what Callender was certain was the direct order of Governor Monroe, had threatened him with unemployment and ostracism when he dared to make his demand for the repayment of his fine and his claim on the postmastership. They paid him a pittance for articles as long as he behaved. Now that he had kept silent during his year in the political wilderness, they believed they could drop him with impunity. Let them think that. Their republican *Examiner* now had no officeholders to denounce; its readers subscribed largely out of habit from the anti-Federalist days. The *Examiner* was vulnerable to personal attack.

December 22, 1801

"Mistress Examiner" was the headline in the newly strident *Recorder*.

The lavish living and growing demands of publisher Jones's black mistress, Callender charged, was causing financial embarrassment at his newspaper. Jones had set up the beautiful slave in an apartment of her own and had been seen at black dances and horse races with her on his arm. Callender placed himself as a witness in the article: "I have heard him, at his own table, and before his own lady, boasting that he never had any pleasure but in a certain kind of woman. And that it was the custom of his family to be fond of the 'other color.' Moreover, it is known that the sable wench wears a miniature portrait of the lascivious editor around her neck."

Stunned by Callender's attack, Jones in the *Examiner* responded by charging that Callender was a disgruntled *Examiner* writer, fired for drunkenness.

Next day, the newspaper war, as residents of Richmond called the action of their suddenly combative press, saw Callender deal decisively with Jones's statement that the reason he had fired Callender was drunkenness. "My career at the *Examiner* ended," he wrote, in a countercharge that was repeated all over Richmond, "when I mistakenly entered my employer's

Scandalmonger

bedroom and discovered that with Mrs. Jones out of town, 'Mistress Examiner' was occupying the room."

January 3, 1802

Jones could challenge the truthfulness of only one of Callender's charges: he claimed never to have given his black mistress a portrait of himself to wear around his neck. The denial of that detail was believed in the spirited conversations in Richmond's taverns, casting some doubt on the more serious matter of the sexual intermingling of the races. Callender took that lesson to heart: henceforth, he would avoid publishing details he heard about in passing but was not fairly certain were true, or at least could not be proven untrue. Never stretch for a detail, he told himself, that could be used to discredit the rest of your accusation.

In less than a month, the *Examiner* was crumbling under the *Recorder*'s sustained attack. "Men disposed to sacrifice private confidence that was offered in a spirit of benevolence," wrote Jones about Callender, his former occasional employee, in an anguished article, "to satisfy their revenge, and who array trifles in the harsh language of crimination, may always make unpleasant assaults."

Callender shook his head in wonderment at the *Examiner*'s weak responses. "Pusillanimous. Jones lacks the talent of selecting, of combining, of charging home his information," he told Pace. "He lacks the firmness that fights for the last inch of ground. Can you imagine how Porcupine would have reacted to an attack from another editor? It's a good thing Cobbett's far gone."

"Jones has surrendered," his partner noted happily. "Who do we make war on now?"

"No politicks." Callender was firm. "I think we have awakened the good people of this city to the social evil under their noses. There are plenty of hypocrites yet to be found."

"Do we have to name them by name?" asked his partner, apparently thinking about libel.

"Not the boys and the bachelors," Callender replied. "They will take liberties. But every member of the set of wealthy plantation owners who has a white wife and a black concubine will have to buy a copy of the *Recorder* every week to make certain they and their African merchandise are not named in it."

That did his Calvinist soul as much good as it did his newspaper's circulation. The *Recorder* was now selling a thousand copies a week, taken from the republican *Examiner* as well as the two Federalist weeklies. Just as important, even without the postmastership that Callender thought he would need for social standing, the sheet was adding advertising. He wondered if the commercial interests merely wanted to sell their wares in the newspaper that all Richmond was talking about or were worried about exposure of their own moral lapses.

Chapter 34

GEORGE HAY

February 8, 1802

"Callender? I'm George Hay. Do you remember me?"

The editor rose and extended his hand to one of the lawyers who defended him at his sedition trial. "You were good enough to accompany Governor Monroe to visit me in prison. Of course I remember you. Please have a seat."

Hay ignored the outstretched hand, saying, "This is no social call. I think what you are doing to this city and state with your scurrilous sheet is a damnable disgrace."

One of those gentry with a guilty conscience, Callender thought. "If you'd like to write a letter—"

"I have no intention of seeing my name in your filthy publication." Hay took a seat across the wide writing table from Callender, hands on his walking stick set firmly between his legs. He fixed a glare on the editor. "I'm here on behalf of the many upright citizens of Richmond who don't wish to see their names blackened and their families shamed and their lives ruined."

"You were not this irate in Justice Chase's courtroom, Mr. Hay."

"I do not like the questions you have been asking about my friend, Peter Carr, or myself. What we do, who we do it with, and how we entertain ourselves and our friends is no business of yours."

"Carr lives at Monticello, does he not? A nephew of Jefferson's?"

"I am not here to answer questions, Callender. I'm here to give you fair warning." He brandished the walking stick in the editor's face. "A libel suit that would take years to cripple you is the least of your worries. I can get a recognizance from the court to keep you from publishing anything that defames the character of any Virginian."

Callender whitened. "What virtuous character has ever been destroyed by this paper? If seduction and miscegenation and hypocrisy have become the South's new code of morality and virtue—"

"Don't talk of morality to me! You've been wallowing in the gutter all your life, you and all the other immigrant drunks that befouled the republican cause. We're well rid of apostates like you."

"The men presently in office," Callender tried to explain, "are more dangerous than the remnant of the Federalists. That's not apostasy. I still have my republican principles, uncorrupted by the seductions of high office."

"You fugitive scum don't know what principles are. And you think you're safe because you're not a man of honor and no gentleman will stoop to challenge you to a duel. We have another way to deal with the likes of you—horsewhipping." Hay strode out, slamming the door.

Henry Pace and one of his beefier printers' helpers appeared at the doorway, heavy clubs in hand. "Friend of yours?"

"Only my lawyer." Callender was trying to treat it lightly, but he was shaken by the threat of physical abuse. "He's the author of the 'Essay on the Liberty of the Press.' "

"Do you suppose Governor Monroe sent him?"

"Hay came on his own, I think. He's one of the gambling crowd." Now that the confrontation was over, he felt his anger rising. "But I think it's time to send Monroe and his friends in Washington a message. And time to stir up my old colleagues in the republican press."

He would not give in to his fears. No editor or governor or great man was in control of him now. He had proven his impartiality, and enough time had lapsed to weaken the charge that he was a disappointed office-seeker. Though it was earlier than he had planned, Callender decided to put a shot across the republicans' bow. He would make public some of Thomas Jefferson's financial support of the Adams Administration's most severe critic in the years before he became President. That was how the *Recorder* would reach out beyond Richmond to attract the attention of all the papers in the nation.

He planned it to unravel in two stages, much like his extended exposure of Hamilton. Nobody knew better than Callender how to hold back parts of a story until the target committed itself to answering the opening salvo. He would assert Jefferson's sponsorship first, with no specifics. He would wait for the lapdog republican press to come at him. At the same time, he could count on the Federalist press to play with the charge that Jefferson, as Vice President and professing to be above all party wrangling, secretly collaborated in the hated republican newsmonger's vilification of George Washington and John Adams.

Then, after a month or two in which Callender produced no damning proof, the Jeffersonians would assume he had none and issue their irate denials, which Duane would trumpet in his *Aurora*. And finally the editor of the *Recorder* would spring his trap: he would print his letters from Jefferson urging him on and giving him money through third parties. In that way, Callender figured, he could stretch the controversy out over three months, becoming once again the most feared and famous journalist in America.

The thought of Hamilton—the man who portrayed Maria as a blackmailing whore to save his financial reputation—reminded him of Cobbett, that former Treasury Secretary's warmest admirer. Curious, the Scot observed to Maria when he took dinner with her that night, that James Thomson Callender, of all people, should be the one to take from the routed

Porcupine the role of leading critic of the hypocrisy of Thomas Jefferson.

He returned to the *Recorder*'s print shop and, candle in hand, walked up the stairs to his room. He set a second candle on the writing table, reached for a knife in the drawer and slowly sharpened a quill.

Chapter 35

ABIGAIL ADAMS   THOMAS JEFFERSON

July 4, 1802
WASHINGTON, D.C.

A band was blaring "Yankee Doodle" outſide his window, giving him a headache, and Abigail Adams was the last person in the world Thomas Jefferson, at that moment, wanted to see. But she had appeared at the President's house, where she had been the first hostess, and there was no denying a cordial reception to the former President's wife.

He recalled that when John Adams served as America's first Minister to London, at the time Jefferson was serving in Paris, the often-imperious Abigail had been not only gracious but motherly to his motherless daughter Martha and her companion Sally. The two never forgot that comfort in a difficult time, nor would he. Jefferson had never adequately expressed his gratitude to Abigail for that and her intelligent friendship when he came to London to collect the girls, and it was too late now. The estrangement that began in the early days of George Washington's Presidency had widened.

Jefferson and the Adamses, warm old friends in historic times, had not had a private chat in more than a decade.

The "Duchess of Braintree," as the republicans liked to call her, had come to the capital to represent her family at an Independence Day celebration. Her husband, whom Jefferson had bade a strained farewell the year before when he first entered this house, did not accompany her.

The President welcomed her in his writing room. As soon as the lady was seated, she heard a chirping coming from the corner and said, in the bright and forthright way he had always admired, "What in the world is that?"

"That's my mockingbird," Jefferson told her, indicating a large cage in the corner. "It keeps me company here. Its name is Dick."

She gave the bird a curious look, made the proper inquiries about Jefferson's daughters, and reported the good health of her husband John. He was now carrying on extensive correspondence with a variety of friends from their home in Massachusetts, but Jefferson had not received any communication from him and was not inclined to initiate any. Their parting, after the acrimonious election and the midnight judges, had been too painful.

"One act of Mr. Adams's life, and one only, ever gave me a moment's displeasure," he told her regretfully, taking the offensive lest she bring up his dismissal of John Quincy Adams, their son, from a political post in Boston. "I did think his last appointments to office personally unkind."

After Jefferson's election by the House, and just before he was sworn in as President, Adams had surprised and dismayed the incoming republicans with the appointment of judges that threatened to bedevil the government for decades. That provided sinecures for a host of Federalists, many of whom would now oppose Jefferson from the Judiciary. Worst of all was the new Chief Justice of the United States—his longtime rival in Virginia, the Federalist John Marshall—who connived with Adams by candlelight to pack the Federal courts. According to Jones at the *Richmond Examiner*, "General Barbecue"—his sobriquet for the socially active Marshall—had been seen at the offices of Callender's *Recorder*, hatching a conspiracy to vilify Jefferson. The President hoped that was just another falsehood generated in that fierce newspaper war, but he did not trust Marshall.

"Those appointments," he told her, "made at the last minute, were from my most ardent political enemies."

"This was done by President Washington equally," she replied levelly, "in the last days of his Administration so that not an office remained vacant for his successor to fill. No personal unkindness was intended. Mr. Adams had no idea of the intolerance of party spirit at the time he left office."

That last was surely untrue; party spirit was intolerant of Adams even within the Federalist ranks. But Jefferson remained silent, suspecting what brought her to him.

"I have never felt any enmity towards you, sir," she said, "for being elected President of the United States. I considered your pretensions much superior to Colonel Burr's, to whom an equal vote was given."

"I am glad to hear that, madam."

"But the instruments you made use of, and the means by which you brought about the change of administrations, have my utter abhorrence and detestation. For they were the blackest calumnies and the foulest falsehoods."

The woman never minced words, he had to admit. "Perhaps there are certain facts," Jefferson said mildly, "that have not been presented to you under their true aspect."

She paid no attention to that. "And now, sir, I will freely disclose to you what has severed the bonds of our former friendship."

He sighed and nodded for her to go on.

"One of the first acts of your Administration was to liberate a wretch who was suffering the just punishment of the law."

She meant Callender, of course. He dreaded hearing more of this.

"This person had committed crimes of writing and publishing the basest libel, the lowest and vilest slander, which malice could invent against the character of your predecessor."

"I didn't 'liberate' Callender; he had already served his sentence," the President pointed out. "And I discharged every person under punishment under the Sedition Law, because I considered that law to be a nullity, as absolute and as palpable as if Congress had ordered us to fall down and worship a golden image."

"The power that makes a law is alone competent to its repeal. If a Chief Magistrate can by his will annul a law, where is the difference between a republican and a despotic government?"

He was unaccustomed to such direct argument. If the President did not have the power to challenge the constitutionality of an act of Congress, who held that power? The President took an oath to protect the Constitution, and no power of any branch of government could be unchecked. "I tolerate with the utmost latitude the right of others to differ from me in opinion without imputing to them criminality." He swung back to the main subject in the newspapers that caused his personal embarrassment. "I realize that my charities to Callender are considered as rewards for his calumnies, but—"

"The remission of Callender's fine was your public approbation of his conduct," she said, driving home her point about the pardon and remission. If she only knew the trouble that $200 owed to that rascal had caused him, and the time it took from himself and the Secretary of State and the Governor of Virginia when they all had more important matters to attend to.

"If you, as Chief Magistrate of the nation," she pressed, "give countenance to a base calumniator, are you not answerable for the baleful influence that your example has upon the manners and morals of the community?"

"As early, I think, as 1796, I was told in Philadelphia that Callender was in the city, a fugitive from persecution and in distress," he explained wearily. After Callender revealed his financial support from Jefferson in his *Recorder* a few months before, the tale had been explored at great length in the nation's newspapers. As Jefferson had remained silent, the agitation was worsened by his friends' denials of letters from Jefferson—which the rascal then unexpectedly produced and spread before the public. Callender entrapped them all. "I had read and approved his book. I considered him as a man of genius, unjustly persecuted in Scotland. I knew nothing of his private character and expressed my willingness to contribute to his relief and to serve him." Lest she catch him out in an incomplete explanation, he added, "I afterward repeated the contribution."

"Until I read Callender's seventh letter," she persevered, "containing your compliment to him as a writer, and your reward of fifty dollars, I could not believe that you resorted to such measures." He blanched; were there seven letters? He had lost track. "This, sir, I considered as a personal injury."

The President felt small and tired. Did John Adams have to put up with this every day? "When he first began to write," he assured her, "Callender told some useful truths in his coarse way. But nobody sooner disapproved of his writing than I did, or wished more that he would be silent." Monroe had warned him about making such a disavowal, as it was unlikely to be considered credible. But that was Jefferson's version of the facts, and he had repeated it often enough to come to believe it. "My charities to Callender were no more meant as encouragements to his scurrilities than those I give to the beggar at my door are meant as rewards for the vices of his life."

She swept that argument aside with a wave of her gloved hand. "And now he has published the letters from you. The serpent you cherished and warmed bit the hand that nourished it." She leaned forward and tapped her finger on his desk. "In no country has calumny and falsehood stalked abroad more licentiously than in this. No political character is secure from its attacks. No reputation is so fair as not to be wounded by it—until truth and falsehood lie together in one undistinguished heap."

Enough. "I was as far as stooping to any approbation of the falsehoods that writers published against Mr. Adams as he was respecting those of Porcupine," the President told her. "Cobbett published volumes against me for every sentence vended by Callender against Mr. Adams." Many republicans were certain that Cobbett's *Porcupine's Gazette* was a favored outlet of the Federalist government. Jefferson made his next charge subtly, through indirection, that a mind like Abigail Adams's would surely grasp. "But I never supposed Mr. Adams had any participation in the atrocities of that editor."

"How can you even equate your financial support of Callender with—"

"I never supposed that any person who knew either of us could believe that either of us meddled in that dirty work." That placed both Adams and Jefferson in the same boat, equally innocent of the slander uttered by their champions in the press.

"You do Mr. Adams justice in believing him incapable of such conduct." She emphasized the "him," skewering Jefferson with what she left unsaid.

"My motives for contributing to the relief of Callender might have been to protect, reward and encourage slander," he told her slowly, so that she would remember his words and transmit them back to the former President. "But they may also have been those which inspire ordinary charities to those in distress. And my motive for liberating sufferers under the Sedition Law may have been from the obligation of an oath to protect the Constitution, violated by an unauthorized act of Congress. Which of these were my motives must be decided by a regard to the general tenor of my life—and not on the testimony of Porcupine."

Abigail Adams rose. "There is one other act of your Administration that

I take as personally unkind, but I forbear to say it." That, he knew, was the dismissal of her son John Quincy, but Jefferson was not about to change his mind and in any way advance the arrogant young Federalist's career. "I bear you no malice. I cherish no enmity. I will not, sir, intrude any further upon your time."

That was fortunate, as the band had struck up again and made conversation difficult. The indomitable lady stopped before the birdcage on the way out and said, "And goodbye to you, Dick." The startled mockingbird remained silent.

Chapter 36

August 1, 1802

RICHMOND

"*I* brought you a cafe of the fineſt Jamaican rum," said John Beckley, standing in the doorway with his arms full, breathing heavily from the climb up the stairs. The printing shop was closed on a Saturday afternoon, but one of the burly devils told him the editor of the *Recorder* could be found in his room above.

Behind the startled Callender he could see a comely woman. This did not surprise him because Madison had said that the reason Callender was so driven to seek money and a respectable position was that he was in love. Presumably, this was his affection's object, wearing a light dress with bare arms on a hot day. Beckley judged her a more attractive woman than he ever thought his old political ally would be able to win, but Callender now had more to offer than a soulful poet's eyes; he had become a successful editor at last.

"This is my friend, Mary Clement," he said, introducing him as "John Beckley, the man who made Jefferson President." She went to the cupboard, brought two glasses to the table and the men sampled the gift. "I'm glad you wrapped these in the Northern newspapers. The new postmaster here holds up my deliveries."

Beckley did not miss that reference to the political appointment that Callender thought he deserved. "I get all the papers in Washington," he hurried on, "in my new job."

"I heard it was your old job, Clerk of the House," Callender said, gathering up some sheets of paper with his crabbed writing on them and laying them aside. "I was disappointed for you. After all that work for Jefferson, carrying Pennsylvania for him twice, you deserved a greater share of the spoils than that make-work for Governor McKean."

True enough; but because Beckley had earned the hatred of the Federalists, Albert Gallatin, the Treasury Secretary who dealt out the patronage, had been reluctant to give him anything at all. After eighteen difficult months passed, republican House members took pity on him and let him have his old job back. Beckley tried to make light of it: "I was a factionalist, all right, and you know what the President says about the baneful effect of party spirit. Can't blame him. Protecting the Federalist officeholders was part of the deal Gallatin made with Bayard to stop Burr."

"Didn't Jefferson swear he made no deals?"

"He didn't make it; Gallatin did. And I suppose it's best to cool all the old passions. But James, you're worrying our friends. They say you're a renegade, an apostate."

"That's not all my former friends say." Callender picked up a local paper and began to read aloud with great amusement. " 'The damning facts of your ingratitude, cowardice, lies'—this is Jones in the *Examiner*—'venality and constitutional malignancy, Callender, glare you in the face with the petrifying lividness of an imp of the infernal regions.' Imagine, John—me, God-fearing Calvinist that you know me to be, pictured as a demon right out of Hell. Poor Jones—not even his African mistress will talk to him any more."

That was one of the matters Beckley had been told by Monroe to prevail on Callender to stop stirring up. "Your interest in the mingling of the races doesn't become you, Jimmy. It's been going on for generations, and has nothing to do with politicks."

"It has everything to do with gambling, prostitution, miscegenation and a general moral decline." At Beckley's jaundiced look, Callender added a practical reason: "See what my exposure has done to Jones? I already have half his readers, and when he is forced to close down, I'll get most of the rest."

Beckley decided not to pursue the racial argument. If the Scot thought a moral crusade would sell his newspaper, so be it; Beckley's primary task was to dissuade him from harping on the political duplicity of Jefferson and Monroe. "I thought *Examiner* readers were republicans," he said. "Do they want to read your attacks on other republicans?"

Callender replied in the voice of a professional newsmonger. "Although they are republicans, *Examiner* readers will turn to a newspaper that brings them excitement. Revelations, like the news of Jefferson secretly supporting me when I was calling George Washington a debaucher of the republic."

Beckley knocked back his rum and poured himself another, noting that Callender was sipping slowly. Evidently, the tall woman with the long brunette hair and bare arms had a moderating influence on his old conviviality. "That's what I came to talk to you about, James." This was not going to be easy; McKean and Monroe did not understand the long-smoldering resentment in this man. "It's getting out of hand. I can understand your irritation, nine months in jail and all, and nothing to show for it, but remember your principles. You may not be happy with everything that people on your side do, but James—we are on the same side."

" 'We are all Federalists, we are all Republicans,' you mean?"

Beckley sensed the weakness in his argument, considering the way his own loyalty had gone unrewarded, but that made him press harder. "You don't want to besmirch the political reputations of those who believe in the same things about the rights of man as you. You don't want to stop us from picking up thirty of the new seats in the House this fall. For God's sake, you don't want to help the damned Federalists come back and create a monarchy."

"Be calm, Calm Observer," Callender said, recalling the pen name Beckley once used. "Both parties require a great deal of watching. There is not a prodigious difference between the moral characters of the one and the other."

"Be sensible, James. You're getting us all into a lot of trouble."

"I'm making a decent living for the first time in my life. In six months I should have enough to afford a place big enough to put up my boys, and the money to feed and clothe them. And I'm making a difference again, the way I did when I brought Hamilton down, thanks to you."

Wincing at that last note of gratitude, Beckley handed over a newspaper. "I want to show you what Hamilton's editor, Coleman, is writing in his *New York Evening Post*. See? He republished all your articles accusing Jefferson of being your secret backer. And Coleman says that it was Jefferson who incited you to expose Hamilton and Reynolds, which turned the public against Hamilton and cleared Jefferson's path to the presidency."

"I don't know if this fellow Coleman will be a good editor," said Callender, "but he sure is an accurate historian."

Beckley exploded. "Damn it, Callender, don't be such a fool! Don't you see the damage you're doing? Don't you realize that if public sentiment shifts back to the Federalists, and they win, you'll be back in jail for the rest of your natural life? Jesus!" He took out a bandanna and mopped his face. "Excuse my language, madam. I cannot bear to see my friend here become a tool in the hands of our enemies. Believe me, Alexander Hamilton will stop at nothing." At her sympathetic nod, he went on: "When he's not stirring up mischief between Jefferson and Vice President Burr, Hamilton's quoting James Callender. Never thought that day would come. Maybe he's getting old. I hear he wears spectacles now."

Callender casually handed the *Post* over to his woman friend to read and said, "You have nothing to fear, John. I'll never tell who gave me those documents six long years ago. That would truly go against my principles."

Beckley seized on the offer. "I have your word on that, then? If they ever did tie me to you, I'd never get a job in the government. It would look like a payment to me for helping you do in Hamilton."

"It would, that," the editor agreed.

" And I have my eye on a new position that Harper—he's now on our side, you know—created just before he left Philadelphia. Librarian for the Congress. It pays only two dollars a day, but I could do it in my spare time. They don't have many books."

"You have my word," Callender assured him, "which has been good for all these years. Do you bring any more documents with you? I've shown you I can keep a secret about my source."

"No. I'm here as your friend, to call you back from the brink of destruction. There are men out there just as passionate as you, just as filled with vengeance as you, who can write and do terrible things."

"Gallatin? Or that gentleman dandy at the *National Intelligencer,* who was nowhere to be found in the years we were the Outs, who's now getting all the government's printing business?"

"No, no, nobody close to Jefferson. I mean the fury of some of your own émigrés, the wild Irishmen and English who came from the old country and believe in what Paine wrote and took up the fight for the rights of man. Duane in particular at the *Aurora*. They're furious with you, more than Porcupine ever was."

"I see you've rid America of Cobbett."

Beckley nodded. "Governor McKean promised Judge Shippen he'd make him Chief Judge of the State if he'd ruin Cobbett with the biggest libel judgment ever. He did, and now he's Chief Judge, and Cobbett is back in England where he belongs." Beckley had a hand in those judicial dealings and was proud of it, especially the way he assembled a republican jury. "But I want you to know this, James. Jefferson and Madison and Monroe dealt badly with you, I know that. But you got even with them. You've had your vengeance. Now the score is settled and that's enough."

Callender twisted around and looked at the woman. "You think that's enough, too, don't you, Mrs. Clement?"

"I have often pointed out the biblical injunction, 'Vengeance is mine, saith the Lord,' " she said to Beckley. "That it is not for mortal man to seek revenge."

"Listen to her, Jimmy, she's right." Beckley was glad to see that she was not merely a good-looking woman but a sensible, God-fearing person who might be a restraining influence on the suddenly powerful editor. "We've got no more control over what some of the newsmongers on our side write than we ever had control over you." He thought that was an especially strong point, not least because it was true; James had always gone his own way, usually too far, in Jefferson's cause. He never needed to be told what to write or who to attack, not even in prison. Now that Porcupine had been silenced, nobody in the press was as adept at inflaming the public as James Thomson Callender. That's the figure of speech Jefferson liked to use, too: "the flame of public opinion" needed to be lit by the incendiary newsmongers.

"You mustn't let this get out of hand," Beckley pressed. "When they react and lash out at you, as some of our old firebrands in the press are bound to do, just tell yourself you've already won and let that be an end to it. Don't blame Jefferson."

"If that's what the President of the United States sent you down here to tell me, my old friend, I've heard you. He ought to give you a better position for riding all the way down here and delivering this rum."

"Wasn't him sent me." That was true.

"Monroe, then, on his behalf."

Beckley chose silence.

"General Washington spoke of his 'hatchet men,' " Callender went on, "the Indian scouts who would cut a path through the thickest woods so Washington's troops could follow. Monroe is Jefferson's hatchet man."

Beckley upended his glass of rum, nodded to Callender's sensible companion who seemed absorbed in the *Evening Post,* and trotted down the porch steps to his horse. He would be able to report little or no progress with this quietly angry man. He hoped, for everyone's sake, that Callender's wrath, soon certain to be rekindled, would be somehow contained.

"Be sure my books are in your library," Callender called after him.

Maria was troubled by the surprise visit. Her anonymity was important to her. Callender's visitor from Washington had never seen her before and could not identify her as Maria Reynolds, but if he were to describe the woman in the editor's room to Monroe or someone else who had interviewed her, a suspicion might arise and her identity might no longer be secret.

Callender kept unwrapping the bottles of rum. She was pleased to see he was not interested in the liquor but in the wrapping, glancing quickly over the latest newspapers, tearing out items of interest, passing the remainder of the papers on to Maria when he was finished.

"Why didn't they reward Beckley, James?"

"John grew up in Virginia and the gentry let him be Mayor of Richmond, which gave him pretensions of aristocracy. But he came over to America as an indentured servant when he was a boy, and no matter how he puts on airs, the gentry will never let him into their set. They use him but they wash their hands afterwards."

She took up the open rum bottle and screwed in the cork. "Hamilton came here from the Indies," she said. "He never knew his father, an itinerant ne'er-do-well, and they tell mean stories about the morals of his mother. And yet he's considered an aristocrat."

"He's handsome. He is a brilliant orator. He carries himself like a gentleman. And Hamilton's a rich lawyer now, or at least he lives as if he's rich, and he looks down on other aristocrats, which intimidates them. Even so, everybody knows Adams called him 'the bastard son of a Scotch pedlar.' It sticks."

She returned to the new newspaper and pretended to read the *Evening Post*. It gave her the chance to ruminate privately about something Beckley said about Hamilton wearing spectacles. They were all getting older.

Maria remembered Colonel Hamilton's boy, Philip, and his sister, Angelica. They played in a grassy commons in New York City near Hamilton's home, not far from the cramped quarters James Reynolds provided for his new family. The Hamilton children were about six and five years old when her daughter Susan was an infant. Maria's handsome husband was doing some financial work for the Colonel and had introduced her to Hamilton one day in the park with all the children. She spent the mornings there regularly; the Colonel took to accompanying a servant on walks to the commons with Philip and Angelica.

She was then not yet seventeen and was desperately unhappy. She loved James Reynolds and had broken with her family when they refused to countenance him, but after financial mishaps he had taken to drink and then to beating her. She remembered how the handsome young Hamilton, though a great and famous man, took a sincere interest in her welfare. That led to a meeting without the children and a dinner in a fine tavern with rooms upstairs. He seduced her. Maria felt that was a fair statement of what had taken place, though she may have shown an interest that he interpreted as encouragement. She recalled clinging to him for what seemed like hours afterwards, in her shame at becoming an adulteress. He was a lover as she had never known, his mood flickering from fierceness—when he discovered bruises inflicted on her body by Reynolds—to tenderness, when he said she reminded him of his lonely and courageous mother in Jamaica.

During those enchanted few months together, another politician accosted Maria who seemed to have some reason to suspect she was seeing Hamilton. That was Colonel Burr, whose agents sometimes followed Hamilton. She knew that he, too, sought her affections, and she rebuffed his advances until Burr told her the terrible truth about Hamilton and her husband. Burr told her the equally terrible truth that Reynolds knew full well that his wife was secretly seeing the powerful financier but did nothing to stop it; indeed, he was using the fact of their sinful relations to extract concessions from Hamilton in various financial deals. It was not overt blackmail, Burr explained to her, but merely a case of taking advantage of a man who was taking other advantage of him. Maria, learning the ways of that world, said nothing to either her husband or her lover, but began to see Burr regularly as well. Reynolds stopped beating her; Hamilton gave her money; Burr promised nothing but offered a genuine friendship.

Her involvement with three quite different men at the same time ended when President Washington called Hamilton to serve him as Treasury Secretary in Philadelphia. In parting, Hamilton told her he knew of her acquaintance with Burr and warned her that he was both a trimmer and a voluptuary. She dared to disagree, and was glad now that she had; Hamilton had no right to be angry that the woman he lured into adultery would engage in that sin with a political rival.

Reynolds, within weeks of Hamilton's departure from New York, promptly abandoned her and their child and followed the new Treasury Secretary to Philadelphia. Maria was grateful to this day that Burr, a widower, took care of her and Susan in New York when her family turned them away. But she missed Reynolds, and forgave the drunken beatings as the result of his financial defeats and melancholy. When she heard that the father of her child was becoming wealthy, she decided to move to the nation's capital and find him. That was a great mistake; he had fallen in with a fallen woman and a gang of thieving financiers.

That was when she paid a visit to Hamilton's home on the sunny afternoon that changed her life again. She had really only wanted enough money to return to New York with Susan and pick up the remnants of her life there. She knew that Hamilton's wife was at home and assumed he had money in his house. He had no need to arrange to see her later. But then when he bounded up the stairs, they could not stop themselves.

She had trusted him to help her, and presumed he would have, for years. But then his true beloved—not his mistress or his wife, but his cherished financial integrity—was challenged, and he chose to use Maria as a human shield. At their final meeting, Hamilton tried to explain that only because he was a patriot had he been forced to concoct the story that she and her husband were blackmailing him. To reassure the new nation's public that its Treasury was above reproach, Hamilton had been willing to embarrass himself to his political rivals—never thinking they would use it to ruin his future. He had been certain none of it would come out. He persuaded her that he concocted the tale of blackmail because he assumed Monroe and Muhlenberg were gentlemen of honor and would never reveal a sordid affair that would embarrass a man's family. He had sacrificed his moral reputation with two presumably discreet men to save the financial reputation of the nation. He told her he had never meant to shame his wife or publicly blacken Maria's name.

That was all very logical and understandable, but the result was precisely what he had not intended. Thanks to the equally intense, less good-looking, usually impoverished, vengeance-driven man whose affections she now shared—and to today's visitor who brought the rum and the warning—Hamilton's false story had been forced out. As a result, Hamilton felt the need to bolster it with forged letters, and Maria Reynolds was now the best-known blackmailing whore in these United States.

She looked over at the writer who was both her exposer and defender. Callender was avidly consuming the papers in which the bottles had been wrapped. Maria was surprised at the way she had come to have a genuine affection for the brilliant and vulnerable Scot. Thanks to her, he had cut down his drinking and reduced his level of hatred for the world, and she prided herself on that visible improvement. He was more like a son to her than a lover—nobody matched Burr, not even Hamilton—but he could satisfy her, and she enjoyed the way he worshipped her. But when James Thomson Callender found some inviting target in his sights, and became consumed with the need to bring down the reputation of the high and mighty, his passion transformed him, if just for a few hours, into the man of power that she had come to dread.

Though she feared its consequences, Maria Lewis Reynolds Clingman Clement took pleasure in the rejuvenation of the man she had met as a suspicious reporter and came to know was a frightened and lonely newsmonger. Thanks to the additional money he took home from his much-talked-about *Recorder*, he would soon be able to afford the rental of a house with rooms for his sons. As a woman forced to hide her daughter in a seminary to protect her, she felt a deep void in her life; his boys would need a mother.

Callender broke her reverie by shaking the paper in his hand. "Maria, listen to this. From last month's *Port Folio*, a Federalist literary sheet in Philadelphia. It's a ballad, in Negro dialect, unsigned, sung by a black named 'Quashee.' Starts out with 'Massa Jefferson' saying all men are born free, and then a few verses down, it says:

> "For make all like, let blackee hab
> De white womans . . . dat be de track!
> Den Quashee de white wife will hab
> And massa Jefferson shall hab de black."

He dropped the paper. "Somebody's onto it."

"On to what?" She did not understand the dialect. "What does it mean, 'Jefferson shall hab de black'?"

"Somebody's onto a secret I've kept for years, ever since that black told it to me in jail, before Monroe hanged him." There was a glint in Callender's eyes that she did not admire. "I knew it when I went to see little Jemmy Madison for that postmastership, and I had to bite my lip to keep from warning him I'd use it."

"What story?"

He seemed on the verge of telling her, then drew back. "It's something I've wanted to hold until the next Presidential campaign. That miserable Marshal Randolph, who wouldn't give me back my two-hundred-dollar fine, first let it slip to one of my friends. I'm not sure of all the details yet, but I've been picking them up little by little. Nobody will believe it—not even you, Maria—unless I have the details."

She knew better than to press for an answer. He would tell her in due course, when he needed to confide in someone, and when he trusted her completely. Perhaps she would pass it on to Burr in advance. When Callender strode out of the house to walk off his worry, she picked up the *Port Folio* and read it again:

> Den Quashee de white wife will hab
> And massa Jefferson shall hab de black.

William Safire

Chapter 37

August 15, 1802

RICHMOND

*C*allender had firſt heard rumors *of* laſcivious goings-on at Monticello from the condemned black in the Richmond jail. Years before, he had seen a hint of the white fathering of slaves in Jefferson's house in *Rind's Federalist*. At the time, as the foremost expositor of republican thought, Callender had been infuriated at the depths to which the Tory hirelings in the press would sink in the attempts to vilify the republican leader. In the Richmond jail, he at first had dismissed what he heard from the doomed slave. The editor had thought it likely that the talk of the off-spring of sexual debauches at the Jefferson plantation was directed at Peter Carr, Jefferson's nephew who lived at Monticello. He was a habitué of the black dances, along with the excitable lawyer George Hay.

But one night at the City Tavern, Callender had a few drinks too many with General Henry Lee, the former Virginia Governor, who let slip some high-gentry gossip about "Dusky Sally," one of Jefferson's slaves, and her white son Tom. The editor knew that Lee's reputation had fallen far down from the gallant "Light-Horse Harry," eulogizer of Washington as "first in war, first in peace" and the rest of it. The former Revolutionary cavalry leader was in financial trouble on some land speculation and loudly blamed Jefferson and Monroe for failing to help him in his hour of need.

In his cups that night, the embittered Lee spilled a detailed confirmation of the black rebel's story to Callender. Though he had to match his companion glass for glass and became tipsy himself, he remembered enough to add the substance of names to his bits and pieces of gossip about miscegenation. Not for immediate use, of course, with Jefferson's popularity on the rise in mid-term, the result of his muddying of differences and carrying out his deal with Bayard to protect Federalist officeholders. But it was wise to accumulate ammunition for exploding a good scandal in 1804, when Jefferson would be standing for re-election.

In his *Recorder* office above Pace's print shop, the Scot worried about someone else getting the juicy details about Jefferson's black offspring and publishing the information prematurely. The trick was to hit with a charge,

[*328*]

built around some kernel of truth—and especially a charge that could not be readily disproved—in the heated final months of a political campaign. He also wanted the accuser of Jefferson to be not some literary Federalist editor who might panic and retract at the first heated denial or visit from an angry advertiser. He wanted the accuser to be James Thomson Callender, the sedition-scarred editor whose previous revelations had been at first denied and then shown to be accurate. Callender's new charge, he was sure, would soon be reprinted by Federalist newspapers around the country, and then given greater currency by the furious denials in the republican press.

Were the reports of mixing blood true? He had no way of knowing. Nor was he so impetuous as to go to the neighborhood of Monticello himself, where Carr and his highborn fellow ruffians would probably thrash him. He had to wonder: What about the literary set in Philadelphia who published the verse in the *Port Folio?* Whoever wrote that doggerel had picked up the Virginia gossip about Jefferson having a black "wife," but Callender assumed the dialect poet had only a suspicion. And nobody, not even he, would have the gall to inflict such a libel on the President of the United States unless at least a few undeniable details were available to make the charge credible.

He decided to let the hint in the *Port Folio* pass and hope it would not be taken up by anybody else. For the next year or so, he would keep his ears open, watch for any sales of slaves from Monticello, make acquaintance with other gentry in the area. Light-Horse Harry Lee, who despised Jefferson, was an entry point. Callender would pick up bits of the string of gossip and tie them together until they could be rolled into a large ball. Besides, it would not do to mar the homecoming of his four young sons with the explosion of a controversy. He would, as his Scottish mother used to say, "possess his soul in patience."

That resolution lasted until the courier came into the office that day with a copy of Duane's *Aurora.*

He looked at the masthead of the Philadelphia newspaper that had once employed him: *"Aurora General Advertiser,* published (daily) by William Duane, successor of Benjamin Franklin Bache, Eight Dollars per Annum, Wednesday, August 25, 1802." Eight dollars for a daily; Callender's *Recorder* charged about the same, two dollars a year for twice a week, and his circulation was now over a thousand. But where the *Recorder* could boast commercial support, the *Aurora* was thin. Duane surely was pleading for government advertisements; Callender was sure the *Aurora* editor had expected much more support than a three-inch notice from Tench Coxe, U.S. supervisor for Pennsylvania, warning drivers of carriages to pay the tax on their vehicles on pain of penalties. He smiled at the advertisement for "A striking likeness of Thomas Jefferson, President of the U. States, on a Silver Medallion." Every good republican home should have one.

He turned the page and his eye caught his own name. Smiling, he sat back to read Duane's "Letter IV to J. T. Callender." He and his former friend had been exchanging diatribes in print, enlivening both publications and delighting the Scot, whose barbs were envenomed with embarrassing facts. Duane was on the defensive, vainly trying to explain Callender's accusations of support by Jefferson of his years of vilification of Washington and Adams. "There is nothing to be found in your paper concerning me," wrote his rival up North, "but such scurrilous ribaldry as you have applied to every man who has chanced to fall in your way. You are found uniformly at war with your species, hateful to yourself, and impious even to your Creator."

That was typical of Duane, sounding off with no facts to entice the reader. At the next paragraph, however, Callender sat up.

"A case occurs to me of a person caught in the act of stealing mahogany," wrote Duane. "You know the person."

The person, of course, was Callender. When he left Philadelphia for Virginia, having entrusted his children to Leiper and paid his final rent, he had been accused falsely by his landlord of taking some mahogany furniture. "He who detected the theft conceived it to be his duty to send the culprit to saw marble in prison," went the *Aurora* charge, "for which his muscular frame was better calculated than for a life of laziness and intemperance."

Duane regularly accused Callender of drinking too much, just as Porcupine used to concentrate on imaginary fleas. This annoyed but did not seriously bother the Scot, and the charge of stealing the furniture amounted to little. He rather liked the "muscular frame" reference. "But the man who caught the robber Callender was a republican, and the robber had attached himself to that party, and the honest man hesitated."

The next paragraph pulled Callender out of his seat. "He found that the poor wretch Callendar had a wife at that time overwhelmed by a created disease"—that meant a venereal disease—"on a loathsome bed, the disease given to her by her carousing, drunken husband." His jaw literally dropped. He could not believe anyone would make such an infamous, disgraceful charge, let alone print it.

"Their numerous children," Duane went on, "were all in a state next to famishing, actually existing on the private contributions of the charitable, while the wretch Callender himself took daily for his morning beverage a pint of brandy." He found it hard to comprehend the print before his eyes. "Pity for such a combination of wretchedness and vice," Duane concluded, "and the discretion of a political partizan, suffered the thief of mahogany to escape."

Callender flung the paper against the wall and howled in rage. "He lies! He lies!" He felt himself choking and felt pain in his chest.

He raced downstairs and cried to Henry Pace, his partner: "My dear wife died of the yellow fever. Dr. James Reynolds, Rush's man, knows that. To say that I befouled her bed with a loathsome disease, and watched her die in filth—how can, how can—" He could not finish the sentence. "I'll get those blackguards—"

Pace sat him down lest he have a seizure, flung open the window and told him to take deep breaths of air. He tried, but a wave of nausea overcame him and he vomited out the window, then slumped to the office floor. His partner lifted him into a chair, murmuring silly soothing like "It's too outrageous to be taken seriously" and "Nobody reads the Saturday *Aurora.*"

As soon as he could speak, Callender said, "That's why that bastard Beckley came down here. They sent him to warn me that Duane would do this if I didn't mend my ways. They wanted me to think it was all Duane's idea, but that's a lie—he just writes what they tell him. Thomas Jefferson and his lickspittle Jemmy did this." The vision of his faithful, loving wife, dying a lingering death in his arms, overpowered him, and he began to sob. That people should remember her as infected by him with the disease God sent to punish sexual sinners was too much to take.

Soon after he regained his breath, their apprentice arrived from his daily run to the post office. Henry Pace took the mail and found a letter in it that he hesitated to hand to Callender. "It's from Thomas Leiper in Philadelphia, James. I'll open it."

Callender heard him say, "Oh, my God," and then "this had better wait until tomorrow."

"Read it," Callender said dully.

"He writes, 'Your children have read with great dismay and horror the article about your terrible misdeed that resulted in the shameful death of their mother.

" 'They have decided, and I cannot blame them, not to move to Richmond to live with you. The years may assuage their anger, but I advise you not to communicate with them now by letter or in your scurrilous sheet.' The scum. He finishes, 'I acknowledge receipt of your 100 dollars for past board, and am required to raise the rate to 125 for the coming year, as their appetites increase with age.' "

Benumbed, he took the letter from his partner's hand and stared at its words. Leiper, the Jefferson ally, would make certain that the minds of his children were poisoned by the lies of republican editors assigned to vilify their father. "They've stolen my boys," Callender said.

"What will you do?"

"I need to talk to Maria first."

She cradled him in her arms as, for the first time since she had known him, he cried. After a bit, he stopped and sat bolt upright. "I'll write to the doctor who treated her," he said. "I'll prove it a lie."

"Do you have his address?"

"No, no, I won't write him a letter; he'd ignore it. He's a Rush acolyte, a Jefferson appointee to some medical board. God, Porcupine was right about the damned bleeders. I'll write him a letter he can't ignore. Maybe somebody will show it to my boys."

"What's his name?"

"Dr. James Reynolds."

"Not—"

"No, no, a well-known republican doctor, one of Benjamin Rush's men." It was a coincidence that he had the same name as Maria's husband. He had never thought of it as an evil omen.

"Dr. James Reynolds, Philadelphia

"Sir,

"In the summer of 1798, you attended my family in Philadelphia, as a physician. I entreat you to mention in a letter to me whether you perceived, in any person there, symptoms of a complaint which it is hardly decent to name.

"I think myself entitled to demand, as an act of justice, that you will give your opinion on the case. I choose to address you through the medium of the press, in preference to a manuscript letter by post, because I have no confidential communication to make or solicit. On this subject, I am all open.

"The secrecy and delicacy which may be required from a professional man must give way to the request of his alleged patient. I invite, I welcome, I solicit the honest assertion of the truth in this case that the Supreme Being and your own conscience dictate.

"Your most obedient servant,

"James T. Callender."

"He'll surely answer that," Maria said. She had been with James when he was angry, but his face was twisted as she had not seen before.

"The doctor will never answer it. Rush won't let him."

"How can you be sure?"

"Because it will appear in the same issue of the *Recorder* that reveals the true nature of Thomas Jefferson."

"The President did not write what appeared in the *Aurora*, James." Jefferson never told Callender what to write, either, when the writer vilified Washington as a traitor and Adams as a hoary incendiary. She felt it was unfair to hold one man at the top responsible for every excess of his supporters.

"He sanctioned it," Callender said, eyes cold. "He had it in his power, with a single word, to have extinguished the volcanoes of reproach. But with that frigid indifference that forms the pride of his character, Jefferson stood neuter."

She silently stroked his hair, knowing better than to argue with him when he was in this state.

"To charge a man as a thief," he went on, "that causes him to pose as an adulterer, as I did Hamilton, is of itself bad enough. But when Jefferson, through his lackey Duane, charges me with an action that is much more execrable than an ordinary murder"—the bile rose in him and he choked it back—"then that is the time to wreak vengeance."

Vengeance is mine, saith the Lord, not yours, she said to herself but not to him. Nobody could stop this man, estranged from his boys by a lying scandalmonger, from wreaking vengeance of his own.

Chapter 38

Governor James Monroe was the firſt to receive his copy of the *Richmond Recorder.* He read it in horror.

"It is well known that the man, whom it delighteth the people to honor," wrote Callender in the edition of that morning, "keeps and for many years has kept, as his concubine, one of his slaves. Her name is Sally. The name of her eldest son is Tom. His features are said to bear a striking though sable resemblance to those of the President himself."

Miscegenation by the President, stated as bald fact. Was it true? Not necessarily. To Monroe's eye, Callender's phrase, "though sable," suggested the boy was brown; the Governor knew that Sally Hemings's eldest, like all her children, could easily pass for white. That meant Callender had never seen the slave he said the others called Young Tom. He read on:

"The boy is ten or twelve years of age. His mother went to France in the same vessel with Mr. Jefferson and his two daughters. The delicacy of this arrangement must strike every portion of common sensibility. What a sublime pattern for an American ambassador to place before the eyes of two young ladies!"

The Governor winced at the thought of Jefferson's daughters reading this today. Had the savage Callender no feeling for the children of the people he slandered? He knew that the writer had at least one of the details askew: the slave Sally had gone to France later, accompanying his younger daughter as her maid. But the account was uncomfortably close enough to the truth. He judged Callender's estimate of the boy's age to be off by a couple of years; Young Tom, if that was what they called the slave, was about fourteen. Monroe hoped Jefferson had not entered his birth in his property records. His neighbor, with his tidy sense of history, had a tendency to record everything.

"Some years ago, the story had once or twice been hinted at in *Rind's Federalist,*" wrote Callender. "At that time, we believed the surmise to be an absolute calumny." Monroe grunted; that was when Callender was on the republican side. "One reason for our thinking so was this: A vast body of people wished to debar Mr. Jefferson from the Presidency. The establishment of this single fact would have rendered his election impossible. We reasoned that if the allegation had been true, it was sure to be ascertained and advertised by his enemies in every corner of the continent. The suppression of so decisive an enquiry shows that the Federalist party's interest was overruled by Divine Providence.

"By this wench Sally," Callender's article continued, "our President has had several children. There is not an individual in the neighborhood of Charlottesville who does not believe the story, and not a few who know it."

Monroe had often stood with Jefferson at a window on the heights of Monticello looking across the fields and down at the town of Charlottesville. Did the people there whisper about intercourse between white and black on the plantations?

Monroe, who had never struck or caressed a slave, had heard such rumors—not only about Jefferson, but from Meriwether Jones, editor of the *Examiner,* about John Marshall, too—and had set them aside as idle gossip. But no such gossip had ever seen public print. What drove Callender, the damnable seditionist, to publish such a libel? Granted, he had to wait for his fine to be returned, but he ultimately got his $200 from the government, and never returned the $50 advance from Jefferson. And granted, Callender could say he had been half-promised the postmastership, but he was prospering now without it. What was eating at his v?

"If Duane sees this account," wrote Callender, "he will not prate any more." The Governor nodded; that must be it. William Duane in the *Aurora,* answering Callender's charges of support from Jefferson, had gone to the extreme of accusing his former colleague of killing his wife by infecting her with a venereal disease. Monroe had instructed Beckley to tell Duane to put a shot across Callender's bow, but had intended nothing so severe. Duane should have known better than to provoke a man like Callender into an unreasoning rage. He forced himself to read on:

"And do you know how all those republican printers of biographical information will be upon this point? Mute! Mute! Yes, very Mute! Behold the favorite, the firstborn of republicanism!" exclaimed Callender. "The pinnacle of all that is good and great! In the open consummation of an act that tends to subvert the policy, the happiness, and even the existence of this country!" Monroe shook his head; now the man was getting hysterical. " 'Tis supposed that, at the time when Mr. Jefferson wrote so smartly concerning Negroes, and when he endeavored so much to belittle the African race, he had no expectation that the Chief Magistrate of the United States was to be the ringleader in showing that his opinion was erroneous; or that he should choose an African flock whereupon he was to engraft his own descendants."

Today it was the talk of Richmond; in a few days, the gossip would be all over the country. Hamilton's *New York Evening Post* would spread its slander throughout that city, much as it had been a Northern sounding-board for Callender's claim that Jefferson paid for his repeated assaults in print on Washington and Adams. And the vicious Scot had made no attempt to conceal his political purpose: "We hear that our young Mulatto, the President's son, begins to give himself a great number of airs of importance in Charlottesville, and the neighborhood," he wrote. "Jefferson, we presume, cannot, and Madison shall not, if we can help it, be the next President. The republicans must make haste and look about them."

Monroe pursed his lips. If Jefferson became so disgusted at this calumny that he left public life, to whom would republicans turn? Madison would be Jefferson's choice, though he would be wiser to support Monroe. Albert Gallatin might find backing, but Virginians would not want the Chief Magistrate to be a Pennsylvanian and a foreigner. The most likely contender for Jefferson's mantle would be the Vice President, Aaron Burr. Monroe returned to reality: low gossip must not determine the course of America's history.

Prominently displayed on page 3, the page that most readers turned to first, was a poem in Negro dialect reprinted from the *Port Folio*. That a Philadelphia literary publication, with the gentry as its readership, hinted at the same rumor lent credence to the *Recorder*'s article.

This had to be dealt with. The Governor sent for George Hay, now a widower with an interest in Monroe's daughter Hortense, to direct him to find the mulatto "Young Tom." If such a slave existed, Hay was to spirit him northward, essentially freeing him but not with any damning documentation of birth. Jefferson would probably object to the loss of a property worth several hundred dollars but Monroe would persuade him that it could not be avoided.

What if other slaves in Monticello were redheaded and bore a resemblance to the master? Monroe decided that Hay's bachelor companion, Peter Carr, was the natural choice to be designated as the progenitor: he was Jefferson's blood nephew, lived at Monticello, could be seen at all the "black dances" and was a notorious consort of beauteous black prostitutes. With such a philandering reputation, Carr could be assumed to have dallied with every comely quadroon on the estate.

Then Monroe sent for Meriwether Jones of the *Examiner.*

"Come forth thou hideous and fateful mortal," strained the editor of the rival newspaper to the editor of the *Recorder.* "Thou clot-hearted Scot. Thou art a thief."

Monroe ran his eye past Jones's empty fulminations down to the denial that would have the merit of plausibility. "That this servant woman has a child is true. But that it is Mr. Jefferson's or that the connection exists, which Callender mentions, is false. I call upon him for evidence."

That was a stupid suggestion. Callender was sure to take up the challenge. Monroe cursed all journalists, friend and foe alike. First Duane, instructed to assail Callender in the *Aurora* for simple thievery of fine mahogany furniture, plunges ahead into allegations of Callender's infecting his wife with sexual disease, sure to provoke the most salacious response. Now here was the *Examiner* calling for Callender to produce fresh evidence of Jefferson's black progeny. What if he could? That, Monroe knew, was a favorite trick of the Scot's—to hold back information until the story was denied, or until he was challenged, and then to launch a fresh attack in response, offering new slander with pious regret, as if only to demonstrate his innocence.

"Is it strange that a servant of Mr. Jefferson's at a house where so many strangers resort," asked the defending editor, "who is daily engaged in the ordinary vocations of the family, like thousands of others, should have a mulatto child? Certainly not! Mr. Jefferson has been a Bachelor for more than twenty years. Not a spot tarnished his widowed character until this frightful sea calf Callender, in his wild frenzy, thought proper to throw his phlegm at him."

Monroe assumed Callender would not welcome the prospect of physical violence, unlike his former Federalist counterpart, the sturdy and combative Cobbett. Though his frame was hard and wiry, Callender had suffered at least one thrashing and had let it be known he was ready to flee from another. Monroe looked in the *Examiner* for the anticipated dire warning to Callender, which came at the end of Jones's overheated defense.

"Are you not afraid, Callender, that some avenging fire will consume your body as well as your soul? Stand aghast thou brute, thy deserts will yet o'ertake thee."

September 6, 1802

WASHINGTON, D.C.

"It's all that maniac Duane's fault," Beckley told Madison. "I knew it the minute I saw that diatribe of his about Callender killing his wife with a shameful disease. It's not true, you know—I spoke to the doctor in Philadelphia, and he said it was the yellow fever. He bled her and the treatment failed. I made certain he would not answer Callender's open letter demanding exoneration." That had been easy because the man was a protégé of Dr. Benjamin Rush and feared losing a prestigious appointment. "It was Duane's slander about the dead woman that set Callender off. I could have restrained him otherwise, but not after that."

The Secretary of State showed his concern about the effect of this incredible charge of fathering slaves on Jefferson's daughters, Maria and Patsy.

"It's awful," Beckley agreed. He said nothing about the effect of Duane's vengeance on Callender's sons because he did not want to appear to be giving the turncoat scoundrel a decent motive for his revenge. He assumed that Madison and Monroe had known for years about Jefferson's living arrangements. The President's wife died when he was not yet forty, and as the story went, on her deathbed he pledged not to remarry. Rather than burn, Beckley assumed, Jefferson kept his solemn promise and took as his bedmate the nubile fourteen-year-old maid of his youngest daughter.

Jefferson's choice of this particular female slave as his partner struck

Beckley as quite understandable. Sally Hemings, he knew from Monroe, was the offspring of Jefferson's wife's father, John Wayles, and one of his mulatto slaves. That made Sally the half-sister of Jefferson's wife, dead these twenty years. "Dusky Sally," as Callender was now calling her, was a quadroon, one-fourth Negro, her skin almost completely white; graceful and gentle, she closely resembled her half-sister. What could be more natural? Perhaps there was something in the Bible that would justify that.

Beckley had heard in Richmond that Sally was also "a good breedin' woman," productive of healthy children, which had to secretly please Jefferson, who enjoyed being surrounded by offspring. There was a practical aspect as well, known to every plantation owner who impregnated his household slave women: the brood was destined to become valuable property, worth nearly $400 a head when trained to household service. Some flippant poetaster in the *Boston Gazette* had written a lyric about this to the tune of "Yankee Doodle" that was now on too many children's lips. None of this, Beckley knew, could be admitted. Callender had to be personally discredited and his charges not only denied but denounced. But not by the President.

"I recommend that the President not dignify it with a denial," he told Madison.

"He won't. Long ago he told me he would never answer the calumnies of the newspapers, for while he should be answering one, twenty new ones would be invented." The angry denials and cries of "scurrility" were to come from the newly respectable republican press. "Where is Callender getting this?" Madison asked. "Is he making it up out of the whole cloth?"

Beckley assumed that Callender must have spoken to some of the highborn Virginians jealous of Jefferson, as well as some of the talkative dealers in slaves. He was also nearly certain that Madison, a frequent visitor to Monticello, was aware of his lifelong friend's living arrangements. Beckley passed along a counter-rumor: "Jones of the *Examiner* tells me that 'General Barbecue' has been seen at the office of the *Recorder* recently."

Madison frowned. "Isn't that the sobriquet of John Marshall?"

"Jones says there is some person behind the curtain who directs the operation of the *Recorder*," Beckley reported. "He means Chief Justice Marshall, as you know, who attends just about every barbecue and picnic in the State of Virginia." Beckley wished Madison would do more of that to maintain touch with the people. "Jones claims that the influence of this

'General of the barbecues' is connected to the influence of Hamilton in New York. The *Examiner* believes that Marshall has been furnishing Callender with matter for detraction, and joined wits with him to bring forth the information about Sally."

Madison shook his head and refused to believe it. Beckley didn't quite believe it either, but felt he had to give Madison some countervailing rumor to take to Jefferson. The Clerk of the House, who was also now styling himself "Librarian of Congress," drew out of his pouch a copy of the current *Examiner*. "At Governor Monroe's suggestion, Jones denounced Callender two weeks ago, but now I fear the attack grows feeble. You must remember that Callender excoriated his rival at the *Examiner* for having an African mistress, which explains this. It's a defense we could do without." He handed the Secretary of State the paper folded to the relevant page:

"That this servant woman Sally has a child is true," admitted Jones. "But in gentlemen's houses everywhere, we know that the virtue of unfortunate slaves is assailed with impunity. Having no defender, they yield most frequently. Is it strange therefore, that a servant of Mr. Jefferson's at a home where so many strangers resort, should have a mulatto child? Certainly not."

Madison read it and closed his eyes in pain. Beckley said he would suggest to Monroe that he have the *Examiner* drop entirely the subject of anyone's use of slave women at Monticello.

Chapter 39

Detail from 1807 etching

October 11, 1802

RICHMOND

*M*aria's long strides took her from Dr. Mathew's houſe to the offices of the *Richmond Recorder* in ten minutes. Before another installment appeared in the press, she wanted to see what Callender was writing about the scandal that had all the doctor's patients gossiping.

Delighted by her midweek visit to his office, Callender pushed toward her the pages filled with his tight scribbling. She read it all, standing.

"You cannot say this about her, James."

"The Negro whore? That she's called 'Luscious Sally'? Why on earth not?"

"First, because she is not called that. You just made that up."

Callender looked sheepish. "Poetic license. My uncle in Scotland was a poet."

"And second, why do you heap your hatred of Jefferson on her head? She's a slave, not, as you say here, 'a whore common as the pavement.' She's his property to use as he wishes. Sally has nothing to say about what he does with her."

"You don't understand." Callender began pacing about the room, wringing his hands and pulling at his knuckles. "I was rushed just before the first story about Sally, and I've been told by someone who knows that some of the details were wrong. Sally did not go to France in the same vessel with Jefferson. He sailed first, with his elder daughter. The younger Miss Jefferson went afterwards, in another vessel, with the black—all right, 'wench,' if you prefer—as her waiting maid. I'll have to straighten that out in the next *Recorder.*"

Maria nodded; "wench" would be better than "whore." But she wanted him to stick to that word, which he had already used in his first article, and to stay away from the word that had been applied so cruelly to her after Hamilton's Reynolds pamphlet. "Won't those mistakes cast doubt on everything you've written?"

"No. My corrections will show I have more information coming in by courier and by post and by packet, which is true, you know. One must be scrupulous about correcting errors; it drives them crazy. And the readers get the feeling they are learning new facts along with you. They don't expect me to be perfect, only honest with them."

"But why cast blame on the poor woman? He's the immoralist, not her." Maria did not feel comfortable discussing morality, sinning on Saturdays as she was with this man in Richmond, while secretly enamoured of the Vice President in Washington, and while still renowned throughout the land for an illicit affair with a great man now in New York.

He changed the subject. "Beckley says that Madison called the miscegenation story 'incredible,' " he said excitedly. "I'll use that as their weak defense. Shows how fair I am. And I'll also write that Harry Lee called my article a falsehood. Costs me nothing, and protects him. He's worried that he'll be blamed for being the one who told me."

She refused to let him ignore her point. "None of this is the slave's fault. She had no choice but to share his bed. If she did not submit to him, Jefferson could have her whipped." She thought of her first husband. "Or he could beat her himself. He has the absolute right as her owner to make black Sally do anything he wants."

"Talk about your 'rights of man.' I wonder what Thomas Paine thinks about his favorite American now." Maria kept looking directly at him and Callender reluctantly had to address her objection. "But don't you see? I have to give them something new. A description of Sally as 'luscious' is what the reader wants. And who knows, she may be as luscious as—"

She assumed he was about to say "as luscious as you" but wisely

changed his mind. Hard work around the doctor's house and in his garden
was keeping her figure slim and she could still wear the clothes Burr had
given her years ago.

"Sally can hardly be unattractive," he observed, appealing to her mother
wit. "Jefferson would not have her around all these years. I mustn't call her
'dusky Sally' any more, or the 'Sable goddess,' because that's a mistake—
I'm told she's not dark at all. But nobody can say she is not delectable, to
him at least."

" 'Luscious,' then. But not a 'whore common as the pavement,' as you
have here," she said, tapping his manuscript. "He's the villain in this, not
her." And she was not so sure about Jefferson's culpability, either; if the
man, twenty years a widower, wanted to bed the image of his long-dead
wife, what was so villainous about that? Especially if he treated the slave
well, and cared for their children, as she suspected Jefferson did. Sally was,
after all, the daughter of Jefferson's father-in-law; that gave her family
standing. Yet Maria was not ready to assume nobility in the man's character; Hamilton had told her about another episode long ago with a neighbor
named Betsey that reflected badly on the young Jefferson's moral judgment.

"Oh, Maria my love, it's a wondrous thing to see. All of Jefferson's
friends in Richmond set out with a sturdy denial of Sally's existence. They
had been in Albemarle County their whole lives. They said they never heard
a word of her. How then could Callender, that outsider, that fugitive from
faraway Scotland, get hold of the story?" He put on a Virginia gentleman's
pompous voice: "Depend upon it, sir, the whole thing must be a lie. It cannot possibly be true, a thing so brutal, so disgraceful! A thing so foreign to
Mr. Jefferson's character! That scoundrel Callender has been disappointed
and affronted, you know, and this is the slanderous way he seeks revenge."

She noticed that the wave of hatred that had passed through Callender
at the publication of Duane's sacrilege about his boys' mother had receded.
Getting his own back by striking hard at Jefferson with what he liked to call
"the hammer of truth" in print had tempered his mood; he was at home at
the center of controversy again.

"Jefferson's friends are still insisting your article is a lie," she reminded
him.

"Ah, but so much more carefully. And the great man himself, of course,
says nothing because a denial would give it even greater currency. Yet there

is another side to the coin of silence: many take his silence as confirmation that it is true."

That did not seem to Maria to be fair; in Callender's trap, Jefferson was damned if he denied, damned if he stood mute. She had been in a similar position herself in the Hamilton affair, unable to speak, relying on others to defend her. In that case, only "that scoundrel Callender," as they all called him, had tried to clear her name. Now here he was, America's leading calumniator.

"Jones in the *Examiner*," he went on, still pacing, "with his own black whore on his conscience—and that's what that one is, no doubt about it—is fairly crawling away from this subject. He cannot deny there is a Sally. Her five children are in the record of the census taker, and they live at Monticello. Visitors have seen the whole brood, with their light skin and Jefferson red hair." He paused in thought. "I need to get their ages, and see if Massa Jefferson was at home nine months before each of their births. That may be difficult, but it's worth it."

"Where are you getting your information? You've never been near Monticello or anywhere in Albemarle County."

"The trick, Maria m'love"—that was the second time he used that phrase lightly, but she noticed it, as she was sure he intended—"is to make yourself into a kind of magnet. That way you attract information, the way a magnet pulls in metal filings. Once you become known as the one with the courage to publish," he said, looking out the printing-office window at a great maple tree turning gold, "and you are called 'scandalmonger,' people who are angry or oppressed come to you. Or more often they send you anonymous letters in the post. A scandal feeds on itself. Look here—" He took a letter out of his pocket. "Remember how I reprinted that Negro poem from the *Port Folio*? It was signed 'Asmodio.' "

Maria had wondered about that. Usually, the writer who chose one of those mythical or historical names was giving a hint to his identity to those in the know. Hamilton did that all the time—Publius, Camillus—as did Burr.

"I can figure out every one of those ancient pseudonyms," said Callender, "but that one in *Port Folio* was a mystery to me. But here's a letter from a biblical scholar. It seems that the Hebrew word *asmodeus* in the Book of Job means 'destruction,' and in the legends of Solomon, Asmodio is the 'evil angel.' My correspondent says that in the Talmud, this evil spirit is represented as being in love with Sara, a beautiful woman who married seven times, and Asmodio killed each of her husbands on the wedding night."

Maria made a horrified face. "What is that supposed to mean?"

"The diminutive of Sara is Sally. And Asmodio, the writer of the ballad, is in a sense killing Sally's 'husband,' Jefferson, by exposing this miscegenation." He smiled in wonderment. "What this tells us is that the writer of the poem in *Port Folio* is an erudite person, probably a biblical scholar himself. Perhaps he's a preacher in Albemarle County furious at Jefferson for being an atheist, or a deist, or whatever he is. Or maybe our *Port Folio* poet is also the writer of this letter, which would explain it all." He examined the envelope for some evidence of its origin; there was none. "Damn," he said. "It makes a good story anyway."

"You should have been a teacher, James." Maria meant it; her vision of contentment was one of a home with this man and his boys, and Maria and Susan together in the early evenings, reading and explaining poetry and ancient history. That studious side of him was directly contrary to his chosen life as feared and hated scandalmonger. She imagined how much he missed being able to teach his boys what a famous poet's nephew had learned in his Scottish school and in his lifetime's reading.

Callender suddenly looked bleak at the thought of the life of scholarship and teaching that he never had. Then he shook off the shadow and plunged ahead. "You remember I told you about Jefferson's secretary, Captain Lewis, who passed me the fifty dollars and called it charity? The one who became all offended when I called it not charity but hush money? Well, Jefferson got Congress to appropriate twenty-five hundred dollars and sent him off with much fanfare to find the Pacific Ocean or something." He displayed another letter enclosing a cutting. "Here's a verse the *Boston Review* prints about this fellow Lewis, our new Columbus: 'Let dusky Sally henceforth bear / the name of Isabella; / And let the mountain, all of salt / Be christen'd Monticella.' "

He slapped her knee in delight. "And do you know the best part? This fellow says the anonymous writer of that doggerel is John Quincy Adams, the President's son, the young Federalist that Jefferson fired from his government post in Boston. Oh, delicious. I'll reprint that, too, though I mustn't say young Adams wrote it until I can be sure. You see? Even the reverberations of the article become part of the continuing saga, carrying it along." He spotted some children walking along the street. "Come quick, follow me." They hurried outside and Callender asked one of the boys, no more than ten: "Have you and your friends heard of Sally?"

The boy looked at his friends and giggled.

"You don't read the newspaper. You didn't learn about her there."

"From the song," the boy said. To the tune of "Yankee Doodle," and joined by the others, he sang:

> "When pressed by loads of state affairs
> I seek to sport and dally,
> The sweetest solace of my cares
> Is in the lap of Sally."

Callender clapped his hands and joined in the verse:

> "Yankee doodle, where's the noodle?
> What wife were so handy?
> To breed a flock, of slaves for stock,
> A blackamoore's the dandy!"

Maria stamped her foot and shut them up. She took James by the arm and marched back into the printer's shop. "You ought to be ashamed."

"I didn't teach it to them. It's all over, a dozen verses. You want to hear my favorite—"

"No. Ridiculing the President this way is dangerous."

He became subdued. "I suppose it is. But I'll bet my own boys are singing it now."

She worried about his safety. "You'll be careful, James?"

He seemed not to hear. "Our circulation is up to fifteen hundred, thanks to Luscious Sally, America's foremost—"

"Wench."

He scratched his head and suggested a compromise. "Slut?" She shook her head firmly and he shrugged and smiled. "Wench, then. A favorite word in Shakespeare's plays. No, wait. I can do better than 'wench.'" He wrote out a line with a flourish, and showed it to her. "Officiating as house-keeper at Monticello is THE AFRICAN VENUS."

Her disapproving look did not discourage him. As she strode off to go back to work, she could hear him humming "Yankee Doodle."

Scandalmonger

Chapter 40

Monroe guided his horse across his field of corn stubble to the neighboring plantation of Thomas Jefferson. He knew that Madison was already at Monticello for this meeting before the President and Secretary of State returned to Washington. There in the nation's capital they would learn the results of that fall's congressional elections.

One problem to be discussed was Napoleon Bonaparte. Monroe had reason to suspect that the ever-more-powerful Frenchman was making a secret arrangement with the weakening Spaniards to take over Spain's possessions in the Floridas and the vast Louisiana Territory. The jewel in this crown of retrocession was the port of New Orleans. That spelled danger for America.

Our Minister to Paris, Robert Livingston, was in the dark about this; he spoke no French, and even if he did, that would have done little good because he was deaf. His unhappy selection had been necessary; with it, Jefferson broke the influential Livingston family away from Burr in New York. But Napoleon was known to have dreams of world empire and the military genius to make them come true. He had already sent 20,000 troops to the island of Hispaniola and used a flag of truce to trick the leader of the slave revolt, Toussaint L'Ouverture, into surrendering. Once he gained New Orleans, Napoleon would control trade on the Mississippi River. He could then use his force, now based in the Indies—though reduced by yellow fever—to take over much of the New World.

Monroe's political sense told him that such a move by France's dictator would surely revive anti-French furor from the XYZ affair, wounding republicans here and giving the Federalist party new life. On top of that, a thrust by Napoleon would strike fear into the republicans in Kentucky and Tennessee, farmers and trappers dependent on the Mississippi River for their trade. The frontiersmen would then turn to Aaron Burr, long popular in the West with his notions of expansion southward through Mexico. Vice President Burr could then use his new frontier influence to counter the Livingston and Clinton interests in his native New York, and to join with Federalist New England to defeat Jefferson in the election of 1804. That presumed that Jefferson, who had to be heartsick at all this newspaper furor, would want to expose himself further by standing for re-election.

Another concern to Monroe was the growing spiritual movement that called itself "the second Great Awakening." This was a surge of religious enthusiasm among the more Calvinistic of the Congregationalists, along with the "gospel" Methodists and Baptists. They resented the secular deism of the Jeffersonians, and indeed suspected the President of being a secret atheist allied to the infamously irreligious Tom Paine. Monroe made a mental note to urge Jefferson to begin to be seen attending church regularly in Washington.

More immediately, there was the matter of Callender. His reports of payments to him by Jefferson to support the slashing attacks on Washington and Adams had stung; not even republicans believed the feeble answer that monies passed to the writer had only been charity to a starving artist. Then came Callender's sensational accusation of Jefferson's breeding of a mixed-race family. Seemingly overnight, "Luscious Sally" had become the most famous woman in America. Studiously ignoring the scandal—and the Governor had to admit to himself that "scandal" was not too strong a word—had not stopped its spread. Not with Callender's savagery being distributed by post to every anti-republican paper in the land, stimulating the caricature of "a philosophic cock" and an adoring black hen, inflaming his Calvinist cohort with its indictment of Virginia's hypocrisy about the rights of man and the rank immorality of its leading citizens.

The boy who took his horse as he arrived at Monticello was white enough to pass for white. One of Sally's? The Governor tried to put that thought out of his head. It could not be the one known as Young Tom, Sally's eldest, for Beckley had reported he was not at the plantation. Either he never existed or had been safely removed; Monroe did not want to know. But that was as far as Jefferson was willing to go in defense of his reputation; how would any close friend of Jefferson's suggest that this handsome family of house-trained slaves be sent to the fields, hidden or even quietly sold? There was no doubt in Monroe's mind that Sally's children were uniquely favored among Jefferson's hundred slaves. His wife had told him that two months ago, during the outbreak of measles that swept Virginia, Jefferson—fearful of his daughter Maria's baby becoming infected—had ordered all slave children removed from the area. All but Sally's.

Monroe strode through the two-storied entrance hall, with its busts of the French economist Turgot and the philosopher Voltaire, and terra-cotta plasters of Washington, Franklin, and Lafayette. He made his way through the dining room to the adjacent tearoom. It was the coolest room in the house, its bow windows facing north and offering a commanding view from atop the six-hundred-foot hill. Monroe was familiar with the surroundings; Jefferson used this room often for writing and small gatherings. His revolving Windsor chair on rollers with its attached writing arm was in a corner; in that, visitors were told, he wrote his draft of the Declaration of Independence. Madison was already seated at the square tea table, looking worried. Jefferson lounged on the upholstered Burling sofa and looked terrible.

"Are you all right, Thomas?" He was sometimes afflicted with the sick headache, a recurrent malady that felled him for days at a time.

"An excessive soreness all over," the President replied, "and a deafness and ringing in the head. From riding in the fog, I suppose. You'll have to speak up."

"New Orleans," said the Secretary of State to the Governor. "We wanted your thoughts, as the former Minister to Paris, about what Napoleon and Talleyrand are up to."

"The Spanish intendant has stopped our river traffic," Monroe answered, "revoking our right of deposit. It's a direct treaty violation. I suspect he was told to do this by Madrid on orders of Napoleon, who plans to force retrocession on Spain and to occupy the island."

"There is on the globe one single spot," said Jefferson grimly, "the possessor of which is our natural and habitual enemy. It is New Orleans, through which the produce of three-eighths of our territory must pass to market."

"You're suggesting that France could soon become our enemy," said Monroe. For Jeffersonians, Francophiles to a man for the past generation, that startling notion was a form of heresy.

"The day that France takes possession of New Orleans," said Jefferson, "fixes the sentence. It seals the union of two nations who in conjunction can maintain exclusive possession of the ocean. From that moment, we must marry ourselves to the British fleet and nation."

Madison, Secretary of State but with little diplomatic experience, shook his head as if slapped. Monroe knew that Jefferson and his foreign minister must be aware that an alliance with Britain was not possible; that seafaring power rightly saw her former American Colonies as competition to her dominion of world commerce.

"Neither the government nor the nation of France has any remains of friendship for us," Jefferson pressed, put in a bad mood by thinking about Napoleon. "On the contrary, an unfriendly spirit prevails in the most important individuals of the French government towards us."

Monroe understood it was necessary to get that new Presidential mood across to the newspaper editors of the West. Madison, meanwhile, would hint to the French Minister that an alliance of America with Britain was not impossible. When word of that got to Talleyrand, that wily diplomatist would see through our bluff, of course—but perhaps Napoleon needed money to sustain his European conquests. Madison's notion was to offer to buy New Orleans from France as soon as Napoleon snatched it away from Spain. Jefferson had confided to Monroe that he was even harboring the dream of buying not just New Orleans, but the entire Louisiana Territory halfway across the continent. That was one reason he had sent his secretary, Captain Lewis, off to explore it. Monroe supposed that the faithful secretary and Albemarle neighbor much preferred the rigors of opening a vast continent to the dirty business of paying hush money to a disgruntled newsmonger.

That, and the arrival of a tea tray, reminded Monroe of the domestic concern.

The tea service and cakes were brought in by the woman he recognized as the slave known as Sally Hemings. Jefferson graciously permitted her the use of a family name, uncommon in the slave culture. Her service was deft and graceful, her demeanor quiet and confident. Monroe judged the lovely woman to be about thirty and presumed that Jefferson took up with her in Paris when she was half that age. Was she aware that she was at the center of a storm? Not that Monroe could tell. Jefferson smiled his thanks at the cup of tea and declined the plate of cake, much as he would with any household slave; of course he did not introduce her. Madison took his tea and said, noncommittally, "Um." Monroe, who had routinely said "Thank you, Sally" in the same situation scores of times over the years, chose to incline his head slightly and limit himself to "Thank you."

What the likes of Callender would never understand, he knew, was what the gentlemen of Virginia, and especially their ladies, would see as the real scandal at Monticello. Forget the uproar in the North about the hypocrisy of the man who wrote "all men are created equal" using a slave woman for his sexual pleasure, and the Yankees' foolish fears of mixing races. The problem to the propertied voters of Virginia was not that Jefferson was using an attractive slave as a bed wench; every planter considered that to be the plain right of a property owner, and the ensuing impregnation was seen as an enjoyable way of adding to the stock.

On the contrary, the shocking part of Jefferson's behavior to the ownership class, and particularly to its wives, was the permanence and apparent mutual affection of the arrangement at Monticello. Jefferson was treating Sally almost as a wife, not merely a slave, conferring a dignified status on her that surely contributed to dangerous pride in others. To wealthy Virginians, the most galling detail in Callender's account was the way the supposed oldest offspring, "Young Tom," had been acting like a member of the master's recognized bloodline, lording it over the other slaves around the estate. That was why it was so important he not be found.

It was a lucky thing, Monroe thought, that the contumelious Scot referred to Jefferson's quadroon concubine as a "luscious wench" and an "African Venus." That suggested that the female house servant was merely a delicious morsel to be regularly ravished—rather than the respected, longtime mate that Monroe, Madison and other nearby plantation owners knew her to be.

After the gentle Sally withdrew, Monroe observed obliquely that the President must be under great strain from matters other than the challenge at New Orleans.

"With the aid of a lying renegade from republicanism," Jefferson said bitterly, "the Federalists have opened all their sluices of calumny. Every decent man among them revolts at Callender's filth."

Monroe looked at Madison, who nodded in relief; the use of "lying" by the President was direct refutation of the charge that Sally was a concubine and that Monticello was overrun by Jefferson's miscegenated offspring. A filthy lie it was and would be so branded, though the denial was never to come directly from the President. So long as it was forthrightly scorned and could never be proven true, Monroe concluded, it did not matter how widely it was believed.

"Those among them not so decent," Monroe told Jefferson, "will try to take advantage of the libels. Politically—"

The President waved that away, certain of his support among the people. "There cannot be a doubt," Jefferson insisted, "that were a Presidential election to come this day, the Federalists would have but three New England States, and only about half a dozen votes from Maryland and North Carolina." He was confident that the public would rally to him against the gossips. "Federalist bitterness increases with their desperation. They are trying slanders now which nothing could prompt but a gall which blinds their judgments as well as their consciences."

"How shall we respond?" Madison asked. Monroe was certain that the Secretary of State believed that the best response to calumny, even when true, was silence.

"I shall take no other revenge," Jefferson vowed from the sofa, true to form, "than by a steady pursuit of economy and peace, to sink Federalism into an abyss from which there shall be no resurrection."

"Here, here!" Monroe applauded the political piety coating Jefferson's admirable determination to destroy the opposition. Provided that Callender kept stressing the purely sexual nature of the relationship, republicans from established families in the South would direct their umbrage at the disloyal ranting of immigrant radical writers. The egalitarian views of these alien imports like Cobbett and now Callender had always been an embarrassment to the wellborn of the South. Jefferson properly could take the high road of prosperity and peace to sink his political opponents; other Jeffersonians, organized by dedicated republicans like Beckley and Monroe's man Hay, would use more direct means to protect a great man from defamation by the detestable foreigners.

Jefferson added a few choice words for the press. "Nothing can now be believed which is seen in a newspaper. Truth itself becomes suspicious by being put into that polluted vehicle."

"Still, the people must be informed," Madison put in. Monroe rolled his eyes; the man must have been reading his own amendments.

"The man who never looks into a newspaper is better informed than he who reads them," Jefferson shot back. "He who knows nothing is nearer to truth than the man whose mind is filled with falsehoods and errors."

Monroe was glad to see the President's views maturing in office; Callender's dirty work, too painful not to be true, had its effect on Jefferson, who had previously been all too prone to defend the liberty of the press. "I'll take my leave and wish you well in the capital," Monroe said. "Be careful about riding in the fog, with your catarrh."

He rose and examined a few of the miniature portraits on the wall of the tearoom. Two were of Jefferson, brought back from Paris, and a grouped trio was of Revolutionary War generals: Gates, Dearborn and Clinton. He tapped the frame on the portrait of George Clinton, now "the Old Incumbent," nine-time Governor of New York. "Think about him for Vice President," he said, despite knowing that Jefferson had little regard for the man. Clinton would block Burr in New York and be too old to get in the way of Madison or himself as Jefferson's successor.

Walking his two closest aides to the door, the President returned to the subject of the difficulty of dealing with foreign potentates like George III and Napoleon. "Sometimes accident gives us a place in history for which nature has not prepared us by corresponding endowments," Jefferson observed. "It is the duty of those about us carefully to veil from the public eye the weaknesses, and still more, the vices of our character."

Monroe chose to take that wise observation to apply not to Virginians but to King George III. He bade his fellow Virginians farewell and waited on the porch, with its distinctive pillars introducing an architecture that never seemed to get finished, for the young slave to bring his horse. He recalled that Jefferson had assured them months ago that nothing in his past could cause embarrassment; presumably he meant that the stories about Sally would never reach the public eye. What more damage could the vicious Scot do?

He recalled a threat that Hamilton had made years before to reveal an episode casting obloquy on Jefferson. But Callender would be the last person in the world to have contact with the New York politician whose political future he had ruined. What other attacks were likely? The charge that Jefferson had been a coward in the Revolution had been made and had not stuck. The imputation of atheism was one the Virginians would have to live with but was a matter of the mind and could never be proven by the fanatical preachers. Financial chicanery? Jefferson had property in land and slaves but no money to speak of. Perhaps this accusation of an African harem was the last stone in the scandalmonger's sling.

The stable boy brought his bay horse around and handed the Governor the reins. Monroe mounted and spurred the animal across the field toward home. The alert, fine-looking boy bore no special resemblance to Jefferson, the Governor decided, other than the light skin. And the red hair. And the self-assured, languid way of carrying himself.

Chapter 41

December 20, 1802

RICHMOND

*M*aria heard the shouts outſide and threw open the front door of Dr. Mathew's house. Staggering up the path was James, head pitched forward, bleeding all over his jacket, supported by his partner Henry Pace.

"George Hay, the bastard," grunted Pace, easing Callender onto the couch in the doctor's dispensary. "Barged in to Darmstadt's store and bludgeoned James over the head four, five times before I could get to him."

"Hat," James seemed to say, mouth filled with blood. Maria sent a slave to fetch the doctor. She wet a towel and gently dabbed at the Scot's injured skull and face.

"I couldn't find a cart so we had to limp all the way here," said Pace, looking on glumly. "Nobody would help. Thought he was drunk again, some said as much. The coward Hay, he just came up behind him where he was trying to find the translation of a document in Dutch, and damn near knocked his head off, yellin' all the time, 'Dusky Sally! Dusky Sally!' Like to have killed him unless one of our devils got to him in time."

"What are you trying to say, James? Just whisper to me." She leaned close to the battered ear.

"Hat," he whispered hoarsely.

"It's this hat," Pace explained, showing her the hat stuffed in his kit. "It's stiff and heavy, and he wears it all the time, in the stores, even at the type table. Proud of it, he is. Saved his life when the bludgeon hit him, I think. Stayed on for two or three of the blows at least." He handed to Maria the blood-soaked headgear that had served as a helmet. She had given him the hat as a present on his birthday in November because she didn't want to see him hatless in the cold. She could hardly see it through her hot tears.

"You can go now, Mr. Pace. Here's Dr. Mathew now. We'll take care of him."

"Mayor," Callender said urgently to Pace.

"I'll go to the Mayor's office now to get an order binding over Hay to

Scandalmonger

keep the peace," the partner told her. "Mayor Foster's not a republican, thank God. He won't worry about Hay's courting Governor Monroe's daughter." He looked dubiously at the editor, groggy but not from grog. "I don't suppose you will be able to write about this for the next issue. I'll try my hand at it."

She could feel James start up in protest, wince in pain and then sag against the doctor. "You'd better wait until he can write it, Mr. Pace."

Her employer dipped the towel in the reddened water in the basin and dribbled it over his emergency patient's head. "That's a nasty crack you have there, young man," Mathew said. "Breathe deep. Don't talk."

James continued to try to talk. He seemed to her more confused than angry at this latest outrage. This time she was the one who felt the surge of fury.

December 22, 1802
RICHMOND

"You're not going to believe this," Pace told Callender, whose head was still wrapped in a large bandage, sitting up in bed in his room, "but Hay is counter-suing us. He's got a Jefferson judge in Henrico County to cite us for being 'evidently common libelers of all the best and greatest men in our country.' "

"That's a compliment."

Pace wasn't so sure. "You have to put up a surety of fifty dollars that you won't attack Hay in revenge."

"Never." Callender started to shake his head but quickly stopped.

"I'm to put up twenty dollars, because the complaint says I'm 'more insignificant, being totally destitute of talents.' "

That drew a rueful smile. "The word 'totally' is too strong."

"You're a kind man, James." Pace took some bills out of the drawer. "I'm going to pay the twenty. One of us has to stay here and put out the paper."

Callender struck him as profoundly discouraged, but the habit of defiance had not abandoned the Scot. "I'll never pay. Let them put me in jail for contempt."

"They'll do that, James. They're serious and they have the Governor

[*355*]

behind them and the President behind him. None of them want to see any more articles by you." Pace had scheduled the next issue to come out the day before Christmas, and it included a good run of merchant's advertising. "This is not a good time to be shut down, James."

"When I'm in jail, put a black border around the front page," Callender told his partner. "Make it read 'From My Old Quarters in Richmond Jail.' That will show the republicans up for a pack of hypocrites."

Despite his aching head, he took up a quill and wrote the story in advance. "That such a paper as the *Recorder* should long be suffered to exist, in the centre of riot, of assassination, and of despotism, is what no rational being can be supposed to expect."

Pace, reading over his shoulder, found that attitude distressing; was Callender thinking of quitting?

"If the torch of the press is not extinguished in the blood of its editors," Callender wrote, "as it almost has been, we shall probably find it advisable to seek an asylum somewhere else. We shall attempt publication and look for protection in some happy corner of America, where the phantom of justice does not flutter upon the knots of a club, or the lock of a pistol."

Pace took the pages and read them in dismay. "This is the sort of thing Cobbett wrote when he ran back to England."

"I know how he felt, the royalist wretch."

"But we're adding twenty subscribers a week. At that rate we'll match the circulation of his Porcupine someday."

"I'll be straight with you, Henry. I don't want to go to jail again. You don't know what it's like to be in the dungeon with blacks singing to split your ears, or to face a mob outside led by the hotspur kin of Monroe and Jefferson."

"Then put up the fifty dollars."

He thought about it, at least, before saying "Never. I'll rot in that hell first."

January 5, 1803
RICHMOND

Monroe was surprised that Callender chose jail. He was irritated that the blackguard could generate sympathy for himself by publishing a black-bordered edition the day before Christmas, with its four extra pages of advertising. Even Duane in the *Aurora*, whose excessive attack on Callender for killing his wife with a loathsome disease had probably driven him to reveal "Luscious Sally," could not stomach the re-jailing of the man who had suffered for the Sedition Act. "The press has indeed been prostituted to the basest purposes by Callender," that editor wrote, "but the method taken to correct the evil will have the contrary effect."

The Governor was concluding his term of office. President Jefferson needed him to go to France as special envoy to head off Napoleon's designs on New Orleans. If that mission failed, the Federalists would call for war to defend the Mississippi trade and political power would flow back to them. These were great matters of state that would affect the nation for decades to come; why, then, did he have to concern himself with the beating and suing and jailing of one miserable newsmonger?

Because, he reminded himself, he had seen the effect of Callender's martyrdom on the stupid Federalists two years before. Monroe was determined that the same technique of suffering behind bars not be used against the republicans now. On one of his final orders as Governor, a new bench of magistrates had met on January 4 in Henrico County, reversed the previous judgment and dismissed the charges against Callender. They left the $500 bond in force against his assailant, which the public viewed as only fair, since Hay had been the man with the bludgeon. Monroe's daughter carried on about penalizing her suitor, and his wife sided with her forcefully. But Beckley had told Monroe's acolyte to intimidate Callender only privately, not to assault him in public. The idea had been to teach him a lesson that would make the editor think twice about continuing his campaign of lies, not to make a martyr out of him. Monroe thought his prospective son-in-law Hay was a hotheaded fool.

January 13, 1803
RICHMOND

Maria sensed that the savage beating and the one-week jailing had taken more out of Callender than he would admit. Not merely physically, though he moved more slowly, but the intensity had gone out of his eyes. She wondered if what he had written about "seeking asylum somewhere else" had been more than a play for sympathy. He was drinking more now, insisting that at least a pint at breakfast was needed to dull the pain. She did not believe that. He despaired of ever seeing his sons and confided to her his fear that they would grow up as field hands taking in Leiper's tobacco crop, all the while hating their father for killing their mother. She believed that.

"And I am out of ammunition, Maria. You cannot fight a war without gunpowder."

"What does that mean?" They were in the kitchen of the Mathew house.

"For three months now, the artillery of the press has been thundering upon my *Recorder*. The republicans are as zealous as the aristocrats." He poked at a stack of newspapers on the kitchen table. "You cannot open a single one of them without seeing a personal attack on me. As you know, all at once there has been cast open every porthole of scurrility, falsehood and execration." He pulled himself out of his chair and tried to warm himself at the wide fireplace. "In all other disputes of this kind, an editor was certain to have a posse of like-minded editors to support him. But the situation is now that every printer of both parties has thought it necessary to begin his performances by declaring 'Callender is a rascal!' Nobody in America or Scotland has ever had to endure such a terrible tempest of papershot."

She could understand the melancholy brought on by the constant derision by newspapers on both sides, on top of the physical battering and the threat of more such attacks from others in the angry gentry. But his demeaning self-pity and his sudden dependence on the bottle was too much for Maria to take.

"And so you want to give up and run away? Go home to Scotland where they're waiting to put you in jail? Go out West and get besotted every day and live with the savages?" That sat him back; she had never talked that way to him, or any man, before. "You talk about the artillery of the press. I know what it was like to have that artillery trained on me, and be defenseless against it. But you, you have the biggest gun in all that artillery. You can silence anybody—the *Aurora*, the *Examiner*, anybody—with your own barrage."

"So long as I had the ammunition." He explained his predicament. "Long ago, I had the shot from Beckley to use against Hamilton. After the election, when they cheated me out of my postmaster office, I was able to thunder back with Jefferson's letters transmitting money to me through

Madison and Monroe. And then when they sent Duane after me with his horrendous lie about my dear dead wife, I had the information about black Sally to blaze back against Jefferson."

He began to pace, more slowly than usual, but cracking his knuckles as before. "That information was the hair of Samson. That made me as powerful as the high and mighty, but now, Maria, I am shorn. They sent a man to beat my head in, and they waited to see how I would respond. All I could do was to insist on going to jail, which embarrassed them, but they must know that was just a trick. They want to see what I have left." He spread his palms. "But now I have nothing left, just some leads that will take months to explore. My readers will see I have no ammunition in my fine artillery and they will go elsewhere for their news. What is a scandalmonger without a scandal? Only the threat of some new exposure wards off the men in power. When they see me helpless, they will silence my paper and then come and kill me."

Maria shook her head, no; she could not stand to see him in despair. "I know where there could be a tempest of papershot, as you call it." She thought about what she could do to provide him the protection he needed. "Tomorrow is Saturday. You stay at home and rest. I will borrow the doctor's horse and carriage and pay a visit to a woman I was told about who lives in Albemarle County." Long ago, when Colonel Hamilton needed a threat that he thought might stop Jefferson's men from exposing the Reynolds affair, she had heard him mention the woman's name.

Chapter 42

January 20, 1803
ALBEMARLE COUNTY, VIRGINIA

*T*he tall young woman in the fine wool coat who drew up to the front door driving her own black carriage was obviously a lady. Though the name on the card she sent up—Mrs. Maria Lewis Clement, with a London address—meant nothing to Betsey Walker, the mistress of the mansion readily told one of her house slaves to admit the lady to the parlor.

She identified herself as Maria Clement, a former New Yorker related to the Livingston family. She was presently resident with her husband in London and on an extended visit to Richmond at the home of a family friend, the eminent physician Dr. Thomas Mathew.

"I could tell that your dress was not made in America," Betsey told her visitor, motioning for the slave to bring tea with biscuits and jam. "It's elegant."

"It was made in France a few years ago," she replied modestly. "I fear these bows at the hem are no longer the style."

"Your kinsman is our Minister there," Betsey Walker offered, who recalled having heard her husband say something about "that republican fool Livingston" representing us in Paris.

"It cannot be easy for him, not knowing the language as his predecessors did, and being hard of hearing as well. Mr. Jefferson and Mr. Monroe were fluent in French, I understand."

Betsey let her displeasure show, as she did on most occasions when Jefferson's name was mentioned. "Mr. Walker and I are not admirers of either the President or the Governor. A facility with foreign languages is no indicator of character." With the leaves now off the trees, she could see Monticello from her bedroom window upstairs. She often looked at it and imagined the worst of what had gone on there.

"In truth, that is what brought me here, Mrs. Walker. A friend of mine in New York, a great and famous statesman, once told me of an ignoble action taken by Mr. Jefferson many years ago. It was in regard to a respectable young lady here in Albemarle County."

Betsey felt her heartbeat speed up and put her hand to her breast. She had hoped someone would ask her about this for years.

"By coincidence," Mrs. Clement continued, "only a few days ago a writer I know mentioned that he had heard of a similar incident. He said it reflected poorly on the character of our President."

"And that it most certainly did," Betsey blurted out. Then she thought it would be more ladylike to be discreet, at least at first. "I mean, I think I know what you are referring to."

"Because of the delicate nature of the matter, and your position as a lady of honor and high reputation, I did not want to mention your name to him until discussing it with you. I hope you don't find my coming here too intrusive."

"Who is your writer friend?"

"James T. Callender, editor of the *Richmond Recorder,*" her charming visitor said forthrightly.

"Dusky Sally!" Betsey clapped her hands. "Everybody in the county clear to Charlottesville knew about her being Jefferson's concubine. She dropped a colt nine months after whenever the great man came back to Monticello. Must be half a dozen of their little octoroons running around, and they lord it over all the rest of the blacks."

"Then it's true?"

"Everybody knows it. But nobody had the courage to write about it until Callender did. We are subscribers to the *Recorder,* Mrs. Clement. It prints the truth."

"But that shocking matter about the slave is not what drew me here," said Mrs. Clement. "I really don't know how to begin—"

"It started back in 1768, before the Revolution." She drew her chair closer to her guest. "The year before, I had married Jack, who was Tom Jefferson's best friend. Tom was one of his bridesmen at the wedding, for God's sake. Jack's father was Tom's guardian and the executor of his father's will."

"Your husband's father was Mr. Jefferson's guardian?"

"They all couldn't be closer. We were living at Belvoir, just a stone's throw from Tom, who was still single then, no more than twenty-five, at Shadwell." She took a deep breath as the memory came back vividly. "Then Jack was asked by the Virginia Commission to go to Fort Stanwix to draw up a treaty with the Indians, and he asked Tom to watch over me and my new baby. He looked after us, all right." She stopped. Should she be telling this to a total stranger?

"What happened then?"

It was not really a secret any more, Betsey Walker decided; Harry Lee, who knew about it ever since he married Betsey's niece, despised Jefferson just as much as she and her husband did. Light-Horse Harry must have told a dozen Virginia neighbors of this evidence of the character of our new President, with Betsey's tacit approval. With no names mentioned, it had even been hinted at in *Bronson's Gazette,* the *Bee* and obliquely denied in the *Examiner.* She tore out the articles and saved them all.

"Tom Jefferson came to our house in Belvoir. With my new baby sleeping upstairs, mind you, he made advances toward me."

"Are you certain, Mrs. Walker? As we know, sometimes a man can be affectionate, or avuncular, without—"

"He wanted to take me to bed with him. He took hold of me, and Tom's big, you know—I was little, then, with a waist like yours. When I pushed him away, he wouldn't stop. It wasn't until I picked up a scissors that he finally backed away. And I was his best friend's wife." She wasn't really sure about the part about the scissors, but she vaguely recollected it, and she had told the story so often over the years that the scissors had become real in her own mind.

"When your husband came home, did you tell him what Jefferson had done?"

"Of course not. Mrs. Clement, you're from the North, so you may not be familiar with our code duello. A gentleman whose wife has been so insulted must demand satisfaction or a public apology. Jack would have had to challenge Tom to a duel and one of them would have been killed. I didn't want that. And I had made myself absolutely clear to Tom. I was sure he would never bother me again."

"Did he? Ever bother you again?"

Her visitor was surely persistent in her questioning. She found it good to talk about this with a lady so interested. "There was the time, a year or so later, Tom pressed a note into the cuff of my sleeve. I showed it to my husband and he ordered Tom out of our house."

"What did the note say? You kept it, of course—"

"I tore it to pieces after the first glance. It sought to persuade me of the innocence of promiscuous love. Can you imagine? Trying to make it seem that there was nothing wrong with—with adultery?"

The word hung in the air. She hoped she had not shocked Mrs. Clement by using it.

"Adultery," repeated Mrs. Clement in a whisper.

"Yes. But the note wasn't so specific that it required a duel. After that— but I've said too much already. None of this, of course, is to be repeated in the press."

"It's hard to keep these things quiet," Mrs. Clement replied, "especially when so many people in Albemarle know it. Let's leave it up to Mr. Callender. He's most careful to preserve a lady's reputation, even when he castigates dishonorable men."

Betsey Walker was not so sure. "He didn't preserve the reputation of the Reynolds woman. She could never show her face again."

"James Callender tells me that was Colonel Hamilton's doing in that awful pamphlet, and not his own. Indeed, as I remember it, Callender was the only defender of Mrs. Reynolds's virtue."

"I forgot that," said Betsey. She paused; if Mrs. Clement was friendly with the famous writer, perhaps she knew some delicious details of that old scandal. "Do you suppose that Hamilton—"

"Colonel Hamilton as an adult was no more a gentleman than the Jefferson you knew as a young man, Mrs. Walker. Some handsome and ambitious men believe they are above all morality, and a woman's virtue becomes a mere challenge to them." She added, "At least that's what I hear from the editor of the *Recorder*. And I respect his writing as highly as you do." The young woman frowned, thinking, as she finished her cup of tea.

"There is something else on your mind," Betsey said. "I can tell. Out with it, now."

"After your husband saw the improper note that Mr. Jefferson put in your sleeve, Mrs. Walker, did you mention his previous attack on you?"

Betsey sighed and shook her head, no. "Not for years. But then when

Jefferson sailed for France to be our Minister, Jack told me he was going to name Tom the executor of his will. I pleaded with him not to, and was forced to give the reason. It was awful."

A rejuvenated if still somewhat battered James Callender read and re-read the notes that Maria made of her conversation in Albemarle. She wrote clearly and in a fair hand, reporting in detail as much as she could remember of what had been said. One day, he thought, she would have to write a pamphlet of her own answering Hamilton.

He sent a message to his adversaries with a single line of type in capital letters in the *Recorder.* It read: "NEXT WEEK: MRS. WALKER."

Then he went to the tavern to find and compare notes with Light-Horse Harry Lee.

Chapter 43

*J*ames Madiſon was puzzled. "What does he mean, 'Next week: Mrs. Walker'?"

Monroe had ridden to the capital to consult first with Madison and then with Jefferson about his mission to Napoleon Bonaparte in Paris and the latest threatened calumny from Callender. "He means Jack Walker's wife Betsey, Jemmy, and that concerns me. Do you know her?"

"Of course. She was a great beauty in her day," Madison recalled. "She and Jack Walker were close friends and neighbors of the Jeffersons for years. But then it cooled for some reason."

"There is some rumor about that reason," Monroe told him.

"I know Jack wanted to stay on as Senator and thought he had our support," said the Secretary of State, "but we needed you in the Senate in Philadelphia. The Walkers were put out about that, I remember."

"That is not why Callender is interested in Betsey. You may recall that Betsey's niece married Harry Lee."

"Oh. Harry is in financial trouble, and no friend of ours."

Madison apparently still did not grasp the import of the single line of bold type in the *Recorder.* "I suspect Harry Lee was Callender's source of the lies about—" Monroe reached for a suitable phrasing—"the living arrangements of the slaves at Monticello. And Lee may be talking to that blackguard again, this time about Betsey and Jefferson."

Madison seemed to shrink into his coat, fluffing out the ruffles on his shirt with nervous fingertips. "What about them?"

"When Muhlenberg and I were investigating Hamilton—hard to believe it was ten years ago—I recall some message Hamilton wanted me to take to Jefferson. If we made public his financial scandal, he supposedly would reveal some scandal involving the Walkers."

"I had no idea—"

"I don't involve you in everything, my friend." Madison was a political naïf; he never should have transmitted money from Stevens Mason to Monroe for Callender years ago, but he did, thereby directly involving Monroe in the benighted payment. Preserve us from the blunders of innocents, he thought; they caused more trouble than the sins of the guilty. "I transmitted Hamilton's message to Jefferson at the time, but he assured me it did not worry him." As he said that, Monroe recalled how Jefferson was filled with certitude more recently that he was impervious to Callender's charges. The President, confident of his rectitude, was blind to his vulnerabilities. "We need to warn the President of the impending slanders. Will you come with me?"

The Secretary of State, looking miserable, rose and followed the retiring Governor out to cross the street to the President's palace. "I want to talk to you about your mission to France," he reminded him. "We cannot recall Livingston; his family is too important to us in New York. But if you could talk to Talleyrand about the purchase of New Orleans, we could assure France we will make no claims beyond the west bank of the Mississippi. Those troops of Napoleon's on Hispaniola—"

"Some of our slaves say the French force there has been decimated by the yellow fever," Monroe reported. "If that means he cannot conquer the New World, he may want to sell us New Orleans." He hoped to get around Talleyrand to speak to Napoleon himself, explaining that it would be in the interest of France to have America as the commercial competitor of Britain. "But we'll worry about Talleyrand later. This Walker matter is more pressing."

"It is true," Jefferson confessed. "I plead guilty to one of his charges. When young and single, I offered love to a handsome lady."

They did not look directly at Jefferson or he at them.

"I acknowledge its incorrectness," the President said painfully. "It is the only one founded on truth among all their allegations against me."

The first thought to race through Monroe's mind was that it was nearly twenty months until the next election. If this youthful indiscretion was revealed now and could be laid to rest quickly, all the diatribes in the Federalist press about Jefferson's "character" would have dissipated by election time.

"It was thirty-four years ago," said Madison in sympathy. "You were single."

"Unfortunately, Mrs. Walker was not," Monroe reminded him, returning the group to reality. This was not a matter to be ignored, like the Sally slander, nor dismissed as a mere act of charity, as were the payments to Callender when he was serving the republican cause by calumniating Washington. The Walker affair could not be truthfully denied, and it could not be publicly acknowledged without great political risk. It had to be dealt with in some other way. Jefferson's use of the word "incorrect"—rather than "wrong" or "improper"—suggested it could be treated as a social error, an indiscretion perhaps misunderstood and exaggerated in retrospect. In that light, friendly observers might not construe it as sinful behavior.

"It was without premeditation," Jefferson offered in extenuation, "and produced by an accidental event."

The explanation that they just fell into each other's arms would not set well with Federalist editors, in Monroe's judgment. Much depended on what the lady would recollect today; if the talkative Betsey could be induced to remain silent, perhaps by her husband, who could be promised anything, the matter would fade away in a few months. But Monroe knew Betsey; she loved being the center of attention. She would delight in basking in the interest afforded someone who had been maddeningly attractive to the young man who later became author of the Declaration of Independence and President of the United States.

"Did you correspond with either of the Walkers over the years?" Monroe knew Jefferson faithfully kept copies, or at least notes, of all his letters. He could recall no correspondence with either of the Walkers.

"Perhaps you would ask your secretary to search your records."

"How can we keep this quiet?" Madison wondered.

"These people," said the President about his press enemies, "slander for their bread. As long as customers can be found who will read and relish and pay for their lies, they will fabricate them for the market."

Jefferson was missing the point; by his own admission, this was not a lie. Monroe thought a few moves ahead into the new year. First, there was the danger that Callender had the story Hamilton had alluded to. After that, the danger lay in public corroboration from Betsey. After that was the danger of reverberation in the *New York Evening Post* and elsewhere. And finally the greatest danger of all: the near-cuckolded John Walker being forced by public exposure to demand satisfaction from Jefferson on the field of honor.

Nobody wanted that; not Betsey, not Jack, certainly not Jefferson. But the code duello often forced Virginia gentlemen into inescapable corners. If Walker were forced to issue a challenge, Jefferson would be forced to take it up; he could not afford to be labeled a coward. Monroe recalled how close he had come to a duel with Hamilton when Callender published the Reynolds letters. Thanks to the insatiable lust for vengeance of that same scoundrel, Jefferson could soon be in mortal danger. "Next week: Mrs. Walker." Monroe feared that this could get out of hand.

Chapter 44

[Vol. II.] **READING IMPROVES THE MIND** [No. 72.]

THE RECORDER;

PRINTED BY HENRY PACE, & JAMES T. CALLENDER, RICHMOND, VIRGINIA;
PUBLISHED EVERY WEDNESDAY MORNING. SUBSCRIPTION TWO DOLLARS PER ANNUM, IN ADVANCE.

February 3, 1803
RICHMOND

Mrs Walker

CIRCUMSTANCE BETWEEN A
CERTAIN GREAT PERSONAGE
And a lady in Albemarle County

First, the public have a right to be acquainted with the real characters or persons, who are the possessors or candidates for office.

Second, an enemy cannot refute the right of being attacked with his own weapons. Everybody must well remember the noise which was made by the republicans in Summer, 1797, concerning a personage of the Federalist party, who said he had fallen into an illicit commerce with another man's wife. *Sauce for the goose, sauce for the gander,* says the proverb.

Third, we have been badly accused in the past week of a design to attack the character of a most respectable lady, whereas such a thing never once came upon our heads. Instead of arraigning, we are going to vindicate the lady's character, if indeed a character so uncommonly respectable and amiable could be supposed to stand in want of a vindication.

Without any declamation upon the sanctity of the Seventh Commandment, or the guilt of seduction, or such trite matters, we shall tell a plain story that is universally believed, and that ought long since to have been published.

Mr. John Walker of Albemarle is a gentleman of independent fortune, and a most irreproachable character. His lady is universally represented as worthy to be the pattern of her sex.

A Great Personage, who resides at some distance from Mr. Walker's, and who had been at school with him, had, after Mr. Walker's marriage, been received in Mr. Walker's family with that cordial hospitality for which a Virginian country gentleman is so proverbially distinguished.

The return to this friendship was an attempt, as foolish as it was infamous, to injure the virtue of Mrs. Walker, and the happiness of her husband. He was repulsed with the contempt he deserved, and his intended *exertion of his ENERGIES for the multiplication of our species,* was, in this instance, disappointed.

The lady, at the request of the Great Personage, consented to the concealment of the proposal. She did this on the promise of better behavior in time to come. Matters remained in that situation, for a certain period, how long we do not exactly know.

We did not suspect that the Great Personage had possessed that *ardor of constitution,* which was necessary for the renewal of so detestable, and so desperate a scheme. However, we have been, within the last fortnight, almost overwhelmed with reputable affirmations that a second attempt was made, by slipping a billet into the lady's hand.

In the commission of the very same crime, circumstances may lessen or augment the proportion of guilt. There is not, perhaps, any vice, where the degrees of guilt admit of a greater diversity than in that which is the subject of the present article. Upon a topic so delicate we decline the hazardous office of endeavouring to expatiate. We only say that, in combining the circumstances of this Albemarle conspiracy, there is not a single point of alleviation.

Whether the Great Personage was, at that time, married, we do not pretend to say. We have, in relating this affair, adhered to a generality of expression, to prevent the little contradictions of our precious public printer.

On the receipt of the billet from the Great Personage, Mrs. Walker took her husband aside. She put the paper into his hand, and told him of the former attempt that she had conditionally promised to suppress. The Great Personage received immediate permission to *quit the house.*

Mr. Walker never mentions the name of the Great Personage but in epithets of the most ardent detestation. We have been assured that he received from the Great Personage either one or more letters of *deprecation.* If any great clamour shall be raised by the republicans, these letters, or that letter, will be produced to burn upon the indignation of mankind.

Now, don't give us any more challenges to *publish letters.* You have had quite enough of *that.* Don't give us any more defiances to do all that *we can do.*

If you had not violated the sanctuary of the grave, SALLY and her son TOM would still, perhaps, have slumbered in the tomb of oblivion. The vile attempt to seduce a best friend's wife would still, perhaps, be whispered about among the Virginia gentry. But there is reason to bring these scandals into the light of public scrutiny.

To charge a man as a *thief,* and an *adulterer* is, of itself, bad enough. But when you charge him with an action that is much more execrable than *an ordinary murder,* is the party injured not to repel such baseness, with ten thousand-fold vengeance upon the miscreant that invented it?

PART IV

The Libel Scandal

Alexander Hamilton, bookplate:
Viridis et Fructifera, "Green and Bearing Fruits"

Chapter 45

*H*amilton, returning from a regular meeting *of* the Society for Manumission of Slaves, read the reprint in his *Evening Post* of Callender's latest exposé with considerable satisfaction. Jefferson's youthful attempt to seduce the wife of his best friend had finally caught up with him; such a revelation about his lifelong adversary's character, he believed, was long overdue.

Ten years before, under the pseudonym Catullus, Hamilton had written that Jefferson was "a concealed voluptuary hiding under the plain garb of Quaker simplicity." He liked the word "voluptuary," with its Latin root "pleasure, sensual gratification," and applied it to both his major rivals, Jefferson and Burr. He supposed they could both have applied it to him, though no longer fairly, despite all the talk about an affair with his delicious sister-in-law, Angelica Church.

In 1792, his estimation of Jefferson's two-facedness had been based on his political rival's advances toward Betsey Walker, his best friend's wife. He had not known at the time of the man's Negro concubine. Surely Jefferson had read the "concealed voluptuary" attack; when he did, and Monroe relayed to him Hamilton's threat to make unspecified sexual charges public, Jefferson might have assumed guiltily that Hamilton knew about both scandals. And yet the reserved Virginian did nothing to stop Monroe, five years later, from providing Callender with the Reynolds papers. Hamilton wondered why. Did Jefferson assume that he was immune from retaliation—that his own illicit amours with the wife of his best friend and with the slave companion of his daughter would never be exposed?

The man was shameless, Hamilton concluded, or self-deluded about his immorality. Or—and this, curiously, was a good augury for the Republic—the man now President was possessed of more sheer audacity than anybody previously imagined. The New York lawyer was glad to have had nothing to do with the original publication of the Walker story, but delighted that Jefferson's egregious misconduct, after all these years of hypocritical moralizing by its perpetrator, had been dragged by the press into the light of day.

He assumed that Harry Lee was the source of Callender's information. He remembered Light-Horse Harry, during the Revolution, as the sort of disciplinarian who decapitated deserters. That was contrary to Washington's orders; although beheading set a stern example to others in the ranks, it smacked of savagery. Years later, during the Whiskey Rebellion, Washington had sent Hamilton with Lee into western Pennsylvania and told him to make certain the hotheaded cavalryman did not execute anyone not in armed revolt. And never under any circumstances by chopping off his head.

His wartime comrade had told him in those days of "whispers that I have heard" about Jefferson's improper approaches to the beautiful Betsey Walker just after she had first become a mother. Her husband, Jack, who had won an interim appointment as Virginia Senator in 1790, had been ruthlessly thrust aside by Jefferson to make a seat for Monroe, and Jack had complained to their Albemarle neighbor Harry Lee, who passed the sordid tale on to Hamilton. He asked himself: should he have carried out his threat, sent through Monroe to Jefferson, to expose the affair if the republicans made public their investigation of him in 1792? He had been tempted to five years later, when Monroe stabbed him in the back by giving the documents to Callender. But he was glad now to have restrained himself. Burr would have used it to win the presidency. Better that the Walker affair not come out until now.

What Hamilton found hard to understand was how Jefferson had been able to maintain, through all these sordid revelations, his hold on the public sentiment. Despite all the suspicions of preachers about his supposed atheism; despite the sea change of opinion in America that turned against the bloodthirsty French radicals; and despite the growing distaste in the North at the way the author of "all men are created equal" continued to support human slavery—the President seemed to float above it all. Why?

Perhaps it was because most of the country was so productive and the population was growing so rapidly. Jefferson had cut the odious tariffs on imports previously needed to support a navy—indeed, acting on an end-of-term initiative of the perfidious Adams, he had sold off a portion of the navy to private bidders. That act of tax reduction lowered many prices to farmers and mechanics. It made the republican President a hero to many in the Federalist rank and file, though in Hamilton's view it weakened the nation.

As a result, Jefferson rode a crest of national confidence and gained much of the affection that Washington had steadily enjoyed but had been denied to Adams. In the recent Congressional elections, thirty of the thirty-three new House seats had been gained by the republicans; worse, in the Senate, Federalists had lost seven; republicans now outnumbered Federalists in the upper body by three to one. In the Presidential election ahead, however, Jefferson's reputation would have to reckon with the vicious investigative talents of James Callender, and no public servant, Hamilton reckoned, could withstand such a sustained onslaught on his character. Public sentiment would surely turn into public outrage and be directed against him.

He summoned William Coleman, his editor of the *Evening Post*. "Callender is a scoundrel," he told the young man when he appeared, breathless and eager. Hamilton tapped the edition that reprinted Callender's sensational *Recorder* story. "I want you to put a notice in the next issue of the *Post* that I was not consulted before you reprinted this offensive story. Get this down, young man"—he pushed forward a quill and inkwell—"that I am adverse to airing in the press the private business of all personalities, not immediately connected with public considerations."

"But this is news, General. The city is abuzz with it. Some fool republican will be sure to deny it, which will give the *Recorder* cause to run another damning piece next week."

"Which you will display prominently," Hamilton directed, "again without consulting me." He smiled. "Be prepared to be rebuked for your impetuosity." Coleman's work pleased him; the young editor had driven Noah Webster's *Commercial Advertiser* out of business.

"I know how you despise Callender, sir, for his calumnies about you years ago," Coleman said. "But in everything he's written about Jefferson recently, that Scotsman has been dead accurate. The charge that Jefferson and Madison and Monroe paid him secretly was denied, but then he printed their letters to him and proved himself right."

"What about the innuendo about consorting with his slave?"

"His articles about 'Luscious Sally' and his mulatto children were denied, too," said Coleman, "but I have corresponded with less biased editors in Virginia. They have been talking to people on the rich plantations, and they inform me that what Callender has written is probably true. And now this Walker affair—I know it's about a youthful indiscretion of thirty years ago, but it does reveal character, and don't you think it has the ring of truth?"

"Harry Lee will verify it, but don't tell him I said that," Hamilton said, being certain to add with a frown of disapproval, "Scurrilous. Public men should not have to endure this."

"Callender suggests here"—the editor pointed to a passage in the article the *Post* had taken from the *Recorder*—"that he has letters to authenticate his charges. He all but dares the Jefferson men to deny the article."

"He could be bluffing," Hamilton replied, recalling his previous experience with the scandalmonger. "Or the letters could be forged, or possibly false 'copies' of what had never been written." The thought of libel crossed his mind. "How do you suppose Jefferson and his friends will react to the *Post*'s republication of Callender's work?"

"You know how he has talked about the liberty of the press," Coleman noted, "but he's not above letting the States do his dirty work." Hamilton nodded; the First Amendment to the Constitution held that "Congress shall make no law" abridging the liberty of the press, but placed no such restriction on the State governments. Jefferson set great store by the rights of States. He showed that disunionist bent in his anti-sedition resolutions that threatened to nullify the Federal compact. Hamilton suspected that Jefferson was the secret author of the inflammatory Kentucky Resolution that sowed dangerous seeds of secession.

"There is not a syllable in the New York State Constitution concerning the liberty of the press," said Hamilton, a point he had made more than fifteen years before, writing as Publius in the Federalist papers. But at that time he was arguing against the need to festoon the Federal Constitution with a bill of rights. He believed then that no fine declaration in any document denouncing any freedom—excessive taxation, or violating the liberty of the press—would secure the people's rights. Liberty of the press altogether depended on public opinion, on the general spirit of the people and their government, he had been certain then. Now he was less sure. There was a bill in the state legislature to shield editors, and even talk of amending the New York State Constitution to ensure press freedom. If Jefferson, Madison and Monroe achieved a stranglehold on the national Presidency for decades to come and intended to make State Courts their instruments of suppression of criticism, such protective action by individual States might be necessary. Public opinion was not showing itself to be a dependable guardian.

"McKean in Pennsylvania has been cracking down in State court there," Coleman reported, feeding his fears, "and the Attorney General here is moving on the *Wasp* up near Hudson."

The *Wasp* was a lampooning weekly of insignificant circulation published upstate, near Albany. Hamilton asked what it had done to draw the fire of the state's chief law officer.

"Harry Croswell, the editor—no more than a boy, in his early twenties—has been printing every word Callender writes," Coleman replied. "And it's the home newspaper of Attorney General Spencer. We did an article about his suit against the *Wasp* for seditious libel."

"Why did he swat the insignificant *Wasp* and not the *Post*, if we're reprinting Callender, too?"

"The republicans are afraid of coming after you in a New York City court, what with your legal acumen, sir." Hamilton noted the editor wisely did not mention his employer's influence with New York City judges, many of whom owed their appointments to him. "But they want to make an example out of somebody, to intimidate anyone else who reprints Callender."

That piqued his interest as both lawyer and newspaper owner. The republicans had let the Federal Sedition Law lapse, which was good, but could State law that currently punished seditious libel also be overturned, or at least modified? The republicans had marshaled public opinion against the Federalist's Sedition Law, to their great political benefit; could Federalists now turn the tables and marshal public opinion against State libel law? "Keep me informed about the progress of the New York State action against Croswell." Only a few years before, Hamilton had successfully sued a newspaper for libel and driven its editor to the wall, but the times and his position had changed. He was now a publisher and in political opposition, and the opposition press needed all the protection it could get.

Coleman left him alone in the office. Before packing up his papers to take to the Grange, his new home ten miles north, in Harlem, Hamilton allowed himself to ruminate about the strange effect of the news.

Even miserable miscreants like Callender, he was forced to admit, served a public purpose in checking a too-popular government's power. But the apathetic public reaction to the editor's string of exposés struck the owner of the *Evening Post* as hard to explain. His paper and even the republican press dealt with the salacious doings daily, to the benefit of their circulation, but the public reading it avidly did not seem incensed by it. Why?

He presumed one reason for the absence of outrage was the division and disheartenment of the Federalists. Their main supporters in New England were worried about the effect on their commerce of new hostilities between England and France, and concerned that their political influence was being diluted by westward expansion. But that only partly accounted for the national ennui. Perhaps a greater part was the reluctance of republicans to join in the jeering at their vehicle to power; it was not that they loved the flawed Jefferson more, but that they loved the imperious Federalists less. Adultery, the admission of which had dashed Hamilton's dream of the highest office, seemed not to shake the foundations of Jefferson's hold on the people. To the contrary, although Hamilton always thought of his rival as womanish, these scandals about Sally and Betsey were evidence of vigorous manhood, imbuing the man in the new President's house with a new reputation for virility.

He was aware of the way seemingly minor events could upset great plans. Callender had not yet published the gossip that a romance actually had been consummated between Jefferson and Betsey Walker. What if the spread of that suspicion—which Hamilton did not think was so far-fetched—were to force Jack Walker into a demand for satisfaction of his honor? Men were often killed in duels. Hamilton's heart sank at the thought of his son Philip, killed at nineteen in a duel that his father stupidly failed to prevent, a failure that would surely depress his spirit throughout his life. Hamilton and Monroe had been on the verge of a duel in which the life of one of them would have been cut short, and only the cool intercession of Aaron Burr, of all people, had averted it.

Burr. If Walker were driven to demand satisfaction under the code duello, Jefferson could not in honor refuse. If Walker then shot him dead, Vice President Burr would become the acting President of the United States.

Hamilton sent for Coleman to return for new instructions. The *Evening Post* would reduce its reprinting of Callender's latest scandal. The atmosphere was already too highly charged.

Chapter 46

LIGHT-HORSE HARRY LEE

May 1, 1803
ORANGE COUNTY, VIRGINIA

Light-Horſe Harry Lee was glad that James Monroe had sailed for France, supposedly on some business to buy New Orleans from Napoleon. That seemed to him to be a fool's errand and a weakling's way. Lee's approach to protecting the West was to raise an army, side with the British against the French in their war, and dare the French general to fight it out up the Mississippi Valley.

With Monroe gone, James Madison was the only other intimate that Jefferson trusted enough to deal with the delicate Walker affair. The Secretary of State, Lee was certain, would be a softer negotiator. The talk was that if Jefferson did not choose to stand for re-election next year, Monroe might challenge Madison for the support of republicans. Lee thought Monroe would make a more forceful President, possessed of what Hamilton liked to call "energy in the Executive." He was also more likely to obey Washington's stricture, written by Hamilton, against foreign entanglements.

Lee's fine chestnut mount, a vestige of his former affluence, approached the mansion and acreage the Madisons called Montpelier. The house rested on a plateau where the western slope of Little Mountain leveled off and the great Blue Ridge Range could be seen. This Shenandoah property was becoming more valuable every year, unlike the speculative Greenbrier land that had brought Lee to the brink of impoverishment. He dismounted and turned his horse over to a slave.

John Walker was already in the library with Madison. The aggrieved husband of Lee's Aunt Betsey had asked his wife's nephew to represent him after news of the egregious misbehavior had been galloping from Richmond all across the country for months. The *Bee*'s reprinting of Callender's series of articles had stirred New England, the *Evening Post* was informing New York, and Duane's *Aurora* in Philadelphia spread the scandal by denying it in detail.

Lee's assignment was to assist Walker in obtaining, first, a private acknowledgment of the wrong done to his family by Jefferson, which had after all these years come to public attention. Not only had the barrage of articles in the *Recorder* become a source of great embarrassment, but cast a reflection on Mrs. Walker's virtue and, more to the point, Mr. Walker's honor.

The second object of negotiation was to establish the fact of Jack Walker's written protest to Jefferson in Paris. Because he sent this letter as soon as his wife told him of the attempts to seduce her, this would show Walker had not been remiss in defending his family from a predatory force.

Lee's third and most difficult goal was to obtain a public apology from Jefferson. And not just a murmured plea for forgiveness between old friends, but a public statement that would firmly assert Mrs. Walker's virtue, which she maintained despite her would-be lover's sustained importuning. This last would give moral underpinning to a political cause that Lee and Callender had in common: to discredit the character of the republican leader and make impossible his re-election. As Hamilton had shamed himself out of a potential candidacy with his admission of philandering, so could Jefferson, his character as a youth revealed, be shamed out of standing again.

"Thomas Jefferson will be here soon," Madison said. "It's only thirty miles from Monticello, as Jack here knows. Perhaps we can begin."

"No," Lee told the Secretary of State, "we'll wait for the President." Lee had fought honorably in the Revolution alongside Washington and Hamilton—while Madison and Jefferson had been, to his mind, mere politicians. Like Jefferson, Lee had served as Governor of Virginia, but unlike Jefferson, no blemish of suggested cowardice tainted his three-term record. Like Madison, Lee had recently served in the House of Representatives, but on the Federalist side of the aisle. Though in deep financial difficulty at the moment, Lee would not be awed by the power of his kinsman's adversaries, which he knew to be why John Walker had turned to him, beyond the family tie. His own underlying reason—known only to Callender, and delicious to both of them—was that Lee was the man responsible for the exposure of the wrong.

Such revelation of the scandal, in Lee's disciplined mind, was by no means a sign of disrespect to his wife's kin. Betsey Walker was secretly delighted at all the attention she was getting. At this stage of her maturity, embarrassed by her girth, to be linked to the handsome President in their youth was an elixir to her spirits. Lee suspected that her claim of ten years of travail—keeping the secret of Jefferson's insulting propositions lest her husband be forced into a duel with the assailant of the sanctity of his marriage—was a bit exaggerated. Tom Paine, the atheist friend of Jefferson now visiting America and being feted at the President's house, had observed pithily the month before that the supposed siege of Betsey was longer than the siege of Troy.

Nor did Harry Lee think of himself as being the least disloyal to John Walker in having secretly spread the story. He knew that Walker had enjoyed being Virginia Senator before he was shunted aside by Jefferson to make way for Monroe, and the rejected politician bore his faithless neighbor a lifelong grudge. He had struck his pose of outraged husband, determined to set straight the matter of his wife's challenged but never-compromised virtue, provided—as he told Lee—it did not get out of hand.

Lee was aware that Walker did not want to invoke the code duello any more than Jefferson wanted to take up a pistol. To Walker, the contretemps between himself and the President of the United States increased his importance in the eyes of his neighbors. That was satisfaction enough, of pride if not of honor, but Lee could not allow his client's eagerness to avoid combat show in the negotiation.

Jefferson, looking dusty from his ride and grim at what he was facing, joined them. He nodded in a friendly way to Walker and Lee but did not extend his hand; in this delicate situation, that would have been in error.

"I think the affair between the President and Mr. Walker," said Madison, host of the gathering, to Lee, "can have a happy *eclaircissement.*" Lee said nothing; he did not appreciate the Secretary lapsing into French, but the word sounded like it had something to do with clarification. Lee wanted more than that; his client deserved a public apology. "Of course what is discussed here today," Madison continued, "is for the bosom of those already privy to the affair."

"This is already in entirely too many bosoms," said Lee. He took out a page taken from the most recent *Recorder.* "Listen to this. 'We hasten to correct an error in our earlier story. Mr. Walker was not at home when the attempt was made on his domestic peace. He did not learn the particulars till after the Great Personage had gone to France as an ambassador. He then wrote a letter to this inestimable representative of the New World. The answer has been read by dozens.' That is what this blackguard Callender avers."

"I have been used for some time as the property of the newspapers," President Jefferson responded, "a fair mark for every man's dirt."

"Of course," said Lee to the man he could not forget subsidized the dirt that Callender threw at Hamilton and Presidents Washington and Adams. "My question to you, Mr. Jefferson, and to you, Mr. Walker, is—would you show these letters to Secretary Madison and me?"

Jefferson looked directly at Walker. "I never received a letter from you while I was serving in Paris."

"Perhaps it miscarried," said Walker, as Lee had instructed him. "I have a copy of my letter to you. It's dated May 15, 1788."

He handed it to Jefferson, who read it slowly, shaking his head. "Never came to me. I think its miscarriage unfortunate. Had I received it, I should—without hesitation—have made it my first object to have called on you on my return to this country."

"To what end?" asked Lee, to pin the President down.

"To come to an understanding as to the course we were to pursue," Jefferson replied, "which was the object of your letter."

"And here is my recent letter from you, Thomas," said Walker, "dated April 13, 1803, only last week."

Lee wished Walker would not call the President by his first name. It would not do to re-establish a cordial relationship. "Read it aloud," Lee told his wife's aunt's husband.

Walker did so. "It says, 'Time, silence and the circumstances growing out of them have unfavorably affected the case.' I presume by 'the case,' Thomas, you refer to the unconscionable advances you made over the years on my totally innocent wife. Your letter goes on: 'My best endeavors shall be used to consign this unfortunate matter to the oblivion of which it is susceptible. I certainly could have no objection to your showing this letter to the ladies of your family. My greatest anxieties are for their tranquillity. I salute them and yourself with respect, Thomas Jefferson.' "

"Hardly a proper apology," said Lee. "Not even an admission of guilt. And how, Mr. Jefferson, do you propose to keep all this out of the newspapers in the future?" asked Lee. The anti-republican press led by Callender was enjoying an enhanced readership thanks to the scandal, and the reliably republican papers like the *Aurora*, to keep up, were reprinting all the charges under the pretense of refuting or condemning them.

"If Callender of the *Recorder* and Coleman of the *Post* can be silenced," Jefferson said, "the others are but copiers or answerers of them. They have not pretended to original information, but as long as customers can be found who will read and relish and pay for their lies, they will fabricate them for the market." Apparently, Jefferson considered his allies in the press no better than his foes.

"The *Bee*, one of your republican papers," Walker noted, "has been devoting much attention to this."

"With respect to the *New England Bee*," said Jefferson, "I know not the editor. But through a friend who knows him I can have a total silence recommended to him, probably with effect. Through the same channel, the *Aurora* and *American Citizen* may probably be induced to silence. If their antagonists can be brought to be silent, they can have no reason not to be so."

"As you see, we can quiet the republican papers," Madison said to Lee. "But the Federalist papers—"

"As for the antagonist presses," Jefferson broke in, "I have with conscientious exactness opposed the smallest interference with them, further than to have public documents published in them."

Lee said nothing, waiting for Jefferson's qualifier at his show of virtue. It came.

"The present occasion, however," Jefferson continued, "will justify using the intermediation of friends to direct the discretion of antagonists of principle circulation." He looked directly at Harry Lee, apparently hoping he would volunteer to take on that task.

"That will be considerably more difficult, as they have a lively political interest in pursuing this unfortunate matter," Lee replied. "I can appeal to General Hamilton, who would be able to quieten Coleman at the *Evening Post.*"

"What about Callender?" asked John Walker. "He's the source of all the trouble."

"I don't know the man," Lee lied. "I can undertake to visit his printing shop and say this is the wish of Mrs. Walker. From what he has written, I would say he holds her in high regard."

"Never met him?" Madison asked, then without waiting for the denial Lee was quite prepared to make, went on: "Where do you suppose Callender is getting these documents from?"

"It's likely he does not have them," Lee could say truthfully. "You'll note in this piece about what he calls 'the Albemarle amours,' he writes 'the answer has been read by dozens.' It is apparent to me that the contents have been described to him, but Callender does not have copies. If he does, perhaps I can prevail on him to turn them over to Mrs. Walker."

"It is not enough to try to silence the press," Walker reminded the group. "The honor of my wife and I needs more satisfaction than that."

"You have my admission that I plead guilty," Jefferson said painfully. Avoiding the eyes of the others, he made his carefully phrased confession: "When young and single, I offered love to your handsome lady. My action was without premeditation." Jefferson forced himself to look directly into his former friend's eyes. "I acknowledge its incorrectness."

"It is one thing to confess to us in private your guilt in trying repeatedly to induce Mrs. Walker to commit adultery," Lee said, using with relish the previously avoided word, "but it is quite another to make your behavior clear to a reprehending world. It is Mrs. Walker's reputation for marital fidelity that is at stake, and it is necessary for you to attest publicly to her refusal of your repeated attempts."

Jefferson shook his head, no.

"That is the only satisfaction possible short of a satisfaction of honor under the code," Lee said with care. "I have heard that great events are in train to expand our frontiers, and responsibility weighs heavy on you. But we are all Virginia gentlemen. We all understand that nothing is more important than our sacred honor, for without that we are nothing."

Walker nodded nervously. Jefferson exhibited no expression.

"Perhaps there is a third way," said the Secretary of State. He put forward a plan for Jefferson to write a letter to be shown to a small circle of their friends acknowledging the incorrect action, without reference to its place, frequency or duration. Jefferson's letter would attest unequivocally to the morally indignant reaction of Mrs. Walker, thereby assuaging her irritation and obviating any need for further satisfaction. The letter would then be destroyed. In that process, her social circle would be reassured, her reputation would remain unsullied, and yet the President would not be publicly humiliated nor would the episode belittle the nation in the eyes of the world.

Lee knew this was what his client wanted and more than he thought he could get. The contents of Jefferson's letter would be described to Callender, which was the same as having Jefferson make a public statement. The editor would probably pretend he had a copy.

"A solution worthy of a diplomat," Lee said to the Secretary of State. "I think that might satisfy honor, provided the letter goes to the lady's entire exculpation without mixing in any exculpation of yourself. And to make certain any future claim of it being a forgery can be refuted, the letter must be acknowledged and countersigned by any two of your friends in the world." He looked at his client. "Do you accept that, Jack? If not, I stand fully prepared to be your second under the code duello."

"I accept it," said Walker, Lee thought a bit too quickly.

Madison nodded assent on Jefferson's behalf. He must be thinking, guessed Lee, that it was right and proper for the President to acknowledge his own guilt and totally absolve Mrs. Walker, provided the document was certain to be kept out of the hands of Callender and his ilk. Monroe would not have been so naïve. "There is no need for documents or memorials of any kind on this matter to be preserved," Madison said. "I will countersign the true copy for the President."

"And for my part, I will get John Marshall to attest in writing to its authenticity," said Walker. Lee noted that Jefferson winced at that—Marshall was a longtime political rival of his—but he could not object to sharing this confidence with the Chief Justice, a Virginia neighbor who knew them all.

"And everything said in this room remains within these four walls," agreed Lee.

Jefferson stood up and extended his hand to Walker, who clasped it with solemnity. Lee took his satisfied kinsman by the arm and left the President and his Secretary of State alone.

Jefferson slumped into one of Montpelier's upholstered chairs and hung his head in his hands. Madison had to strain to hear his muffled voice ask, "Do you suppose Harry Lee will get that ingrate Callender to stop?"

"Monroe, before he sailed, told me that he suspected Lee was the one who stirred up the Walker story in the first place."

"I know," said the President. "Years ago, when he was in the Senate, Monroe told me about Hamilton's threat to reveal it. That was during the attack for Hamilton's connection with Mrs. Reynolds. I of course ignored the warning."

"I presume Lee will now go back to Callender," said Madison, "and pursuant to our agreement today, prevail on him to drop this and find something else with which to diminish your political strength. Not because Lee is an honorable man, but because it is in his interest and that of the Walkers." Madison felt the need to add, "Thomas, you appear to be in pain."

"This gives me great pain, my friend. If I thought that Betsey Walker countenanced the publication in the *Recorder,* my sensibility would cease." He shook his head, rejecting that possibility. "But I have to assume she is as innocent in this publication now as she was in the original matter back then."

Madison picked up a copy of the *Recorder* with the latest Callender harangue that had been lying on the table, and fed it into the fire.

At the firelight's sudden brightening of the room, Jefferson looked up and watched the despised publication curl in the heat and turn to ashes. "You know how I feel about the people and the press," he told his friend. "We've seen the firmness with which the people withstood the late abuses of the press, and the discernment they've manifested between truth and false-hood. It shows that they can be trusted to hear everything—both true and false—and to form a correct judgment between them."

Madison nodded, aware that the disclaimer was likely to be a prelude to how Jefferson really felt about the unfair attacks on him.

"And you know, Jemmy, that I deem freedom of the press one of the es-sential principles of our government and consequently will shape its ad-ministration."

"You made that clear in your Inaugural Address."

"Then why is it, I ask myself, that when the Federalists make up not more than a tiny fraction of the nation, they command three-quarters of its newspapers?"

"Because most newspapers are vehicles for advertising and published in seaports and commercial towns," Madison explained. "One would expect them to promote commerce with England and support the mercantile class." He saw from Jefferson's expression that was not what he was get-ting at.

"Because I thought there was not a truth on earth which I feared should be known," Jefferson said, "I have lent myself willingly as the subject of a great experiment. That was to prove that an administration, conducting it-self with integrity, cannot be battered down, even by the falsehoods of a li-centious press."

Madison nodded. "Such an experiment was needed to destroy the pre-text that freedom of the press is incompatible with orderly government."

"That is why I have never contradicted the thousands of calumnies propagated against myself." The President rose, took up a poker, and rus-tled the ashes of the newspaper among the logs in the fire. "But since we have shown that the press is impotent when it abandons itself to falsehood, I leave to others to restore the press to its strength by recalling it within the pale of truth."

"And how shall we induce others to do that?" Madison knew the answer but did not want to be presumptuous.

"As you above all others know, we deny that Congress"—he empha-sized the name of the legislative branch—"that Congress have a right to control the freedom of the press. We deny that."

" 'Congress shall make no law abridging,' " Madison recited, agreeing.

"Correct. At the same time, we have asserted the right of the States, and their exclusive right, to control freedom of the press. The States have accordingly—all of them—made provisions for punishing slander."

The rationale for his counterattack, Madison saw, was taking shape.

"We have come to a dangerous state of things," said Jefferson, warming to the subject. "The press has been pushing its licentiousness and its lying to such a degree of prostitution as to deprive it of all credit, and it ought to be restored to its credibility by the States. A few State prosecutions of the most prominent offenders would have a wholesome effect in restoring the integrity of the presses."

"Not a general prosecution—"

"No, no, for that would look like persecution. Instead, a selected one." He went out into the hall, took a newspaper out of his overcoat, and put it on the table. Madison saw it was the *Port Folio* of Philadelphia, the literary sheet that had so delighted in foul doggerel about "sooty Sal" to the tune of "Yankee Doodle." That sheet was now turning to the Walker affair to further Callender's predations.

"I think I'll write a confidential note to Tom McKean," said Jefferson.

Madison knew Pennsylvania's McKean had unsuccessfully tried William Cobbett for libel, but later as Governor had manipulated the courts to drive Peter Porcupine out of Philadelphia and ultimately out of America. McKean, if encouraged, would not flinch from making an example of those at the forefront of this latest wave of attacks. Madison noticed that the President, after this painful personal trial, now seemed more like his normal, optimistic self.

Chapter 47

June 18, 1803
RICHMOND

"*Y*ou're as bad as Porcupine," said Beckley, throwing down a copy of the *Political Register*, the weekly edited by the banished British Tory. He was now publishing his outrageous opinions in London, with editions printed in Dublin and Philadelphia; there was no escaping the man. "Cobbett has no principles either."

Beckley watched Callender eagerly scan the latest production of his longtime rival. The *Register,* a few months behind the times, denounced the peace agreement between Prime Minister Pitt and Napoleon Bonaparte known as the Treaty of Amiens. To Cobbett, British attempts to appease the French Consul-for-Life would only embolden him; the newsmonger preferred a continuation of the war until Britain prevailed.

"You see?" Beckley, on his Jeffersonian mission to Callender in his printing shop, wanted to appear almost gleeful. "Porcupine was a great Tory voice when he was here. He went back home and Pitt embraced him as a fearless British patriot standing up to the Frenchified Americans. The government probably financed his new paper, and now it's the only one being printed on both sides of the ocean. And what thanks does Pitt get?"

"Cobbett appears to be attacking Pitt's government mercilessly," the Scot remarked mildly, turning the page.

"You newsmongers are nothing but oppositionists." Beckley was certain he had solved the riddle of Callender's original betrayal. "You cannot stand to be loyal followers of your own cause. You are all sail and no ballast and you jump ship the minute it gets to port. You live only to be against."

What made him that way? To the mind of the self-styled Librarian of Congress, the slowness of the repayment of Callender's fine had been merely an annoyance to the editor. The denial of the deserved postmastership, concededly more infuriating, was not in itself enough to make a turncoat out of a principled republican. Not even Duane's lie in the *Aurora* about the drunken editor killing his wife with a loathsome disease, though it understandably provoked a fierce broadside, could not explain the Scot's sustained, passionate campaign to bring down the President.

The greatest impetus to Callender's savage betrayal, Beckley was convinced, was the man's innate discomfort with being on the winning side. Callender was a born resister, a hater of authority, and a rebel against anybody in power—a disloyalist in his bones who found perverse satisfaction only in tearing down great men.

Beckley came to Richmond to find out what other scandals Callender had in store, and whether he could be reasoned with before he brought a mob's violence down on his head. That would reflect badly on the republican cause.

"Look at this, John," the Scot said, poring over Cobbett's lively international paper. "A French émigré editor in London is being tried for seditious libel. He dared to criticize Napoleon in his paper, *L'Ambigu.* Cobbett says the craven British press ought to be ashamed of themselves for not coming to the courageous émigré's defense. Good for Porcupine, the pompous bastard, for going against the lapdogs and lickspittles that call themselves the English press. I wonder how many he sells."

"Four thousand, and now he's starting a French edition. They should close him down everywhere soon for trying to foment war." Beckley came to the purpose of his visit. "James, I have been seasick for a day, sailing from Alexandria to Norfolk and then up the James River to here for one reason: to prevail on your good sense. Enough of this about 'Luscious Sally' and Mrs. Walker, even if you think it may be true. We're all human, even men who later rise to the Presidency. Come back to the republican fold. Uphold the principles you believe in."

"The first thing I believe in," said Callender, "is that Thomas Jefferson does not have the requisite moral character to be President of the United States. If you ask a married man what he would say if his closest friend attempted to dishonor him by seducing his wife, he would declare that he did not know whether such a wretch was fittest to be hanged or drowned—but was surely not fit to be chief magistrate of the nation. I am going to prevent Jefferson's re-election."

"There is no accusation you can make," Beckley stated, gorge rising, "that will have the slightest effect on his re-election." Because Callender always insisted on fresh, specific information, he gave him some: "Your Calvinist divines with their charges of atheism and sermons about slave concubines may deny him Connecticut, and Delaware is always doubtful. But in the past three months I've been in almost every other state, testing the sentiment, and I tell you true—Jefferson will sweep them all." He calculated swiftly in his head, adding, "Yes, even Massachusetts."

"Your count has been right before," the editor observed. "Who will run against him for the Federalists?"

"Nobody. Charles Pinckney is said to be the most likely sacrificial lamb. He won't even run second."

That piqued the newsmonger's interest. "Who will get the second-highest vote?"

Beckley saw no harm in telling him what he really believed. "Not Burr.

Nobody trusts him. Governor Clinton of New York will be Vice President."

"The Old Incumbent? George Clinton is tired and sick."

"That's why he'll be chosen. Jefferson wants Madison to remain Secretary of State and then succeed him in '08. And after him it will be Monroe's turn. That is the way it is destined to be, James, republicans all, Virginians all. There is absolutely nothing you can do to stop it."

"Is that what they sent you down here to tell me? You know what Little Jemmy calls you, don't you? 'The ablest clerk in America.' They all despise you, John, those highborn Virginians, because you came here no better than a slave. That's why, after all your work getting them elected, you were put in charge of a couple of trunks full of books."

Beckley, seething inwardly, kept his temper. All that contained a grain of truth, of course, like so many of Callender's barbs. By virtue of his political exertions and his experience with numbers—the "ablest clerk" had written Monroe's analysis of Hamilton's Treasury predations in 1792—Beckley was eminently qualified for the job he sought, Comptroller of the Treasury. But Jefferson had told Gallatin to give it to a scion of a Virginia plantation who would better grace the genteel republican court of sycophants around Jefferson. The snub rankled, but Beckley refused to let it embitter him. Politicks had lifted him out of the gutter; he recognized that not even his early service as Mayor of Richmond could help him part the Virginians' social curtain.

After having plied Callender with sound political information, Beckley felt entitled to know the editor's plans. Not only Madison in the national capital, but also Monroe's eyes and ears in Richmond, the bellicose George Hay, had been pressing him to find out what other scurrilities lay in store. "No way can you affect Jefferson's re-election," he repeated.

"The agonies of Erebus agitate their bosoms," said Callender. Beckley made no pretense of having had a Greek classical education; he said nothing.

"Erebus was the son of Chaos, the brother of Night," Callender instructed. "He is the personification of darkness. The ominous presence of Erebus causes your patrons the agony they feel, John. They sent you here to find out what fresh scandals await them as my light is cast into the darkness of Jefferson's past."

"Admit it: there are no more scandals, James."

"Perhaps your Great Personage will recollect a letter he wrote to his favorite nephew, Peter Carr, wherein he advises him to question the existence of a Supreme Being."

Accusations of atheism had long been aimed at Jefferson, but had no evidence behind them other than his association with the avowedly godless Thomas Paine; to counter the rumors, the President was regularly attending church for the first time in his life. Beckley was proud to have been the first to publish Paine's *Rights of Man* in America, but recently argued against Jefferson's receiving the old radical in the President's house because his atheism had become a political embarrassment. The existence of a document, in Jefferson's handwriting, that suggested the President did not believe in God would fuel the anger of the religionists of New England. "You're not serious."

"Do not fancy that I am in jest," said Callender, wagging a finger. "The particulars will appear in my next paper. Next, you may wish to intreat your Great Personage to recollect the message that was sent him in May 1800, by his private secretary, Meriwether Lewis."

Captain Lewis was unreachable, far out on some exploration of the West. "What message?"

"You will die of curiosity before I tell you one more word of that episode. Or another, of the accounts of the expenditure of public money by the Executive Council." The Scot pointed to a stack of letters in a chair by the fireplace. "Gentlemen are sending me packets of information—by hand, not through your postmaster—with the injunction that if their names are called for, they may be printed."

Beckley swallowed to clear the dryness in his throat. "You're giving me hints of terrible things to come, but so far I see nothing for the government to worry about."

"You have no idea the grand harvest the *Recorder* of this summer will offer to the curiosity of the public," said Callender, at last giving Beckley the information he sought. "For a subscription of a mere two dollars per annum, they will have the transcendent enjoyment of hearing as how a certain ambassador to France borrowed five hundred pounds currency of a gentlemen during our glorious Revolution. And then how he proposed to repay when Revolutionary certificates had dropped in value—but the lender would not accept a repayment of good hard Peruvian silver with rotten republican Revolutionary paste-board dollars."

He swallowed again; that sounded specific enough to be troublesome. It went to the subject of financial dishonor, which moneyed interests in New York and Boston considered far more nefarious than enjoying the favors of a Negro concubine or dallying with a neighbor's wife.

"And then I will correct a mistake in my story about Mrs. Walker," said Callender, licking his thin lips. "I will print an apology and a correction, to protect my reputation for being scrupulously accurate."

Beckley braced himself.

"I have written that the Great Personage put an amorous billet into the hand, or sleeve, of Mrs. Walker, even after she repelled his first obnoxious advance." Callender shook his head and made a clucking sound in mock self-reproof. "But I have since found that the billet was wrote, and really put into the hand of another married female—not Mrs. Walker. The Walker dalliance was not an isolated episode. This lusting after other men's wives was apparently a habit of the young Thomas Jefferson's."

"What proof—"

"And if this is denied—perhaps, just perhaps, the damning note can be produced, not in a copy but in the Great Personage's most familiar handwriting."

He was bluffing, Beckley figured; pretending to have a damning document was a familiar device of his. But what if he did have some sort of evidence—if some other woman was eager to come forward with a recollection or even an old note? How many low blows of this sort could the President absorb before the people became disgusted with their elected leader? "My God, James, you don't know how—not just unseemly, but how dangerous all this is."

"To the country?"

"No, you damn fool, to yourself."

Callender seemed not to hear. "It seems 'the Albemarle Amours'—that will be my headline—extended to another lady into whose hands Jefferson's amorous epistle was put." He paused, and then as an afterthought: "And then comes all the rest about the mulatto plantation, and about Sally's previous husbands."

"You take pleasure in this, don't you? You enjoy meddling in the private lives of public men."

"Not at all," Callender dared to insist. "It never was my serious intention to meddle with Mrs. Walker, but the President's *felo-de-se* defenders insulted the public with denials of the fact. That compelled me to knock down those denials with the hammer of truth."

The Librarian made an effort quickly to enumerate in his head the scandals to come, lest he forget any in reporting to Madison: (1) the atheism letter; (2) the mysterious message from his secretary Lewis; (3) the Executive Council financial accounts; (4) the Jefferson debt during the Revolution repaid in devalued currency; (5) another neighbor's wife seduced; and almost as an afterthought (6) "Dusky Sally's" several husbands.

Perhaps he had nothing more than rumors. But if Callender wrote one of those half-dozen half-truths every other month, letting the reverberations and denials play themselves out each time, that would take him right through the presidential election next year. Presumably, the publication of those scandals would encourage others resentful of Jefferson to come forward with other truths or hard-to-deny falsehoods. No wonder there were angry men in Washington, and especially on Virginia's plantations, who, like Monroe's acolyte Hay, felt strongly that Callender was a dangerous scoundrel who had to be stopped.

"I cannot impress upon you too strongly, James," Beckley told him with fervor, "that you are playing with fire. I warned you before Duane wrote that terrible lie about your wife, remember?" He was careful to add, "Though I didn't know exactly what that damn fool was going to do beforehand, of course. Now I'm warning you again. There are violent men out there."

Callender took a moment to digest that. "I do not like to see my idols of recent years revealed to have feet of clay," he said finally. "But if there is one thing I have learned, Calm Observer, it is that Paine was right: with authority comes corruption. Republicans, it seems—even the noblest of them—are just as corruptible as the rest of mankind."

Beckley would not sit still for that pretentious self-justification. Callender was besplattering greatness with his mud to satisfy his insatiable rage and to sell his damnable sheet. "You are using that high-minded nonsense to conceal your own lust for notoriety. These scandals you are mongering do not even rise to the level of sedition, bringing government into disrepute. They are personal matters you are using to blacken the name of one great and good man, who may be as human as you or me."

"He has blackened his own name by his actions," said the editor. "I only make them public, as I am at liberty to do."

"Don't you understand the difference between liberty and license?"

"Licentiousness is nothing more than a ricketty, or dropsical, species of liberty," Callender said. "I will grant you that licentiousness—that's what you mean, not mere license—is defined as liberty swelling beyond its proper limits. But if you ask the first ten men you meet, you will find it hard to find four that will agree where such limits are to be placed."

"And so you admit of no limits at all. Every foul rumor comes under your beloved 'hammer of truth.' "

"The public are entitled to know the personal character of the men who would lead them. Jefferson used to say that he refused to believe that there was one code of morality for a public man, and another for a private man."

"Circumstances change and a man's opinions with them, as you well know. Madison tells me the President now thinks he's become a fair mark for every man's dirt. You scandalmongers make a mockery of your liberty of the press, and by so doing endanger it. You're drawn to all this tittle-tattle only to sell your newspapers."

Callender shrugged. "If there were no buyers of newspapers," he replied, "there could be no sellers." He picked up a strange-looking hat and ran his fingers along the brim, turning it as he ruminated. "Have you stopped to think, John, how little difference there is between Hamilton and Jefferson?"

Beckley had the answer and it had little to do with domestic politicks or Britain versus France or personality clashes. "All the difference in the world. Hamilton thinks that man's nature is evil and that he needs strong government to control his passions. Jefferson sees man as essentially good and needs to protect his freedom from the monarch's domination. From that flows all the dissension of our time."

Callender tilted his head in thought.

"And you used to be on our side," Beckley pressed, "with Jefferson and Paine and Locke and the enlightenment of mankind. What's happened to you?"

"I am in neither camp now," Callender said. "It is not that man is inherently good or bad. It's when a man climbs up into the saddle, he is corrupted by the height. It happened to Hamilton, and I fought to bring him down, and now it's happened to Jefferson, and I have to do the same."

"Why, for God's sake? Nobody elected you to be the Savonarola who expels the Medicis."

"True, and as I recall, the Florentines tortured and burned him at the stake for his reforms. John, I do not relish the thought of returning to the jail you built when you were Mayor here, so long ago. Or being run out of this self-satisfied country to face a gibbet in Scotland. Or suffering another attack from Monroe-once-removed, from which this stout hat kept my brains from being beat out. I just think, John," he concluded, "that those on high who have the power to strike fear into people's hearts should live with the risk of having fear struck into their own."

"You've enjoyed your vengeance. You've built up your circulation. That's enough. If you go ahead with this hateful besmearment," Beckley warned him, "tearing down our leaders and making people in this very neighborhood ashamed of the way they live, there will be those who think jail or exile is too good for you."

He left him to think that over, but was fearful that the stubborn Scot would never learn.

Callender was more shaken by Beckley's warning than he had let on. Hay's beating had him looking over his shoulder whenever it grew dark. He always wore the helmet-like hat Maria had given him. He was less worried about the angry republicans than about the fury of the young rakes in town who blamed him for the curtailment of the black dances. It seemed to him that every man's hand was turned against him.

But not every woman's. He locked the door of the printing shop and walked up the muddy street to the tavern near Dr. Mathew's house where he and Maria now regularly took dinner. She was seated at their table near the window where they could smell the honeysuckle. She held a letter in her hand.

"Read this," she said after their kiss.

It was from Aaron Burr in Washington, enclosing a letter from his friend at the Boston seminary where Susan Lewis was being educated. The girl was expressing a desire, almost a desperation, to see her mother again. However, any meeting of the two had to be arranged with discretion lest their relationship be exposed; the seminary would never put up with the notoriety. In his letter of transmittal, Vice President Burr wrote that he had arranged for Susan to sail to Washington for a week's stay at a respectable rooming house in the capital. He presumed that Dr. Mathew would excuse Maria from work that week, and he had arranged board for her also at a separate place in Washington.

"You're going, of course," said Callender. "When do you leave?"

"Day after tomorrow on the packet. I hope she's all right. It's been over a year."

He understood. "It must be wonderful to have a child who wants to see you."

"Oh, James. You and your boys will be reunited one day soon, I know it."

He had come to doubt that. Even if they showed an interest in coming to Richmond, he could not provide a home that guaranteed their safety. George Hay and all his friends were on his mind.

"You look worried," she said. "Was it anything Beckley told you today?"

Callender shrugged. "Pack your bag in the morning. Stay with me tomorrow night, and I'll to take you to the wharf and see you off." He stared at the letter from the Vice President and handed it back to her. "You'll be seeing your friend Burr?"

"Probably. I mean yes, of course, to thank him for all he's done for Susan and me."

"Tell him I wish now he'd been more active in snatching that election." That was true; like Jefferson and Hamilton, Burr's past offered a rich subject for a scandalmonger. Callender had a suspicion that Hamilton and Burr were rivals for Maria's affections when one or both seduced her back in 1791, and each despised the other as a voluptuary ever since. But that was a matter too painful for him to ever ask her about lest she tell him a truth he did not want hammering at him every time he touched her. She had been very young; her husband was a rogue and a brute; her lover or lovers were men of wealth and power and good looks. He would judge them but not her. He let himself hope that Burr was now no more than her friend.

Maria smiled at his suggestion of political support of the outcast Burr and then became serious again. "You'll be careful while I'm gone?"

"By that you mean not too much drinking. I'll be careful." He already felt profoundly alone.

Chapter 48

RICHARD HARISON

July 1, 1803
NEW YORK CITY

"*I*f we try this case on the law, General Hamilton," Richard Harison told his famous law partner, "we would surely lose."

They sat on this late-spring afternoon at the great bay window facing the Harlem River; the window behind them had a view westward of the sunset across the Hudson River. Harison knew that Hamilton had bought thirty acres on a $5,000 loan and hired the architect of City Hall to draw up the plans for the Grange. He named the country house after the family seat in Scotland, skipping back a generation past his improvident father and free-spirited mother in the West Indies.

"We would lose," Harison explained, "because our client has clearly printed a libel on Thomas Jefferson."

"The Zenger precedent?"

"In the seditious libel trial of the printer John Peter Zenger," Harison recited, "a jury ignored the judge's reading of the law. The jurors accepted Zenger's unprecedented contention that truth is a defense against libel, and found him not guilty. That was seventy years ago." Ever since, that runaway jury's verdict had been portrayed by publishers as a great victory for liberty of the press. But it was not, in terms of the law. "As we established in your libel suit against the editor of the now-defunct *New York Argus*"—Harison had helped put out of business the republican publication that enraged

Hamilton—"it was the judge's charge in the Zenger case, and not the jury's verdict, that confirmed the legal precedent set by Judge Coke in England."

"The common law is plain?"

Harison was sure of it. "It matters not if a libel is true or false; it matters only that its publication defamed and damaged the plaintiff. Blackstone defines libel as 'any scandalous publication that tends to breach the peace.' "

"Even so, we have undertaken the defense of Croswell of the *Wasp pro bono publico*," said Hamilton, steepling his fingers. "I intend to win it, Richard. But win or lose, I intend to expose a foul act that sought to demean President Washington. How do you suggest we proceed?"

Harison presumed that his partner had a dual purpose in taking time from his lucrative law practice to defend the hapless Columbia County editor. The political purpose was to spread far and wide the accusation that Jefferson had hired James Callender to vilify and distract President Washington; that is what Callender had alleged and Croswell reprinted. The second, nobler purpose was to build public support to stimulate the New York State legislature to pass a bill, already pending, to change the libel law and enshrine well-motivated truth as a defense.

An element of Hamilton's self-interest was present even in that nobility of purpose: a new judicial precedent or a new law that discouraged libel suits would build a wall of protection against the spate of State prosecutions that Jefferson's men were launching against opposition newspapers across the country. Everyone in the Hamilton firm knew that the coordinated republican use of State libel actions to suppress the nation's unfriendly press would ultimately reach the General's *New York Evening Post*. Harison saw the ironic symmetry in the reversal of roles: just as the Jeffersonians had exploited the public's outrage at the Federalist's Sedition Act, Hamilton would try to whip up public resentment against republican State libel laws. It was not that most of the American people trusted the press more, but that they trusted government—any government—less.

"My recommendation is to do what Zenger's counsel did," Harison advised. "That is, to make a dramatic appeal to the jury to defy the judge's instructions and to nullify the law."

Hamilton nodded and waited.

"The drama would have to be more than oratorical," the experienced counsel continued, knowing that not even Hamilton's renowned skills as a courtroom advocate would likely carry the day without an additional strong element of theater. "You would need to call the one witness that nobody would expect you, General, to call. A witness who would make everyone on the jury gasp with astonishment."

"James Thomson Callender," said Hamilton with relish, "the most scurrilous scoundrel of them all."

Harison allowed his partner a few moments to consider the use of his Nemesis, the writer who ruined a great statesman's career in politicks. Everyone in the courtroom would remember the Reynolds affair, a national titillation that eclipsed even the current Walker affair because the adulterer had so publicly confessed. To see the scandalmonger at the root of exposing both cases joining with the object of his first attack to defend a sacred principle of liberty might well inspire the most timid juror to depart from a judge's pettifogging instructions.

"Harry Croswell is charged with"—here Harison looked at New York State's indictment—" 'deceitfully, wickedly, maliciously, and willfully traducing, scandalizing, and vilifying President Thomas Jefferson and representing him to be unworthy of the confidence, respect and attachment of the people of the United States.' The key word is the first word—'deceitfully.' "

He picked up a copy of the *Wasp,* the unimportant weekly that was chosen by the State Attorney General to become an example to any editor who dared to heap obloquy on republican leaders. "The prosecutor will introduce as evidence this article in the *Wasp,* reprinted from the *Richmond Recorder.* In it, Callender accuses Jefferson of having paid him hundreds of dollars over a four-year period to subsidize his pamphlets, books and newspapers. It includes copies of letters from Jefferson encouraging these publications and enclosing money—"

"—Including slanderous attacks on President Washington," Hamilton chimed in, "calling him a traitor, a robber, and a perjurer, which may have contributed to the rapid decline of his health. I can recount to the jury, firsthand, Washington's reaction to the vicious attacks that Jefferson hired Callender to level at him. I saw with my own eyes how debilitating it was to that great man in his final years."

"That would be persuasive. The indictment also says," Harison pointed out, "that Callender also called President Adams 'a hoary-headed incendiary.' "

That last did not seem to bother Hamilton, who permitted himself a small smile. "The scoundrel has a way with a phrase."

"We will stipulate that Croswell did indeed print Callender's account,"

Harison suggested, "and treat that central element of the prosecution case as insignificant. We will never put Croswell on the stand. Instead, we—you—will call Callender as our witness."

"The State will object, of course, at our attempt to use him to establish the truth," Hamilton said. "And the judge will rule that 'truth is no defense.' "

"We can assume the prosecution will do everything to prevent Callender from taking the stand. We don't know who the judge will be, but the Attorney General chose the Claverack, New York, venue to get a republican jurist, I'm sure. As you suggest, the judge will probably refuse to allow Callender to testify."

"We sit that scoundrel Callender in the front row facing the jury for the whole trial," Hamilton said, smiling at the prospect. "I could say, 'That man—whose contumelious lash I can still feel on my back—was not allowed to confirm the truth in this case to you.' " He liked the sound of it. "Yes, it would outrage the jury."

"Perhaps not 'contumelious.' " Harison feared that Hamilton's vocabulary went beyond the understanding of the average juror.

"You're right. 'Vicious.' 'Savage.' "

"And Callender would write his account of the trial in a manner censorious of the prosecution—"

"Oh, he'll vilify the judge in letters of vitriol," Hamilton was certain.

"—which Croswell could then reprint locally, as the poor young fellow has little more to lose. And there would be other members of the press in the courtroom to talk to the famous Richmond scandalmonger."

"Assume on the other hand, Richard, that the judge does allow us to put Callender on the stand—"

"The witness, under oath, would then go into great detail about how Jefferson, even while serving as Washington's Secretary of State, supported his attacks on the revered late father of our country." Harison stopped. "You know, as I think about this, General, I suspect that the prosecution would drop the case at the first sign that Callender might be our witness."

Hamilton agreed. "Our strategy has to be, first, to assert the truth of the published information as a defense against prosecution for libel."

"You'll be overruled on the law."

"Right, but I'll challenge that. Second, we will argue that for libel to be a crime, it must be maliciously committed. No intent of malice, no crime."

"Overruled," said Harison, playing the judge.

"Let him. Finally, we will argue that the jury has a say in the interpretation of the libel law."

"Overruled again. The jury decides the facts, but the judge rules on the law."

Hamilton nodded again. "But by challenging that, too, I may embolden the jury to emulate the Zenger jurors of the last century."

Harison could only blink and shake his head in wonderment at their daring. Here was Hamilton planning to argue against centuries of English precedent that defined libel, true or false, to be any publication that breached the peace. And on top of that, he had in mind to empower the jury at the expense of the judge.

Harison was about to point out the audacity, if not the foolishness, of such a courtroom course. But then he asked himself: why not? With Madison and Jay, Hamilton was the man who wrote *The Federalist Papers*, making the definitive case for the Constitution. This aide to Washington, Revolutionary hero, first Treasury Secretary—by dint of his genius for articulation did more to persuade the States to ratify the Federal Constitution than any man alive. Even political enemies acknowledged him to be, along with John Marshall, among the most brilliant legal minds in the nation. Who was to say this man could not stretch the boundaries of the received wisdom about the common law, or give the musty traditions a new construction? Certainly not his law partner.

If they did not win at trial, perhaps on appeal; if not then, perhaps Hamilton's argument would be taken up by the State legislature and the law would be changed. If New York's constitution precluded that, it could be amended, and State constitutions across the land would follow, thereby thwarting Jefferson's plan to use State libel laws to silence sedition throughout the nation. It was a heady thought, mixing politics and law on a grand scale.

"I take it, General," said Harison carefully, "that you are inviting these fundamental controversies as a way of dramatizing—not just to the jury, but to the general public—the import of what the witness Callender has to say about Jefferson's betrayal of Washington. What you call 'the foul act.' "

"Surely it is not an immaterial thing," Hamilton acknowledged, looking pointedly at a portrait of Washington on his office wall, "that a high official character should be capable of saying anything against the father of this country. It is important to our country, to us all, whether the charges made by Callender, and reprinted by Croswell, be true or false. It is important to the reputation of Mr. Jefferson, against whom Callender's charges are made, that they should be examined." They sat in silence for a moment, until Hamilton concluded, almost in a whisper, "It will be a glorious triumph for truth."

Harison was pleased to see Hamilton almost his old vigorous self again. Ever since his son Philip was killed in a duel and his daughter Angelica went mad, the fire had gone out of him. The energetic executive who roused his countrymen to great enterprises had seemed enervated, as if at sea for too long; this case strengthened his spirit and stimulated his mind.

The partners both assumed the Jeffersonians would anticipate that Callender would be called the moment they learned the Hamilton firm had taken the case. Not many other law firms would have the daring, or the wherewithal, to bring a witness nearly five hundred miles up the coast. Croswell's original attorney, William Van Ness—known to be a friend of Aaron Burr's, but a sound lawyer—had expressed the worry that republicans might try to intimidate or suborn Callender to prevent his appearance. Perhaps they thought a postmastership would buy his silence.

Hamilton directed his partner to go to Richmond the following week, to bring Callender to New York and put him up in a secret location here at whatever the expense. He said to advise him that as a witness in a court action, the editor ran no risk of libel in reporting all the proceedings daily, especially including his own testimony so damning to the high-placed slanderers of Washington.

Harison knew that Hamilton could make much of the piquant irony in all this. President Jefferson had ostentatiously pardoned everyone convicted under the hated Federal Sedition Act, to great public applause, but now—in power—Jefferson was encouraging States to circumvent the spirit of the Constitution's First Amendment, drafted hardly a decade ago by Madison, now his Secretary of State. But General Hamilton, long denied the attention of the nation, was now allied with Callender, his former tormenter, in the newsworthy defense of an appealing young journalist. Hamilton would have an unparalleled forum to expose his lifelong rival as a thoroughgoing hypocrite.

"I'll see what ship is scheduled for Baltimore or Washington, and from there on to Richmond," Harison promised. As he rose to go, he could see fresh dirt dug up in a patch just outside the window. "You're planting?"

"Charles Pinckney was good enough to send me some melon seeds," said the new country squire. "A garden, you know, is a very useful refuge for a disappointed politician." He indicated a large birdcage in the corner of the room. "And he sent those Carolina paroquets for Angelica. She is very fond of birds."

Harison swallowed at the sad reference to the troubled young woman and hurried out to his carriage. It was important to get to Callender before any of Jefferson's allies tried to bully him or buy his silence. His witness would make all the difference.

Chapter 49

AARON BURR

July 10, 1803
NEW YORK CITY

Richmond Hill was widely reputed to be the most elegant home in the State of New York. Its private library numbered 6,000 volumes; not as extensive as Thomas Jefferson's famed collection of books at Monticello, but impressive to most visitors of intellect. English and French furniture graced the spacious rooms; the stables housed blooded Arabian horses. Its upkeep was driving Aaron Burr toward bankruptcy.

The cost of living at his second lodging, in Washington City, took up the $5,000 a year he received in salary as Vice President. Knowing he was, in a word, strapped, Burr put Richmond Hill on the market for $150,000. When that drew no takers, he was forced to turn to his daughter Theodosia's husband for a substantial loan.

More distressing to him than his financial predicament was his political position. He was aware that Jefferson and the republicans distrusted him profoundly, as a result of the awkwardness surrounding the tie vote in the 1800 campaign. All he had done was to refuse to close the door to a possible Presidency; what politician in his right mind would have done differently? At the same time, Hamilton and many of the fragmented Federalists despised him cordially, a sentiment he returned with cool ferocity.

Both political roads to the presidency in 1805 thus appeared closed to him. His informants told him that Jefferson, seeking a Vice President who would pose no challenge to his Virginia dynasty, was inclined to pick George Clinton, the intermittent Governor of New York, who was all too pleased at the prospect of stepping into that semi-retirement in the eddies of the stream of power currently occupied restlessly by Burr.

However, that would leave open the Governorship of New York. With republicans set to make the City's current Mayor their candidate, and Hamilton certain to block Burr's chances for the Federalist nomination, that meant Burr would have to stand as an independent, unaffiliated with any organized faction. If he won—and Burr still controlled the Tammany Society, which would place him in contention—then he would be in a position to listen to the rumblings from discontented Federalists and resentful republicans throughout New England.

Some leaders there had confided in him a daring plan: Massachusetts, Connecticut, Pennsylvania and New York, which controlled most of the nation's manufacturing and commerce, had little in common with the Virginia and Carolina farming aristocracies. The issue of slavery also separated the sections of the agglomeration of Colonies. These States were far from "United"; why not separate into nations of the like-minded?

He looked at Hamilton's *Evening Post* on the table in his library. Even as Burr had been mulling this idea of secession of the Northern States to form a New England nation, the stunning news of Monroe's coup in Europe broke in the newspapers.

Jefferson, Madison and Monroe had been secretly negotiating to buy the City of New Orleans from Napoleon. But the French leader astounded them, and the world, by offering to sell out his complete position in the New

World. The sheer size of the offer was staggering. What drove him to it? Some said the would-be Emperor needed to finance his European conquests; others held that the yellow fever had so weakened France's force in the Indies that invasion of the North American continent was impossible. Burr suspected that the dictator of France thought that he could create a new commercial competition between Britain and its radically expanded colonies so fierce that France would benefit. If that was his strategy, the much-feared Frenchman was a dunce who had just given up for a pittance the most valuable mass of property in the world.

The deal was struck for 80 million francs, or $16 million. Monroe insisted it included Florida, although Spain disputed that claim. Burr knew that the Spaniards had hoped that France, in the great western expanses of the Louisiana Territory, would block American expansion toward their Mexican colony and the rich realm to the south. Napoleon betrayed the Spaniards' trust. Whatever the boundaries were, the size of the United States was at least doubled overnight, and total control of the Mississippi River fell unexpectedly into the nation's hands.

Even Hamilton's *Evening Post* was agog at the development just brought back from Europe. Vice President Burr saw the irony that so many would surely miss: financing from the United States Bank, which Hamilton had formed over Jefferson's repeated objections, made it possible for the United States to make a purchase that meant Jefferson would be harder than ever to beat in the coming election.

Who could best administer this vast new territory, incorporating into the United States? Burr had persuaded himself that he was the best man for that post; he had only to persuade President Jefferson of his ability to fasten the new land tightly to the nation. At the same time, Burr could make private plans to ultimately make it an independent nation.

Alternative vistas opened for the isolated Vice President. As New York Governor, he could become the leader of a secession of New England to form a new and more cohesive Union. The other way was as master of the Louisiana Territory, leader of another new nation that would soon conquer the Spaniards and strike down through Mexico to open another continent. That Western alternative, combining secession with conquest, piqued his sense of adventure. Burr doubted that Jefferson could be persuaded of his loyalty, but before challenging Jefferson in New York by running for Governor, he would see him to make the effort to win the post with headquarters at New Orleans.

"A Mrs. Clement to see you, Colonel. The lady says you are expecting her."

Maria was as statuesque and striking as he remembered her, the level blue eyes still challenging, but her face was pale. She held herself stiffly; he presumed her back was painful again, which often happened when she was deeply worried or harried. "The voyage must have been exhausting," he said, taking her hand when she did not offer her cheek.

"The James River packet to Norfolk was delayed," she reported, "and I missed the connecting ship to Baltimore and New York. But I got here last week in time to receive Susan from Boston."

"How is your daughter?"

"Susan is upset," she said. "We're so grateful to you for making it possible for us to meet privately. This week has been hard, but I think we helped each other."

He was aware that the girl was in difficulty. His friend at the seminary had informed him that Susan Lewis was morose at times, defiant and insubordinate at others. Burr presumed that the years of secret shame with her mother—and the continuing need to lie about her identity—combined with the natural turmoil of a girl at her stage of life to produce considerable mental strain.

Burr had his own worries about his motherless daughter, Theodosia. After the two friends shared their trials of single parenthood, Maria expressed a desire to return to Richmond quickly.

"I had hoped we could spend some evenings together while you were here," he said. She was as attractive at thirty-two as she had been to him at nineteen, when he secretly shared her favors with the voluptuary Hamilton. His feeling for her had deepened and mellowed over the years. Maria and he had been through different but equally hot crucibles of political fire, remaining constant friends and occasional lovers.

"I would like that, of course," she said, "but I must get back. I've written you about the man I've been seeing. He's alone and in danger, I fear, of slipping back into a bad habit."

Burr had read of Callender's reputation for heavy drinking; Porcupine had often branded him a drunk. But Maria did not know that the danger he faced was greater than that from a bottle. He thought it odd that she wanted to be faithful to him; Maria had many attributes, emotional and surely physical, but conjugal fidelity had never been one of them. They were both getting older.

"A close associate of mine needs your help," Burr told her. "His name is William Van Ness and he's upstairs right now. He and your old friend Hamilton are working together on a legal matter that could embarrass the President. It could involve Callender, and we need your advice. I have no public involvement in this at all, you understand."

She could keep a secret. He sent for Van Ness.

She extended her gloved hand. Van Ness was a young man who struck her as a bit too well dressed and self-assured. Burr introduced him to "my long-time client, Mrs. Clement, who is now resident in Richmond. She counts among her friends there James Callender, a man you are interested in."

"We're thinking of calling Callender as a witness for the defense in a libel suit," said Van Ness. "What sort of witness do you think he'd be?"

"If he is called as a witness, James will tell the truth. Perhaps more than you want. He often says he regards the truth as a kind of hammer."

"That's an interesting figure of speech, Mrs. Clement. What does he mean by it?"

"He says he uses the truth to smash barriers of lies," she replied. "There is no stopping him. I don't think he can stop himself when he gets that hammer in his hand."

"Would you say he would appear to the average person—a juror, in this case—as a man filled with hatred?"

"There is some of that in him," she said, "but not so much directed at this man or that man. What angers him most is the way men are corrupted by the lust for power." She looked at Burr. "That frightens and disappoints him, and I think he hates to find himself frightened and disappointed."

"Someone who has seen him recently tells our friends that Mr. Callender claims to have a half-dozen more scandals ready to publish," said Van Ness, in what Maria thought was an unctuous tone; nobody ever called the notorious scandalmonger *Mr.* Callender. "Have you heard your friend say that to people?"

"I have. Most of them are just suspicions on his part. He acts as if he just needs a little more information to finish his article and publish, but that is only to encourage people to tell him more. It's his way."

"Do you know if he has documents in his possession—not copies, but in Mr. Jefferson's handwriting—of the transmission of money to him from Jefferson, as he has claimed in his newspaper?"

She looked at Burr, who nodded at her to encourage an answer. "Yes. He has shown them to me. They are not signed, however, and I have no way of knowing if the handwriting is the President's." Burr kept nodding; she knew that he knew she had previous experience with forged notes that Hamilton attributed to her.

"And where does he keep these letters and documents?" Van Ness probed.

Maria shrugged; James used to keep them under his mattress, but the month before gave them to her for safekeeping in Dr. Mathew's house. The documents were now under her mattress in an envelope sealed with wax. That was not this lawyer's business; she would not even tell her trusted friend, Burr.

"The reason he asks," Burr put in, "goes to one reason that I wanted you here rather than in Richmond. His life, and anyone close to him, may be in danger."

She felt a constriction in her chest in addition to her back pain. "He knows that all too well."

"There are those in New York and Washington City," Van Ness continued, "who for political reasons do not want him to be a witness at this trial. There are others locally in Richmond, more hotheaded and prone to violence, who do not want him further exposing the practices of plantation life involving the mixture of the races."

"I know. He gets threats all the time. I've seen some of the letters that contain threats to horsewhip him."

"Has he been drinking a lot?"

She started; that seemed slightly off the subject. "No more than usual, a half-bottle or so a day. It makes him quiet, but it does not interfere with his work."

"Does he talk of suicide?"

"Never."

"The reason my friend asks," Burr interjected, "is that we hear rumors here and in Washington—and I suppose you hear them in Richmond, too—that he's been getting drunk all the time, and talks about suicide. The deliberate spreading of that rumor could mean that he is at risk of being beaten or even killed, and his office and house ransacked, possibly burned to destroy evidence. That is why it would be better for you to remain in New York a few weeks."

Maria could not stop tears from starting to her eyes. She looked through them to Burr: "You are Vice President of the United States. Can't you protect him?"

Van Ness was the one to answer. "My co-counsel in the defense of the editor of a small newspaper called the *Wasp*," said the attorney, "who is a law partner of Alexander Hamilton, has already left for Richmond to bring Callender to the courthouse in Claverack, up in Columbia County."

"Is he likely to come?" Burr asked her.

"To testify against Jefferson? You can't be serious. He'll be eager to come." She blinked away her tears, genuinely frightened now. She wished James knew of the urgency of the need for him to get out of Richmond.

"You'll remain here in New York, then," said Burr with finality.

"If you would like to attend the trial, Mrs. Clement," said Van Ness, "I would be pleased to make sure you are seated where you can hear all the proceedings."

Chapter 50

July 17, 1803
RICHMOND

Callender knew his drinking limit. He could down one bottle of rum in a day without falling down. He would stagger a bit and his tongue would be too thick for his words to be understood, but he could manage to get from the printing shop to his room on his own, especially in the light of a summer's evening.

He finished the last of his bottle with a small bit of food at a lonely dinner at the tavern where he and Maria customarily met to talk and dine. He spread his hands on the table, leaned his heavy head forward and prepared to push himself into a standing position when he heard a couple of voices coming at him.

The voices were friendly, which surprised him a little because when he looked up he hazily saw George Hay, the Monroe aide who defended him at the sedition trial and later attacked him with a club, and a man who looked like Peter Carr, Jefferson's nephew whom he had observed more than once at one of the infamous black dances. A third man, a big fellow, he did not recognize and was in no condition to remember his name when he said it.

They brought their own bottle to the table and said there was no reason for them all to be enemies. Callender, though suspicious, agreed to that. They poured him a drink and he said no, he had reached his limit, but he toasted their health with an empty glass. Maria would have liked to see that.

Next he knew, they were talking about business and Callender complained about Henry Pace owing him, $1,800. They were partners, and the writer was responsible for the success of the *Recorder,* but the printer had invested the capital and kept a tight fist on the profits. His table mates agreed that was unfair. They went on and on about the 80 million francs being paid to Napoleon for all the land west of the Mississippi, and Callender was not so sure the wilderness was worth it. He said he could not remember how much it was in dollars and held out his glass, which was refilled.

A while later he made to get up and go home but could not push himself up. So he stayed, silent, drinking with his companions, half-listening until the big man had a splendid suggestion that they go fishing. Callender perked up at that. He liked to fish in the shallows of the James River, he told them as best he could, because the water was warm and the fish were biting in the evening and the morning, whichever this was.

He let them help him off the bench, through the tavern and onto the road outside. Several strangers passed by and, weaving forward, he waved cheerily at them, saying "Fishing."

Time slipped past during which he thought he saw Henry Pace's angry face arguing about the money, but he may have imagined that. Then he heard the buzz of insects, smelled the river water, and felt the hard board of wood under his seat. He was in a rowboat, going fishing. What a fine idea. Callender wondered what he would do for a pole and a string and a hook. Only one man was with him now and he was rowing out into the shallows. Callender had the urge to wade out into the warm water, which he knew would only come up to his hips. He took off his shoes.

His friend helped him overboard. The mud felt wonderful in his toes and the water was hardly above his knees. To escape the mosquitoes, he waded out further and ducked under the water for a moment. That refreshed him a little and he looked about for the rowboat, but it was dark and nowhere to be seen. He hoped the fellow would not get lost. He was up to his waist and, arms extended, relaxed his weight onto the welcoming black water and felt himself happily passing into a dream.

July 18, 1803

The lawyer from New York peered through the shuttered window of the *Richmond Recorder* and could make out a man inside in printer's apron who seemed to be counting a large mound of type. He rapped on the shutter. The man—young, in a begrimed apron—unlocked the door of the newspaper.

"We're out of business," he said. "Go away."

"I am looking for Mr. James Callender," the lawyer said. "I was told he is the co-owner of this establishment."

"You were a friend of his?"

"I am associated with Alexander Hamilton in a legal matter in New York."

"You just missed him," said the printer. "He's supposed to have drowned yesterday."

Richard Harison took a step back. "What do you mean, 'supposed to have drowned'? Is Callender alive or not?"

"Oh, he's dead all right, and the whole town couldn't be happier. They hated the little Scot immigrant, especially the plantation owners around here. They hated to have to read him."

"You say he drowned?"

"In three feet of water, over at the James River, if you believe that. Ask the coroner down the street in City Hall. They had the inquest this morning, lasted all of five minutes. They wanted him in the ground in a hurry."

"Who's 'they'?"

"He had enemies. You're not the first fellow from New York come down here asking after him. The Federalists up your way hated him for all the years he made President Adams furious. The republicans down here hated him for digging up the truth about President Jefferson and Black Sally. You here with a libel charge? You're too late."

"It does have to do with seditious libel," the lawyer said. "Three feet of water, you say? You can stand up in that."

"He was drunk, they say, too drunk to get up."

"You don't believe that, though."

"Callender was always half-drunk, even when he was writing, and never drowned himself before. That man could hold his liquor."

The lawyer wanted to ask about the other fellow from New York asking after Callender, and about who discovered the body of his witness, but the printer closed the door.

He walked down the main street of Virginia's capital to City Hall, identified himself to the coroner as Richard Harison, Esquire, former United States Attorney in New York, and asked the cause of death and whereabouts of the body of James Thomson Callender.

"The damn scandalmonger was a drunk," the coroner said, "and booze finally killed him. No doubt about it. He was wandering the streets here late yesterday, bottle of rum in his hand, bothering the good people on the street in front of the tavern. A dozen folks could swear they saw him drunk last night."

"The cause of death?"

"Lungs filled with water. He staggered off near the river, fell face down and that was the end of him. Burial took place this noon at the Methodist church, where the Scots go."

"Who brought him in?"

"Couple of kids fishing, spotted his hat in the water, then the body."

"Any bruises about the head?"

The Richmond coroner, a tall man, rose to his full height. "And what is your interest in the deceased?"

"I am a law associate of Alexander Hamilton in New York. We were interested in bringing Mr. Callender to New York to appear at a trial to testify as a witness in a seditious libel action. You did not, I take it, examine the body for evidence of foul play?"

"Of course I did. Callender was a notorious drunk. He passed out and fell on his face in the water and drowned. He lived on mud and died in mud. I held my inquest and it's closed."

"Who identified the body?"

"I did. Know that mean face anywhere, even all bloated the way it was. Doctor bled him but he was long gone." He paused before dismissing his

Northern visitor. "And why should Alexander Hamilton, of all people, be interested?"

"A matter of principle. Did he leave a will, or any documents at the bank or with any friend?"

"No. Died intestate. Didn't have anything to leave anyway, except a claim against his partner, and Pace is probably out of town already."

"Where can I find the place he lived?"

"You can look, but you won't find much. He lived alone in a rooming house with no other roomers. I hear there was a fire there this morning, destroyed all his things." The coroner volunteered a little more information: "Some talk of Callender being a suicide. He was pretty miserable, his own kids hating him, everybody sore at him. I didn't go into that, though, because it only makes things awkward at the funeral."

"Who was at the funeral I could talk to?"

"Meriwether Jones, editor of the *Examiner,* was there. He'll do an obituary. Dead man's partner, Pace, never showed up. I expect the *Recorder* won't publish any more."

Harison made to take his leave, but as a seeming afterthought, added: "I'm told another fellow from out of town was asking for Callender the other day. Perhaps I know him. An attorney, too?"

The coroner stared at him stonily and did not respond.

At the *Examiner* printing shop, Harison found Jones. He was a mild-looking man not as censorious of Callender as a competitor so personally vilified might be expected to be.

"He was endowed by nature with the most admirable talents," said the rival editor, "including an unconquerable bias toward political discussion."

"What made him so mean?"

"Persecution both in his native country and in America seems to have soured his temper," said Jones. "That produced the falsehood, detraction and personal abuse that more or less characterized all of his writings."

"How did he meet his death?"

"Some say suicide. For the past week or two, Callender threatened to end his existence by drowning himself. It could be that in an intoxicated frenzy, he put a miserable end to a miserable life."

Harison caught the skepticism in his tone and said, "But you don't believe it was suicide. Or an accident."

"If you want my opinion," said Meriwether Jones, "I think he was murdered. His monstrous partner, Henry Pace, cheated him and had a man drown him lest he collect what he was owed."

Harison took that to be the story the republicans would adopt if the explanation of an accident was met with skepticism. The death of their most dangerous tormenter would be blamed on suicide or murder by a partner motivated by money. "What about the fire that destroyed his room? And the absence of any will or personal effects, or documents he may have been assembling to use in articles?"

The *Examiner* editor shrugged; he had no answer for that.

Chapter 51

THE WASP.

By Robert Rusticoat, Esquire.

Vol. I.] " *To lash the Rascals naked through the world.*" [No. 6.

HUDSON, AUGUST 30, 1802.

FOR THE WASP.

COMMUNICATION.

THE democratic printers are altogether at a loss what to do with James Thompson Callender, author of " The Prospect Before us," a book written with great ability, and much more wickedness—reviling not only Adams and Hamilton, but even Washington himself—and that not during Washington's life only, but

furiated man seeking through (the) blood and slaughter of other men's fame, the long desired Presidency. —Hot gall was poured upon the ashes of the immortal Washington, and to this wretch it was luxury to snuff the rich incense. Language fails here. When will the people open their eyes. When will they learn that the sweetest talker—he who is continually trying to persuade them, that he, and he alone, is almost perfection—when will they learn that such an one is the deadliest of hypocrites? When will they learn—to despise these word-mongers—to detest these magicians of the infernal?

July 21, 1803

CLAVERACK, COLUMBIA COUNTY, NEW YORK

*T*he bailiff called out the name of the case at trial as "In the Great Cause of the People versus Harry Croswell." But Maria Lewis Reynolds Clingman Clement, clothed in a decorous black dress and her anonymity, and seated in the tenth row of the county courthouse, knew it in reality to be Jefferson versus Callender.

"May it please the Court," said William Van Ness, co-counsel with Alexander Hamilton for the defendant Croswell, "that James Thomson Callender, of the State of Virginia, is a material witness for the defendant. Without the benefit of his testimony, we cannot safely proceed to trial."

The judge was Morgan Lewis, Chief Justice of the State of New York, a republican appointee of Governor Clinton. He asked, "Where is this witness?"

"Until a few days past, Your Honor, we had good reason to believe that Mr. Callender would attend as a witness at this Court. We expect to be able to procure the voluntary attendance of this witness at the next circuit court in two months' time. He will bring with him two letters from Thomas Jefferson, now President of the United States, to the said James Thomson Callender, wherein Mr. Jefferson expressed his approbation of a certain publication then about to be printed by Callender."

"What do you expect to prove with this absent witness, and with those letters, if such exist?"

"We will prove," Van Ness told the judge, "that Thomas Jefferson, Esquire, well knowing the contents of said publication, called *The Prospect Before Us*, paid to Callender the two several sums of fifty dollars. The first to assist him prior to publication, and the other subsequent thereto as a reward, showing his approval thereof."

Van Ness held up a copy of the Callender pamphlet. "In this publication that Thomas Jefferson caused to be published, George Washington, late President of the United States, deceased, is charged in effect with being 'a traitor, a robber and a perjurer.' John Adams, late President of the United States, is herein expressly declared to be 'a hoary-headed incendiary.' "

Some jurors moved uncomfortably in their chairs and looked at one another. The judge's expression remained impassive. "And what would the testimony of your witness and the production of his letters be intended to prove, counselor?"

"It will prove the truth of the statement we are prepared to stipulate was printed by the defendant Croswell in his newspaper the *Wasp*," said Van Ness. "We will prove that Jefferson paid Callender for calling Washington a traitor and Adams an incendiary. By so proving the truth of that printed statement, we will demonstrate that the defendant Croswell did not, as the indictment states, 'most grossly slander the private characters of men who he well knew were virtuous, to the great scandal and infamy of the said Thomas Jefferson, President of the United States.' "

"Truth is not a defense against libel in common law," Judge Lewis declared. "That English common law, so clearly and forcefully expressed by Lord Mansfield in the case of the Dean of St. Asaph, is the law of the State of New York. The testimony of your witness, even if produced, would be irrelevant. Therefore, application for delay is denied." He turned to the State Attorney General. "Let the prosecution begin."

"May I ask what brings a beautiful lady like you to listen to this case?" The man seated on Maria's left was idly curious.

"I had nothing to do today," she replied, "and I heard that General Hamilton will speak. And you?"

"I represent this district, Columbia County, in the State legislature. The Federalists have a bill pending to make it harder to prosecute libel, and I'm to speak against it next week. We republicans are now a majority, you know."

She nodded politely, feigning womanly ignorance about politicks, and turned to listen to the Attorney General make the case against the press.

"We contend that the rights of reputation are as sacred as those of property," said Attorney General Spencer to the Court, "and it is the duty of all to equally respect both. The common law of England is the basis of the laws in force in the State of New York, congenial to the spirit of our Constitution. That law, laid down as Your Honor reminds us by Lord Mansfield, holds that libel, slander and calumny are breaches of the peace—whether or not the facts they contain be true or false."

He turned to the jury, his longtime friends and neighbors, which Maria had been told by Burr was the main reason this venue was chosen. "I trust the day is now arrived in which, by your good judgment, every citizen will lay himself down with the pleasing consolation that his character, as well as his property, his peace of mind as well as his family, are equally protected by law."

Spencer was able to move quickly through the facts in evidence because the essence of his case had been freely admitted, even asserted, by the defense: Croswell had, indeed, published and sold the edition of the *Wasp* that contained the statements cited in the State's indictment. Those words, the Attorney General argued, defamed and sought to bring into public contempt two Presidents of the United States, thereby breaching the peace and producing disorder. He quoted Britain's Lord Bacon: "The frequency of libels is a sure forerunner of tumults in a state." It was for the jury to recognize those undisputed facts and—contrary to the miscarriage of justice in the Zenger case—to listen to the charge of the judge on the law requiring conviction in this case, which could not be clearer.

"A libel is punishable criminally not on the intent of the perpetrator," Spencer told the jury, "for that is no ingredient of the crime, but simply because holding our leaders up to scorn and blackening their names breaches the peace. Were a man to knock me down, it would be no defense to say he did not mean to hurt me. An unlawful act implies a criminal intent. A libel, whether true or false, exposes a public man to public hatred and invites disorder. Indeed, all the venerable sages of the law—Lord Coke, Blackstone—have made clear that 'the greater the truth the greater the libel.' If falsity be not the offense, then truth cannot be the justification."

He pointed to the defendant Croswell, seated between Van Ness and Hamilton. "A libeler creates a tribunal unknown to the law of the land. In his self-erected jurisdiction, the accuser, judge, jury and executioner may be united in one malignant wretch. The first notice of the proceeding given to the unfortunate accused, in this worst of inquisitions, is the publication of the sentence in the newspaper. Is this freedom of the press, the boasted prerogative of a free country?"

He walked to the defendant's bench. "I did indeed read a statement by one of these calumniators by trade, Callender by name, that 'public men were fair game.' " He stared not at young Croswell, the defendant, but at Hamilton. "If that principle of the scurrilous Callender becomes the maxim of the land, it will force all men of merit to quit the walks of public life. Why? To save their lives. Because calumny and slander, propagating injurious reports—whether true or false—plant and nourish the seeds of anger, create that ferment and excite those passions that provoke to personal hostility and acts of violence."

·   ·   ·

"That's what happened to Hamilton five or six years ago," the legislator whispered to Maria. "I don't see how he can defend it now."

"What was that about a Zenger case?"

"It's when a jury went beyond the facts, ignored the judge's charge and took the law in its own hands. The Attorney General wants to make sure it doesn't happen in Columbia County."

"It is asked, however," Spencer said, to anticipate a defense argument, "by defenders of the so-called liberty of the press—are we not to know by whom we are governed? Yes, I answer, but to obtain this knowledge, calumny and abuse, slander and detraction, are by no means necessary." Spencer pointedly turned away from Hamilton and toward the spectators. "We want to fill our offices with the most virtuous characters. But we all know that even the best of these have their failings, their little foibles, and—as they are men—at times their occasional sins." Hamilton remained expressionless, toying with a quill at the defense table.

"If each of these indiscretions is to be dragged forth into public view the instant they step forth in the public service; if their reputations are to be the preparatory sacrifice for public favor; if their names are to be offered up at the shrine of this Moloch of scandal, they will fly from the public employ, leaving only men without shame."

The Attorney General walked to the jury box and leaned on the railing. "You will drive the good men from the seats of power and justice. You will place in their stead none but the abandoned, the case-hardened and the callous. Creatures without remorse; lost to all sense of feeling; equally despising and despised, they will use the sacred trust deposited in their hands to barter their nation's honor for gold or to secure the means of expanding their own power."

The Attorney General turned back to Hamilton. "Those who argue that the power of libeling is necessary to the freedom of voting will find it ever more endangered. In a republic, it is not the spirit of liberty that we have to keep alive, but it is the spirit of faction—the enemy of our liberty—that we have to repress. I ask the eminent counsel for the defense: do you really want to create a haven for the calumniator, a sanctuary for the civil incendiary who uses as his firebrands scandal, slander and invective, and thereby kindles the flame of party spirit?

"If you do, General Hamilton, the chief of every band, with a servile, hireling press at his back, will vomit out slander on his opponents and panegyric on himself. Every candidate and voter will be the object of abuse. The good, the decent, and the quiet will be driven from our polls. A headlong mob, with the bludgeon and the dagger for their qualifications, will give us tomorrow's rulers, until the people, worn out with anarchy, will with joy behold some American Bonaparte arise."

Having reminded the courtroom of old whispers about Hamilton's secret desire for a monarchy with himself at the head, Spencer again addressed the jury. "These are not the chimeras of a lawless imagination. Would to God that they were. They are the inevitable consequences of a factious spirit, engendered by hate-filled pamphlets and calumniating newspapers in the periodical slanders of the day."

Matthew Lyon, sitting in the back of the courtroom with his son Jim, didn't know what to think. He was now a Congressman from Kentucky, having moved west to make his fortune in postal contracts and settlements of the corrupt Yazoo land deal. Because he needed a smart partner, he was in New York to see Aaron Burr to interest him in running for office in Tennessee instead of wasting his time trying to become Governor of New York. Burr was equivocating—Spittin' Matt assumed he was still more interested in power than money—but told him of this libel trial in Claverack. The former Vermonter, who shared a distinction with Callender of having served time for sedition, brought his editor son along to see how the republicans were now embracing State seditious libel law.

"He makes a powerful case, Father."

"The aristocratic bastard may win. I never thought I'd be praying for the likes of Hamilton to save us from Jefferson's men."

Lyon wondered why Callender wasn't here. It would be a perfect place for him to make a splash in all the newspapers in the country. Probably couldn't afford the fare.

ALEXANDER HAMILTON

"Surely it is not an immaterial thing that a high official character"—Hamilton, speaking for the defense, did not have to pronounce the name of Thomas Jefferson—"should be capable of causing to be printed anything against George Washington, the father of this country. It is important to have it known to us all whether what he said was true or false—whether Washington was a traitor and a perjurer. It is important to the reputation of him against whom the charge is made, General Washington, that it should be examined. It is important regarding the character of the present head of our nation; for if the truth, as stated in the indictment, can be established it will be a serious truth, the effect of which it is impossible to foresee. We stand at the threshold of a glorious triumph for truth."

"He's putting Thomas Jefferson on trial here, for God's sake," Matt Lyon said to his son. "For libeling Washington. He wants the jury to think it's not about Croswell repeating Callender's libel of Jefferson. That's why Hamilton took this case, to turn it all upside down and make Jefferson the defendant in the public eye. Oh, the dog."

"Brilliant," said his son.

"I never did think that speaking or writing the truth was a crime," Hamilton said quietly, his tone causing jurors and spectators to lean forward to hear. "I am glad the day has come in which it is to be decided, for my soul has always abhorred the thought that a free man dared not speak the truth. I rejoice that this question is now to be decided." He took a sip of water. "Before I advance to the full discussion of the questions in this trial, let me define the liberty for which I contend, and which the doctrine of those who oppose us are calculated to destroy."

He began with a concession to establish his reasonableness, a technique Maria remembered in many discussions with him. "In speaking for the freedom of the press, I do not say there ought to be unbridled license. I do not stand here to say there should be no shackles to be laid on such license." He nodded, as if in agreement, to the Attorney General. "I consider the spirit of abuse and calumny as the pest of society. I know—I know as well as any man here—that the best of men are not exempt from the attacks of slander."

He pointed to the portrait of George Washington on the courtroom wall, high over the judge's bench. "Though it pleased God to bless us with the first of characters as our first President, and though it has pleased God to take him from us, I say that falsehood eternally repeated by this band of calumniators and their secret supporters would have affected even his name. Drops of water in long and continued succession will wear out adamant. This libel on Washington, therefore, cannot be endured." He pointed to his client, the young editor. "Those who exposed the source of the scurrilous attacks upon our late President must not be punished. It would be to put the best and the worst on the same level."

His voice grew stronger. "I contend for the liberty of publishing truth, with good motives and for justifiable ends, even though it reflect on government, magistrates, and private persons."

Hamilton noted that the Court had stated that the common law is the basis for our law of libel, and the prosecution had entered into evidence a list of precedents from the English bar. With a sweep of his arm, Hamilton rejected them all.

"The doctrine that truth is no defense is not rooted in the common law. That doctrine originated in one of the most oppressive institutions that ever existed—the Star Chamber. It was a court where oppressions roused the English people to demand its abolition, whose horrid tortures and judgments cannot be remembered without freezing the blood in one's veins. The source of the doctrine trampling on liberty of the press is foul. It warns us against polluting the stream of our own jurisprudence.

"The Star Chamber was abolished not merely for failing to use the intervention of juries. That cruel court was abolished because its decisions were tyrannical, because it bore down the liberties of the people, and because it inflicted the bloodiest punishments. Shall we today be shackled by its precedents—extraneous bodies grafted on a fine old trunk, rejected in the very country where they were formed?"

Hamilton, without consulting a note, then ticked off six cases before and after the Star Chamber that established justification by truth. "Zenger's case has been mentioned here as an authority—a judicial decision in a fractious period and reprobated at the time." He glared at the judge, who seemed to wither in his chair. "The little, miserable conduct of the judge in Zenger's case kicks the beam supporting justice, just as the popular spirit of inquiry is crushed by a servile tribunal."

So much for the prosecution's precedents. He called up a more recent precedent in England's Parliament not ten years before that established truth as a defense. He noted that even in the much-maligned Sedition Act in America, now lapsed, truth had been established in our law—specifically declared by a wise Federalist Congress, as a concession to a protesting republican minority—as a defense against sedition.

"To those who say that truth cannot be material in any respect," he said, voice rising, "I say: No tribunal, no codes, no systems can repeal or impair this law of God, for by His eternal laws the materiality of truth is inherent in the nature of things."

This was not legal argument, the lawyers and jurors sensed; Hamilton, who had been the most forceful advocate of the nation's fundamental law, was setting forth in this small courtroom the bedrock moral philosophy on which that Constitution was based. He fell silent, then looked directly at the Attorney General. "I call upon those opposed to us to say what a libel is."

Spencer stood up and said without hesitation, "A libel is a scandalous publication that breaches the peace."

"So you say," said Hamilton, treating the answer by the Attorney General as the rote recitation of a book-learned schoolboy. "My definition is this: a libel is a slanderous or ridiculous writing, picture or sign, with a malicious or mischievous design or intent, towards government, magistrates or individuals. Intent is central. Every crime must include intent. Murder consists in killing a man with malice propense, but killing may be justifiable—even praiseworthy, as in defense of chastity about to be violated."

Hamilton paused and looked toward his co-counsel Van Ness, as if to consult him on the example he was about to use. "In dueling," he said bleakly, "the malice is supposed from the deliberate acts of sending a challenge and appointing the time and place of meeting. But natural justice dictates that no man shall be the avenger of his own wrongs, and the law forbidding dueling assumes the malicious intent that makes it a crime."

"Why did he bring that in? He must be thinking of his eldest son," said the legislator to Maria.

"I know." And the tragic consequence of a deadly duel to his daughter, too.

"When a printer, however," Hamilton continued, "denounces a public official with no intent to breach the peace—without, in another word, malice—there is no crime. When a man breaks into a house, it is the intent that makes him a felon. It must be proved to a jury it was his intent to steal; the jury decides that, not the judge."

"He's trying to do what Zenger's lawyer did," the legislator told Maria. "To get the jury to defy the judge on the criminal law. Won't work with this jury. I know these people, good republicans all."

"But I thought a judge could overturn a jury verdict."

"Only a guilty verdict. No judge can reverse a jury's acquittal."

"I do not deny the well-known maxim 'The jury decides the fact, the judge determines the law.'" Hamilton gave the maxim first in Latin to impress the lawyers in the room, Maria assumed. "But every permanent body of men, judges included, is liable to be influenced by the spirit of the existing administration." He faced the men in the jury box. "A jury, on the other hand, is chosen by lot, as each of you know. I freely confess that in difficult cases, it is your duty to hearken to the directions of a judge, and with great deference to his learning in the law. But on matters of intent—on the judgment of malice—that is a combination of fact and law that only you have the right, and thus the power, to decide."

"I object, Your Honor." The Attorney General rose. "Does not the Court day after day grant new trials when the jury attempt to decide contrary to the dictates of law? It is the height of presumption in men ignorant of the law to venture on expounding what they do not understand." He turned to his opposing counsel with a smile. "I have heard in this era, General Hamilton, of newfangled doctrines, that men were born legislators, but never yet have I heard it hinted that they were born lawyers."

"Damned snob," Lyon snorted in the direction of Spencer, his fellow republican. "You lose me on that one."

"Whose side are you on?" asked his son.

"Both. Neither. The bad men are on the right side."

"The true legal doctrine is this," Hamilton replied with the authority of the main author of *The Federalist Papers.* "In the general distribution of power in our Constitution, it is the province of the jury to speak to fact, yet in criminal cases the law and the fact are always blended. The citizen is safe only when the jury is permitted to speak to both. Were I to sit as a juror, as you are today, I would respect the opinion of the judge—but from which I should deem myself at liberty to depart. I would die on the rack rather than condemn a man I thought deserved to be acquitted. Wouldn't you? This I believe to be the theory of our law."

Neither the prosecutor nor the judge saw fit to reply.

A door in the back opened and shut. Maria saw a man with a large, stiff envelope tied with red-tape, the mark of an attorney, walk down the aisle and seat himself next to Van Ness at the defense table. There was some whispered consultation; Hamilton slapped his knee in anger. Van Ness addressed the court.

"I am informed by my co-counsel, Mr. Harison, Your Honor, of a sad turn of events. The witness we had hoped to bring before the court to testify to the truth of what Croswell reprinted in the *Wasp* is dead."

Harison addressed the judge. "The body of James Thomson Callender, editor of the *Richmond Recorder,* was found last Tuesday on the bank of the James River. He had been plied with liquor and drowned in only three feet of water under what some on the scene told me they believe to be suspicious circumstances. He was buried the same day. There was no investigation and none of his papers were found at his office, which had been ransacked, or at his home, which was destroyed by fire."

"What is your contention, counsel?"

"We contend, Your Honor, that there may have been a deliberate attempt to prevent testimony and suppress evidence."

The Attorney General objected, and the judge ordered the jury to ignore the defense counsel's speculation.

"Madam, are you all right?"

Maria was pitched forward, her hands over her face. She straightened, eyes reddened, mouth set. James could not be stopped any other way. He was the destroyer who some planters and politicians or a rival newsmonger were determined to destroy. They would say he was drunk and fell out of a boat or committed suicide, but she knew that James could hold his liquor, and he was a strong swimmer, and he was grimly looking forward to exposing half a dozen new scandals. He had no business on the banks of the James River.

She took an envelope from under the folds of her dress and held it in her hand for a long moment. It contained the two letters from Jefferson that Callender had at first stored under his mattress, and then, concerned about foul play, gave her for safekeeping. She stood up and slipped past the legislator into the aisle. She walked down to the defense table past Hamilton and Harison and the defendant and deposited Callender's envelope in the hand of Van Ness. He recognized her from their meeting at Burr's house but said nothing to indicate he knew her. She wondered if Hamilton was aware that Van Ness was collaborating behind the scenes with Burr in this case.

All four men at the defense table rose. Van Ness and Harison hurriedly broke the heavy wax seal and opened the envelope to examine its contents and show them to the senior counsel. Defendant Croswell looked confused. Hamilton, before turning to the documents, looked at Maria in welcoming wonderment. The subject of his Reynolds pamphlet looked directly into Hamilton's eyes, now behind spectacles, much less confident than she remembered them, and nodded curtly. She told him, "You will notice that these letters are originals and not forgeries. Callender was always telling the truth." Before he could respond, she returned to her seat.

"We have heard that we must guard against the spirit of faction," Matt Lyon listened to Hamilton saying. "Divisiveness is a great bane to community, and disunion is a mortal poison to our land. All great men consider the spirit of faction to be a natural disease of our form of government, and therefore we must restrain it."

Lyon knew he was alluding to the writing a decade ago of Madison, before Jefferson's anti-Federalist movement shattered the innocent illusion of a polity without partizanship. Madison had been mistaken about that, and thank God he was, thought Lyon, because such sweet civility would have left no room for strong argument and fierce opposition to the all-powerful clique under the sway of Hamilton. Not until he was one of the lonely Outs did that man see the danger of power perpetuated by the Ins.

"We have been careful that when one political party comes in," continued the famed counsel for the defense, now a minority of a Federalist minority in dwindling opposition, "that victorious party shall not be able to break down and bear away the others. If this be not so, in vain have we made constitutions, for if it be not so, then we must go into anarchy and to a despotic master.

"Against this terrible end," he said, his voice growing stronger, "there is in our republic an almost insurmountable obstacle: that barrier is the spirit of the people. They would not submit to be thus enslaved. Every tongue, every arm would be uplifted against it; they would resist! And resist! And resist— till they hurled from their seats of power those who dared make the attempt!"

Quieter again. Lyon strained forward to hear him. "To watch the progress of such sinister endeavors is the office of a free press. To give us early alarm is the office of a free press. To put us on our guard against the encroachments of men in power is the office of a free press. This cherished office, then, protects a right of the utmost importance, one for which, instead of yielding it up to any State's law of seditious libel, we ought rather to spill . . . our . . . blood."

Lyon whispered to his son, "My God, the man talks like Tom Paine." This was the way the passionate young Hamilton must have sounded when they were all Revolutionary patriots, when he was fighting the King as General Washington's aide-de-camp and then fought for a strong union in the Constitutional Convention, in the years before the bitterness set in.

Resuming a tone of calm reason, the man designated by Washington to be the effective head of the first standing army of the United States assured the jurors, "Never can tyranny be introduced into this country by force of arms. The spirit of the country is not to be destroyed by a few thousands of miserable, pitiful military. An army never can do it.

"It is only by the abuse of the forms of justice that we can be enslaved. Only a servile tribunal can crush down the popular spirit of enquiry. Our freedom can be subverted only by a pretense of adhering to all the forms of law—all the while breaking down the substance of our liberties." Hamilton approached the jury box. "How would that subversion of our freedom begin? By making one wretched but honest man the victim of a 'trial' in name only. The subversion would continue by taking that citizen off to jail, and ultimately, in some cases, by public executions.

"The sight of this, of a fellow citizen's blood, would at first beget sympathy. This abuse of the forms of justice, in good time, would rouse the people into action—and in the madness of their revenge, Americans would take up those chains destined for themselves and break them upon the heads of their oppressors!"

William Van Ness laid his hand on Hamilton's arm and rose to stand beside him. "May it please the court, the defense places in evidence two letters to James Callender transmitting to him sums of money. These letters encourage him in his invaluable efforts to inform the public, first in the publication of his book entitled *The Prospect Before Us,* and later during his time in the Richmond jail writing for a newspaper. The letters to Callender are unsigned, in an attempt to becloud their authorship if intercepted in the post. But they are in the well-known and unmistakable handwriting of Thomas Jefferson."

At Hamilton's nod, the young attorney placed the letters in the hands of the marshal. "These we submit are proof of the truth in the statement origially printed in the *Richmond Recorder,*" said Van Ness. "They were wrongly called a libel when reprinted by Mr. Croswell in the *Wasp*. They are the late Mr. Callender's proof that he was hired by Mr. Jefferson to attack—in a slanderous, scurrilous and indeed libelous manner—Presidents Washington and Adams."

"And in consequence of this proof of truth," concluded Hamilton, "we ask you, the jury, for an acquittal."

With those words, the defense would ordinarily rest, but Hamilton, speaking beyond the courtroom and beyond the moment, had a last point to make. "The liberty of the press consists in publishing the truth, from good motives and for justifiable ends, no matter how severely it reflects on government, on magistrates, or individuals. That is the principle we defend here today."

Maria was unsteady as her back pain flared up and she let the legislator help her down the four steps in front of the courthouse. "What do you think the jury will do?"

"They'll take longer to convict than they would have," the Assemblyman said, "but this jury was chosen with conviction in mind. I doubt the prosecution will ask for a jail term or much of a fine. That wouldn't be popular at all."

"Can't Hamilton appeal?"

"He will, of course, but the appeals panel is split two to two, republicans and Federalists, so I imagine a guilty verdict will stand."

"We've lost, then," Maria said. "Hamilton and his client, and Callender, too."

A florid man behind them on the steps, in a Western woodsman's jacket, put in, "The hell they lost. What do you suppose will happen to your libel protection bill in the State legislature?"

"The press shield will pass, Congressman Lyon," said the legislator. "It has my vote, after this, and the courtroom was filled with State legislators today, listening like me. You heard how Hamilton defined press freedom? 'Publishing the truth from good motives and for justifiable ends.' That means, I think, a jury has to find malicious intent, which isn't there if the publisher thinks what he prints is true."

"Just fixing the State libel law won't do," said Lyon. "Laws can be repealed overnight."

"You're right. I'll introduce an amendment to the New York Constitution beginning 'the legislature shall make no law abridging . . .' May take a while, but that will pass, too."

Spittin' Matt handed him a card with his Congressional business address written on it. "When you get that amendment drafted, send it down to me in Kentucky. I'll pass it around." He turned to the young man following him and said, "The man saved my life once, and they drowned him in three feet of water." He punched his son affectionately in the arm. "Now I'm about the only man alive in America served jail time for sedition."

The young attorney Maria had met in Burr's office, Van Ness—the one who arranged for her seat at the trial—came hurrying up to her.

"Excuse me, Mrs. Clement, but General Hamilton asked me to say he would like a word with you, if you have a moment, to express his appreciation."

Maria stared at him through her reddened eyes and, as if uncomprehending, shook her head no.

"As you wish," Van Ness said. "In a different regard, I know that our mutual friend in the District of Columbia is eager to learn your impressions of the trial."

She shook her head again, with more certainty this time, as the tension in her spine began to ease. "Tell the Vice President I am going to take the packet to Boston. There I will remove my daughter Susan from the seminary. Then she and I will go home."

EPILOGUE

WHAT HAPPENED LATER

A brief hiſtory *of* what happened later to the characters in *Scandalmonger:*

 ADAMS, JOHN. After his split with Hamilton and his out-reach to France made a second term as President impossible, the energetic Adams retired to Braintree (now Quincy) Massachusetts to twenty-five years of quiet reflection and correspondence.

Though he thought it served no purpose to blacken President Jefferson's reputation, his letters show Adams accepted Callender's story about Sally Hemings without question, calling it "a natural and almost unavoidable consequence of that foul contagion in the human character—Negro slavery." In 1805, he wrote to Dr. Benjamin Rush, a republican he had appointed to be head of the Mint, of his interest in reconciliation with former friends and political adversaries. That led to a remarkable, extended correspondence that brought the two founders, Adams and Jefferson, close in their declining years.

He died on the Fourth of July in 1826; his last words reportedly were "Thomas Jefferson still lives." The second President was mistaken; his successor, Jefferson, also died on that day, the fiftieth anniversary of the signing of the Declaration of Independence.

BECKLEY, JOHN. Blocked from an appointment in the Jefferson Administration because its main patronage dispenser, Treasury Secretary Albert Gallatin, considered him too partisan a republican, Beckley returned to his post as Clerk of the House of Representatives. Madison supplemented his income with a job as the first Librarian of Congress at $2 a day. He owned some heavily mortgaged acreage in western Virginia; a town is named after him in that area of what is now West Virginia. He died in 1807 at the age of fifty, disappointed at his treatment by the Jeffersonians.

 BURR, AARON. When his bid to take charge of the Louisiana Territory was turned down by a distrustful Jefferson, Vice President Burr ran for New York Governor as an independent in 1804. Hamilton disparaged him to Federalists and was instrumental in his defeat. As a result, Burr challenged his lifelong adversary to a duel, and at Weehawken, New Jersey, on July 11, 1804, after Hamilton discharged his gun into the air, Burr shot Hamilton in the mid-section and he died the next day.

Indicted for this crime in New York and New Jersey, he fled southwest and pursued a plan his accusers later called "the Burr Conspiracy." This was supposedly to establish an independent nation out of several of the United States and to then invade Mexico and seize Spain's possessions in America, including Florida. He was captured in 1807 while leading troops down the Mississippi, and tried for treason in Richmond in a trial presided over by Chief Justice John Marshall; to Jefferson's chagrin, Burr was acquitted.

Burr went to Europe for five years and was befriended by William Cobbett, who wanted him to stand for Parliament, but Burr's application for British citizenship was denied. He tried to enlist Britain and France in further adventures in Mexico; when that failed, Burr returned to New York and lived twenty-four years in disgraced obscurity, short of funds and long on enemies. He claimed vindication when Sam Houston defeated the Mexicans in 1836 and established the independent Republic of Texas: "What was treason in me thirty years ago is patriotism now."

CHASE, SAMUEL. The Federalist Supreme Court Justice, in his partisan charge to a Baltimore grand jury in 1803, opined that universal suffrage would "destroy all protection of property" and cause the Constitution to "sink into a mobocracy." This was too much for President Jefferson, who wrote a House leader: "Ought this seditious and official attack on the principles of our Constitution . . . go unpunished?" Republican House members, who thought Chase's intemperate and biased conduct of the Callender trial was "indecent and tyrannical," responded to the President's wish by launching an inquiry into impeaching Chase. Hamilton's *Evening Post,* to protect the Federalist Justice, denounced the "Inquisitorial Committee."

During the inquiry, a witness swore that he heard Chase discussing the case in the lobby of Stelle's Hotel in Washington with Bushrod Washington (the late President's nephew) and John Marshall, and that Chase said if he had known Callender would turn out later to be such an enemy of Jefferson, "he would scarcely have fined him so high." Chief Justice Marshall deposed that the conversation had taken place but was not to be taken seriously; Federalists were disappointed that their champion was more interested in judicial independence than in convicting an abusive republican judge.

The Chase impeachment was tried in the Senate in February 1805, Vice President Aaron Burr presiding in his last official appearance. By the time the impeachment came to trial, however, the Jefferson men considered the long-dead Callender a vicious turncoat and the other radical republicans an embarrassment. Albert Gallatin, following the Jefferson-Madison policy of conciliating with Federalists, passed the word that the impeachment of Chase was unduly partisan. On the single Baltimore jury count, a majority of the Senate voted to convict, but well short of the two-thirds needed. On the five counts voted by the House accusing Chase of abuses at Callender's trial, the hard-to-define phrase "high crimes and misdemeanors" was construed narrowly and not a single Senator voted to convict Chase. Acquitted, the chastened Chase became temperate and nonpartisan on the bench. He died in 1811.

COBBETT, WILLIAM. The most despised Tory in Philadelphia became the most feared and despised radical in London. Spurning government aid, he started the weekly *Political Register* in 1802 and denounced Pitt's peace treaty with France signed at Amiens. He exposed the corruption of rotten-borough elections, railed with the Luddites at the spread of industry into the rural countryside, vilified the government of Ireland and denounced the cruel flogging of soldiers who had protested the thievery of their officers.

This last landed him in Newgate Prison from 1810 to 1812, but he came out as a radical champion of the poor and unemployed. To avoid the heavy taxes that controlled newspapers, he put out an irregular "two-penny trash" publication that reached an astounding circulation of 70,000; the essayist William Hazlitt later wrote that Cobbett's mutton-fisted style and common touch made him "a kind of Fourth Estate in the politicks of the country."

Threatened by further prosecution for sedition as a "leading malcontent," he fled to Long Island in America in 1816. From there, he continued to write and edit his *Register,* turned out a best-selling English grammar, treatises on gardening and the cultivation of corn, and a fond memoir of an America he came to appreciate. He also wrote a short biography of General Andrew Jackson, envisioning that future President as fearlessly populist and more representative of American democracy than Jefferson or Madison.

He returned to England in 1819 with the bones of Thomas Paine in a box to call attention to his unabashed radicalism. He toured the countryside writing pieces that infused his opinions with firsthand observations of life that had not been reported, which became his masterpiece, *Rural Rides.* After flaying and being jailed by the Tories, he turned on the Whig government when farmworkers rioted and was again prosecuted for sedition; as his own counsel, he argued his way to acquittal. Cobbett's long fight for parliamentary reform succeeded in 1832; he was among the reformers who won election to Parliament.

He died in 1835 at age sixty-nine, remembered as a fearless oppositionist, a wildly inconsistent thinker, a colorful and freewheeling stylist, and the first media giant.

DUANE, WILLIAM. The New York–born editor of the *Calcutta Indian World*, who returned to America in 1796 to succeed Benjamin Bache as editor of the *Aurora*, in Philadelphia, was by the turn of the century Callender's rival as foremost republican writer. When the Federalist Senate in 1800 sought to try him for contempt of Congress, Duane defiantly refused to appear, despite Monroe's wish that the editor, like Callender, martyr himself for the cause by being convicted and suffering imprisonment.

Duane remained a Jefferson supporter despite the radical *Aurora* being replaced by the temperate *National Intelligencer* as the favored republican newspaper in 1801. Duane sought a Pennsylvania Congressional seat in 1807, though his long sojourn overseas in his youth placed his citizenship in doubt. Because he strongly supported Irish immigration, nativists who thought cheap white labor would undermine slavery joined moderate republicans to overwhelm him. Jefferson gave him a lieutenant-colonel's commission in 1808 and he served as adjutant-general in the War of 1812. He stepped down from the *Aurora* in 1822 and took a sinecure as Chief Clerk of the Pennsylvania Supreme Court until his death in 1835.

HAMILTON, ALEXANDER. When Burr ran for Governor of New York as an independent in 1804, it appeared he would take enough Federalist votes to win. Even the editor of Hamilton's *New York Evening Post* defected and editorially supported his owner's nemesis. But Hamilton vigorously urged enough Federalists to vote for Morgan Lewis, the State's republican Chief Justice who had ruled against him in the Croswell libel case. After Burr lost, never to run for office again, he challenged Hamilton to a duel over a published remark that Hamilton held a "despicable opinion" of Burr.

On July 11, 1804, at Weehawken, New Jersey, near the spot where his eldest son Philip had fallen in a duel, the despondent Hamilton met on the "field of honor" Aaron Burr, whose second was William Van Ness, Hamilton's co-counsel in the Croswell case. Hamilton shot first, and as he wrote for posthumous delivery to his wife, missed intentionally; Burr's answering bullet made a mortal wound. By his death, which he may have sought in this fashion, he killed Burr's political future.

Many decades later, an aged former President James Monroe visited Betsey Hamilton, who lived into her nineties. He said that since both were nearing the grave, he hoped past differences could be forgiven and forgotten. Hamilton's widow replied: "Mr. Monroe, if you come to tell me that you repent, that you are sorry, very sorry, for the misrepresentations and the slanders and the stories you circulated against my dear husband; if you have come to say this, I understand it. But otherwise, no lapse of time, no nearness to the grave, makes any difference." Her nephew, who was in the room with them, reported, "Monroe turned, took up his hat and left the room."

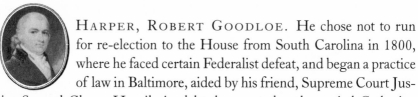

HARPER, ROBERT GOODLOE. He chose not to run for re-election to the House from South Carolina in 1800, where he faced certain Federalist defeat, and began a practice of law in Baltimore, aided by his friend, Supreme Court Justice Samuel Chase. Heavily in debt, he courted and married Catherine Carroll, daughter of the Marylander of great wealth who signed the Declaration of Independence as "Charles Carroll of Carrollton." His fortunes improved in 1805 when he served as chief defense counsel in the Senate impeachment trial of Chase.

Though the former Federalist leader opposed Madison in entering the 1812 War against the British, Harper became a general, comported himself admirably in the defense of Baltimore and was given a suitable parade when he died in 1825.

HAY, GEORGE. Hay's assaults on Callender, both physical and in a pamphlet urging libel prosecution titled "Essay on Liberty of the Press," earned him Jefferson's appointment in 1803 as U.S. Attorney in Richmond. This gave him the opportunity four years later, with Jefferson's approval, to prosecute Aaron Burr for treason, but with meager evidence and inadequate legal skill he failed to win a conviction. He lost his standing with the local republican leadership, known as the Richmond Junto, when he supported James Monroe against James Madison for the presidency in 1808, the same year he married Monroe's daughter Hortense. During Monroe's presidency, George and his wife lived in the White House. In 1822, Hay ran for Governor of Virginia and lost. Though his father-in-law refused on ethical grounds to give him a political appointment, his successor, John Quincy Adams, granted him a Federal judgeship. The vindictive and pompous Hay occupied that post until his death in 1830.

HEMINGS, SALLY. For three decades after Callender's stories first appeared about her lifelong liaison with Thomas Jefferson, the most famous non-white woman in America lived quietly at Monticello. Callender's report that she had five children appears to have been accurate. One (called "President Tom" by Callender) may have died, or run away, or been banished after the publicity broke, or never existed; two, Beverly and Harriet, were allowed to leave when they reached twenty-one; the two youngest, Madison and Eston, remained as slaves on the estate. On Jefferson's death in 1826, Madison was freed and his nineteen-year old brother's manumission soon followed, some say as a part of a promise he made to Sally Hemings when she agreed to return with him from Paris. No other slave family on the plantation was as favorably treated.

Probably because Jefferson did not want to draw further attention to Sally, he did not set her free or otherwise mention her in his will; if he had, he would have had to petition the Virginia legislature to allow her to remain in the state. A couple of years after his death, Martha Randolph, his daughter, freed Sally Hemings, who went to live with her sons in a rented house in Charlottesville. A census taker in 1830 listed the three of them as white. She died in 1835, described then as a "quadroon" but officially a free white woman, at the age of sixty-two. Recent DNA evidence indicates a strong probability, though not a certainty, that Thomas Jefferson's genes were passed on to her descendants.

JEFFERSON, THOMAS. "The artillery of the press has been leveled against us," the re-elected President said in his Second Inaugural Address in 1805, "charged with whatsoever its licentiousness could devise or dare. These abuses ... might, indeed, have been corrected by the wholesome punishments reserved to and provided by the laws of the several states," and although he had no time for that, "he who has time renders a service to public morals and public tranquillity in reforming these abuses by the salutary coercions of the law." As for himself, he said he preferred "the censorship of public opinion."

His first term was marked by the nation-doubling Louisiana Purchase and its related Lewis and Clark Expedition, and he extended American power globally by sending a naval force to pursue the Barbary pirates "to the shores of Tripoli." His second term, less successful, was spent avoiding being drawn into the war between England and France. His Embargo Act, using American trade muscle to apply "peaceable coercion" to Britain, failed and was repealed by Congress.

In 1809, he turned the reins over to his friend and chosen successor James Madison, and retired to Monticello to write, to collect books and works of art and furniture, and to create a center of learning in Charlottesville. He placed a life-sized marble bust of Alexander Hamilton facing a larger-than-life-sized bust of himself in Monticello's entrance hall, and liked to say to visitors "opposed in death as in life." In life, Jefferson opposed the tyranny of monarchy and central power as Hamilton opposed disunion and anarchy.

Before his death at eighty-three in 1826, the founder with the most careful eye to his place in history chose the epitaph for his grave site. He avoided the obvious "first U.S. Secretary of State" and "third President of the United States" and chose instead three themes that go to the heart of the American Dream: "Here was buried Thomas Jefferson, author of the Declaration of American independence, of the statute of Virginia for religious freedom, and father of the University of Virginia."

LEE, HENRY. The cavalry leader Light-Horse Harry's land speculation left him financially ruined during the Jefferson years, and he was confined in debtors' prison in 1808. Defending an anti-war editor during a riot in Baltimore in 1812, he was severely injured, left Virginia and moved to the West Indies to regain his health. He died on the way home in 1818. However, his major contribution to American history came in 1807, when his second wife gave birth to a boy they named Robert Edward.

LEWIS, MERIWETHER. Jefferson's personal secretary, who read the President's State of the Union message to Congress in December 1801, was given the assignment to explore an overland route to the Pacific. With William Clark as co-leader of the expedition, Lewis set out in 1804 to examine and map the recently purchased Louisiana Territory. The two-year expedition was a stunning scientific, geographical success and supported claims to the Oregon country. Lewis died in 1809, possibly by his own hand. Jefferson, told of the death, wrote, "Lewis had from early life been subject to hypochondriac affections. It was a constitutional disposition in all the nearer branches of the family."

LYON, MATTHEW. After Jefferson's victory, Lyon took his family and Vermont mechanics to the Kentucky frontier. Thanks to his republican political connections, he became the Commissary-General of the Western Army, making his fortune in barge traffic and shipbuilding while becoming a Congressman from Kentucky and furiously rejecting newspaper criticism of his conflicts of interest. He had a brush with Burr's "conspiracy" and agreed with fellow Congressman Andrew Jackson that Burr was unjustly prosecuted by Jefferson for treason.

By 1812, "Spittin' Matt" had turned against President Madison and opposed war with Britain, which cost him his republican seat. His commercial fortunes also turned awry, as one of his ships sunk in the Mississippi, bankrupting him. He was driven to petition Congress to remit the fine imposed on him under the Sedition Act but, unlike Callender, had no leverage and did not succeed. President Monroe in 1820 took pity and assigned him a minor post supervising trade with the Cherokees in Spadre Bluffs, Arkansas, where he soon agitated for a cotton gin to help develop Indian farming. Lyon soon ran for Congress from that territory but lost because voters considered him too sympathetic to the Cherokees.

MADISON, JAMES. The mind that matched Hamilton's in shaping the U.S. Constitution and creating the Bill of Rights was that of a thinker, not a leader. Madison was only an adequate Secretary of State to Jefferson and inherited the Presidency against little opposition in 1809. An agreement with Napoleon on neutral rights led him, unprepared, into war with Britain, and he turned to Monroe for needed, practical executive support in his Cabinet. In his second term, Madison abandoned Jeffersonian principles and embraced Hamilton's idea of a national bank and protective tariffs. When he returned to Montpelier in 1817, Washington sorely missed its popular hostess, Dolley Madison.

MARSHALL, JOHN. As President Adams intended in his final major appointment, Marshall remained a force for Federalism against the Jeffersonians, and remained so throughout the twenty-four years of the Virginia republican dynasty of Presidents Jefferson, Madison and Monroe.

When in 1803 one of Adams's "midnight appointments," William Marbury, sued Secretary of State Madison for delivery of a duly signed commission as justice of the peace, Marshall's Court ruled against the Federalist, giving Jefferson's men a seeming victory; but the grounds for Marshall's ruling was that the 1789 Judiciary Act under which the suit was brought was unconstitutional. By giving his longtime Virginia adversaries their minor triumph, Marshall seized for the Supreme Court the power to decide which branch was to interpret the Constitution.

He presided over the controversial treason trial of Aaron Burr in 1807 in which Burr was acquitted by a jury that could find no overt treasonable acts. In *McCulloch* v. *Maryland,* taking up Hamilton's argument that Congress had powers implied though not enumerated in the Constitution, he upheld its creation of the Bank of the United States. More than anyone, he established the Judiciary as the third co-equal branch of government in the U.S. He died at eighty in 1835.

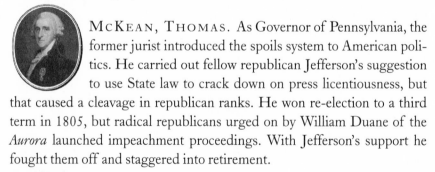

McKEAN, THOMAS. As Governor of Pennsylvania, the former jurist introduced the spoils system to American politics. He carried out fellow republican Jefferson's suggestion to use State law to crack down on press licentiousness, but that caused a cleavage in republican ranks. He won re-election to a third term in 1805, but radical republicans urged on by William Duane of the *Aurora* launched impeachment proceedings. With Jefferson's support he fought them off and staggered into retirement.

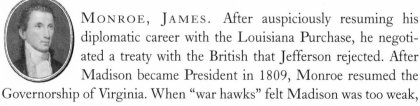

MONROE, JAMES. After auspiciously resuming his diplomatic career with the Louisiana Purchase, he negotiated a treaty with the British that Jefferson rejected. After Madison became President in 1809, Monroe resumed the Governorship of Virginia. When "war hawks" felt Madison was too weak, Monroe joined his Cabinet as Secretary of State and was Secretary of War during the less-than-successful War of 1812 against the British. Elected President in 1816 against a disappearing Federalist minority, Monroe presided over an "era of good feeling" that capped the Virginia dynasty of twenty-four years. With Secretary of State John Quincy Adams eager to block Spain from Latin America, the dour Monroe declared that the American continent was no longer open for colonization and that the United States would not interfere in Europe, a policy many Europeans believed doctrinaire.

MORRIS, GOUVERNEUR. The peg-legged dealmaker of 1801 remained a high Federalist after leaving the New York Senate and became a driving force behind the construction of the Erie Canal. He condemned the War of 1812 as "Mr. Madison's War," supported the idea of New England's secession and died in 1816.

RUSH, DR. BENJAMIN. Although an ardent republican supporting Jefferson, the Philadelphia physician who had signed the Declaration of Independence was appointed treasurer of the Mint of the United States by President Adams and served in that sinecure until his death in 1813. Through his mediation, former Presidents Adams and Jefferson were reconciled. Dr. Rush's son Richard became Treasury Secretary in the administration of President Adams's son, John Quincy.

Although Dr. Rush's notions on the efficacy of bleeding were later discredited, his 1812 book *Medical Inquiries and Observations on the Diseases of the Mind* was the pioneering work on the subject, in the United States, which is why some call him the "father of psychiatry." John Adams wrote him approvingly that his book proved "us all to be a little cracked."

VAN NESS, WILLIAM PETER. The New York City attorney, under the pen name of "Aristedes" (after Aristides the Just), late in 1803 wrote a widely read pamphlet defending his friend Aaron Burr from accusations that he had intrigued to steal the 1800 election from Jefferson. In 1804, as Burr's second at Weehawken, he probably loaded the gun with which Burr killed Hamilton. The republicans later named Van Ness to a Federal judgeship.

WOLCOTT, OLIVER. Hounded out of his Treasury office in 1800 by attacks in the republican press, Hamilton's loyal friend became a business leader in New York until 1815, then returned to his home in Litchfield, Connecticut, to run for Governor as head of the "Toleration Republicans." Like his father, Oliver Sr., and his grandfather Roger, he served as Governor of that state, emphasizing its economic growth. He died in New York City in 1833, a Hamiltonian to the end.

REYNOLDS, MARIA LEWIS. After Aaron Burr arranged for her 1793 divorce in New York from James Reynolds, she married Jacob Clingman. They lived in Alexandria, Virginia, until after Callender broke the story of Hamilton's shady dealings with Reynolds and the former Treasury Secretary countered with his "Reynolds pamphlet." Maria and her daughter probably accompanied Clingman to Hull in Britain where he became a chartered accountant. An unpublished memoir by a Philadelphia merchant who befriended her in 1802, when she was thirty-two years old, recounted roughly the rest of her life story:

When her marriage to Clingman ended and Maria returned to the United States, she sought help again from Aaron Burr. He supported her, discreetly arranged for the education of her daughter Susan in a Boston seminary, and obtained employment for Maria Clement, a name she adopted, as housekeeper and nurse in the home of the Philadelphia physician Dr. Thomas Mathew, whom she married in 1807. (Maria Reynolds and James Callender never met.) Her daughter Susan married twice, drank heavily and came to an impoverished end in New York, leaving her daughter Josepha to her mother to bring up. Maria Lewis Reynolds Clingman (Clement) Mathew, a respectable and religious lady of Philadelphia, died in 1832 at the age of sixty-two. Her memoir, which she claimed she gave William Duane of the *Aurora* to publish, never saw print and disappeared.

Historians sympathetic to Hamilton rely on his pamphlet and a supporting letter from one of his friends to condemn Maria as at least an adventuress, probably a blackmailer and possibly a whore. However, Julian Boyd, the compiler of the Jefferson papers, in a detailed analysis found Hamilton's account a cover-up and her disputation of it credible. If that recent interpretation is true, the notorious subject of "the Reynolds pamphlet" has been unduly maligned by defenders of Hamilton for two centuries.

CALLENDER, JAMES. After his body was found in three feet of water in the James River on July 17, 1803, his death at age forty-five was attributed by the coroner to accidental drowning as a result of inebriation. For nearly two centuries, historians denounced him as "the most outrageous and wretched scandalmonger of a scurrilous age" and, slightly more evenhandedly, as "drunken, vicious and depraved, albeit talented."

However, three of the scandals he unearthed were confirmed contemporaneously. First, Hamilton was forced to explain his payoffs in his Reynolds pamphlet; second, copies of Jefferson's letters transmitting money to Callender were produced; third, Jefferson was forced to admit in writing having "offered my love to a handsome lady" who was married and admitted its "incorrectness."

Callender's Sally Hemings series was angrily derided through two centuries and was the source of most historians' loathing for the journalist. However, recent scholarship accepts that Jefferson may well have fathered at least one of her children. This substantial vindication of his reporting, along with a sympathetic biography by the Australian historian Michael Durey, suggests that a reassessment of the first American muckraker is in order.

One of Callender's sons, Thomas, became a tobacconist and later a newspaper editor in Nashville, Tennessee; a grandson, John Hill Callender, served as a surgeon in the Confederate army and married a great-grandniece of Thomas Jefferson. A living member of the Callender family in the United States informs the author that the descendants of the "scurrilous, scandalmongering scoundrel" are numerous and thriving.

THE UNDERBOOK

NOTES AND SOURCES

*W*elcome to the place usually labeled "Notes." Here is where this novelist levels with the reader about what parts he has imagined, and where I cite sources for specific quotes and add facts to back up my judgments about characters and events.

In this book, as in *Freedom,* my novel about Lincoln and the evolution of the Emancipation Proclamation, the approach is somewhat different from most historical fiction. I am not placing characters of my imagination in a historical setting or mixing real and fictional characters. Rather, I am trying to use a dramatic form to simulate past events and to bring long-ago lives to life. When I use a novelist's privilege to manipulate the timing of an event, or place a character in a scene to be the reader's witness, my aim is to present a close look at what I conjecture was actually going on among those real people.

Historians try mightily to get inside their subjects' minds. They enliven the written record with intuitive judgment after subjecting it to rigorous professional discipline. I adopt much of that discipline, but use the fiction writer's freedom to take an occasional speculative leap in hopes of getting so "inside" as to re-create reality.

In this Underbook, the reader has access to what we know happened, what we can legitimately guess happened, and what we know did not happen. In my book, departures from fact must have a reason: for example, the purpose of the fictional romance in this book between Maria Reynolds and James Callender is to present my view of their real characters. Most historians do not share my largely sympathetic view of both; on the contrary, the somewhat judgmental words most used by otherwise sobersided scholars is "scurrilous wretch" for him and "blackmailing whore" for her. Readers who check out my sources can come to their own conclusions.

Slanted or sensationalized docudramas disserve history. Perhaps this way of dramatizing documents more fairly represents the participants in our past and better illuminates an era. And frankly, tweaking history's plot with a little imagination (fully disclosed in this Underbook) makes a serious look into the long-ago more fun to write and more interesting to read.

A note about style in prose, spelling and punctuation. In the narrative about life in the generation after the American Revolution, I generally try to avoid anachronism. Therefore, nobody talks about "running" for election; rather, the British usage of "standing" for election is preferred, especially because the pose struck by candidates at the turn of the nineteenth century was that of a man modestly making himself available, not of an ambition-driven man racing after a prize. Because "Congress" was construed as plural, characters may be quoted saying "Congress have." Newspapermen, who often called themselves "newsmongers," did not write "stories," but articles. Because news was not separate from opinion, the noun "editorial" was not used.

On capitalization, I have for the most part embraced the modern style and dropped many capitalized words to lowercase. However, in the case of "Negro," then not capitalized, I have moved in the opposite direction. Because the modern reader would find the older style disconcerting, I changed all the "negroes" to "Negroes" with one majestic keystroke on the word processor. The Federalist and anti-Federalist parties are capitalized, but "republican" and "democrat" are usually not, as they were descriptions of a new ideology and not yet party names.

On archaic words, I have left a few in for spice: *contumelious* was a favorite Hamilton synonym for "slanderous" and *flagitious* for "villainous," and Callender used *poetaster* to mean "an inferior poet" who dabbled in doggerel. Some seeming anachronisms are not out of time's joint at all: "boozy" and "tipsy," for example, were common at the time.

On spelling, I have usually modernized, while leaving Adams's derogation of Hamilton as "the bastard brat of a *Scotch pedlar,* " rather than correct it to *Scottish peddler.* Because I think this century was mistaken to change *partizan* to *partisan,* I have left the old spelling, which is closer to the pronunciation. And though it offends logic, I have left the flavorsome *politicks* and *arithmetick* with a *k* while removing it from *logick.*

To calculate yesteryear's money in today's terms, multiply Hamilton's dollar by thirteen to get a rough approximation of buying power. Thus, the $200 fine for sedition that Callender demanded be remitted to him was not such a trivial sum, and the $8,000 levied against Cobbett in the libel suit was enough to break him.

Quotations of Jefferson, Washington and Madison are almost verbatim, Hamilton and Monroe sometimes less so. I have taken long sentences from letters and broken them in half to simulate speech, and sometimes substituted proper names for pronouns to clarify a point. Although dramatic licenses were issued, I identify them back here; for example, in the scene in which Abigail Adams confronts Jefferson, all dialogue is from their exchange of letters, but they were not face to face. This dramatizes but does not distort history. In the same way, I delayed the return of William Cobbett to England by nine months because I needed him around as continuing counterpoint to James Callender, his ideological adversary and vituperative soulmate. The biggest infusion of fiction is the romance between Maria Reynolds and Callender; unfortunately for the lonely Scottish aginner, they never met, but the reader can witness some revelatory scenes through her eyes. (Madison's letter about his falling in love with some Richmond lady is verbatim.)

A short Bibliography is appended of those sources directly cited in this Underbook. These include the sources of the letters to and from Jefferson, Madison, Hamilton and Monroe. The hard-to-find books most useful to me were the two by Michael Durey, a professor of history in Australia: *With the Hammer of Truth,* his 1990 biography of Callender, and his 1997 *Transatlantic Radicals and the Early American Republic.* (Like him, I began by writing about Cobbett until I came across the trail of Callender.) The best book on freedom of the press in the Federal period is fifty years old: James Morton Smith's *Freedom's Fetters.*

To acknowledge a support system for this book: Michael Korda was the editor who understood from the start that my goal was to dramatize without distorting the origins of muckraking journalism in America. He encouraged me to research more thoroughly the background of Maria Reynolds and pressed the idea of illustrating a novel about real people with their portraits and surroundings from the Federal period.

In the tracking-down of caricatures and engravings, some of them rarely published, I am grateful to my longtime amanuensis, Ann Rubin, and to Kathleen Miller, Natalie Goldstein and Shirley Green. Sometimes their assistance was subtle: the 1799 engraving by William Birch of Philadelphia's Second Street, looking north from Market Street, which introduces the prologue on p. 10, shows on the far right the building from which William Cobbett was printing and selling his *Porcupine's Gazette.* It was there, opposite Christ Church, that he faced down a mob enraged by his inflammatory Toryism. A portrait of Matthew Lyon was tracked down to the Vermont State House and is published here (p. 174) probably for the first time.

Only three characters in this book are bereft of illustration. One is John Beckley, the first Librarian of Congress; his successors grimly search for a portrait or sketch or caricature of him to no avail. Another is James Thomson Callender, the scandalmongering protagonist; his only graphic appearance was as a snake, or the tail of a lizard, at the bottom of a cartoon savaging Thomas Jefferson. The detail is on p. 341. The last is Maria Reynolds; though a stock line drawing of a woman in a hat was published in an edition of Hamilton's Reynolds pamphlet, the image had nothing to do with the real woman. She is represented on p. 47 by a profile of an unknown woman created by a "physiognotrace," a technique perfected by the

THE UNDERBOOK

French artist Charles de Saint-Memin while in America at the turn of the nineteenth century. The silhouette is appropriate to Maria's mystery.

Simon & Schuster's Associate Director of Copyediting Gypsy da Silva assigned the task of wrestling with the prose of a word maven to copy editor Fred Wiemer, who helpfully fought me all the way and was right to insist on putting more cited sources in the Bibliography. (The title of one of my *New York Times* language columns, "Let's Kill All the Copy Editors," was a Shakespearean allusion not to be taken literally.) The design of type and layout that gives the book its period flavor was the work of Amy Hill.

Tom Ray, senior cataloger of the Virginia Newspaper Project at the Library of Virginia in Richmond, was invaluable in digging up copies of the long-defunct *Richmond Examiner* and *Richmond Recorder.* Laura Beardsley at the Pennsylvania Historical Association, at my request, went through the 250-page unpublished manuscript of a Philadelphia merchant who revealed the untold story of the life of Maria Reynolds and her daughter after they seemed to disappear from history. Selections from that memoir are published here at the end of the Underbook and cast a new light on her extended relationship with Aaron Burr. It may also enrich the mystery surrounding Hamilton's account of her adulterous affair with him, which was probably true, and of her supposed blackmail, which I think was untrue.

Now to the backup of each chapter.

Prologue: 1792

The three main primary sources concerning the "Reynolds affair" are these:

1. James T. Callender's *History of the United States for the Year 1796,* published in June and July 1797, which charged former Treasury Secretary Alexander Hamilton with speculation in government securities in conflict of interest;
2. Alexander Hamilton's *Observations on Certain Documents Contained in No. V & VI of "The History of the United States for the Year 1796," in which the Charge of Speculation Against Alexander Hamilton, Late Secretary of the Treasury, Is Fully Refuted. Written by Himself,* published in August 1797; and
3. Callender's surrebuttal in his *Sketches of the History of America,* published in 1798, in which the disbelieving editor wrote, "So much correspondence could not refer exclusively to wenching" and "that Mrs. Reynolds was, in reality, guiltless."

That frames the central question raised in the Prologue: Did Hamilton fall for the seductive charm of the twenty-two-year-old Maria Reynolds, only to be roped into a scheme to blackmail him, as he contended? Or, when caught in a financial conspiracy with James Reynolds, did the former Treasury Secretary concoct a blackmail story around an affair with his co-conspirator's wife—and by confessing to a phony sin, hope to conceal a real crime?

The most extensive historians' analyses of the still-mysterious affair are:

1. Broadus Mitchell, in his 1962 *Alexander Hamilton, The National Adventure, 1788–1804,* pp. 399–422, with notes on pp. 704–714, was inclined to believe Hamilton that the letters he quoted from Maria in his "Reynolds pamphlet" were authentic, partly because the historian found Maria's appeals so irresistibly fetching.
2. Harold C. Syrett et al, *The Papers of Alexander Hamilton,* vol. 21, pp. 121–285, is agnostic: "No one has yet devised a way to put together an account that not only answers all the questions that have been asked but also even meets the standards that are usually required for research papers submitted by college seniors."
3. Julian P. Boyd, ed., *The Papers of Thomas Jefferson,* vol. 18, pp. 611–688, "Appendix: The First Conflict in the Cabinet." Boyd makes the scrupulously detailed case that Callender had it right and that Hamilton fabricated letters from Maria to conceal his shady dealing. "Even the confession of private guilt remains in doubt, with the word of Hamilton balanced against that of Mrs. Reynolds and the scales perhaps tipped in her favor because the documents he brought forward in proof of adultery do indeed sustain her charge of fabrication."

Sources in detail:

PAGE

11   *"The man now in jail"*: This is based on the memorandum written by Speaker of the House Frederick A. Muhlenberg in the second week of December 1792, reporting on the beginning of an investigation into alleged speculation in securities by Alexander Hamilton. He wrote that his former clerk, Jacob Clingman, frequently dropped hints to him that James Reynolds, presently in jail pending prosecution, "said, he had it in his power to hang the Secretary of the Treasury; that he was deeply concerned in speculation . . . I conceived it my duty to consult with some friends on the subject." See pp. 209–210 of Callender's *History of the United States for 1796,* in which the first charge against Hamilton was made.

11   *"Reynolds claims to have proof"*: This is based on Clingman's memo of December 13, 1792: "Mr. Reynolds also said, that colonel Hamilton had made thirty thousand dollars by speculation . . ." and both James and Maria Reynolds had told him Hamilton "had book containing the amount of the cash due to the Virginia line [of former soldiers] at his own house at New-

York, with liberty to copy, and were obtained through Mr. [William] Duer," a corrupt Treasury official, later jailed.

14 *For months, in general terms:* Boyd, p. 638. "The Treasury Secretary countered that TJ was an incendiary promoting disunion." Boyd, p. 640.

15 *"Is this man one of the Virginia Reynoldses?":* Monroe was careful to record that he thought the jailed man was a constituent. "Being informed . . . Reynolds, from Virginia, Richmond, was confined . . . we immediately called on him . . . We found it was not the same man we had been taught to believe, but a man of that name from New-York. Being there, however, we questioned him . . ." Callender, *History of 1796*, p. 210.

16 *"I verily believe him to be a rascal":* Boyd, p. 632.

17 *" 'It is utterly out of my power' ":* Hamilton, Reynolds pamphlet, app., p. vi.

18 *"I am Frederick Augustus Muhlenberg":* The Congressman who accompanied Monroe to the interview with Reynolds in jail was Abraham Venable, not Muhlenberg; I have eliminated Venable, the third member of the investigating team, for simplicity's sake. Hamilton, Reynolds pamphlet, app., p. iii.

20 *Interview with Maria Reynolds:* Mitchell, p. 404; Boyd, p. 635.

22 *Dialogue in scene with Maria and Clingman:* Deduced from Clingman affidavit, Callender, *History of 1796*, pp. 213–215, and Monroe's addendum, p. 218.

24 *Dec. 18 scene with Clingman showing note from Wolcott:* Boyd, p. 641, changed by a day.

25 *"Hush money," attributed to Muhlenberg:* A phrase in common use, cited later in TJ letter to Monroe, May 29, 1801. "Blackmail" was not then current in America; "extortion" was the term. The President was then called the Chief Magistrate, not the Chief Executive.

27 *He was determined:* from AH letter, March 19, 1789.

29 *who Hamilton was convinced:* See TJ memo, 1792, 17, Dec. including details crossed out by TJ, in Boyd, p. 649.

31 *AH and Maria dialogue:* Fictional, but Clingman on p. 215 of Callender, *History of 1796*, quotes Maria quoting AH.

32 *Description of Maria:* Boyd, p. 628 notes that in the printed version of AH's Reynolds pamphlet he gives neither her appearance nor the sum he gave her. In AH handwritten draft, he wrote, "I put a thirty dollar bill in my Pocket and went to the house . . . It required a harder heart than mine to refuse [other means of consolation] to ~~a pretty woman~~ Beauty in distress." In this editing, Hamilton moved away from the particular pretty woman to a general "Beauty" in distress. AH's "the variety of shapes that this woman can assume is endless" is in A. Hamilton, *Observations on Certain Documents* (hereafter, the Reynolds pamphlet), p. 31, and is his most vivid assertion of her talent in duplicity.

35 *"difficult to disentangle myself":* In AH draft of pamphlet but not in printed version. ". . . demonstrates the delicacy of my conduct in its public rela-

tions," on p. 19 of A. Hamilton, printed Reynolds pamphlet. This may be the earliest use of the phrase "public relations," though not quite in its current sense.

38 *TJ and Mrs. Walker:* TJ later told William Burwell, his secretary, that AH sent word to him through Monroe that he knew of Mrs. Walker. Burwell wrote in a memoir that "Hamilton about the time he was attackd [*sic*] for his connection with Mrs. Reynolds had threatened him—with a public disclosure." Boyd, vol. 21, p. 134, n. 49.

39 *Monroe internal dialogue:* My speculation. When I have him wondering if the blackmail story was a cover-up of "nefarious abuses of the public trust," it should be noted that Hamilton was, in historian Richard B. Morris's estimation, "without question the least affluent man to hold the office of Secretary of the Treasury in American history." In *Alexander Hamilton and the Founding of the Nation,* Morris recounts on p. 587 a remark attributed to the French diplomatist Talleyrand, who happened to pass former Secretary Hamilton's law office one night on the way to a party and saw him drafting a legal paper by the light of a candle. "I have just come from viewing a man," said the amazed Frenchman, "who had made the fortune of his country, but now is working all night in order to support his family." (Keep this amazement at integrity in mind when we come to Talleyrand's corrupt role in the XYZ affair.)

41 *"screwing the hard earnings out of poor people's pockets":* Austin, p. 68. Cobbett (from now on, sometimes "PP" for Peter Porcupine) note to TJ, in Spater, vol. 1, pp. 42–43.

41 *Scene on dock:* Fictional, though both JTC and PP arrived at about that time.

43 *"You'll see":* Green, p. 122.

43 *"It's wonderful what you can say":* Durey, *With the Hammer of Truth,* p. 91.

43 *"No man has a right to pry":* Durey, *With the Hammer of Truth,* p. 93.

44 *" 'the six or eight hundred years of botching' ":* Durey, *With the Hammer of Truth,* p. 37.

44 *"I am an Englishman":* Green, p. 131.

45 *JTC story about Charles II's horse:* Callender, *American Annual Register, 1796,* also known as *The History of the United States for 1796,* pp. 218–219.

PART I: THE HAMILTON SCANDAL
Chapter 1

49 *PP's call for a "hempen necklace" for "a mangy little Scotsman":* In his bestselling pamphlet "*A Bone to Gnaw, for the Democrats,* reproduced in Cobbett, *Peter Porcupine in America,* pp. 92–93.

49 *"He leans his head toward one side":* Cobbett, *Porcupine's Works,* vol. 9, p. 216.

51 *"Citizen Callender":* This epithet hung around the Scot by Cobbett in his 1795 pamphlet *A Kick for a Bite,* in *Porcupine's Works,* vol. 2, p. 92.

51 *JTC letter to James Madison to find schoolmaster job:* May 28, 1796, in Ford, p. 325.

52 *TJ and JTC meeting:* When the *Virginia Gazette* in Nov. of 1802 wrote, "When Mr. Callender introduced himself to Mr. Jefferson, with his Political Progress of Britain as his passport for favor," JTC responded in the *Richmond Recorder* of Nov. 1802: "It was Mr. Jefferson that introduced himself to me. He called at the office of Snowden and McCorkle in Philadelphia, in June, or July 1797, asking for me. I was then printing the History of 1796. Whatever may since have passed between Mr. Jefferson and myself, it is only doing him justice to say that he did not excite me to begin to write on American politicks, although, from the date above mentioned, he was one of my warmest supporters."

52 *"The work contained":* Cobbett, *A Bone to Gnaw,* in *Peter Porcupine in America,* p. 92.

52 *His plea to Madison:* JTC to Madison, May 28, 1796, in Ford, p. 325.

53 *"I'm concerned that the republican press":* TJ to Madison, April 26, 1798, in Ford, p. 9.

53 *"In my note I tell Adams":* TJ to Madison, May 9, 1791, in Boyd, vol. 20, p. 293.

54 *"And perhaps there is some assistance":* JTC to TJ, Sept. 28, 1797, in Ford, p. 326.

55 *"the first of the bricks":* Cobbett, *Porcupine's Works,* vol. 5, p. 420.

56 *"I'm staying at Francis's Hotel,":* TJ to Madison, May 18, 1797; and see JTC to TJ, Sept. 28, 1797, "when I had the honor of seeing you at Francis's hotel," in Ford, p. 326.

56 *"He gave me a joe!":* JTC's account of this first meeting is not disputed by the many historians who otherwise denounce him as a "vile wretch." Two months earlier, in the *Richmond Recorder* of Sept. 22, 1802, JTC wrote: "In the summer of 1797, the vice president called at the office in Philadelphia, where I was then printing the History of 1796. He gave me a joe." A "joe" is a shortening of "Johannes," a Portuguese gold coin then worth about $16. This is corroborated by a notation by TJ in his June account books of payment to Callender of $15.14 for copies of his *History of 1796.*

Chapter 2

PAGE

56 *"Put James Madison down for twelve copies":* Berkeley and Berkeley, p. 164. On June 25, 1798, Madison marked "without authority" on the bill and refused to pay.

58 *"Washington could no longer be viewed as a saint":* Aurora, August 22, 1795. JTC added, in the wake of the Jay Treaty, "Instead of being viewed as the father of his country, we behold him as a master." JTC on a "nation . . . debauched by Washington," Durey, *With the Hammer of Truth,* p. 95.

58 " 'Calm Observer' ": Berkeley and Berkeley, p. 129. PP: "fretful moans of a weak mind," Berkeley and Berkeley, p. 161, from Cobbett, *Porcupine's Works*, vol. 5, pp. 419–420. See also Syrett, July 1797, p. 132.

60 *Beckley as a source of material:* A survey of most historians' judgment that Beckley was the probable source is in Durey, *With the Hammer of Truth*, pp. 99–100. JTC, in 1798 still an avid Jefferson supporter, absolved TJ as his source of the Hamilton documents: "Mr. Jefferson had received a copy of these documents" but "never shewed them, nor ever spoke of them, to any person. In summer 1797, when the vice president heard of the intended publication, he advised that the papers be suppressed . . . but his interposition came too late."

Chapter 3

62 *"We now come to a part of the work":* Callender, *History of 1796*, pp. 220–223, condensed.

64 *Beckley said yes:* On December 17, 1792, two days after Monroe's meetings with AH, TJ wrote: "The affair of Reynolds and his wife.—Clingham Muhlenb[erg]'s clerk, testifies to F. A. Muhl[enberg,] Monroe[,] Venable—also [Oliver] Wolcott and [Jeremiah] Wadsworth. Known to J[ames] M[adison], E[dmund] R[andolph]d.d[John]Beckley and [Bernard] Webb." Crossed out in TJ's journal was the next paragraph: "Reynolds was speculating agent in the speculations of Govt. arrearages. He was furnished by [William] Duer with a list of the claims of arreages [*sic*] due to the Virga. and Carola. Lines and brought them up, against which the Resolutions of Congress of June 4, 1790 were leveled. Hamilton advised the President to give his negative to those resolutions."

Monroe evidently kept TJ informed immediately. Both concluded that AH's advice to Washington would benefit his "speculating agent," James Reynolds, in a conspiracy with William Duer, a close associate of Hamilton who had the list of which veterans had claims for their arrearages. The corrupt plan was to buy the claims cheap, knowing that the government was planning to pay them in full. We do not know if AH knew what his associates were doing or if he profited by it.

65 *Hamilton informed us of a particular connection:* Callender, *History of 1796*, p. 217.

Chapter 4

68 *In the month of December 1792:* A. Hamilton, Reynolds pamphlet, pp. xxix, xxx.

71 *Maria Reynolds had obtained a divorce:* This is based on a letter from John Beckley dated June 22, 1793, probably to James Monroe: "Clingman . . .

informs me, that Mrs. Reynolds has obtained a divorce from her husband, in consequence of his intrigue with Hamilton to her prejudice, and that Colonel Burr obtained it for her: he adds too, that she is thoroughly disposed to attest all she knows of the connection between Hamilton and Reynolds." Syrett, editor of *The Papers of Alexander Hamilton,* notes on p. 141 of vol. 21 that "there is no record, however, that she ever attested to 'all she knows.'" See a reference in the memoir of Peter Grotjan, quoted at length at the end of these notes, to a pamphlet she prepared and gave to William Duane, editor of the *Aurora,* which he never published and which has disappeared, if it ever existed.

Burr did very well for Mrs. Reynolds in her divorce award. On August 6, 1793, her case was brought before the New York Supreme Court where its minutes, on file at the New York City Hall of Records, show that "the Jury without going from the Bar Say that they find for the plaintiff Three hundred pounds damages and Six pence Costs." An award of 300 pounds was substantial; the token "Six pence Costs" suggests that Burr handled the case for no fee, which lawyers even then rarely did without a personal interest in the client. Syrett adds "that she and Clingman were subsequently married, that they were living in Virginia in 1798, and that at a later time they moved to England."

71 *He sat down:* The leather couch symbol is fictional. The admission by AH that he conducted many of his assignations with Maria in his own home when his family was away especially dismayed his supporters.

Chapter 5
PAGE

72 *In his suddenly bustling office:* This chapter closely follows the account in Syrett, vol. 21, pp. 121–145.

Chapter 6
PAGE

78 *Who? David Gelston:* Monroe chose republican Congressman David Gelston, not his friend Aaron Burr, to be his witness at this confrontation with Hamilton. Gelston made three closely written pages of notes of the meeting just after it ended, the factual basis for this scene; I am grateful to the Historical Society of Pennsylvania for these notes from its Gratz Collection. Afterward, because the danger of a duel still existed, Monroe chose Burr to be his second. Burr ameliorated the dispute, helped Monroe avoid the duel, and perhaps saved Hamilton's life for the day he and Burr were destined to meet in Weehawken, N.J., for their own duel.

I chose to make Burr the reader's witness in this scene, so vividly described by Gelston, not only because I did not want to introduce a one-scene character, but because Burr was Monroe's later choice for negotiations with

Hamilton's brother-in-law, John Church. (Hamilton's wife's sister, Angelica, was married to Church, and was a woman who both Hamilton and Jefferson found attractive. Angelica's letters to Hamilton became less affectionate during AH's eighteen-month affair with Maria.)

79 *"a crooked gun"*: In Jefferson's Anas, in Peterson, *Writings*, p.227. In that same journal (on p. 693 of *Writings*): "I had never seen col. Burr till he came as a member of Senate. His conduct very soon inspired me with distrust. I habitually cautioned Mr. Madison against trusting him too much."

80 *"a respectable character in Virginia"*: see Boyd, app., p. 664, from AH's Reynolds pamphlet reprinting a letter from Monroe to AH, July 17, 1797.

81 *"malignant and dishonorable"*: AH to Monroe, July 22, 1797.

81 *"I fought a duel last year"*: According to AH's grandson Allan McLane Hamilton, in his 1911 *Intimate Life of Alexander Hamilton*, p. 409, the pistols used in the Burr-Hamilton duel of 1804 "were purchased by Mr. Church in London, in 1795 or 1796, and used by him in an English duel."

82 *"your postscript implied"*: AH to Monroe, July 22, 1797, in Syrett, vol. 21, pp. 137–138.

82 *"From that I infer a design"*: Ibid.

Chapter 7

84 *"The most pitiful part"*: JTC to TJ, Sept. 28, 1797.

85 *"Burr can be everybody's friend"*: Shortened from a letter by Beckley cited on p. 141 of Syrett, vol. 21.

85 *"I believe Maria Reynolds"*: Callender, *History of 1796*, p. 211.

86 *" 'a superabundance of excretions' "*: From Lomask, p. 258, citing John Quincy Adams, *Works*, vol. 9, p. 277.

88 *"that impudent vagabond juggler"*: PP's tart opinion of Noah Webster in *Porcupine's Political Censor*, March 1797.

88 *"When we view the second magistrate"*: Referring to the Vice President, July 1797, from *Porcupine's Works*, vol. 6, pp. 316–317.

90 *"Sweet vengeance for my recall"*: Monroe's comments are based on his letter to Burr of Dec. 1, 1797, quoted in Syrett, vol. 21, p. 133.

90 *"Burr inspires me with distrust"*: TJ Anas, Jan. 26, 1804, in Peterson, *Writings*, p. 693.

91 *"Finding the strait between Scylla and Charybdis"*: TJ to John Taylor, Oct. 8, 1797, cited in Berkeley and Berkeley, p. 169.

92 *"The one against you is a masterpiece of folly"*: Madison to TJ, Oct. 20, 1797.

Chapter 8

93 *"You are acting in opposition"*: The Lyon quotes from Austin, pp. 96–97.

97 *Griswold-Lyon incident*: Austin, p. 100, using Griswold's description.

Chapter 9

100 *Wolcott-Adams conversation:* From Page Smith, *John Adams,* vol. 2, p. 955.

101 *"You know, it's a very painful thing":* Abigail Adams's report of her husband's feeling, from Page Smith, *The Shaping of America,* vol. 3, p. 260.

102 *"You know I love and revere the man":* From letter of April 15, 1808, in Page Smith, *John Adams,* vol. 2, p.1084.

103 *"This shall not be made the headquarters":* Ibid., Feb. 25, 1808.

104 *"Why is the President afraid to tell?":* Durey, *With the Hammer of Truth,* p. 107.

104 *"People begin to see their madness":* From the *Aurora,* in Schachner, *Thomas Jefferson,* p. 600.

104 *"petrified with astonishment":* Page Smith, *The Shaping of America,* vol. 2, p. 260.

108 *"Marshall reports here":* John Marshall on liberty of the press, from Jean Edward Smith, *John Marshall,* pp. 229–230.

109 *PP-Harper relationship:* Spater, vol. 1, p.104.

110 *"We do not wish to divide":* Porcupine's Gazette, July 27, 1798.

111 *"That I was no trout":* PP on Talleyrand, from *Porcupine's Gazette,* May 6, 1797.

112 *"The press is the engine":* TJ to Monroe, Feb. 5, 1799; see also TJ's account of his support of republican newspapers to Monroe, July 17, 1802. Comparison of height of Madison and Adams, from Brant, p. 277.

113 *"Its inevitable effect":* This line and "In several places the people have turned out with protests" are rephrased from Madison to TJ, April 22, 1798. I had a source for TJ's "Adams's message arming our merchant vessels is insane," but I cannot find it.

113 *"Public sentiment":* Madison to TJ, April 29, 1798.

114 *"Party passions are high":* TJ, May 9, 1798, cited in Peterson, p. 599.

114 *But Porcupine gives me:* TJ to Madison, in Peterson, p. 603: "Porcupine gave me a principal share in it [the Logan mission], as I am told, for I never read his papers."

114 *" 'Watch, Philadelphians' ":* "Watch, Philadelphians, or the fire is in your houses . . ." Ibid., p. 602.

114 *"The success of the war party":* Madison to TJ, May 5, 1798.

114 *His face bore a sour expression:* Cobbett's description of James Madison at this period of his life is recorded in Daniel Green's *Great Cobbett,* p. 164: "Madison is a little bow-legged man, at once stiff and slender. His countenance has that sour aspect, that conceited screw which pride would willingly mould into an expression of disdain, if he did not find the features too skinny and too scanty for its purpose. His thin sleek hair, and the niceness of his garments are indicative of that economical cleanliness . . . which boasts of wearing a shirt for three days without rumpling the ruffles." Callender later would agree.

114 *Monroe's questioning and observations:* Fictional.

115 *"This curious office . . . Adams . . . wants so badly to be his own man":* TJ to Madison, Dec. 27, 1797.

116 *"Though not one twenty-fifth of the nation":* TJ to William Short, Jan. 23, 1804.

116 *"We must marshal our support":* TJ to Madison, April 26, 1798, cited in Mott, p. 28.

116 *"As you know":* TJ, May 23, 1793, cited in Mott, p. 20.

116 *"Hamilton's life has been":* TJ, cited in Brookhiser, p. 5.

117 *"For heaven's sake":* TJ to Madison, April 5, 1798.

117 *"At a very early period":* TJ, August 22, 1798.

117 *"When he came to importune me":* JTC to Madison, Sept. 22, 1798.

117 *"There's a monster of legislation":* Madison to TJ, May 20, 1798.

117 *"That's a detestable thing":* TJ to Madison, May 31, 1798.

117 *"worthy of the eighth or ninth centuries":* TJ to Thomas Mann Randolph, May 9, 1798.

118 *"lay his purse and his pen under contribution":* TJ to Madison, Feb. 5, 1799.

118 *"There is now only wanting":* Lipscomb, vol. 10, p. 32.

118 *"Perhaps there is enough virtue":* Madison to TJ, May 5, 1798; a rephrasing of the line "It is to be hoped, however, that any arbitrary attacks on the freedom of the press will find virtue enough remaining in the public mind to make them recoil on their wicked authors."

Chapter 10

119 *Description of yellow-fever protections in Philadelphia in 1798:* From Matthew Carey, *Miscellaneous Essays, 1830;* collected in *Library of American Literature* (New York, 1889), vol. 4, pp. 162–163.

120 *his sick wife:* The reader may note that no name is given for Callender's wife. Biographer Durey found none; the only name unearthed for any of the four Callender sons is that of the youngest, Tom.

121 *"Fortunately, you applied for citizenship":* It is not known for certain that Callender's U.S. citizenship was fraudulent, but that accusation was made by Federalist editors and a Federal prosecutor. "In consequence of this act (alien)," Callender wrote in *The Prospect Before Us,* "I have been menaced with prosecution and imprisonment by David Call, that sorry understrapper of Federal usurpation." At any rate, he was sufficiently documented to avoid deportation as an alien enemy.

121 *"A great man":* Beckley's assessment of Dr. Rush comes from Berkeley and Berkeley, p. 172.

121 *"He's one of that aristocratic junto":* Quoted in Stanley E. Flink, *Sentinel Under Siege,* p. 92, citing G. Warner, *Means for Preservation of Public Liberty* (1797), pp. 13–14.

121 *Cobbett's trial:* An account of the libel trial of PP by Judge McKean is in Cobbett's *"The Democratic Judge,"* a 1798 pamphlet; the view from the other

side of the bench is in G. S. Rowe's biography of Thomas McKean, pp. 300–303. McKean's view was that the case, though based on civil libel ordinarily held before a Federal court, involved criminality and thus was subject to State law.

122 *"He is demonstrably small"*: This and other PP quotes in this chapter from Cobbett, the *Political Censor* for Sept. 1796, p. 54.

125 *" 'If ever a nation was debauched' "*: From the *Aurora*, Dec. 23, 1796.

125 *motioned for Callender to stand*: Callender's presence in the courtroom, and that of Lyon and Beckley, is fictional.

125 *"If a man is attacked in the press"*: and subsequent quotes of Callender are from his comments on this case in *Sedgwick & Co*, p. 18, and the *Richmond Recorder*, Oct. 20, 1802. See also Durey, *With the Hammer of Truth*, p. 108, and Spater, vol. 1, pp. 95–100.

126 *"the mask of patriotism"*: *Aurora*, Dec. 23, 1796.

127 *Callender-Cobbett conversation*: Fictional. Did they ever meet? Philadelphia was then a town of about 60,000 and PP's bookstore and printing shop was infamous. It is possible that its two most vituperative journalists did meet; however, if they had, one or the other would probably have written caustically about it.

130 *"When I see you flourishing with a metaphor"*: Cobbett, *Kick for a Bite* pamphlet (1795), in *Porcupine's Works*, vol. 2, p.75.

Chapter 11

PAGE

131 *"treacherous in private friendship"*: Paine letter derogating Washington, dated July 30, 1796, printed in *Aurora* a year later; see Freeman, *Washington*, one-vol. condensation, p. 705.

131 *"Making allowances for the asperity of an Englishman"*: George Washington wrote this to David Stuart on Jan. 8, 1797. Fitzpatrick, vol. 35. Washington used semicolons, which I have changed to commas, and he spelled Cobbett with one *t*.

131 *"How Tom gets a living"*: Hawke, p. 321.

131 *"Some of the gazettes"*: The GW quotations through "I shall pass over them in utter silence" come from the draft in Washington's hand of his Farewell Address, which he called "a valedictory message." He sent it to AH for rewrite. Hamilton killed this passage in redrafting.

132 *"A powerful faction"*: Flexner, p. 392, citing James Hamilton, vol. 6, pp. 289–290.

132 *"It is the most flagitious"*: AH, writing under the pseudonym of Titus Manlius, in James Hamilton, pp. 259, 318.

132 *"One would think"*: Fitzpatrick, vol. 36, pp. 248, 254

133 *"Open war is likely only"*: Ibid., p.271.

133 *"During the Revolution"*: Ibid., p. 457.

134 *It was Hamilton's dream:* For AH on American empire, see Schachner, *Alexander Hamilton,* pp.380–381, and McDonald, p. 346.

134 *"In many instances aliens are sent":* Freeman, p. 731.

134 *"Although the mass of aliens":* AH to Pickering, June 7, 1798, cited in J. M. Smith, *Freedom's Fetters,* p. 55

135 *"Let us not establish a tyranny":* AH to Wolcott, June 29, 1798.

135 *"Colonel Burr is a brave and able officer":* Holmes Alexander in *Aaron Burr* (New York, 1937), p. 126, cites this Washington quote from James Parton, *The Life and Times of Aaron Burr,* p. 240.

Chapter 12

135 *Maria Reynolds in 1798:* In *Alexander Hamilton,* Broadus Mitchell quotes a letter from Richard Folwell citing the whereabouts of Maria Reynolds in 1798, five years after her marriage to Jacob Clingman. Syrett, vol. 21, p.141, also refers to Folwell's placing her in Alexandria, VA. Folwell sent Hamilton two letters in the handwriting of Maria Reynolds, but AH did not use them to authenticate her writing of letters to him when Callender challenged him to show they were not forgeries. This was one reason that Jefferson historian Boyd concluded that the purported letters showing a blackmail plot were "palpably contrived documents" in which Hamilton "tried to imitate what he conceived to be the style of less literate persons."

The Berkeleys, in their Beckley biography, p. 171, note that Jacob and Maria Clingman then "went to England, where they settled at Hull. By January 1801, Clingman was a partner in the prosperous commission firm of Clingman and Gill." Footnote 31 on that page says that in letters to Monroe on Dec. 29, 1803, and Jan. 7, 1804, Clingman "was having passport troubles." Meanwhile, Maria had returned to the U.S., according to the Grotjan memoir.

136 *Maria letter to Burr:* Fictional. My speculation about her Burr friendship is based on the Grotjan memoir quoted at length at the end of these notes. For other speculation about Maria sharing a relationship with both Burr and Hamilton, see Rogow, pp. 153–156, 263–264.

137 *"Sincerely your friend, Maria Lewis Clingman":* Concerning her maiden name, Milton Lomask in his 1979 Burr biography states that "she was born Maria Lewis in New York State," probably based on AH's Reynolds pamphlet, p. 17: "With a seeming air of affliction she informed that she was a daughter of a Mr. Lewis, sister to a Mr. G. Livingston of the State of New York, and wife to a Mr. Reynolds . . . who for a long time had treated her very cruelly, had lately left her, to live with another woman . . ."

Chapter 13

138 *"George Washington is with us"*: Harper to Hamilton, April 27, 1798, in Syrett, vol. 21, p. 449. "The only principle by which radical republicans could be governed is fear" was said by Harper lieutenant Uriah Tracy, but said "Democrats" rather than "radical republicans"; I use "republicans" throughout to avoid confusion. See Elkins and McKitrick, p. 715. Cobbett-Harper conversation fictional.

139 *Gallatin-Harper debate:* This was actually a debate between republican Edward Livingston of New York, a Gallatin ally, and Federalist "Long John" Allen of Connecticut, a Harper ally. For dramatic simplicity's sake, I have substituted Gallatin for Livingston and Harper for Allen throughout. Source for the quotes, including the translation of Juvenal's poetry on p. 144, is J.M. Smith's *Freedom's Fetters,* pp. 112–130.

PART II: THE SEDITION SCANDAL

Chapter 14

148 *"You heard the sad news"*: Benjamin Franklin Bache died on Sept. 9 at the age of twenty-nine.

149 *"There's no more safety"*: JTC quoting Leiper to TJ, Sept. 22, 1798, in Ford, p. 328.

149 *"I hope that this pestilence"*: JTC to TJ, Oct. 26, 1798.

150 *"You will find Mason"*: On Oct. 11, 1798, TJ wrote to Senator Stevens Mason: "I received lately a letter from Mr. Callender to which the inclosed is the answer . . . After perusing it, be so good as to stick a wafer in it and (after it is dry) deliver it. You will perceive that I propose to you the trouble of drawing for 50 D. for Mr. Callender on my correspondent in Richmond, George Jefferson, merchant. This is to keep his name out of sight." Ford, p. 329.

150 *"He hung three of the paintings"*: The story about paintings in TJ's front parlor and AH's reaction are recounted by TJ to Benjamin Rush, Jan. 16, 1811.

150 *First, down in Virginia:* Callender's intention or dream of returning to Scotland is in his letter to TJ of Sept. 22, 1798.

151 *He started south on foot:* JTC to TJ, Nov. 19, 1798.

152 *"When the occasion requires"*: Porcupine's Gazette, June 1, 1798.

152 *"people had better hold their tongues"*: Austin, p. 106.

153 *"The public welfare is swallowed up"*: Ibid.

154 *"old, querulous, toothless"*: This characterization of Adams is complained of in Abigail Adams's letter to Mary Cranch, April 28, 1798.

Chapter 15

156 *"You remember what Ben Franklin"*: Madison to TJ, June 10, 1798.

157 *"The judge said that made it worse"*: Beckley narrative based on J. M. Smith, *Freedom's Fetters*, p. 238.

158 *"This is an experiment"*: TJ in Peterson, p. 611, unsourced.

158 *"I don't know what mortifies me more"*: TJ to John Taylor, Nov. 26, 1798; quote not exact.

159 *"Yet the body of our countrymen"*: TJ to John Taylor, June 4, 1798.

159 *a fine stone house:* The Nourse house in West Virginia, "Piedmont," outside of Charles Town, is now the home of Mr. and Mrs. Jim Lehrer.

159 *"The right of freely examining"*: Virginia Resolutions of Dec. 21, 1798; see Banning, p. 386.

160 *"It's not as if"*: The $2 million in internal property taxes proposed by Harper is discussed in Dall W. Forsythe's *Taxation and Political Change in the Young Nation*, p. 53.

161 *"Congress was not a party to"*: TJ on nullification; see Banning, p. 387. TJ believed that the several States did not unite "on the principle of unlimited submission to the General Government."

162 *Madison's substitution of "interpose" for TJ's "nullify"*: Ibid., p. 389.

Chapter 16

164 *Mason the Senator:* This article comes directly from *Porcupine's Gazette*, not in October but the edition dated Sept. 8, 1798. See Cobbett, *Porcupine's Works*, vol. 9, pp. 215–217. Some sentences have been shortened for clarity and a few phrases cut or added.

166 *The long scene with Maria and JTC:* Fiction; Callender never interviewed Maria Reynolds. The information underlying the dialogue is true.

Chapter 17

175 *"It is quite a new kind of jargon"*: Triumphal parade, Austin, pp. 115–127.

177 *"I paid one thousand dollars"*: Mason dialogue with jailer, who was Jabez Fitch, fictional.

178 *"Come take the glass"*: J. M. Smith, *Freedom's Fetters*, p. 245. In 1840, Congress refunded Lyon's fine to his family.

179 *"Do gentlemen say opinions can be false?"*: Gallatin and John Nicholas of Virginia presented the case for Lyon against Bayard of Delaware's move to expel. Austin, p. 127. Gallatin pointed out that the Sedition Act included a provision that truth was a defense, which had been put forward by Bayard, who now argued that an opinion could be false. Conversation between Lyon and Gallatin, fictional.

Chapter 18

PAGE

181 *no common railer:* "Not a commonplace railer" was Callender's self-assessment to Jefferson.

182 *JTC's internal monologue:* My speculation.

184 *The north end of Monticello:* Domeless Monticello described in Malone, *Jefferson and the Ordeal of Liberty*, pp. 241–242.

184 *"The violence mediated against you":* TJ to Callender, Sept. 6, 1798, in Ford, p. 447.

184 *"I'm concerned about your welfare":* Ibid.

185 *"sever ourselves from that union we so much value":* That sentence continued "rather than give up the rights of self-government which we have reserved." TJ's views on what he called "scission," or secession, were expressed to Madison in a letter of Aug. 23, 1799, which included "The Alien and Sedition Acts is an exercise of powers over the states to which we have never assented." Madison apparently thought it was too intemperate to answer in writing, because he noted on Jefferson's letter that a visit "took the place of an answer to the letter." He wanted to "leave the matter in such a train as that we may not be committed absolutely to push the matter to extremities." See J. M. Smith, *Republic of Letters*, vol. 2, pp. 1109, 1072.

186 *"I would dearly like to find fifty acres":* JTC to TJ, Sept. 26, 1799. TJ's "I thank you for those proof sheets. Such papers as yours cannot fail to produce the best effect. . . . We have to inform the thinking part . . . When I correspond with you . . . keep myself out of the way of calumny"—all from TJ to JTC, October 6, 1799, in Ford, pp. 448–449. This was the most encouraging, personal and conspiratorial letter Jefferson sent to Callender.

186 *"Georgia, North Carolina:"* TJ's political analysis and comment on New York on this and the following page is in his letter to Madison of March 8, 1800. He thought Burr and Livingston in New York too optimistic: "We must make allowance for their sanguine views."

188 *"I fear no injury":* TJ Anas, April 15, 1806, in Peterson, *Writings*.

188 *"To preserve the freedom":* TJ to William Green Mumford, June 18, 1799, in Schachner, *Thomas Jefferson*, p. 624.

Chapter 19

PAGE

189 *PP's conversation with Harper:* Fictional.

190 *"General Hamilton thinks the President":* From Page Smith, *John Adams*, vol. 2, p. 1000.

191 *"Of the four grand departments":* The analysis of a press conspiracy to help overthrow the government is in Durey, *Transatlantic Radicals*, p. 252. He based it on JTC's note on p. 130 of *The Prospect Before Us*, that "Duane and Cooper completed this imaginary triumvirate, who were said to have subdi-

vided among themselves the direction of the presses of anarchy." I have added a fourth: Matthew Lyon in the North.

193 *"I started* Porcupine's Gazette": *Porcupine's Gazette,* Jan. 13, 1800.

194 *"Is there no pride in American bosoms?":* Durey, *Transatlantic Radicals,* p. 256.

194 *"He calls me a 'precipitate old ass' ":* Cobbett, *Peter Porcupine in America,* p. 34.

195 *"But I will not take revenge":* Page Smith, *John Adams,* vol. 2, p. 1001. The Adams-Hamilton meeting in Trenton took place in October 1799; for accounts see Syrett, vol. 23, pp. 546–547; Stewart Mitchell, ed., *New Letters of Abigail Adams, 1788–1801,* pp. 224–225. See also McDonald, pp. 347–348; and Brookhiser, p. 144.

197 *"a degraded wretch":* Cobbett, *Peter Porcupine in America,* p. 231, citing PP's pamphlet, *The Republican Judge.*

198 *"The style of* Porcupine's Gazette": *Rush-Light 3,* in *Porcupine's Works,* vol. 11, pp. 311–313.

198 *"The* Aurora *printed something":* Aurora, Dec. 14, 1799, in Rosenfeld, p. 725.

Chapter 20

200 *"The entire nation is in mourning":* The scene depicted in this chapter is fictional. Before these notes are finished, I will provide some fresh evidence to buttress my belief that Maria had a longtime, close friendship with Aaron Burr.

200 *"first in war, first in peace":* These words were first spoken in the House by Rep. John Marshall, later Chief Justice, delivering the Congressional eulogy on the morning after Washington's death. "The phrase, however," writes Jean Edward Smith in her 1996 biography of Marshall, "was actually written by Henry [Light-Horse Harry] Lee, who had given it to Marshall the night before. Lee had anticipated speaking, but recognized that this would be inappropriate because of the rules of the House, so he deferred to Marshall who had the floor. Marshall, for his part, always did his best to see that Lee was credited for the words."

202 *"Cobbett says Dr. Rush is Dr. Death":* Cobbett, *Peter Porcupine in America,* p. 230. Burr's explanation of how Presidents are chosen comes from McDonald, p. 348.

Chapter 21

206 *it was surely Hamilton's indiscreet over-reaction:* In a letter to Burr, who was his potential second in a duel with Hamilton in 1797 after Callender's accusations, Monroe wrote: "I had no hand in the publication, was sorry for it— and think he has acted, by drawing the publick attention to it, & making it an aff'r of more consequence than it was in itself, very indiscreetly." Cresson, p. 169.

207 *"the flimsy, scurrilous papers of Scipio"*: Letter to TJ from Monroe, cited in Cresson's *James Monroe* but with no date. This was the pen name of Federalist Uriah Tracy. Scipio, the legendary Spanish commander who "dismissed the Iberian maid" in Milton's *Paradise Regained,* fell in love with a captive princess, but when she wished to remain faithful to her betrothed, rewarded her fidelity by paying her ransom as a wedding present. They're not using pseudonyms like that any more.

209 *"I'm firing through five portholes at once!"*: JTC to TJ, March 14, 1800, in Ford, p. 451. He added, "They cannot blame me, if the most enlightened people in the world are as ignorant as dirt."

210 *"To the downfall of His Majesty"*: Callender, *The Prospect Before Us,* cited by John Chester Miller in *The Wolf by the Ears,* p. 151.

210 *"I am always afraid of saying a great deal"*: Callender, *The Prospect Before Us,* pp. 3, 4.

211 *"the curiosity of the post offices"*: TJ to JTC, Oct. 6, 1799: "You will know from whom this comes without a signature; the omission of which has rendered almost habitual with me by the curiosity of the post offices. Indeed a period is now approaching during which I shall discontinue writing letters as much as possible, knowing that every snare will be used to get hold of what may be perverted in the eyes of the public."

Earlier in that letter, TJ supplied JTC with detailed answers to questions about the Barbary negotiations for use in *The Prospect Before Us,* and added: "All who were members of Congress in 1786 may be supposed to remember this information, and if it could be understood to come to you through some such channel, it would save the public of reading all the blackguardism which would be vented on me, were I quoted; not that this would weigh an atom with me on any occasion where my avowal of either facts or opinions would be of public use; but whenever it will not, I then think it useful to keep myself out of the way of calumny." This later became known as "not for attribution."

213 *"I'll raise such a tornado"*: JTC to TJ, Nov. 19, 1798, in Ford, p. 333. "I would then be ready to give our readers such a Tornado as not Govt ever got before, for there is in American history a species of ignorance, absurdity, and imbecility unknown to the annals of any other nation."

Chapter 22

PAGE

215 *"The reign of Mr. Adams"*: From JTC's *The Prospect Before Us,* cited on pp. 339–342 of J. M. Smith's *Freedom's Fetters,* taken from *U.S. v. Callender,* in Wharton, *State Trials,* pp. 688–690.

215 *"You will choose in this election"*: Ibid.

215 *"Marcellus"*: Ibid.

216 *"If the author has afforded room"*: Ibid.

216 *"They should have hanged him"*: From J. M. Smith, p. 343, drawn from *The Answer and Pleas of Samuel Chase . . . to the Articles of Impeachment* (Washington, D.C., 1805), pp. 44, 63–64, 219–223.

216 *Dialogue between JTC and attorneys*: Fictional dialogue, but the scene took place at the jail with JTC and the three named lawyers.

217 *"The Governor asked the Vice President"*: Monroe to TJ, May 25, 1800: "Will it be proper for the Executive to employ counsel to defend him, and supporting the law, give an éclat to a vindication of the principles of the State?" TJ replied the next day that Callender "should be substantially defended, whether in the first stage by public interference"—that is, by State counsel—" or private contributions."

218 *"I know that sometimes it is useful"*: TJ to Monroe, March 16, 1800.

220 *Callender trial*: "The Trial of James Thompson [*sic*] Callender, for a Seditious Libel. In the Circuit Court of the United States for the Virginia District. Richmond 1800" can be found in Wharton, pp. 688–721. A good summary of the trial is also in the *Report of the Trial of the Hon. Samuel Chase . . . Before the High Court of Impeachment* (Baltimore, 1805). Another summary is in Frederick Trevor Hill's *Decisive Battles of the Law* (Harper, 1907), which concludes: "Five years later Chase was impeached before the Senate for oppressive and vexatious conduct during the trial, and indecent solicitude for the conviction of the accused." (Chase was acquitted by the Senate.) A contemporary account of Chase's sentencing lecture was in the *Virginia Gazette* of June 1800, reprinted in Ford, pp. 453–455. The most complete summary of Chase's abusive sedition trial of Callender is in J. M. Smith, *Freedom's Fetters*, pp. 343–358.

Historian Henry Adams wrote in 1880 that "so far as license was concerned, 'the Prospect Before Us' was a mild libel compared with Cobbett's . . . cataracts of abuse" against Jefferson. Over a century later, Chief Justice William Rehnquist told a C-Span interviewer that "the third basis for Chase's impeachment was his conduct at the trial of a fellow named James Callender . . . a kind of poison pen artist who had a most unappealing character, and he wrote a book called 'The Prospect Before Us' . . . Whatever the opposite of a page-turner is, that was it . . . Callender over and over again charged John Adams, who was then President, with being a toady to the British monarchy. Under the Sedition Act, a person could be tried for that. It's unthinkable today with our First Amendment rulings."

228 *JTC's inner dialogue*: My speculation about what may have been going through Callender's head at the trial.

230 *"blacker colors than Sejanus himself"*: Sejanus, title-role villain of Ben Jonson's 1603 play, was the commander of Rome's Praetorian Guard under Tiberius who killed all of the Emperor's children and grandchildren as his route to power, but who was strangled and thrown into the Tiber.

231 *"I understand that government officers"*: Callender did not say this at the trial;

he wrote it in the Richmond jail in Jan. 1801, in *The Prospect Before Us,* bk. 2, pt. 2, pp. 36, 96.

Chapter 23

PAGE

232 *Gallatin-Beckley dialogue:* The conversation is fictional, set about two months before the events occurred. The Berkeleys write in their biography of Beckley that "someone in New York, probably Burr, had sent him a copy of a 'letter,' actually a pamphlet, with the title 'The Political Conduct and Character of John Adams, Esq., President of the United States,' written and signed by Hamilton . . . On October 22, the *Aurora* began publishing a series of excerpts from Hamilton's pamphlet, even before some of its intended recipients had obtained their copies."

233 *"Cursed of thy father": Aurora,* Aug. 8, 1800.

239 *his "religious duty":* AH wrote to George Washington, Sept. 26, 1792, about Burr: "Embarrassed, as I understand, in his circumstances, with an extravagant family, bold, enterprising and intriguing, I am mistaken if it be not his object to play the game of confusion, and I feel it to be a religious duty to oppose his career." This was during the time AH was having an affair (later admitted) with Maria Reynolds—which, I suggest, may also have been the case with Burr.

239 *Burr and the pamphlet:* How did Burr obtain the pamphlet in advance? Writes Lomask in his Burr biography, p. 257: "One of several unsubstantiated tales attributes his procurement of the copy to the good offices of an agreeable young woman well known to both him and Hamilton. According to another, the colonel, an early riser, was out walking one morning when he saw a boy heading for Hamilton's house carrying a basket with a cloth over its contents. 'What's in the basket, son?' 'Only papers, sir,' was the reply. Burr asked to have a look, and a second later a copy of Hamilton's letter-contra-Adams was in his hand. However he got it, he knew what to do with it. He released extracts to the press."

Chapter 24

PAGE

240 *JTC and Bowler:* Callender wrote to Jefferson from the Richmond jail about his talk with Bowler, who was a lieutenant of Gabriel, the free black who planned a slave insurrection on the night of Aug. 30, 1800. "The plan was to massacre all the whites . . . then march off to the mountains with the plunder of the city." JTC to TJ, Sept. 13, 1800. Unlike most of the radical immigrant writers, Callender blamed the blacks for corrupting the morals of the whites who fraternized with them. He favored transplantation of the slaves to "a sequestered part of the continent" where they might live "without intermingling with the whites." Durey, *With the Hammer of Truth,* p. 138.

242 *Monroe-Callender dialogue:* Fictional; Monroe did visit Callender in jail.

Chapter 25

246 The Cannibal's Progress, *had reached 100,000:* Sales of 100,000 in a population of 4 million is equivalent to 7 million copies in today's U.S. population of 270 million. But it was paperback, and there was no other mass medium than print.

246 *Cobbett-Hamilton dialogue:* The scene is fictional, though Cobbett did meet with Hamilton in New York.

246 *"I am a farmer's son":* Daniel Green, in *Great Cobbett,* p. 170, cites this passage from Cobbett's *"Peter Porcupine," The Democratic Judge* (also published as *The Republican Judge*—the words were synonymous). PP noted that "every farmer's son is, in some degree, a practical phlebotomist."

249 *"If there be a man in the world":* Syrett, vol. 25, p. 275.

249 *"No man has a right":* Cobbett, *Observations on the Emigration of Dr. Priestly,* preface (1794), in Cobbett, *Peter Porcupine in America,* p. 52.

Chapter 26

251 *"The contrivance in the Constitution":* TJ to Tench Coxe, Dec. 31, 1800.

252 *"Maybe we could get Burr":* Madison to TJ, Jan. 10, 1801. Madison did not use those introductory words; he wrote that though "not strictly regular" under the Constitution, a joint proclamation calling the new Congress into session might work: "the irregularity will be less in form than any other adequate to the emergency."

252 *"I'll write Burr a letter":* The letter offering a Cabinet post, TJ to Burr, Dec. 15, 1800. Burr reply to TJ, Dec. 23, 1800. See Schachner, *Thomas Jefferson,* pp. 651–657.

252 *"Many attempts have been made":* TJ to Monroe, Feb. 15, 1801.

253 *"You are right about Hamilton":* Signing himself "Aristedes," Noah Webster of the *Commercial Advertiser* answered Hamilton's published letter with a defense of Adams as "a man of pure morals . . . and by far the best-read statesman that the late Revolution called into notice," whose "occasional ill humor at unreasonable opposition and hasty expressions of his opinion are of little weight." In contrast, wrote Webster in this open letter to Hamilton, "Your conduct on this occasion will be deemed little short of insanity." See Page Smith, *John Adams,* vol. 2, p. 1045.

254 *"talk perfect Godwinism":* Syrett, vol. 25, pp. 315–323.

254 *"I admit that his politicks":* AH to Bayard, Jan. 16, 1801.

255 *"Burr has no principle public or private":* AH to John Marshall, Dec. 26, 1800. Marshall of Virginia was opposed to Jefferson, replying that "the morals of the Author of the letter to Mazzei cannot be pure," referring to a publicized private letter of TJ's that denigrated Washington, but Marshall respected Hamilton's judgment about Burr, whom he had been inclined to support:

"Your representation of Mr. Burr with whom I am totally unacquainted shows that from him still greater danger than even from Mr. Jefferson may be apprehended." He agreed to remain neutral. See Smith's biography of Marshall, pp.13–14.

255 *"Les grandes âmes"*: AH to Bayard, Jan. 16, 1801.

257 *"Many attempts have been made"*: TJ to Monroe, Feb. 15, 1801. Jefferson denied ever having made this deal, and recounts his meeting that day with Morris in his Anas, April 15, 1806.

258 *"Men never played"*: AH to Morris, Jan. 20, 1801.

258 *"Harper is telling us"*: From Morris, *Diary and Letters of Gouverneur Morris,* vol. 2, p. 397. Other South Carolina Federalists disagreed sharply with Harper.

260 *"Are the republicans then ripe"*: Malone, *Jefferson and the Ordeal of Liberty*, p. 504.

260 *"A new Constitutional Convention will be called"*: Schachner, *Thomas Jefferson,* p. 657, based on TJ to Monroe, Feb. 15, 1801. Did Jefferson agree to the terms of the deal proposed by Hamilton through Gouverneur Morris? He later denied it; Bayard and Smith swore he did; whether he did or not, TJ honored its terms.

260 *"Here ends the most wicked"*: Gallatin to his wife, Feb. 17, 1801, in Schachner, *Thomas Jefferson,* p. 658.

261 *Beckley leaped to his feet:* James MacGregor Burns writes in *The Vineyard of Liberty,* p. 154: "Ingenious mediators worked out an artifice that enabled Jefferson to be elected President without a single Federalist voting for him. A number of Federalists cast blank ballots, and a single congressman from Vermont now cast his state's vote for Jefferson. That congressman was 'Spitting Matt' Lyon. The crisis was over—Thomas Jefferson was elected President of the United States."

PART III: THE JEFFERSON SCANDALS

Chapter 27

PAGE

265 *Cobbett trial proceedings:* This account of Cobbett's Pennsylvania trial for libel is taken from his embittered and biased *Rush-Light* series, published in March 1800 as an act of vengeance from the relative safety of New York. See pp. 12–123 and 167. In my account, two trial dates are telescoped into one. Judge Shippen's complete charge to the jury can be found in Cobbett, *The Life of William Cobbett,* pp. 80–82.

269 *"A ruinous and therefore a rascally judgment"*: was said not by Hamilton but by republican Mahlon Dickerson of New Jersey, later Governor of, then Senator from, that state. Spater, vol. 1, p. 104–106, describes Harper's double-cross of his client. Daniel Green in his Cobbett biography, p. 175, writes that

PP "consulted Alexander Hamilton about the new libel actions threatened against him. Hamilton offered, if and when they came up, to defend him in court and take no fee for doing so. He did, however, beg Cobbett to keep that fact secret." AH did not want to be seen publicly supporting a much-despised alien that Adams might well deport.

270 *"I never thought much"*: AH, *Federalist Paper* 84, cited in Flink, *Sentinel Under Siege*, p. 94.

271 *"Harper, that walking ball"*: Cobbett's excoriation of his lawyer, Harper, is in a footnote on p. 151 of the *Rush-Light*. "Let Mr. Harper . . . resolve, before he undertakes another cause, never to seek to preserve his popularity by traducing the character of his client . . ." The "lump of tallow" derogation was directed at Samuel Bradford, a printer, and was cited by Callender in his *Annual Register,* p. 178, as typical of Cobbett's "violent stile."

272 *"I knew an Englishman"*: From "Progress of a Ploughboy," in Cobbett and Cobbett, *Selections from Cobbett's Political Works,* p. 83.

Chapter 28

273 *Tom Paine:* Thomas Paine, Callender's pamphleteering hero and Jefferson's good friend, whose *Rights of Man* Beckley published in the U.S., wrote a "letter to George Washington" in 1796 berating him as "treacherous in private friendship . . . and a hypocrite in public life; the world will be puzzled to decide whether you are an apostate or an imposter; whether you have abandoned your good principles or you ever had any." Cobbett responded in a pamphlet: "How Tom gets a living, or what brothel he inhabits, I know not . . . Like Judas he will be remembered by posterity. Men will learn to express all that is base, malignant, treacherous, unnatural, and blasphemous, by one single monosyllable—Paine."

Washington in retirement, as the novel notes later, sent both to a friend, saying of Cobbett: "Making allowances for the asperity of an Englishman, for some of his strong and coarse expression, and a want of official information on many facts, it is not a bad thing."

274 *JTC and Maria:* JTC's association with Maria Reynolds Clingman in this and subsequent chapters is fictional. The dinner in Richard Price's Tavern in Albemarle County was held soon after Callender's release on March 2, 1801. The toast by Capt. Edward Moore on p. 275 is cited in Durey, *With the Hammer of Truth,* p. 142.

276 *"You and I know"*: JTC in the *Richmond Examiner,* Oct. 31, and Nov. 25, 1800.

276 *"Those of us who have been the victims"*: Ibid., Sept. 23, 1800.

Chapter 29

278 *Callender-Madison meetings:* JTC visited Secretary of State Madison in his office three times in 1801. Callender's side of the dialogue in this scene is drawn primarily from his angry letter to Madison of April 27, 1801 ("I now begin to know what Ingratitude is") which was followed by an obsequious follow-up on May 7, 1801 ("I am exceedingly ashamed and sorry for laying such a disagreeable tax upon your time"). Ford, pp. 153–156. Madison's quotations are supported by letters among Madison, Monroe and Jefferson cited hereafter.

280 *"My views about the liberty of the press":* Brant, p. 298.

281 *"I can remember Jefferson saying":* TJ to William Johnson, June 12, 1823.

283 *"You would not take the chances":* JTC to Madison, in the *Richmond Recorder,* Sept. 1, 1802.

284 *"I am not going to set myself up":* JTC in the *Richmond Recorder,* Feb. 9, 1803, recollecting that meeting.

285 *"Inform Mr. Callender, Captain":* Based on TJ to Monroe, May 29, 1801: "Callender is arrived here . . . Understanding he was in distress I sent Capt. Lewis to him with 50 D. to inform him we were making some inquiries as to his fine which would take a little time, and lest he should suffer in the meantime I sent him etc."

286 *Meriwether Lewis's visit to Callender:* Reported by TJ to Monroe on May 29, 1801: "His [JTC's] language to Capt. Lewis was very high toned. He intimated that he was in possession of things which he could and would make use of in a certain case; that he received the 50 D. not as a charity but a due, in fact as hush money; that I knew what he expected, viz. a certain office, and more to this effect."

Lewis's account of his meeting with Callender evidently upset Jefferson considerably. "Such a misconstruction of my charities puts an end to them forever," he continued. "He knows nothing of me which I am not willing to declare to the world myself. I knew him first as the author of the political progress of Britain, a work I had read with great satisfaction, and as a fugitive from persecution for this very work. I gave to him from time to time such aids as I could afford, merely as a man of genius suffering under persecution, and not as a writer in our politics. It is long since I wished he would cease writing on them, as doing more harm than good."

286 *TJ, and Callender's fine:* TJ had already sent a check to Monroe for $50 to pass through his cousin George Jefferson to pay for one-fourth of Callender's fine.

287 *"I lost five years of labor":* JTC's recollection of this meeting from the *Recorder* of Feb. 9, 1803.

Chapter 30

287 *"I am really mortified"*: This and other TJ quotes in this chapter from TJ letters to Monroe, May 26 and 29, 1801.

288 *"It gives me concern"*: This and subsequent quotes, TJ to Monroe, July 15, 1802.

289 *"According to the Scot"*: From Callender, *Richmond Recorder,* Nov. 3, 1802 (see first note for p. 52).

289 *TJ's account of two letters to JTC:* In TJ to Monroe on July 15, 1802, and July 17, 1802. Monroe's irritation at the Lewis payment to Callender is based on his letter to Jefferson of June 1, 1801: "It is to be regretted that Capt. Lewis paid the money after the intimation of the payer of his ruin etc." S. M. Hamilton, vol. 3, p. 289.

291 *"In case he comes to Georgetown"*: Monroe to Madison, May 23, 1801. Having reported to Madison six days before about the difficulty of getting the Federalist Marshal in Richmond to remit the fine, Monroe wrote at length about two visits from Callender, who "spoke of the ingratitude of the republicans who after getting into power had left him in the ditch . . . He asked the loan of some money to enable him to go on the next day to Washington." Monroe advised against giving him anything toward the remission of his $200 fine: "I do not think he wod.acquit the Executive tho' five times the sum shod.be advanced him, and that in case he attacks the Ex: he might state these circumstances or advances, to the discredit of the govt. & its friends."

   Monroe's advice was to let Callender complain: "I wod.rest on the ground of principle & meet his attack. Be assurd that the President & yrself cannot be too circumspect in case he comes to Georgetown in yr. Conversations with him; for I think nothing more doubtful than his future political course." Monroe's counsel was not followed.

292 *"I have heard that Harry Lee"*: Monroe to Madison, May 23, 1801.

293 *Madison letter:* This is the letter Madison wrote to Monroe on June 1, 1801. I have cut about 30 percent of the letter, but all spelling and shortening is left as written by Madison; only paragraphing was changed. It appears in Brugger, vol. 1, pp. 244–245.

Chapter 31

295 *Cobbett's return to England:* PP sailed home from New York on the *Lady Arabella* on June 11, 1800, a year earlier than this scene is dated.

296 *Cobbett had frequently turned down:* *Porcupine's Gazette* was never supported by the British government; see PP to Thornton, Sept. 4, 1800, in Cole, *Letters from William Cobbett to Edward Thornton, 1797–1800.* However, Hamilton was said to have arranged for the consul Thornton to pay his libel judgment.

296 *mutton-fisted style:* "Mutton-fisted" was the description of PP's prose by the

British essayist William Hazlitt in 1821. "One has no notion of him as making use of a fine pen," wrote the great stylist, "but a great mutton-fist; his style stuns his readers . . . He is too much for any single newspaper antagonist; 'lays waste' a city orator or Member of Parliament, and bears hard upon the Government itself. He is a kind of *fourth estate* in the politics of the country. He is not only unquestionably the most powerful political writer of the present day, but one of the best writers in the language . . . wherever power is, there is he against it; he naturally butts at all obstacles, as unicorns are attracted to oak-trees, and feels his own strength only by resistance to the opinions and wishes of the rest of the world. To sail with the stream, to agree with the company, is not his humour . . . He has no satisfaction but in the chase after truth, runs a question down, worries and kills it, then quits it like vermin, and starts some new game . . . with the rabble yelping at his heels and the leaders perpetually at fault. This he calls sport-royal." See *Spirit of the Age,* pp. 219–229. In this, Hazlitt may have coined "fourth estate" as a description of the press.

296 *"Let me remind you of the fable":* Cobbett, the *Political Register,* April 10, 1830.

297 *"live and let live":* Callender letter to the *Examiner,* Sept. 18, 1801: "In the spirit of charity, he [JTC] wishes those good folks to let him alone . . . *Quiescat.* "

299 *"I'm sorry we delayed":* PP to Thornton, May 27, 1800.

299 *"The Governor himself?":* PP to Thornton, June 11, 1800.

300 *"As I have long felt":* Cobbett, *Porcupine's Works,* vol. 12, pp. 109–110.

Chapter 32

301 *Callender was relieved that Maria:* The entire chapter is fictional.

305 *"a dose of salts to the human body":* The Paine quotation comes from *With the Hammer of Truth,* Durey, p. 150. Paine added that both political parties "bear a great deal of watching; . . . there is not a prodigious difference between the moral characters of the one and the other," a position that Callender adopted.

Chapter 33

307 *"We shall neither calumniate nor flatter":* Callender, *Richmond Recorder,* March 6, 1802.

307 *"If we seem to bear hardest":* Ibid., Oct. 27, 1802; in Durey, *With the Hammer of Truth,* p. 151.

308 *Next day, the newspaper war:* PP, in his 1795 pamphlet *A Bone to Gnaw,* had said, "The parties concerned in a paper war, usually bear an infinite resemblance to a gang of sharpers: a couple of authors knock up a sham fight to draw the public about them, while the booksellers pick their pockets." How-

ever, the *Recorder*'s attacks on the *Examiner* in 1802 were properly described as "a newspaper war."

309 *"No politicks":* Callender tried a touch of irony: "Reading Improves the Mind" was the *Recorder*'s surprisingly mild masthead slogan.

Chapter 34

PAGE

310 *"Callender? I'm George Hay":* George Hay's angry visit to Callender in Pace's print shop is recounted in Durey's *With the Hammer of Truth*, p. 164. Because Hay had insulted Pace in a floor debate in the Virginia House of Delegates, Callender had sent word that Hay would receive a "serve" in the *Recorder.*

Chapter 35

PAGE

313 *Jefferson meeting with Abigail Adams:* The physical confrontation between TJ and Abigail Adams did not take place; the dialogue in this chapter is based on an exchange of lengthy and spirited letters between two old friends bitterly estranged by politics.

It began with a heartfelt condolence note dated May 20, 1804, from Mrs. Adams to TJ "to shed the tear of sorrow over the departed remains of your beloved and deserving daughter,"—concluding, from one "who once took pleasure in Subscribing Herself your friend Abigail Adams."

Moved, TJ wrote back on June 13, 1804, to avow his friendship but felt the need to add "a frank declaration that one act of his [John's] life, and never but one, gave me personal displeasure, his midnight appointments. If respect for him will not permit me to ascribe that altogether to the influence of others, it will leave something for friendship to forgive."

Abigail replied on July 1, 1804, that President Washington did the same thing to her husband, and reminded Jefferson that when the appointments were made "there was not any certainty that the Presidency would devolve upon you." She then launched into "One of the first acts of your administration was to liberate a wretch," Callender, for "crimes of writing the lowest and vilest slander, which malice could invent, or calumny exhibit . . . the remission of Callender's crime was a public approbation of his conduct." She was pleased that "the serpent you cherished and warmed, bit the hand that nourished it."

TJ responded on July 22, 1804, on the subject of Callender that "I considered him a man of genius, unjustly persecuted. I knew nothing of his private character . . . When he first began to write, he told some useful truths in his coarse way; but nobody sooner disapproved of his writing than I did, or wished more that he would be silent. My charities to him were no more meant as encouragements to his scurrilities, than those I give to the beggar at my door are meant as reward for the vices of his life."

TJ then went on the offense: "I was as far from stooping to any concern or approbation of them, as Mr. Adams was respecting those of Porcupine. . . . who published volumes against me for every sentence vended by their opponents against Mr. Adams. But I never supposed Mr. Adams had any participation in the atrocities of these editors . . ." He explained that he pardoned everyone, not just Callender, convicted under the Sedition Law "I considered to be a nullity, as absolute and as palpable as if Congress had ordered us to fall down and worship a golden image." He then appealed "to that Being who sees himself our motives, who will judge us from his own knowledge of them, and not on the testimony of Porcupine . . ."

An unfazed Mrs. Adams fired back on August 18 with, "If a chief Magistrate can by his will annul a law, where is the difference between a republican and a despotic government?" She added, "In no country has calumny falsehood and revileing stalked abroad more licentiously, than in this . . . No reputation so fair, as not to be wounded by it until truth and falsehood lie in one undistinguished heap." She apparently did not believe Jefferson's disclaimers of responsibility for what Callender wrote, pointing out acerbically that her husband "has never written a line in any newspaper to which his name has not been affixed."

The mockingbird "Dick" in Jefferson's writing room is described in Schachner, *Thomas Jefferson*, p. 768. The cage purchase is cited in TJ's account book for Dec. 8, 1803.

Chapter 36

PAGE

318 *"I brought you a case."* The meeting between JTC and Beckley is fictional.

319 " *'The damning facts of your ingratitude' "*: From the *Richmond Examiner* of Aug. 14, 1802. At that time, Coleman of the *New York Evening Post* and other Northern editors were reprinting JTC stories of subsidy by Jefferson for attacks on Washington and Adams. *The New York Herald* wrote: "It must be allowed that [Callender] certainly has a faculty at 'hitting that particular knack, which is the soul of a newspaper.' " See Durey, *With the Hammer of Truth*, p. 155–156.

321 *"It pays only two dollars a day":* From Berkeley and Berkeley, p. 239.

323 *Maria was troubled by the surprise visit:* The internal monologue of Maria Clement is my speculation about what took place in her life in 1791. In vol. 2, p. 142, of his Hamilton biography, Robert Hendrickson asks, "When and where did Hamilton first meet James and Maria Reynolds? When did his affair with her really begin?" He answers: "Circumstantial evidence places their first meeting well before her 1791 summer visitation to his house[,] the time Hamilton suggests." Her association with both Hamilton and his political rival, Burr, may well have begun in New York, as her husband Reynolds first made contact with Hamilton there and followed him to Philadelphia.

Soon afterward, Burr also moved to Philadelphia, as New York Senator. Hendrickson does not agree with Jefferson scholar Julian Boyd that Hamilton forged Maria's illiterate letters to conceal his dealings with her husband, but suggests instead (p. 157) that Burr helped the illicit romance along to ensnare Hamilton.

My interpretation makes Maria the victim of Hamilton's need for a defense, and perhaps the willing subject of Burr's manipulation. In light of the Grotjan memoir, excerpted later in these notes, it seems to me a more reasonable reading of the conflicting evidence than one that simplistically condemns her as a blackmailing whore.

327 *"And massa Jefferson shall hab de black":* Port Folio, Philadelphia, July 10, 1802.

Chapter 37

330 *"Letter IV to J. T. Callender":* William Duane's letter to JTC in the *Aurora,* August 25, 1802.

331 *"It's from Thomas Leiper":* The letter from Leiper is fictional. The Callender children, however, did not join their father.

332 *"In the summer of 1798":* JTC letter asking Dr. Reynolds to tell the truth about his wife's terminal illness in *Richmond Recorder,* Sept. 22, 1802.

333 *"To charge a man as a thief":* Based on the May 28, 1803, *Richmond Recorder,* cited more specifically in chap. 44 excerpt from *Recorder* of that day.

Chapter 38

334 *"It is well known":* Richmond Recorder, Sept. 1, 1802.

337 *"Come forth thou hideous and fateful mortal":* Richmond Examiner, Sept. 25, 1802.

339 *"Long ago he told me":* TJ wrote this to Samuel Smith on Aug. 22, 1798.

339 *"Jones says there is some person":* Durey, *With the Hammer of Truth,* p. 161, citing *Richmond Examiner,* Sept. 1, Sept. 15, and Nov. 6, 1802. After Pace and Callender signed affidavits that Chief Justice Marshall had never been to their offices and was not a subscriber, the *Examiner's* Jones hinted that Marshall himself was "not invulnerable" to charges of miscegenation similar to those Callender made against Jefferson.

Chapter 39

341 *"You cannot say this about her":* The dialogue between JTC and Maria in this chapter is fictional.

343 *"Depend upon it, sir":* Richmond Recorder, Sept. 22, 1802.

345 *"The diminutive of Sara is Sally":* Brodie, p. 540. n. 28.

345 *"Here's a verse"*: Brodie, pp. 540–541, n. 57. John Quincy Adams was embarrassed in the campaign of 1828 when his authorship of this verse was disclosed.

346 *"When pressed by loads of state affairs"*: From the *Boston Gazette*, n.d., reproduced in Peterson, p. 708.

Chapter 40
PAGE

349 *Monroe strode through the two-storied entrance hall:* Room and furniture descriptions from Susan R. Stein, *The Worlds of Thomas Jefferson at Monticello* (New York, 1993), pp. 88–92.

349 *"An excessive soreness all over"*: TJ to Martha Jefferson Randolph, Oct. 7, 1802.

349 *"The day that France takes possession"*: TJ to R. R. Livingston, April 18, 1802.

351 *"With the aid of a lying renegade"*: TJ to R. R. Livingston, Oct. 10, 1802.

352 *"There cannot be a doubt"*: Ibid.

352 *"I shall take no other revenge"*: TJ to Levi Lincoln, Oct. 25, 1802.

352 *"Nothing can now be believed"*: TJ to John Norvell, June 11, 1807

353 *"Sometimes accident gives us"*: This statement was written by TJ in January 1776 about King George III, and it is a fictional stretch to put it in his mouth in October 1802, but the ironies are in the fire. See Boyd, vol. 1, pp. 283–284, and 284 n.

Chapter 41
PAGE

354 *Staggering up the path:* For an account of George Hay's bludgeoning of JTC, see Steven H. Hochman's "On the Liberty of the Press in Virginia" article in *Virginia Magazine of History* (1976), pp. 437–440; the *Richmond Examiner,* Dec. 29, 1802; and *Aurora,* Jan. 5, 1803.

356 *"If the torch of the press"*: Callender, *Richmond Recorder,* Dec. 29, 1802

358 *"For three months now"*: Callender, *Richmond Recorder,* Sept. 1, 1802. This was in response to Duane's charge in the *Aurora* of infecting his wife with a loathsome disease, and appeared in the issue in which JTC broke the story of Sally Hemings. The metaphor "artillery of the press" was picked up by Jefferson in his Second Inaugural Address.

358 *JTC-Maria dialogue:* Fiction.

Chapter 42
PAGE

360 *Maria Clement at Betsey Walker's:* A fictional scene; Maria and Betsey never met. The first mention of the Walker affair appeared in *Bronson's Gazette of the United States,* and was picked up and developed into a national scandal by Callender.

The account of young Jefferson's attempt to seduce his best friend's wife, an act he later admitted was "incorrect," is in Brodie, pp. 73–79, and 374–375,which includes John Walker's complete 1805 letter to Harry Lee telling his story of TJ's years of harassment of Betsey Walker. In Charles Royster's 1981 biography *Light-Horse Harry Lee and the Legacy of the American Revolution,* the historian writes: "He drafted John Walker's first-person narrative of Mrs. Walker's charges that Jefferson had propositioned her repeatedly for eleven years . . . In later years, when John Marshall tried to explain the sources of 'the bitterness displayed' toward Lee in Jefferson's writings, Marshall included among its causes 'the part he took in the affair of Mrs. Walker.' "

Dumas Malone, in *Jefferson the Virginian,* (Boston, 1950), p. 97, and in the later *Jefferson the President, First Term,* pp. 216–219, derided the Walker letter as "a disgusting tale which bore the marks of wilful exaggeration . . . all we can be sure of is that Jefferson made advances of some sort to his neighbor's wife . . ." Schachner, *Thomas Jefferson,* has a balanced account, pp. 762–766.

Chapter 43

PAGE

365 *"When Muhlenberg and I were investigating":* William Armistead Burwell, who succeeded Meriwether Lewis as Jefferson's secretary, wrote a memoir in 1808, on file in the Library of Congress, in which he noted that Jefferson "told me the affair had long been known & that Hamilton about the time he was attacked for his connection with Mrs. Reynolds had threatened him with a public disclosure." See Gerard W. Gawalt, "Strict Truth: the Narrative of William Armistead Burwell," *Virginia Magazine,* Jan. 1993, p. 120.

365 *"he never should have transmitted money":* Based on Madison to Monroe, Nov. 2, 1801: "General Mason has just requested me to forward the enclosed 100 dollars to be put in the hands of Mr. S. Pleasants for Mr. Callender."

366 *"I plead guilty to one of his charges":* Burwell memoir, Library of Congress, p 119.

366 *"These people," said the President:* TJ to John Walker, April 13, 1803.

Chapter 44

PAGE

368 Recorder *article:* This chapter is taken 85 percent verbatim from the *Richmond Recorder* of October 27, 1802.

PART IV: THE LIBEL SCANDAL

Chapter 45
PAGE

373 *"a concealed voluptuary"*: Sept. 29, 1792, Syrett, vol. 12, p.504.

374 *"whispers that I have heard"*: Hendrickson, vol. 2, p. 401.

375 *"Which you will display prominently"*: Ibid., p. 591.

376 *"There is not a syllable"*: A. Hamilton, *Federalist Papers*, 84.

Chapter 46
PAGE

380 *The gathering at Madison's:* The action in this episode stretched to 1806 but is telescoped here to a scene in 1803. Most documents concerning the Walker affair were destroyed, but Harry Lee kept some records; his son, Robert E. Lee, four decades later, recounted the matter to President Tyler.

382 *"I think the affair"*: Madison to Monroe, April 20, 1803, parts in code.

382 *"I have been used"*: TJ to Peregrine Fitzhugh, Feb. 23, 1798.

383 *"It says, 'Time, silence' "*: TJ to John Walker, copy certified on May 13, 1806 by James Madison (for Jefferson) and John Marshall (for Walker). The copy is at the Virginia Historical Society; the original, as well as other letters about this affair, were destroyed, probably deliberately.

383 *"If Callender of the* Recorder*"*: Ibid.

383 *"With respect to the* New England Bee*"*: Ibid.

384 *"The present occasion, however"*: Ibid.

384 *"When young and single"*: On July 5, 1805, TJ wrote the agreed-upon letter to his Attorney General, Levi Lincoln, with a copy to Secretary of the Navy Robert Smith. The original letter disappeared or was destroyed, but the covering note to Smith remains: "The enclosed copy of a letter to Mr. Lincoln will so fully explain its own object, that I need say nothing in that way. I communicate it to particular friends because I wish to stand with them on the ground of truth, neither better nor worse than that makes me. You will perceive that I plead guilty to one of their charges, that when young and single I offered love to a handsome lady. I acknowledge its incorrectness. It is the only one founded in truth among all their allegations against me."

Although some historians include the Sally Hemings charge among "all their allegations," and thus construe it to mean that Jefferson denied his relationship with her, a narrower construction holds that he referred only to the several charges made by John Walker, including an accusation that TJ forged a letter about an old debt to Walker's father, his guardian. TJ admitted only making a pass at Betsey Walker, and did not admit any other of Walker's charges. He was silent about the Callender story of Sally Hemings, which was no part of this business.

See also his secretary William Burwell's memoir, Library of Congress:

"what Mr. J. declared to me." TJ told him, "It however gave him great pain, & it was only by his knowledge that Mrs. W. herself countenanced the publication in the N.P. [the *New-England Palladium* in 1806] his sensibility ceased."

386   *"You know how I feel"*: TJ to Judge Tyler, 1804, Foley, p. 717.

387   *"Then why is it"*: TJ to William Short, Jan. 23, 1804.

387   *"That is why I have never contradicted"*: TJ to Thomas Seymour, Feb. 11, 1807.

388   *"We have come to a dangerous state"*: TJ to Thomas McKean, Feb. 19, 1803. TJ wrote the republican Governor of Pennsylvania whose judiciary had successfully driven Cobbett out of the country: "The press ought to be restored to its credibility if possible. The restraints provided by the laws of the states are sufficient for this if applied. And I have therefore long thought that a few prosecutions of the most prominent offenders would have a wholesome effect in restoring the integrity of the presses. Not a general prosecution, for that would look like persecution, but a selected one . . ."

He enclosed a paper that seemed to him "to offer as good an instance in every respect to make an example of." Dumas Malone suggests, in *Jefferson the President, First Term,* p. 230, it was the *Port Folio* of Philadelphia, which was ultimately charged with a libel. That was the magazine that first hinted in dialect poetry at his miscegenation. Malone, a most sympathetic biographer, wrote "the counsel he gave Governor McKean marked the lowest point of his faith and the highest of his fears in his first term."

Chapter 47
PAGE

389   *"Cobbett appears to be attacking"*: Most of the quotations attributed to JTC in this part of the chapter are from the *Richmond Recorder* of Nov. 17, 1802.

393   felo-de-se; Latin for "a crime against oneself," or suicide.

395   *"one code of morality for a public man:"* TJ to De Feronda, Oct. 4, 1809, in Mott, p. 24.

395   *"a fair mark for every man's dirt"*: TJ to Peregrine Fitzhugh, Feb. 23, 1798.

396   *JTC and Maria:* This final scene in the chapter is fictional.

Chapter 48
PAGE

398   *Harison and Hamilton at the Grange:* Richard Harison (one *r*), a Tory loyalist during the Revolution and former U.S. Attorney for New York, was the Hamilton law partner who worked with him on the Croswell defense.

With the exception of p. 402—"Surely it is not an immaterial thing . . . It will be a glorious triumph for truth," which is from the Croswell trial record—all the dialogue in this chapter is fictional. Its purpose is to provide the reader with the reasoning behind the arguments later presented at trial.

[*479*]

Hamilton worked behind the scenes with William Van Ness, lawyer for Harry Croswell, editor of the *Wasp*, in the trial; later, Hamilton appeared as lead counsel in the appeal. To intensify the drama and to save space, I telescope trial and appeal into one scene.

Hamilton participated in planning to bring Callender up to New York to testify to the truth of the matter charged as a libel. Thomas J. Fleming, writing "Verdicts of History IV: 'A Scandalous, Malicious and Seditious Libel' " in *American Heritage*, Dec. 1967, noted: "The defense now made a most significant motion—a request for postponement in order to bring from Virginia James Callender himself, who would testify to the truth of the libel. Attorney General Spencer sprang to his feet, quivering like a wire. Under no circumstances would he tolerate such a procedure."

398 *The description of the Grange and its financing:* From Brookhiser 1999 biography of AH, p. 204.

404 *"And he sent those Carolina paroquets":* Ibid.

Chapter 49

405 *More distressing to him:* This is my analysis of the political choices available to Burr in mid-1803. His own papers were later lost at sea, and after his exile in England and his return to the U.S. he wrote no memoir. That is one reason that so much of his biography is guesswork. Judgments about his character during the period of this novel (1792–1803) were largely based on Washington's coolness toward the youthful Burr's "intrigues," Jefferson's suspicion of his passivity in the 1801 election, and Hamilton's unalloyed hatred of a personal and political rival. Through these years, Madison and Monroe regarded Burr highly, but because of Jefferson's antipathy, not publicly.

406 *The deal was struck for 80 million francs:* Napoleon's distress sale of Western America was a property blunder greater than the apocryphal sale of Manhattan Island by the Indians.

407 *"The James River packet":* Fictional dialogue, with comments about her daughter Susan's enrollment in a Boston seminary based on the recollections in the Grotjan memoir at the end of these notes. William Van Ness, then twenty-seven, was a Burr partner and protégé. He worked with Hamilton on the Croswell libel case and later served as Burr's second in a duel at Weehawken, N.J.

408 *Maria, Burr, Van Ness meeting:* Fiction.

Chapter 50

410 *Circumstances of JTC's drowning and burial:* Historical conjecture. Hamilton biographer Hendrickson writes in vol. 2, p. 600: "A hastily impaneled coroner's jury found that James Thomson Callender had been drowned—in water three feet deep. His many enemies did not mind saying that the corpse

was found face down 'in congenial mud.' They added that it had been drunk. He was buried the same day in Richmond Churchyard, though if any burial record were made, it has disappeared . . . No one in town seemed to give much credence to the coroner's verdict of accidental death by drowning. Most seemed to take it for granted that Callender's sudden demise had been hastily arranged and hushed up as some kind of a cover-up."

Callender biographer Michael Durey disagrees, finding the murder theory unlikely. "Callender's life was certainly miserable enough by then to suggest suicide as a possibility," he writes me from Australia, "but on balance I prefer the obvious (non-conspiracy theory) answer: he drowned while dead drunk. He was certainly seen wandering around drunk earlier that night."

414 *"He was endowed by nature"*: This and subsequent quotes of Meriwether Jones, from the *Richmond Examiner,* July 27, 1803.

Chapter 51

415 *"The People versus Harry Croswell"*: The most detailed account of the Croswell appeal in Claverack, Columbia County, New York, was by George Caines, associate counsel to New York State Attorney General Ambrose Spencer. He printed his own prepared remarks verbatim and summarized the arguments of the others in a pamphlet titled *The Speeches At Full Length of Mr. Van Ness, Mr. Caines, the Attorney General, Mr. Harrison* [sic] *and GENERAL HAMILTON in the Great Cause of the PEOPLE against Harry Croswell, on an indictment for LIBEL on THOMAS JEFFERSON, President of the United States.* It was printed in 1804 and reprinted by the Arno Press in 1970 from a copy in the Rutgers University Library Rare Book Collection.

For dramatic simplicity's sake, I have incorporated Mr. Caine's remarks in the speeches of Attorney General Spencer. An even greater liberty with the facts was taken in compressing the Croswell trial and subsequent appeal into one scene. Judge Morgan Lewis presided at both. William Van Ness represented Croswell at the trial, though Hamilton and Harison helped in his preparation; after the trial jury found Croswell guilty of libel, Hamilton, with Harison and Van Ness, argued the appeal.

No verbatim transcript exists of this historic appeal. Caine's notes (excepting his own speeches, herein put into Spencer's mouth) are summaries. Because Hamilton spoke for hours longer than a reading of these notes indicate, I have felt free to set Hamilton's arguments in a more organized sequence, and to rearrange some sentences. I do not add to Hamilton's words nor tamper with the substance of his speech before the court.

On p. 667, a fictional contention was put in Harison's argument "that there may have been a deliberate attempt to prevent testimony and suppress evidence." That was implicit in the refusal to allow Callender to be called at the trial, and in his subsequent death, but was not in the Caines notes.

424 *"I do not deny"*: "I do not deny the well-known maxim, 'the jury decides the

fact, the judge determines the law' . . . [but] on the judgment of malice—
that is a combination of fact and law that only you have the right, and thus the
power, to decide." In other notes taken by one of the appeals judges, AH
went on to say that "in criminal cases, the law and the fact are always
blended" and if, in the jury's judgment, "the law is different from what the
Court advances, they are bound by their oaths and their duty to the Creator
and themselves, to pronounce according to their own Convictions."

Here we have Hamilton in the Croswell case justifying jury nullification
in seditious libel, just as Jefferson in his Virginia and Kentucky Resolutions
justified State nullification of a Federal Sedition Act. Though poles apart in
their concept of Federal power, Jefferson was prepared to challenge the Executive, as Hamilton was to challenge the Judiciary, in urging States or individual jurors to resist or ignore sedition law.

Maria Reynolds Clement was not present at the trial, nor was Matthew
Lyon or his son. The dramatic production of Callender letters is fiction,
though such letters transmitting money from TJ to JTC exist and were cited.
The unnamed state legislator is fictional, but the information he conveys is
true: as a result of Hamilton's argument, a State law was passed restricting the
abuse of libel. Truth as a libel defense was enacted into the New York State
Constitution in 1821, setting the pattern for many other States. In 1961, not
only was Hamilton's requirement for the showing of evil intent reaffirmed by
the Supreme Court, but even if a defamatory charge was untrue, the plaintiff
in a libel action against public figures had to show that the publication acted
"with actual malice" and "in reckless disregard of the truth."

428 *"It is only by the abuse of the forms"*: An example of my revision of the notes of
the trial is this: The paragraphs beginning "It is only by the abuse of the forms
of justice that we can be enslaved . . ." and "The sight of this, of a fellow citizen's blood . . ." constitute a straightening-out and dramatic rendering of
these obviously hasty notes: "It is not thus that the liberty of this country is to
be destroyed. It is to be subverted only by a pretense of adhering to all the
forms of law, and yet by breaking down the substance of our liberties. By devoting a wretched, but honest man as the victim of a nominal trial. It is not by
murder, by an open public execution, that he would be taken off. The sight of
this, of a fellow citizen's blood would first beget sympathy; this would rouse
into action and the people, in the madness of their revenge, would break upon
the heads of their oppressors, the chains they had destined for others."

The quill-penned note-taker caught the gist of Hamilton's argument, but
not its logic and eloquence, which I have tried to restore.

What is the basis for my speculation that Maria Reynolds and Aaron Burr had
a longstanding relationship? That they knew each other is an established fact: Burr
represented Maria in her divorce from James Reynolds in the mid-1790s. Since
she had no money, it had to be for little or no fee—probably the token sixpence in

"court costs." Perhaps this free lawyering was done out of friendship, or a common detestation of Hamilton, or as the natural action within a continuing love affair. But more telling evidence of their lengthy association is in a memoir in the possession of the Historical Society of Pennsylvania from which excerpts have never been published at length.

Julian Boyd, the Jefferson historian, noted that after Hamilton's pamphlet appeared using Mrs. Reynolds as his shield, only three sources "seem to have voiced the opinion that, far from being the aggressor, [Maria] herself was the victim of a cruel and slanderous fabrication." One was Jacob Clingman, who married her; another was James Thomson Callender, the polemicist; and "another was Peter A. Grotjan, a Philadelphia merchant who wrote long after the event and in such a mixture of verifiable fact and implausible recollection tinged with romanticism as to make his account usable only with extreme caution."

With that caveat, let us examine the sections of Grotjan's memoir that deal with Maria Clement, the name she assumed. The memoir was written in 1846, intended not for publication but for the study of his Philadelphia family. Of its 40,000 words, about 2,000 deal with Maria and her daughter. They are the only evidence unearthed so far that they returned to America, and that they were helped by Aaron Burr. Here it is in print for the first time, written by an old man about events that took place more than four decades before. The reader can decide if it has the ring of truth.

Selections from Memoirs
of Peter A. Grotjan

You have often my dear children solicited me to give you a sketch of the adventures of my past life and I have often promised you, that if my time, circumstances, and situation would permit, I was willing to undertake this agreeable task. This period has at length arrived. The term of my public services has expired, and my present age (nearly 70 years) admonishes me, that I have arrived at that period of life at which I can without censure withdraw from the turmoils of it.

In the spring and summer of 1800, Mr. Edward Addicks and Frederick Brauer, two particular friends of mine, the latter being a fellow boarder, rented some rooms at a farm house on the margin of the Schuylkill River near the Falls, with a family the name of Culp, in order to enjoy the summer afternoons and evenings at this rural and truly romantic retreat, where I often visited them by general invitation and spent many a delightful evening and Sunday. It appeared that a lady of very retired habits, also had rooms there and a permanent residence for the summer. I had not yet seen her and it appeared that Messrs. Addicks and Brauer had only met her at the dinner table. However, I was shortly afterwards introduced to her one evening, and a walk on the banks of the river proposed.

She went by the name of Mrs. Clement, was remarkable [*sic*] handsome, and particularly interesting, in consequence of a shade of melancholy visible in her countenance. She was well bred and well informed, and although of rather a romantic turn of mind, she was free from affectation or pretensions.

The acquaintance of this charming person was a great acquisition to our social circle. But notwithstanding the great propriety of her conduct, there was a mystery attached to her situation and lonely seclusion, well calculated to awaken the curiosity of persons of our age. Messrs. Addicks and Brauer who had more frequent opportunities to converse with her than myself, had learned that her history was somehow or other connected with that of Aaron Burr and General Hamilton but further their knowledge did not extend. Having recently read a pamphlet published by General Hamilton in justification of some bitter political controversy between him and Aaron Burr, in which the former exposed the character of a Mr. Reynolds and his wife, but especially traducing the character and reputation of the surviving widow of Mr. Reynolds in the most glaring manner, the idea struck me that this lady might be Mrs. Reynolds under the assumed name of Mrs. Clement.

Without communicating my impressions to her or anyone else, I notwithstanding had many opportunities during our conversations to allude to various parts of her history, as if speaking of another person. I frequently perceived her astonishment and surprise and found that she gave me credit for more knowledge of her affairs than I actually possessed. My uniform friendly and delicate conduct towards her, had won her regard for me, and one evening, when alone accompanied by a flood of tears, she begged my friendship and confidence. She said she felt herself irresistibly impelled to make me acquainted with her sad history, and if my advice could not better her condition, my sympathy would assuage her sorrows.

She then gave me an outline of her history, up to the time of our conversation, which I will endeavor to narrate as faithfully as the lapse of forty-four years will permit. Having from that period until her death (which took place about 10 or 12 years ago—1832 or 4) been a true and disinterested friend to this lady, many circumstances have occurred after the year 1800, which will connect her with the thread of history.

She informed me that her maiden name was Maria Lewis, that she was born in New York and was married very young to a Mr. Reynolds. This person was an active politician of the Federal party, and as such the friend and co-adjutor of Hamilton, deeply initiated in all the intricacies of political maneuvering and as such employed by the General in the execution of various plans. In the meantime Hamilton became deeply enamoured with the charms of the beautiful Maria and succeeded in seducing her affections from her husband.

The various political maneuvers did not remain unobserved by the sagacious Aaron Burr, who sought the acquaintance of Mr. Reynolds, whom he by some means convinced of his political errors. The consequence was a disagreement between him and Hamilton which ended in breaking up their connections and throwing the weight of Reynolds secret knowledge into the scale of Aaron Burr. Hamilton and Burr, both men of powerful intellect, both crafty and ambitious, had been for years political opponents and this circumstance greatly widened the breech [sic] and increased their personal dislike.

However, Mr. Reynolds soon afterwards died, and left his widow with one small child, a daughter, named Susan. In due time she consoled herself for the loss of her husband by marrying a gentleman by the name of Clement. [Did Clingman change his name to Clement?] Of this person she gave me very little information, except that he got into great pecuniary difficulties, and left her and the child without protection. She stated that she had never heard of him since. From that moment Mr. Burr befriended her, and extended his support to her and her child for many years after.

In 1799 [1797-ed.] some political scheme of General Hamilton's having been counteracted and foiled by the tactics of Aaron Burr and several severe animadversions having appeared in the public prints against the General, he published in pamphlet form a refutation, wherein he exposed his intrigue with Maria Reynolds in colors, the most glaring. Depicting the character of Reynolds as base and unprincipled, he accused him of having been privy to his intimacy with Maria and did not spare Aaron Burr's character as a political maneuverer. This pamphlet created considerable sensation but was a death blow to the reputation and prospects of the unfortunate Maria.

Dragged so ungenerously before the public by her seducer, pointed at as a vile prostitute, her situation was lamentable in the highest degree. Shame and remorse nearly annihilated her and but for the assistance of Aaron Burr, she would have fell an early victim of despair, instead of living for many years after as a highly respected married lady. As this period of her story, which I have greatly condensed, she was so overcome by agonizing feelings, that she could not proceed for many minutes.

Under these dreadful circumstances, Mr. Burr provided a place of education and board for the child in Boston under her mother's maiden name as Susan Lewis, and advised Mrs. Clement to retire for a while to some other place in the deepest seclusion and privacy. She followed this advice, removed privately to Philadelphia and lodged with a poor but respectable widow whom she had known in the days of her prosperity, until she accidentally heard of the family of Mr. Culp and their retired situation on the banks of the Schuylkill, where she expected to remain secluded and unobserved during the summer.

She added that her leisure time had been devoted to write a pamphlet in answer to that of Hamilton in which she had given a faithful history of the arts and wiles employed by him for her ruin. This pamphlet she had placed in the hands of Mr. William Duane, editor of the Philadelphia *Aurora,* for publication and that it was her desire and request that I should peruse it. I made several efforts to that effect, but could not obtain it, Mr. Duane, stating that in the event of certain political movements, it should be published, but before that time he did not wish to communicate the contents to anybody. It was never published. Thus passed the summer of 1800, at the close of which she returned to the humble dwelling of her friend, and I only heard from her occasionally.

This was the first year of Th. Jefferson's administration and laid the foundation of a long and permanent ascendancy of Democratic government and measures. The Alien & Sedition Law, the Stamp Act, (under which I became a naturalized citizen) the Window Tax, and many other obnoxious and anti-republican laws were repealed but not without great opposition and bitter feelings from the Federal Party, who to give vent to their disappointed feelings showered their unmitigated abuse, both in public and private on the head of Thomas Jefferson. He was a Jacobin, A Visionary—An Atheist. They accused him of being in love with a negro woman under the euphonious title of "Black Sall," a lampoon in verse, to that effect was published and widely disseminated, the composition of which was attributed to John Quincy Adams. Aaron Burr who had been elected Vice President, also got his share of abuse, but being rather of a cunning and intriguing disposition was not so heavily persecuted . . .

I discovered in the beginning of this year [1801] that the situation and pecuniary circumstances of Maria Reynolds (who had now reassumed the name of her last husband Clement) were very embarrassing and precarious and offered her my services to make her circumstances known to Mr. Burr. This formed the commencement of my correspondence with that celebrated person. Whatever may have been the failings of Aaron Burr, I have always found him to be a man of the highest intellectual character and of a humane and generous disposition towards those who suffered.

He shortly afterwards visited Philadelphia and sent me an invitation to see him at the Indian Queen in Fourth Street. I found him a lively and very agreeable man in conversation. He informed me that the daughter of Maria, then about 14 years of age, who he had placed in a Seminary in Boston, with the assistance of some of his friends at that place, under the name of Susan Lewis had informed him that she was very anxious to see her mother but that under present circumstances it could not be, with propriety, affected, unless she could be respectably introduced into Society, without revealing her parental history. I was fully impressed with the existence of these difficulties, but still felt desirous to gratify her innocent and natural wishes, if it could be done with propriety and safety to the persons immediately interested . . .

Some short time previous to this event, Maria Clement had consented to superintend the household affairs of a celebrated old French Doctor by the name of Mathew who had been made acquainted with her history, and her situation was comparatively much more respectable and comfortable . . .

From January 1, 1806 to December 31, 1807

During my endeavors to settle my affairs in the most advantageous manner, I in some measure retired from at least Gay Society, and practiced the strictest economy, consistent with comfort. I rented an office in Walnut near Front Street, a small two story brick building with one sleeping room on the second floor. Here I kept Bachelor's Hall, that is to say breakfast supper and lodging, and dined at a boarding house. My intimacy with Dr. Mathew and Maria Reynolds (now Clement) then his housekeeper and still under strict incognito as to her adventures; remained uninterrupted . . .

I remained at St. Jago to await the arrival of Capt. Grafton with whom I intended to return. He arrived in January 1807, and the first information I received of him from Philadelphia was the intelligence that my friend Dr. Mathew had been married to Maria Reynolds or Clement, or rather as she was only known by her maiden name, to Maria Lewis. It pleased me much, but did not surprise me. She was highly amiable and handsome, she was besides an exemplary housewife, and personally as well as from gratitude much attached to the Doctor . . .

Susan Lewis married to a Mr. Wright at Boston . . . and had one daughter by him. It seems however that they could not agree and were divorced by mutual consent. Her mother, Mrs. Mathew, wishing to have her daughter near her to come to Philadelphia (which she accordingly did in 1808) and lived with her mother for several years, when on a visit she made to some friends in New York, she got acquainted with a Mr. Phillips a merchant in that place, and a native of Scotland whom she married and resided with him in New York until his death. This was probably the happiest period of her life, as he was an amiable man, much respected and in prosperous business. She had by him one daughter named Josepha . . . Mr. Phillips died suddenly and unexpectedly of an affection in the brain, I believe in the summer of 1818 or 19, and sometime after his widow and her daughter came to Philadelphia and resided with her mother (Mrs. Mathew).

From this period forward, she brought on by degrees, her own subsequent misery and degradation. I have often pondered and reflected on the probable causes, which could have eventuated in so deplorable an issue; and am strongly of the opinion that the desultory manner of her early education, the knowledge of the shame and exposure of her mother during the most interesting time of her youth, the secrecy and deceptions she was forced to practice in early life had greatly contributed to give a wrong direction to a mind naturally virtuous, innocent and amiable.

It is with sincere grief that I have to call to my mind the direful end of this once lovely and beautiful creature, who under all circumstances, looked on me to the last, as her over sincere friend, and affectionate brother. It is not my purpose minutely to describe the conduct of her latter years. Suffice it to say, that vanity by degrees led her on to utter ruin step by step. She was married again to a young man of irreproachable character, but in less than a year afterwards gave him cause to declare that he would live with her no longer. I was applied to by her mother and herself to heal this breach, and had an interview with her husband for that purpose. All that he chose to communicate to me on that delicate subject was that the nature of her conduct and behavior was such that no consideration should induce him to live with her any longer. They then parted by mutual consent. From that time forward she added to her misery the vice of intemperance and became fierce and unmanageable, even by those whose opinions she had hitherto respected, until she became unfit for decent society. She subsequently went on to New York, where sometime afterwards she died in misery and poverty, amongst a wretched class of human beings. Her daughter, Josepha remained under the care of her grandmother until she grew a lovely woman and was married. She is now a widow (1846) and the single remnant of that family.

Dr. Mathew and his wife the celebrated Maria Reynolds having both paid the debt of nature a number of years ago. Mrs. Mathew, soon after she was married to the Doctor experienced a great change in her mind. She became serious sedate and religious without hypocrisy. She joined the Methodist Church, but retained all her former gentleness of manner. Her former life and adventures being only known to a few of her sincere friends, who had long ago buried the knowledge in oblivion; she enjoyed both for her own sake, and as the wife of a highly respected Physician, a well deserved rank in society, and the love and good will of all who were acquainted with her.

Apparently this memoirist was smitten with Maria, too. Historian Broadus Mitchell summed it up for all who look closely at that scandal-bedeviled period in American history and one of the enigmatic women central to it: "The entreaties of Maria were calculated to fetch men less responsive than Hamilton," wrote the Hamilton biographer, "and awake a partiality in the male reviewer to this day when she has so long been dust."

BIBLIOGRAPHY

*T*hese are the sources referred to in the Underbook:

Adams, William Howard. *The Paris Years of Thomas Jefferson.* New Haven and London, 1997.

Ammon, Harry. *James Monroe: The Quest for National Identity.* New York, 1971

Austin, Aleine. *Matthew Lyon, "New Man" of the Democratic Revolution, 1749–1822.* University Park, Pa., and London, 1981.

Banning, Lance. *The Sacred Fire of Liberty: James Madison and the Founding of the Federal Republic.* Ithaca and London, 1995.

Berkeley, Edmund, and Dorothy S. Berkeley. *John Beckley: Zealous Partisan in a Nation Divided.* Philadelphia, 1973.

Bernhard, Winfred E. A., ed. *Political Parties in American History, 1789–1828.* New York, 1973.

Bowers, Claude G. *Jefferson and Hamilton: The Struggle for Democracy in America.* Boston and New York, 1925.

Boyd, Julian P., et al., eds. *The Papers of Thomas Jefferson.* Esp. vol. 18, pp. 611–688, *The First Conflict in the Cabinet,* Princeton, 1950.

Brant, Irving. *The Fourth President: A Life of James Madison.* Indianapolis, 1970.

Brodie, Fawn. *Thomas Jefferson: An Intimate History.* New York, 1974.

Brookhiser, Richard. *Alexander Hamilton, American.* New York, 1999.

Brugger, Robert J., et al., *The Papers of James Madison: Secretary of State Series.* Vols. 1–3. Charlottesville, Va., 1986.

Burns, James MacGregor. *The Vineyard of Liberty.* New York, 1982.

Callender, James Thomson. *The Political Progress of Britain; or, An Impartial History of Abuses in the Government of the British Empire in Europe, Asia and America from the Revolution in 1688, to the Present Time; the Whole Tending to Prove the Ruinous Consequences of the Popular System of Taxation, War and Conquest.* Philadelphia, 1795.

———. *The American Annual Register; or, Historical Memoirs of the United States for the Year 1796.* Philadelphia, 1797.

———. *The History of the United States for 1796; Including a Variety of Interesting Particulars Relative to the Federal Government.* Philadelphia, 1797.

———. *Sedgwick & Co; or, A Key to the Six Percent Cabinet.* Philadelphia, 1798.

———. *Sketches of the History of America.* Philadelphia, 1798.

———. *The Prospect Before Us.* 2 vols. Richmond, 1800.

Cobbett, John M., and James P. Cobbett, *Selections from Cobbett's Political Works, Being an Abridgment of the 100 Volumes Which Comprise the Writings of "Porcupine" and the "Weekly Political Register" with Notes, Historical and Explanatory.* London, n.d.

Cobbett, William. *A Bone to Gnaw for the Democrats; or, Observations on a Pamphlet, Entitled, The Political Progress of Britain.* Philadelphia, 1795.

———. *"Peter Porcupine," The Democratic Judge; or, the Equal Liberty of the Press.* Philadelphia, 1798.

———. *"Peter Porcupine," Political Censor; or, Monthly Review of the Most Interesting Political Occurrences Relative to the United Sates of America.* Philadelphia, 1796.

———. *The Scare-Crow; Being an Infamous Letter, Sent to Mr. John Oldden, Threatening Destruction to his House, and Violence to the Person of his Tenant, William Cobbett, with Remarks on the Same by Peter Porcupine.* Philadelphia, 1796.

———. *Porcupine's Works, Containing Various Writings and Selections Exhibiting a Faithful Picture of the United States of America; of their Governments, Laws, Politics and Resources; of the Characters of their Presidents, Governors, Legislators, Magistrates and Military Men; and of the Customs, Manners, Morals, Religion, Virtues and Vices of the People; Comprising Also a Complete Series of Historical Documents and Remarks, from the End of the War, in 1783, to the Election of the President, in March, 1801, in Twelve Volumes.* London, 1801.

———. *The Life of William Cobbett, Dedicated to his Sons.* Philadelphia, 1835 (from the 2nd London ed.).

———. *Peter Porcupine in America: Pamphlets on Republicanism and Revolution.* Edited and with an introduction by David A. Wilson. Ithaca, N.Y., and London, 1994.

Cole, G. D. H. *The Life of William Cobbett, with a Chapter on Rural Rides by the Late F. E. Green.* London, 1947.

————, ed. *Letters from William Cobbett to Edward Thornton, 1797–1800.* London, 1937.

Cox, Joseph W. *Champion of Southern Federalism: Robert Goodloe Harper of South Carolina.* Port Washington, N.Y., and London, 1972.

Cresson, W. P. *James Monroe.* Chapel Hill, N.C., 1946

Currie, David P. *The Constitution in Congress: The Federalist Period, 1789–1801.* Chicago and London, 1997.

Dabney, Virginius. *The Jefferson Scandals: A Rebuttal.* Lanham, Md., 1981.

Durey, Michael. *With the Hammer of Truth: James Thomson Callender and America's Early National Heroes.* Charlottesville, Va., and London, 1990.

————. *Transatlantic Radicals and the Early American Republic.* Lawrence, Kans., 1997.

Elkins, Stanley, and Eric McKitrick. *The Age of Federalism: The Early American Republic, 1788–1800.* New York and Oxford, 1993.

Ellis, Joseph J. *American Sphinx: The Character of Thomas Jefferson.* New York, 1997.

Fitzpatrick, John C., ed. *The Writings of George Washington.* 39 vols. Washington, D.C., 1931–1939.

Fleming, Thomas J. "Verdicts of History IV: 'A Scandalous, Malicious and Seditious Libel." *American Heritage Magazine,* 19, no. 1 (Dec. 1967).

Flexner, James Thomas. *George Washington: Anguish and Farewell (1793–1799).* Boston and Toronto, 1972.

Flink, Stanley E. *Sentinel Under Siege: The Triumphs and Troubles of America's Free Press.* Boulder, Colo., 1997.

Foley, John P., Ed. *The Jefferson Cyclopedia: A Comprehensive Collection of the Views of Thomas Jefferson Classified and Arranged in Alphabetical Order Under Nine Thousand Titles.* New York and London, 1900.

Ford, Worthington C., ed. *Thomas Jefferson and James Thomson Callender.* New Englander Historical and Genealogical Register 51 (1897): pp. 19–25, 153–158, 323–328, 445–458.

Forkosch, Morris D. "Freedom of the Press: Croswell's Case," *Fordham Law Review* 33 (1965).

Forsythe, Dall W. *Taxation and Political Change in the Young Nation, 1781–1833.* New York, 1997.

Freeman, Douglas Southall. *Washington.* An abridgment in 1 vol. Norwalk, Conn., 1968.

Goebel, Julius, Jr., ed. *The Law Practice of Alexander Hamilton: Documents and Commentary.* Vol. I, pp. 775–808, New York and London, 1964

Gordon-Reed, Annette. *Thomas Jefferson and Sally Hemings: An American Controversy.* Charlottesville, Va., and London, 1997.

Green, Daniel. *Great Cobbett: The Noblest Agitator.* London, 1983.

Hamilton, Alexander. *Observations on Certain Documents Contained in No. V & VI of "The History of the United States for the Year 1796" in Which the Charge of Speculation Against Alexander Hamilton, Late Secretary of the Treasury, Is Fully Refuted. Written by Himself* [familiarly known as "the Reynolds pamphlet"]. Philadelphia, 1797.

Hamilton, Allan McLane. *The Intimate Life of Alexander Hamilton: Based Chiefly Upon Original Family Letters and Other Documents.* New York, 1911.

Hamilton, Stanislaus Murray, ed. *The Writings of James Monroe, Including a Collection of His Public and Private Papers and Correspondence Now for the First Time Printed.* New York and London, 1902.

Hawke, David Freeman. *Paine.* New York, 1974.

Hazlitt, William. "Mr. Cobbett." *In The Spirit of the Age,* pp. 219–229, New York, 1846.

Hendrickson, Robert. *Hamilton,* 2 vols. New York, 1976.

Hochman, Steven H. "On the Liberty of the Press in Virginia: From Essay to Bludgeon, 1798–1803." *Virginia Magazine of History and Biography,* no. 84 (1976).

Jellison, Charles A. "That Scoundrel Callender." *Virginia Magazine of History and Biography,* no. 64 (1959).

———. "James Thomson Callender: 'Human Nature in a Hideous Form.' " *Virginia Cavalcade* 29, no. 2 (Autumn 1979).

Levy, Leonard W. *Emergence of a Free Press.* New York and Oxford, 1985.

Lipscomb, Andrew A. ed., *The Writings of Thomas Jefferson.* Washington, D.C., 1903.

Lomask, Milton. *Aaron Burr: The Years from Princeton to Vice President, 1756–1805.* New York, 1979.

Malone, Dumas. *Jefferson and the Ordeal of Liberty*. Boston, 1962.

———. *Jefferson the President: First Term, 1801–1805*. Boston, 1970.

Mattern, David B., et al., eds. *The Papers of James Madison*. Charlottesville, Va., and London, 1991.

McDonald, Forrest. *Alexander Hamilton: A Biography*. New York, 1979.

Miller, John Chester. *The Wolf by the Ears: Thomas Jefferson and Slavery*. New York, 1977.

Mitchell, Broadus. *Alexander Hamilton: The National Adventure, 1788–1804*. New York, 1962.

Mitchell, Stewart, ed. *New Letters of Abigail Adams, 1788–1801*. Westport, Conn., 1973.

Monroe, James. *A View of the Conduct of the Executive in the Foreign Affairs of the United States, Connected with the Mission to the French Republic, During the Years 1794, 5 & 6*. Philadelphia, 1797.

Morris, Anne Cary, ed. *The Diary and Letters of Gouverneur Morris*. 2 vols. New York, 1888.

Morris, Richard B., ed. *Alexander Hamilton and the Founding of the Nation*. New York, 1957.

Mott, Frank L. *Jefferson and the Press*. Baton Rouge, La., 1943.

Nichols, Roy F. *The Invention of the American Political Parties: A Study of Political Improvisation*. New York and London, 1967.

O'Brien, Conor Cruise. *The Long Affair: Thomas Jefferson and the French Revolution, 1785–1800*. Chicago and London, 1996.

Pasley, Jeffry L. "A Journeyman, Either in Law or Politics: John Beckley and the Social Origins of Political Campaigning," *Journal of the Early Republic* (Winter 1996).

Peterson, Merrill D. *Thomas Jefferson and the New Nation*. New York, 1970.

———, ed. *Writings, Thomas Jefferson*. The Library of America, 17. New York, 1984.

Rogow, Arnold A. *A Fatal Friendship: Alexander Hamilton and Aaron Burr*. New York, 1998.

Rosenfeld, Richard N. *American Aurora: A Democratic-Republican Returns*. New York, 1997.

Rowe, G. S. Thomas McKean: *The Shaping of an American Republicanism.* Boulder, Colo., 1978.

Schachner, Nathan. *Alexander Hamilton.* New York and London, 1946.

———. *Thomas Jefferson: A Biography.* 2 vols. New York and London, 1951.

Schwartz, Barry. *George Washington: The Making of an American Symbol.* New York and London, 1987.

Smith, James Morton. *Freedom's Fetters: The Alien and Sedition Laws and American Civil Liberties.* Ithaca, N.Y., 1956.

———. *The Republic of Letters: The Correspondence Between Thomas Jefferson and James Madison.* Vol. 2, 1790–1804. New York and London, 1995.

Smith, Jean Edward. *John Marshall: Definer of a Nation.* New York, 1996.

Smith, Jeffrey A. *Franklin & Bache: Envisioning the Enlightened Republic.* New York and Oxford, 1990.

Smith, Page. *John Adams.* 2 vols. Norwalk, Conn., 1962, 1988.

———. *The Shaping of America.* Vol. 3. New York, 1980.

Spater, George. *William Cobbett, the Poor Man's Friend.* 2 vols. Cambridge, Eng., and New York, 1982.

Syrett, Harold C., ed., with Barbara Chernow, Joseph Henrich and Patricia Syrett, *The Papers of Alexander Hamilton.* Esp. vol. 21, pp. 121–144. New York, 1976.

Wharton, Francis, ed., "Trial of James Thompson [*sic*] Callender, for a Seditious Libel in the Circuit Court of the United States for the Virginia District. Richmond, 1800." In *"State Trials of the United States during the Administration of Washington and Adams,"* pp. 688–721. Washington, D.C., 1849; reprinted 1970.

PICTURE CREDITS